Mere Mortals

Book II

John Andrew Myers

JAM Press, LLC

Published in the United States by JAM Press, LLC.

ISBN(paperback) 9781734348620

First Edition: 2024
Copy editing by Tammy Salyer
Proofread by Miranda Paige
Cover illustration by John Andrew Myers

Visit www.meremortalssaga.com for exclusive downloads, gear and additonal information on UnEarth and the world of Mere Mortals.

Mere Mortals Social:
@ MereMortalsSaga

Dedicated only to
the worthwhile dream
inside so many of us
of finally sitting down
and writing a book.
Don't wait. Start now.
Even if it sucks.

Mere Mortals II

TRIVIUM CITY

Smooth . . . Soft.

That's all Alex could think as his left cheek was smushed into the shiny, doughy, bioluminescent mass of the creature before him.

Also, kinda wet.

He'd gotten used to being angry and scared around UnEarthlings. *That's a given.* Most of them were ugly, mean, and usually wanted to pull him apart limb by limb. But the one currently hugging him, squeezing him into her whole being—standing around seven feet high—showed no signs of letting him go anytime soon. And he liked it. He liked it very much.

What body parts am I up against? Is it her chest? Part of her stomach? Ah . . . who cares.

The small, paw-like appendages on her person might have been mistaken for breasts when folded inward to their "prone" state, but their designation or purpose was not important. All Alex knew was that he was feeling true warmth and love for the first time in a long dark while. A deep desire to drift to sleep on her squishy mounds of jellyfish-like flesh flowed from the top of his head down to the tips of his toes. No pillow had ever been so giving. If only for a moment, he found himself nearly happy and almost comfortable. His thoughts of Melissa were fading, along with the fire raging inside him.

But I don't want to forget her. I'll never forget you, sweetheart.

Alex was not the only one enveloped by the sumptuous cuddle. No-no. Next to him, Bennett—also ensnared—was having the opposite reaction to Alex's bliss and a hard time getting his unease and dissatisfaction across. Muffled noises escaped the burly, tattooed, freshly shaven former soldier that would have clearly conveyed a desire for freedom to most people or things. But the message was lost like a paper boat in a tsunami on a creature from Nashwyn, particularly one of her species, called by many names but primarily the Mal-Drimo. Their shade of Eve was created on Earth by numerous emotions and actions: obsession, pleasure, gift-giving—but above all else, love of the physical variety—or, more simply, plain ol' fuckin'. With comically large puckered lips, a scent like all Earthly flowers rolled into one, skin the color of a shallow Caribbean tide, and a gigantic heart-shaped ass, it was hard not to feel enticed by her and all others in her genus.

Curved flaps flowed out from the sides of her head, beginning from her dramatic brow, stretching outward and upward before curving back down and connecting behind her head. A thin layer of skin inside the band created a tall umbrella canopy. From this canopy, grooved flesh tendrils flowed down, hanging clear to the ground like a cluster of fat jellyfish arms. These were what had grabbed Alex and Bennett when they first entered the shop.

The hug continued, seeming as though it would go on forever, when off to the side, a bristly voice chuckled warmly to itself.

Izaiah, their pseudo guide, wearing his green coat and gray knitted cap, hunched sloppily over his emerald-topped cane, couldn't seem to help but giggle while watching the affectionate welcome unfold. His snickers were likely brought on because he knew something the Wyst didn't: the duo she was currently greeting with such tenderness were real live humans—something never before seen in Trivium. Moreover, these were not just any humans pressed between her knolls, but the delegates recently chosen by the Senate to catch the nameless demon in the Joseph Mandate. Everyone had been talking about it from one corner of Trivium City to the other: Alex and Bennett Hunter's recent debacle, including their selection by Izaiah, and the events in Africa on Earth, where a temple of ultimate evil had been discovered. Three stones found inside, known as the Gehenna stones, were filled with concentrated sin, capable of causing a chain reaction that would destroy all life. This and a myriad of other horrors had recently emerged. Yet what scared the citizens of UnEarth more than anything was the Ire, which until a week ago had gone by another name: Alexander James Barker.

He had almost no memory of becoming the maelstrom, but what the teacher could remember continued to haunt him. As a living ball of hellfire, he'd done what no others could: he'd defeated the monster. The stones of Gehenna had melted in his hands, and Wraith Chloe was destroyed. Life was saved. Part of him thought he might finally get to be a hero and stand in the light. But because of what he'd become, he would never be able to. He was a fugitive, a menace, the myth they'd long feared—public enemy number one. It seemed the people of UnEarth had already forgotten the nameless demon, his union with the human Mason Royans called Joseph, or his crusade to wipe out all life.

Luckily, the chances of being caught were low, as nobody in Trivium City actually knew what Alex looked like. The image adorning the wanted banners strung up all over town, bearing his and Bennett's names, was a fantastically terrible rendering. And thanks to the Eve inside them, they could blend into the crowds in the city. Imbued with Wrath, Alex simply appeared to be a Human Archfiend (*or demon, or imp, or fiend—lots of names*). This suggested he had been stripped of his Eve in the Purge and sent to live on Earth as punishment. Bennett, with his Rapture signature, appeared to be a Purged Celestial—or angel.

It's all pretty confusing. I'm still trying to catch up. We're basically incognito on Trivium, Alex thought.

He'd learned much in the past couple of weeks, such as how his soul existed on a higher material plane than Earth's universe. All life—even trees and grass, and even rocks and minerals to a certain extent—gave off this energy, which had coalesced into a new universe called UnEarth. This reality, it seemed, was as close to the afterlife as anything got. It also proved everything Alex believed and thought he knew had been dead wrong. He had not been a studious Sunday school student, but he knew the basics. If he were honest with himself, he would admit most of his current Bible trivia knowledge was remembered from the Charlton Heston movie *The Ten Commandments. Why was he white? I look more like what Moses would've looked like, and my ancestors were thousands of miles from Egypt. Bangladeshi, just in case you . . . you know, were . . . you know.* The Ten Commandments were easy. Ten commands. Simple. Up, good, Heaven. Down, bad, Hell. Easy peasy. But in this new reality, Heaven and Hell were not actually Heaven and Hell. Those were names given to them recently by Earthlings, similar to North Americans' use of the name China even though the Chinese primarily call their country Zhongguo. Heaven was Hywyn, and Hell was actually Arros. And there weren't just two. Seven worlds made up UnEarth, each born from a different shade of Eve—*Or, soul.*

Alex wondered if he still had his. Since his "death," he hadn't been sure what was inside him. Was it really his own soul, or had he faded? *That's the true death—when none of your essence remains.* It could have happened to both him and Bennett, and considering all the physical changes he'd been going through lately, he never would have known about it.

Presently, Bennett did what Alex had no desire to do and managed to free his face from the wet hug. "Please, um . . . lady, let us go."

The Wyst, who was also the shop owner, released them and smiled down on him, staring through shimmering black lenses and puckered lips. Keeping one cyan tentacle supportively on each of their shoulders, she massaged the humans' muscles and nodded in slow spirals, speaking with a dragging cadence.

"Of course. It's so wonderful to meet you, you sweet Archfiend and Celestial. Welcome to my shop. My name is Indya-Belaruse-Rayne. If you have any questions, even the tiniest, most smee-mie-meemie, please don't hesitate to ask, you wonderful people. You sweet Wrath baby." She caressed Alex's face and made kissy sounds with her vast lips. "And you—you stunning Rapture baby." Bennett dodged away before she could get at his face.

"No thank you! Just here to browse." With a quick boost, the soldier retreated into the shop.

Alex nodded appreciatively at Indya-Rayne and said, "Thank you," speaking with a cracked, broken voice he no longer recognized as his own and vehemently hated. *Melissa would have, too.*

"I need not your thanks, as I live to love," Indya-Rayne said, kissing the air they left behind. Turning to greet the next customer entering her shop, she gave them the same treatment, smothering them with love and tentacles. "Welcome to Rayne's Paradise, you wonderful thing. If there's anything you need, please let me know, no matter how small. I would do anything for you. *Anything*. You impeccable child of Fovos. You sweet Dread baby."

The Human Scythe looked as uncomfortable as Bennett had, but tolerated the hug in a way that suggested this was everyday behavior around here. Nothing new. Accepting Wyst affection was part of the Trivium social contract.

Free to look around, Alex found the store reminded him of a new-age market on Earth, but one mixed with a gothic S&M sex shop. Speckled with bits of color from crystals littering the shelves, the moody atmosphere was dark, broken by tiny water fountains flowing with neon liquids every five or six feet. Clouds of potent UnEarth incense wafted through the air, and music played overhead that might have been soft and calming by UnEarth standards but unfortunately made the hair on the back of Alex's neck stand up, as though his baser instincts had been activated. The music featured what sounded like hundreds of birds calling, angry reeds thrashing in a thicket, water rushing, a wind instrument shrieking like a tornado, and so many soothing sounds clamoring over one another that it became a cacophony. Still, it was better than whatever was playing over the PA system outside in the streets of Trivium, which sounded like a thousand war drums out of sync with one another and an equal number of lead-singer howler monkeys tweaking on rancid ecstasy.

It seemed there was nowhere he could find calm—not even where they supposedly sold it in the land of extremes. Though this *was* the closest he'd gotten to it, mostly thanks to the hug from Indya-Rayne. She and her store were giving him a glimpse of peace, letting his skin gradually cool and his thoughts come under his control enough to sift through them.

But his progress was halted when he spotted two UnEarth Humans staring from a dark corner. Whispering to themselves, they were partially hidden behind a pair of blue-and-green-dominated scarf racks. Each appeared human, except for the left's circular, bug-like eyes and the one on the right's scaly orange skin and horns. He didn't know why, but something gave Alex a surefire impression they weren't shopping for peppermints and incense.

Do they know who we are? Is that what agents of the Senate look like?

Keeping his hood low over his burnt face, he forced his gaze down, trying not to appear suspicious, pretending to look over stacks of lavish bowls in front of him. A nearby info card stated they were created from nevrose, a metal that made Eved foods more neutral for a less intense experience. *Hmm . . . have to remember that.*

Usually the vigilant one, Alex's partner was too distracted trying to fix a plate he'd broken by accident to notice the possible stalkers. As Alex tried to alert Bennett silently, Izaiah moseyed up to them, carrying a straw shopping bag.

"How you fellas doing? Look what I found!" Reaching into the bag, he revealed what must have been a decorative piece of art shaped like a potato with elephant feet sticking out from different sides—two feet high, emerald green, and tackier than Alex's grandma's decorating.

She's fond of indoor sundials.

"What do you think? That's real Winnie glass!" Izaiah stated proudly while grazing the thing with his fingertips.

"We don't know what that means," Bennett grunted, stymied by the broken plate he couldn't fix.

"You know, from the Winnian Mountains," Izaiah said. "Near Pichie-Pichie Lake! On Lanwyn—wait, what am I saying? Of course you don't. Silly me. Really is a lovely place, though. One swim in the Pichie-Pichie and you'll be giggling for weeks."

"Sounds exhausting." Bennett was now trying to balance the chunk long enough so he could walk away and pretend he'd never seen the plate.

Alex nudged Izaiah and motioned toward the suspicious duo he'd spotted in the corner. "Izzy, don't look, but I think we're being followed."

"Huh?" Izaiah asked, lifting and twisting his head around like a groundhog poking its head out of a hole. He searched, squinting. "You think . . . nah, we've kept a low profile. You've both stuck to the false identities I gave you, right?"

"Nobody's asked," Bennett answered. The broken plate chunk fell again, hitting another dish on its way to the ground with a clang. He stood up straight and turned toward the shopkeeper like a kid caught with his hand in the cookie jar.

Indya-Rayne waved his worries away. "Don't you fret, you enchanting Celestial wonder of life! We'll clean that up and make everything all better . . ." The shopkeeper cupped her mouth and shouted, "Vindley!"

A moment later, a creature like a five-foot, spiky red frog came shuffling out of a pair of swinging double doors. He was an Archfiend, Alex could tell right away, but not like any he'd seen before. The bulbous gut protruding from Vindley was covered by thick, cracked, lizard-like skin. Like the other demons, he had no wings, but unlike them, he couldn't float, so he was forced to shuffle forward on his two front legs instead, which were like thick tree trunks, capped at the bottom by clawed feet. Poking out of his backside was a petite set of limbs that offered little in the way of mobility.

The stout creature lumbered to a halt near Indya-Rayne and re-leased a steamy, labored sigh. "What? Kinda busy here."

Indya-Rayne waved as though shooing a fly. "One of our exquisite guests has made a mess. See to it. And don't break anything on your way with that ungainly thing poking out below your head!"

Vindley took a quick glance down. "You mean my body?"

"Chop-chop," Indya-Rayne replied, clapping like a dog trainer.

"Right. Totally worth my time. What was I thinking gettin' filled with rage for being called out here like a mutt?" The Archfiend nodded his bulbous head, covered in spines and barbs, and grumbled hateful slurs as he toddled toward Alex and company. Steam poured from his snout as his brow collapsed farther inward with each step.

"I'd like to leave," Bennett said, sliding away.

"I agree," Izaiah said. "We don't need the attention, and I don't know about you fellas, but I could go for some lunch."

"Now you're talking!" Bennett made sure to pass behind Indya-Rayne on his way out to avoid whatever her goodbye hug was like. But her tentacles could not be avoided and managed to snag him anyway.

Before leaving, Alex checked on the two UnEarth Humans he'd suspected of spying near the scarf rack. They were now nowhere to be seen. *Maybe it was all in my head?* Reluctantly, he followed Izaiah and Bennett to the exit, wishing he could have stayed a little longer in the semi-tranquil shop. Nearing the door and the chaotic, sprawling metropolis outside, he tried to prepare himself mentally and emotionally. *Here we go.*

When he stepped out, the energy of the city struck him like the morning sun in his eyes, but across every inch of his body. His ability to sense (*or see*) the Eve was now a permanent part of him and had been since his return from his time as the Ire. But unlike his eyes—

his body had no lids to close. Most buildings in Trivium City had walls made of materials that hindered Eve, but that only made the sensation all the more jarring whenever he stepped outside.

The cleanup effort underway was impressive, spearheaded by the Celestials and their dominance in the realm of construction. Many mounds of piled debris created by Hannah and Joseph's fight had yet to be cleared away, but the progress made so far was astounding, especially considering how slowly Celestials moved. *Angels, guess you'd call them. Very angular. Big, blue—look like naked people made of glowing rock. Wings for days. Not super friendly, if you ask me.*

When Alex was here last, the city had appeared dead and gray. Now, there was life. The people were back, and they'd brought their strangely shaped bodies with them. Some appeared mostly human, with a deviation or two, such as an aquamarine tail or an extra set of limbs. Vests were a favorite, but no hats, as heads were never covered here, at least not by those whose bodies had a proper "head." However, the UnEarth Humans only made up about thirty-five percent of the population of Trivium. The rest were "pures," who possessed all their Eve. This meant bodies ranging from insect-like, fear-inducing forms, such as the Fovosians; to the smooth, stunning sea creature forms of the Nashwynites; to all the variations and shades in between and beyond. These, the people of Trivium—or creatures (*same thing—"creature" is not derogatory here*)—came big, small, every color of the rainbow, all vibrant and all astounding. However, from his meager height, Alex perceived only mammoth shapes engulfing him, and body parts—most likely butts of a kind—cooking up a stench casserole that proved impossible to avoid.

Feel like I'm walking with a bunch of zoo animals . . . hope that's not offensive . . . to zoo animals or to UnEarth creatures.

"This place'll be in tip-top shape in no time," Izaiah said. "The people of Trivium are mighty resilient. Look around! Out of tragedy—magic is happening. I'm so glad you both chose to come and see it. Now, I think it would be wise to go over our cover story once again." Izaiah pointed at Bennett. "You, the Rapture man— who are you?" The Medolian waited a moment, then started snapping his dirt-encrusted fingers at Bennett. "Come on—come on! Someone approaches you and says, 'Nice to meet you. I'm so-and-so.' You reply . . ."

Bennett groaned. "Ugh . . . Ian Billbrody. At your service."

"Outstanding. And you?" Izaiah turned to Alex.

You're going to make me say it out loud? Alex checked to make sure no one nearby was listening. "Barnebus Molm. Nice to meet you."

"Very good!" Izaiah exclaimed. "Make sure you remember the last name, Alex. *Molm.* That reveals your former clan. Very important for all Human Archfiend. Remember those things and we'll be fine. I'm quite proud of the new identities I've made for you. Now, don't forget, according to our story, you both are Purged UnEarth Humans visiting Lanwynite friends in town on a graphite card allowance, which means you can stay for a small period of time before going back to Earth. I should have your forged documents soon. They're . . . in transit."

"What counts as a small period of time here?" Bennett asked.

"Three hundred years."

"Hopefully, we have our situation figured out by then."

"With any luck!" Izaiah exclaimed before quieting himself and looking around with suspicion. "We're going to need it. I know those names may seem unnecessary, but they're for your own protection."

"Protection from who?" Bennett asked. "Your Medolians?"

"Officially, we have not been given the order to hunt you. The Tribunal has us tending to other matters at the moment."

"So, who?"

"Them, actually." Izaiah pointed at the far end of the street, where two bulky blue shapes with folded wings rising from their backs were powering through the crowd. Citizens made way as best they could, just like pulling over for a cop. A few unlucky souls caught in the Celestials' path were slowly bowled over. The march of the gemstone creatures didn't seem to be out of hate, but more driven by a blind, robotic sense of duty.

"The Barium Guard," Izaiah said. "The stony hand of the Iolanze. Stay low, keep quiet."

The crowd around them grew silent and parted, squishing Alex into the mass as the Celestials neared. For once, he found himself quite happy to be small and easily hidden from view. Through gaps in the crowd, he watched them stomp by, their silver helmets and armor singing like bells struck with soft mallets with every step. In their right hands, each carried a spear a few feet taller than themselves, which Alex guessed to be around nine feet. With their wings, another five feet were added to their overall height, and no telling how much longer those were when fully opened.

So . . . that's what's hunting us? Great. Though elegant and statuesque, Alex hoped to never be this close to another Celestial again. Judging by the hushed crowd, the people of Trivium felt the exact same way.

Bennett groaned, mashed between two globular creatures—one forest green and slimy, the other the color and coarseness of Egyptian sand. "Sorry, friendo," the big yellow creature said, turning a baby seal face and puppy-dog eyes down on Bennett.

The human soldier's upper lip curled as he turned away from the giant, bashful creature to face Izaiah. "You'd think in all your years, you guys would've figured out how to thin your crowds."

"Being near your fellow creatures is a good thing, Mr. Hunter!"

Izaiah said. "Learn to live with them and learn *from* them. No matter where you are, they have something to teach you."

"Don't care. Hate it all," Bennett muttered.

"Surely you must have traveled during your time on Earth," Izaiah said. "Perhaps found something worthy of your reverence on that wondrous blue ball?"

"I traveled," Bennett said confidently. "Went lots of places. Killed lots of people in all of them. Found out everywhere but America sucks. Once I got back, kicked off my boots and stayed put."

"Oh dear," Izaiah said, as though watching a toddler spill a pail of freshly drawn milk on the lawn. "Mr. Hunter, I think this is going to be a much-needed experience for you."

Once the Barium Guards had passed, the crowd refilled the lane while Bennett's gaze remained fixed on the "angels."

"Hannah was one of those before the Purge?" he asked. "I just don't see it."

"She was," Izaiah said. "Many of the Guard served Hywyn under Hannah in the war before turning to policing. I expect most of 'em are awful upset right now, having lost their former commander. Though they'd never show it. Celestials are what you might call inexpressive, except, of course, when it comes to whatever it is they're building."

"Why are the people here so spooked by them?" Bennett asked.

"The Guard are dangerous warriors, trained in the techniques of the Ou-I, which I know you've seen in action firsthand."

"Hannah?"

"Bingo. The Guard answer to only one-third of the Trivium government, and the other two branches are without an arm to speak of. Their power lies in politicking. So, you can imagine the authority the Guard wield. Let me tell you, they take their duty to maintain order very seriously. They're authorized to do whatever it takes to see their mission through. If one spots you and recognizes you, you run—and don't look back. Got it?"

Bennett and Alex shared a troubled glance. *Starting to sound like coming with Izaiah wasn't such a great idea . . . again.* Alex wanted to go back to the new-age shop and get another hug from Indya-Rayne.

"Don't worry! I'm sure your paths will never cross with the Barium Guard's again!" Izaiah sang. "Let's get a move on. I want to show you the Oal district on the way to lunch! Won't take long!"

What sounded like a quick detour turned into several hours of walking and talking, as Izaiah took them on a foot tour of the city, pointing out every small detail he could. The number and variety of businesses in Trivium were as staggering as how similar those businesses were to those found on Earth. *Guess I thought their society would be stranger somehow.* Turned out the things humans wanted and needed were not universally exclusive. Food and drink, entertainment, and home improvements were necessary no matter what frequency you lived on. There were Nashwyn spas, which doubled as brothels. "Very loose laws in that regard," Izaiah said. "You'll find Trivium folks quite accommodating." Archfiend demolitionists could be hired to destroy anything in need of destroying. Lostros moving companies offered the services of the big sad lugs, who apparently could carry just about any object capable of being carried. Fovos hounds could be rented at kennels to deal with rodent infestations or patrol as guard dogs. But nearly two-thirds of all businesses in Trivium were eateries or taverns.

Walking past a café advertising twice-baked bruno snout, Alex found himself hungry for the first time since he'd become the Ire. Doloros food smelled the best: forcefully comforting, somehow. The scent reminded him of his grandma Roshni's Bangladeshi cooking, which only piled on more homesickness.

"How much longer?" Bennett moaned, having been complaining about his own hunger to deaf Medolian ears for several blocks.

"Not far," Izaiah said. "You can make it a few more hours, can't you?"

"No!" Bennett screamed frantically. Pointing at a rotating sign above a nearby restaurant, he said, "What about this place? That says chili. We can eat that! I love chili."

"That's Ostra chili—Wrath food. You might not be ready for that," Izaiah said with a hearty chuckle. "But if you were starving, all you had to do was say so! We'll take a shortcut. This way! Not far."

Bennett kept on his heels, and Alex followed, holding his gaze on a lone Celestial at a table as they took a bite from their chili bowl. Steam sprayed from their mouth, and a soothed smile crossed their face before they heaped up another spoonful.

Izaiah's shortcut took them through a sprawling mall filled with pedestrians on white-and-gold-tiled garden walkways, and vendor carts slinging food and wares. Planters throughout the promenade were framed with translucent gold and contained vibrant trees and bushes of every shade, from blood red all the way to shimmering violet and blue. At the mall's center sat an enormous building, a sixty-story explosion of silver. Pointed streaks blasted out in all directions, bubbling and swirling on the sides, as though time had frozen a millisecond after a huge detonation occurred, and a shimmering structure had been built in its place.

"That there's the Bibliotheca," Izaiah said. "The library. Operated by the Celestials. They're a little touchy about organization and keeping things all pristine, so they float around the stacks and get the books for whoever's borrowing 'em. And boy, if you don't return them in tip-top shape—whooo . . ."

Alex wished he had his watercolors and an easel. *This would make one heck of a nine-by-eleven.* His thoughts returned to home. The ache and emptiness reminded him of . . .

No. Don't do this. Not here.

His chest was already heating up. He needed a distraction. Fortunately, his attention was quickly drawn by rows of sculptures decorating the plaza, placed in dedicated squares every fifteen feet or so. He passed by a few, staring in awe. Unlike any sculpture he'd ever seen on Earth, these pieces looked different from every angle—strange colors, impossible shapes. Each one could've taken a lifetime to analyze. Their construction was completely alien. *How would you even go about building something like that?* The urge suddenly struck to try and make something similar in his woodshop back home. Inspiration wanted to reenter his purview, but had to be shut down before being given a chance. *You don't have a woodshop anymore. Remember?*

With bitterness filling him, Alex moved on to meet Izaiah and Bennett at the end of the lane.

Walking another three or four blocks through crowded Trivium streets, the trio soon came upon a dank eatery with dark blue walls covered in rich green moss. The sign overhead blinking every two seconds was written in an alien language that looked as though a six-year-old had been handed a marker and told to draw wind. Alex took a deep breath. *Guess I found that smell.* For several blocks, he'd been wondering where this particular stink had been coming from. *But it's much more than a scent. That word's not enough. This is like if all the fishing piers Grandpa and I ever visited jammed their way into my nose all at once.*

"These guys have the best soushue in Trivium," Izaiah said, striding onto the patio with open arms and taking it in with a deep, proud sigh. "You know, all their sous are hand-caught, which is far more sustainable and eco-friendly."

Alex was about to ask what that even meant but decided he'd likely loathe the answer. Instead, he asked what food from Earth their lunch most resembled.

"Hmmm, maybe escargot?" Izaiah replied.

I should learn not to ask questions.

The tables and chairs on the outdoor patio came in a variety of shapes and sizes. Those made for humans were relegated to a section near the outskirts. "Wait here," Izaiah said, picking out an open table. "I'll go put our order in. You're going to love it. I know it!"

He hurried away to the order window, and Alex waited with Bennett. But unease soon crept in. The patio felt too exposed, especially after that glimpse of the Barium Guard. *Stay calm. They were on patrol. Not searching for us. They'd never suspect we're on this planet. Right?*

A trio of Archfiend at a corner table caught Alex's eye. Two of them looked similar to the Aili clan, the demons he'd seen on Earth, long and stretched like Chinese dragons. But the third one was even longer and skinnier, with twice as many legs. The trio were looking Alex's way, laughing and tearing through a barrel of raw meats, letting the flesh cook in their mouths as they chewed.

They don't know who you are. No one does. Don't look suspicious. Stay calm. He rubbed his hands nervously, being careful of the rocky scabs and blisters covering his skin just starting to heal. The moment was too quiet. He again needed a distraction; otherwise he would start thinking about . . .

"Let's have a check-in. Tell me how you're doing," Bennett said out of nowhere.

"Fine," Alex said, nodding as though he were trying to trick his therapist.

"All we've seen today and you're just fine?"

"Don't you think we should keep moving?" Alex's throat continued to burn with each word.

"Try and chill out. Think of this as a well-earned vacation," Bennett said. "If you're ever feeling something coming on, or feeling heated, just—"

"I'll say something. Don't worry. I know every stress-management exercise ever put on tape. You can stop lecturing me."

"Just saying, you and I are alone on this planet. I got your back. Hope you have mine."

"Yeah, I know." Alex wanted to snap back and deliver some snark, but he also knew Bennett was trying his best. They'd both changed a lot recently, and were trying to catch up—not only with one another, but also with themselves.

Soon Izaiah returned, carrying a tray with six white boxes, each the size of an average red brick, which he distributed to the table. "Dig in! Quick, while they're fresh."

Alex opened the box in front of him and was immediately assaulted by a light so bright, and a smell so intensely fishy and vinegary, that he almost threw up on himself. The writhing things inside looked like green-and-silver eels in a mustard-yellow sauce, each about an inch thick. *I don't see any heads.*

"What's wrong, Alex? Still not hungry?" Izaiah asked, slurping up the shimmering, sloppy meat like it were a huge noodle, making his cheeks glow pink. "Yrr gnna nnd t'eat."

"Still not hungry," Alex said, pushing his boxes away.

Bennett stared curiously into his, then with a shrug said, "Eh, whatever. Live like the Romans fuck," and took a pair of small tongs from the tray.

I think he meant "when in Rome," but at least he tried.

Izaiah advised Bennett as he took the eel in hand. "Best to swallow 'em whole, my man."

Once the first wriggling thing disappeared down Bennett's throat, he made a "hmm—not bad" sound and continued eating. Twenty agonizing (*for me—at least*) minutes later, he'd finished two boxes' worth of eels, and Izaiah had polished off the remaining four.

The group's pace was much slower leaving than when they'd arrived, with Izaiah and Bennett holding their glowing guts as though they'd burst.

"They do stop moving eventually, right?" Bennett asked, his voice a mix of satisfaction and terror, followed by a belch.

"Nope, they'll keep squirming 'til they come out the other end," Izaiah answered with a giddy hoot.

The soldier froze in place. "You're kidding, right?"

"Not this time." Izaiah strolled on cheerfully. "But don't worry—they'll give your insides one heck of a cleaning!"

Bennett lifted his shirt. The glowing worms were clearly wriggling their way through his intestines. He looked to Alex for some sort of support, but the teacher could only laugh, then followed Izaiah, leaving Bennett a few minutes to himself before catching up a bit later.

By the time they left the city's hub, the Trivium sky was growing dark, transitioning from a rich burgundy to a deep purple. When the sun finally set and the stars came out to play, the night sky erupted with life, somehow even brighter and more vibrant than during the day. All the stars normally seen from Earth were present, twinkling white, but joined by hundreds more, each blazing with different, colorful shades of Eve. *Other planets with Eve . . . makes sense.*

In close orbit, a brilliant yellow moon dominated the sky.

"Doloros looks lovely tonight," Izaiah commented.

On the other side of a quiet, sparsely populated road, the city's atmosphere changed as they entered what seemed like a suburban neighborhood of single-family homes. The pavement under Alex's feet grew softer as they walked, reminding him of the fancy tennis courts he and Melissa used to play on while visiting her uncle in Oklahoma. The dwellings of Trivium again showed a great—if somewhat disappointing—similarity to those on Earth. Front doors, back doors, windows—most of the basic elements were present. The only glaring difference between them and Earth was in how drastically the style of the homes shifted every three blocks or so, ranging from hard edges and silky-smooth planes to literal treehouses swathed in craggy vines.

As they reached a neighborhood with tall, thin houses resembling brownstones, but made in a colorless retrofuturism style, Izaiah suddenly started chuckling to himself and took out his green notebook to write something down.

For many blocks he walked, snickering gleefully. "Do humans find jump ropes particularly funny?" he asked, letting his tongue hang out as he tapped his chewed-up pencil on his gray-bearded chin.

"I wouldn't say so. No," Bennett replied.

Izaiah frowned and looked back over what he'd been writing. Shrugging, he said, "I don't care. I've always found them quite funny."

Continuing to stew, he glanced up several blocks later, only to realize they had walked too far and needed to backtrack. Reaching a gray home, inconspicuous among the many, with a broad, flat face and lifeless windows and awnings, the Medolian breathed a sigh of relief.

"Told you I'd find it! Here we are—Ten Forty-Eight Alesia Lane. Remember, his name is Winston. Shade is Dread, and though he may seem like the worst person in the world at first, he's really a softie. Loves humans. Fights for 'em like a—I recently heard this expression and love it—'tooth and nail.' Do you know this term? A tooth and a nail?"

"We do. Are you sure your guy is okay with us staying here?" Bennett asked.

"Very okay. Always ready to help a fellow creature. I do want to impart one word of wisdom, though—don't mention the weird thing you'll be thinking about when you first lay eyes on him."

Bennett's eyebrow peaked. "A thing? I love things. What thing?"

"You'll know it when you think it. And you'll think it every time. Trust me."

Before Izaiah could knock, the front door swung open, revealing a face with leathered skin like wrinkled laundry. The right half of his head was bald, including eyebrows and facial hair, while half of his lips and mouth were gargantuan in size, giving Izaiah's giant ears a run for their money. The lower lip, in particular, stuck straight out, making the man look like some feeble bigmouth bass with an attitude.

Izaiah opened his arms and approached him. "Hello, old friend! So good to—"

"I said back door, you idiot!" The wrinkled man slammed the door in Izaiah's face, who turned back to Alex and Bennett with a pleasant smile.

"Like I said. Softiepants." Izaiah pushed past them, back down the walkway. "Guess we'll head to the rear."

At the end of the lane, they circled around and made their way down a tight alley behind the row of homes. On the left, the walkway was pressed in by a wall of blue-leafed bushes glowing softly, giving the path a dreamlike or nightmarish quality, depending on the traveler's disposition. Reaching 1048, they entered through a stout back gate and moved up an overgrown stone path surrounded by patches of radiant green grass. Two cracked tree pots made of a glistening silver metal sat empty in the corners. Half-buried orange rocks of varying sizes—the only items not glowing—lay scattered throughout the yard. Climbing the porch, Izaiah knocked on the back door three times.

A muffled voice called from inside, "What's the password?"

Izaiah scoffed. "You just saw us at the front. We're here. Let us in, Winston, you big dumb idiot."

"Password!" Winston shouted.

Izaiah rolled his eyes as well as his head. "Augustus sucks! Happy?"

The curtain in the small window popped open and closed before a lock was released and the door swung inward.

"Finally," Izaiah said.

"Augustus sucks?" Alex asked as the group approached the doorway.

"Just a reckless, wine-induced bet I made with this ugly weirdo that he's never let me live down. I'll tell you about it some other time."

Stepping inside, Alex, Bennett, and Izaiah found the curmudgeonly Winston crammed against the entry wall, hidden in shadow. "Don't like being seen." His giant lip flapped up and down as he spoke, like some inflatable pool toy being stomped on.

So . . . that's what Izzy was talking about.

Once his visitors were inside, Winston slammed the door and locked it. Stepping into the light, he appeared mostly human, a little taller than Alex, wearing a beige bathrobe and slippers. However, his entire right side was nearly impossible to look at without staring. Besides being completely hairless, Winston's right half was about fifteen percent larger than his left. His foot, hand, leg, head, arm, torso, ear—even his right shoulder—were all disproportionate, giving him an unfortunate Quasimodo-like hump. *He looks like two different-sized people were cut in half and sewn together.* But his most ill-fated feature was undoubtedly his face, which was perpetually scrunched on the left and swollen on the right, making it look as though he were forever smelling fetid farts.

Tightening his bathrobe, Winston slumped into his kitchen, letting his fur slippers clomp on the dusty hardwood floor, which reverberated like driftwood. "You're late."

Judging by the looks of the place, he preferred to live humbly and by his own rules. A definite bachelor—if not a full-blown gutter-dwelling hoarder—his counters were covered in pots, pans, utensils, messes, and stacks of books, papers, and scrolls, with nary an appliance in sight. A wide slot in the wall resembled a brick pizza oven, and in the corner, under a pantry shelf, sat a barrel raised on three legs, its spout covered in a caked-on orange sludge. Empty and half-empty mugs of the stuff were scattered throughout the home.

"We're not *especially* late," Izaiah said.

"You said Sunday! It's Tuesday!"

"No it's not, you ignoramus! It's Wednesday."

Winston did not respond, instead grasping a stack of newspapers and crinkling them furiously. He was seething, his misshapen teeth exposed.

"I had to show the fellas around," Izaiah continued, unaffected. "This is only their second time in town. Speaking of, it's impressive what the Builder Corps has been doing out there. The restoration is going quite well, don't you think? T.C. will be back and bustling before we know it. Maybe even better than before."

Winston slumped with an exhausted groan into a chair at his kitchen table, illuminated by a lime-green light. "You mean the restoration needed because of the destruction you and your people brought to my city?"

Izaiah chortled. "Your city? When did you start paying taxes? Also, I wouldn't call Hannah one of my people. She's more of a free agent."

"Don't you dare try to feed me that nonsense about a battle with a Celestial and a Fiend," Winston said. "I saw the damage with my own two eyes, and I can tell you it wasn't from any Eve explosion."

"No explosion?" Bennett asked. "Guess you missed the giant fireball going boom in the sky."

"What boom? I was in my room that entire night watching the show. When that last flash went off, there wasn't anything but a big woof, like a blanket got tossed over the city. A low tone. That's no discharge."

"And I suppose you know exactly what it was, instead?" Izaiah asked.

"Sure I do!" Winston cried. "The Tribunal's been trying out new weapons for tens of Ks. They were testing them on their own before putting them into use in the field."

"You do know how ridiculous that sounds," Izaiah said.

"You think you're smart, but you can't see the berries on the bush you fell in. I saw that crater the next day before they had a chance to cover it up. There weren't no explosion—that hole was an implosion crater."

"What's the difference? It did the same thing. Why does it matter?" Izaiah asked.

"It matters, you infinitesimally small rodent, because truth matters. No matter what anyone says, I'll never believe General Hannah and the nameless blew themselves up. Too convenient. Not believing it until someone proves it. And maybe not even then . . ."

"Huh, good thing that doesn't really matter," Izaiah said. "Regardless of how it all happened, I'm glad the Tribunal is being rebuilt. It'll be splendid, I'm sure."

"No one can figure out what to do with it," Winston said. "Everybody wants to fix her—they just won't get off their butts and do anything about it! Got some committee in charge of it or something, I don't know. I don't get it. It was an ugly building before—it'll be an ugly building after! Nothing you can do about it. Just leave it the way it was."

"Maybe people see this as an opportunity to change and adapt and grow," Izaiah suggested.

"Eh, why do things always need to change?" Winston snarled.

"'Cause otherwise, nothing would ever happen."

Winston shuddered as though Izaiah's joviality was freezing his inner organs. "Things happening is overrated."

"Guess that explains why you haven't changed a bit." Izaiah pushed aside a pile of newspapers and trash with his foot, as though it helped the place look less ghastly, before ushering Alex and Bennett out of the rear entryway. "Come on in, fellas. Don't be shy. Get comfy. I want you nearby when I give Winston the gift we got him as a way of saying thanks for letting us stay. Ain't that right?"

They stepped into the murky kitchen. "Uh, absolutely," Bennett said.

Alex nodded, not wanting to speak.

Izaiah reached into his shopping bag and presented the emerald-green gift with both hands. "Ta da!"

Winston gawked. "What is it?"

"A candleholder. Don't you like it?"

"You seem to greatly misunderstand our relationship."

"Sure you do! Where should we put it?"

"In the garbage."

"You're such a kidder! But sure, we'll make that decision later. It's a big one." Izaiah left the thoughtful gift on the table. "It's right there whenever you need it. So . . . aren't you going to ask how I've been?"

"No." Winston spotted Bennett leafing through one of the stacks of newspapers on the counter and swatted the air as if he were accosting a raccoon. "Hey, don't touch those! They're for important research. I don't want your human diseases getting all over them, smudging the ink and such."

"Diseases?" Bennett asked. "I thought you guys lived forever."

Winston glared at Izaiah with scorn. "*Some* of us seem to, but most of us die eventually. Thank the Eve."

"You'll have to excuse Wincy, fellas," Izaiah said. "He sees the world through a rather paranoid Dread-colored filter. He doesn't even eat real food, he just drinks that Ungh-kli paste over there."

"Do you know how ignorant you sound? Ungh weed is incredibly nutritious!" Winston barked. "You don't need any of the crap they sell you in Glikleck Main to sustain yourself."

"But where's the fun in your way?" Izaiah asked.

"Some of us don't have the liberty of fun when things are the way they are. Just because I don't believe you and your government cronies when you say everything is fine doesn't mean I'm paranoid. It just means I know the truth. I know what's not in the papers. I had to piece it all together. And it's coming along—their great plan. The Tribunal's final solution."

"And what's that?" Izaiah asked. "You'll have to excuse my ignorance—I'm a government employee, after all."

"A *top* government employee . . . no, wait, I just figured it out. Of course they didn't tell you! They knew full well you'd ruin everything. *Hrmf.* Poor, dumb Izaiah. I've got some things you should read that might enlighten you—the *real* truth in word. Do you even know how corrupt the *Exodus* has become? Nothing they print is factual—just lies to keep us blind."

"Sounds like you and my uncle Adrian would've gotten along great," Bennett interjected. "Dude could go on about the deep state for hours. What's the UnEarth equivalent of chemtrails?"

"We don't know what that means," Izaiah said. "But speaking of blinds, Winston, when was the last time you opened a window and let a breeze in here?"

"And give them a chance to see inside? No, thank you." The wrinkly, half-fish-lipped hermit folded his arms and sank further into his chair.

"You're on the run too?" Bennett asked.

"Not like you, son," Winston said. "Don't speak like we're the same. Mankind knows nothing of us."

Izaiah drew open a window and waved in some fresh air. "Wincy, the only reason you're stuck is because you chose to be. Maybe one day you'll accept that and move on. Maybe *before* you die."

"Here we go again," Winston said. "I'm never going to go live on your Earth, so you can stop suggesting it. Ya hear me? I'd rather relocate to Mallum Bay."

Izaiah smiled. "There's always a spot for you on the Sentries."

"Again, Mallum Bay."

"You're a Medolian?" Bennett asked Winston. "*Huh.* Thought you were a Scythe."

"Only a Medolian by definition," Winston said. "I'm born of Mallos, which means I see things clearly."

"And apparently, you're the only one of us who does," Izaiah said. "Winston here was part of the new class, born after Inferius. But unlike the others, a life of public service didn't appeal to him."

"It's slavery!" Winston cried.

Izaiah carried on, "So, I gave him a choice—be a Sentry and help the people—steady the proverbial boat—or live off the grid, as humans call it. He chose exile, which is fine, but that doesn't mean you needed to stay inside for *all* of it!" Izaiah took off his gray knit-ted cap and slapped Winston over the shoulder with it.

"Spare me, you toothless idiot," Winston coughed out. "I'm per-fectly happy here. I got everything I need. It's been a delightful fourteen hundred years. That is . . ." His misshapen eyes narrowed viciously at Alex. "Until this one came along."

"Me?" Alex's gut dropped, already knowing what Winston was about to say.

"You're the Ire boy. The one who fell in the hole."

"That's enough," Izaiah said, stepping in to block Winston's path to Alex. "I'm sure Alex doesn't want to talk about that."

"Doesn't matter!" Winston spat out. "Nobody gets what they want, do they? Like this one. I can't believe the Ire could ever be a man so . . ." *Small?* "Plain. The people say you became the mindless force, the doorway to all the power of Arros. So tell me, if you were the Ire, how did you come back from it? If you're here and no lon-ger a burning mass of death, I'd say that points suspiciously in the direction that there never was any Ire, and never will be."

"Man, what the fuck are you talking about?" Bennett shouted. "No Ire? I was there. I walked into the damn thing!"

No Ire? Alex couldn't grasp the implications, while Winston seemed quite comfortable with them, leaning back in his chair, a smug grin on his face.

"Hey, fellas," Izaiah interrupted. "Why don't you head into the living room? Winston'll make us some tea, and we'll meet you in there. Just need to chat with him for a bit."

"Now you want my tea?" Winston shrieked, sounding close to needing a paper bag to breathe into.

Izaiah shooed the humans into the living room, where the air felt stuffier than stuffed, suffocating, thick with the scent of rust and age. It was as if this room hadn't circulated air for centuries, the stale atmosphere heavy and dull like gasoline fumes. The high-walled chamber exuded an English-manor-ghost-story vibe, but instead of browns and burgundies, it was adorned in yellows and oranges, coated in a layer of ultrafine dust that marked every foot-step and shifted object from the last few millennia.

Alex and Bennett wandered the room, examining Winston's clutter as the Medolians continued their discussion in the kitchen, their voices clear since there was no door between the spaces.

"You can insult me all you want, but don't insult the fellas," Izaiah said sternly. "They've done nothing wrong."

"That's not true, and you know it. Every human commits wrongs to remain alive. It's part of their culture! Most of them are handed a baby when they reach adolescence and have to suck out its inner flesh to continue receiving government bonds."

"What in the name of the Eve are you yapping about?"

"You think it's not true? I know it's true. Just like their attempts to inseminate the Earth animals! That's why their world is the way it is!" Winston shouted. "You're so blind, Izaiah Ezekial. Just *see* it already. For the good of the world. See it."

"What would you know about humans, *hmm?* You're always going on about them, like you're some kind of authority. But when was the last time you actually talked to one?"

"I hear things, okay?"

After ten minutes of relentless arguing, Izaiah and Winston rejoined the humans in the living room. Winston grumbled as he carried a tea tray toward Alex and Bennett, who had bravely claimed seats on the grimy couch.

"Okay, fellas," Izaiah announced, "Wincy wants you to know he couldn't be happier to have us and that you should take the upper bedrooms while he and I make do with the sofas down here."

Winston scoffed. "You malodorous little—! I never agreed to—"

Izaiah cut him off. "Just make sure you leave the laundry for him to do in the morning. He'll be happy to take care of it."

Winston's face swelled with beet-colored rage. "Yep. Happy to be of service." He slammed the tray onto the table, causing cups and tiny spoons to clatter as tea splashed over the sides. "Serve yourselves, you little rodents." With an uncivilized snort, Winston stalked toward the basement staircase in the corner. "Now, if you'll excuse me, I'm off to bed—going to sleep in a cellar, where I apparently belong in my own house! If I'm lucky, I may never wake up." Clenching his fists and muttering to himself, he disappeared down the steps. "After tonight, we're done, Izaiah. You hear me? Done!"

"Good night, Mr. Winston!" Bennett shouted. "We'll keep it quiet. Promise."

A door slammed downstairs, plunging the room into silence. Izaiah exchanged a glance with the humans that seemed to say, Check this place out, huh? "I think he likes you!" he whispered loudly. "I've never seen him so obliging."

"I don't think we can trust this guy," Bennett said.

"I used to think that too. But if Winston is so willing to be disdainful on the outside, then he must actually be a good guy deep down, right? It's sound logic! Besides, if there is one thing that defines that man more than anything else—he absolutely, infinitely, stupendously does not trust or in any way associate with the government. He'd rather die than expose himself. Don't worry so much. Just take some time to relax! Have some tea. This is going to be your home for a little while, but for now, just try and get a good night's sleep."

"Did you say sleep? Fuck yes. That's my thing. Where do I lay my body?" Bennett was already on his feet. *Guess he doesn't want tea.* For once, Alex agreed with him.

Izaiah led them upstairs to the second floor, where he showed them their rooms. Each featured a mound of interconnected sofa pieces near its center, effectively turning half of the space into a bed.

"God in Heaven." Bennett moaned, his eyes wide. "Dibs!" He charged into his favorite room, the one down the hall to the right, leaping onto the bed area in a cloud of dust. Sprawling out, he tossed aside books and newspapers cluttering the space. "You're right, Izzy, this was a good idea." With his arms spread wide and eyes closed, he settled in.

He looks awful comfortable after having gone through what we did. Though it's not like he lost anyone close to him, is it? Must be nice.

"Brushing your teeth?" Alex asked, keeping his words to a minimum to save his voice.

"I haven't done any of that shit since we died," Bennett said. "Have you?"

Actually, now that I think about it . . . Alex had tried to maintain some hygiene during his saga with UnEarth, but he'd only had access to running water a few times and hadn't brushed his teeth or washed his hands in more than a day. The last time he showered was back in Prescott, after the Ire, when he'd "found" a half-used bar of soap near a homeless tent camp. Under the cover of darkness, he'd used a hose behind a LubeItUp to wash off. The cold water felt blissful on his scorching skin, still cooling like lava rock even now.

Through it all, he'd never actually smelled all that unpleasant, or noticed plaque on his teeth, as he used to. He'd washed and brushed out of habit, nothing more. It seemed being imbued with Eve meant he no longer needed things like self-care. *Guess my Wrath burns it all away, and Bennett's Rapture sanitizes everything. Huh.* The former teacher marked it down as the first benefit he could remember getting from all this. *One point to Wrath. Fine. Whatever.*

Izaiah regarded Bennett with eyes full of pride and scruffy cheeks flushed with warmth. "Guess that about does it. I'll leave you fellas to your devices. Make sure to have a pleasant night. If you need anything, come wake me. Though you'll have to shout pretty good to get me up. Once I'm down, I tend to stay down. Don't be afraid to flog my nog, if you gotta." Izaiah hobbled back down the wooden staircase. "Until next time, fellas, welcome to Trivium."

"Night, Izaiah," Bennett said, muffled by the bedsheet over his face that he was too lazy to move aside.

Alex stayed quiet.

"How about you?" Bennett asked Alex once they were alone.

The teacher shrugged in response.

"Yeah, it's going to be strange getting used to this, but I think we'll be okay," Bennett said.

Easy for you to say. Alex didn't want to argue or use his voice, so he nodded and grabbed the handle to shut the bedroom door.

"I mean it, Al. You and me, we're gonna be able to get through this—move past it. Just because something takes time doesn't mean it won't happen. You just gotta have faith."

That was one of the last things Alex expected from him. *It must have been something he picked up from Hannah.* It looked as though Bennett's Celestial mentor had taught him well, whereas Alex had been sidelined with the clean demon, Felix—*who took off without a goodbye.*

He nodded and shut the door before moving down the dark hall to his own room. Once inside, he sat down to take a breath, now surrounded by salmon-colored walls. *So, this is life.* The room's enormous bed area stretched all the way to a window capped with mildew-ridden drapes. Other than a tall dresser and a vanity against the left wall, all the remaining space was covered in stacks of books, newspapers, and trash. *Just lovely.* After trying for a few minutes to tidy up, Alex realized its futility.

The hundreds of blankets on the bed stank relentlessly of mold. Digging past the top layer, he found a blanket that looked and smelled fresher and lifted it to the surface. Crawling inside, he curled up, closed his eyes, and took a breath—in through his nose, out through his mouth—feeling little comfort or calm taking shape. Staring at the ceiling, not feeling the slightest bit tired, he decided to roll over and try reading one of the newspapers scattered around the bed to pass the time. Grabbing what looked like the most recent issue from a stack, he found the banner headline typed in many languages, including English: "Tribunal: UnEarth Census to Resume as Planned." While not especially interesting, looking it over was better than letting his mind wander. *Because it always wanders to the same place…and probably always will.*

How long had it been since he'd lost his love? A lifetime? Three days? The snap of her neck coursed through his body, through his bones, making him tense and shake. The quilt-wrapped ceiling above him seemed to be spinning. *Is this all real? I still can't believe it, even while living it.* He didn't want to be in a strange bed in a strange house in a strange city. He didn't want fire hands, or hugs from jellyfish women. Not really. He wanted his bed, the one he'd known weeks ago. He wanted his life. To him, Heaven was not Hywyn, or even the one in the Christian Bible, if it existed somewhere out there. To Alex, Heaven was lying in bed on a Saturday morning with his wife, the sheets and their love weighing them down, keeping them in place both out of want and need—unlike the unreasonable weight of despondency holding him down now. But that Heaven was gone, no longer ahead of him by any possibility.

The night droned as Alex tried to calm his mind, tossing and turning, until a clang outside pulled him out of bed. Moving to the window, he drew the blinds. Across the horizon, Trivium was a silhouette speckled with dots of soft color. *Diet Vegas.* Another clang called his gaze to the backyard, where a dark shape was crawling out of the basement window directly below. Winston stood up into the moonlight and cracked his back before slumping toward the gate, glancing around nervously. *Where does he think he's going? Wait . . .*

Alex got a bad feeling just before the moonlight above was ripped away by multiple shadows soaring through the air. Wrath shot up his veins, reacting to an incoming freight train of Rapture. *Back!* He launched himself off the balls of his feet as monstrous dark shapes crashed through the entire window wall, obliterating it. At the same time, the roof above him caved in, forcing Alex to dive for cover under the sheets of the giant bed. The blare was deafening. A gale-force wind stirred the room as he crawled toward the bedroom door, a deluge of wood shards and glass showering the bed. His ankle was pinned by a heavy chunk. Something sharp landed on his shoulder, missing his skull by an inch.

Two pairs of dense feet landed somewhere in the room and stomped toward him, then another—*BAM BAM BAM*—the crashing wouldn't stop. Pulling his legs free, Alex kept crawling. *I think the door was this way!* He burrowed deeper, as though the blankets might protect him, barely missing a spear to his right. Another stabbed to his left. The Rapture coursing through the spears pervaded his senses like an ice-cold punch. His Wrath kicked into a higher gear, smothering the blankets around him, blinding him and filling his lungs with smoke, which they didn't seem to mind.

You want a fight? Fine! Diving out of the blankets, he narrowly dodged a third spear about to impale him and rolled onto the ground to face his attackers. Their large, swift, and terrifying wings flapped, churning a storm of wood shards and dust into the air. Among the floating artifacts, the blazing blue eyes of three Celestials coursed toward him. Alex then remembered what Izaiah had said about situations like this.

Run.

Abandoning the desire to attack, he turned and leaped toward the door, smashing his fist into the wood. With a blast of Hellfire, it exploded and he sprinted into the dark hall, his blazing hands lighting the way. The whole house sounded as if it were being struck by an earthquake and indoor thunderstorm at the same time, drowning out his cries for help. The Celestials were right behind him, crashing through the doorframe as if it were papier-mâché.

Alex spun in time to see a spear tip coming for him. His Wrath responded, broiling his chest and lighting his scars. He ducked. The spear sailed overhead, down the hall, impaling itself in the wall near Bennett's room, where the bedroom door blasted open and a man in glowing blue medieval armor was hurled out. Bennett crashed into the wall, left embedded and wriggling for freedom, cursing like his life depended on it as two huge armored Celestials exited his room.

Too small to stand any sort of chance, Bennett's fight didn't last long. The glowing blue bodies overtook him and smashed him into the ground just as Alex was tackled from behind by a force like a semi-truck. Rolling over, he tried to fight off the huge, stony warrior but was forcefully held down by a single broad, icy-cold hand.

The Celestial raised their other fist, ready to pulverize Alex, when an apple-green sphere surrounded him, encasing him safely. Another formed around Bennett. The Celestials pounded at the spheres as the humans were airlifted toward the stairs and to Izaiah, who looked as if he were still waking up. His hands were high, though, ready to fight, his right clutching his cane and his left fingers clawed, feral. "Those boys are under my protection, and I ain't scared of you. So, who sent you, huh? I know this ain't Tribunal business!"

The five Celestials halted their advance, spreading out and studying Izaiah, whom Alex had never been happier to see.

"You folks are dealing with the Warden Sentry, Izaiah Ezekial. Now state your business—" He was cut off by a sound so loud that it blotted out all senses but one.

Like a spout of liquid nitrogen had been opened behind Alex, the Rapture signal forced him to his knees just before the wall behind them exploded, obliterating a nine-foot-by-fourteen-foot framed landscape of a Fovos swamp hung across it. A torrent of broken wood bits sprayed the area as Izaiah, Bennett, and Alex were struck to the ground from behind by members of the Barium Guard.

Izaiah's emerald-topped cane flew through the air, vanishing into the rubble, while Bennett shouted from somewhere on the right, "Al, go Ire! Smite these assholes!"

The colossal weight on Alex's back forced the air from his lungs. He struggled to find his Wrath—fought to remember what had ignited the power. *It was her. Of course it was. Seeing what I saw.* He thought of Melissa—but found no rage—only emptiness. Unable to move, he twitched as a subzero metal object was jammed into his back. Alex screamed under its weight as his arms were forced into freezing, rifled slots. Rigid clamps came down on his hands, wrists, and forearms, locking them in place, followed by a stinging pain in his ribs as six spikes stabbed into his flesh, locking the device to his body. Hot blood ran down his abdomen, pooling around him on the floor, mixing with the dirt.

When the device was lifted into the air, Alex came with it, releasing an agonized shriek. The guard left him dangling as another Celestial approached holding a bumpy, craggy, hand-hammered metal mask with no eyeholes. A wave of despair washed over him as the mask was slid over his face. *All this is for me? Why? What do they think I am? I didn't choose to be this!* The hefty mask's locking mechanism clicked, echoing within it and encasing him in darkness. His skin almost reveled in the cold chill of the metal as his Wrath was siphoned away, extinguishing the fire around his hands and in his veins.

Sweetheart, where are you?

"That's completely unnecessary! Take that thing off him!" Izaiah's shout came through, muffled by the mask covering Alex's head. "Bennett, stop! It's done. They'll kill you. Stand down!"

Bennett must still be fighting back.

Alex couldn't see anything but could still sense Eve enough to feel the encroaching wall of Rapture around them. The Guard were standing proudly over their prisoners. The shortest figure among them, radiating the most potent signature, stepped forward and spoke to Izaiah in a surprisingly high-pitched, delicate voice for a Celestial.

"Mr. King Medolian. Welcome back to Trivium."

"Loredosai," Izaiah grumbled with a loathsome turn. "What is the meaning of this? Where is Captain Hwyllahs? Who are you to attack a civilian home in the middle of the night? Have the Guard sunk so low?"

Loredosai's smugness was crystal clear, even though Alex couldn't see his face. "Harboring humans wanted by the Senate—this we were informed of. I found the rumor easy to believe."

"What? That's ridiculous! These are just two of my friends, Ian and Barnebus. Come on, guys, tell them who you are!"

"We require no story. We know who they are," Loredosai stated flatly.

A scream echoed from the lower halls. "No! Put me down! I have a deal!" Winston's faint Eve signature approached, being dragged by another Celestial. "You idiots are breaking my whole house! Who's going to pay for all this?"

As Winston reached the second-floor landing, he was released and stumbled toward Loredosai. "What the heck is going on? You said this would be a silent operation!"

"Was this not . . . discreet?" Loredosai asked, sounding suspiciously sardonic.

"It was you?" Izaiah shouted at Winston. "You told them?"

Imagining the pained look on Izaiah's face was easy, but focusing on the situation was becoming arduous. *Getting so . . . tired.*

"Did you not hear anything I said?" Winston shouted back. "I hate you! I've always wanted you in jail. I've told you so many times!"

"I just figured you were as good at joking as I am!" Izaiah's voice cracked, sounding rattled to his core.

"You're not good at jokes! They're awkward and simple and—frankly—embarrassing. Everyone thinks so."

"What are you saying?" Izaiah pressed.

Winston screamed, "I'm telling you I hate you! You brought humans into my house! Humans like that!" Even without sensing it, Alex knew Winston was pointing at him. "You made a monster and expect me to help you clean up your mess? No. I'm done with that. I'm done with you!"

Izaiah scoffed, his signature turning canary yellow. "You know, I'm starting to think we were never friends at all."

Winston screamed again. Alex imagined he was pulling out the remaining hair on the left side of his head. "I want you people out of my house! Everyone!"

"We are leaving," Loredosai said, then feebly shouted a command at his team. The troops responded with booming Celestial voices that dwarfed their captain's squeaky tenor.

"Thank the Eve." Winston began heading back toward the stairs, his slippers clomping on the floor. "So, when do I get my reward?"

"Soon, Medolian," Loredosai said.

A Celestial stepped in front of Winston, blocking his path. "What are you doing? I had an agreement with Speaker Binahq herself."

"Speaker Binahq knows the agreement. Speaker Binahq is wise, unlike you . . . who is not." Loredosai turned and led the way back to Alex's room, his troops following with the prisoners in tow. "The agreement will be upheld. You will come to the Tribunal."

Winston bawled throughout his abduction as the Celestials took off through the ceiling one by one. With cold indifference, the guard carrying Alex hoisted him by the contraption attached to him, straining his arms and shoulders, yanking at his impaled abdominal flesh. With a deafening whoosh, they were airborne. The Celestial's wings rose and fell as they climbed higher over Trivium, passing through pockets of hot air amid the freezing night. Feeling more helpless than ever, Alex wanted to cry from sadness, but that emotion had also been sucked away by the mask, leaving him numb.

Izaiah's muffled voice cut through the wind just enough to be heard. "Alex, Bennett, I'm so sorry! This wasn't supposed to happen. But I'll fix it! We'll figure this out, don't you worry!"

Don't worry? thought Alex.

CHASING GHOSTS

"Leigh?" Casey called, met only with silence, telling her instantly she'd made a terrible mistake by coming here. The London flat belonging to her former boss felt abandoned. A gut-wrenching realization washed over her, draining every promising and positive thought she'd built up over the last sixteen months. The air reeked of rotten food and old laundry. The lights wouldn't turn on. A stifling, callous feeling lingered like a fog.

Case, why did you have to come back? Why?

It didn't take long to conclude that Leigh hadn't been home for some time. Essentials were missing—clothes, toothbrush— suggesting she had left voluntarily rather than been kidnapped. The fridge was empty and dead, along with the other appliances. Mountains of takeout garbage and dirty dishes littered the kitchen counters. The only clean surface was the table, covered with a plastic sheet topped with computer electronics parts and tools, including a soldering kit. Next to it sat a dried cup that likely contained bleach and water, with a paintbrush nearby. Bits and pieces

of circuits were scattered everywhere, alongside frayed black Kev-
lar straps.

In the main parlor, Casey found the entire south wall plastered
with a hectic collage of newspaper clippings and photographs—
something one might expect from a conspiracy theorist who'd decided to just go for broke. Clippings of old animal attacks bore urgent notes in red ink: "*UnEarth animal? Which? Scythe claws?*" and
"*Portals? Alignment timeline? Emergence points?*" Lists overlapped,
suggesting potential UnEarth Humans masquerading as real people, including a few celebrities. *No way. Not Kenny Loggins. There's
no way he's a Wyst. Leigh better be ready to back that up.* At the top,
a lone card read "*Gabriel,*" with another below it marked "*Lucifer.*"

I think I might faint.

Coming here was probably the most boneheaded of moves she
could have made in a lifetime filled with them. Things had finally
been going well for Casey. Her months of therapy following the
Joseph incident had been showing results. She'd managed to get
off her parent's couch and back to work, starting part-time at a
jewelry counter in the mall, preparing to make her way back to
the world of archaeology. After months of rejected applications at
universities around the States, she had finally landed an interview.
It didn't matter that it was back at UCL—a place she'd promised
never to return to. The job was a project manager position at a dig
in Nepal. The opportunity couldn't be missed.

Her problems seemed behind her. The interview was going well.
The job seemed hers to lose, right up until the moment Thomas,
the man interviewing her, brought up her former boss.

His comment could have been ignored. Casey could have continued toward her dream job, potentially leading to financial stability and—oh, who knows—maybe one day a family. But one off-
hand remark, likely intended as a compliment, toppled that fragile

house of cards. Thomas, smooth as a greased toupee, noted how pleased many at the university were to see her break away from the professor. "I mean no disrespect, but very few of us in archaeology at UCL were fans. Your previous boss was brilliant, but also came with a lot of baggage. And—"

But Casey had to stop him, suddenly taken aback. "I'm sorry, I'm sure it's nothing, but I noticed you're referring to Leigh in the past tense. Is there a reason for that?"

"I only meant Professor Evans has had her time in this field, which I'm sure you agree."

"Actually, I'm not sure what you mean."

"No credible institution will ever touch her again. I hope that doesn't come as a surprise to you, or I may have to reconsider this entire interview."

"I'm so sorry, but I think I'm missing something. Did something happen to Leigh?"

"Good heavens, you mean you don't know?" Thomas closed his notebook. "The professor is a thief. A manhunt is underway to locate her at this very moment."

A gasp escaped Casey. "Can you . . . please explain what you mean?"

"Five days ago, she was caught on closed circuit television entering this school. After breaking and entering, she disappeared multiple times before reappearing in the collections warehouse. The police are baffled—they assume her extensive knowledge of the layout and security must have helped her, but I call that rubbish. Most of the staff, myself included, know this place top to bottom, and none of us can see how you might sneak around so successfully without setting off alarms or being caught on camera. Remarkable, really. She was only identified because a student's desktop was left streaming after an online tutoring session. Last I heard, they believe her to be responsible for a string of recent artifact robberies throughout the country."

"But why did she do it? I mean, what did she steal?"

"I don't believe I'm forbidden from telling you she took several items with no apparent connection—some gold and silver bits, a few pieces of jewelry from the Spanish conquistador collection. But the key item seemed to be a Sumerian bowl. No one knows why she wanted it. We're all baffled. Not to be too insensitive, but we feel she's plunged into the deep end, as it were."

Thomas refused to answer any further questions and insisted they proceed with the interview, which felt moot at that point. Casey knew how little a chance she had of getting the job. The interview had been arranged two weeks before Leigh's theft. Given how intertwined their names were, both professionally and personally, it now seemed miraculous she'd even been allowed inside the building.

I'm so tired of this. Why can't I escape her shadow?

After bumbling through the rest of the interview, Casey found herself outside, sat on a bench, gazing at the ground. Some tears needed to be wiped away. Her mind couldn't stop racing. How could Leigh have done what Thomas said? And what else was she capable of? As much as Casey didn't want to believe her former boss—and once friend—could fall so far, it wasn't hard to imagine. *Not after the frenzied emails she's been sending me for the better part of a year. Obsessed would be a mild word to describe what she's got going on with UnEarth. Unlike me. I never think about it. Not ever. Not once. Especially not in the shower.* While Casey had tried desperately to put what happened behind them, Leigh had never entertained the notion. The two women had experienced something earth-shattering together, something that tore apart the fabric of what they knew and believed. It was naive to think they could ever return to a normal life, not after Casey's near sacrifice at the hands of the Wraithians. Not after Leigh lost her voice. Not after Joseph.

Anxiously, she scanned the campus. The very real possibility that UnEarth agents were lurking about, ready to strike, had taken root in her psyche months before. According to Leigh's contacts in UnEarth resistance circles, Bennett Hunter and Alex Barker had been arrested on Trivium and were set to go to trial. If those two were considered convicts in the land of spirits, it stood to reason the same people who had arrested them might know about Casey and Leigh and consider them a part of the Joseph debacle as well. Since this dawned on her, Casey had avoided dark alleys and doorways, generally staying inside unless absolutely necessary, leaving her parent's house only during the day.

It's only paranoia if the thing you're afraid of doesn't exist. Right?

Leaving the country now was the best option. Michigan was safer—it had to be—and the professor was no longer Casey's problem. Her former boss had always been self-interested and condescending. If Leigh had gotten herself into trouble with both UnEarth as well as human authorities, that was on her. Casey couldn't help. No way.

After calling a taxi, she froze when the driver asked where to. The airport was obvious, but what good would it do going home if she wouldn't be able to sleep? *Oh God, I'll probably never sleep again, huh?* Casey knew herself too well. If she didn't find out the truth or make sure Leigh was safe, she wouldn't find peace. Ignoring Thomas's words was impossible. Other people might have been able to manage it, but not her. First, she tried calling Leigh—no answer.

I'll just swing by her place and see if she's home. If not, I'll hop on the next flight home. Easy as pie.

She asked the driver to head north to the outskirts of the city.

Using a spare key left over from her days as the professor's assistant, she let herself in when there was no answer at the door.

What she found did not shock her, unfortunately. By the looks of the place, Leigh could have easily been in some kind of trouble. In the bathroom, Casey found six empty two-gallon containers of bleach. Residue coated the walls, and the stench was overwhelming. *You really did drink the Kool-Aid, didn't you?* According to Leigh's "literature," which had flooded Casey's inbox over the months, bleach was a natural retardant of Eve energy. It appeared Leigh had been using the bathtub to sterilize her belongings and likely anything brought in from the outside world. Next to the bottles were tubes and plunger devices.

What were you planning?

Rushing to the office, the most crucial room to search, Casey found Leigh's desk cluttered with papers and notes. Sifting through them would take too long; any important information wouldn't be left lying around. Reaching down the side of the desk, Casey's fingers grazed a raised wooden tab. She pressed it, and a click echoed within the desk framework, releasing a foot-long section. The panel pulled away, revealing a secret compartment. Inside was a worn college-ruled notebook, nearly every page filled with scattered, overlapping notes in Leigh's handwriting.

Double-checking the mess on the desk for any planners or calendars, Casey noticed most of the scattered notes seemed to engage in back-and-forth dialogues, possibly between three or four different voices, peppered with a particular name scrawled in loud letters, sometimes crossed out with furious red ink: Aluqa.

Right. Her.

Ever since the events of the Joseph Mandate, the mysterious benefactor who had funded the dig that unearthed Gehenna had remained elusive. Casey had tried to contact Aluqa Morinnean several times through her companies, only to be given the run-around with endless calls on hold and the same answer: "We're sorry, that's not our department/sector/company." Leigh was most definitely holding a heavy grudge against the magnate—*at best*.

An atlas dominated the office's right wall, featuring long-winded Post-its mentioning the Medolians, usually beside a major historical event—mostly disasters. Judging by the looks of it, Leigh blamed the Mallos users for almost everything bad that had ever happened, suggesting Izaiah Ezekial and the others had been altering events on Earth for ages.

Books about UnEarth with poorly designed covers were scattered about, likely self-published by the same people who sold volumes on their personal alien-abduction stories. Casey glanced over a few to find them earmarked and highlighted heavily, inundated with notes in the margins. One particularly worn book featured another lengthy back-and-forth discussion regarding the ways to kill UnEarth creatures. *Heaven help you, Leigh.* The books were stuffed into Casey's backpack, if only to keep them from falling back into their owner's grasp.

Before leaving, she sat on the corner of the couch and flipped through the college-ruled notebook. At the very back, on the bottom of the last page, she found a note that looked like an appointment to see someone named *Oyel Pattel* at the *Klaas Fete*. It was dated just a couple of days before. That boded well; Leigh was probably still alive and kicking. *Klaas Fete? What kind of a place is that? And what sort of name is Oyel Pattel?* The clue wasn't much, but unfortunately enough to get Casey's mind cranking, trying to imagine what a fete—or market—of UnEarth would look like.

But I'm not going to go after her. No way. She's on her own. Whatever she's doing. No way. Casey would have sooner taken a bath in the bleach-soaked bathtub than go after Leigh, even if it meant making sure she was okay and not a possible danger to herself and others.

She's not my responsibility anymore! She never should have been! Getting mixed back up with Leigh would mean getting mixed back up with UnEarth. That was the last thing Casey ever wanted.

Right? That's true, right?

It would make perfect sense. After all, she had nearly lost her life the last time she was embroiled in the world of the spirit and the Eve. But if that were really the last thing she wanted, then why had she spent nearly every moment of the last sixteen months thinking about UnEarth and the creatures that lived there? Why did she find herself doodling Archfiend and Wraithians on receipts while bored at work at the jewelry counter? The things she'd seen and learned had taken over her psyche and no matter how many therapy sessions she aced, there was no denying it. Casey knew this. That's why she could only mutter angrily at herself as she stuffed the notebook into her backpack and slipped it on.

When she called another taxi, she continued muttering during the entire ride to the internet café, where she set about learning all she could about the Klaas Fete, including where it might be located. The name did not come up in any mainstream sites. Only the back-alley web knew about the Fete, which she learned was located somewhere near People's Park and the River Suir in Waterford, Ireland. When she found what she was after, Casey sighed, devastated that she had been given a direction to go in that wasn't headed back home, toward her nice, comfy bed and pillow. *Why do I do this to myself?*

Two days later, following a brief flight and a forty minute train ride, she was walking through an outdoor bazaar that stretched from the city center to the wharf. Idling down a stretch, her curly medium-length hair dancing around her eyes, Casey fought to find a balance between looking around too much and too little. Agents of UnEarth or unfriendly eyes were far more likely to be about here. *Stupid. Stupid. What am I doing?* Though so far, everything was not only perfectly ordinary but also quite charming. If signs of UnEarth were about, she had yet to see them.

All I want to do is shop here. Some of this stuff is so cute!

The merchant tents filling the skinny stone lanes sold everything from furniture and groceries to clothing and wicker crafts. Moving past a deli cart that was offering miniature sandwiches, and while wondering just how much cash she had left in her pocket after getting breakfast at the airport, Casey's attention was suddenly drawn to a path on her right. She stared down the alleyway, which led to additional merchant tents. It appeared to darken as it went along—due to a lack of humanity and downright hope, if she had to guess.

Hate to say it, but that feels like the way to go.

As she started down the new path, the low rooftops above seemed to close in around her, blotting out more and more sunshine, perhaps trying to scare her into going back where she'd come from. The few locals she stopped to ask about the Fete mostly said they'd heard the name but didn't know exactly what or where it was, while some simply gave her a rough side-eye before moving on.

Leaning on her backpack against the corner of an ornate, brown-bricked building, Casey pressed the back of her head against the wall. Filling her chest with air and letting it out slowly, she noticed that the section of wall behind her head felt especially cold—winter cold. Stepping away, she found a plaque dusted with frost. The faded plate, having long lost the bulk of its luster, read: *Klaas Plaza. Est. 1791.*

This is it? This is it! It's gotta be here, somewhere. Suddenly giddy, she marched parallel with the plaque, starting down a brick path into yet another, somehow murkier segment of the market. No obvious reason jumped out as to why this particular section was so macabre. All she knew was that it felt like she were in some sort of live-theater haunted house version of a farmer's market. The air became denser, as though filled with invisible fog, engulfing her and making it tougher to catch a breath.

A couple passed by with shopping bags. Both were wearing sunglasses despite the day's waning light. In Leigh's notebook, she had mentioned that UnEarth Humans sometimes kept their energy raised, which in turn made their eyes glow. To cover this up and walk safely among humans, sunglasses were an easy fix. The proof was not incontrovertible, but if Casey's theory were true, that would mean she had just walked past two UnEarth Humans. *Okay . . . sort of terrifying.*

Casey pulled out her phone. Flipping through her contacts, she stopped at the number for Fabian, the Medolian. *Been saving this.*

The hefty man with a bushy beard, wearing yellow Kurdish clothing, had been excited to exchange numbers at UCL when they met following the Joseph attack. Having the personal number for a powerful (*and surprisingly polite*) creature from the spirit world was one of the only things that had kept Casey from having a nervous breakdown every time she went outside. The Medolians were strong and would be able to protect her. She could call in the cavalry, so to speak, at any time. But that was also proving to be a major temptation and mildly intoxicating. So much so, Casey had to assure herself repeatedly that the number was only to be used in emergencies. *UnEarth emergencies. Not human. Just for demons who want to eat me and my soul parts.*

But what about now? Nothing had happened yet, but that didn't mean it wouldn't.

I'm just going to get it ready, in case things go south.

She typed a message to Fabian, informing him that an emergency was taking place and exactly where she was, and put the phone in her right front pocket. A breath of relief followed.

Approaching a dead end, she searched desperately for the strangest thing she could find, but nothing stood out. As she stopped at the last two merchant tents at the end of the cul-de-sac, one on either side, their kindly owners smiled and held aloft their products, looking for a sale.

That's it?

What did she miss? There had to be some sort of secret entrance or passage—some sign. She couldn't have passed the Fete already. The stretch of market she had passed through was abnormal, sure, but not UnEarth weird.

With a ding, a small mass of people exited the general store capping the end of the cul-de-sac. All were wearing sunglasses, and many among the group had vests of varying colors, with nary a hat to be seen, just as Leigh had described UnEarth Human culture. *Bingo.* Just above them, subtly posted on the doorway, were UnEarth symbols marking Eve shades. No human—such as a building inspector—would have taken a second glance, assuming they were either graffiti or part of the already busy signage.

Pretending to look over bracelets in one of the merchant tents, Casey waited for the group to pass by. Once the coast was clear, she planned on going inside the general store to snoop around. *It's just a store. I can't get into too much trouble. They have candy bars and chips—that means it's safe. Right?*

Marching for the door, she peered through the un-postered sections of the murky windows but could see little more than a few jumbled aisles. When she stepped onto the welcome mat and took the door handle, a voice suddenly spoke from behind, stopping her hand—*and maybe my heart!*

"Michaela?"

The voice itself was not terrifying, but still unnerving due to its somewhat nurturing tone. The name was wrong, but the voice was clearly speaking to her. Casey initially resisted halting, but the possibility that such an action might get her into more trouble loomed large. Turning, she faced the mystery figure, revealing herself to be a woman in her fifties with salt-and-pepper gray hair and lively brown eyes. The black vest she wore was faded and dirty, looking like it had been torn and sewn back together many times. It was a similar story with her dark pants, but the springtime-yellow dress shirt she wore looked fresh off the rack.

"You're going the wrong way, Michaela," she said, staring at Casey with a seriousness that felt almost deadly, her tone carrying a tinge of "play along or you might die in the near future."

Casey considered correcting her, but something told her that wasn't a good idea. Instead, she stared like a lemur caught in a spotlight.

Good going, Case. Just had to go and get yourself involved, didn't you?

THE INVITATION

Perched on a narrow ledge fifty feet in the air, tucked precariously between two vertical steel slabs, Leigh felt not even a trace of terror. She hadn't for more than a year now. From this height, after a fall, she would likely suffer merely a slow and agonizing death after the splat, staring at her bones protruding from her body, taking her time left alive to imagine all the things she'd done wrong to get there. Tonight's mission could find her dead in numerous ways other than falling: shot by a security guard, crushed by a tumbling crate, or even being eaten alive by an UnEarth animal on guard duty that she hadn't spotted during her reconnaissance. Yet, for all the dangers and all that could go wrong, her heart was as still as a frozen river in the dead of a Montana winter.

It seemed that following her time with Joseph she'd lost what others might call their humanity, which meant fear was now a thing of the past. Leigh had feared bad weather at the age of six, the possibility of volcanoes at nine, and being caught smiling with her braces at thirteen. *Also, scorpions and knives.* Running away from home at sixteen, never to return until after her mother's passing, was itself an act of utter fear. Keeping her head in the sand as an archaeologist the rest of her life had been the result of something similar, digging for treasures from the past rather than looking living people in the eye today.

Her current hiding place high in the rafters of a warehouse beside a shipping dock, would have absolutely terrified her in her previous life. *One of the reasons I chose a profession that kept me below the ground, not above it.* But the fear of heights was gone, as were all others, and with them had disappeared all self-doubt. Fear was not the only emotion absent, either. Every visceral reaction and sensation—including joy and sorrow—had been wiped clean from her perception. Without them and their ridiculous, illogical decision-making, Leigh felt—in a manner of speaking—utterly free. *And never more efficient.*

She readjusted her earbuds and turned up the volume of her heavy metal until it thumped down to her shoes. Bobbing her head to the snare, she visualized everything about to happen. She knew the routes and schedules, the ins and outs. All that was needed was for the treasure to arrive.

So I can take it.

As the day grew late, her nook was draped in utter darkness. She should have been shivering; it was near five degrees Celsius in the warehouse, and the warmest piece of clothing she wore was a thin black hoodie. But the cold did not bother her—possibly thanks to the fifteen pounds of muscle she had put on in the last year. Under her hood, she wore a black baseball cap, and her shoes and socks were pro-athlete grade. *More expensive than I liked, but they seemed necessary.* In the dark expanse below were stacks of crates, pallets, polypropylene cases, and metal boxes of varying sizes, all being stored before auction. From the street, any day of the week, this rustic warehouse would have seemed like it contained nothing worth a second glance: just a Swiss commercial enterprise with good parking and ample storage. But sometimes, this perfectly normal building hosted objects whose origins were not of this world. Any facility could be prone to unknowingly storing UnEarth artifacts from time to time, but only a select few, such as this one, handled them so regularly.

Maybe because the co-owner is a Human Scythe.

The "Brincedro Brothers," as they advertised themselves, were an odd pair. One was human, while the other was a Human Scythe. Dealing in UnEarth artifacts was a huge moneymaker for the Purged, and the brothers had gotten away with it successfully for over sixty years, partly thanks to how low a profile they kept. Their overall philosophy seemed to be "don't look like you're asking for attention, and you won't receive any." This could have helped explain why their security was so lax and why they had no real working surveillance cameras, only props. Another explanation could be that the Scythe who co-owned the place was also a member of the Isleum Swarm, and the last thing an organized crime syndicate wants is a record of their comings and goings.

Information on the Swarm was scarce, but Leigh had found enough to know that dealing with them came with an ominous warning. *Makes the mob look like a bunch of baby goats tipping over in a sandbox.* The Swarm's reputation for unnecessarily violent reprisals alone ensured that no one would dare mess with them or their belongings. *No one except me, apparently.*

Another voice in Leigh replied—anesthetized, yet firm, and still very much her own.

[*Though it seems unlikely they would ever be able to track me, and the piece is being melted down tomorrow morning. We will both vanish without a trace.*]

Even considering the reputation of the Swarm, breaking into the warehouse was surprisingly easy. At four p.m., when security was at its lowest, she leaped from the storage facility next door—*the one with no security whatsoever—go figure*—and crawled to a window that had been propped open, one she'd spotted with binoculars earlier in the week. A short climb utilizing metal structures near the ceiling brought her to an impeccable hiding nook walled by slabs dotted with industrial bolts painted over so many times they looked welded on. Settling in just before security doubled for the night, she crouched down and began her vigil, which—if all went to plan—would last until nine thirty. *Five and a half hours.*

Yet another voice responded, this one closer to the derisive inflection she possessed as a teenager.

(no biggie)

Throughout the day, the warehouse crews came and went, loading and unloading, never suspecting a thief lay above them, watching from the shadows. Leigh tried to keep her mind from racing, to stay clear and in the moment, but the memories of the last year and her upcoming plans found their way in, as always. Every moment she'd spent with Joseph replayed in perpetual slow motion, drawn out as though they contained hidden messages her subconscious was trying to get her to decipher but that she was too stupid to grasp. The months she spent locked in her flat after returning home—not out of fear but of common sense—pulled on her like chains dragging trash cans full of sand behind her. *It was so much lost time. One of the things I truly despise.* As she spent weeks marinating like an old hunk of prime rib, studying and learning all she could, the history of the world as she knew it—and her very being—began to change with every new bit of information gathered about UnEarth.

The day she discovered the Roman Empire was destroyed by rebel bands from Fovos and Nashwyn fighting a proxy war was equally as horrid as a night spent in Joseph's company. And yet, news like that was merely the tip of the iceberg. UnEarth and its agents had been slithering through the shadows of mankind's history since long before *Homo sapiens* even evolved. A trusted source had even informed Leigh that the Medolians were responsible for the Hindenburg explosion and the near extinction of the panda bear. *Still a mystery, but the going theory is that pandas need to be tempered to restrict the planet's Rapture and Jubilee. In short, they are too lovable to let live.*

The juvenile responded, *(what kind of fucked-up is that?)*

For too long UnEarth had been robbing humanity of its autonomy. But Leigh would make those who committed crimes against her species sorry they did. She would right the wrongs of history and dismantle the system while finding peace and justice for what had been taken from her. With her own soul as her witness, she would make them pay. Though Joseph was now dead, along with Chloe, and couldn't suffer penance, there was a whole reality out there worthy of taking their place.

And I'm going to see it done.

UnEarth's grip was tough but not absolute. Based on what she'd seen and learned, it was possible to put a decent-sized wrench in their gears and watch the machine crumble. The only real advantage the Eve creatures had was that their people could pass freely between the different worlds and realities, whereas Leigh and all other humans were relegated to their home world. *All except for Hunter and Barker. Hope they're enjoying UnEarth jail.*

She was stuck in a battle that was seven worlds to one, and the lone participant could not even touch the others. *(talk about a fucking fair fight)* For now, at least, she would have to settle for doing the best she could to defend Earth from this side of reality. [*Which sounds quite insane when you say it out loud.*]

But I didn't say it out loud, so I'm not nuts.

[*No, of course not. Everything I have done, I did because logic dictated it.*]

Leigh nodded in the darkness.

That's the only true sanity, right? I mean, you're only sane if everything you do makes sense.

[*Precisely, which means I am the sanest of all. The everyday things normal people do make no sense in any capacity.*]

(and that's exactly why i can wage this muthafuckin' war myself)

Hundreds of renegades have waged successful solo wars over the centuries. Look at William Walker, Narciso López, and Rani Lakshmibai. Of course, most of them resorted to using soldiers eventually.

(but i won't be like them. i'm doing this shit alone)

[*Still, the renegades were only effective once they attained the right tools and the right resources.*]

Which is why I spent so many long nights perfecting my tool chest.

Many jobs in her string of burglaries over the last year were committed in order to grow Leigh's arsenal. Her first attempt—to steal a bracelet made of Jubilee-imbued metal—was a total failure. Ripping off a street merchant selling out of the back of a van proved far deadlier than anticipated, nearly getting her shot and ending her crusade before it could even begin.

Gotten a lot better at it since.

[*More efficient, as well.*]

Electronics were the easiest to pilfer, and Leigh had grown quite fond of tinkering with them. Over the months, she had perfected a custom-built, portable computer she'd designed from scratch and dubbed her Gauntlet. *One of my little projects.* What began as a portable voice box to communicate with those who didn't know sign language perpetually evolved until it became the Gauntlet she was now wearing. Built into it was a Bluetooth transceiver—a relatively new technology that acted as a replacement for cables and wires, working especially well with portable electronics, allowing her to use wireless headphones.

The current model of Gauntlet could not only speak but also included a portable toolkit and the ability to connect to the internet, interface with local electronics, scan radio frequencies for police chatter, report her biosigns and health, and print out lines of text like a label maker. It even held a fifteen-foot cartridge. After extensive practice, Leigh could now type up to forty words a minute with her right hand, either to print out or speak with the computer's codified voice. She'd even installed a touchscreen, another new technology similar to—*and objectively better than*—the groundbreaking LG Prada, a mobile phone set to debut in the summer. *They're calling it a "smartphone."*

[*A rather uninspired name, if one were to ask my opinion.*]

(*tell me about it*)

Not to be ignored, her right wrist was gilded with a bracelet adorned with many colorful charms. Appearing to be an eccentric (*and tacky if I'm honest*) piece of jewelry, each fragment had a useful function and was derived from a mineral of Eve, granting Leigh access to a host of new tools and abilities.

In her pocket she carried two Jubilee crushers, which were extremely hard to come by. Each could give her a sudden burst of speed if she needed to make a getaway, though she had never tested them on herself and did not know what the experience would be like. They were to be used only in the most severe of emergencies.

But the greatest tool she possessed—the one that she alone wielded—was the prize she had retrieved from the desert where her hell began. The Wraithian dagger, successfully recovered from Gehenna, was also wholly untested. Its serrated blade was unique in its ability to extract the Eve from the one it cut, and neither she nor anyone else knew what might happen if she absorbed a concentrated shot.

[*I believe I could handle the surge. It would not pose a problem.*]

But I'd rather not be filled with the revolting essence of UnEarth. I'm staying pure human to the very end.

[*It is the only logical thing to do. Unless my life is threatened, of course.*]

Of course.

Taking in an UnEarth creature's spirit was daunting, even to someone who'd lost their fear. Doing so could not only prove agonizing to her unprepared flesh but also stood a good chance of killing her, *stopping my mission in its tracks.* [*So . . . illogical.*] Leigh did not dare take the blade out on nights such as this, just in case she might use it on an UnEarthling on accident. As anxious as she was to reveal it, the dagger's time would come, but it wasn't now.

And it'll remain safely hidden away until that time.

Tonight was yet another attempt to bolster her toolkit. A hot-ticket item had recently popped up on the UnEarth black market and caught her eye: an ancient Germanian metal crown belonging to a conqueror in the far reaches of antiquity named Archaextrix. Unbeknownst to its original creators, the crown was naturally imbued with Rapture and considered a cursed item by the ancient peoples, who entrusted it to their king as a symbol of the responsibility they carried—never to be worn. It was set to go to auction in two days, but Leigh wasn't planning on making any bids. A hunk of Rapture-soaked metal like that could be turned into any number of useful things. *And I don't see why it shouldn't be mine.*

Presently, it was 9:14, and she didn't have to go to the bathroom yet. *(thank Christ!)*

Sitting for hours in the dark was actually quite peaceful, even while fighting off a cramp in her lower abdomen. Thankfully music helped with not only the boredom but also the pain. An assault of Rammstein, Cannibal Corpse, Slayer, and other metal staples on her "guitar gods" playlist helped her meditate and prepare. The playlist—which she hadn't updated since its initial creation as a set of burned CDs nine years before—had become her primary psyche-up agent when doing a job. *Wish there were more contemporary bands I liked. Does that mean I'm old now?*

[*No. Old is a construct.*]

The last time she'd added anything to her regular musical rotation was Slipknot's self-titled album in the summer of '99, and she was still warming up to that one. *Great energy, but they literally repeat phrases in multiple songs. Can't tell if it's lazy or genius.*

At 9:28, a wall lamp next to the ground-level door turned on. The door opened and a young man stepped through—the early one, the gofer, here to turn on the lights and open the roll-up door for the incoming truck, which soon started down the ramp, beeping in reverse just as he finished locking the chain to the wall. Passing through the door, the truck's flashing lights reached Leigh's hiding spot. *Thought this might happen.* Adjusting the bracelet on her wrist, she pinched one of the charms—a golden orb—suddenly feeling like she was packed full of static electricity. As she did, her body was rendered translucent to any and all observers.

Forgot how uncomfortable this is.

The golden orb was more than a pretty addition to her bracelet; it was an UnEarth device known as a tone, one she'd recently stolen from UCL. To the creatures of UnEarth, a tone was a household device used to temper one's Eve. When held tightly, Mallos flowed through them, providing a deep-tissue massage's level of relaxation. But when Leigh, a human, pinched one between her fingers, the Mallos that pumped through her made her form nearly invisible. She could still technically be seen and heard, but she was much more likely to be brushed off as a figment of one's imagination. Most importantly, however, she was rendered invisible to all UnEarth senses.

The added stealth came with the catch that the Mallos made her clench up as though she were being subtly electrocuted. To keep the connection and the energy flowing, she needed to continuously pinch the tone firmly with two fingers.

If I slip even a tiny bit, the connection will break.

(and then probably my ass, too. these guys don't play around)

Below, the crew opened the truck's rear door and began unloading its contents, which were taken down the aisles of stacked goods and sorted away, disappearing into the shelves that reached all the way to the ceiling. Ten minutes later, the truck was empty, and the cart movers disappeared. The driver closed the rear door and entered the cab to drive off, leaving the gofer alone to lock up, checking items off his clipboard on his way to close the roll-up door. Two minutes later, he was gone, and the warehouse returned to placid darkness.

And a one-two-three-four . . .

Leaving the metal blaring, Leigh slid over the small ledge where she stood and climbed down. Ten feet up from the ground, she leaped onto a stack of moving blankets, rolled to a stop, and waited for any possible signs she was spotted before commencing. Hurrying down the lane of crates and boxes, she kept low, her eyes scanning the numbers at the foot of the lanes, zeroing in on the crown's cubby.

As she started blindly around a corner, a pair of footfalls caught her ear. Freezing, she held her breath. The smell of cheap cologne wafted toward her. The steps grew nearer, just around the corner. *Damn. Two of them.*

There was still time if she hurried.

Reaching into her right hoodie pocket, she found a small plastic case. Opening it, she dumped out its only contents: a blue puck of Rapture ice, a device of her own creation. Rather than hit the ground, the disk bounced and wobbled before coming to a peaceful hover an inch above it, like an air hockey puck. At its center was a shallow, thumb-sized bowl. The disk sizzled and released plumes of blue mist, remaining perfectly still, as though awaiting instructions.

Removing her backpack and water bottle, Leigh quickly drizzled a few drops into the bowl, which instantly began sizzling and jittering. *Do your thing, little guy.* With a light kick, the puck zoomed down the lane without resistance. Bouncing left to right, back and forth, never actually making contact with the crates, it worked its way toward the guards, who took immediate notice, shining their flashlights on it.

Leigh pressed her back against a crate, waiting for this to work.

"Was ist das? Hat jemand in der Nähe etwas verloren?" one guard called in German.

He pulled his radio off his belt but did not use it. A handful of seconds passed during which Leigh heard only the sizzling of the puck.

So far so good.

Come on, guys, let's see some curiosity. Five, four . . .

"Dies ist ein seltsames Gerät," the other guard said with a slight chuckle, sounding amused.

Three, two. . .

Boom.

Then came the blast, sounding like the air was let out of a huge tire. *One.* Leigh stood and turned the corner. The lane was awash in blue mist, shrouding the guards, who were stuck in a frozen pose while attempting to block the blast. A thin layer of blue ice filled with coursing violet waves covered them and all nearby crates. As Leigh approached, a frigid, invasive cold ran up her legs and spine, making her teeth chatter. It also felt like the Earth's gravity had suddenly increased, and she got the strangest urge to build a house with her bare hands for the homeless man she'd seen on the street that morning. This was not the first time she'd used a Rapture disk; she'd tested them before, their compound perfected, but she still hadn't gotten used to the overwhelming effects of being near pure Eve, especially not the essence of protection, creation, and endless growth.

Stepping past the guards—whose eyes were stricken by slow motion—Leigh found her target: cubby 7A. The crown was as good as hers. Removing a gem from her bracelet, a red one with firelight within, she cracked it open over the lock before backing away. The gem, packed with a fluid form of Wrath, released bright liquid fire that ate through the metal faster than any lava. Once the lock had dripped onto the ground and formed a puddle, the crate door opened. Sifting through its contents, Leigh found a twelve-inch cube, perfect for housing the crown. Opening the black case, she found a beautiful wooden box inside, carved along every face with an intricate assortment of symbols and right-angled shapes: *Hywynite script.*

(come to mommy)

She took the box from the case and froze, as near to panic as she could currently achieve. Something was wrong. The box was too light. *Way too light.*

[*The crown of Archaextrix was said to weigh fifty-four pounds.*]

(so, what the fuck?)

Before she had a chance to check inside, a bone-chilling wail soared across the warehouse. Something living—and very deadly sounding—had let itself be known. Leigh did not recognize the roar, but the nails-on-a-chalkboard nature of it made her feel that whatever it was, it was likely Fovosian in nature. *Those tend to be deadly.*

The thing was still far away, but there wasn't much time to get out, and the box was coming with her. It was the only clue as to what was going on and what might have happened to the crown. Keeping low, Leigh dashed for the far wall from which she had originated. Her free hand fought to find its way into her pocket as she ran. The Jubilee crushers were meant for moments exactly like this. But moving made it too hard to collect one from her pocket. With no other recourse, she committed to a full sprint.

[*There were never any UnEarth animals when I checked the warehouse previously.*]

And with the crown missing, this can't be a coincidence.

[*Did someone beat me to it? That seems highly unlikely, at least.*]

Does that mean this is a setup?

[*It would explain why it was so easy to enter the building.*]

Another roar from the creature echoed, shaking the shelves surrounding her as rapid footfalls began to thump and shake the floor. It was much nearer and apparently much larger than it had sounded before. Leigh pushed herself to her max, making her fancy footwear carry its weight as she bolted back to the window wall she had used to enter the warehouse and climbed, never looking back. [*The only logical thing to do.*] Once outside, she dashed across the roof to the raised edge and leaped toward the building opposite, hearing a fading cry from the creature that was likely too big to climb after and exit the building.

Landing on the opposite roof, she charged into the darkness beside the exit stairwell and stopped to catch her breath. As she stared back at the warehouse roof, her weight centered on the balls of her feet, ready to run, she expected to hear another roar from the monster. Instead, a voice emerged from the darkness behind her, from beside a rooftop fan. A youthful, Portuguese-accented sweetness filled it.

"Can I just say . . . wow. I mean, come on! You're the whole box of bananas, aren't you?" Heavy boots clomped toward Leigh and the light. A person with androgynous features who couldn't have been older than twenty-two became clearer as they neared, with long, bright, neon hair of magenta. The newcomer's clothes, including a vest, shirt, tie, and pants—all faultlessly professional and top of the line—glowed as though dusted with UV light.

Leigh almost ran. Was this a member of the Swarm? Regardless, it was way too early in the game to start picking fights with neon strangers. Checking her bracelet, she found that the smallest gem attached to it—a particularly sensitive rock made of Grief—was not reacting. If it had been glowing, it would have meant she was in the presence of an UnEarth creature. *They're human. That's good, at least. But how did they get up here? And what do they want?* The person's body language was enigmatically relaxed, and they seemed rather curious, hoping to get closer. Sensing no immediate danger, Leigh chose to hold still and wait.

"I was watching you. And I have to say, I had a lot of fun. I don't normally say that to the people I talk to, but escaping a tolinmek on foot? Get outta here! Yeah, really enjoyed getting to see you in action. Finally." The mystery Brazilian stepped forward, their clothes subtly changing color with the shifting fabric. "I apologize—I'm not being my usual professional self. Going on and on like a cryptic merry-go-round. You'd think I would have learned that lesson by now. Mamãe, ay, look at the mess you made. My name is Pahlanksha Luga, senior director of recruitment for the Surface. It is an honor to meet you, Professor Evans." With grace and clarity, Pahlanksha signed their last words using ASL, spelling out their name in under two seconds.

[*That is a pleasant surprise.*]

(*y'know, more and more people are learning sign language all the time*)

If this person really was the head of recruitment for the Surface, that meant Leigh and her efforts were already being noticed. But it also meant that she had been under surveillance by the largest independent group of freedom fighters on Earth. *And for how long?* The Surface had been around for more than one hundred years and had a membership rumored to be in the hundreds, if not thousands. Anyone who knew anything about UnEarth knew they were the main deterrent keeping the Purged creatures on Earth in line.

(*the Coca-Cola of anti-unearth organizations*)

But what do they want with me? I never contacted them. We have completely different conflicts going on.

(*i'm serious—if they're here to stop me and my plans, i'm gonna beat this person's ass so hard*)

Leigh remained docile, revealing nothing, letting Pahlanksha begin whatever this was.

"My employer is sorry she has not been able to contact you until now. Your eighty-seven texts and messages were not ignored. Please understand, Miss Morinnean has strict instructions designed to limit her interaction with the outside world. She's quite busy, as I'm sure you know."

Leigh typed into her Gauntlet. The robot voice spoke, "Aluqa?"

Pahlanksha smiled and bowed their head. "For more than two decades I have been responsible for maintaining the health of the organization. Feeding it—plumping it—if you can imagine." *Two decades? How old is this kid?* "It is my life's passion and my avenue for growth. Our leader, Aluqa Morinnean benefits from my talents because I believe in her, as well as the cause."

Leigh's toes curled.

Aluqa? That's who's in charge of the Surface?

[*Of course. It makes perfect sense.*]

It was Aluqa who'd hired Leigh's team for the dig in Chad, then severed all contact once the door to Gehenna was opened. The entrepreneur had sent many dig crews all over the world in search of the temple, but it was Leigh's crew who won the prize of actually discovering it, hired as contractors by a now disbanded business with no paper ties to Aluqa. The woman was harder to gather intel on than even the great lords of UnEarth, despite being a public figure and face of several nonprofit charity groups. Email and snail-mail correspondence with her many businesses was a joke, and the courts were a null option for someone with Leigh's legal standing.

But if Aluqa was truly the leader of the Surface, it would add an entirely new dimension to everything she'd ever done. [*How had I never considered it before?*] Was it possible she was also a freedom fighter, trying to end UnEarth's hold on humanity? If so, did that mean her actions were also driven by logic, even if inconvenient to Leigh?

That would make them easier to understand.

(not like i could point blame)

Leigh typed into her Gauntlet, letting the computer's voice speak for her. "What does Aluqa and the Surface want with me now? She left me to die and evaded my attempts at communication."

"She was keeping her distance, but never stopped watching you. Even when you were with Joseph, we were keeping an eye on you. And before."

"Before?" Leigh signed.

"Professor Evans, my job is to scour the world looking for the next brick to add to the wall that keeps UnEarth at bay. Unfortunately, the best bricks are rarely searching for something greater to be a part of. They're fine existing as a beautiful brick by themselves in the sunshine. But a single brick could never withstand a lifetime of rain, wind, snow, and hurt. Only when part of a collective will it endure every storm."

Leigh typed into her Gauntlet. "You have nothing to offer me." Turning to walk away, she heard Pahlanksha's hefty boots clomping after her.

"Because you have the dagger? Believe me, the blade of Gehenna isn't going to be enough to accomplish what you're planning."

Leigh slowed and glanced back.

"What?" Pahlanksha asked. "You think she couldn't have gone and found it herself following the Ire? She wanted you to have it."

"Why?" Leigh signed.

"Because I recommended so, and she trusts my judgment. It was a sign of good faith to show you we trust you and hope you will do the same . . . to begin to see the light. The dagger is yours. Aluqa doesn't want it unless you'd give it up willingly."

Leigh signed, "Then tell her I said thank you," and continued leaving.

Pahlanksha clambered after her. "We can get you into UnEarth."

Leigh stopped flat and turned around gradually.

"Ooh, that's what you really want, yeah?" Pahlanksha asked. "Think I found your açúcar."

"What is this?" Leigh signed. "What do you want?"

"I don't want much these days. But you—if you want to cross the barrier, if you really want in . . . we're your only chance. And this is a one-time offer. Once you and I step off this roof, it's gone, and you'll never hear from us again."

"Why me?"

"Just look at how far you've come! I'd say you've grown quite a lot and made yourself a player, whether you want to be or not. In fact, you've done so well that Miss Morinnean has requested a private audience with you, which, I can assure you, has never happened before."

What angle could Aluqa be playing here? Why wait until now, just when things are starting to get going for me?

"What for?" Leigh signed.

"She wishes to finally meet face-to-face. I assumed you wished the same."

Of course I do! Without thinking, Leigh nodded.

"Splendid! Then we're shipshape. She'll be so happy to hear it. For now, I will bid you farewell. But before I go, would you mind checking inside the box?"

The box? Leigh had almost forgotten about it. She looked at the wooden box on the ground. Picking it up and opening it, she found a small square envelope inside along with a pen. Written on the front in delicate script was her name. Inside the envelope, she discovered a foil-lettered invitation to a preservation benefit gala hosted by Ashbury, Inc., one of Aluqa Morinnean's nonprofits.

"I can take your RSVP now," Pahlanksha said with a coy smirk.

Leigh typed into her Gauntlet. "I'll need to check my calendar. I can drop this off—just leave me your address."

Pahlanksha waved a playful, *naughty-naughty* finger. "This has been a courtesy I have never made to another recruit in the history of our organization. Make a choice, Professor, before I—and your chance to be in the same room as Miss Morinnean—disappear forever."

Leigh studied the invite for any hint of a clue, finding none.

She signed messily, "You've actually found a way to get humans into UnEarth?"

"There's only one way you're ever going to find out."

Leigh took the pen, closed her eyes, and checked the "will attend" box. After signing the invitation, she placed it back in the box and handed it to Pahlanksha.

What did I just do?

"Wonderful! I know she'll be pleased. And now . . . I believe you wanted this."

From behind their back, Pahlanksha revealed a wooden box—an exact double of the one Leigh had stolen from the warehouse. With suspicion, she took it. The weight was correct. Inside, she found a headdress made of blocky metal the color of deep ocean: the crown of Archaextrix.

When she looked up, Pahlanksha was all but gone, walking away in the shadows, their clothing and hair illuminating them like a distant carnival. "Until next time, Professor, you box of bananas . . . and welcome." Pahlanksha continued their march until they stepped right over the edge and plummeted out of sight, sending the rooftop back to earth-toned darkness.

Closing the box, Leigh climbed down from the roof and walked away, thinking about all the things she was going to ask Aluqa now that she would finally get the chance. For so long she'd hoped to force her to tell her why she had wanted weapons as powerful as the Gehenna stones in the first place. *But I won't join her little club. No matter what she says. If that's the price, it's too high.*

[Besides, it would be a waste of my time.]

(i don't play well with others, and i never have)

But . . . if she really does have a way into UnEarth, I'll listen.

[Nothing wrong with listening.]

BRICK

Bennett had been in worse jails—certainly danker and more dangerous—but never a more boring one. *If I'd been staring at a single sheet of blank paper for the past eighteen months, I would have gotten more neural stimulation.* Doing push-ups had gotten old. Tossing a ball of trash in the air had gotten old. The few people he ever saw regularly in the jail became uninteresting after the first day. The novelty of UnEarth creatures and their alien appearances had worn off long ago. The smells they secreted made him gag. They were also ugly and annoying and he hated them and they sucked.

His cell's bunk was rectangular and gray, along with his ceiling, which was also gray. The floor was like smooth, slick cement—perfect and straight as could be, and also gray. The bars of the cell, a matte perimeter enclosing him within a muted nightmare of—you guessed it—gray, were perfectly spaced, creating a square so flawless that a vector-software program would swoon. Originally built to house Celestials, the cell's walls were well over fifty feet high, featuring three platforms at different heights where the blue gemstone creatures might perch. The width was approximately thir-ty-five feet (*sometimes I do sprints*), and the bulky bed allowed him to fully stretch out and then some, though that didn't matter much when it was only as comfortable as a concrete slab.

The "bathroom" consisted of a bench and a shit bucket in the far corner. *No plumbing in the Tribunal. UnEarth folk do things the old-est-of-fashioned ways.* Privacy didn't seem a priority either, as there were no walls or curtains. Not that Bennett minded; he'd defecated in front of plenty of people before. *Not proud . . . just true.*

Apparently, the different creatures in Trivium took so many dif-ferent kinds of shits in so many different ways that it was simpler just to have workers scrape up whatever was deposited in the des-ignated areas. UnEarth society long ago figured out they might as well get something out of their collective wastes, and so the Tribu-nal began collecting and processing it into a number of new ma-terials. *Good. Recycle. Super important.* More than half of Trivium City itself had been made out of reprocessed UnEarth bio-waste. *And if that's not progress, I don't know what is.*

Even if it was just a bucket, bench, and rag, it was still the best craproom Bennett had ever been gifted while doing time. He'd even come to respect his shit bucket and, in doing so, had become slightly attached to it. His wiping rag, too, was by now considered a dear, beautiful friend. Its shade of blue reminded him of the logo for the Corpus Christi Islanders, a football team in South Texas whose games he used to attend with his dad and older brother while on vacation. *The women there, oof. Good stuff. Lots of bellies out. Very fun for a young man on a family trip. Also, one of my few fond memories of spending time with Dad.* The jail's provided wip-ing rag was also soaked in Rapture and smelled exactly like what sailing a pleasure yacht in the Arctic with the two sexiest Greek goddesses—who were also bi and always wet and naked—must have smelled like. No toilet paper had ever treated his ass with such love and care. No dookie could stand up to the rag, as they were instantly vaporized on contact—gone without a trace. Once a turd, next a cloud.

Bennett loved to play with his poop and find new ways to make it evaporate. Sometimes, his bucket would be empty at the end of the day because he'd simply "ghosted" all of its contents. Curiously, one of the stranger things about the disappearing poops was that they left a smoke trail of Eve. Turned out, they were a source of neutral Mallos. *Who knew?*

Playing with his dung was childish, but Bennett had nothing better to do and was in no short supply of it, for which he primarily blamed the food—the only thing he was not bored of. His meals in this jail were perfectly tolerable. Many items were often far too sour, salty, or plain disgusting to ingest, but there was always at least one edible item. UnEarth food—even jail-quality UnEarth food—filled him so completely that there was never any reason to finish a full serving of anything. One or two bites of glowing mush and he was set for a day, if not several. Thanks to his human physiology, he'd never been hungry during his stint.

But the real joy came on Bennett's favorite day of the week, what he called 'treat day,' when his meal tray would include an illicit item. The treats, usually little hard candies that coated every molecule of his tongue in heavenly goodness, were impossibly hard to describe. Some were buttery and smooth while others were tangy and crisp, but all glowed with colors ranging from Pacific blue to deep apple green to wheat-field gold, injecting him with so much Eve that he might as well have been on hard drugs. Stupid bliss, overwhelming serenity—Bennett had never had better trips. He'd seen jailbirds get similar treatment before, which could only mean he had friends in high places. Friends he didn't know but for some reason wanted him comfortable.

On a handful of occasions, the treats had gone missing from his tray. Bennett initially thought nothing of it, not caring enough to rat anybody out. *Didn't feel like making trouble for once.* However, when pressed by his lawyer—a creature who could sense lies—he told the truth. The suspected Celestial guard was discharged. Since then, for fifteen consecutive weeks, Bennett had not been without a treat.

If it weren't for his boredom, the last eighteen months could have been mistaken for a magical getaway on the level of a rockstar bender in the Dominican Republic. With a seemingly invisible shield of protection provided by his legal team, Bennett didn't even feel in danger when it came to the other inmates. *I should be terrified at recess. What kind of jail is this?* He'd never walked the yard with fear, and everywhere he went, the others seemed to drop their eyes in his presence, and it wasn't because he was so humbling. *They're all giant fucking monsters. Of course they're not afraid of me.* Most seemed only to be staring at the buckle on his belt.

Or my junk. Lots of people do.

It seemed the story of Hannah's belt buckle was even more infamous than the story of his and Alex's entry into UnEarth. *They all want it. I can feel it. Want to take it, but they can't. Fear and respect of Hannah keeps them from doing it.* Just seeing the way they acted in the presence of the buckle gave him a tiny glimpse of what it must have been like for her during her life. *My guess is she never liked the idea of celebrity. But she was one, whether she wanted to be or not.*

When Bennett and Alex had been paraded through Trivium upon their arrest, graffiti across the city read *"Hannah lives!,"* *"She did it for nothing,"* and more. Inmates and guards alike talked about it whenever Bennett was near. Most echoed what Loredosai, the head of the Barium Guard, said the night he arrested him: "I don't understand. What did she see in you?" To them, Bennett was lucky scum. Mentorship from Hannah seemed like a golden ticket he had been using as a bookmark.

Would she actually be ashamed to know I have her buckle? I still don't know why she tried to teach me to control my Rapture in the first place. She seemed so tired by the time I met her, like an old tree or something. He hadn't thought much about it at the time, but yes, she was in fact an angel—*superficially, at least.* He didn't deserve her time or what she'd given him. He didn't deserve the belt buckle, yet he had it, and no one was contesting. What no one else knew, however, was that Hannah had not given it to him; Izaiah had, which Bennett had always questioned.

How desperately he wanted to stop thinking about the toothless Medolian. So far during their stay in jail, the joke-attempting idiot had been silent. *Which makes no sense. Isn't he supposed to be some kind of heavy hitter? Can't he just put a stop to all this?* Every inmate said the same thing: there was no way Izaiah could be held against his will, which meant he was allowing himself to be incarcerated for reasons unknown.

If he really cared about us like he claims—if he really cared about Al—he'd get us out of here.

The majority of Bennett's stay in the cell had been spent thinking about Alex, in constant worry about what kind of place his adopted brother was in, both physically and mentally. If the rumors were true, he had been taken to a section of the Iolanze called the Weya-Vein, or "UnEarth Death Row." Apparently, even without a proper sentencing, his future had been all but spelled out. According to the stories, the Weya-Vein was a putrid place, void of light and hope, where Alex stood little chance of being treated like a human being. *Then again . . . maybe he will. If the guy gets pushed far enough, he might even become a walking Wrath monster again.* Every day Bennett expected the planet to go up in flames because some idiot looking to feel tough found a new button to push on Alex. *But could he actually become the Ire again? I mean, what else could set him off like that? It's not like there are two Melissas out there.*

Bennett had never known such unending remorse, which meant his Rapture should have been surging, but no power of Hywyn was left in him, likely because he was so furious all the time. Much like seeing an old friend and reverting to one's old ways, being in jail had taken him back to his days before he'd started living life within the confines of empathy. No matter how he tried, as the weeks turned into months and then to more than a year, he couldn't help but be wrathful. Too much annoying shit had happened. The ice had not been on his chest since his first night in Trivium. The wing scars on his back had not lit up with brilliant cobalt-blue energy. By now, he'd nearly forgotten how he'd activated the Rapture in the first place.

Presently, the time was nearing one p.m., which meant Bennett was about to have company. A rustling in the cellblock grew over the next hour, just as it always did around this time, because the average UnEarth daily schedule only contained one true "thing"— one event, one item, one appointment, or activity around which the whole day was built. These daily events were universally centered on two p.m. *It's a fantastic idea when you think about it.*

Today, Bennett would have not one but two visitors, the second being his lawyer. *He's supposed to have news. There's been movement on the trial, finally.* But before his lawyer arrived, he would be visited by his only friend in the entire jail. For this, he was genuinely excited.

At 1:15 p.m., Bennett sat cross-legged in front of his cell door.

At 1:45 he rose, so giddy he could squeal. Soon after, a shuffling approached down the hall.

It's time!

Seen through the skinny gaps between the bars, a short blue creature approached, waddling up to the cell. He appeared to be a miniature, stubby version of the High Celestials, standing around four feet tall, and a lighter shade of blue. Essentially one big slumped-over hunch, the creature's body appeared perpetually overcome by moroseness and fatigue. The simple majesty of the Celestial species appeared to have eluded his genus, even when it came to their wings. Like their larger, dominant brethren, the Psera Celestials had rigid folded wings made of blue gemstone, but unfortunately theirs looked far too tiny to fly with. *I think they're just for decoration.* A protruding stone brow above his eyes slanted down on the sides like some dramatic wailing theatre mask, fitting painfully well with how miserably the Pseras were treated by UnEarth society at large. Bennett had seen many of them both outside in Trivium and throughout the prison, and nearly every time they appeared to be doing grunt work or serving another.

Shuffling up to the outer track of the cell gate, the stout Celestial carried a bucket twice his size on his back and a ring of keys in his right hand. Unlocking the gate with a low-pitched *dong*, he entered the outer track of the cell.

"Hey, Brick, how you doing?" Brick was not his name, but Bennett had never gotten an answer when he asked for his real one, so he'd gone with the first thing that came to mind when he saw him. Brick's body would have been deadly catapult ammo, with hard angles and smooth planes—similar to a—*Brick. They get it. Moving on.*

From the outside track, Brick was able to empty out Bennett's shit bucket fluidly, like a robot, never stopping or stuttering, using hands that had likely completed the task millions of times, utilizing another near-invisible feature of the cell: a Lazy Susan that could only be operated outside the bars.

"So, what ya been up to lately? Scoopin' some Scythe shits? I bet those are nasty. I tell you, one time I took a shit so big . . ." Bennett proceeded to tell Brick about the largest shit he had ever taken for what must have been the sixtieth time. Not only was it one of his favorite stories to tell—involving the restroom of a Dayton, Ohio, Carl's Jr., a frisbee duct-taped to a feathered bang wig, and two boxes of Stouffer's Thanksgiving stuffing—he also had nothing else in common with the little guy. *And I cannot resist talking to him.*

The Celestial had tolerated his verbal diarrhea well enough so far that Bennett felt he wasn't doing any permanent damage. *If he didn't like it, he could've said something months ago.* As his more mundane and immature tales began to run dry, he'd started turning to his war stories, recounting all of his favorites, and then eventually some that he had forgotten completely, only remembering them as they began spilling from his mouth. He wasn't sure why he did it. Perhaps because he hoped war was enough of a consistency to act as a bridge between his and his shit collector's cultures. Feeling he could admit anything without being judged for it, Bennett confessed to some of his most horrid deeds, which seemed to spring free from time to time in the presence of the sad-looking Celestial. *The guy also probably doesn't understand anything I'm saying.*

"Did I ever tell you about the time we were in Fallujah, late 2002, and got pinned down?" Bennett said. "One of my last firefights. They had just taken the building across from us—used to be a dress factory or something, which we thought was secure. Turned out our local 'friend'—this guy from the area we brought along—had ratted us out. First and only time that ever happened. They're usually cool as shit. And this was two weeks before I was supposed to go home, too. The fight was nasty, but we ended up coming out of it all right. But man, I tell you . . . me and the guys . . . the anger. I mean . . . our guy, our local. He was supposed to be helping us, you know? Me and the guys, we were just so furious. Then we found him. Little shit hid around the corner in a trash can. But we . . . well, we took him to a . . . You know, you never think about stuff when you're that angry. You know, Brick? I mean, he had his reasons and didn't see us as the heroes we thought we were, but me and the guys, we . . . just had to make him see his error. You know? Had to punish him. We thought it was . . . well, no we didn't think. I don't know why, and so we . . . Because, you know, I keep that guy—the one I used to be—in now. The one who hurts people. The one covered in blood—"

Bennett had lost himself in the story so fully that he didn't realize Brick was actually facing his way, listening. *Whoa . . . seriously?* But when the story stopped, the Celestial turned and began waddling toward the exit. *Wait!* This was a breakthrough.

"Hey! You ever seen any action? Huh? Brick?" Bennett kept pace along the cell bars. "Were you in Unos? Or was that war too long ago? I get confused with UnEarth timelines. Maybe Inferius? That wasn't so long ago. Three thousand years, right? Give or take."

Come on, correct me. Say something! Brick was about to step out of the cell.

"Can't you stay a bit? Do you know any games? If not, I could teach you! You ever hear of slug bug? No . . . that wouldn't work. What about I spy?"

The empty diamond eyes of Brick in their crystal sockets stared, not blinking, before he calmly opened the outer cage to step out.

"Good talk, buddy. See you tomorrow."

As Brick was closing the door behind him, a slew of thumps filled the hallway. By now Bennett knew that sound meant his lawyer and his entourage were approaching. *They're early. Didn't know Celestials could do that.*

Stepping out of the way, Brick held the door for the towering parade. At the center was a thin Celestial protected by two bulky High Celestials on either side. Roland—Bennett's counsel, the one in the middle—was a race of Hywynite with a longer face, ears, and neck than most Celestials. His breed also featured a unique protrusion jutting from the tops of their heads. Though these appeared suspiciously like hair, they were merely a continuation of their gemstone bodies, each unique in shape. While one might appear like a woman's sixties crop top, another might, by happenstance, look as though they simply had a traffic cone sticking out of their head. *It's occasionally fucking hilarious.* The thin-limbed Faire Celestials, colored a deep royal blue, already stood an average of three feet taller than the High Celestials, and oftentimes this "hair" could add an additional two feet to their height, making their genus the tallest of all UnEarth creatures.

Roland's own head protrusion was shaped like a stylish mane one might expect on a stockbroker in the eighties with expensive shoes and suspenders attached to his slacks. But the big slicked-back curves were not naturally occurring, as Roland was one of the many UnEarth creatures who'd recently come to know the human innovation of plastic surgery. It seemed he'd gone for the deluxe package, including the complimentary horse's smile to go with it, creating what looked like a cartoon used-car salesman had a baby with a politician.

He was draped in a mess of loose-fitting purple cloth, and his many gold necklaces on his neck and rings on his fingers hung just as freely on his neck and fingers. *He looks like gangster Socrates or something—I don't know, I was bad at history.* Every step taken or movement Roland made was accentuated by the robe, billowing and flowing freely. Along with his wings, the whole package added up to a garish display, accurately heralding the bulk of the attorney's disposition.

When his entourage entered the cell, one of the High Celestials accompanying Roland bumped into Brick with their wing, sending him to the side. The shit bucket attached to him spilled over the walkway and over his head, covering the small-scale Celestial from head to toe. The taller one's wing fluttered once to remove any particles, but that was the only sign they had even sensed their smaller counterpart's presence in the slightest. Bennett's eyes narrowed. *You two just booked VIP spots on my shit list.* The three with Roland passed under the cell doorway and began to close the gate. Meanwhile Brick got to work cleaning up the mess in the hall. The gate then slammed shut, cutting him off from Bennett's vision. *Sorry, buddy.*

Now in the outer track of the cell, Roland folded his wings and assaulted Bennett with a smile through the bars. "Hunter! Babe! Applesauce! How's the flow?"

UnEarth lingo. Means 'How is your Eve flowing?' I don't get it, either.

Roland sat on the bench outside the bars and placed his bag of scrolls on a cubic table as his associates settled into a motionless vigil behind him.

"I'm doing fine, Roland. Thank you." Bennett sat down across from him, continuing to ignore the moniker "applesauce," knowing Roland didn't mean anything by it; he was just excited to have a human client and was doing his best to be accommodating. Roland had done his research on modern human speech and social decorum, and hadn't done that bad a job of it, especially compared to the way pure Celestials usually interacted with Bennett. *Buncha stuck-up dicks.* After all, it wasn't as though Roland were being paid for his services. *Sort of low on UnEarth cash. Guess I can give the guy a break.*

"Everyone treating you okay?" Roland asked. "No more treat stealing or wiggin' out?"

"No wigging. Treats have been fine. Thank you. Any word on getting some of those down to Al?"

"My clients get only the best treatment. Especially when they're innocent heroes. Like you, applesauce."

"Please stop calling me a hero."

"But you are, babe!"

Despite how much Bennett disliked him, Roland had only ever shown him admiration and affection. Smiling with his four-inch teeth every time he saw his client, he'd usually say something like, "Babe, there he is! The human who defeated Joseph, Chloe, and the Ire all in one night!" Thus began Bennett's constant struggle to remind him it wasn't he who'd stopped Joseph and Chloe, but Hannah and Alex. All he'd done was calm Alex down afterward. But no matter how many times Bennett tried, the lawyer continued to insist he was the one who'd saved them all and therefore could never be convicted. The statement was intended to make him feel better but always fell dismally flat.

"Tell me where we stand today," Bennett said.

"Really well, applesauce. Truly, completely well. This is a quick trip for me, but a good one! That's why I'm early. So sorry for that, by the way. I figured with you being human and your time being so limited, you wouldn't mind. We're on the fast track to freedom now."

"But it's already been a year and a half, and I haven't even been formally charged."

"Things are moving incredibly fast for UnEarth. Trust me, bubblegum. Never seen the public this hungry for a trial. Babe, have

I sent you astray yet? Not a chance. That's why I've won so many cases and lost so few, aka none." *He actually said aka, not A.K.A.* "You're in our world now. Things run slower than what you're used to, but I will still see you walk free, my man."

"And Alex?"

"Why do you insist on bringing him up every time I visit? Are you really *that* worried about the Ire boy? I mean, he's of Wrath—you're of Rapture. They don't mix, babe."

"His name is Alex, and I told you, I don't want freedom unless he gets it too."

"And I told you that was crazy!" Roland stroked his head extension, as though to cool himself off. With a huff, he started again. "Let's move on to the big news. The first official hearing for your case is next week. This is not the trial itself, but a precursor, only attended by counsel and judge. This will be where the official charges will be brought against the defendants and the ground rules of the trial decided."

"Ground rules? It's not being treated like every other case?"

"I have demanded your unique physiology be taken into account and the trial be hurried as much as possible. That being said, I do expect you to withstand the many hours of talking that will occur and to do so with grace. After all, you're representing those of Rapture. You must appear blameless at all times, thoroughly noble, a being that could never be garish. Gabriel likes things placid. Let us both impress him by staying as still as possible. Though I know that is hard for you sometimes. Such a fidgety bunch, humans."

"He's coming to the trial? Gabriel?"

"His advisors tell me he's taken a keen interest in your case. Rumor has it he may come to the later proceedings. Such a thing has never been done by a lord of Hywyn. They usually remain in Ayel, the Celestial citadel, wasting away their tenure on the throne, never coming down. The more inert, the more noble. Gabriel has been trying to catch up to Ki the Highest's record. Quite a somber fellow, Gabriel. I'd be truly surprised if he attended the trial, almost as surprised as if Lucifer made an appearance. Then again, we're making history here. There will be many texts about this. I'll feature prominently, I'm sure. Now, the other thing to remember about these hearings is that Judge Axios is from Fovos. That means she likes things dark and quiet. She is old and wise, and little gets past her, so don't try. Axios is the key to all this. There will be no jury, so if we win her, we win the case. Luckily, she loves me, and did I mention I've never lost? So, to reiterate: us, good guys; Judge Axios, important; Gabriel, possibly coming and changing both of our lives; you, sitting quietly and listening. Don't make too many of those human facial expressions. In fact, none—none would be great. Ariel Van-Mortus will be leading the opposition, representing the people of UnEarth, and she is a cunning adversary who could turn a drop of sweat into a sealed confession. I do, however, remain confident."

"Sounds good. Glad to have the support. Again, what happens to Alex in all this?"

Roland sighed. "Frankly, cherry cake, it's bad news. I've received word Arros has pulled all support from human Alexander Barker and given the responsibility of his counsel to a Veen proletariat, which I assure you is an insult. The Veen are helpers for the Counselors—clerks. I don't know a single one of their names, let alone any details concerning the chosen counsel of Mr. Barker."

"You're telling me there's no way he can win? No chance?" Bennett had figured something like this would happen last minute. *The Man always finds a way to screw you.*

"With this list of charges? Doubtful." Roland reached back to his entourage and was handed a scroll. "Looks like they are trying to get human Barker for seven hundred or so counts of reckless use of the Eve, more than a thousand counts of endangering UnEarth's source world, and one count of attempted creation of the Ire."

"Attempted?"

"It's never actually happened before. It's supposedly sort of an Armageddon thing, so there are no laws for completing the Ire, as we'd all be dead. Again, supposedly."

"Are you kidding?" Bennett scoffed. "This place sucks more and more. What about Joseph? Or Chloe? What about the ones who didn't come to help? Alex is the most innocent person in all of this. I mean, what about me? What am I being charged with?"

"I feel I can talk your charges down to two counts of destruction of public property."

"Look, I'm not ungrateful, but I don't deserve that. I was in this just as much as Al. In fact, I sort of pushed him into it. You gotta put something on both of us or neither of us."

"You? Breadcrumb, we don't put away heroes. The people are already quilting canvases of you. 'Human Bennett: the honorable and brave.' Hywyn wants to make you a prime example of how Rapture in action is best for all. It's an effective campaign, if I do say so. With any luck, soon you may be a free man and get to enjoy the fruits of our world."

"And Alex?"

"I would assume the death penalty."

"They can't do that!"

"They can. Frankly, it's the cleanest solution. It also gives the people what they want. If there's one thing Celestials like, it's things tidy and the people content. Of course, I'm dearly sorry for any sorrow this brings you."

"I won't accept that."

"Well . . . I . . . don't know how to respond to that. Let's worry about things when it's time to worry about them. *Hmm?* We're not Scythes after all. Don't tell anyone I said that. Oh, and before I forget." From his briefcase, he took out a glass jar the size and shape of a powder makeup kit. "These should get you to next week."

Inside the jar were translucent balls, reminding Bennett of the bright orange fish bait he'd used as a kid, but blue. He knew well by now what these little suckers, called Lyllup Dragons, did. Because of their effects, Bennett had nicknamed them Soul Spheres, after his favorite video game as a kid, *Doom*, and the energizing Easter egg power-ups hidden throughout levels. But whereas the glowing spheres in the game were the size of a basketball, Lyllup Dragons were baby-pea size and more pleasurable than any candy. If Bennett had somehow gotten a supply of these before the Rapture and Hannah, he would have wasted his life away as a junkie. *Oh, for sure. No doubt.*

To the people of Trivium, the treats were on par with a box of Skittles, but for Bennett, each pill was like zoo-grade Vicodin cut with extra-concentrated espresso, sans the jitters, panic, or heart palpitations. Their effect made him feel invincible, able to take on a horde of demons. Often, he desired to build something grand. Other times, to do nothing but clean, even if there wasn't a speck of dirt to be found. No guilt or paranoia was associated with the high. *Best I've ever had. Bar none.* Guilt *did*, however, come on after sobering up, and it always came on strong, usually the moment he remembered Alex.

Bennett thanked Roland once more, and soon the cell door was closed and he was alone, exhausted. He considered eating a Dragon to feel better but decided against it. Not tonight. He'd save his treats from now on and find a way to get them down to Alex. *It could work. Not like I haven't done it before.* If this were the Fourth Avenue jail in Phoenix, he would have passed the goods through the bathroom window and paid someone to deliver them, but here it would take more finesse. Even with his preferential treatment and powerful Celestial lawyer, he couldn't surmount the people's hatred of Alex.

Lying on his concrete bed, Bennett tried to calm down. The trial was finally here, and Roland's words—"death penalty"—hung over him like thunderheads. If there was some sort of god, he hoped that meant there was a miracle waiting to get Alex's neck out of a noose. *Maybe he'll only get life behind bars and I can visit him a lot? That wouldn't be too bad.*

Bennett lay still for a long while, never falling asleep despite his radical fatigue. He then realized it was not so much his thoughts keeping him awake but a pulse of energy nearby. Looking down, he found his belt buckle was the source. The metal oval with seven spheres across its face was faintly glowing in a pattern, and if he didn't know better, it was acting awfully as if it were trying to communicate. This was not the first time it had done so, either. Initially, Bennett figured it was reacting to the Eve floating around that he couldn't see—*like a solar flare or something*. But tonight, the glow was particularly intense, and the tone coming off the buckle was like a wet finger rolling across the rim of a crystal glass the size of a bucket.

Was it simply doing what objects do when saturated with Eve? Was it reacting to Bennett and his thoughts? Or perhaps the buckle was simply angry because it wasn't with its true owner? Bennett was sure it was calling out somehow but didn't know what it wanted or how he was supposed to respond. When he reached down to touch it, the buckle went dark just before his fingers grazed its surface.

Whoa. Spooky.

DOUBLE TROUBLE

"This way," the woman with the salt-and-pepper gray hair said, leading Casey back down the cul-de-sac from which she came. Soon they passed the cold corner plaque and made their way into the more "legitimate" section of the market. Walking farther out of the bazaar was a long and galling trek, retracing Casey's hard-earned steps. Several times she called to the gray-haired woman, but the mysterious stranger seemed not to hear her (*or pretended not to*) over the hubbub.

"Excuse me, where are we going?" Casey called. "I really do need to go to the Klaas Fete." She then stopped altogether. "Uh, ma'am. Sorry—but I'm heading back. Okay?"

The woman halted at a crosswalk. "Best we get as far away as possible before havin' the talk I think we're about to have."

"Just tell me what—"

"Uh-uh. I know your secret, darlin'. Just a little bit more silence please, for your own good. That's all I ask." When the crosswalk was clear, the woman headed toward People's Park, an expansive and lush civic space.

Casey froze. This could have been exactly what she long feared. The gray-haired woman could have been an UnEarth agent on the hunt for her and Leigh. *Maybe Leigh isn't missing at all. Maybe she was captured, and they set a trap knowing I would be looking for her?* But like it or not, following the gray-haired woman was the only path at the moment, so Casey hurried to catch up. Finally, the woman slowed down beside a tall lamppost not yet lit and an empty park bench.

"Please, take a seat," she said, still refusing to turn and face Casey, who loathed receiving orders from the back of someone's head. But she took the seat all the same.

"Nice place, isn't it?" the gray-haired woman asked. "The store you were headed into."

"Has a lived-in charm, I suppose."

"It's called the Tou-Nam-Ion. Did you know that? Owned and operated by the Tou-Nam family for generations."

"Oh, interesting."

"There's no point in playing dumb with me, dear. No one goes into that store alone unless they're an UnEarth original, which you aren't. So, why don't you tell me your story?"

"What gave me away?"

The gray-haired woman finally turned around and smiled, revealing dozens of cheerful wrinkles she'd been hiding. "A lot, to put it plainly." She sounded on the verge of laughing at Casey as though she'd brought a bikini to the North Pole. "In fact, I'd say not one thing is right. Most of all your shoes. New shoes are rare where you're trying to get. Eevees don't give a damn about shoes and often go without."

Casey was mildly insulted, but also fascinated. *Eevee? Eve creature? Hmm, good to know.*

"Sorry, luv, I know I came on strong. Just seemed you could use the help," the woman said.

Casey was unable to deny it. "I suppose so."

"Do you have any idea what you were doing? Not trying to be rude, just confirming."

"I do."

"I see, and what does Rapture mean to you?"

"Sorry, I didn't get your name," Casey said bluntly.

"That's because I didn't give it. Answer the question. Rapture, what does it mean to you?"

Casey huffed and blew away her bangs. "The shade of energy that created Hywyn."

"Good, but that one was easy. How many worlds of UnEarth are there?"

"Seven, including Trivium."

"Wrong. Eight. Never forget the Earth, the birthplace of everything, including you."

Casey felt stupid at that, but the question was also a tad sneaky on the woman's part. "Did I pass your test? Or fail?"

The woman chuckled and sat beside her on the bench. "Good enough. Scoot over." Settling in, she placed her hands on her knees, as though suddenly carefree. "Bet this is all a tad much for you, isn't it? UnEarth creatures, underground clubs and black markets—the lot. Doesn't seem fair we have to know about it. You're so young. You remind me of me, actually. Oh, the things I could've been if I hadn't been such an . . . anyways, forget it."

Casey realized her jaw was hanging and shut it.

"Bet you're wondering why I stopped you from going in," the gray-haired woman said.

"I am."

"I did it because I learned to help others out when they need it, as well as when they don't know they need it."

"You want to help me? Can you?"

"Yes. But only if you tell me what's going on, and soon. We're about to start attracting attention."

"Does that mean you're an . . . UnEarth—" Casey began, but the woman cut her off.

"No. I'm not, dear. I'm just a human who won't hurt you, born on this planet because my parents had sex. But that place, where you were trying to get to . . . no one else is."

"You've never been inside?"

"Plentya times. But only because I know how to do so safely. Sounds like your friend does too. At least I hope so, or else your search could be for nothing."

"She can handle herself," Casey said. "Too well, sometimes, in fact."

"It's not about that. Nothing goes according to plan when you're dealing with life from the afterlife. Believe me."

"Why are you saying this to me?" Casey asked.

"What makes you think your friend is in there?"

Casey saw no point in lying about that. "I found a note. She was meeting Oyel Pattel. It's the only lead I have."

"Makes sense," the gray-haired woman said. "Oyel runs an Eve gem shop, and he'll do business with whomever he can. I'll help you get in, but that's it. After today, I never met you. Fair?"

"And what are you getting in return for all this?"

"Nothing, I guess. Just dealing with what life threw at me today. There's really no need to thank me. As far as I know, I'm sending you to your death." She reached into her blouse and pulled out a golden gem on a necklace chain. From within the rock came a soft glow, like sunlight streaming through amber. "First thing you're going to need is an Eve source. To get anywhere in UnEarth, really." The woman took off the gem. "It gives the wearer a signature large enough to appear to be an Eve creature. Humans are usually close to invisible to those of UnEarth. With this, you're just . . . one of them."

Casey was instantly struck by the gem's simple grandeur. Seeing one in person for the first time was far more formidable than she'd expected. "Where did you get it?"

"All of us who infiltrate the workings of UnEarth need one."

Us? What does she mean by us? I don't do this sort of thing regularly. I'm just trying to save my friend. After that, I'm out of here. You guys, whoever you are, can go fight UnEarth all on your own.

"Make sure you find your shade and start wearing it as much as possible. Gotta get used to it. A few weeks should do it. Soon you'll be able to pop in and out of 'Eve mode,'" the woman said as though it were a joke she made at every orientation for new hires in her department. "I hardly notice mine anymore."

She cupped her hands over the gem like it were a heated stone warming them in a blizzard. "Just don't let anyone catch you with it. Here—" She held it out to Casey. "To find your friend."

"I can't accept that," Casey said. Its worth was too obvious.

"It's either that or you turn back. Your choice. But if you're caught with it, I didn't give it to you. Oh, you'll also need these." She produced a pair of black sunglasses from her pocket and handed them to Casey. "Your eyes don't glow."

With the sunglasses in her right hand, Casey slowly reached out to take the Eve gem with her left. As her fingers neared it, a crackling of static electricity stiffened the hairs on the back of her neck. Just by taking the chain, she felt it: a heavy and morose energy seeping into her being. Her knees shuddered. *I feel like I just drank six chardonnays.*

"No easy way to do it, dear," the gray-haired woman said. "Best to just put it on and get it over with. Quickly, before someone sees you with your Eve in your hands and not in your heart."

Taking the necklace chain in both hands, Casey slid the gem over her head and was taken over, body and soul, by the deepest and most pure emotions she'd ever experienced. It was as though she'd just read a thousand tragic romance novels while the thunderstorm of the century outside killed all of her millions of cats. Meanwhile, her imaginary boyfriends—twenty or so of them—had just broken up with her, all while they sliced a field of onions into purée with the sharpened bones of nice people's grandmothers. The weight dragged her mind into the pits of her deepest despair, while her spine became heavy and bent, collapsing her posture. Her lips and brow quivered, ready to release a stream of tears. The dam wall quaked. *Everything is so sad! There's no point to anything, and everything is so sad!*

The weight of the gem and the feelings railroaded her, sending Casey tumbling to the side, steadied just in time by the gray-haired woman. "Easy, dear. I know—I know. You're just going to have to fight through this first one."

Like a mother pushing her kid's bike as they rode off on training wheels, the woman urged Casey along while holding her hand. "If this must be done today, then it's going to be difficult. Accept it."

Casey nodded appreciatively while fighting a tremor in her neck. Shivers came and went. Her mind seemed to roll in and out of consciousness, and suddenly the woman, whoever she was, had left her alone on a different park bench, undone by moroseness. Casey wasn't sure where the woman had gone to or when, all she knew was she'd never felt more isolated or heavy in all her life. A wailing sadness contorted her face wildly, while thoughts of the gray-haired woman clung to her mind. *Wish I knew her name.* As much as she wanted to, Casey did not immediately go back to the bazaar. Finding a public bathroom, she hid in a stall and took off the gem long enough to gather some composure. A few times she tried to put it back on, but in each instance needed to get away from it quickly, like a bath still too hot to get into. *Or too cold.*

After a few more tries and many shed tears, she was able to put it on and leave it. Removing her shoes and stuffing them into her backpack, she started for the Klaas Fete, somewhere within the Tou-Nam-Ion general store, if the gray-haired woman was to be believed.

First out of the bathroom stall, then to the bazaar, and finally all the way back, fighting a horrid battle with her heartache the entire way, Casey entered the general store, finding it smaller inside than she'd thought, as well as more dilapidated. Only a few overhead lights were providing steady light, and just a handful more flickered intermittently. *Don't know why I expected UnEarth stuff to be more "high end." Guess that's egg on my face.* The dusty air in the shop seemed to put everything behind a hazy filter of burgundy and gold. She approached the elderly couple at the front. *Ah, you must be the Tou-Nam family. You're both so ugly! That's so sad!*

With his stare locked on the TV to his right, Mr. Tou-Nam paid no attention to Casey when she entered. The football match he was watching was tied at one with twenty minutes left. Mrs. Tou-Nam, seated in a neon-green lawn chair behind the counter, was facing the opposite direction of her husband and appeared to be watching the exact same match, but on a handheld TV she'd propped up on a lower shelf. Fanning herself with one hand and sipping an iced tea with the other, she had also not looked up when Casey entered. *I can't believe they won't pay any attention to me! Why not? Can't they see how SAD I AM?*

She cleared her throat.

"What ya needin'?" The man's white mustache wiggled as he spoke, while his eyes refused to be pulled from the screen.

"I'm so, so sorry to disturb you . . . Can you help me?" Casey asked. "Please? I'm looking for Oyel Pattel."

"Of course you are," Mr. Tou-Nam said with a banal, stock reply. "Know the password?"

Without thinking, Casey blurted out, "I do know the password," then locked down her face. *Password? Nobody said anything about a password!* She tried to think, but her brain was too inundated with sad thoughts to rifle through her memory.

I can't remember! I'm too close to bawling!

The old man chuckled and broke his gaze with the TV long enough to take a glance her way. "Oh, boy. You believed us? How long's it been since you were here? We don't have a password." He casually kicked the bottom of his wife's sandal, who chuckled enough to appease him.

"We've never seen you before, have we?" Mrs. Tou-Nam asked, gazing up at Casey through neon-pink-framed glasses.

"Not for a long time. Just like he said," Casey responded quickly.

She felt good about her delivery of the lie, but Mrs. Tou-Nam did not look convinced. This obviously meant things were going south and Casey was as good as dead. *My life was terrible! Just let it end now!* The lingering pause before the couple's response was torturous, but after sharing a brief glance, both Tou-Nams shrugged.

"Not our problem," Mrs. Tou-Nam said, waving away any responsibility and returning to the match and her iced tea.

Lifting a glass tip jar from the counter, Mr. Tou-Nam revealed two buttons embedded in the desk. Without looking away from the match, he pushed the smaller button, and with a heavy metallic clang, a cooler door in the rear of the store opened, revealing an open entryway. Casey nodded at the Tou-Nams with appreciation, but both had already moved on, likely having already forgotten she'd ever existed.

"Thank you. Have a good night."

When her comment drew a puzzled glance from Mr. Tou-Nam, Casey hightailed it for the open doorway before he changed his mind. Once she was through the threshold, a mechanism activated, and the wall section closed automatically behind her. *That's fine. I'm fine . . . No, I'm not! Nothing is fine. This is the saddest stairwell I've ever seen and I'm going to die!* Walking down the stairs beyond the door, Casey sniffed, trying to hold back the tears welling in her eyes. Many curious smells found her. There was a sour stench mixed with the electric scent of coming rain, but also concentrated age, whether from the warped wooden planks overhead or the walls made of a material she couldn't identify in the dim light. Along with the musky smells similar to an archaeology site, there was another scent she couldn't quite identify, but it triggered a memory nonetheless of being near UnEarth creatures.

Dark at first, the stairwell gradually filled with light as she neared the bottom. Reaching a landing, she stepped through the door.

Laid across a broad basement so wide she couldn't see the walls, the Klaas Fete ceiling soared twenty-feet high, supported by square pillars throughout the space. A lower-level parking garage came to mind, but instead of rigid concrete and steel, the place had a lived-in warmth about it—*almost grandparentesque.* Energy and movement filled every inch of the market, and yet there was not a single streetlamp or overhead light. The subterranean world gleamed with Eve-filled illumination from every corner, whether from the people, the buildings themselves, or the goods and products within them. Most shoppers let their eyes blaze freely with neon brilliance, while only a few continued to wear sunglasses.

At the entrance were several food carts run by UnEarth Humans with extra limbs and the occasional tentacle. The smells, which included a coppery bitterness that reminded her of the taste of blood, were so overwhelming that she had to fight not to puke her guts out. Normally, Casey would have been exhilarated and terrified to experience all this, but thanks to the Grief gem around her neck, all she could feel was terrible sorrow. *That's awful! That's worse! Think of the poor little animals in the stew!*

Something written on a passing T-shirt reminded her of her mom, and she had to fight not to cry. Luckily, that was a fight Casey had been waging most of her life. *I can do this. I can carry on. What's a little sadness?* The hardest thing to control was her jittery feet. *Keep it cool.* With her eyes on the ground in front of her, she stomped forward, determined to find Oyel Pattel without drawing any attention.

Passing a cluster of shoppers gathered around a small group of musicians, Casey spotted a short woman with wild yellow hair covering half her body. She was playing the hell out of a pair of triangles, as well as a shaker, all with her four arms. Behind her, a tall, pale man in a black vest grooved with a form of stand-up bass, larger and with thicker strings, producing notes so low they slapped at the chest and loosened the bowels. The man up front, with hairless aqua-blue skin, played a form of xylophone seemingly made from fish scales, using his main upper arms as well as a much smaller set protruding from below his chest. Each hand held two mallets, making eight in total, all playing independent parts. Adding to the beautiful, alien quality of the music, it seemed two different compositions were layered over one another, each with a unique tempo. *It could even be more. Hard to tell.*

Around the next corner came the scraping of an enormous object being pulled across the ground. Casey turned to find a mammoth sand-colored shape at least nine feet tall and round all over enter her view from behind a vendor. The rough-skinned creature was littered with fat folds. A line of purple spines ran down its back to its stout tail, which dragged behind it like a heavy bundle of knotted chain. The lumbering UnEarth creature's face looked much like a harbor seal's, looking stricken by constant sadness, thanks to their frown and puppy-dog eyes. Upon seeing them, Casey felt an instant connection, as though she'd found a long-lost best friend.

Oh my God, it's a Lostros.

This was it: Casey's first pure Eve creature in the flesh since the demons in Montana more than a year ago. The creature of Grief, who must have weighed many thousands of pounds, was walking with two large human-shaped creatures, all chatting away as they neared Casey, who tried not to blatantly stare. They each gave a smile and a nod as their paths crossed, and Casey nodded in return, trying not to cry. When they had gone, she felt even more sadness in the Lostros's absence. *I think I love them!*

She approached a large junction, the crowd and the noise thickening. Many were stopped to watch an attraction: what sounded like a cage match. The snarling and roaring of the combatants was apparent, but the crowd was too thick and frenzied to clearly see them or the ring. Distracted by the commotion, Casey stepped into a large man with a thick beard and glowing blue eyes, who stopped and looked down, gaping as though he had just found a mouse at his feet. "*Argh!* Almost missed ya. Try boosting your signal, aye?"

Something about him reminded Casey of a preformed Bennett Hunter. "I will. I'm so sorry."

Fixing her gaze back on the floor, she walked away as quickly as possible, while the man muttered under his breath, "Fucking Los-tros, can't you guys toughen up a little?"

Casey continued on from the chaos of the junction and began searching every tent for any sign of Oyel Pattel. Thankfully, the rear of the market was a much quieter shopping experience than the front, removed from the food and the fights. Many of the merchants sold jewelry, clothing, and fine rugs, while others had closed doors and guards out front. *Must be by appointment only. Maybe massages? Some of the sounds coming out of these tents would be frightening if I wasn't so sad.*

While perusing signage, Casey found a bright cyan tent with the word *"Pattel"* written in heavy yellow cursive. *This must be it.* Hurrying to the shop's entrance, she double-checked the message she'd typed for Fabian on her phone. With any luck, she'd never be forced to send it. The phone went back in her front pocket with the screen unlocked. Feeling as ready as she ever would, she stepped through the tent doorway filled with strings of beads.

The colors were the first thing to catch her eye: everywhere and shimmering—blues and oranges and fiery yellows. Blistering gems lit from within sprayed the walls with lines of color like a chapel packed with stained glass. The rocks lining the shelves came in all manner of shapes, some behind glass cases as though they were rarer or more expensive. Directly in front of Casey was the main counter. Behind this was the store's keeper, as well as additional shelves with more gems inside decorative display cases.

Emotions filled the tent the same way aromas from candles and perfumes would. Simple gold-hoarding avarice flowed through her like a memory, then giddiness, then guilt. Spurts of relief were quickly followed by moments of anger or determination. Rampant horniness showed its face for the first time in years before disappearing altogether and being replaced by severe panic. The fight to remain calm was more exhausting than either of the times she'd trained for a half-marathon.

A tall man with a droopy nose and a chin apparently too heavy to let him close his mouth, the shop's keeper wore a visage of perpetual boredom, as well as a black leather vest trimmed with silver. He leaned on the counter and spoke to the only other customer in the shop: a man Casey couldn't fully make out, but could tell was wearing dark clothing down to his feet and was quite large in the midsection.

"I don't know what to tell you. I'm dry," the shopkeeper said following a prolonged yawn.

"You can't be. We had a deal!" The mystery customer was obviously trying to stay quiet but doing a poor job controlling himself.

Rolling his eyes, the shopkeeper turned away from his conversation to motion at Casey. "Be right with you, friend. Have a look around in the meantime." He offered just enough energy to not seem irritated before returning to the mystery man, whom Casey was beginning to suspect was not a customer at all.

Using her stature to her advantage, she lowered herself to disappear among the shelves, pretending to shop while closely listening in.

"I don't have what you want," the shopkeeper said. "No one does. My suppliers are dry. Their suppliers are dry. High shade rocks are an endangered species. It's a complete mystery. I haven't seen a good-sized Rapture rock in more than half a dime."

"And you call yourself a businessman," the round mystery man grumbled. "Just give me whatever you have in the back, and I'll be on my way, never to return again."

"Those are reserved. But you're welcome to help yourself to my selection on the show floor before you go." The shopkeeper folded his hands one over another and smiled overtly.

"These? Bits for jewelry and mood stows? That's not enough and you know it!" The mystery man no longer seemed to care if an audience viewed his display.

"Then I don't have enough," the shopkeeper said. "Supply and demand. You're on Earth now, or did you forget? Buy it all or nothing, just stop wasting my time."

"You Wyst idiot. Talked yourself out of a fortune. I'll be telling my superiors about this. Who knows what might happen to your little shop then?"

"Tell your bosses! I want no part in whatever you people are doing. You've spoiled things for business owners like me, not helped us. I'm guessing what you're up to is no good at all." He lowered his voice for the next part, which Casey couldn't make out.

Whatever was said sent the mystery shopper storming toward the exit. "You'll regret thinking that!"

"Don't forget, you promised never to return!" the shopkeeper called as the man exited the shop. Casey was still unable to get a good look at him but confirmed he wore a tattered blue cloak over a dark shirt and pants, as well as gold-rimmed glasses.

"You finding everything all right over there?" the shopkeeper called to her, still out of sight below the shelves. At first, she said nothing. "I apologize for my previous customer's outburst. He will never be welcome here again. You can come out now."

Rising to her feet and stepping out from behind the aisle, Casey gave a small wave. "Hello."

"That's better, isn't it?" the shopkeeper said. "No reason to be shy. Now, what can I do for you, Miss . . ."

"Lipmayer. I'm looking for Oyel Pattel."

"Congratulations, Miss Lipmayer, you're in luck! I take it this means we're meeting each other for the first time, so before we get started, let me introduce myself and my shop. Yes, my name is

Oyel, but my friends call me Oi! Of which I have many, because I am a very friendly person. In this shop, everyone is my friend, and today I give you my promise—we will find whatever suits *your* individual needs. That's what I do. I satisfy needs. At the moment I can see you're in need of relaxing, so you can take that Grief gem off. You don't need it anymore, and I can tell it's causing you distress."

"I don't need it anymore?"

"Ain't that a shame. A humie thinking they got the best of me. Give Oyel some credit. Just because there's a secret entrance up front doesn't mean we're not on Earth. This is *your* species' planet as far as I'm concerned. I'm just a visitor here against my will. Some of us seem to forget it, but me? I'm not picky and try not to judge. I'll sell to anyone who's paying."

"I don't know what to say."

"Do you think you're the first human to try this?"

"You sell to us regularly?"

"If a curious humie is getting their first taste of UnEarth, I'm usually who they start with. Or someone like me. A handful of humans have always known about us and our world, and quite a few of them want to play along, get a taste. Doesn't do any harm, really. Besides, business is lord on this planet and an immigrant needs to adapt, yeah?"

Casey considered running away. His story seemed genuine, but then again, it could have been the perfect way to get her to incriminate herself. With a heavy sigh, and seeing no other way, she took off the gem.

Oyel held out his hand, asking her to hand it over. "Please."

She did.

"Ah yes. I remember this one well. They all sing a unique song.

This one I sold to Bree. Figures she would help you. Always was too soft."

"Actually, she didn't give me her name."

"Interesting. If she wanted to remain a mystery to you, I won't spill any of her secrets. Just be thankful she felt pity for you. Me? When I see pitiful, I get angry. Then again, with humans, they're all about pity, aren't they? Which I mean nothing personal by. In fact, you seem a mild surprise as far as sapiens go." He handed her back the gem. "I assume you need a new one so you can return this. I can already tell that you and Grief had no problem sinking into one another. That might be a good place to start. Maybe Dread, too. I could see either working."

"Grief or Dread? Could you please . . . elaborate?" Casey's eyes scanned the brilliant rocks in the case below Oyel.

"Look, it's not as easy as buying a gem and getting off scot-free into any UnEarth establishment you like," Oyel said. "Your gem should match your primary shade—the tint of the stuff you've already got inside you that you'll release when you die."

"I see. That helps explain the Eve." Casey looked at her chest as though hoping to see her own within her. "To be honest, I still don't really get it."

Oyel laughed and presented his shop. "Would you believe I personally know every gem I've ever sold? Your species doesn't understand what it's like for us Eve creatures. When we feel another's signature, we see so much more than your human emotions. We can see another's whole being, even from a distance. We feel their feelings and know their desires. Especially my species."

"What is your species? If you don't mind me asking."

"Not at all. I'm a Poa-Lo-Fey. Passion flows through my veins. In my case, I find solace among stones that sing to me. Also, in money. So, help me find the stone that sings to you, and then pay me handsomely for it. Sound like a deal?"

"I'm sorry, but I'm not in the market. Not now, at least."

"You're not here to buy? Then what do you want?"

"Information."

"I see. You're an even bigger mystery than I thought. Very well, ask away." Oyel, obviously now less interested, used the opportunity to straighten out the jars and boxes of gems within the counter display case.

"I'm looking for someone. A friend," Casey said.

"And how can I help?"

"I think she came this way. A human like me. She would not have used her real name and may have gone by 'the Professor.'"

"I haven't had many humans lately." Oyel's tone was suddenly six degrees cooler. "What did she look like?"

"She's tall, dark-skinned, curly hair. Last I saw her, she'd let it grow out."

Oyel's long nose pointed at the ground as he leaned closer to Casey. "Evans?" His upper lip began to curl.

"Yes! So she did use her real name. I can't believe it!" Casey was beaming, but Oyel was not smiling along with her.

His upper lip revealed his teeth, which reminded Casey of a whale's—spaced out and curved—while his brow clenched over his eyes. "The human Evans stole from me and almost killed a Fete custodial officer while escaping. I've had a party out for her capture ever since, but this party recently went silent. Disappeared."

Casey's gut dropped. She chuckled nervously while Oyel's charmless stare assailed her. "Wow. What are the odds we'd both be looking for the same person?" She began to back away as slowly as possible. She then heard the wet slap of a tentacle on the floor behind the counter below Oyel, along with what sounded like enormous slithering snakes. Chuckling again, she said, "I've wasted enough of your time. I'll be going." Wanting only to run and disappear into the crowd, she knew any sudden movement might set him off. *I have to play this extremely carefully.*

"I can excuse being human," Oyel said, his newfound contempt bleeding through, "but I cannot excuse what the human Evans did. She—and likely you—are treading a dangerous path going after UnEarth. You might find that's a sleeping giant you'll regret waking up. Things have been peaceful between our peoples for millennia—why do you want to ruin that?" His eyes were beginning to glow with cyan fire.

Casey's phone with Fabian's number and a message ready to send was still in her pocket, behind a barrier of cotton that might as well have been titanium. *You idiot! Why didn't you hold on to it?* Her hand made its way up her leg, ready to slide in and grab her phone. *But my pockets are impossible to get into smoothly! How am I going to do this?*

Oyel's open mouth hissed like a cobra, spraying green-tinted saliva into the air and sending a panic through her, followed by a frigid chill. They both reacted, with Casey reaching for her phone and Oyel launching over the counter, revealing that the lower half of his body was not human at all but a mess of shimmering blue tentacles. The flapping limbs propelled him like a slingshot, sending him onto her, pinning her to the wall with slimy aquamarine suction cups. Casey's thumb stabbed at the Send button on her phone in a panic as a wet tentacle wrapped around her arm and wrist, forcing her to drop her phone, unsure if the message had gone through or not.

Two more tentacles slithered over her, making six in total holding her in place. Squirming for freedom as one slid over her mouth and around her head, she tried to pull away from Oyel's loose-lipped face, which grew closer, transforming into an aquatic nightmare. A deep cyan color spread from his chest to cover the rest of his body, while his eyes drifted slowly apart toward the sides of his head. Somehow, even stranger was the smell, like car grease mixed with cheap, salty seafood.

Taking the cell phone from the ground, Oyel's tentacle delivered it to his right hand, and he chuckled dismissively. "These modern creations—such a joke. Peons will never learn how inferior all their technology is. No message could be fast enough to help you now, which is a shame. I liked you. But I cannot let atrocities against my people and place of business go unanswered. In the absence of the professor, her payment will be taken out of your hide."

Oyel's tentacle seized Casey's other wrist, and with a heavy pull, he began to drag her over the desk toward the hall behind his shop. She felt helpless, like a baby antelope being hauled away by a lioness to be feasted on under the shade of a tree. *It's been fairly nice to be alive.* As her hips passed over the counter edge and she began praying for a quick death, a bright flash lit up outside the tent. A gust of wind rushed into the Fete, blowing debris aside. Oyel froze in place when a wonderfully welcome voice shouted from outside, "Medolian Sentries! Nobody move!"

Muttering curses in an alien tongue, Casey's captor redoubled his efforts. Thanks to Fabian's arrival, she found enough strength to fight back against the Wyst and stymie his attempt to haul her away.

Casey?" Fabian called from outside, popping his turban-topped head into view just before she was taken beyond the threshold into the tent's rear section.

"I don't know why I've put up with you stupid humans for so long." Oyel's words were stained with abhorrence. "Nothing but a headache. You have no idea what you just did. No idea."

Fabian quickly spotted Oyel and Casey and moved toward the counter with both hands raised peacefully. "Hey, buddy. Oyel, right? Remember me? Didn't we—we ate lunch together, right? At the Reesu café around a thousand years ago?" His round face offered a timid smile.

Oyel had not stopped hauling Casey away but *had* slowed down, which was nice.

"Yeah, I remember. But a brunch isn't going to stop me from killing this human if you come any closer. Back off! Or her death will be on your conscience, Medolian."

"And you'll be in the Murag," Fabian said like he was speaking to a toddler in timeout.

"For a human? As if they'd send a Wyst to an Arros prison. But it'd be better than living down here, playing servant to these ignorant sapiens." Oyel's tentacles wrapped tighter around Casey, squeezing the air out of her. *Fabian . . . whatever you're going to do, do it fast!*

"Just to be doubly sure, you're saying you intend to kill that human, yes?" Fabian asked. "Because I'll have you know, I'm quite fond of her."

"If I have to," the Wyst responded.

"That'll serve the paperwork just fine." Fabian glanced over Oyel's shoulder and nodded.

The tension in Casey's body suddenly released, and Oyel's head reared back. A shocked gasp escaped his throat before he collapsed to the floor with a thud, like a sack of moldy tangerines. Sticking out of his back were four red-handled daggers. Blue-green blood began to pool on the ground around him as Galinthia stepped out of the dark. With a wave of her hand, the daggers extracted themselves from the body and flew into their sheaths on the sash draped over her.

Casey's ass cheeks instinctively clenched in her presence. She had forgotten how savage and intimidating Fabian's Wrath-tinted partner was, with her bare, muscular arms, face pierced like a pincushion, and arsenal of cutlery.

Stepping over Oyel, Galinthia addressed Casey without meeting her gaze. "Woman, peon, I remember you. Why are you here? This is a place for those not of the Earth."

Suddenly, a blast of light and wind struck, and Casey screamed, turning to see Fabian emerging from a Shift, having jumped six or so feet to join them in the hall. He approached her with arms spread wide for a hug.

"Miss Casey! You messaged me! You really did!" His broad arms enveloped her, squeezing like a grizzly bear. After eventually setting her down, he held her in place, one hand on each shoulder. "For several dimes, I've wondered what it would be like to receive an electronic transmission from a human—an electronic mailing, a real, true text. Thank you for showing me! What a joy!"

"Uh, sure. No problem. Anytime," Casey said. "Thank you for coming to my rescue."

"Make her be quiet," Galinthia said. "You told me we were traveling to eat. I didn't know we were saving your little pet from the Mandate."

"Hush now, you rude little person. We're going to eat, don't worry, but we also had the added benefit of rescuing our friend, Casey Lipmayer—five five five, two nine eight three." Fabian turned to Casey. "I apologize for my partner and her lack of manners. We both get a little agitated when peckish. Speaking of which, you're welcome to join us for a meal."

"You mean you don't want to know why you just killed that guy?"

"No!" Galinthia was sniffing the air vigorously and moving in the direction her nose indicated. "This way."

As they stepped out of Oyel's gem shop, Fabian stuck his nose into the air as well. "Mmm, right, there it is. I remember it now—that thing they've got here—Wydon rib. Blackened. Thresh sauce. Two kinds of mokie slaw. Can you smell it?"

He stopped a passerby, a stout bald man with glowing blue eyes and an orange vest covered with colorful buttons. "You there, good citizen, my name is Fabian, and I am a Medolian Sentry."

"You think I don't know that?"

"We have just conducted business on these premises. Can you please inform the custodians that a man's deceased body has been deposited inside this tent here?" He pointed at Oyel's shop. "Please tell them it was an official A-six dash four Medolian erasure and to log the proper scrolls with the IOA. They will take it from there."

"I don't have to do what you say," the man muttered. "I know my rights."

That drew a growl from Galinthia, who took a step toward the man, forcing him to back away.

"Okay, fine, sure. Yeah."

"Fantastic!" Fabian exclaimed, moving on. "Thank you for your help." He patted the man on the back with his huge paw, sending him tumbling toward Oyel's shop.

Casey couldn't help but notice the crowd beginning to gather, likely wondering why a pair of Medolians were present along with a human—and what had just happened to Oyel. A few people charged into his tent as Fabian and Galinthia began a steady march away, their business concluded. Neither seemed to pay the slightest attention to what was going on around them as they passed through the crowd, completely carefree, never noticing how the people parted or stared from the corners of their eyes, suggesting the Medolians were either revered like movie stars or hated like a rich countess strolling through a ghetto.

The growing agitation of the crowd was palpable, forcing Casey to stick close to Fabian, never leaving his or Galinthia's wake and never risking a glance back. If an attack were coming, she didn't want to know about it.

Fabian stopped at every eatery to sniff and drool, each time being pushed along by Galinthia. "No. Wydon rib. Keep moving." After passing the underground cage match, which came to a standstill to allow the Medolians to pass, they arrived at the dining patio of a red-bricked eatery. The patrons on the patio scattered, leaving their food and drinks behind. As though a buffet had just opened for their enjoyment, Fabian and Galinthia drifted about the tables, sampling bites from all the different trays and comparing notes, sometimes sharing something noteworthy.

"Mmm! It's just as I remember!" Fabian said gleefully with a messy mouthful of what looked like barbecue spareribs spilling from his lips.

From the service window of the eatery, the owner looked on as though they were a farmer watching their chickens being slaughtered by coyotes. A single tear dripped down their face. *Hope this doesn't kill their business.*

Casey couldn't believe what she was seeing. The food that the Medolians were stuffing into their faces was not only abhorrent, but its sheer volume baffled her. *Where are they putting it all?* After twenty minutes, she began to feel faint.

I need to figure out what I'm doing here. How do I get out of this?

A glance at the walkways around the patio revealed no escape route. She would be an easy catch—and an even easier meal—if she tried to go anywhere alone. Somehow, she needed to get the Medolians to leave and take her with them.

But why stop there?

A couple of powerful Eve creatures seemed like a good thing to keep around, both for protection and also because their powers might have been able to help locate Leigh. *If I can convince them to help me, maybe their "Shift" thing can find her?* When Casey last interacted with Medolians, she'd been taken through a teleportation of sorts, and the direction of the flow had been dictated by her thoughts. *Maybe if I think only of Leigh, I'll be taken directly to her?*

She needed to act fast; the trays of food on the patio were quickly emptying, and there was no telling where the Medolians might go once they finished. There was a reasonable chance they might just Shift away and leave her to fend for herself.

Approaching Fabian, she said, "Listen, I know a place with even better food than this."

The big guy stopped chewing and turned, his cheeks bulging. "Rr-lly?" He swallowed the bite. "Better than wydon? What is it? Is it mandelbren bread?"

"Nope. Even better."

"Salsheenis root?"

"Better."

"Well, now I must know! Tell me."

Casey shook her head. "I can't. It's a secret. If I say it out loud, everyone will know, and then the secret will be ruined."

Fabian wiped a mess of sauce from his mouth. "You promise? That much better?"

"I understand if you're too full to try it now—"

"No!" Fabian tossed the hunk of meat aside. "I don't know the meaning of the phrase. We'll depart for this eatery at once! Gale!" She looked up from her own meal, a gob of sauce spilling from her mouth. "We're leaving."

She slurped up the morsels and swallowed. "But I'm not done yet."

"We're moving to course number two. Miss Casey has promised something grand."

Galinthia dropped her food and stood up. "Okay."

As the Medolians descended on her, Casey started to wonder if this wasn't such a good idea. *They wouldn't harm me for lying about something as insignificant as a meal, would they?* But the looks on their faces revealed creatures somehow still in the throes of hunger. As they placed their hands on her shoulders, they locked their gray eyes onto hers.

"I trust you remember how this works?" Fabian asked.

"Yeah, I just need to think of the place and then you'll take us there."

"This meal better be all you say it will be," Galinthia grumbled.

"Here we go," Fabian said as a familiar and deeply unsettling feeling began to permeate Casey.

She tried to prepare herself for the Shift, but there was no way to truly do so. The main thing she needed to focus on was getting to Leigh, keeping a clear head, and maybe—just maybe—she would be able to bring her friend home before she got herself hurt. But when the brilliant flash of white overtook her, and she felt herself stretched like taffy, she couldn't hold onto the thought. The image of Leigh was scratched from her mind as a stretching and tearing pain coursed through her body.

Casey's thoughts scattered like dead leaves. Despite her experience directing the destination of a Shift, this was the first time she'd ever done so while wearing an Eve gem, which seemed to only increase the chaos. As the light began to fade and she felt her body re-forming, she knew something had gone wrong. When the Shift ended, she was standing on her parents' front lawn, back in Michigan, and her gut dropped to her feet.

No, I didn't. How could I have . . .

What might have been a welcome sight in any other instance brought only despair, and with nothing to do with the Eve gem.

My life and their world cannot meet. They just . . . can't. How did this happen?

She had tried to think of Leigh and only Leigh, wherever she was. All Casey wanted was to bring her home, but instead of her friend, there stood a monstrous brown building with seven bedrooms, three bathrooms, an unfinished basement, and a four-car garage. Behind the house was an industrial wood mill within a warehouse big enough to house a midsize commercial jet. Surrounding the property and mixed throughout was lush pine forest.

"What is this place?" Galinthia asked, starting toward the home. "Curious. Your mind was aflutter until touchdown. Therefore, it must be a great secret. Good! Better food I imagine."

"Wait!" Casey ran to block her path, drawing a—likely rare—stunned glance from Galinthia. "I'm sorry, but no. You can't go in there. You have to leave now, before my family—"

"Family?" Fabian sounded spirited as he sped past Casey's blockade. "Oh, I love families! Gathering for meals. Listening to one another's problems whether they want to or not. Indentured love is forever. I've always longed for such things!" He nearly made it to the porch when Casey grabbed his gray cloak and pulled as hard as she could. The Medolian halted, turning with a grave expression.

"Miss Casey! A Medolian's cloak is not to be handled in such ways. Creatures have been slaughtered for much less."

She clasped her hands together and pleaded into his gray eyes. "Please. This was a mistake. We need to leave. I didn't mean to bring you here. I was trying to find my friend."

"You attempted to deceive us?" Galinthia growled.

"She's in danger and you two are my only chance at finding her."

"Miss Casey, you should have spoken with us about such things,"

Fabian said. "We'd be happy to help you find your friend, but first, we'll taste these foods you spoke of."

"No, you don't understand, I—"

But Fabian wasn't listening. Turning to the house once more, he found a small figure standing in front of the door. Casey's nephew, Brandon, was wearing a plastic fireman helmet, gazing up at the Medolian with a slack jaw.

"Hello, little one," Fabian said. "Do you have the ability to communicate? I'm from a foreign land, and it is necessary I check. One blink for yes, two for no." He waited patiently as Brandon continued his quasi-blank stare.

"Do you like oranges?" the boy finally asked.

"Yes. I like oranges very much," Fabian said. "Do you have any?"

"No."

"Oh."

"Hey, Brandon," Casey said to her nephew. "Whatcha got there?"

He held up a toy lizard. "Spined dinosaur lizard."

"Right. Um . . . I know this is a dumb question, but is anyone else home? Maybe they left you alone on accident?"

Brandon's blank stare bounced between the newcomers.

A voice then came from the other side of the screen door. "What's this about leaving people behind?" Casey's father, Lloyd, stepped into view. Through the grime of the screen, she could make out his thick gray mustache and heavily bagged eyes, looking like a detective in a bleak noir. *Dad, what happened to you? Did I do that?*

Lloyd, wearing jeans and a heavy button-up flannel shirt, stepped onto the porch, his demeanor shifting to a defensive readiness as he studied the incoming group. "Case?"

"Yeah, it's me. Hi, Dad," she answered, her heart pounding.

"You're back from your trip?"

"Surprise! Hope you're happy to see me." She hugged him, but he returned it only halfway, his arms stiff.

"We didn't know you were coming. Had us pretty worried when we didn't hear from you . . . **again**. Did you make it to the interview?"

"Yeah, Dad. They said no this time, but maybe I'll get the next one."

"Okay, well that's something, I guess. You look tired." Lloyd's gaze lingered on her companions. "And who are these people?"

"Dad, don't be rude. This is Gale and Fabian."

"It's Galinthia. Call me Gale at your peril."

Lloyd swallowed nervously as he shook Galinthia's hand, squeaking when his knuckles popped audibly. "Nice to meet you."

"Casey was kind enough to offer us a portion or two of your legendary meals," Fabian said, enveloping Lloyd in a bear hug.

Lloyd coughed and collected himself. "That's our Casey. I'm not sure if that's such a good idea, though."

"Of course it is," a stern, smoke-charred, yet tender voice said from the door.

Everyone turned as Casey's mom, Holly, stepped onto the porch. The vibrant sweater she wore, decorated with a mountain scene of leaping deer in tall grass, flowed around her, almost three sizes too large. Her permed blonde hair, darker and grayer at the roots, framed her face, complemented by a thick shell of shimmering red lipstick. The poise and presence she carried were as reassuring as a fireplace in a winter-cabin, elating Casey when she saw her, but also bringing on a gross helping of shame with every step her mother took down the porch stairs.

Holly approached Galinthia first, who instinctively took a cautious step back. "I apologize for my husband's manners," Holly said, smiling and extending a hand. "Did I hear right? Galinthia and Fabian?"

"Uh, yes, ma'am," Fabian replied.

Galinthia took the hand and shook it firmly.

"'Course we'll feed you," Holly said. "That's what we do here." She then shook Fabian's hand, her smile wide and welcoming.

"We will find a way to return the kindness," Fabian offered.

Holly ushered them inside. "I'll hear nothing of it. It's not the first time Casey's brought home strays, and I'm sure it won't be the last. After a while, I started stocking up, hiding some goodies around the place. We've got enough, so come inside and make yourselves comfortable. I get the feeling you three have got some story to tell."

As the group followed her up the porch stairs, Casey could only watch, a growing despair knotting in her stomach, even after she'd taken off the Grief gem.

Good going, Case. You might have just killed your family.

MEAT AND GREET

Leigh's taxi crossed a short stone bridge and arrived on Slovanský ostrov, an island in the Vltava River in Prague. Almost immediately, the driver was forced to stop at a wall of red lights, now in the rear of a line of cars waiting to drop off passengers in front of Zofin Palace, an international conference venue. Seeing as the island was not much bigger across than the building that stood on it, Leigh decided to walk the rest of the way. After paying the driver and getting out, she hoofed it up the driveway.

Five steps in, she stumbled across a patch of grass, barely catching herself. *(friggin' heels)* Trying to walk in her brand-new single straps, she felt like a chicken with backward knees. Yanking her foot free, she scraped off the lawn and adjusted her hem. *(can't believe i'm doing this. i feel like an asshole in this stuff)*

[*But it was necessary to look the part.*]

Her dress was gold with purple accents, shimmering, glittery in the dark and anything but stealthy. It also did wonders for her hips, and she liked the way it showed off her shoulders. Leigh figured if she was going to be watched the whole night, might as well make it easy for Aluqa's people to find her. The dress was also technically the only one she owned, given to her by Casey when they attended a banquet hosted by a potential investor over ten years ago.

Formalwear was not her first choice of clothing to be going into a situation like this—where a group like the Surface would be involved—but it would have to do. Leigh had no idea what to anticipate from tonight. All she was carrying was a clutch purse with her ID and credit cards inside. Being without a backpack or pickax, she felt rather naked, though it helped knowing she had her Gauntlet and bracelet along.

As she moved past the driveway and into the gravel-filled plaza surrounding the palace, she took note. The six-story building was both flat sided and modest, as well as ornately detailed, subtly Neo-Renaissance at its edges, corners, and intersections, all of it laced with white fringe.

(looks like a big yellow wedding cake)

Photographers' flashbulbs lit up the front of the building as they shot the celebrities and elite making their way down a long white carpet leading to the front entrance. Leigh passed by the photo area unnoticed and stepped into a short line of guests waiting to have their names checked by a pair in black suits at the palace door. When her turn came, the pair's eyes locked onto her and seemed to smile.

"Professor Evans. Welcome. Your table has been prepared," the woman said. "You are Miss Morinnean's guest of honor. We hope you enjoy the gala. And, Professor, don't forget to take a program of the evening's events."

Leigh took the program and met the seating attendant at the doorway. After passing through a short entry room, they entered the ballroom, three stories high, dimly lit, but enlivened by crystal decorations and crisp light being thrown onto every surface like confetti. The dining area was freckled with broad round tables, which the seating attendant navigated smoothly. Leigh followed as they passed guests gathered in clusters, eating hors d'oeuvres, sipping cocktails, and chatting before the evening's main event. She didn't know why, but something about the scene reminded her of the Temple of the Beast in Gehenna, filled to the brim with Wraithians. But these were not Wraithians. These were worse: European socialites and bureaucrats.

As the attendant continued toward the front, Leigh wondered when he would finally point to a chair. Reaching the second table from the podium, he stopped and pulled out her seat. "Here we are."

Leigh thanked him with a nod and sat. After the attendant left, she studied the room for an emergency escape plan. Even though she'd done her homework on the venue, security forces, attendees, and the catering company, unfortunately she had no control over the evening's decorations or where she'd eventually be sat. Being this near to the front prohibited her from making any dynamic moves. *Good and controlled.* Worst of all, she had no information on the Surface's role in all this. The group's secrecy and lack of online presence made them extremely hard to gather intel on. Most of what she knew about them was rumors, such as the numerous undisclosed bases they had all over the world, or that their leader was supposedly a great hunter of UnEarth creatures: someone even the Celestials and Archfiend feared. If that actually turned out to be the woman Leigh would meet tonight, there were more than a few questions she wanted to ask her.

The lights soon dimmed and the presentation began. Leigh declined joining the others in applauding a man in a white suit with a blue bowtie approaching the podium, who began by welcoming everyone to the gala. The speaker then gave pertinent information such as the location of the restrooms and asked that all cell phones be turned off. Following a brief history of Zofin Palace and the island on which it was built, he laid out the course of the evening's events.

"The presentation will last forty-five minutes." *(sweet Jesus, what have i done?)* "Now, please sit back, relax, enjoy the show, and most of all, open those hearts and those wallets. Without further ado, ladies and gentlemen, allow me to introduce the woman of the evening, Aluqa Morinnean!"

Rising to their feet in riotous applause, the audience's chaos made it hard to tell which direction they were aiming their reverence, until a figure was revealed via spotlight to the left of the podium, emerging out of the fluctuating crowd. Her height was above average, skin luminous olive, and head bald and glistening. In a somewhat preposterous coincidence, her dress was strikingly similar to Leigh's, but instead, a bright silver with yellow accents.

As she traveled, her eyes locked onto Leigh, the vibrant brown in them seizing the light and glistening like copper. There was something familiar about them, or at least it seemed so. Aluqa's gaze carried a weight with it, as though burdened with innumerable secrets she wanted to release but knew she never could. A sensation then passed through the professor, as though she were meeting an opponent at a weigh-in before a title match.

Reaching the podium, Aluqa turned her attention on the audience, her face glowing. Clasping her hands, she mouthed her thanks, flashing an honest and disarming smile. Pausing to soak it up as the applause died down, she folded her hands on top of the podium and let her stare drift over the crowd as she spoke with a soft, scratchy, mesmeric voice, pulling in the ear and tickling the gut.

"Thank you—thank you. I can't tell you what that means to me. It is so wonderful to see my fellow warriors-for-change here tonight. We're gathered on this beautiful island because we all share one common vision—the preservation of our natural world, and with it, our fragile history."

A smattering of applause broke out. Aluqa went on to briefly describe the slideshows and videos to be shown. "But first, I would like to recognize a special individual who traveled a long way to be with us here tonight."

[*Oh, dear.*]

"Tonight's guest of honor is a research professor of archaeology,"

Please don't.

"Her tireless efforts have seen the collection and preservation of more than six thousand priceless artifacts and treasures of humanity's past."

(is this shit supposed to embarrass me?)

[*That is exactly what it is supposed to do.*]

Aluqa's gaze locked on Leigh again. "My fellows, I give you Professor Leigh Marie Evans." The crowd cheered. "Professor." Aluqa clapped toward her with narrow eyes, suggesting she rise. The crowd agreed.

Great. Leigh rose and waved. *This what you wanted? Happy?*

"Professor Evans's work in the world of societal preservation is incredible," Aluqa said. "If I told you even half her story, you wouldn't believe me. But trust me when I say, none of us would be here tonight if it wasn't for her. A toast to Professor Evans!"

After playing along for what she thought was a reasonable amount of time, Leigh sat down.

The applause subsided. Aluqa went on, speaking about the non-profit and the work it had accomplished to preserve Czech culture. More applause. The presentation then continued with a slideshow narrated by Aluqa. When Leigh found herself admiring the dig sites and restorations on the screen, she had to remind herself not to be taken in by the slick messaging.

Don't forget what she did. Don't forget the plan.

[*I am not here to make friends.*]

When the presentation ended, Aluqa thanked everyone for coming and wished them a pleasant evening. "Drink lots and give even more!"

The DJ then started into their set, and the room filled with movement and discussion, which turned to laughter and backs being slapped. Those in attendance moved outside, ready to begin the debauched portion of the evening. But Leigh's focus was still on the podium.

Aluqa was facing her, a frozen statue among a flurry of guests and caterers. Her expression was hard to read, living perfectly between all emotions. Seeming to move in slow motion, she approached Leigh at her table. When near, she signed with grace, "May I sit?"

"Of course," Leigh signed back.

Aluqa took the seat and spoke, her sandy voice like a cold wind whistling through a cracked window. "It's wonderful to meet the prodigious Professor Evans after all this time. We should have done this sooner. I am a fan, after all."

Leigh signed, "That why you hired me?"

Aluqa grinned subtly. "You must be mistaken. I've never hired you. You were brought here tonight for your contributions to the science of archaeology. Nothing more. Our foundation is . . . truly in your debt. However, I have many affiliates, so perhaps you happened to work for one of them? It's a small world, isn't it? I can't be blamed for—"

"I'd rather not," Leigh interrupted, using her Gauntlet's voice computer. She typed again. "I didn't come this far to be mocked."

"What did you come here for?"

"Answers."

"I'm on the search for those myself. You're better off looking on your own. Seems you've been doing a great job of it so far." Aluqa's friendly air had gone away. Leigh was now sitting across from a person whose programming had a more pragmatic sense of priorities. "A busy little beaver, aren't you?"

Leigh wouldn't let herself be sidetracked, beginning to sign, "I want to talk about—"

"I know what you want to talk about. Those conversations would have happened should I have deemed them necessary. You ought to be grateful I decided they were not. You have a chance to be free of all of it, to live the life you've always wanted. There's no reason to step into the darkness. You'll find only horrors there. You, my wondrous friend, have the chance to break down barriers here, in what they call the real world. A mute, mixed-race archaeologist who found international greatness at the top of her field? Now that . . . sounds like history being made. That is someone I could not have gone a lifetime without meeting."

Leigh signed, "You baited me here. Now I want to know if you can actually do what you said you can."

"I never said a thing. I do what I do out in the open. There are no secrets with me. But if you want to know the deep truths of the Earth—the things that will take you to the bottom of the well— then you will need to work for it, as did all who brought about real change. You would have to dig harder than you ever have before. I'm not so sure that's what you're looking for."

(this bitch is trying to get under my skin)

[Or more appropriately, into my head.]

(but . . . i don't tolerate that kind of bullshit. don't care who you are)

Leigh scanned the room and party guests. She typed, "How many here are yours?"

"The majority are mine in some fashion," Aluqa answered. "My threads run long and deep. Helps keep things in perspective for all involved when the pyramid has only a single stone on top. Why do you ask? Planning on doing something audacious?" She waved to a passerby with her political smile before rejoining her conversation with Leigh, the robotic expression returned. "You know, I meant every word I said up there. I admire you and your work. So much so, I want to help you in any way I can."

Leigh typed, "Then work with me. We both want the same thing."

"You seem to misunderstand. I don't work with others. They work for me. Speaking of . . ." Aluqa motioned to one of her staff keeping watch from a distance. They hurried over and handed her a small black pouch. Inside was a pen and checkbook. "I would be honored to help fund your next dig. No need to thank me, it's the least I can do for Professor Evans. Now, who should I make this out to? Possibly your company? Or Miss Lipmayer? How is she, by the way?"

"You've got to be joking," Leigh signed, wondering what the hell was going on.

"Of course, silly me, it goes to you." Aluqa began writing the check, her eyes glued to the pad. "Now let's talk business-business, how much do you want?"

"Do you think I want your money?"

"You drive a hard bargain. Very well, I'll only go as high as five million." Aluqa finished scribbling, tore the check out of the book, and set it on the table, face down. "Think of it as an apology." With her finger pressed into the slip, she leaned forward just enough to pull in Leigh's gaze to meet her own. "An apology for all the time you spent waiting for this meeting."

This can't be why she brought me here. There has to be more to it.

Before she had a chance to tell Aluqa where she should stick the piece of paper, Aluqa said softly, "Think . . . before you say anything. I'm going to leave this here and we're going to talk. I advise you not to make a decision about the money yet. Now"—she put the candleholder on top of the check and leaned back with a playful smile—"tell me about your parents."

"Why?" Leigh signed.

"Because I want to know you. I want to see beyond the vengeful professor out to settle a score. That character bores me. I want to hear about the little girl who ran away from a loving home. A failing mother and a distant father? Mmm, classic. Our relationship with our parents makes us, doesn't it? What relationship is more important?" The politician smile was back along with Aluqa's scratchy, tickling voice. "Tell me how you became you."

"Sounds like you already know it all," Leigh signed.

"I want to hear it from you. Whether from your own hands or by that machine you've created on your wrist, which I must say is very clever. You seem to have a handle for all things cutting edge."

"Thank you."

Leigh started into what was supposed to be a brief story about her parents, signing the words, as it was easier for long-winded discussion. She described her father as a free spirit, at least in early life, and an artist from limited means. Her mother was the opposite, a devout evangelical bookworm and daughter of a career politician who ran away to a foreign land looking for adventure.

Aluqa stopped her. "No, I know all that. Tell me what they meant to you."

Leigh hesitated before letting loose. "My father was an ass. A selfish man. My mother? I feel like I didn't know her. Either of them. They loved music and God, usually more than me. It's what got them together. But they didn't love each other. What cemented their relationship was me. I wasn't planned and they never wanted more than one. When my mother was diagnosed with MS, our home divided. Dad fell further away from his trust in God, and Mom gave herself over to her faith in a desperate bid to foster a miracle. I left shortly before my mother's death, and my relationship with my father has been nonexistent ever since."

"And now he's cleaned up and moved on to become a successful community planner," Aluqa interrupted again. "I suspect more a business partner to you than a father at this point, yes? Connected superficially by blood and law."

Leigh didn't like this. Aluqa was overpowering her. She had to push back. She signed, "I'd ask about your parents, if the stories are true, but I'm not sure I'd get a truthful answer."

Aluqa paused, then chuckled like a kid caught in a lie. "There aren't many I share myself with. Aren't many I trust in the first place. This world is a cold and unforgiving one, child. I advise all I meet to take the path of least resistance. Save yourself in this life and enjoy what you can before it's gone."

"You don't really believe any of that," Leigh signed.

"Just because I tell others to do something doesn't mean I'll necessarily do it myself." Aluqa lifted the candle off the check and slid it the rest of the way across the table. "I hope you kept an open mind." Her tone made it clear she was about to stand up and walk away.

"I want to go someplace private and talk," Leigh signed, keeping the desperation out of her hand movements.

"This was our talk. Tonight is all the time you and I will ever have, as much as I hate to say it. I really meant it when I said I'm a fan." Aluqa checked her watch. "And it looks as though that time is up." She rose and extended a hand.

Wait, we can't be done!

[*I still do not know if she can really get humans into UnEarth or not.*]

When Leigh took the hand, Aluqa gripped hers with a stone grip, cracking some knuckles, and turned her arm, studying the bracelet on her right wrist. "Fascinating." Her unblinking gaze remained fixed on the gems for several overwrought moments before she released Leigh's hand, seemingly satisfied. "Tonight was my pleasure. Take care of yourself, Professor."

Before Leigh could type or sign anything in response, Aluqa was turned around, headed toward the darkened rear of the room and her waiting staff. Leigh watched her leave, for the first time in a long while not knowing what the next move was.

(was that how i wanted it to go?)

The check was on the table, ink still fresh. With the money, her solo operation could be funded for years: an option she'd never even considered. Aluqa and the Surface would not be a problem. Her own plans could continue unabated.

[*It is one of the best possible outcomes. I largely get away with everything I desired.*]

Yeah . . . mostly . . . but not the big thing. Not the thing I'm really after.

[*It is highly likely that if Aluqa has uncovered the secrets to entering UnEarth, she would not share it with an outside party so easily. Doing so would prove a poor stratagem.*]

Of course! Then the Surface would lose any advantage it had.

[*Only those in Aluqa's organization will ever be close enough to utilize the technology. Only those who plead loyalty.*]

But I can't join them. I won't! I need to do this on my own. There's no other way.

[And yet, it is being proven again and again how difficult a solo excursion will be.]

I can't swear fealty to another, though.

[Even if they are the genuine article?]

Leigh watched Aluqa. There was no doubt a captivation about her that pulled on the professor's curiosity. *(does she really hunt unearth creatures?)* No one Leigh had ever met had seemed quite as impressive in so short an amount of time. *Just on handshake alone.* Nobody had ever stumped her so resolutely in a dialogue. No one had ever presented themself as such an obvious authority of not only their own lives, but also those around them. Aluqa seemed a towering ship that had come out of the darkness in a storm, ropes and buoys to grab on to and be pulled to security and safety in abundance.

Taking the check, Leigh found it was made out for ten million—double.

I don't know what to do.

The rigid voice responded quickly. [*I think the choice is obvious.*]

Balling the slip up in her fist, she tossed it toward Aluqa. The ball sailed over her bald head and landed on the ground a few feet in front of her. Leigh's attack revealed two nearby secret guards, who reached into their jackets for weapons. Once the danger had passed, they returned to their roles as party patrons. Aluqa picked up the balled-up check and faced Leigh. The political smile was back. "Not enough?"

Cautiously, Leigh moved to meet her, signing, "Fine. I'll play your game. I'm in."

"Game? I thought you were smart. If you think uttering such a word is a sound idea, you may wish to think harder. In fact, I ought to just leave you here in the mud with nothing, where I found you."

"You already did. And now I'm here. Here. Your fault, by the way. So, what's it going to be?"

Aluqa's face contorted into a sharp, shaking mess, as though about to explode, until she relaxed and let out a bellowing laugh. "I knew I had good taste. Even without a voice it seems you can talk your way out of anything. Or into it. But I mean it when I say this isn't something to play with. This . . . this thing that you're asking for . . . it will be different. It is something you can never talk your way out of. Your world will be left behind and you will be assimilated into the fabric of the greatest conflict our species has ever been a part of, yet never known about. Once you are inside, I will not be able to help you, no matter how much I may want to. You will either rise, or fade."

"I've gotten this far on my own."

"Professor, if you take this next step, you will never be alone again for the rest of your life. Not for one second. Like I said, your world will be left behind."

Leigh nodded.

"Once made, the choice cannot be unmade."

Leigh typed into her computer. "Made."

Aluqa softly closed her eyes and smiled, as though savoring pure satisfaction pouring through her veins. "I knew you were the one. I always did. This way. Time to follow."

Into the rear recesses of the palace, Leigh walked a few steps behind Aluqa as she commanded her way through the darkness. The farther they went the more guards joined the parade. No one spoke. A tight corridor, large bodies in suits, and the sound of shoes on tile surrounded Leigh. It wasn't clear where they were going, only that she should just walk and not ask questions.

"What a mixture of shades you must have built up over your life." Aluqa's voice echoed in the hall. "You'll add a hardy mix to the Eve, I'm sure."

Was that sarcasm?

[*I believe it was a compliment.*]

"Sometimes I think it's a shame we can't just shut down our feelings and stop giving life to that wretched world which oppresses us. Wouldn't that be divine?" Aluqa said.

Leigh typed into her Gauntlet. "Joseph said I had Fervor, Dread, and Wrath."

"Dear, if I may suggest something . . . fuck every word that lowly Archfiend ever said to you." Aluqa reached a door at the end of the hall below an exit sign. "You are a creature superior to that coward in every sense. Never forget it."

Leigh hadn't thought about Joseph in that way in more than a year, as though she'd forgotten how to hate him. Lately, the nameless demon had been more a subject for mental dissection and analysis than that which she loathed like nothing else. *(you're right. fuck that sniveling little shit)*

Stepping outside, they viewed the rear car park of the palace, where three black SUVs waited. Aluqa and Leigh walked toward the car in the front of the line. "I sent out hundreds of missions, you know? Looking for Gehenna," Aluqa said. "Chad was only one of a thousand possibilities. If it hadn't been you, it would have been another. But I know you'll believe me when I tell you that I had no idea about the nameless demon. I would never have put anyone in a situation like that knowingly. Especially you."

Leigh wondered if Aluqa would be willing to put someone in a "Joseph situation" if they had agreed to it first. As they approached the SUV, Aluqa opened the rear passenger door. Leigh sat down, ready to slide over, but the door was shut behind her.

"You're not coming?" she signed through the open window.

"I'll be right behind you." Aluqa tapped the car door and started back into the palace.

It was only when the SUV drove off that Leigh noticed the three security guards in the back with her, so silent and darkly dressed they seemed to blend in, one with the car. She checked her bracelet. The little Grief gem was not glowing.

All human. Good.

The drive lasted half an hour. Even if she weren't mute, Leigh would not have tried to make conversation, wondering what she'd just gotten herself into for the duration of the trek. They were soon arriving at a warehouse in an industrial zone. With the car windows tinted nearly black and the driving as smooth as a standing escalator, she'd gathered no idea of the direction they'd headed. *Thirty minutes from the palace in any direction . . . Not too narrow a field. If I get out of this alive, I'll have to add a GPS system to my Gauntlet.* The SUV parked at the front of a large orange warehouse with white lettering. The guards in the back seat did not move or say anything upon arrival, so Leigh wasn't sure when it was okay to move. For thirty seconds she sat, debating what to do, when the door finally opened and a familiar Brazilian face decorated with thick-rimmed glasses poked their head inside. Pahlanksha's long hair had been recolored into a bright springtime green.

"Professor, so glad to see you made the right choice," they said with the warmth of a restaurant host. "If you'll just come with me now, we'll begin your initiation, or as I like to call it, sampling of punch."

Leigh stepped out of the car and looked around. The Dickensian bleakness of the warehouse and industrial zone countered wonderfully with Pahlanksha's softly glowing multicolored three-piece suit.

"The festivities will be inside," they said. "I'm afraid we're a little ahead of schedule and may have to wait. This way." Turning, they marched into the warehouse.

Leigh followed them through a large doorway. The interior was dark and smelled horribly like old eggs and rotten grass. Pahlank-sha chuckled. "Apologies for the unpleasant stench. It's quite horrid, isn't it? Reminds me of my mother's moqueca baiana, but I didn't say that. Someone who was standing right here must have said it and run off. I would never badmouth my mother's subpar cooking like that. She taught me too well. This is why I try to make the opening ceremony for all new recruits as pleasant an experience as possible. But, of course, some things we can't control. And certain orifices we can't close. Don't worry, though, we won't be here long."

Passing into another hall, Leigh took a glance at her Grief gem. Still no sign of Eve. *(no creatures hiding to eat me. i like that)* They entered an open area. The outskirts of the room were filled with heavy-duty landscaping machinery. At the center of the room, below a skylight, were two empty folding chairs facing one another.

"I assume one of those is for me," Leigh signed.

"Just as bright as they all say," Pahlanksha signed back, then said, "First, a little business. Part of my duty as the head of recruitment for the Surface is to inform newcomers that all of their financial assets have been immediately seized and are ours now and forever, goodbye. The organization thanks you for your contribution."

Leigh had not anticipated that, but now felt foolish for it.

"And that's the conclusion of the business portion of the evening." Pahlanksha released a surprising giggle.

Walking past the first chair, Leigh stood near the one facing the entrance. She signed, "I'll stand until the meeting begins."

But her words were squashed by a booming voice from the shadows engulfing the room. "SIT." The word was a wave of force, an all-encompassing presence, yet flowed over her as though no vibrations occurred along with it. Leigh sat down, feeling suddenly so cold she might shiver, searching for the source, but no one was in sight.

"That's the Cardinal," Pahlanksha said, generally unaffected and typing in their phone. "He likes to watch. Make sure everything is in order, which is ridiculous because," they shouted at the darkness, "*I'm* here! The one who should be. And he isn't!"

Watch? So that came from a speaker somewhere? But it felt like whoever that was . . .

[*Was right beside me.*]

Trying to solve that puzzle made Leigh's mind as wobbly as the chair underneath her. Her memory contained nothing on the name Cardinal, which was cause for alarm. Until now, she'd been working under the assumption she'd done her due diligence.

Not such a great start, all things considered.

Pahlanksha's phone dinged. "Oh, one moment." They disappeared out the entrance, and Leigh was left alone with the darkness—no real surroundings to study, no escape plans, no data. *(seat of the pants. wish i was wearing some)*

For three minutes she sat in silence with no idea what was going to happen, expecting the booming voice of the Cardinal, whoever or whatever he was, to rise again and chastise her. When Leigh's ears began to get their first hint of commotion outside, her eyes were drawn to her wrist. The Grief gem was beginning to show signs of life.

From outside there came many sounds: SUVs pulling up aggressively and car doors opening and slamming. Pahlanksha's was the only voice to be heard among hushed footfalls, which grew louder toward the entrance hall. As the other voices drew near, the Grief gem on Leigh's bracelet burned brighter. Through the doorway there came movement. The first to enter were two average guards in dark suits. Next was a tall man in torn, messed clothes, possibly once a three-piece suit, now smeared with sizzling green blood. His arms were tied behind his back, and a black bag was over his head.

The one leading him into the warehouse was a woman wearing a thick-strapped dress that showed off her comically large shoulders and triceps. Leigh recognized her as Sophia Skraga, whose name was well known and respected among UnEarth enthusiasts. For many years, Skraga had fought a solo war against UnEarth, much the same as Leigh hoped to, her greatest success being the take-down of an underground UnEarth nightclub via nothing more than a phone call to the state-level police, who were the least likely to be corrupted by UnEarth.

Included among her posts on UnEarth forums were pictures of the author: a woman unsure of her place in the world, with a delicate build and sunken cheeks. But the woman escorting the supposed prisoner into the warehouse looked like she could have rolled a boulder up a mountain and would have been notable marching in a parade beside major heavyweight wrestlers. Leigh had seen medical records confirming Skraga was a regular human, born in Auckland, but her current appearance seemed to confirm the rumors that she had undergone some sort of transformation at the hands of Aluqa, which boded well for the possibility that the leader of the Surface had actually found a way into UnEarth.

With a seesawing bounce in her shoulders, Skraga led the bound man toward Leigh and the chairs in the middle of the room. "This her?" she asked with a heavy Kiwi accent.

Leigh remained sitting, watching with no expression whatsoever.

"Hey! Professor!" Skraga pointed and shouted with the unex-pected energy of a bleach-blonde Malibu surfer. "Good to finally meet you. Heard lots about you. Here—welcome present." She dumped the bound and hooded man into the chair opposite Leigh. The Grief gem was fully glowing now.

Drifting back and forth at first, his head finally slumped to the side and he went practically still—alive, but barely conscious. A soft sizzling could be heard as smoke drifted up from his wounds and the green blood slowly dissolved his clothes. Only one kind of UnEarth creature's blood could eat through material like this, like sulfuric acid, which meant the man must have been a Human Archfiend. The scene was enough to set off every internal alarm Leigh had. Things were headed nowhere logical fast.

At the entrance, Aluqa appeared, marching with lively steps. A smile was fighting to cement itself onto her face. "My dear professor, that took much longer than I thought it would. My most sincere apologies. Oof! I do feel out of practice, occasionally."

Skraga steadied the unconscious man before stepping away and letting Aluqa take over, putting her hand on his shoulder and gripping it like a vise.

"What is this?" Leigh signed at her.

"You know exactly what this is," Aluqa said. "You've made a request. Same as many. But unfortunately, the first lesson is . . . you don't get what you want. No one does. I can't give you anything other than a purpose, if you choose it."

Leigh remained stoic. Aluqa continued, "Those who find out what it takes—those who realize that they must lose that which they hold dear in order to do anything of worth—that is we. No single cell ever created or ended life on its own. No single creature ever transformed their environment. It is only through collective strength that real change can occur."

"I understand."

"To join the Surface means giving up everything you want. No personal battles or individual trials. These are now shared. With this comes responsibility, and trust. All who work with me trust me explicitly. So, tell me, can you be ears to only one, and neglect all other voices?"

Aluqa motioned to the darkness. Pahlanksha stepped out of the shadows and handed her a knife that she regarded with playful abandon, like a child's toy: fun, but expendable. Taking it by the tip, she then handed it to Leigh. The blade was six inches long and curved, with a cheap handle made of black acrylic, scratched top to bottom, producing rough, jagged lines that stuck painfully into her hand if gripped too hard.

"Our organization requires a level of commitment that cannot be faked," Aluqa said. "We need to know how truly you believe in our cause."

Leigh stood and approached the man in the chair, the knife loose in her grasp. The dull blade refused to gleam in the darkness.

She typed into her Gauntlet, "Who is this?"

"It doesn't matter."

"He is an UnEarth creature. Could matter a great deal."

"He is your enemy. You want to help Earth, yes? Humanity? To preserve our way of life? There is a war coming, and we need to take every advantage and gain every foothold." Aluqa approached Leigh and stood just to her left. "To do anything less would mean human lives lost." A gentle hand was placed on her shoulder. "In addition, it is I who is asking."

Is it really down to this? Am I actually going to kill for the cause? I know I've thought about it, but . . .

[*What kind of war did I expect to fight, if not one where people die?*]
It's true, but to stare at it . . . it's a leap I haven't taken yet.

The Human Archfiend in front of her groaned. She typed, "Is he guilty of a crime?"

"The man is a demon from Hell. He was born a crime."

Leigh did not want to kill him, Archfiend or no, though she had no real reason not to. Falling to the floor, her gaze stayed there, fixed. There were no options. Her tricks and tools offered no help.

Likely sensing trepidation, Aluqa slowly stalked around the chair. "When I was a child, a horror forced its way into my village, and into my life—a creature of the darkness that consumed only at night. Many were killed. We would not have survived another year. It was too big, too fast, they said, hunting any who ventured alone into the woods. Legs rising into the sky and a mouth split up the middle. Able to eat anything smaller than a child whole. Our village was doomed . . . until one day, a little girl went in pursuit of the creature. No longer the hunted. The hunter climbed a tree and waited for a sign, not eating, not sleeping until she saw it. The creature was there, stalking through the vegetation below.

"Knowing this was her chance, the little girl pulled from her bag a shard of broken bowl. This was a very special bowl, given to her by her poor grandmother. The little girl believed in the shard, and so believed in herself when she held it. Amazing thing—faith—and the strength it provides. The beast never expected to be attacked from above, and when the girl leaped and plunged the shard into its body, she killed it, saving the village. That creature was an Aidaas of Fovos. An invader in our world. The first of many."

"So, it is true?" Leigh signed.

"Everything they say about me is true, even the bad things. Maybe especially. But a long time ago, I began putting the creatures invading our world into the ground and I've been doing it successfully ever since. This man will expire, as all things do. Remember, a single life does not matter, only what it can help accomplish. Make your life mean something. Make a choice. Take a side."

That all made sense, but reason was still hard to find in the act of murder. Leigh had no desire to take life. *(human life that is . . . and he's no human)* Perhaps that was it, the required ammo that could persuade her to do it. *He's a demon. And this guy was chosen for a specific reason, right?*

[*She would not ask me to kill a random person. He must have done something truly wicked to end up like this.*]

There's no way he's making it past tonight. He's dying no matter what I do. And if I don't kill him . . . I'll be the next one sitting in the chair.

It was true, and all the proof she would need. In order to push forward, this was the price.

[*I told myself this was coming. I knew it would eventually get this far.*]

But I never thought I would do it because someone else told me to.

Fear wasn't a factor, but her logic circuits were fighting her feet as they stepped toward the chair. The man then groaned, starting to wake, but Leigh didn't want to hear his voice or words. She no longer wanted to know anything about him or why he was chosen. In this situation, only ignorance could bring bliss.

Feeling Aluqa's gaze on her, she gripped the handle and took a handful of the black bag and the shaggy hair underneath it. Forcing the man's head down, she put the knife under his neck. *Forgive me, Mom.* In a swift motion, she drew it across his flesh, trying to tear as much as possible. The blade was too dull to give a clean cut, so being thorough seemed best. The sooner he bled out, the better.

When the knife lifted away, the man released a short gasp, enough to hint what he might have sounded like. But it was quickly replaced by the sound of someone choking on their own blood, legs kicking and head quaking side to side. The display lasted for more than four minutes before he stilled, and it was all over. A pool of dark green blood forming around the chair sizzled as it slowly ate away the floor and everything it touched.

Leigh stared for what felt like a long while, watching the overhead lights mold and bubble in the expanding puddle. *There. It's done. No more emergency exit.*

Suddenly, Aluqa was beside her, slowly taking the knife from her hand, its blade dissolving from the Archfiend's blood. "Well done." A comforting hand was laid on Leigh's shoulder. "How do you feel?"

Feel? No, I . . . don't. Something was happening. Leigh couldn't be sure. Her thoughts were lost. Were these emotions coming back? Perhaps hints of panic? Then she figured it out. The hint was the faint call of an emotion she'd long forgotten: satisfaction.

Aluqa's eyes, now appearing somehow more honest and open, and seeming to have shifted to a brighter shade of brown, found her. "Welcome to the Surface, member two three two four."

Leigh nodded as a warmth spread in her belly.

Turning away from Leigh to face the darkness, Aluqa asked, "What do you think?"

The booming voice of the unknown Cardinal responded from the shadows of every corner, a low canyon resonance. "Agreed. Ready. This is she."

DRINKS & PRELIMINARIES

The noise and commotion of the outside world were all but silenced within the sleek, silver-and-blue interior of the BAT train car, which glided so smoothly that Mara often forgot she was on a moving platform. *Perfect. As designed.* Her gaze was fixed on the window as she awaited her favorite part of the route. Soon, the track inclined, and—like a curtain being pulled away—the tunnel vanished, revealing the glistening Trivium skyline. *There you are.* The city turned like a monstrous carousel as they raced toward the broken Tribunal at its center, still magnificent despite its recent maiming at the hands of the nameless demon. The Pilomine Mountains loomed behind it, bathed in sunlight and the glow of Doloros. As Mara tried to soak in the view, a cynical scoff from the man beside her—whom she was handcuffed to—cut into the moment.

Her prisoner fidgeted, tugging on her arm. "I can sense you enjoying the view—ugh, that even tasted gauche coming out of my mouth."

Nigel Roe's nose was tilted at a high angle as he scrutinized the city he couldn't see. The towering man's bone-thin frame swam in an ensemble of khaki shorts and a T-shirt—something Mara would expect a human from Jacksonville, USA, to wear, not a haughty Fovosian who considered himself a beloved dignitary and political warrior of his people.

"Such a drab color, if memory serves," he continued. "The peaks of the Pilomines all look the same. Nobody will admit it, though. I may be blind, but their Eve signature is as boring an assortment of shapes one could ever hope to assemble. It's a wonder people live here at all."

Wanted for questioning in the Joseph Mandate depositions, Roe had not responded to the Tribunal's hails for more than a thousand days, prompting the Sentry Force to collect him. It was common knowledge he was hiding at Madam Daphne's fortress, where no Medolian could enter safely without express permission—something that had never been granted. But in a twist of fate, for the first time in six hundred years, the madam responded to a message, informing the Tribunal that he had been banished from her club and to stop bothering her. She also mentioned the Scythe had last been seen heading for South America, narrowing the search considerably.

Though a younger Sentry could have handled the task just fine, ever since Mara had taken over as Warden, every mandate passed down by the Tribunal had been accomplished by her, solo, as perfectly and promptly as possible. *Two hundred ninety-eight, so far. It's been . . . busy.* Much like the general public's, her trust in her team had waned enough that she hadn't even attempted to contact any of them yet, let alone give out any orders. Based on the respect Izaiah had received during his tenure, there was no reason to believe her orders would be taken seriously, anyway.

It only took a few hours to find Nigel hiding in a Brazilian fishing port, trying to pose as a local worker gutting fish, despite his dull gray complexion resembling burned newspaper. *Seeing him gave me my first good laugh in a while.* Collecting the Human Scythe was, as North Americans say, a "piece of cake," since he was no longer under the protection of Yusay'ne, the retired Niel Nulus, who had abandoned her employer after his cowardice in battle with Alex Barker.

Too bad—it would have been nice to see her.

Presently, as Mara continued to ignore Nigel's lamentations, she watched a human-bodied couple play on a bench across from her, tickling each other's arms and caressing fingertips. One was a Human Archfiend with a flowy tongue; the other was a Human Beaubon with bright green hair like a hyena's mane. Their sexes were female, assigned when they became human following the Purge, yet they easily traded dominant and submissive roles, reminding Mara of herself and Hannah when they'd first met. *But shouldn't. Stop it! Be a professional.*

"Oh, my head," Nigel groaned. "I can't believe you. The audacity. The things you people do . . ."

"You shouldn't have run."

"You failed to properly identify yourself! How was I supposed to know who you were? If the Tribunal had simply sent a declaration through the proper channels—"

"They did."

"I would have turned myself in! My lawyers will tear this charge parcel into a thousand pieces!"

"Great. In the meantime, could you please be silent?" She closed her eyes, trying to enjoy the ride. There were still a couple more stops before arriving at the Tribunal.

"I'm not even sure what you've detained me for," Roe continued. "I smell a multitude of civil suits coming your way."

"As you've surely heard, there's a trial about to happen, rather large and public. You spoke to both Joseph and Barker before each attempted to destroy a planet. Do the math."

"Unfortunate timing! Speculation at best."

"That's for the lawyers to decide." She kept her eyes closed. Nigel scoffed and tried to fold his arms, struggling while handcuffed to her.

"Well, of all the . . ." he muttered.

A few stops later, a jingle played on the overhead PA as the train pulled into the BAT central station. A voice welcomed the train's passengers in all five primary UnEarth languages, as well as the common Trivium tongue—which was, strangely, English. *That's a recent change—made because humans assigned it as the language of air traffic communication. I guess UnEarth thought that meant all humans would be speaking it from now on.*

"This is us. Get up," Mara said, hoisting Nigel to his feet. They exited the train, his flip-flops clopping on the cobalt-and-ash-colored walkway. At a junction, they turned up a wide staircase that led into a hallway sixty feet wide and one hundred feet tall. Navy-blue carpet covered the center, leaving the outer sections of gray concrete exposed, worn smooth after eons of use. UnEarth creatures capable of flight zoomed overhead, while those that preferred to swim sped through canal tubes embedded in the walls, ceiling, and floors.

"Really, I can walk myself," Nigel protested.

"I'm assisting the elderly."

"I'll have you know, five thousand is considered youthful for my species. Please, you would surely catch me, should I run. Allow me my dignity."

Mara kept her grip on his arm as they ascended a shallow ramp into the bright hub of the BAT central station. Stained glass windows rounded the walls, transforming the sunlight streaming in into a multitude of colors that draped the interior of the Gothic-analogous station in chromatic brilliance.

Fifteen minutes later, after weaving through dense crowds, they reached the Iolanze, one of the four primary sections of the Tribunal, containing the jail and the Pro-Stasia, or Barium Guard central command. Approaching its fifty-foot door framed with blocky blue brilliance, Mara had to step aside when several members of the Barium Guard stomped out. When the last Guard passed, they allowed the door to slam shut behind them with a bang.

Thanks for holding it.

Stepping inside, Mara stifled a gasp at the wall of brilliant blue flanking her on either side. At least twenty High Celestials stood as still as statues in the lobby. *This has never . . . what could you all be waiting for?* All at once, their heads turned to regard her and Roe, who flushed with Dread at the sight. Even he seemed to recognize the magnitude of this show of force, with Commander Loredosai of Hywyn's armed forces—recently elevated to command of the Guard—seemingly having returned from Hywyn with reinforcements. Mara was sure there were scrolls that needed signing for such a thing, and she wondered if anyone was investigating the legality of these additions. When she had left for Earth, the Guard was already patrolling the city twice as often as before the Joseph incident, which had clearly unsettled the populace. No one had informed her of any imminent threats that would warrant these recruits, and with all the turmoil running across the UnEarth worlds, it was hard to imagine anyone stirring trouble on Trivium.

Forcing Roe through the giant double doors, she pushed him toward the counter. The clerk behind it, Kiji, who was a Yoduk—a larger, darker-furred version of a Beaubon—looked up, beaming with an explosive smile. With hands like hydraulic presses at the ends of their brawny upper arms (*two of four*), and a constant can-do attitude, the Yoduk were prime candidates for many trades in Trivium, including the hauling in of bad guys after an arrest. Smiling with their three-inch teeth and wide saucer irises, Kiji stomped around the desk, their padded feet slapping the ground as they rushed to meet Mara.

"Warden Sentry! Yabuk-tabuk!" they growled happily. "News from Earth realm, yes! So good to see you. So good! What have you brought us today? Let Kiji see! You know me! Is it something elusive? Dabble-d-dee!"

Nigel Roe turned as cold and stiff as a gravestone, his feet suddenly refusing to move. "You're not going to leave me with one of *them*, are you? Have mercy, I beg you."

"Greetings, Kiji. Wonderful to see you," Mara said, pushing Nigel forward, letting the blind Scythe find his own way. "You know who he is. You know why we want him."

"You're not even coming with me?" Nigel pleaded. "After all, I am your prize."

"No, you were my ten o'clock." She gave Kiji another wave and an appreciative smile. "Apologies, Kiji. Thank you for booking him."

Kiji waved away her worries with their fourteen-inch-wide hand. "Apologies, boo! Say no more! What a promotion you're dealing with! So good! Isn't that right, Nigel?"

Taking Nigel by the hand and swaying back and forth, Kiji dragged him toward the rear of the station. "Did you congratulate her, Nigel Scythe? If you didn't, you still can. Whenever you want! Tiggi-Jiggi! That's the great thing about friends, Nigel Roe. Friends—tiggi—so good!"

"Uh . . . yes . . . friends," Nigel muttered, his tone that of someone being led to their doom. As they toddled away, Kiji continued to ask cheerful questions, soaking the Scythe in unease, and giving Mara a deep, satisfying sense of accomplishment.

Needed that.

Making her way to the ground floor of the Tribunal, Mara hurried to catch the 1:10 southbound train. Even if she could have Shifted while on Trivium to save time, she was too exhausted. Technically, there was an Eb Ring within the Tribunal, but that gate was supposed to be a secret and required special permission to use. Mara still wasn't sure why she lacked that permission but had stopped caring about such bureaucratic nonsense centuries ago.

Soon she was in the south end of Trivium, making her way northwest on foot, toward a district called Port Wynass Lunsai. A strange name, considering there was no such thing as a natural body of water on Trivium; the water used by the city was pumped from the core. However, with a heavy Wyst population, and given that the district consumed nearly ninety percent of the planet's liquid water, it bore the same name as many Nashwynite municipalities.

As she ventured deeper into the neighborhood, the sound of rushing water grew, echoing through the lanes between buildings. The system of tubes that UnEarth creatures swam through, called the Hydro-Vel, became dense, rising and falling above the streets, sometimes so tangled that Mara could hardly tell where one tube ended and another began. Pools and moats began to replace front lawns and patios, some adorned with giant waterlilies buoyant enough to support two-hundred-pound creatures called drakki. Here, the buildings were not made of concrete but grown from a transplanted living environment, built off vines and tree trunks the size of oil pipelines—or larger.

Approaching her destination, Mara sensed the shimmering, alluring frequency of the Louiuolopa, a resort hotel and the crown jewel of the district. Its influence on her mood and Eve had been significant well before she turned the corner of Tufts and Wald to view its artificial waterfalls and babbling brooks, framed by a wall of green-and-turquoise magnificence. Now, in full view, the intensity of the Eve signal became deafening. Wet boulders clustered into formations, reflecting the hotel's extravagant light with glistening clarity. The canopy serving as its roof was only occasionally thick enough to provide cover from the sun, leaving much of the property open to the elements and prying eyes—privacy and modesty being foreign concepts to those from Nashwyn.

Mara stepped off the sidewalk and onto a narrow blue walkway. The plants lining the path bobbed and moved, releasing plumes of intoxicating scents toward her as she passed. A mixture of tangy, salty, and sugary aromas filled the air, making her feel like she could finally take a clean, real breath, her lungs fuller than they had been in a long while.

Sliding through gray-green doors that squished open, she entered the lobby, filled with smooth surfaces rippling in broad waves. Sinuous, glowing moats ran the length of the building, painting every surface in blue-green light. These were home to various wildlife: frog-like creatures, insects with enormous sexual organs, flowers with lips and teeth, and myriad fish, some of which were more flowerlike than the blooming buds up in the air, and also had enormous sexual organs. Passing through cyan vines with white florae crawling up the walls and into the tight cracks of an open doorway, Mara glimpsed a sparkling party filled with merriment, music, and laughter.

She approached the doorway and its keeper: a Human Wyst named Cione, stationed at a podium, dressed in a white suit with cyan accents.

"Warden, on time as usual," Cione said, blinking with fish-lensed eyes.

"Where is he?"

"His usual table. Senator Bo is several drinks in and in a rather chipper mood. Should be good company."

"I'd agree if we didn't have to work later."

Before she could pass, Cione stepped in front of Mara, blocking her path.

"We like you—our Medolian friend—here at the Louiuolopa. We want to help you enjoy life. Truly enjoy it. I see the weight you carry. Your tensions constrict your every movement." He held out a green four-inch glass case. Mara sensed Fervor within the glowing syringe tucked inside. "Normally you would need to purchase the deluxe package to get these, but you're a special guest. Compliments of the house."

Mara shook her head and walked away. "I don't use artificials."

"It's pure. One hundred percent liquid Fervor." He called after her, "Come on, I'd fight a tillian to see you cut loose sometime, Warden. We all would."

Mara stepped through the cave-like entrance filled with leaves and vines into the next section, where cyan and gold remained the motifs. On her right was a foot-soaking lounge and accompanying bar. The bar top and all the surrounding chairs were made of green glass textured like moss. Ignoring the flowing drinks and frivolities of the quainter, far more desirable area, she took the left path, framed by huge rings every five yards, making her feel, as always, like she were traipsing inside a monumental green rib cage.

A display of light rays danced on the ceiling, projected through the door at the end of the hall. Stepping through, she entered the pool area: a perfect replica of a Nashwyn resort, designed to invoke an unreasonable amount of passion in the viewer. Multiple natural structures rose several levels, letting vibrant aquamarine water flow wildly over the tropical playground, creating waterfalls wherever it pleased. The liquid was then recycled back to the top by huge green tubes curving over the area, large enough for creatures to traverse and deposit themselves at the top of the structure, where they could either ride the cascade back down, or simply jump.

Hundreds of guests were scattered across the patio, many Human Wysts, but at least one of each type of pure creature was present—*except for the Clavus Celestials. Violets don't play well with others.* Nearly every shade could appreciate what the Fervor world had to offer, including the sworn enemies of the Wysts: the Scythes, who were known to frequent Nashwyn brothels. *And who could blame them?* Mara herself had considered visiting one recently but had decided against it. There was no time for happiness right now. Maybe later, but not now. Possibly, not for a while.

She quickly found her mark among the angels, demons, and everything in between. Senator Mau-auvt Bo was not hard to spot, deep behind a velvet rope, surrounded by adoring parasites and well-wishers. As a senator, he'd been forced to purge his Eve, appearing human. Like Bo, his personal guard were also UnEarth Humans, *and there seem to be more of them than ever.*

The more unabashed creatures of UnEarth often embellished their appearances with hairstyles, body paint, and wrist and ankle bracelets. However, none could rival Bo's ostentation, as he wore so many feathers he resembled a giant bird of prey flitting among the crowd, tickling guests with witty remarks. *The man loves feathers. Loves—them.* When he spotted Mara, he waved her over, his feathers fluttering.

She passed under the rope into his two-hundred-square-foot VIP section as Bo hurried to meet her. "My Warden, you're looking triumphant today!" They joined hands and kissed each other's wrists in greeting. Bo then turned and marched into his party. "Inside. Now! Sit. We have thresh provided by my new friend, Kalice-Tria, from the Caverns of Ulchfulg. Also, reagen gourd. All fresh. Chef Rigohil killed and mashed the gourd not five minutes ago. Such a sight to see if you manage not to blink. Nothing quite like it. Come-come-come."

"Thanks, but I'm fine." Mara settled into the open seat across from Bo. "I thought we were going to the hearing."

"We are."

"But for some reason, you thought 'drinks'?"

"Sentry Loren, shame on you—excuse me, Warden Sentry Loren. Naughty thoughts! You and I have discussed calming down and relaxing so many times that I—" He scoffed, biting his hand as if it might contain an impending implosion.

Mara stifled a growl. "Right, and I told you it was unwise to tell me to calm down."

"Yes, fine. Digressed. But maybe just this once? If I may, you know, make a suggestion? The idea of calm—it helps in meetings, trust me, especially when it might be one's first time doing a certain task while in a certain new position. So, I offer this as an, I don't know—a lease on life. Sign here if you will—LACIOUS! Hello!"

Bo suddenly waved toward a far-off corner of the VIP section. "The scrolls you sent were brilliant! Memo my secretary. We'll do a twilight feast."

"You're drunk, aren't you?" Mara said.

"Jumping right to the highest ledge, are we? Never considering I might take it nice and slow and enjoy the journey? *Hmm?* Ever hear of just getting a little drunk?"

"Who's paying for this?"

"Now that you're in the highest echelon, young one, I suggest you familiarize yourself with how things are done as quickly as possible. Don't be a dud like your predecessor. You're one of us now. And don't forget, people know of our friendship, which means my reputation is tied to yours. I trust you'd do nothing to sully my image."

Grabbing a handful of Dread party mix from a bowl, Bo stuffed it into his mouth and washed it down with a large gulp of apple-green moss. Wiping his face with his arm, he continued, "You think we don't deserve a few drinks and baskets of fruit from time to time? We are the ones who keep Trivium—and all of UnEarth, really—flowing. Come-come-come. Eat—EAT! You must be hungry living on a Med's salary."

"Speaking of which, I haven't been told what my new salary will be. And my coronation hasn't been scheduled."

"I didn't realize. *Hmm*, does it need to be? I mean, it's not as though you didn't get the job."

"It's customary. Izaiah received one, as did his superior. I should receive the same."

"Oh, who has the time? You have your title—what else do you want? You'll receive all the same glitz and glamor, all the pageantry. Don't worry, you have the power, even without the fancy banquet. You are my favorite and the right hand of the Senate. We don't function without you, and the members recognize that."

"You're welcome."

"Don't be so hard on yourself, young one. After all, you've just suffered a terrible . . ." He paused.

"What?"

"Nothing. Just with your personal . . . I'll say 'situation.'"

"Go ahead. Loss? Is that what you're thinking? I assume you're referring to my former relationship. Hannah and I separated many centuries ago. So, no, I am not suffering."

"It's okay to be in denial."

"I'm not in denial!" The chatter in the VIP section quieted momentarily. Mara lowered her voice. "I'm not going to argue with anyone who wants to mourn the general, but I'm personally not going to. Is that okay with everyone?"

"Sounds like you don't think she's gone. I mean, come on, you saw the hole. You felt what we all did. I'm sure you felt it even more, even while on another planet. In times like this, moving on is important, but it can't be real until you accept the world for what it is."

Mara would have stormed out if anyone else had said that. The senator had been her only friend and ally in the political landscape of Trivium for more than a millennium, the only one to extend condolences following Die Muneris, the Day of the Gift. *Maybe he's right?*

She took a breath. "Fine. Now, what do you say we move out?"

Finishing his drink with a final swig, Bo clapped twice. "Wonderful idea!" Collecting his belongings into a satchel, he added casually, "Oh, darling, one more thing before I forget: do you have that letter I asked for?"

Mara hesitated. She was hoping he wouldn't request it until after the hearing, when she could question him further before handing it over.

"Yes, I do. But I was wondering if we could—"

"Wonderful." Bo held out his hand, his gaze still fixed on his satchel. Mara suddenly wished she had never written it. *I should have lied and said I'd forgotten it at home. Good going, Warden.*

Reaching into her side pouch, she retrieved the scroll case. "Tell me, once more . . . what prompted this particular request?"

"The Counselors are collecting testimonies from all parties for the archives. They'll have no bearing on the case. The archives are a neutral account, as you know. Likely locked away for millions of years, or simply never to be seen again. Nothing nefarious."

Bo finished packing his bag and looked up at Mara, his free hand still outstretched, waiting for the letter. His smile was fixed, as though stuck.

"It's just," she began, "the questions you asked seemed slightly outside the purview of—"

"Again, it's only for the archives. Nothing to worry about. Have I ever led you astray? Look where you are now. Who made you Warden Sentry? *Hmm?* You're amazing, Mara Loren, but you've got to work on your trust issues. You asked me to be your mentor, yes?"

"I did."

"Then trust me. Everything you've said will remain confidential—you have my word."

Mara placed the letter in his hand. Bo snatched it up and tucked it into his satchel before tying it shut. "Great. Now let's move with haste. One should always strive to arrive early, yes?"

After a brief hike to the train station and a twenty-minute ride west, Mara, along with the senator and a handful of his coterie, briskly strolled along a narrow red path leading to the interim Tribunal, situated at Mullen Tados, the largest thresh distillery in Trivium City. The walkways were lively, reminiscent of the bustling halls of the Tribunal when the Senate was in full swing.

As they approached one of the five colossal buildings dominating the compound, Mara admired the copper-colored steel that ran along their lengths, gleaming with a brilliant sheen and casting a sepia-toned haze over the area. The windows of the still houses were jagged and caked with centuries of grime.

They passed Distillery House Number 4, which housed the interim Senate chamber. Today's hearing, however, would take place in a smaller conference room in Distillery House 3, further down the lane. Mara followed Bo and two of his assistants inside, while the rest of his crew broke away toward the thresh tasting room to enjoy free samples.

The distilleries within House 3 were engineering marvels, encased in glistening crimson-and-copper metals that spiraled and twisted like marble. Tubes of various sizes, adorned with pressure gauges and valves, snaked around the enormous vats—large enough to store thousands of gallons of boiling-hot thresh. *It was impressive on first sight. Gotta admit. Hannah tried several times to get me to join her on the tour. Said she thought I would have enjoyed it. Don't know why I never said yes.*

"This way," one of the Senate proletariats said, a Psera with an echoey voice like a glass jar scraping over a sidewalk. The stout creature waddled between two steaming vats, leading Mara and the others to a tall set of glass double doors. "Inside," the proletariat instructed before shuffling off to repeat the process for the next group of arrivals. Mara thanked them, but the Celestial either didn't hear or chose not to respond.

Upon entering the dimly lit conference room, Mara found most parties already present. In the far corner stood the lead Counselor to the Tribunal, Valio-Malo, a pure-bodied Na-Nala Wyst. Today, he was the chief representative of the Counselors, the bulk of the Tribunal's legal wing. Nearby, Bennett Hunter's attorney, Roland, and his entourage formed a closed circle with their wings, making it difficult for anyone to approach unannounced. Across the table, another Celestial clique gathered around Speaker Binahq, the Tribunal Senate leader. Currently draped in a dazzling blue robe, the honorable speaker was a Human Celestial, her wavy hair as white as fresh snow.

Lurking in the murkiest corner of the room was Claud Malcolm Rowse, the senator from Fovos, lounging in a robe the color of used coal, his five o'clock shadow sharp enough to cut glass. He took intermittent swigs from a large flask, all while digging for a chunk of wax that hung halfway out of his left ear. Also present were Afton Laffler of Lanwyn and Prime Minister Yaddo of Doloros, both dressed in contemporary human three-piece suits, with Yaddo additionally wearing a canary-yellow ceremonial robe. Each senator's cadre included at least one pure Eve creature.

Following Mara and Bo, a Veen Scythe entered the room. Initially, she thought nothing of him; they often assisted the court. The creature resembled a stout four-foot mosquito, vibrant orange and brown, with murky, near-translucent wings. He carried scrolls under his giant housefly-like arms and in his long, curled mouth. A bright orange bow tie, likely cut from a banner in his neighborhood, adorned his (*chin?*) Moving in jittery bursts, each step seemed to be accompanied by soft chirps or comments, such as "whoa there" or "look out," so quiet they soon became background noise.

Approaching the primary table, the Veen did not leave after delivering his papers, as Mara had expected. Instead, he sat in the chair reserved for Alex Barker's counsel.

The rumors are true? Arros actually gave Alex a Veen lawyer. Lucifer and the Archfiend were attempting to nullify their connection to Barker, even though they were the ones who'd imbued him with Wrath in the first place.

Seemingly unconcerned by his surroundings, or the task at hand, the Veen unpacked his satchel, setting out ink and a pen before unrolling a blank scroll in preparation. Mara couldn't help but notice that none of the other lawyers or court mavens were doing the same.

The last party to arrive was that of Ariel Van-Mortus, the senator from Arros. Gliding through the door ten minutes before the meeting began, she might as well have been fashionably late. With eyes glistening with inner demonic fire, she was clad in a skintight, sleeveless red dress that rose to her chin, currently hidden behind a gray scarf. Her deep brown hair, pulled into a tight flower-shaped bun, pulsed with an orange glow, like the embers of a dying campfire. She and her floating Archfiend assistants made their way to the large round table at the center of the room, where the duo helped her into her seat. Both were of the Ostra clan: Archfiend on the smaller side, with boar-like faces and only four limbs. Spiked round shells shielded their backs as their arms and legs hung limply, like wet socks.

After completing their duties, the Ostra drifted to a line of chairs against the wall, their spiny shells puncturing the seat cushions with a series of pops. They settled in, releasing steam from their nostrils and grinning with misshapen mouths.

As the clock chimed the half hour, an UnEarth Human court assistant turned a knob on the wall, dimming the room lighting further. All parties found their seats and fell silent while Mara, unsure of her role, remained frozen near the entrance. Feeling trapped, she didn't want to draw attention. Having never participated in formal proceedings before, she had no idea what her duties would entail. After being denied permission to visit Izaiah in his cell to ask him, she had spent weeks poring over Tribunal charters, hoping to glean some understanding of her role, but found scant information about the Medolians at large. *An anger-inducingly small amount.*

The same UnEarth Human who'd dimmed the lights called loudly, "All will rise for the honorable Judge Nagura Axios."

Those present stood all at once, though Van-Mortus was the last to do so. Two court assistants opened the glass double doors as a tall creature in a dark robe slowly approached, made murky by a veil of orange smoke dancing around her frame. Axios entered the room, her bare feet beneath her robe taking plodding steps, scraping on the stone floor. In the darkness of her hood, deep within recessed eye sockets, tiny, reflected dots of light were the only evidence that she had any eyes at all. The soft lighting of the deposition chamber played on her exposed face, which had skin like cloudy paper pulled tightly over her skull—human enough, but exaggerated, as though crafted by a caricature artist at a carnival.

Axios entered the chamber, her gaze drifting along those present until it landed on Mara, standing only a few feet away. The judge's speckled eyes blinked twice.

"I'm sorry, Your Honor," Mara stammered. "I wasn't sure if I was supposed to . . ."

Without a word, Axios opened her palm to the empty seat beside her own chair—the one Mara hadn't even considered could be hers. *Honestly, I didn't think I'd be sitting at all.*

"Of course. Apologies again, Your Honor." Mara hurried to stand beside her seat, aware that the others around the table were probably mocking the back of her head. *I can feel the Wrath of their petty thoughts.*

OALEEN

"Yes, Mr. Barker," the class said in unison when Alex asked if they had read the chapter the previous night. *What a response!* A quick shot of endorphins coursed through him whenever they answered like that, which had only happened a few times before.

"Thank you, class," he responded, turning to face his fourth graders. They were especially attentive today, which was nice. Alex liked nice. "Since you all seem to have read the chapter and looked over the worksheet . . . who can tell me the answer to question one—the basic building blocks of plants and animals?"

Emily Morgan raised her hand. Always eager and ready for Friday cleanup and whatever chores might earn her extra credit, she was the first hand up, come rain or shine. Since learning he was having a daughter, Alex had hoped she might turn out something like her. *Maybe a little less tightly wound, but still just as much a go-getter.* He often joked to himself that he could set his watch by her hand streaking into the air after a question was asked. But today something had changed in his class—something that made him pause and stare like a deer in some headlights. Today, it was not only Emily's hand that rose into the air, but all his students', rising in a wave from the back.

Alex had never seen this before and didn't know what it meant. *Okay. Wow.* Inundated with choices, he didn't know which hand to pick, so he decided to choose Emily's again. *She was first, after all. But this is strange, even for nine-year-olds.*

She stood at her desk proudly. "The correct answer according to the sheet is cells, such as meat and vascular," Emily half yelled. "I already checked. But I would argue, Mr. Barker, that first we should mention the individual organs. It seems wrong to ignore that level of classification and go all the way down to cells because they're really small—like really small. Way smaller than a heart or a kidney," she emphasized for the rest of the class. "But that's just what I think."

She sat back down. The other kids stared in awe. A few ooh'd.

"Very good, Emily. As usual." Alex crossed out "cells," which he'd begun to write on the blackboard, assuming she would give the answer from the homework sheet, but once again, Miss Morgan had surprised him. He wrote "organs" in the empty space and stared at the word. This kind of moment was exactly what teaching was all about.

"Did you see that, class? Always ask those kinds of questions," he said, writing a sudden flurry of ideas on the board, feeling the urge to impart every little lesson he'd learned in his life, forwarding the data on to this new crop. There were so many thoughts that he couldn't keep up. His hand and the chalk drifted across the board, leaving streaks of knowledge in their wake. After each note was safely on the board, they blurred in his peripheral vision and disappeared from his memory. But he couldn't stop writing. He needed to teach the kids.

"Always look for the thing that everyone else missed, class. Don't go crazy about it, but don't always take the first option you're handed. If something feels fishy, trust that feeling. Ask questions, analyze, think about the future and what events you would like to see happen to get you there. Then think about how to make them happen. This is where the good ideas come from and might help keep you safe in a bad situation. I hate to tell you this, but life will not always go as planned. Something you've done a thousand times can suddenly change on the thousand and first. You could even go out for something as mundane as takeout and—"

"Mr. Barker . . ." Emily said.

"Yes?"

"You're rambling again." She snickered with her friends.

Alex rolled his eyes and bobbed his head. *Sorry, stupid me.* He finished up his frenzied writing of life lessons and broad questions. "Thank you for stopping me, Emily. Sometimes I can't help it. This is just too fun. Don't you think, class?"

"Yes, Mr. Barker," the kids responded again in perfect unison. *Wow, twice in one day.* They smiled, revealing their teeth at the same time as though a rope had been pulled, lifting their lips like miniature stage curtains.

Alex asked a few more questions from the homework sheet. Each time he did, every single hand went up, raised with such enthusiasm that they must have actually known the answers. His afternoon of teaching continued without any issues whatsoever. The chalk in his hand did not dry out his fingers and make him uncomfortable. Jimmy H. did not throw his shoe at anyone. Teresa did not start crying when other kids got to hold the class guinea pig. Ronnie K. smelled like he'd taken a bath. *Which is strange because Rotten Ronnie left my class six years ago . . . The kids made up that nickname, not me.*

But how likely was it that all those things could be going on all at once? Ronnie had always smelled bad—that was a universal constant. And why couldn't Alex read his own writing on the board? An experiment was needed to figure out what was going on. Turning to his class, he asked them if they'd like to stand on their heads and bark like border collies while they spun like tops until they puked their lunches out. The kids responded with a re-sounding, "Sounds fun, Mr. Barker!"

This wasn't right.

This wasn't real.

Alex put the chalk down and backed away toward his desk. His eyes darted around the room. His life wasn't this anymore. It had changed drastically; he knew it but couldn't remember how or why.

I can't be here.

But where did he belong?

A Thai restaurant passed through his thoughts. Next was something called a Medolian safe house in the desert: a gray haven. Alex's chest erupted in sudden agony, bringing him to his knees with the return of a searing sting in his hip, traveling into his torso. He couldn't remember why his chest was burning as if hot coals had been stuffed into his flesh, but the feeling carried a familiarity. His mind ached and burned. Why couldn't he remember? This life was wrong. The kids were still smiling, waiting at their desks for more knowledge, but Alex had none left to give, and there was no reason to.

Because I'm not here. I can't be—because I'm dead.

A harsh, squawking buzz penetrated his ears and sliced deep, pulling him brutally from his half-sleep, tearing the classroom away. Blackness and light switched, yanking his mind around as if it were attached by a rope to a pickup truck taking off at full pow-er. His previous location was replaced with a damp, lifeless cavern engulfed in cold shadow. The frigid, motionless air clawed at his skin, creeping over him from one spot to the next. In his weakened state, he could have thrown a stone in any direction and not hit any of the walls in the distance.

With a scrape, a metal grate hanging precariously above him opened, releasing a cascade of slop onto a wet mound a few yards away. The smell hit him without delay—a musk like human shit and rotten milk filling his cell, reminding him where he was and how stupid he was for denying the perfection of his dream. *Why? Why can't I just let myself be happy?* During his days waking hours he often tried to imagine the place he had just been. Today's dream was the clearest his classroom had ever been realized, and like an idiot, he had pushed it away. Though the debate was moot when one considered that no sleep—however cozy—could resist the noise of the meal alarm.

"Enjoy your feast, Ire boy!" A low, hate-filled voice echoed across the cavernous cell, coming from an intercom system built into an unseen nook in the rock.

Alex leaned forward to see the food pile—ultimately a pointless waste of energy. He knew what was over there: always the same and never good—far worse than the slop he used to give his dog, Oliver, when he was a kid. Every day he wished for the headless eels in paper boxes Izaiah had offered him the day they were arrested by the Barium Guard.

Whenever he did muster the courage to eat, he nibbled only on the "freshest" stuff at the top of the ever-growing, festering pile of abandoned meals, and avoided the rest. Always on the verge of throwing up yet never able to, he had lost so much of his body weight that he could clearly see and feel his ribs, making him thankful he had no mirror in his cell. Though Alex didn't need to see himself to imagine what he looked like: weak and helpless, worthy of pity, yet also in chains so extensive you'd think he were some gigantic, terrifying beast—something even more monstrous than King Kong.

His cell did not have bars: only rock walls so thick they could have withstood a Tomahawk missile strike. There was no visual of the hall except for a small window on the door, which was at least ten yards away—merely a cube of light in the vast darkness around him. The place was a titan's cage, but its current occupant was simply a fourth-grade teacher from Prescott, Arizona, named Alex Barker. *Go Diamondbacks.*

The perception surrounding the "Ire boy" had its own built-in celebrity. Tours were led through his cellblock regularly by the guards and workers in the Weya-Vein, letting their curious friends and acquaintances catch a peek—to peer into the cage and maybe see the rage or some billowing smoke, or an earth-rending heat that scalded the eyes. Yet all looked disappointed when they leaned into the window and saw the man inside, slumped over, obscured by chains, with no trace of color in his eyes.

Alex waited as long as possible between feedings and ate as little as he could—only enough to stay alive—but today he would have to put his dignity aside. If he passed out in his current state, he wasn't sure if he would ever wake up again. There was no reason to believe the guards in the Weya-Vein would provide him medical care if he stopped breathing; he'd been injured plenty of times—usually by the guards themselves—and they'd never shown the slightest concern before. Eating would be a gruesome experience, but at least it would prolong his life a bit. Alex wouldn't let himself die on the floor of an UnEarth jail. He couldn't die again. Not yet, not when so much of him still believed he would see his wife again when he did.

And I don't have an answer yet as to why I let her die.

Crawling on all fours to the pile under the pipe, forced to fight against the chains attached to him, which rose into the ceiling and disappeared into the blackness above, Alex collapsed near the slop to take a bite of the food, favoring the fatty bits that provided good energy and had the most tolerable texture. Muscling his way through a few bites, he tried to open his throat so the mystery meat covered in Fovosian vegetable sauce would slide down without much resistance. He told himself that, luckily, he wouldn't have to ingest much. This meal would sustain him for a week if he kept his activity to a minimum.

Shouldn't be a problem, but I'll check my calendar anyway.

The chains on his wrists and ankles were beginning to hurt. He'd been away from the pedestal for too long, and the tension on them would not ease until he returned. The spring nature of his restraints was part of the cell's design, which had been built for colossal behemoths that wreaked havoc on the worlds of UnEarth, as well as Earth. *One guy told me there used to be giants on Earth. Unfortunately, they got into it with Hywyn. Bad idea—because, then—poof—no more giants.*

The cell was officially designated number four but had earned the nickname the Sackulli-Karni, Arrosian for "Executioner's shitbox." It was so named because this was the only cell within UnEarth death row where the occupant was not required to be currently sentenced to death in order to occupy it. The great Archfiend general Molm'Ursuth had been held in the cell following his arrest for crimes against UnEarth, thus ending Unos, the first UnEarth war. If the rumors of his size were to be believed, he would have filled the entire cell and likely been able to view the ceiling, which was far too high for Alex to see.

A giant of Ursuth's size and destructive capabilities had never been seen before. Presumed guilty well before his trial, nobody had any reason to believe he shouldn't be immediately placed on death row. When his sentencing came through, it turned out the people were good guessers. Thus began the tradition of especially heinous offenders being sent to the Sackulli-Karni preemptively.

Another famous occupant was Kleegex-Noi-Va, a Wyst and political prisoner who fought for seven millennia to break Hywyn's
grip on the Tribunal and paid the ultimate price for it. Kleegex also
helped spawn over one hundred progressive political parties within local UnEarth governments. Alex was still hazy on the details,
but she sounded like the Eve equivalent of a populist revolutionary
deserving of having her face put on a stamp.

But there was another name he could not get out of his head:
that of a former occupant of the cell and an UnEarth criminal who
was unrivaled—and would be for all time. *At least if the Bible has
anything to say about it.*

On the day of his arrival, the other prisoners had shouted it into
his face with all their might: "Lucifer's cell! Aveyl's cell! Poor Ire
baby's sleeping in the Fallen One's wake!"

Having any connection to the contemporary symbol of evil was
more than Alex could stomach. He desperately wanted not only
out of the cell but to rid himself of the Wrath within him. *Permanently. I don't care what it takes or what else I lose.*

But at the same time, he feared being without it. There was a
longing buried within him for his anger's return. The emotion had
been like a sports car he'd only begun to test-drive. The strength
he'd felt in his spine when fighting the Aili clan and the Wraithian
cult could not be easily dismissed. Never in his life had Alex been
able to go out into the world without woe or fear, knowing that
whatever came at him, he could take it—and it had all been thanks
to his burning hands. But his fingertips were now as cold as night,
and he had already forgotten how to reignite them.

Grandma Roshni would often joke that Alex had been born
without the anger gene. *And any time I showed even the slightest
trace of it, she'd shut it down real quick.* His whole life he'd kept it
under his thumb, even when things never went his way. He never

got angry. Even when both his parents were killed while on a trip to Asia when he was a boy, he didn't complain. The next twenty years of his life were filled with nosebleeds, no girls in sight, and dealing with being the only biracial kid in his class—and the awkwardness that came with it—both mean and nice—right up until high school. *Even then, there were only three of us.* Yet, he still did not complain. All six of his applications to Ivy League schools had been put on waiting lists, but Alex did not think the odds were good enough that one of them would pull through. At his grandpa's behest, he had not applied to any other colleges.

"Nonsense!" Grandpa Parai had shouted boisterously. "You don't need to go beg at a lesser-than college. All six of those idiot schools are going to call us back and beg for you to go to their piece of shit school. Mark my words! Mark them! You will see."

But none of the universities called, and before the summer was over, Grandpa Parai was dead from a pulmonary embolism. Still, Alex did not complain. He did not get mad. He stayed silent and strong, standing by his grandmother's side, feeling like a weak mess beneath it all. The thought of being mad never even entered his mind. In all his memories, Alex could find no instances of rage, not even in the moment his own wife had been murdered.

Any other man would have taken Chloe out right then and there—that's what Alex believed. Stopped the murderer. They would have taken control of the situation and avenged their wife immediately. Maybe even gotten one of their Rapture-imbued friends to heal and save her, killing every bird in the tree with one big badass rock. But that wasn't what Alex had done. When he'd seen his love taken from him . . .

I sat there on my knees, gaping like the failure that I am.

He still wasn't even sure when the Ire had taken over. His being had frozen, but he was still aware, still awake, his body simply wouldn't move or obey commands. Then, just like falling asleep, he faded away without ever seeing it coming.

Most anger I've ever experienced, and I don't even remember how it felt.

Since that night, the pit in his chest had only grown deeper. His longing, misery, and hopelessness were so deeply ingrained in him that not even the chains made of nevrose could strip him of those emotions. He missed his wife so much it made every muscle fiber in his body ache. It rattled his mind with the same thoughts over and over—his greatest enemy forcing him to relive memories he never wanted to see again. Fighting to hold onto the good times was a losing battle. The images could have been of Melissa and their baby, feeding Patty and smiling, enjoying parenthood. Instead, he saw the Medolian Chloe, possessed by evil incarnate, holding his wife. Her illuminated face bore a pain that clawed at his already mangled psyche.

"Eve alert!" a scratchy voice called sarcastically from the hall outside his cell, finishing with a mousy chuckle.

Oh, great. Alex's every thought was halted. *I thought you were asleep . . . hoped you were.*

The voice belonged to his closest cell neighbor. Though a rock wall separated them, thanks to his ability to sense Eve, he could always see her magenta-colored form—a puff of color that brought on a multitude of feelings just by viewing it, none of which were particularly pleasant.

He hated himself for accidentally creating what must have been an infinitesimally small amount of Grief for her to notice. *How does she do that so fast?*

"Is that Grief?" his neighbor asked. "You know how much I hate that stuff."

Her name was Oaleen, a Human Archfiend and once a member

of the Vostrus clan, carrying the honorable name Vostrus'Oaleen. But that was before her Purging and subsequent arrest. It turned out she enjoyed killing a little too much, which translated into her being a direct threat to her own teammates. Once a battle was over, Oaleen had a difficult time settling down and would often continue killing anything still moving, including her own. The only thing she seemed truly proud of was her body count—a number so large Alex assumed she had to be pulling his leg.

"Can't believe they convicted me!" she'd shouted numerous times. "I'm a Wrath user. I mean, what do they expect? It's the Archfiend way!"

She was also perpetually livid that a human was being held in the Sackulli-Karni instead of her. "Should be me in there before they lop my head off. I earned it! I'm a bigger threat to them than you could ever be!"

No argument there.

"How was your meal?" she asked him presently, her voice loaded with derisiveness. There were seven other prisoners in the upper wing, including two Archfiend, three Scythes, and two Wysts. None of whom showed the same level of interest in humiliating Alex daily as Oaleen.

But he was too tired to answer today.

"*Ch-ch-ch*, bet you got the good stuff, huh? Yeah, *ch-ch-ch-ch*, bet they gave the Ire boy his dessert before his meal. Maybe it'll help you grow? Does that sound nice?"

The chattering of her speech was not an impediment, but rather something that seemed rooted in her very nature. Alex guessed her species used to do it as a way to frighten their prey, and it sometimes leaked out. Not that she seemed the least bit embarrassed about it.

"Hey! Hey—Ire boy! I'm talking t-t-t-to you."

I don't want to do this.

He hated speaking with her, but Alex couldn't help responding every time she threw a new insult at him or tried to ruin his day, despite repeatedly swearing to himself he wouldn't. *What is wrong with me?*

"What would dessert even look like in a place like this?" he asked, thinking he'd found a clever comeback.

"You're a quick-witted little humie, aren't you?" Oaleen's voice echoed clearly in the hall. The acoustics between cells was miserably effectual. "So, where'd you drift off to, huh? *Ch-ch-ch-ch*, thinking about your dead wife again? I bet you were. I can always tell when you are. Your shade gets even more pathetic."

Just don't listen to her. Don't listen to anybody.

"Not talking today, huh?" she asked. "Guess that's all right. Makes sense, being such a terrible week for you, what with your trial about to start. At least they're sending your lawyer down."

That's today? Alex thought it was Wednesday, not Friday. That meant today he was set to meet his counsel, a Veen—whatever that meant. A jolt of hope sped through him, filling his cold belly. Being in limbo without a lawyer was a constant stress, and he'd been looking forward to this day for a long time—the day he would finally meet the one soldier he had on his side in the fight.

"You didn't forget, did you?" Oaleen asked, even though Alex knew she could tell the answer just by looking at his signature.

He tried lying anyway. "No. I remembered."

"What was that?" she said, sniffing vigorously. "Smelled an awful lot like hope. Don't go getting any funny ideas about freedom and due process." She snarled. "You do know you're getting the death penalty, right? Have I mentioned that before? Seems like I have."

"You've mentioned it," Alex said softly enough he hoped she wouldn't hear.

"Oh, good. Wouldn't want you going in unprepared."

"You're so kind."

"Yeah, that's just the kind of gal I am." She had the carefree air of someone lounging on an apartment stoop with friends, smoking cigarettes. "Say, did you notice anything special in your meal today? Maybe a secret ingredient? Try and guess! Ah, never mind. It's Lostros rawk'we! That means snot! A little gift from us in cell-block W.V.1. to commemorate the start of your trial, or klawkoln, as I call 'em. Compliments of Marvaney down the hall, of course."

Marvaney, a Lostros, grunted from his cell three doors down.

Alex didn't have the energy to care. Besides, he really hadn't noticed. If Marvaney's muck poisoned him and he died, so be it. Being murdered might have been a good way to get some last-minute sympathy points before meeting whatever almighty he still desperately wanted to believe in.

Oaleen grunted like a frustrated boar. "Nothing? Not a peep? I tell you I fed you snot and you just sit there? Man, you're worse off than I thought. I mean, look on the bright side—you're already on death row, so you can't get any lower. You should count yourself lucky, if you ask me. In fact, I think you should apologize to me."

"I'm sorry."

"Thank you. I don't forgive you, but I feel we can move on from it regardless."

Alex had no idea what he'd just apologized for. Oaleen continued, "You complain too much. Have I told you that? I bet you haven't even seen the inmates on the other side of the Vein. How packed in and miserable they are. Look how much space you've got! You could run around, play like a child, have a ball. Try and soak it up a little. Make the best of it! This is the one place where the more dangerous you're considered, the better your accommodations get."

"Where I come from, people don't get special treatment for who they are. Crime equals time," Alex said.

"It's adorable how you believe that." Oaleen's tone, so casual and sure, made Alex instantly feel like a dolt. *Guess she's right when you think about it for a second.* This was yet another example of the rough-handed wisdom of Oaleen. Her ideas, deeply rooted and constructed, always seemed to come down to some form of "You can't make an omelet without cracking some eggs." Other times, her advice to Alex steered him more toward the simple need to toughen up. "I bet you didn't walk tall even before they put those chains on you." "There's lots of things you could do to make yourself less pathetic. Threaten people every now and then. You're way too polite to the guards when they come to get you." Et cetera. The advice went on and on.

Always nice to hear how everything about me is wrong and should be better but I just won't do anything about it.

Presently, she barked at Alex, "Hey! Don't doze off on me. I ain't in the habit of talking to myself. Unlike you, little Mr. Help, I Can't Find Her! Where's Melissa? I need my wifey-woo!"

Must have been talking in my sleep again. "Sorry you have to hear that."

Oaleen growled. "*Ch-ch-ch* that word! That strengthless word! I swear, if you say it one more time, I'm going to break through this wall and your chains so I can snap your neck."

Alex was far too drained to try and push it with her today. He settled on not replying. The silence only lasted a moment before Oaleen spoke again.

"Hey! I'm serious. Speak up! All I can hear is your misery, it's annoying. Like a tiny wet tentacle in my ear. Lighten up! Things could be worse, you know. You could be in a prison on Arros. They wanted to send you there. Did I tell you that? Trust me, you'd rather be sentenced to death than end up in the Murag. Did I mention that? They wanted to let the Archfiend hold you while your case goes through. Can you imagine that? *Ch-ch-ch-ch*—No, of course you can't. You have no idea. You've proven humans are just as dumb as I was expecting. More so. And adorable." She coughed and gagged. "Like a weak little *ch-ch-ch-ch* baby creature! A baby creature I can't stand! Yuck! Babies! So glad my world doesn't have them."

"Yeah? Could a baby kill Chloe?"

"Ha! You didn't kill Chloe. The Ire did."

"You have no idea what you're talking about," Alex snapped back. "You always look at other people and try to find inadequacies and triggers just for your own amusement. Well, I think it's sick and brought on by your own weakness because you can't deal with your problems."

Oaleen's chuckle filled the cellblock hallway. "There was a pinch of strength. Sounds like you wish you had it but just aren't quite there. Don't worry—I hear you can't be a baby forever."

"Shut up!"

Oaleen left a pause, probably so she could analyze whatever Eve he'd created with that outburst. "Woof," she eventually said, sounding more disappointed in him than anyone ever had in his life. "Not a trace of Wrath. Not a puff. You're not capable of kill-ing a Medolian. You're no eradicator. You were a vessel. A puppet. Nothing more than a science experiment from Hell."

"Leave me alone." Alex couldn't plug his ears or get away from it. Nor could he feel anger.

"You should listen," Oaleen said. "I'm forced to listen to your whines, your bull and your sleep talking. Forced to feel your timid energy all day long."

One of the inmates down the cellblock row shouted, "Right on!"

Another started a rounding chant: "Melissa! Oh, Melissa! I can't find her!"—much to the delight of the others. Alex was glad he couldn't see them with his eyes because listening was bad enough.

"Do you have any perspective on what your life has been, little man?" Oaleen asked him. "*Ch-ch-ch-ch*—You've been living the sweet life on the only planet in this solar system truly pleasant to live on, without knowing thousands of years of boredom. *Ch-ch-ch-ch-ch*—Do you know how hard it is to pass the time? Humans have it so easy that you could n-never persuade me to feel sorry for you. If you saw my home world, it would alter your perception like nothing ever has. I was on Earth up until a couple hundred years ago. *Ch-ch*—I know what the humans call my world. I know how much the thought of it spooks your brethren. I know what they think of King Lucifer-Aveyl."

"I want to be done with our talks," Alex said.

"The effect of his name on you says it all. He controls your every thought almost as much as your wife."

"Does not."

"Does so."

"I said I want to be done with our talks!"

Oaleen chortled. "The only way that happens is if one of us dies."

"Then hopefully one of us gets the chair soon."

"What chair? I hate chairs," she said.

Alex sighed. "Never mind. Do you know if the mail has come by yet?"

"Did you hear anything I just said?"

"Yes, I'm trying to change the subject. I need to know if the mail carrier has been by yet."

Oaleen hissed. "*Ch-ch-ch-ch*—they did. While you were passed out."

That means it's around two-thirty. My lawyer should have arrived by now.

"Thinking about why your lawyer hasn't shown up yet?" Oaleen asked, slightly softer around the edges.

"They should have been here by now."

"Guess that means they abandoned you."

What could be keeping them? I thought people in UnEarth were punctual.

When the expected knock on his door finally came, Alex felt a swell of excitement. The sound meant good things were about to begin happening. The door to his cell was about to open, and he was about to meet his counsel. They would be tall, impressive, and mighty, and he would remember what relief felt like.

But none of that happened. Instead, the small window on his cell door was opened and filled by the glowing blue face of a Celestial guard. Their mouth was out of sight below, as their diamond eye filled the window and focused on him.

Alex knew what it meant the instant he saw them.

"I have a message for prisoner Barker. That one's meeting with his counsel has been canceled. The Veen was called to Tribunal work. That is the message." The guard started to close the window.

"Wait!" Alex shouted. "Will the meeting be rescheduled?"

"I have completed my task." The guard closed the window and stomped off.

Alex sat in silence for a moment. His chains seemed to gain weight by the second, dragging his shoulders somehow lower.

"They're really going out of their way to screw you, huh?" Oaleen said with the air of someone suggesting you check your car's fuel gauge when the battery is dead. "That's too bad."

STAND, ACCUSED

"Go get 'em, peon," one of the fellow creatures in the cellblock, Bahlah, an Ostra Archfiend, said as Bennett was led out in shackles.

Shuffling down the dim, cold, gray cellblock, he passed the other prisoners at their bars, facing out. Even Angry Eddie, as Bennett liked to call the Poa-Lo-Fey Wyst at the end of the row, stood up and did not spit at him as usual. Instead, he offered chirps of encouragement and grunts of solidarity. With the great meal he'd just ingested, Bennett's day was turning out to be not so bad. At least not so far, which was very likely to change soon, as today was the commencement of the Joseph Mandate trial.

Exiting the jail via a grand exit gate, the Iolanze guards and Bennett came upon a waiting carriage made of opaque blue bricks. A pair of enormous creatures, like giant brown beetles—but more tall than wide—stood at the front of the transport, attached to it by thick leather straps. A blazing line of orange light coursed through the harnesses wrapped over and around their spined bodies. In the darkness below the hoods jutting out like sunshades over their faces, numerous eyes twinkled like wet stones in a moonlit creek. Their armored shells were craggy and spiked with jagged prongs and razor-sharp hairs. From the looks of them, no one would ever dare touch one, let alone try to ride it.

After being loaded into the carriage, Bennett was made to wait. Forty minutes later, just as he was about to drift off despite the irritating chants of the people, a low rumbling arose that reminded him of an Abrams tank on the approach. From his cushioned seat in the carriage, he peered out the window. Something was coming. The crowd could feel it too and gradually grew quiet.

When the doors to the Tribunal opened, a robust slab of stone on large wheels was rolled out. Attached by a mess of chains was Alex, accompanied by a slew of guards, creating a garish show of strength. A door panel from the carriage was removed, and the slab was placed into the slot, locking him inside. The mask over his head prevented Bennett from seeing his face or whether he was even conscious. *But I can sense him. His signal is barely there.* All warmth had been washed away from the elementary school teacher over the past eighteen months. His meat and stored fat were gone, revealing his bones, filled in between by thin shadows. It was clear that it was only thanks to the chains holding him up that his frail body didn't slump to the carriage floor.

"You okay?" Bennett asked.

"Fine," Alex replied with lifeless energy.

"It's good to see you."

"Wish I could say the same," Alex said, likely referring to the mask over his head and not a hidden hatred of Bennett. *But who knows?*

The carriage left the jail, accompanied by a squad of Barium Guards marching in seamless formation. Traveling through Trivium, the caravan absorbed abuses from the citizenry, most of which were generally aimed at Alex. "Get the Ire boy out!—Kill it now!—Don't bring it here!"

As the caravan picked up speed, the cacophony outside grew more intense, and Bennett couldn't help but grab hold of the gold handle on his left for stability. *Starting to feel a little like a transport mission in Iraq.* Household objects used as projectiles crashed against the carriage with shocking intensity, breaking and splintering on the sides, adding to the madness.

The caravan then came to a sudden stop.

Celestial cries—a whole different kind of booming—overtook the atmosphere. Outside the window, wildly colored figures obscured by hoods rushed out from the crowd. *An ambush.* Likely, they were after Alex, who seemed not to have noticed anything yet.

A Molotov cocktail burst against the carriage door with a glass-breaking shriek. Another landed on the opposite side, splashing fire through the window grating. Green flames dripped to the floor between Bennett and Alex. But the teacher still did not stir.

Yep, something way too familiar about this! An explosion laced with Wrath rocked the carriage, drawing fierce bellows from the Fovos beetles. The chaos pulled on Bennett's mind. His feet were suddenly not where they should be. His body was in the desert as far as he knew, a gray high-powered rifle in his hands. Precious time was bleeding away and there was someone out there who was supposed to be dead. Finding this man and ending his life was Bennett's task. If he didn't do it, no one would. What then? Who else will get hurt because of this man? No one. Bennett would stop him by doing what he'd done time and again in the Marines: find something and kill it.

Snap out of it, you idiot!

The fantasy filtered away. He was back. The green fire scorching the carriage stank like welding fumes. The chants outside continued. Whoever was attacking was organized; that much was clear. Their shouts were full of passion, glory, and purpose, likely aimed at taking back their home from invaders.

"Uh, can we get out of here? Like, now?" Bennett shouted at the driver, tired of the weak-ass pandemonium surrounding them.

As though the throng outside had heard him and acquiesced, a denouement in the chaos followed, and near silence washed over the area. Looking outside the window, he saw that the Barium Guard had made quick work of the troublemakers—*the only thing they do fast*. Once the last of the rebels had been stabbed through the chest with a spear and shushed, and the streets were stained with the multicolored blood of the public offenders, things were brought under control. Bennett studied one of the dead on the ground. They were a Wyst; he could tell simply because they looked like they belonged underwater. Oblong and rotund, covered in a soft-skinned shell and with a face nearly obscured by luscious lips, their branch of Wyst, called the Na-Nala, was one he hadn't met in person yet. So why did they fear and despise him and Alex so much? What did these people believe, and who had told it to them? *I want to know because I hate that person.* His Rapture weakened. *Damn, not hate. What about blissfully dislike?* The strength returned. *Cool.*

"You doing okay?" Bennett asked Alex as the carriage picked up speed. The clatter of the Fovos beetles' feet on cobblestone streets echoed down the tight corridor.

"Am I doing okay?" Alex responded with a bit of bite. "You know what . . . yeah. There's not a whole prison's worth of chains holding me down. And I can actually breathe a little, even with this mask on. I mean, the smells down there . . ."

Can't blame the guy for sounding bitter. But I know just what will make him feel better. Reaching into his pocket, Bennett produced a single Lyllup Dragon, the bite-sized candy given to him by his lawyer.

"Here. I snuck this out for you. A little something, courtesy of Rapture. Check it out." Bennett held out the treat, understanding he was offering it to a man in a metal mask, but figured since Alex could sense Eve, he might be able to spot the treat through any material. The former teacher's head swiveled toward the Dragon, but he didn't say anything for an uncomfortably long time.

"You don't want it?" Bennett asked, unsure if this gesture was backfiring.

"I can't see. How am I supposed to grab it?" Alex asked.

"Right . . . my bad." Bennett took Alex's hand and placed the Lyllup Dragon in his palm. "Thought you could see it."

"The mask stifles Eve," Alex said blandly. "It's all a dark haze to me." He perused the treat with his fingers. "Where did you get it?"

"Doesn't matter. It will make you feel great. Looks like you could use it. And there's plenty more where that came from." Bennett wished he hadn't added that last part.

Alex delivered another long silence before asking, "So you've had a constant supply of feel-good candies this whole time?"

"No, not this whole time. I only—"

"I bet they taste amazing. I can already tell. What else did you get?" Bennett chose to hold his tongue. "Thanks," Alex said finally, managing to push the Dragon into his mask through one of the small mouth holes with his limited arm movement.

The remainder of the trip was spent in silence. Bennett hoped it would stay that way and that Alex was enjoying the high and riding the wave, feeling free to ignore the world around him. *Maybe find a little bit of happiness before these fucks—sorry, silly people—take it all away.*

Unimpeded, the convoy traveled the rest of the way. Passing

through the Molm Distillery gate, Bennett saw protesting faces he wished he had not, and was glad Alex was unable to. There were snarling Archfiend spitting fire, as well as giant insectoids and angry fish people wagging furious tongues and eyelashes at him and the so-called Ire boy.

Guess we really pissed some folks off.

Rolling inside the compound, the carriage traveled down the main lane between the primary office and maintenance building. The public's cries had been reduced to a dull roar, but the brief pause was slowly ended when a wall of flowery, orotund string music drew close. As their destination neared, Bennett spotted a new crowd waiting outside the building, which reminded him of an early twentieth-century factory, but much larger than whatever you were imagining. The sight was terrific but also demoralizing, made all the more so by the pomp and circumstance of the procession of the accused waiting for them—likely, the work of the Celestials.

Dancers pranced around the perimeter of the carpet leading to the entrance. *That's dumb.* An inappropriate number of flags and banners hung overhead. *That's dumb too.* The ceremonial "band" playing a tune was more an overbearing wall of sound rolling over Bennett like a river he had waded into and decided to plop down in while drunk. *Dumb, dumb, dumb.* A Bai-Shalk Wyst to his right was dancing seemingly to their own tune in their head. The performing artist was also a mime, apparently, or at least shared similar makeup with those of the Earthly profession. *Whoa—big dumb.*

Arriving at the end of a wide blue carpet, the carriage driver halted, the door facing the path leading to the interim courthouse. When Bennett looked out over the grand entrance to Distillery House 4, he felt as though he were arriving at a Hollywood movie premiere. There were no flashing bulbs, but what were clearly press flocked like hummingbirds, pointing blocky blue devices at him with glowing rings on the front where a traditional camera's lens might be.

Stepping out of the carriage, Bennett noticed he was being escorted by the same High Celestial who had slapped on his cuffs and carried him away from Winston's house the night of his arrest. He still didn't know their name.

"Hey, how's it going?" Bennett asked, but the Celestial did not answer. "That's cool. Got a name?" Still nothing. "Well, in that case, I'm going to call you Wiener Whistle. Is that okay, Wiener Whistle? I might shorten it to Wiener or Wiener Whiss, but not until we're really comfortable with each other. How's that? Sound good? Awesome. Just let me know if you ever want a rematch, Wiener Whistle."

Bennett was sure that would elicit a response from the stoic guard, and for a moment they remained silent. But after fifteen seconds, the ten-foot angel responded, "A pointless exercise."

With a giddy sigh, Bennett couldn't help but smile. *Yes. Thank you, Wiener Whistle.*

When Alex's slab was released from the carriage, the crowd gasped and recoiled defensively, providing Bennett another much-needed laugh. *These alien people clutching their pearls is so goddamn funny. I might pee.*

When they were so close to the entrance that Bennett could have long jumped to it, there remained one final, grand presentation. The song, sung by a Scythe, lasted thirty-four minutes and featured more passion and ferocity than any opera from Earth could ever hope to muster. *It feels like my face is being melted off. Kind of gnarly.* But only after it finished, just before Bennett could take no more and was about to start whining and moaning and kicking and screaming, were they allowed to cross the damn threshold into the building.

Once inside, he was surprised to find almost no sound, but the amount of Eve around him had skyrocketed, thanks mostly to a few powerful sources. The many spectators came from all walks and shades of UnEarth life. In many ways, the sensation was similar to Joseph and the Medolians' battle. But this time there was no raucous movement or noise. Not so much as a dull roar of whispers between spectators or counsel could be heard, and even the proletariats scurrying about on errands for the high-profile creatures did so as softly as plastic bags skimming along the ground. *I wonder if this is what the OJ Simpson trial felt like.*

Inside the courtroom, an additional choir was singing in the background. Bennett hadn't paid them any attention until their tone changed the moment Alex was wheeled in. Every head in the room turned to the door. In an instant, the place grew even more still than it had been before, while tinges of Dread popped up everywhere. *They're afraid of him. Weak fucks.*

Where the judge's bench would normally be stood a huge structure that blotted out most of the wall, with odd gaps resembling a shadowed mountain. The pointed top was high enough that he needed to crane his neck to see it comfortably, and at the base of the structure was a multitude of desks, none of which looked particularly special or judge-like. Standing at the front of the desks was the Medolian Mara, keeping watch over the gallery, clad in her dark gray, cyan-trimmed cloak. Her gaze was locked forward, as still as a rock, and she did not acknowledge Bennett when he tried to get her attention. *Probably for the best. She might not be too happy to see us.* Lifting his gaze above the disorganized mess of oddly shaped desks on the ground, Bennett found six empty balcony seats, all human-sized. Insignias representing the six independent worlds of UnEarth hung above them, each with a special entrance leading into the back wall.

Looking even higher above the balcony seats, he finally spotted the judge's bench. The enormous chair behind it, made of black wood and ratty leather, matched the desk perfectly, resembling a frayed macabre nightmare—an omen of grisly justice doled out by whoever sat in it. *Not stoked to meet whoever that is.*

Forced to march alongside Alex's rolling slab, Bennett was led straight to the defense table by Wiener Whistle. There, he found Roland already seated, flanked by Mayon and Kahli, the assistants Bennett had put on his shit list when they bumped into his friend, Brick. Sitting behind them were two additional Human Celestial assistants and a Psera Celestial standing perfectly still, their arms outstretched, holding a stack of scrolls like a living file cabinet.

To the right of them, at the end of the defense table nearest the aisle, sat what looked like a five-foot brown housefly with pointed, jittery orange wings. His nose, curled into a spiral like a butterfly's, jutted out from between his bulging, faded-disco-ball eyes. In his largest right and left hands, he held ink quills, both scribbling away simultaneously on separate scrolls. Bennett made out slight mutterings from the bug man as he wrote, hearing at the end of one breath, "Whoa, that's looney."

So that's Al's lawyer? Hmm . . . No idea what to think there.

The bug man stopped writing when Alex was wheeled next to him. His voice did not amount to much in volume or presence, reminding Bennett of the noise it made when he and his brother were kids and used to talk to each other with kazoos in their mouths.

"Ah—Hello, Mr.—Barker! Hello! Hi! AH!" the man screamed, pointing behind Alex. "There it is! Right there!" Before Bennett could look, the bug man rescinded his scream. "No, wait. Sorry—

no. Nothing. Nothing! Nothing is there. We are here. Alexander, I'm sorry we haven't been able to meet before today. Yes! It was out of my hands. My name is Jobaya. Jobaya!"

"It's fine," Alex said, his face and voice still muffled by the metal mask. "Good to meet you."

They're not going to leave that thing on him the whole time, are they? Bennett wondered.

"I want you to know I'm going to do—I'm going to do—my best for you! To help you. For you!" Jobaya shouted, rapping his right fingers on his left knuckles.

"I have no doubt you will," Alex said as politely as a man asking for no ketchup on his hamburger but who wouldn't be upset if they forgot and put it on anyway.

Looking as though he were fighting a heavy shake in his legs, Jobaya turned to the Celestial guard overseeing the defense table. "G—Guard! Hello. Yes." Jobaya cleared his throat. The Celestial guard turned to the small insect man to see what he wanted. "Guard, please release my client from this—*mmm*—mask! This mask here. Yes." Jobaya lost his battle with his shaky legs. "Yes! I am his counsel. I c—can—can—request it. I can!" He raised a single finger on all of his right hands for emphasis, dropping them as quickly as they had gone up. The Celestial guard stared blankly for a moment, as though processing, before complying and removing Alex's mask with the movements of a production-line robot. As he was revealed, the teacher winced from what must have been an overwhelming wave of Eve striking him all at once.

Even emaciated and colorless, Alex's face was a relief to see. His eyes remained shut initially as he let them adjust, and when he finally looked around, he showed no signs of emotion, staring like an animatronic on a boat ride at Disneyland. Bennett then remembered he'd also given the teacher a good deal of psychotropic substances, likely contributing to his general reaction—or lack thereof—to the moment.

Soon after, another parade from outside the building reached the courtroom entrance. Izaiah had been transported in his own carriage and given his own special walk of shame, escorted by Loredosai. When he stepped into the chamber in handcuffs, the crowd began to hiss and boo.

Led to the defense table, Izaiah quickly spotted Alex and Bennett, waving and smiling with his near-toothless grin. "Fellas! Hey, fellas! Over here!" He settled into his seat. "Boy, is it good to see you both. How have you been? They treating you all right? Alex, I dare say you need to eat better. I tried to sneak in some leftover pashinum sandwiches, but they took 'em and fed 'em to the hounds."

Bennett didn't say anything, just stared at the guy in disbelief. After a beat, Alex replied, "Hi, Izaiah."

"Don't worry, fellas, I'm doing okay. Hope you haven't been sick about it. But we'll talk later." Izaiah cheerfully clapped his hands and rubbed them together as though he were about to see the opening of a Broadway musical.

Soon, every seat in the house—some four thousand—was filled, and the people of UnEarth waited patiently for the trial to begin. Loredosai flew to a perch beside the judge's bench and, with a voice far less impressive than his High Celestial counterparts, declared himself the speaker of the court. He then introduced the senators from each of the UnEarth worlds.

When Van-Mortus was announced, she entered through a ground-level door behind the Counselors' desks at the room's front. Wearing a sleeveless black dress and a burgundy boa that looked like charred strips of bacon, she walked with heavy yet smooth steps, exuding a rough grace. The instant she entered, it was clear she commanded the room, every bit as awe- and terror-inspiring as the stories claimed. Clinging to her wake were two Human Archfiend and two pure Archfiend, the latter being ugly spuds that Bennett found humorous in a floating-pinata-at-the-ready sort of way. Reaching her seat, the senator from Arros remained standing.

Only one introduction remained: the one who would be overseeing the whole thing. Loredosai made a grand call in all five primary UnEarth languages for all to rise. "The most honorable, High Judge Nagura Axios."

Above the crowd, atop the crookedly built judge's loft, a door draped in shadow opened with a whoosh, as though the space beyond had been a vacuum that filled at the breach. A figure in a cloak of brown and black stalked through the void at the end of a short hall, her steps echoing like bones clacking against rock. Bennett couldn't tell exactly when she emerged into the light. *Maybe it's too scared to land on her?* Under her hood, he caught a glimpse of a face like a sketch: black and gray with sharp, frizzled lines forming a visage akin to a skull, but with a swollen mouth full of tall, rotten teeth.

The judge settled into her enormous chair, looming over all, and Bennett felt a chill. *That's who's presiding? I've never seen anything so metal.* With a crackling from her vertebrae that resonated throughout the silent room, Axios placed her gavel—a petrified ferrule of charred wood shaped into a short-handled hammer—on its stand. It was called Çilrex, which Bennett would later learn meant "the sower of silence."

Axios's gaze drifted over the gallery. When it landed on the defense table, her eye sockets fixed on Bennett, filling him with utter fear, stripping him bare. All that was his was now hers, leaving him naked. He felt her in his flesh, in his head, crawling through his gut, analyzing and devouring him while sitting two hundred feet away. The relief was immense when her stare shifted to Alex, as though a literal clawing weight had been lifted from his shoulders. He took a sudden deep breath, tasting the sweet-sweet air of freedom from the stare.

Curling her long index finger, the judge summoned Loredosai to her bench and spoke in a whisper. Nodding, he swooped down to the defense table and gave the posted guard orders. The guard raised a fist of solidarity. Loredosai reciprocated before flapping his wings and soaring back to his roost beside the judge's bench.

Picking up Alex's metal mask, the guard placed it back on his head and locked it shut. This time, Alex's lawyer did not protest.

"I'm s—sorry—yeah—Mr. Barker," Jobaya stammered as Alex's face disappeared behind the mask once again. "I guess the j—judge has spoken—oken."

"Guess so," Alex said.

With that matter settled, Axios nodded to Loredosai, seemingly satisfied. The Celestial called, "We will now observe piety."

The entire gallery then suddenly turned and faced the statue of Michael the Great in unison, as though this were the obvious part of the day where people did that kind of thing. For the next twenty minutes, long-voweled chants were directed at the statue during an eerie ceremony. *You people ever hear of toxic hero worship?* Once the praising of the former lord of Hywyn had concluded, Loredosai retrieved a scroll that, when opened, unrolled clear to the ground. "We will now read the rules and standards of conduct for the trial, as decided by the Counselors."

For the next three and a half hours, Loredosai read off the rules one by one. When finished, he was handed a glass case with yet another scroll inside. After punching his fist through and retrieving it, he handed the document to Axios. "I give to you, Your Honor, today's proceedings."

Proceedings? Does that mean we're going to actually proceed? Taking the file, Axios drew out a long knife with a red handle and cut it open. Her crackly fingers unraveled its contents. After reading for a moment, she looked out over the gallery. When she spoke, her words seemed to emanate from a planetary body, as though nature itself were talking—or a creature of equal authority. The sound of the judge's vocal cords was not just a chilling assault on the ears; it actively drove away all hope with its touch, butchering joy in the process. To hear it was to sense that something nearby, somehow, was absolutely wrong.

"Many charges. Even for defendants three." Her eyes scanned them one by one.

"The accused will stand!" the Barium captain shouted.

Bennett's lawyer pulled him to his feet, then did the same with Izaiah. Both stood with as little effort as possible. *Guess Izzy and I both feel the same way about this thing.* Alex, of course, was exempt, as he was chained to a slab. They waited for Axios to finish reading. Every turn of the page was audible. Her neck crackled like corn cereal, coming in waves, as though the weight of her head caused it to lose strength, only to regain it again. The tension in the room was palpable. Bennett thought that if he listened closely enough, he might hear the atoms in the words reacting as Axios's vision passed over them.

At one point during the lull, Loredosai turned to the judge, about to speak, but a long, silencing finger was raised first, stopping him. The Celestial bashfully turned away, waiting with everyone else. Around fourteen minutes later, Axios closed the file and finally looked up.

"I've read the final charges. Do you, Izaiah Ezekial, Bennett Hunter, and Alexander Barker, all creatures of planet Earth, being of sound mind, understand why you are here?"

Bennett was about to shrug but stopped himself. The three of them nodded in sloppy unison, Bennett adding a second nod. *But why? God, I'm getting weird.*

Axios nodded back. "The charge parcels will now be read. Izaiah Ezekial is charged with four counts of breaking official Tribunal orders, two counts of endangering UnEarth and its power source world, eight counts of misrepresenting the Tribunal and its members and the Senate, and one count of deliberate false witness. Human Bennett Hunter is charged with two counts of reckless use of Eve while on Earth, as well as one count of reclemne, the attempted revealing of UnEarth society to the population of Earth. Human Alex Barker is charged with seven hundred forty-one counts of reckless use of Eve, twelve hundred and ninety-eight counts of endangering UnEarth and its source world, and one count of willful attempted creation of the Ire."

When the last charge was read, Bennett shot up from his chair. "That's horseshit! Al didn't do anything willfully. You assholes put that shit in him! All he did was watch his wife get killed! Who are you to—"

A scream rang from the gallery, loud enough to stop Bennett in his tracks. More followed. The crowd fell into disarray. With a wave of her hand, Axios discreetly said, "Quiet," yet her voice resonated clearly in every ear. The gallery immediately sat back down and fell silent.

A gigantic, rock-solid, royal-blue hand rested heavily on Bennett's shoulder. "What are you doing, pumpkin pie?" Roland asked, his voice ripe with the mostly unaffected worry of a Celestial.

"How dare the human speak so out of turn!" Loredosai boomed from above. "You shall be held in contempt!"

Axios quieted her bailiff with an extended hand. The silence lingered while her gaze remained fixed on Bennett. Eventually, he folded his arms and looked away, admitting defeat.

Moving past the disruption, the trial continued, and the lawyers were given their chance to make opening remarks. Van-Mortus, as the lead prosecution, was allowed to choose the order and opted to go first. Her trek to the podium could have been mistaken for a performative art piece; she seemed intent on conveying the gravity of the trial even before saying her first word.

Reaching the podium, she spread her arms wide and addressed Axios, the Counselors, and the gallery. "With permission from the Counselors . . ." Van-Mortus locked eyes with the bulbous Wyst seated at the largest desk among those at the front of the room. He nodded with respect. She continued, "Your Honor, my fellow creatures, it is an honor. I'd like to begin by thanking the Molm Distillery for going to such lengths to accommodate us. We know it is beyond such a business's usual means, yet you did the impossible. Mr. Molm, wherever you are, thank you." She started a round of applause that quickly fizzled out. "Though I do look forward to when the Tribunal is repaired to its former glory. These trials will not feel the same until that day." She then thanked the Celestials working on the repairs, congratulating them on their efforts, making sure to mention it had been funded thanks to a bill she dutifully cosponsored.

"I stand before you today as a representative of the people, for whom I will fight. To find justice, yes, but also to alleviate the pain of those present in this courtroom and those beyond, throughout greater Icthene. Fear not, for you are not voiceless. I will ensure your words and thoughts are heard, delivering them with the ferocity that the great people of Arros expect from their leadership.

"In this trial, I will demonstrate without a doubt that the three accused share equal responsibility for the damages inflicted upon

Trivium City and our beloved Tribunal. I will show you that the events of the Joseph Mandate could have been prevented at any point, had even one of these three chosen to act. You will hear how they, along with the team that Izaiah himself commands—excuse me, commanded—the Medolian Sentries—brought about this unthinkable disaster."

To Bennett's right, Izaiah giggled a little.

"I will also show you that the great world of Arros and its ruler, Lucifer-Aveyl, share none of this blame. My people's words were ignored time and again. In fact, if our advice had been heeded from the beginning, none of the events surrounding the nameless demon and the Ire would have occurred. The great world of Arros recommended Bennett Hunter for the Wrath imbuement. As one who'd spent a lifetime living in anger, he would have been the clear choice to control the shade—"

"I disagree," the giggling voice to Bennett's right said.

"What?" Axios asked Izaiah. "You were speaking as counsel, Medolian?"

"Yes," Izaiah answered. "Well, maybe a little bit of a personal comment, too. Fifty-fifty."

"What is your comment, Medolian?" Loredosai asked.

Izaiah stood up wearily with a grunt. "The thing is, I don't believe what she said is true."

"You poor, dear Medolian. Izaiah, after so many millennia presiding over this court, it seems you've learned nothing," Van-Mortus said. "With no official citation, you will be overruled—"

With a nervous shake and while muttering a hundred affirmations to himself, Jobaya rose out of his chair. "I believe Izaiah is—*AH!*—calling speculation. Speculation! Article seventeen, Your H—Honor. Please. Sorry. Thank you! Ah!" The Veen tossed

a quick glance at Izaiah before sitting down far faster than he had
stood up.

Axios stayed quiet and nodded, her neck crackling like tree
branches bending. Her gaze drifted to Izaiah.

"Yep, that's exactly what I meant! Article seventeen. My favorite," he said.

Axios sighed and shook her head. "Very well. Van-Mortus will
cease speculating."

"My apologies if my statement appeared vague, Your Honor.
I hadn't finished." With uncharacteristically visible frustration,
Van-Mortus approached her team at the prosecution's table and
was handed a scroll. She scanned it as though searching a map. "I
was getting to the facts, such as how Izaiah changed the agreed-up-
on plan and how this brought about the Ire. *Not* the shade of Eve.
Not the energy of revitalization. *He* is the one who threatened our
food and energy supply, not Arros or Wrath."

"Understood," Axios said.

Van-Mortus continued, "The human Alex Barker created the Ire
through his own lack of self-control."

Alex's lawyer stood again. "Interjection. Wait! No . . . I mean yes.
Article two, Your Honor. Two! Mr. Barker's mental state following
his Earth—Earthly—EARTHLY—death has not been analyzed.
No—NONE—conclusions have been drawn. He was obviously—
AH! Over there!—broken by the Eve put inside him. According
to your own dissertation—whoa, look out—Mr. Barker accomplished many feats—many—while in the so-called 'Ire' state. This
would suggest outside motivation. Out! It does."

"No!" Van-Mortus shouted, losing her unshakeable cool for the
briefest moment. "While that is true, Human Barker also—"

"Van-Mortus will cease," Axios said, silencing the senator.

Jobaya sat down at the same time as Van-Mortus and tried to hide his face behind a stack of scrolls.

"She's still looking at me, isn't she?" the Veen asked.

"*Mm-hmm*," Bennett answered. *This little guy is putting quite the target on his back.*

The judge then moved on, allowing the defense a turn to make their opening arguments. Speaking first would be Roland. Before rising, he gave Bennett a heavy pat on the back.

"Don't worry, applesauce. Here's where I shine." Clutching his robe in both hands, he began a boisterous oration. "With permission from the Counselors . . ." Roland waited for the approving nod before continuing. "Your Honor. My fellow creatures, it is an honor. I stand here today in these unprecedented times as a proud member of the Celestial race and representative for all Rapture users—not just the human you see here in the courtroom. For though this creature was once only human, he has since been changed by the wonder that is Rapture. This man is no more guilty than any of us here. He did all that was asked and saved our lives from certain doom at the hands of the miserable cockroach you see chained up next to my client. He, the Ire boy, is the only one who is to blame. Everything you will hear Van-Mortus say about Alex Barker will be true. On him, we do not disagree."

Bennett's gaze filled with hate. *What the fuck is this guy doing?* He was on his feet in a flash. "That's horseshit, too!"

More gallery screams rang out. The Eve in the room pulsed and spiked. The penetrating gaze of Axios was upon him again, stinging Bennett's inner self.

One of Roland's assistants pulled him back into his seat as the lawyer marched over and soon loomed over him. "What are you doing, you little waste?"

Moving back to the podium, Roland attempted to get the crowd back on course. The next five minutes were spent sowing the seeds of sympathy. "This poor man lost his family. His brother to war. His father to the terrible human disease called cancer. His mother, all but lost to him."

Bennett had no idea how Roland knew all this. They'd never discussed his family or life on Earth. *Plus, that's not even true. Just because I hope she doesn't know I exist doesn't mean I don't know where my mom is.*

The show continued, but Bennett could take it no longer. "Stop! I don't want sympathy!" he shouted, interrupting.

Roland's assistant pushed him down in his seat again, this time keeping a hand on his shoulder, pinning him down like a boulder with a death grip.

"Lay off Al. I mean it," Bennett shouted at his lawyer. But this time, Roland ignored him and continued, though much of the wind had been taken from his sails by then.

"You will see that my client is a separate entity and acted accordingly with the requests of UnEarth and as his human military training would have him do. Despite what many in UnEarth have heard, the militaries of the human world have become quite advanced and respectable, relatively speaking. To think my client could be careless and irresponsible is a long jump indeed."

When he finished, Roland thanked the crowd and Axios. Before sitting, he fluffed out his gown and let his wings deflate like balloons down to his side.

Loredosai then pointed at Jobaya. His turn was up.

"The counsel for Mr. Barker . . . Veen, what is your prefix?" Loredosai asked.

The jittery bug stood from his seat, playing with his many fingers. "Ish. YES! If you wish for my professional title, it is Ish Veen Jobaya. It is!"

"Very well, Ish Veen Jobaya. Once you've received permission from the Counselors, you may make your opening remarks. Briefly."

Jobaya waited for the head Counselor to nod slowly and deliberately. The bug man then took a long breath before beginning.

"Th-thank you—thank you, Counselors. Yes. Your Honor, my fellow creatures—NELP!—you give me glory with your ears. I stand—STAND before you today—"

"But not very tall!" shouted a Beaubon from the gallery. The crowd erupted with laughter. Axios reached for Çilrex and all went quiet.

Motioning at Jobaya, she spoke slowly, letting her ghostly voice scrape across Bennett's eardrums. "Proceed."

"Oh, th-thank you!" Jobaya said. "In this trial, my hope—HOPE—is to prove that only one individual in the entire Joseph Mandate—*ACK!*—was without autonomy or his faculties. Alex Barker was a good man set to die-die . . . die a hero in his land, when our world intervened and thrust him down a path—APATHAP-ATH—he not only couldn't control but was not given proper instructions in order to take part in. Due to UnEarth interference, an innocent man was sent to his people's—LOOKOUT!—literal embodiment of all things undesirable. Then, THEN, due to UnEarth inaction, he—"

Loredosai interrupted. "That will be all, Ish Veen Jobaya. Thank you."

"But I haven't finished," Jobaya said. "In fact, I've prepared several other—"

"You've said enough. Inaccuracies have no place in this courtroom, and the government of UnEarth is not on trial—Alex Barker is. You're not here to point fingers."

"With all fingers pointed at him, SKELP!—where is my client to point?" Jobaya asked.

"Make not a mockery of this hallowed institution!" Loredosai moaned.

"I make no mockery! No mockery made! Mockery-less! Just speaking as counsel, the assignment which I was gifted, gifted . . ." Jobaya trailed off with muttered ramblings.

"It is no longer your time to speak, Veen," Loredosai said.

"*Mmmm.*" Jobaya tapped the table a dozen times in quick succession, causing a buzz. The sound was intended to grasp attention but somehow managed to carry a controlled air of respect. "*Mmm* . . . Your Honor . . . great Axios, I must protest."

A pregnant pause followed as Axios considered. Finally, she nodded at Jobaya.

"Noted, but we will now hear from the Medolian."

Jobaya sat down while all eyes fixed on Izaiah, who didn't budge or respond for a moment, then suddenly seemed to come to. Smacking his lips a couple of times, he pushed back his chair and rose to his feet with a series of pained grunts.

"Oh, I guess I don't have much to say. Sorry we're having to get together under these pretenses. Though, the change of scenery is kind of refreshing. I don't know. I'm sorry for a lot of the things I've done. I did my best the whole time. If you still want me to go back to work for you, I will. But first you gotta stop blaming the fellas. The only parts they played were the ones given to them. They're innocent. Nobody deserves blame here but me. Not the fellas. Me. Guess that's all." He sat halfway before standing back up with another labor-filled moan. "Oh, and . . . I feel really bad about the Tribunal blowing up. That's been a big mess for a lot of people. Pretty regrettable. Anyways . . ." Izaiah sat down, his shoulders taking a few bobs to settle.

"Are you making a farce of this court?" Loredosai asked.

"I wouldn't know how to make a farce if I had the recipe," Izaiah said, chortling.

"The Medolian's ease is unappreciated," Axios chimed in, adding a frigid chill.

"I'm awful sorry about that, Your Honor. Truly," Izaiah said.

"You sound sarcastic."

"No, I'm not, Your Honor. I'm very true right now. You can see that, right?"

"Yes. You still sound sarcastic."

"I'm trying so hard not to, you wouldn't believe."

Jobaya cleared his throat and raised his right hands. "Your Honor, if the third defendant has no further remarks—MARKS!—might I utilize his remaining time? After all, opening remarks are usually quite long." Jobaya caught Izaiah's gaze. "As long as that's okay—KAY—with you."

"I can't imagine anything I want more," Izaiah replied.

"You were given your chance," Loredosai said.

"But my case—*rrnnnn*—was designed to provide information at certain junctions," Jobaya said. "I have yet—have yet—to disseminate any of my intended—"

"Does the Veen have trouble hearing directions?" Loredosai asked.

"N-No, sir. I'm a fine listener. That's me! Fine!"

"Then you will cease this nonsense and bring your evidence when you are called to do so."

The Veen lawyer's fingers twiddled like mad. It appeared he was waiting for Axios to disagree with her bailiff, but when she did not, Jobaya sat back down.

Alex's voice, soft from within the mask, said, "Thanks anyways."

The rest of the first day continued much the same, proving Alex was already cemented to the chopping block. As the proceedings carried on, Bennett, who could usually keep near-perfect internal time, was left mystified, unknowing how much of it had passed. His internal rhythm was gone. His mind was a roaming fog drifting in and out, struck periodically by the shades of Eve in the room and the feelings they instilled. Sudden Grief overtook him when he sensed a nearby Lostros. Bennett then looked down and found his knuckles were covered in blood. Someone was screaming.

Then his lawyer was nudging him back into the present and the courtroom. "Stay with us, applesauce. It's early still."

MINE

Despite her travels and her prolonged transformation into someone who no longer spent her days residing in the dirt, Leigh had
somehow found herself back where it all started. There she stood,
the pickax she had just been swinging resting beside her, leaning against a portable generator box. Her shoulders heaved as she
caught her breath. The mud on her clothes was caked in splotchy
patches over juicy sweat stains. The worn work gloves shoved into her back pocket were slightly soggy, soaking her jeans and butt
cheeks.

Yeah, I'm back, go figure. Stills smells bad.

[*Perhaps I never departed in the first place?*]

Clangs and piercing bangs rang out like fireworks dropped by
neighborhood children as the crew in Leigh's care worked away on
a rock pile with hammers and pickaxes, filling buckets with chunks
of rubble and depositing them in the back of an electric cart. The
demolition they had set off that morning was already proving
worthwhile; some of the precious mineral they were after was

spotted during a quick once-over of the pile. The two charges of C-4 had created a far bigger boom than she had expected, loosening more earth than Leigh had imagined the tiny packages could.

As a former archaeologist, she was used to treating sites with extreme care, making sure not to harm any unseen artifacts. Explosives had never been part of the picture. But here, at Surface Station Five, the goal was not to be precious but to extract as much treasure as possible from good Mother Earth by any means necessary.

No one knew exactly what they were mining for, and they were encouraged never to ask, but Leigh had a good guess. This region of Europe was often cited by UnEarth aficionados as a hotspot for Eve-infused minerals, which were naturally occurring but often rare. Since no major studies had been conducted on the subject, no one knew how minerals within the Earth's crust had been soaked in Eve or how their properties had changed. Most of the experts Leigh trusted believed that during the Earth's formation, the enormous energies at play had loosened the barrier between the universes, allowing small amounts of energy to trade back and forth.

The most common of these minerals, found all over the world, was a metal called dolmuk, which was soft and brittle and conducted Eve about as well as rubber soles conducted electricity. Much of the waste scraped off the top of a bucket of molten iron in a smelting plant was dolmuk, unbeknownst to metalworkers throughout history. However, other Eve-infused minerals, such as minillia, were powerful generators of UnEarth energy. This was what Leigh believed the Surface was truly after.

[*It would make sense. Minillia can be forged into mylas, which boosts Eve properties.*]

But minillia can also be tempered into nevrose, which basically kills

Eve. So, I guess I'll just have to wait and see what the fuck Aluqa is really after.

As far as Leigh could tell, she was the only one on her team truly interested in what they were toiling away to collect.

[The others are content to just do as told. An enviable trait.]

Nice and docile. Though most of 'em seem scared shitless, if I'm honest.

Whenever she met a Surface member for the first time, they inevitably shared how they ended up pledging themselves to the cause. Each tale varied but often involved an encounter with an UnEarth creature that either scared or fascinated them to such a degree that it consumed their thoughts and lives. That initial incident usually represented the bulk of their understanding of UnEarth. Initial impressions were everything, and many Surface members ended up dead wrong about various things they believed. *One poor guy thinks UnEarth controls the weather with magnets. Didn't know what to even say to him.*

Proper knowledge or not, those who had crossed over and become embroiled with the world of the Eve often described themselves as videnties, or "those who know better." This was, of course, in stark contrast to the moniker given to those who knew nothing: inanies. *[Classic in-crowd and out-crowd. Usually inevitable if group cohesion is to be maintained.]*

As the ultimate videnty, the others quickly gleaned Leigh's expertise and took advantage of it, asking question after question as they worked alongside her or passed by in the halls. "Oh, I'm sorry to stop you, but is it true that Beaubons can shoot electricity from their eyes?" "Did Hywyn really freeze Arros over, and that's why it's been so quiet lately?" For how curious they were, it was amazing that no members ever took the time to visit the station's library, which wasn't much—and missing what Leigh thought were some of the better books on the subject—but still had plenty they could soak up. [*If only they would try.*]

To be treated as a walking encyclopedia was quite grating—*the one emotion I was apparently left with following Joseph is irritated, go figure*—but there was also something endearing and reassuring about the other Surface members. It turned out Leigh was not alone in her thoughts and beliefs, nor in her—what some would call—foolish mission. The professor was currently among the closest people she likely had to peers. Her dominance in the world of UnEarth trivia had given her a boost of confidence upon joining and helped her get promoted to team leader, or "charge," after only a few weeks. This boded well for her chances to rise to the next level, known as the Higher Surface, and become one among its members called the Cavaliers. *We call them Cavs or Cavvies down here.*

Just like all social groups, the Surface was built on a hierarchy. The lower members, called "rooks"—those who were newer or had not yet proven themselves—primarily worked the mine. Every rook was required to toil at least six hours a day, six days a week, in the tunnels, though more was politely encouraged. This was in addition to their regular duties, which kept the facility running, with jobs ranging from cook to plumber to dishwasher to janitor. Sleep was rare, and even when it came, it was seldom restful. The accommodations for lower members were deficient in nearly every capacity. Pipes moaned and leaked. Basic electrical systems shorted out, starting two small fires since Leigh had arrived. The provided "beds" (*using that term generously*) came four to a room and were stiff and sharp and poke-y at their creases. All this said nothing of the food, a cuisine more suited to a dilapidated prison near some stark Russian border.

But one positive that could not be ignored were the clothes the rooks received: a blue-and-white work jacket with matching pants and T-shirt, as freshly pressed and clean smelling as a flower-blanketed meadow after a rain.

(but good-smelling flowers, because some flowers can actually smell like ass when wet)

[*That is—unfortunately—true.*]

It seemed impossible that an organization as well-funded and globe-spanning as the Surface could not afford better accommodations for its people, which could only mean that the quality of the lower-member barracks and work zones was a deliberate attempt to "break them in" or motivate them to strive harder to climb the ladder. If a rook could show great worth, they might ascend to the elite of Aluqa's army: those who would be on the front lines of whatever conflict everyone around here seemed to think was on its way. The sweet, sweet revenge that came with it was what most everyone was after. *I can't say I'm all that different.* Once in the Higher Surface, the rook would then gain access to the east wing of the station, which was cordoned off from everyone else and a complete mystery. If Leigh had to guess, it was better than the lower facilities in every conceivable way.

You know that's where the really good books are hiding.

[*It is curious, though. Nothing I read about the Surface before joining mentioned such a hard division among its members.*]

And nothing mentioned the Cardinal, either, who seems to be number two around here, even though he hasn't been at the station the entire time I have.

[*I wonder what other useful bits of information I can expect to discover moving forward.*]

The Cavaliers were rarely seen in the lower tunnels, and almost never near the mine. *Skraga comes down from time to time to help out. Watching her lift and chuck boulders with her bare hands is always inspirational.* Whenever the rooks were graced with the presence of a

Cavalier or two, it was often as they were returning from a mission for Aluqa, riding in on the back of a cart or truck, often bloodied and bruised, looking as though they'd just come from a street fight. The lowers could only speculate about the sort of adventures the mighty Cavs had been on. Once pulled into their ranks, all higher members ceased conversing with the lowers and refused to even look them in the eye when passing. Secrets from above were never shared below.

Leigh guessed the truth wasn't all that dramatic; the Highers were likely just Aluqa's inner circle: thugs who did her dirty work. The bags and crates they often returned with were no doubt stolen goods. But if anyone was going to be among the first to use whatever means the great leader had discovered to get humans into UnEarth, it would be them.

So that's where I need to be.

Until she could secure an invitation to the Higher Surface, Leigh would need to do her time in the lower levels among the rooks. Though she'd already sacrificed a lot to join Aluqa's organization— her time, her money, her future plans—the work and pain would be worth it. Once she knew how to get into UnEarth, she could leave the Surface behind and return to her solo mission. But in the meantime, she would become a lackey—something she hadn't been since her teenage years.

Far more exposing than I remember. Makes me rethink a few of the times I spoke to my employees. Oops.

After arriving at the station, Leigh had been forced to remove her Gauntlet and gem bracelet. Pahlanksha, comfortingly, was the one who took them and placed them in a crimson box, telling the professor she would get them back when the time was right, offering a slight but reassuring wink to go along with it. *Felt stupid. I hadn't considered they would take them. At least, not my Gauntlet.*

[*Though it makes perfect sense.*]

Ever since, Leigh had been on her own. Just as Aluqa had told her the night she joined, she had not been given a trace of leniency or special treatment. Eleven weeks had passed, and the leader still had yet to even acknowledge her within the station. Whenever she did appear in the mine, Aluqa did so as a queen among the fortunate peasantry, looming from a high vantage point with scrutiny. A coterie of Cavaliers often glued to her heels seemed to follow her as she glided like rolling mist—a being beyond those who served her. All of this was the point. The display crafted the image of a perfect being, one worth laying down one's life for.

[*And it largely seems to have worked.*]

(oh yeah . . . big time)

The authors of those books I read on cult leaders would do well to study this lady.

Aluqa's rooks worked hard and without complaint. If a rare failure did show itself, they were first warned with a trip down the long dark hall in the south wing to the Ketinolum. No one really knew what happened inside, as none who were escorted in ever came out talking. White faces and shaking lower lips accompanied mumblings and apologies, but not much else. If that first warning, however extreme it seemed, did not work, and the rook continued to break rules—or, even worse, slack off—they were expelled. No one seemed to know if that meant continuing to live on the outside or being permanently silenced by a Cavalier, but upon their discharge, a note would be left on their bed stating that the expelled had failed to qualify to continue serving the Surface—frequently because they'd tried to sneak out or were caught communicating with the outside world: the two largest offenses. There was no way to confirm whether the expelled member had actually committed the crimes or not, but from what Leigh gathered, no one seemed to care. None would dare question Aluqa. The members of the Surface—from the lowest rook to the highest Cavalier—treated their time in the organization as though they'd enlisted in the military to defend their country in a time of war, and she was the boundless general who would lead them to victory.

Sometimes it's endearing, like watching kids play. And sometimes it's really not.

[*I often find myself wondering if their mental faculties are being affected by their time underground. Human physiology does benefit greatly from sunlight.*]

(*true, but i'm doing fine. no friggin' problems with these mental faculties*)

[*None whatsoever.*]

Presently, as Leigh was about to take up her pickax and join the others following her water break, one of the more zealous rooks, Klive, began shouting. "This pile hasn't gotten any smaller! They'll mark us if we don't hustle! Come on! The Cardinal says he needs all he can get! Get to it!"

The screaming Englishman was well into his fifties and had unfortunately blown out most of his hearing while working as a steelman in Sussex. The issue was that he seemed to forget that fact a lot. A general conversation with the man could often be heard from five tunnels over.

"Don't forget, he's coming. He'll be here soon to see how we've done." Klive coughed up a wad of spit and showed it to the ground. "And we shouldn't disappoint him!"

"Yeah, we know he's coming, Klive! Whether we want to or not! Because you won't shut up about it," Daria said calmly, kicking a clump of dust at the Englishman to cover his spit.

"Hey! None of you give our Celestial comrade his dues," Klive protested. "This facility was designed by him!"

"That's not such a great compliment," Daria said.

"You only say that because you've never seen the east wing."

"Neither have you."

"Yes, I have! I told you I saw the Cavvies' barracks."

"Right, and we told you we don't believe you."

"You're all full of it! I don't care if you believe me or not! I don't! Just watch, you'll see I don't!"

Klive grumbled to himself while Daria and the others stifled their laughter poorly.

"You speak of the Cardinal as though he's greater than Aluqa," said Lommie, one of the smaller volunteers.

"I never said that. But he is great," Klive insisted.

"Aluqa is our leader. The head of the Surface," said Lommie.

"I'm not saying she isn't! But there wouldn't be any Surface without the Cardinal. We've all heard the story. She was the greatest Eve creature hunter in the world! When she came upon him, she spared the Cardinal's life. She saw the good in him, and he has since devoted his life to helping the cause. He is our ally."

"The only reason you go around singing his praises is because you think he'll pick you for that special team he's putting together in America," Daria said. "And the reason you've been so much louder lately is because you think he will take you back with him after he visits here."

"Bah! I am not! What a rude thing to . . . do you really think he would?"

The others groaned at Klive and kicked more dust at him.

"You make me sick, trusting anything from that godforsaken reality that hangs over us," Daria said. "I've never understood why Aluqa trusted such a creature."

In five months, the Cardinal was set to arrive from America, though no one seemed to know the reason for the trip. He and Aluqa, it seemed, had a coparenting relationship with the Surface, having maintained it from different continents for more than five years. The separation occurred when the Cardinal decided he needed larger facilities to continue his experiments and develop weaponry to use against UnEarth. Rumors now speculated that he had independent facilities spread across North, Central, and South America.

One of these sites was likely where the technology needed to get humans into UnEarth was being developed, which Pahlanksha had alluded to. If the Cardinal was making the trip to Europe and Station Five, along with a rumored fifty crew in tow, there was a good chance he would be bringing that technology with him.

What other explanation could there be? Unless he's just dropping off some new recruits.

As of now, Leigh had no opinion one way or another about the Cardinal. It was just strange to know so little about someone who seemed to be such a key player—*I'm simply not used to it*—but she had no real reason to distrust him any more or less than anyone else.

With annoyed gusto, she slapped her hands across one another and huffed out her nostrils. The dig team, knowing that was her way of saying "shut up and get back to work," did exactly that. There was no more gossip or bickering for five or six lovely minutes until the shift-change bell rang, echoing through the tunnels.

The second shift change of the day meant she would now need to travel back to her bunk and hopefully get some shut-eye before her late shift in the washroom—her second job in the facility. After her team put away their gear and once the last of them was on their way out, she followed in the rear, keeping a bit of distance.

The replacement team soon passed by, and Leigh nodded civilly as they descended into the tunnel, handing off the day's log as they went.

Reaching the cart junction, the professor declined the first ride; it was a little too full for her taste. Despite her team's protests, she waited for the next transport and rode the ten minutes back to the station alone. Exiting the tunnel, she entered a hall plated in vibrant blue metal. A silver sheen lingered over the smooth surfaces like a fine mist.

Walking briskly, she passed the first of what would be many UnEarth creatures' skulls mounted high on the wall. Taken from a pure Beaubon, this one had three-inch teeth fixed in a clownish smile. The trophies came from Aluqa's personal collection and decorated almost every hall and junction in the station. A handful were from pure UnEarth creatures, like the Beaubon, but most were from UnEarth Humans, their shapes much closer to that of *Homo sapiens*, often exaggerated in various ways, with bloated bulbs or deep divots. Sometimes, they appeared caught in the transition back to their former selves, leaving the skull with insect mandibles, horns, or split lower jaws. The skulls were endlessly fascinating, and Leigh took every free moment to study them. [*There is literally nowhere else with a similar collection.*]

Dozens of bodies clad in the Surface's navy-blue uniform passed by as she made her way from the central core toward the north barracks. Station Five was the supposedly the largest and busiest of the Surface outposts, considered the central hub for those who followed Aluqa. (*makes me feel like i got drafted by the Yankees*)

The halls were especially hectic today. Nearly every rook with a job or task—already demanding in their own right—had seen their duties doubled or even tripled in the last few weeks, as more bodies were pulled away to assist in the mine. With the excitement

surrounding the Cardinal's arrival, along with the still-reverberat-
ing news of Alex Barker's and Bennett Hunter's transgressions in
UnEarth, an electric anticipation had been steadily mounting in
the station, practically quivering through the walls.

When a mess of younger members came scampering down the
hall, likely late to wherever they were supposed to be, Leigh had
to dodge out of the way before making her final turn into the
entrance of the northern barracks, currently housing forty-eight
members. Upon entering, she found her larger roommate, Esma,
sitting in the center of the room between the bunks. With her
tanned legs folded and hands on her hips, she breathed with a
staccato, grunting rhythm. Upon Leigh's entrance, she ceased her
meditation—intended to help awaken her hidden Eve powers
(lol)—and quickly rose to stand as tall as possible, practically on
her tiptoes. The twenty-eight-year-old's desire to govern had been
immediately apparent upon their first meeting. *Her opening handshake said it all.* Esma was the lord of bunk room 227 in her mind
and, she would be respected, come hell or high water.

Leigh's other roommate, Danika, was sprawled across her bunk,
staring intently into a bright orange gem in her hand, as if it
might suddenly reveal the secrets of the universe. When Danika
had introduced herself, she quickly showcased the collection of
shiny rocks she had amassed over the years, convinced they might
contain Eve. This obsession was both her hobby and her passion.
(probably one of the reasons she stays so friggin' cheerful in this place)

At five feet tall, Danika was a perfect example of the type of person the Surface attracted: seemingly ordinary until a run-in with
an UnEarth creature changed their life forever. In her case, it was a
Human Veen Scythe. With no one else to confide in, she eventually found her way to Aluqa. Originally stationed at Station Seven,

Danika had been transferred to Station Five four years ago after Seven was mysteriously shut down.

[*According to her, they were attacked by a woman named Madam Daphne, whose troops overran the base while most of the members were away.*]

But that story clashed with another rumor circulating around, which claimed that Station Seven had been completely flooded when a dam wall burst upstream from its hydroelectric generator, killing only a few while the rest evacuated in time. Both tales were incredible, and there were more where those came from. *Almost none of which I believe.* But it did seem particularly strange that even Danika didn't know the real truth of Station Seven's fate, convinced it was Madam Daphne's doing. *It makes sense, I guess, given she and Aluqa are apparently mortal enemies. But the madam hasn't made many moves the last few hundred years. Don't see why she would start now.*

[*The Wyst is said to be a master tactician. It could be possible she is looking to take advantage of the chaotic situation currently taking place in her world.*]

I know I would if I were her.

When Leigh finished acknowledging her roommates, she found, resting on her own pillow, a white envelope. Its face was blank. Initially, she thought it might be a prank from Esma—*(fucking bitter lady)*—but a quick, suspicious glance at her officious roommate was met with a firm "It wasn't me." Gradually assured this wasn't a trick, Leigh concluded this must be something from the powers above. *It has to be.*

"Looks like you have a good friend somewhere," Esma said with envious grit.

Taking the envelope, Leigh found a card inside. In plain text at its center read: *Door 12.*

[*Twelve? Ah yes, I know where that is.*] The door was located in the rear of the central station core, a place Leigh was familiar with, having stumbled upon it on accident after taking a wrong turn once. *(and while doing a bit of snooping. shh, don't tell)*

The envelope and card could only mean she'd been called—approved to join the Higher Surface. The time to ascend the ladder had come.

Already? It just feels soon. Not that I'm complaining.

Was Aluqa changing her mind? Was this the special treatment Leigh thought she would never receive? Or had she truly earned this spot through tenacity and skill?

(shit, i say i earned it. why the hell not?)

[*I have little reason to think otherwise.*]

The hall where Door 12 was located was a maintenance corridor, where only the electrical engineers worked. The station generator was overall quietest here, but that only made the walls hum louder with the power flowing through them. Finding the inconspicuous wooden door, the professor took the handle. Only now, in her second visit, did she notice there were no signs or indications of what lay beyond the door.

As she opened it, she found a steep set of stairs rising sharply out of sight, engulfed by navy-blue walls.

No handrails, huh? Nothing suspicious about this.

Each step was taken carefully, and soon Leigh reached the top landing and an open doorway. Peering inside, she saw that the space was dim, about ten yards deep. The far wall was lined with white trim that complemented the room's deep-sea hue.

Several electric lamps glowed faintly in the corners, invoking the ambiance of an old Victorian landowner's smoking lounge, though without any seating to enjoy a cigar. Short tables and marble statues were interspersed between stone columns throughout the two-story room, topped with even more statues. If Leigh didn't know better, she'd swear these were UnEarth relics: sculptures created by humankind over the hundreds of thousands of years of history between the worlds. How they had survived intact for so long, and in such fine condition, escaped her.

Inside the display cases throughout the room was the largest collection of UnEarth artifacts Leigh could have ever dreamed of. Each piece rested on a custom, hand-carved base with LED display lights, categorized by world and shade of UnEarth. To her left, artifacts from Arros included bits of Archfiend melee armor and gnarly hand tools designed for destruction.

Is that what I think it is?

Beside a case stood a tall, clunky plant, coated in what looked like a layer of volcanic rock. Steam rose from the cracks in its bulbs and stems, which opened and closed slightly to let it breathe, crackling like a dying campfire to reveal a red-hot core within.

A real, live Kreshin plant? Here, in our world? How is this possible? How are any of these specimens here?

To her immediate right, opposite the Arros exhibition, was a tilted display case with a green velvet face covered in various objects. Leigh approached to find knives, blades, brass knuckles, a mace club, and assorted trinkets and tools of UnEarth design. *What is this, an arsenal for a street fight?* Toward the bottom lay a row of smaller items, including a Crusher, but without a label to indicate which shades would mix if squeezed in hand. Risky, as Crushers could do any number of things based on the combination of Eves inside them—*even explode. More powerful than a hand grenade, just by adding Jubilee to Wrath. Potent little things.*

An empty space in the display suggested that one item was missing: a round object small enough to fit in the palm.

But why just one? What is this? What's going . . .

The realization struck the second after she asked the question: what lay before her was a test, one of choice. In the olden tradition of dueling, she was being given a chance to select her arms. Once a weapon was taken, the contest would likely begin.

Most of the choices were striking weapons—blunt and direct. The most enticing was a red hatchet with a blade that looked as though it had just come out of a furnace, likely thanks to Wrath forged into it. But that couldn't be the right choice. Nothing flashy ever was. Besides, Leigh wasn't interested in bludgeoning; she wanted to win whatever this challenge was and ascend. Her gaze scanned the remaining options, finally settling on a small golden object akin to a Zippo lighter.

A slight gasp escaped her lips.

No, that can't be . . .

The object was an Uvullu'Ye, and from the looks of it, it was in great condition—possibly even working condition. Leigh had only read about them; many thought they were mere myth. She reached for the trinket, drawn by both her curiosity and the tool's potential for serious damage.

I touched it. Guess this will have to do.

Turning in an about-face, she surveyed the room and its three remaining doors. It seemed her next test would be choosing which door to use. Nothing particularly identifying about any of them stood out. *Will there be a different challenger in each? Might as well make a decision at random.* As she considered her options, she felt her pulse elevate and her skin flush. *(my subconscious is freakin' about something i don't even know about)*

[*Yes, something is erroneous.*]

The room then fell unnaturally quiet. Leigh steeled herself, waiting for the test to begin.

The attack didn't come from a doorway but from within the room, which until that moment she had assumed was empty. A muddy shape, blending into the wall, caught her eye due to the way the soft light fell at the corner, signaling something out of place. Then it dawned on her sharply: a *tone*. That's what was missing from the weapons display—the very tool she often used herself. Her opponent, whoever they were, was trying to sneak up and ambush her.

(you can't hit me with my own shit!)

Narrowly avoiding the attack, a translucent body crashed into the wall where she'd just been standing. Leigh raised the Uvullu'Ye and activated it, aiming forward as she released a ball of fierce cyan light. The burst sent her attacker's cells into hyperdrive, igniting a mixture of passion, exhaustion, and an unquenchable desire to flex every muscle endlessly. Such a sensation would be too much for anyone but a pure Wyst to withstand without losing consciousness. *Just hope I'm not fighting one of those!*

Before they could retaliate, the figure of her attacker was revealed on the ground, awash in cyan sparks. The man shrieked in pain, rolling back and forth on the carpet, gripping his groin as though it were a wound that required extreme pressure to stop bleeding. With a final yelp and a whimper, he went still, his lifeless eyes locked on Leigh.

She recognized him. [*His name is Lionel. Another crew leader from the south barracks.*]

As much as Leigh appreciated her victory, she was more concerned with what came next. Who had watched the battle unfold, and what would the repercussions be? Moments later, from the only doorway in the room she wasn't facing, Aluqa appeared, softly clapping.

Unfazed, Leigh turned to her and signed, "Hope that was entertaining."

"Of course! Though I'm glad you knew to stop after just one hit.

If you'd blasted him again, he would have splattered into a patch of goo on the floor. Trust me; it's impossible to get out of a rug," Aluqa chuckled, clearly pleased. Taking Leigh's hands in hers, she found the professor's gaze. The striking brown of Aluqa's irises, with their amber highlights, seemed unnaturally vivid tonight. For a moment, Leigh swore she saw twinkling glints of sky blue scattered within. "I'm so proud of you. That was exactly how I wanted it to go. Simply wonderful. You are . . . *mmm*, I just love it. Whatever it is."

With a giddy squeak, Aluqa dragged Leigh toward the door from which she had appeared. Beyond it was another, much larger door, equipped with a heavy-duty electronic lock. Aluqa pressed her hand onto a plate, and gears activated, opening the door automatically. She ushered Leigh inside. The room beyond was enormous, stretching two dozen yards in every direction.

Lining the perimeter were more artifact display cases, with exotic UnEarth plant specimens interspersed, releasing puffs of colorful gas and soft, moaning sounds from time to time. Noticing Leigh's wandering eyes, Aluqa quickly led her into the room. "I'll show you around later, my sweet. For now, allow me to introduce you to the others." As they rounded a display case, a long table stretching across the back of the room came into view, luminous silver and coated with a glossy finish. Seated around it were seventeen faces, most of whom Leigh had seen before but never spoken with. All were focused on her. The higher members wore expressions of blank indifference, which Leigh actually appreciated. *(all except for this guy up front here. he's sporting a bit of a scowl)*

Standing partly in the shadows near the head of the table, holding a tablet at waist level, was Pahlanksha. Their hair gave them away, now dyed a vibrant yellow that could radiate through the foggiest of nights. The expression on their face was hard to read, living somewhere between boredom and apathy, though they did seem genuinely pleased when their gaze met Leigh's.

Pointing to an empty seat at the far end, Aluqa left Leigh to take her place and glided to the head of the table. Skraga sprang up like a jackrabbit to pull out the chair for her leader.

"Is this out far enough?" she asked.

"It's fine," Aluqa replied.

"I can adjust it if you need me to." Skraga's hands jittered, as though wanting to grab the chair again but afraid to do so just before Aluqa sat down.

"No, really. Here's fine." Aluqa sat and turned to face the table, having only just put on her beaming, diplomatic smile when Skraga spoke up again from over her shoulder.

"If I messed up the distance, I'm sorry. I can make it right. You should be comfortable. I can move the chair with you in it. It's not a problem."

"No, seriously, it's fine. Good. In fact, this spot is great. I always want the chair placed here from now on. Thank you." Aluqa turned a somewhat embarrassed smile toward Skraga. "Member Grassrock . . . you may take your own seat now."

With a few nervous twiddles of her fingers, Skraga nodded and returned to her seat. "Okay, sorry. Sorry, everyone." The hulking woman sat with a thud and kept her bashful gaze fixed on the floor for the next few minutes.

Releasing a gasp that was likely meant to lighten the mood and clear the air, Aluqa looked around the table. "Well, let us begin. Today, we welcome a new member to the Higher Surface. Two believers were chosen, having shown the dedication, sacrifice, and strength needed to join our ranks. But only one passed the final test."

Her gaze locked onto Leigh, which the others followed in turn.

"Rook number two three two four, formerly Leigh Evans, do you know why you have been brought here today?"

Leigh signed, "I have a pretty good idea," causing a handful of Cavaliers to squint, looking slightly confused by her hand motions.

"Huh? What did she say?" Skraga asked Aluqa, her brow furrowed.

"She said she is with us," Aluqa answered. "And I suggest those of you who have not yet studied sign language do so. It will benefit you in more ways than just communicating with our newest member." With a beaming smile directed at Leigh, Aluqa continued, "But before we begin, I will introduce you to the Cavaliers before you."

Aluqa proceeded to go around the table, introducing them one by one—not by their birth names, but by their code names assigned upon ascension. The first few were "Member Rampart, Member Bastion, and Member Steelbrook." The others' code names were similarly imbued with strength and solidity.

When she finished, Aluqa concluded, "These are merely the Higher Surface of this station. Those who have ascended across the globe number in the thousands. Joining these ranks demands utmost sacrifice and dedication. Every cell in your body must be committed, willing to fade if needed in order to see our work done. Those seated around this table fight not for a single country or individual, but for all of mankind. We are the wall protecting everything we hold dear. If you choose to accept this nomination, you will never be able to shift blame or denounce responsibility again. Everything you do will help set the course of humanity's future. Never take this lightly." Aluqa paused, glancing around the table like a proud parent admiring her offspring. "So, rook number two three two four, do you accept this nomination? Or denounce it?"

Leigh signed, "I accept." When nothing seemed to happen right away, she added, "What now? Do I have to take a blood vow or something?"

"You already did. The night you joined." The playful look on Aluqa's face resembled that of someone watching a child unwrap a birthday present they'd gotten them. It also told Leigh the whole story in an instant: the killing of the Archfiend must have been a test normally reserved for those about to ascend. *Of course, it's not like she made every single rook kill just to get in. That's thousands of murders every year.* For some reason, what was normally the final step of initiation had been her first act as a member.

I think I always knew but never took the time to think about it.

[*Or perhaps, I did not want to? But I wonder . . . does that mean I did, in fact, prove myself as a rook? Or was it all a show?*)

But why? Why would Aluqa want me here so badly?

Pahlanksha emerged from the shadows, approaching Leigh with a crimson box. She recognized it all too well. With a grin, Pahlanksha placed it in front of her. Inside was her gem bracelet and Gauntlet wrist computer.

"You'll need these where you'll be going in service to the cause," Aluqa said.

Leigh snatched her tools up and began putting them on, swept up in the realization of how incomplete she'd felt without them. But when she reached for the gem bracelet, a jolt of unease shot through her. One of the gems was missing, and not just any gem, but the largest and most important of them all.

Though she felt no panic, Leigh's heart raced. What could this mean? If the Surface had her Mallos gem, that meant they had stolen not only her greatest tool but also her greatest advantage.

[*Was this all an elaborate trap?*]

"Before we move on to other business, there is one more item concerning our ascended rook," Aluqa said, her fierce gaze fixed on Leigh. "And those in the Higher Surface can have no secrets."

Leigh instinctively held her breath, ready to be swarmed—ready to bolt from her seat, until Aluqa casually revealed the missing steel-gray gem, placing it on the table for all to see.

"My apologies if I scared you," Aluqa said. "But I wanted to speak with you about this particular stone. It's very clever, I must say. Very special. A longsteene stone, correct? From Trivium? The world of UnEarth with the frequency closest to our own."

Leigh typed into her Gauntlet. "And?"

"Most UnEarth creatures cannot focus enough to hide objects within one another. It's a fine skill. Yet you have here a stone with something hidden inside it. I know not what . . . but I have a pretty good guess."

Leigh remained silent, bracing herself.

"It's perfect. I couldn't have imagined a better way for the tale to unfold. You found a fitting way to conceal the dagger of Gehenna and keep it out of the wrong hands—your own included," Aluqa said.

So it's true. That's what this was really all about.

Leigh signed, "So what now? You take it and kill me?"

Aluqa hung her head. "Once again, young one, you show how little you pay attention. It's one of your few flaws." She slid the gem down the table toward Leigh, who caught it. "Let's see it," she said.

Leigh kept still.

"We all wish to see the great tool of the Molochs."

Leigh glanced around the table at the others. [*Aluqa must think I will be more willing to give it up if I am overwhelmed and surrounded. Too bad she does not know that I do not get overwhelmed.*]

That being said, what options do I really have in this situation? The door is shut and locked, and I'm in a room full of Cavvies.

(not even my gem bracelet has enough tricks to get me out of this)

"I know you recovered the dagger. There's no point in hiding it," Aluqa said.

She never wanted me—only the dagger.

Seeing no other way, Leigh decided, *Ah, what the hell.* Taking the gem in one hand, she held her other hand over it, grazing her fingers lightly along its pumice-like surface.

With a deep breath, she concentrated. It took everything she had—more than she'd ever known before training herself to do it. After months of practice, she still needed absolute silence and no distractions to pull the object from the stone. She needed to visualize it, down to every cluster of molecules. If she faltered even slightly, the retrieved object could be mangled or fused with the stone.

The effort was immense. It hurt. There were too many faces here, too many voices that could judge her. Leigh had never wanted to retreat to her bunk and deal with Esma and her shitty attitude so badly.

Amid her struggle, a sizzling sound akin to bacon in a skillet arose. The gem began to glow where her fingers met its surface. A metal object began to emerge from the brilliant light. But just as it started to rise, she felt a hand on her shoulder. Turning, she found Aluqa's warm face just inches away.

"Save it," Aluqa whispered, her voice soothing. Standing and folding her hands near her waist, she loomed over Leigh. "Do you know its name—the blade of the Molochs? I doubt you do, even with all your impressive knowledge."

Leigh shook her head.

"No one knows the name given to it by its creators, but since time immemorial, it has been called Erelerim. Through the sands of time and fate, it has come to you. You are its keeper now," Aluqa said. "I would never betray the will of Erelerim or the fates, nor take the treasure from one who was successful in finding such a thing. It is yours. Earned. But remember, you are now an ascended member, which means you will be put to the test every single day. You will do things you never dreamed of doing. You will be tasked with mastering all forms of UnEarth defensive weaponry. You will protect what we hold dear with everything you've got. You will fight when told to, and die when told to. Nothing will be too much for you, and nothing will stop you from achieving our goals. This is both your pledge to us and our pledge to you. We are all the Surface, and we are all one. All that we are. All that we have. Do you understand?"

Leigh nodded, feeling a little caught off guard and having trouble following. All she knew was she suddenly wanted to agree with everything Aluqa said and make her happy.

"With this, your transference is complete. You are no longer rook number two three two four as of this moment," Aluqa declared. "You will now be known as Member Silverthorn. Welcome to the Higher Surface."

"Welcome," echoed the seventeen other souls seated around the table.

Leaning into Leigh's ear, Aluqa whispered once more, slower and softer, "We're going to have so much fun, you and I."

PAST LIVES

Mists of clouds surrounded her. A chill gust flowed past her cheeks. Mara viewed the landscape below; so far away, it became a beautiful, earth-toned mush. As far as she knew, she was in the sky alone, up where peace could wash over her as smoothly as the wind.

There came a tug on her hand—or so she thought. Was it a dream? It felt so real. She turned to them, whoever they were, but the person holding her hand had no face, no identity, no name. But Mara didn't care. She only cared about holding their hand—as tightly as she could. It would never be let go, so long as she could hold on. This felt right immediately. Here in this land, wherever it may have been, with this person, whoever they were, she had found happiness. The weight of her old life, whatever it used to be, was gone. Her old problems, whatever they were, had vanished.

What's that? I can smell a spring. It's one I know, but I can't remember exactly where. It's a place I used to visit when . . . I can't recall.

With a steady change, the clouds whipped by faster until they transformed into steam, billowing around her until the outside world was blotted out. She tried to ask what had happened and where the mystery person had gone, but no sound escaped her throat. Then the clouds receded, and her hand was suddenly empty. The wind on her face began to sting like reeds whipped across her skin. The voice of Loredosai was suddenly upon her, the syllables of his anemic yet somehow blaring tone striking her like baseball-size hail.

A jolt struck. Mara was awake, present, and freezing cold, standing alone before a crowd of a few thousand. The courtroom was silent, and every eye was upon her.

Oh no, what did I miss? Did something happen?

"The scroll, Warden!" Loredosai shouted, glaring from his lofted platform. Beside him, Axios's tiny orange eyes flared within their sockets with ardor.

Damn it.

Mara punished herself internally. Thanks to her daydream, she had not noticed the item being held out to her by one of Ariel Van-Mortus's assistants. The Human Archfiend looked nervous, as though the scroll in their hand were a raw steak and Mara were the trained wolf ready to snatch it away. A slight smile was on Van-Mortus's face, seemingly soaking up Mara's embarrassment. There was no telling how long the assistant had been like that.

Turned out, much of Mara's role in the trial was simply to be at the ready, maintaining the appearance of order—a balanced, independent presence. Her only real duty as the Warden Sentry was to "mediate evidence,"—a *fancy way of saying I fly parcels up to Axios. Or rather, I fly them up to Loredosai, who then hands them to her.*

The excitement she'd felt upon entering the position on her first day diminished quickly. Hours went by as she waited for someone to acknowledge her as the new Warden, half-expecting a surprise ascension ceremony, maybe one orchestrated by Senator Bo. But no such thing had occurred then or since. At no time was she for-mally recognized, except (*of course*) by title alone whenever she was needed to transfer evidence. Even after all her hopeless devotion to her duties over the last three millennia, Mara found herself dream-ing already of leaving the post

I can't do two thousand years of this like Izaiah or Batia did. I see no point.

Taking the scroll from the prosecution's assistant, she flew it up to the judge's bench and handed it to Loredosai, saying the cere-monial phrase, "Bahc-thuc," Ulhirem for "With honor."

After replying with "Thac-Re'n," Loredosai opened the scroll, which contained depositions from those who claimed to have wit-nessed the Ire. *Except they're all lying. No one was there except me and the humans, and they won't accept any of us as witnesses.* On more than one occasion, Mara had offered to take the stand to set the record straight but had been outright rejected by Axios, a decision that made little sense to her—*similar to a lot of what I'm seeing around here.*

Mara had to give the creatures who lied on the stand points for creativity. The stories they came up with were interesting and sinis-ter, but nowhere near as interesting or sinister as the real thing had been. Mara could see already how the record would be not only incomplete but wholly incorrect. The events surrounding Joseph and the Ire would be wiped away, replaced only by approved truth.

The attacks from Van-Mortus had grown gradually more fero-cious, likely a diversion designed to obfuscate a point recently made by Alex Barker's counsel. During a presentation of witness state-ments, Jobaya implied a shared responsibility on the part of Arros in the Joseph Mandate events, as several eyewitness accounts put members of the Aili clan at the scene on Earth. The rumors put their numbers in the hundreds. If this were true, and the invasion of Earth had been an order from the Arros government, it would have been seen as the first step toward a breaking of the Covenant and a new war. Mara was unsure how she felt about the Veen lawyer taking such steps but couldn't help ultimately respecting it. *He's putting his own neck on the line to do it. Hope he knows that. Seems smart enough to.*

Van-Mortus had not been ready for the accusation and stumbled in her initial response. But in the following weeks, she'd hit back, eventually claiming the Archfiend on Earth were a part of Chloe's army. *Gee, I wonder why they chose to emphasize the Medolian.* The prosecution highlighted that the Archfiend were under some sort of mental spell, brought on by the Abyss, making it much stronger than any known forms of manipulation or mind control.

These tactics by Van-Mortus were generally unsurprising at this point. Just the week before, the Arrosian lawyer had sent an Archfiend to the stand who claimed to have seen Alex as the Ire and stated he "looked exceptionally in control." Mara happened to know the particular demon, as she'd arrested him at least twice that she could remember. He wasn't one of the possessed Aili present on the night in question, but no one else in the courtroom knew that, and Mara was not allowed to tell them, forced to remain a silent ornament.

Throughout the trial, Izaiah stayed silent, except to defend the humans he'd brought into the fold, usually simply repeating, "It's my fault. Blame me, not them." Whenever given the chance to cross-examine a witness, he declined, and at no point did he attempt to mount a defense of any kind, merely offering a smile and a polite, "No thanks, Your Honor," when given the chance. Mara was starting to wonder if he'd finally lost it or possibly discovered the truth that he was a waste and everything he touched turned to more waste. She'd known as much for a long time and had a list of reasons why she hated Izaiah, but that didn't mean she wanted to see him go to jail. He was no longer Warden Sentry. There was nothing else the court could do. Mara felt he should have been released months ago. The point had been made. If Izaiah lived his remaining days far away from her and out of her life, that would have suited her fine.

Presently, a familiar silence caught her attention. A hand was once again in her face—this time, that of an assistant for the prosecution, meaning it was time, yet again, to fly something up to Loredosai. Mara hardly ever glanced at the items she was supposed to deliver, but this time, when the object touched her hand, she felt something new yet entirely familiar. It was herself, as well as Senator Bo. Mara knew the feeling of the paper, the trace levels of Eve soaked into the scroll. She knew the words written on it. The item was something she'd wanted to forget, to pretend didn't happen. It was something of her own creation, which brought utter shame as she'd crafted it. Gripping it now, the shame returned tenfold.

The item was the letter she'd written at the request of Senator Bo of Nashwyn. *They can't. He didn't* . . . She spun and looked up at the senator's high balcony seat, but he was gone, and his entourage had vacated the Nashwyn box.

You left me?

Mara didn't understand. The words in the letter were never meant for public viewing. Every ounce of her fought the idea of handing it over. The issues touched upon in the letter could be used in dangerous and manipulative ways if mistreated. *Why did I write them? Why did I allow myself to be in this position?*

There must have been an explanation. This made too little sense; Bo must have been tricked. Van-Mortus must have blackmailed him or something similar. *He ran in shame. Did he have no idea what this was going to be used for? Bo, how could you be so naive?* Mara paused, unwilling to fly the scroll up to Loredosai, while the court waited in silence.

She resisted until she could no longer handle the wall of Wrath being sent her way by the gallery and the lawyers for the prosecution. Van-Mortus's energy signature became especially concentrated. Far above, Mara could sense Axios becoming Wrath-tinted as well.

With the letter in hand, Mara glided up to the judge's desk, speaking quietly. "Your Honor . . . this item is of a personal matter. May I—"

Loredosai moved to block the path to Axios. "Warden Sentry, this is not your place to speak. Hand over the parcel and return to your station."

"I'm certain this item has not been cleared for use in this trial." Mara was trying to find Axios's eyes, but Loredosai was playing too good of defense.

"It bears the Tribunal imprint." Loredosai gestured at the cylinder.

"But its contents are of an unrelated nature."

"That's a lie!" Van-Mortus called from below, rising from her seat at the prosecution's table. "It directly correlates. In fact, the nameless demon is mentioned thirteen times within this text. All the proper channels and procedures have been adhered to in the greatest degree, Your Honor."

Axios held her hand out, unfurling her fingers, directly asking Mara for the scroll. Loredosai took the hint and backed away.

But Mara did not budge. "Your Honor, this is . . . mine."

"Yours?" Axios asked.

"It was written by me."

"True. Technically," Van-Mortus called, standing again for emphasis. "The Warden Sentry did compose this entry, but as a part of her professional duties. Being a career Sentry of great repute, our own Mara Loren stands as an exemplary character witness and informant. I'm sure all will agree to the level of credence her words will command. The scroll contains valuable information for the prosecution's case, and as such, deserves to be heard and addressed. I move we proceed from this delay and have its existence removed from the record."

"Be not rash," Axios said, stroking her bony chin. Her other hand was raised with a preemptive flat palm to silence Mara, should she feel the need to argue further. The moment spent in silence while Axios deliberated was excruciating. Mara clamped her eyes shut and hoped for a win to come her way. *Something has to stop this. It just has to.*

"It will be allowed," Axios said.

Mara's eyes stayed closed as she handed the scroll over. Like a dead leaf breaking from a tree, she floated back to ground level, sensing elation at the prosecution's table.

Finally reopening her eyes, she took another glance at Senator Bo's empty seat. *How could you abandon me like that?*

Van-Mortus began her presentation at the podium, reading along with a copy of the scroll. "Your Honor, there are several points of interest to discuss in the document. These highlight the many weak aspects of the Sentries, not only regarding their response to the Joseph Mandate but also their many offenses over the previous two thousand years. I reiterate, these are the words of the newly appointed Warden Sentry. If the court would please read aloud the highlighted section."

Axios handed the scroll to Loredosai, who proudly unfurled it and sucked in a huge chest full of air to begin.

But Mara needed to try one more time to stop this from happening. "I protest, Your Honor. The Sentry Force is not on trial here today, and as stated, this letter and its words are of a personal nature. My own. I feel—"

Axios raised a hand to halt Mara's argument in place. "Feelings have no station here." She motioned toward Loredosai, still holding his breath.

"Article ninety-three. Group sigma. Evidence to be read, sections six to eight. Author, Warden Sentry Mara Loren, Medolian," he began, before raising his tenor slightly higher. "'It's true, every wrong move has been made. Under Izaiah's command, the Sentry Force has floundered.'"

Mara's gut dropped hearing which section they'd chosen, where she let her feelings flow free. *Three thousand years I've been keeping a cool head, and the first time I decide to tell the truth . . .* She looked at the mass of people before her, absorbing and ingesting every word as though it were a standalone statement or fact and not merely part of a larger piece. *Why did I ever want this?*

Loredosai continued, "'Who knows what kind of conclusion the Joseph and Chloe conflict could have ended up with? One thing is clear—we would not have lost so much to win.'" He closed the scroll. *That's it? You're stopping there?* Mara wanted him to read the next line, which read, "I might not have lost her."

"Thank you, Lord Bailiff," Van-Mortus said. "Beautifully read." She tucked away her copy of the scroll, seeming quite pleased with herself. "Your Honor, we feel that with this clear and impartial judgment of the Sentry Force, a fourth charge parcel is not only recommended but imperative."

The crowd gasped.

Did she just say a fourth charge parcel?

"*ACK!*—Your Honor." Jobaya stood quickly. "Including

a—*K'NELP*—fourth charge parcel in an already ongoing-going case will add a *g*-great deal of time. The humans, including my—*g-g*—client, have been assured—*IT'S RIGHT OVER THERE*—a swift trial."

"This is why . . ." Van-Mortus moaned with a drop of her head and leaking frustration, "I am proposing a break-off trial, to begin as soon as all Medolians can be collected—sorry—as soon as they can be procured. We see no reason the current leg of the trial should be delayed." She finished with a sly, conniving grin aimed at the defense.

Collected? Mara was fighting the Wrath building in her. *They want to bring us in and interrogate us? What in the Eve is going on here?*

This time, Axios did not need long to deliberate. "Parcel approved."

A shudder ran through the crowd. It seemed they could not believe it any more than Mara.

Loredosai shouted, "Follow up one year from today! Charges shall be drawn authorizing the assemblage of Medolians on Earth for the purposes of the court. Those who refuse these charges will be considered Uraan, or enemies of the Tribunal, and imprisoned in the Iolanze."

This was surreal, like a bad dream. Mara expected next they would order her to return to Earth to collect the others. *Which I will summarily refuse. No one is going to "collect" the Medolians as long as I'm Warden Sentry.*

Loredosai continued, "The Sentries will be contacted and assembled. This, by their own. Sentries Philomena, Omalind, and Asmund, recently made deputies of the Barium Guard, will be they who travel to Earth, thus preserving the Covenant."

Mara's gut dropped at the sound of the names, though not out

of surprise. Omalind, Asmund, and Philomena were the most resolute and devoted to the overall concept of the Sentry Force. They
were also the three Medolians Mara arguably knew the least. We
don't exactly have inside jokes. The trio had been born within a century of each other, all within the broad confines of Eastern Asia,
and so gravitated to one another naturally. A mini gang within the
Sentry Force, they had been the ones Mara most expected to show
up and help when the Joseph Mandate became dire. Yet even after
Izaiah sent out memo after urgent memo, they had not answered,
which had never made much sense. Then Mara discovered that the
trio had not been on Earth for the majority of the Joseph Mandate, nor had they been on Trivium. On both worlds, Izaiah's signal
would have been quite clear. But Eve memos could not puncture
deeper into UnEarth to the six worlds. Early in 2006, Philomena
and the others had been invited to a celebration on Arros, hosted
by none other than Ariel Van-Mortus, enjoying the festivities for
more than a year and a half.

I found it eerily convenient at the time and find it dreadfully so now.

Known as the Embedded Stone in more than one land, in the
first ten years of her life, Philomena had memorized the entire
Sentry Charter (*all ten thousand pages of it*) and had never been
known to deviate from it. Citing Batia as her main influence, the
same as Mara, she was yet another student who had been determined to figure it out all on her own. *Except I actually knew Batia.
I learned from her own words, and even she knew that the rules need
to be bent sometimes to achieve balance. Every situation is different,
and no amount of rules can account for all that you see. What might be
a criminal offense on paper could sometimes be a misunderstanding or
a person who had a bad day and just needed a little compassion.* But
Philomena and her acolytes did not see things that way. The idea
of those three being brought into secret meetings with the Barium

Guard, or Ariel Van-Mortus, opened a fresh barrel of unease in Mara.

She spun to face Axios, shouting, "Your Honor, I don't understand. I am Warden Sentry. The Medolians are under my charge."

"You are too busy to collect your counterparts," Loredosai answered. "This will allow the trial to continue unimpeded. They remain your Sentries but will give first priority to the Guard and its duties."

Before Mara could push back again, the court moved on, just another order of business done for the day. The Barium Guard had gone over her head with ease, and there was no telling how much worse this situation could potentially become. With the deputized Medolians, it was possible they could find the others in no time at all. Most wouldn't even know the Tribunal was behind their fellow Sentries' arrival and might come back willingly. By the looks of things, that could mean they would be walking into waiting shackles, and since no Medolian could be held in chains for long, that would mean an instant death sentence. But Mara wouldn't let that happen. There would be no dead Medolians on her watch. *I have to warn the others, but I can't do that when I'm stuck in this blasted spot!*

The day's session needed to end before she would have a chance to alert them, hopefully before Philomena and her ilk could even be given the assignment. *Luckily, those delivering the orders are some of the slowest creatures in the cosmos.*

Mara's message to the other Medolians on Earth would need to be concise, getting across the gist of the warning while still allowing her the leeway to talk her way out of any trouble she might get into because of it. *I'll need to send it multiple times. Just hope they all hear it at least once.*

While she worked out what she would say in the memos, each moment of the day's session dragged, eventually making her want to claw at her own face until it began to squirt. *By the Eve, this must be what the humans feel like.* When Axios's gavel finally fell, marking the end of the day, it woke Mara from yet another daydream she'd allowed herself to drift back into after several hours, pulling her from the happiness she felt among the clouds with her faceless friend, holding their hand tight, their fingers interlaced.

TAKE THESE BALLOONS

Casey scrolled the pages, right-clicking and opening multiple tabs in her web browser, hoping to find a clue that would tell her if Leigh were even still alive out there. Her keyword was Aluqa Morinnean, who Casey had since learned was the head of an UnEarth resistance organization called the Surface. But most of what she was seeing online was not new. Word was still traveling slowly through the UnEarth grapevine.

Bam! Outside in the backyard driveway, another hit ricocheted off the basketball hoop backboard, followed by a chorus of hoots and hollers. The ruckus from the game made it hard to concentrate. All Casey wanted was to get some work done (*you know, something that might actually help!*), but much like the rest of her life, her family was not going to make that an easy thing to do. Every Lipmayer was down there, down to the last grandchild, the youngest being Isaac at a little over a year old.

For seven unrelenting months, it had been like this. Even her sister Terri and her family, who visited Casey's parents the second least after Casey herself, had barely left the house or driven the six miles back to their own home since the Medolians had arrived. All five of the grown Lipmayer siblings lived within thirty miles of the neighborhood they'd grown up in, and as the years went on and the grandkids got older and careers flourished, the families visited Casey's parents less and less. But that was before Galinthia and Fabian. Ever since, the house had scarcely been empty and never more alive.

As far as the Lipmayers knew, Fabian and Galinthia were European friends of Casey's in a cosplay league just visiting for the season. The Medolians intrigued, perplexed, and entertained them. *They were an absolute hit with the kids.* Lloyd, Casey's father, was the only one among the clan who seemed a little uncomfortable around the pair. Twice, he'd been caught snooping (*more like full-on spying*), sneaking around Galinthia, making sure she wasn't up to any mischief. *It's so embarrassing. There's no way she didn't see him in the bushes.* Deep down, though, Casey knew he was doing his best.

Lloyd answered every one of the Medolians' many strange questions with aplomb, such as what he found so appealing about dusting his elk horn collection or why people used salt and pepper shakers. In fact, most of their questions revolved around human food and American Midwest flavors in general. Despite how much the Medolians ate—each consuming as much as three burly men every day—they seemed baffled by the Lipmayers' provided sustenance. No matter how much seasoning Lloyd put into his cooking, Gale and Fabian could barely taste any of it.

Between meals and snacks, they also found plenty of time to lounge about or roam the forest, sometimes for days on end. Taking the occasional daylong nap was common, making it seem the duo was under the impression that the Lipmayers' home was a complimentary bed-and-breakfast.

Or maybe a better analogy would be a summer camp.

A lover of contests, Galinthia had discovered several new hobbies, meeting her match in Casey's siblings, who had never been able to resist turning absolutely everything into a winner-loser scenario. Not even something as mundane as taking out the trash could be completed without finding out who the best at it was. This suited the Wrath-tinted Medolian just fine. Casey was (*rightfully*) worried about an Eve creature playing sports with her siblings, but upon witnessing their first game of basketball, it was clear that Galinthia was holding back her strength and seemed to be enjoying herself all the same. Hockey, golf, soccer—she was more than ready for them all and even let Casey's brothers think it was a somewhat fair fight, despite winning nearly every match. *Except in golf. She hasn't quite gotten the hang of that one.* As though sensing her unease, one day Galinthia mentioned to Casey that she should not worry, as she "surprisingly desired to harm no one in your mother's brood." Casey was happy to hear it. *Sounds like she's having a pleasant stay.*

When it came time for the brothers' yearly hunting trip, Galinthia accepted their invitation to join. Returning home two days later with the kill—the most impressive buck to have ever been dragged into the rear shed to be prepared—the Lipmayer brothers were stricken with the mumbles and white in the face. "She k-killed it with a single knife throw," Wayne stuttered, sounding as though he'd about peed himself. Galinthia, meanwhile, was a bit perplexed by the whole ordeal.

"It was quite adorable to witness the lower creatures struggle with such assailable prey. The forest beast put up no fight and tripped over itself while fleeing. I was embarrassed to kill the senseless thing," she said later that night. "Though I commend your family unit, considering the overall weakness of your species. No offense is intended, but I have hunted beasts on all six UnEarth worlds, and there are things residing in the dark recesses of the Eve realms that would turn your skin inside out by the mere sight of them."

All in all, Galinthia seemed to be getting along well.

Family life had taken to Fabian, and he to it, with magnificence. Everyone in the home was called by their official title via order in the family, such as "third daughter, second generation" for Amber, or "eldest child, third generation" for Pauline. Casey's dad was called Dad, despite his numerous protests, and her mom was called Mom, which was perfect because that's what she liked to be called no matter who was saying it. Holly had taken an immediate liking to the Grief-tinted Medolian, who enjoyed gossiping with her and Casey's sisters (*he's better at it than I am*) or spending afternoons sitting around the kitchen table gabbing over old family recipes. In the late evening, they could often be found in the front room knitting, watching soaps, and crying together. On a few occasions, Casey had walked in on their conversation, which always ended abruptly. Fabian seemed to go quiet out of embarrassment, while her mother reacted with a cold shoulder. Casey hurried away each time before things got any more awkward for her and she felt even more ostracized in her own home.

Presently, trying to ignore the noise of the basketball game outside her bedroom window, Casey clicked open a new tab: the Un-Human tracker report, an underground source of UnEarth creature migrations on Earth. The hope here was that groups like Aluqa's Surface might be inclined to stick near dense clusters of UnEarth Humans to keep a better eye on their enemies. It was a long shot. Casey still wasn't sure if Leigh had even joined the infamous organization, but if she was still running around as a free agent, there was a good chance she would turn up near one of those hotspots all the same.

Another basket was made outside. The family cheered, having a blast. *But I'm not.*

Casey hadn't had any fun since getting back from Ireland. If a moment wasn't spent trying to avert disaster while the Medolians cohabitated with her family—whether due to some confusion over a simple human custom or by not letting any of their Eve powers slip out—it was spent worrying about Leigh. *No one else is.* The Medolians had promised to help find her in exchange for a place to stay but had so far done nothing on their part. *I thought they would have tools and techniques and special types of eyesight or something that would locate her lickety-split. But they've got bupkis.*

What she assumed would be a busy peacekeeping schedule for the Sentries—protecting the Earth and whatnot—seemed nonexistent. They had no daily goals, no needs, no responsibilities. Lazing about life, they seemed content to spend their days eating, drinking, roaming the lands around the home, and hanging out with the Lipmayer family, who were more than happy to host their eccentric guests indefinitely.

Every time the idea of moving along was brought up to Galinthia or Fabian, they brushed off the need to go. "What's the rush?" Fabian asked one afternoon. When Casey brought up, once more, their promise to help her find Leigh, he brushed it off. "Have patience. That's the best thing. Always is."

Well, my patience has run out!

Casey tried again to study, but when the loudest chorus yet broke out (*probably a three-pointer*), she couldn't help but scream and push away from her computer, as though to protect it from her wrath. Marching to the window, she looked out over the crowd that was her family. They had always been a big group, needing the largest table at every restaurant they visited, and that was before any of the grandkids arrived. For eighteen years, the Lipmayer family had only grown, now twenty-one strong, including babies, children, and spouses.

Nine were on the court, with Galinthia playing and Fabian spectating from the small wooden bleachers hand-built by Lloyd, surrounded by the littlest kids, with two perched on his lap. The game was thankfully coming to an end: a match between Terri, Richard, and Wayne, the most athletic of the Lipmayer adult siblings, versus Galinthia and Pauline, sixteen, Terri's oldest, and Ernest, fifteen, Richard's oldest. Galinthia's team was going to win, as they always did, and Casey's siblings could still not believe they'd been outplayed once again.

Studying her parents' faces while surrounded by their kids and grandkids, Casey felt every ounce of their happiness. The house being so consistently full for the first time in years was bestowing a healing grace upon them, clear as day. That was why it stung to think of what harm it might do them when she finally got the Medolians away. *They can't stay here forever, even if they want to, and even if my family would probably let them.* Without blinking, she suddenly found her mother's gaze locked on her, disregarding everything, eyes simmering with a mixture of concern and motherly judgment. The look said, *We need to talk.* The guilt it brought on was deep and instantaneous.

Casey and her mother had not spoken one-on-one since the night she'd arrived with the Medolians. *Last time we really talked was before I left for London again. Even then, it was a superficial conversation. We discussed tomato soup.* But since returning with two strangers in tow, they had not communicated in any way more meaningful than a quick hello or goodbye as they went about their days. Returned to her ways before retirement, her mother seemed always too busy to stop and say much more than, "Got more mouths to feed, things to look after," or diverting with, "Why don't you go see about your sisters?"

The words felt like both jabs and dodges, and Casey wasn't sure if she should put up a defense or not. Ignoring the situation had so far been her plan. What hurt the most was that her mother's chosen ploy was to do the exact same thing. *She's just pretending everything is normal. Am I not worth the trouble?* But with this current look, Holly had let Casey know she was ready. *Thank God. It's been killing me not to get it all out in the open. Festering feelings make me sick.*

When her mother rose from her chair and started toward the house before the game was officially over, Casey knew it was time. She made her way downstairs to meet her, looking around her childhood home, quaint and cute, filled with warm, gold-tinted light. The stairway was constructed of a bright-toned wood that shimmered like a late afternoon sun off a lake in autumn. Quilts hung over just about every able surface, accompanied by multitudes of candles and things made from pinecones. Christmastime lasted all year in the Lipmayer home, and any space not festive or foresty in theme was dedicated to sports. Memorabilia throughout the house ranged from posters and championship season pennants to full-size cardboard standees featuring every professional team from Michigan, though primarily the Detroit Pistons.

Fifteen minutes later, Casey was sitting in the den on her favorite chair, the extra-squishy olive-green one, opposite her mother. A mug of tea was shaking in her hands as though it wanted to escape. Not the hands, but the mug, which must have become sentient and wanted nothing more than to dance and wriggle free of her grip. *That has to be it. Yeah. Or . . . more likely, I'm just nervous.* The cup was starting to feel heavy. She wanted to set it down, but that might have seemed like she was trying to end the conversation before it had even begun. *Or would it seem like I was finally ready to begin?*

Her mother took a sip and returned to sitting quietly, staring at the wall.

"Why won't you say anything?" The words burst out of Casey like a blast of compressed air. "Aren't elders supposed to take the lead? I feel like they so often don't."

"You think I should be the one to start this off?" Holly asked with searing undertones. "Girl, you might need to rethink that."

"I don't think I'm the only one with something to say."

"But you're the only one shaking like you got a woodpecker in your branches. Case, we both know the 'I'm your momma, I grew you and I can ungrow you' speech. I don't feel like giving it. So just, once and for all . . . tell me what's on your mind."

"I will. I just . . . it's hard. I need to start small. You could tell me if you like the tea. It's the kind I bought you in Marrakesh."

"Right, huh, that's that throaty flavor. I'm waiting for it to cool off before I drink it." Casey's mother leaned back in her pleather chair covered in multiple layers of blankets and padded her permed, billowy locks.

Taking a slow, full breath, Casey said, "Look, I'm trying. Can't you see that? I've *been* trying. But you're treating me like some criminal. It's not like I got a tattoo!"

Her mother scoffed. "You're being ridiculous. I don't think you're a criminal. You wouldn't even jaywalk across the street with us when you were little. We'd all have to wait for little Casey to run to the end of the block to cross all safely and catch up to us."

"Well, you're acting like it! This whole time I've felt like an intruder coming into our family's lives to destroy them."

Holly shrugged. "Guess we feel the same way about that."

Casey almost choked. "You don't mean that."

"What are your father and I supposed to think? We said bye to you plentya times. We were always proud of you, 'cause you were off being brilliant and doing fun things in fun places. Then Professor Evans came into the picture, and ever since, you started coming back different. Just little by little. Two years ago, I said bye to my Case, and that was the last I ever saw of my baby girl. I don't know what happened to her after that."

"That's not true! Why are you saying this?"

"It is true! I don't know you any more than I do those people you brought into our house. But I won't hate, and I won't judge, and I will shower them with love, just like I'm showering you. But that doesn't mean I understand it. It's kind of hard to do that when nothing your kid says to you is true."

"Mom, if I could—" Casey was cut off by her mother's raised hand.

"I always thought of us as friends, you know? All the way through you growing up, you never lied to me. Then all of a sudden they started coming—one by one by one. You think I can't tell every time? I see it, and it breaks my heart."

"Because it's so crazy! You have no idea how radical all of this is, Mom. I'm sorry I hurt you and I love you more than anything, but I also have responsibilities—new ones—and they're sort of a big deal. These people, my friends, they're a part of it, and what we're doing is very important. I know it all sounds ludicrous, but I just need time to sort it out." Casey was just barely staving off hyperventilating.

"You said they were in a cosplay league," her mother said, using the same tone she used to scold Casey with as a teenager. "Whatever that is. And don't tell me, because I don't really care."

"Okay, you want the truth? Here it is. They're part of a special team. Sort of military. A deep reconnaissance outfit that helps keep peace in our . . . sector. We're not allowed to tell people about them or what they do. Literally. We're dealing with a foreign government that will hunt them down if we reveal their secrets."

"So they came out here to eat waffles and shoot hoops in Michigan? Are you hearing yourself?"

"Yeah, sort of."

"We ain't part of any mission, unless you made us into one. If that's what's going on, then that's a whole different conversation, young lady."

"Of course not. But *I am*. Fabian and Galinthia need me, and I need them . . . unfortunately."

"You're not some secret agent, Case! You're my kid who used to eat too much funnel cake and shit herself every year at the tractor pull. Get this stuff out of your head."

"You're still not listening to me. This is as serious as I can get. It's a matter of life and death."

"For you?"

"Not yet, but I can't say the same for Leigh."

Holly waved off the ridiculous claim. "If she got herself wrapped up with some bad crowd, that's on her. Got nothing to do with you."

"She's missing, Mom."

Holly got quiet and sat up in her chair. "Now that ain't a word to throw around lightly."

"I'm worried about her. Really worried. In London I went to her apartment, but it was empty, and the things I found inside . . . it's like she's . . . I don't know how to explain it. But it looked like it had been empty a long time. I'm the only person she talks to, and

I haven't heard from her in months. Her dad doesn't even know where she is."

"And what does this have to do with Gale and Fabian?"

"They've agreed to help me find her in return for the room and board you and Dad have been graciously bestowing on them. Thank you again, by the way."

Holly took a long sip of her tea. "*Rm*, throaty. That's what it is. Yeah. Well . . . okay. Can't really argue with any of that, now can I?"

"I'm sorry, Mom. About everything. I never meant to involve you or the family." Casey choked up a little at the end, enough to make Holly instinctively hold out her arms, inviting her to sit on her lap, which Casey did.

"Come here, baby girl." Holly embraced her and kissed her on the forehead. "All is forgiven. Don't you worry, no matter what, your family always loves you. Always will. No doubt about that. You just . . . do such off-the-wall things sometimes. Guess it's made our lives more interesting at least."

"I don't mean to, honestly I don't," Casey said weakly.

Before Holly could respond, there came an anxious knock from the open doorway into the first-floor hall. Amber was there. "Sorry to interrupt, but I think you should come see this. Casey, your friends are . . . well . . . just come look."

Hurrying outside, they found the rest of the family staring in gaping curiosity and worry at the Medolians, who were frozen in place, their heads aimed at the sky. The littler kids who were sitting next to Fabian on the bleachers were tugging on his cloak, trying to get him to snap out of the trance.

"What are they doing?" Amber asked Casey. "They just suddenly went like this."

"I . . . I don't know," Casey replied. She'd never seen either of them do this before. Was it some kind of spasm or seizure? Was it something normal for Medolians to do? She sorted through the options in her head. If she could reach Fabian's phone, would she be able to call the other Medolians if this didn't stop? A crippling fear was slinking into her gut. *Please don't let this involve my family any more than they already are.*

"I'll call nine-one-one," Terri said.

"No!" Casey cried out, hurrying to check on the Medolians. Upon reaching Fabian, she found his eyes glazed over, completely white. "We can't."

"Something is clearly wrong with them!" Terri shouted. "We have to do something."

"Paramedics won't be able to do anything." Casey waved her hand in front of his face. He didn't respond.

"What do you mean? Of course they will!"

The children were beginning to cry, adding to the growing hysteria in Casey's mind.

She locked eyes with her mother, who'd remained behind on the sidelines. The look she was giving her daughter said, *What didn't you tell me?*

Oh, screw it! Might as well come clean. Casey faced her family. "Paramedics won't be able to help because . . . Fabian and Galinthia aren't human."

The Lipmayers gawked with a colorful mixture of expressions.

"Not human?" Wayne asked. "As in illegal alien? Or . . ."

"No!" Casey shouted angrily at her brother. "As in a different species."

"Like aliens, aliens?" Amber asked. "Because that would actually make a lot of sense."

"The gray eyes," Terri added, waving her hand in front of Galinthia's face to no response.

"No. They're born on this planet but . . . it's hard to explain."

Before Casey could stumble through an explanation, the Medolians came to life with a shudder. Their irises returned, along with obvious worry. Neither Galinthia nor Fabian said a word, but they locked gazes and held the stare as though unaware of the rest of the family, seemingly exchanging thoughts without a word. Based on their expressions, those thoughts were dire.

"Fabian?" Casey asked. "Is everything okay?"

Upon facing her, utter sorrow filled his face. "No, Miss Casey. I don't think it is."

"What just happened?"

"An Eve memo. From the Warden Sentry . . ." Fabian said, sharing another glance with Galinthia. *Even Gale looks scared.*

"And?" Wayne asked. "What did it say?"

"Something that cannot be true," Galinthia answered with a vacant stare. The basketball still in her hands squealed under the pressure she was unknowingly applying until it popped with a shocking bang. The youngest children began to weep even louder.

"Whoa, whoa! Everyone needs to calm down. Let's slow our rolls." Lloyd moved into the middle of the group.

"This does not concern you . . . Dad," Galinthia said.

"Sure it does!" Richard offered. "We can help. The Lipmayers aren't afraid. Aliens or not." The rest of the family cheered and agreed. Brandon held up his toy dinosaur and roared.

"Aliens?" Fabian asked Casey.

"Don't worry about it. But Richard is right—let us help."

"There's nothing you can do, child. The Tribunal has called for the collection of all Medolian Sentries." Galinthia turned to Fabian. "We don't have much time."

"Until what?" Casey asked.

"They could already be on their way," Galinthia said, bypassing Casey.

On their way? Casey caught a glimpse of her worst fear come to life. *On their way here?* If someone from UnEarth was coming, it could only mean her family was about to be in danger. "Who's on their way?" she asked.

"Medolians. The ones who decided they didn't like being our friends anymore, apparently," Fabian answered gravely.

Casey's gut dropped. The idea of evil Medolians brought back chilling memories of Chloe. "So, what do we do?"

"You do nothing," Galinthia said. "But we must depart at once."

"Shifting is a no-no. They'll be able to track it, lead them right to us," Fabian added.

"Shit, if you need to get out of here, I can give you a lift," Wayne offered, patting his pockets, looking for his car keys.

"Language!" Holly scolded him.

As stupid as Casey thought it sounded, the Medolians did not seem to hate the idea of hitching a ride, based on the glance they shared. But there was no time to figure out the logistics.

With a bright flash, a Shift portal opened up on the far end of the yard, opposite the family on the driveway basketball court. Standing there when the portal closed was a broad-framed woman in a gray cloak similar to the ones Galinthia and Fabian wore. Her clothes underneath appeared handwoven, accented with dark cyan, entwined with vibrant, intricate beadwork. The wide salakot hat she wore obscured much of her wrinkleless face, and a sizable wicker bag hung from her right arm.

Her eyes remained hidden under the brim of her hat while Fabian and Galinthia moved to meet her, both parties approaching one another tentatively. The visitor soon called out with a rich yet timid voice in a language Casey didn't recognize, to which Fabian replied in the same tongue. An exchange began that Casey could tell was going to get testy—probably quickly. If this newcomer was here to arrest them, there was no way Galinthia would go quietly.

Gazing at her family, Casey's heart sank. They looked afraid—all except Brandon, who appeared to be having a grand time, holding up his dinosaur as an offering to the newcomer. *They were never supposed to be a part of this. I never wanted them to see any of this!* But it was done, no matter what she wished. The only thing to do now was to make sure nothing happened to them.

The new Medolian was not yet aggressive (*thank the Lord*), and based on her body language, Casey guessed she wasn't thrilled to be standing against two of her comrades. *Maybe she's more of a lackey, and not used to doing this sort of thing. But that doesn't mean reinforcements won't show up.* Casey needed to act fast. Hurrying toward the kids and teens, she tried to corral them as well as calm them. "Everyone! Everyone! I need you to move away. Kids, now! Get back in the house. Terri, Richard, and Wayne, come with me! This way!"

Time to implement Medolian countermeasure C!

Leading her siblings, Casey hurried away to the side of the house to a small tool shed with a heavy deadbolt lock. Opening it, she retrieved a stacked trio of plastic buckets and handed one to each of her siblings. "I need you to hit that lady in the hat with these and don't stop."

Her brothers and sister looked at her like she'd just told them to jump off a cliff with a cocktail umbrella as a parachute. Stacked inside the tubs were water balloons of myriad colors. Each bucket contained about twenty. "Please! I don't have time to explain," Casey shouted. "Richard, you pitched in high school. You never shut up about it. So, use it! Please."

She didn't really expect them to comply. In her entire life, her siblings—all of them put together—had only heard about seven of the words she'd ever muttered. But, in the shock of all shocks, the most broken of new ground, the people who had never listened to her whenever it really mattered did just that and took the buckets. Earnest expressions draped their faces. It was like something out of a dream Casey never knew she'd always had.

"Okay, Case. Whatever you say," Richard replied.

With reassuring nods, he and the others dashed off toward the backyard, toting the stash of water balloons, while Casey shook off her astonishment and prayed this plan would work and not end up murdering her entire family.

It's a simple request.

MEMBER SILVERTHORN

Sitting in the rear of an empty cargo van, Leigh stared at the floor and her shoes, considering retying her laces again—even though she'd already done so three times. There couldn't be any mistakes tonight. If anything went wrong, it wouldn't be because of her. It couldn't be.

The other members of Team One were also silent, some staring at the floor like Leigh, others with their eyes closed, on the verge of drifting off. In the driver's seat was Member Soundkin, whose body was built like a beer-poster girl but whose fashion style was akin to that of an eighteen-forties fundamentalist Swedish grandmother. Her manners and good grace were infectious, making anyone nearby feel instantly at ease—especially with her patented backrubs. Beside her in the passenger seat was Member Forcement, about whom Leigh knew little. Closest to the cab in the rear was Skraga, or Member Grassrock, her brand-new jacket's shoulders already torn at the seams from her ever-growing muscles. Surprisingly, she appeared calm and steady compared to her usual, apprehensive self, perhaps aided by the quick breaks she took every five minutes or so to disappear under her jacket, where a light sniffing sound could be heard. The rest of the team comprised Members Steelbrook, Bulltress, Impressa, and Vasberad.

In her assigned seat, Leigh was next to the rear door, her main responsibility for the first part of the operation. *(doors i can handle. they open, they close. no sweat)* Her fear and anxiety had yet to show themselves, but that hadn't stopped her mind from imagining all the ways things could potentially go wrong. This mission would be perilous, and she had not been allowed to bring a weapon—only her bracelet and Gauntlet. Pain and dismemberment didn't frighten her, but losing a limb or being killed would undoubtedly put a damper on her plans to raze UnEarth. Tonight also marked the first time she would be trusting her life to others—and vice versa—which was something she was still wrestling with. Caring for humanity in general had never been Leigh's strong suit, and her teamwork skills were marginal at best. When Aluqa first approached her about the mission, she thought it was a test or maybe a joke. A snatch-and-grab mission, as the Cavvies called them, was no place for a new recruit. But when a spot opened, it apparently became Leigh's lucky day. Aluqa had tried several times to warn her of the potential dangers, but she jumped at the opportunity regardless.

In a dimly lit parking garage, the Cavaliers of Team One waited, poised to pounce at the go signal. Their target was a freight captain at a shipping company in West Germany. The plan was a straightforward kidnapping: snatch the target off his feet and drive away, Mexico City–style. But the real prize wasn't the freight captain himself; it was the knowledge he possessed—the door codes to the back entrance of an art gallery they were set to rob that night. Time was critical, as the code changed every four hours, and he was due to arrive in thirty minutes to supervise the night's shipment.

(i hope the plunder is worth it) Ultimately, they were after a rare metal derived from Rapture. The majority of UnEarth Human technology was made from this material, which Aluqa needed to maintain a constant supply to keep her operation running and growing. Eve-powered technology was new and mostly controlled by the powers within the Purged community, though rumors circulated that all the worlds of UnEarth were beginning to explore the development of their own. *Just another thing they can take from humanity.*

The timing of the mission lined up well with the arrival of the Cardinal from America, which was now only six weeks away. If Leigh's theory was correct, he would be bringing with him whatever he had discovered or created that could transmute earthly flesh into that which could pass clear to the depths of Arros or Hywyn. *They say he's secured passage on a cargo ship. I hear those can haul pretty hefty loads.* The mineral they were after tonight could have been the final piece needed for an UnEarth-tech machine, though that was still just a guess. Leigh could have been dead wrong, and despite the opinions circulating—most notably that the Cardinal's bases in America had been ransacked and his remaining forces were in retreat to join the European Surface for good—none of the other Cavaliers actually knew the real purpose of his visit and remained just as in the dark.

(hell, for all we know, it's a hostile takeover that's on the way)

Presently, Leigh's earpiece came to life. The go signal came through, and the first phase of the mission began. The team piled out. As reported, their target was within striking distance, obscured behind some pillars. He was a normal-looking man with a combover, wearing a polo shirt, khakis, and a coat, dangling a coffee thermos from his fingers while digging for car keys in his pocket with his other hand. Hardly given a chance to yelp before being grabbed and having a duffel bag pulled over his head, the man fumbled his folders, which scattered, and the thermos clanged on the ground. In seconds, while struggling in vain against Skraga and Bulltress, he was dragged to the van.

Making sure no one was sneaking a peek, Leigh waited for them to haul him inside before moving to collect his things from the ground. *No reason he should lose these. They look important.* Once the freight captain was secured, she hopped in and slapped the van wall twice, signaling the driver. The van took off with a squeal.

They soon reached the bottom of the parking structure and began making their way toward a highway. Lying on his chest like a sack of flour, rocking and rolling with the van's bumps and turns, the freight captain hadn't made a peep, and Leigh began to wonder if Skraga and Bulltress had accidentally broken his neck while loading him in. With the hood over his face, she couldn't tell if he wore any expression or was even awake.

"Well done," a rasping yet silky and enchanting voice said from the front passenger seat. "I'm so proud of you all."

I know that voice . . . what is she doing here?

Leigh couldn't believe it, and yet easily did. The person in the passenger seat, whom this whole time she had thought was a woman named Forcement, turned around, revealing Aluqa's grinning face, glistening head, and dangling diamond-chandelier earrings. The others in the team did not appear shocked, indicating she did this all the time. What baffled Leigh was how Aluqa had gotten into the van in the first place, and when exactly she and Forcement had switched places.

With nothing but open highway before them, Member Soundkin sped away, and phase two began. Over the next twenty minutes, while they drove to the second location, the freight captain was interrogated for the door code. Leigh had been prepared for that; the briefing she'd received—though succinct—had mentioned the extraction of assets from the target. What she hadn't been prepared for was the lengths to which the Cavaliers would go to get it.

Intimidation and idle threats lasted only a few moments, more like a warm-up than anything, before the hood was removed and a knife was revealed to add menace. The Cavaliers then began shrieking threats at deafening levels into the freight captain's ears—things so forceful and violent that they might have made even Joseph take a moment. Yet still, the man remained tight-lipped, impressing Leigh. But when the next tool came out, she wished he would just spill the beans—*for his own sake.*

She recognized it: what looked like a cattle prod, but with a multipronged orange gem at the end. The device was called a brilshak. When a button on the side was pressed, an electric whirring grew to a sound like a broken blender on high, with no lid and a frayed electrical cord spitting out rabid sparks. The idea was the same as with animals on Earth: jab that which you wished to control. The tip of the brilshak was laced with Dread, which would inject pure panic into whatever was prodded. Just a couple of pokes with one, and even some of the mightiest UnEarth creatures would be reduced to whimpering wrecks, ready to jump through any number of hoops. Leigh couldn't imagine what it would do to a human. When the freight captain heard the sound, his legs began bouncing. [*He seems to know exactly what is going on and has been ready for each step of the process. I wonder, could he have been trained to handle situations like this?*]

What at first seemed like a nasty but harmless threat became all too real and jarring when Member Bulltress jabbed the manager, whose face contorted into a mess reminiscent of mummies warped by time and cave-ins. The sound that escaped him was not so much a scream as a clenched gasp, so loud it reached screaming decibels. Leigh was not necessarily opposed to using such an approach to get what was required, but she saw no need for it in this instance. The freight captain's wails of pain were loud enough to be heard outside the van, soaked in primal terror, as though he were being subjected to something unholy. The torture seemed needlessly cruel, even to someone as numb as the professor. *Also, lazy. I know at least three other ways to get this guy to talk without even diving deep into my tool kit.*

Bulltress prodded the man repeatedly, seeming to relish the act. After just a few seconds, the freight captain was ready to spill the beans, weeping wildly and screaming out the door code while begging not to be jabbed again. But Member Bulltress did exactly that when the man quieted down, apparently just to match the grotesque grin on his own face. Leigh didn't understand why. They had already gotten the information; no purpose was served by torturing the victim further.

A few moments after they acquired the code, Member Soundkin pulled the van up to a curb a couple of blocks from the destination. Team Two—comprised of Skraga, Steelbrook, Impressa, and Vasberad—jumped out.

"See you soon," Skraga said. "I promise I'll do my best not to screw this up, Miss Morinnean. But if I do . . . I just . . . I want you to know that—"

"I'm sure you'll do fine, Member Grassrock," Aluqa said, sounding like she wanted to pinch the bridge of her nose, close her eyes, and shake her head. "No need for that. Just . . . close the door and . . . go do the plan. Please. That's all I ask."

"Yes, ma'am! I'll give you my best. I will!" Looking like she was seconds from wiping away tears, Skraga closed the door quietly and led her team into the urban darkness, armed with the code that would grant them access through the rear.

Continuing on, the van soon arrived at a solid black gate. Tall hedges stretched away on either side, dimly lit from below with an orange-to-crimson gradient evoking a blazing sunset. When Soundkin pressed the button on the gate call box, an angry voice responded that Leigh couldn't understand from the rear seat. After a brief back-and-forth, whoever was on the other line opened the gate and permitted them entry. The van entered a lush green courtyard surrounded by hedges, lined with jet-black pathways. Two prominent planters on either side featured what looked like dead trees, glossy as though covered in lacquer. Each bore a mixture of dead-of-night black and stunning white bark. At first, Leigh took them for pieces of art, until she looked closer and found their surfaces—craggy and wrinkled—were writhing, slowly undulating in patchy waves nearly invisible to the naked eye, as were their branches. [*I once read that plants from the Ilkinok region on Fovos can do the same.*]

They're said to be part of the nulnirin, or "living-dead vine" . . . I wonder . . .

Rolling onto a pebbled section of the lot, Soundkin parked the van, and Leigh took a moment to study the building. Its architecture was modern and minimalist but also jagged and unbalanced. The glass front face revealed a gray-and-black showroom inside accented with orange LED lights angled crookedly. Standing at the main entrance were two door guards in black.

The Surface team got out and closed the van, leaving the freight captain passed out on the floor inside. As the others moved on ahead to meet the guards, Leigh remained back with Aluqa, who was dressed in a long, draping, stylish black ensemble with gold accents and a high collar. As usual, she seemed to float with a serene grace through the courtyard.

"I didn't realize we did that sort of thing." Leigh's Gauntlet spoke the words she'd pre-typed while the torture was going on.

"I assume you're referring to Member Bulltress's extraction methods. You'll need to realize all sorts of things if you want to do this job," Aluqa said while adjusting her gloves and the many rings adorned with colorful gems decorating her fingers. *I would bet money those are Eve powered.* "Do you understand, Cavalier?"

Leigh signed that she understood. Aluqa continued toward the gallery without a second glance. "And one more thing. Don't ever speak to me like that again."

"Like how?" Leigh signed at her back.

"Like equals. You ask nothing of me and question nothing I say. My word comes from a place far higher than yours. I already allowed you to beg your way into my organization and did so graciously. That should be enough. Now, do your job, Member Silverthorn, and show me a little gratitude while you're at it."

Done with Leigh, Aluqa moved on, approaching the glass door, where she greeted the guards genially, professing to be a buyer arriving for their appointment. But Leigh heard nothing of the conversation; she was too mentally jammed by what had just been said to her. *She spoke to me like I was a child.* But what at first burned with disrespect gradually softened. There was a good chance Leigh needed to hear tough-to-swallow things like that every now and then. *I can't pretend to be perfect. I'm not—I know that.*

That was not how the egotistical professor *(hey—harsh)* usually thought. *Then again, I'm not just the professor anymore.* She was Member Silverthorn now. So, who was Silverthorn? She could be anybody she wanted, do anything. [*But not truly. Not as long as Silverthorn works for another. There can be no such thing as freedom when you work for another.*] For now, Member Silverthorn would be a mask, one she could use to further infiltrate the Surface.

And it sounds like Member Silverthorn should just do as told and not stir up shit right now.

[*I can do that.*]

Reminiscent of a high-end car dealership, the building's lobby was peppered not with Aston Martins and Maseratis, but rather huge, colorful slabs of rock. To a curious citizen coming in from off the street (*unlikely, as this place is by appointment only*) the slabs might have appeared to be art pieces or perhaps some ultra-high-end home decor. But the minerals they were made of set them apart from anything a normal business might sell. Pieces like the ones here were highly sought after by both Eve artifact collectors around the world and militaries alike.

Following a series of quick footsteps, a man appeared in the showroom, his posture leaning forward with an arched back and—somehow—a protruding rear end. The widow's peak on his head would not quit, and his front teeth stood out prominently from his open mouth like a baffled rat's probably does.

"You must be our eight thirty," he said, his low-toned, nasally voice exemplifying droll.

"We are," Aluqa replied, using her soft, political tone.

"Do you know the password?"

"Of course. Panzure'Flee. Apologies for our early arrival."

"Nonsense. You're better than the Rapture types, showing up right on the dot. This way, please."

The crooked-spined man led the group to the rear of the gallery. "The piece is back here. A bit of a walk. But don't worry, we've got helping hands."

"I've brought some extra hands as well," Aluqa said.

The man showed them to a room lit with green bulbs lining the outer edge of the ceiling. Directly in the room's center was a long, hand-carved wooden table. *(at least i think that shit's wood)* As she drew closer, Leigh noticed little flecks of orange light twinkling like stars within the material. Sitting at the end of the table was a woman dressed in all white, the same level of fancy as Aluqa, straddling "well-to-do Sunday brunch with the ladies from the other oil families" and "European Michelin four-star restaurant host."

"Miss Zito, I presume," Aluqa said.

"Hello," the woman replied, pulling down her glasses as though to say, *Do you know where you are?* In reality, she asked, "Where is Bruce?"

Leigh and Member Bulltress assumed positions behind Aluqa as she sat in the chair opposite the woman in white. Three assistants dressed in black stood at the two doors into and out of the room, each with an identical gentle sway in their bodies as they loitered. With a bow, the crooked-spined man departed into the rear of the gallery.

Taking her gloves off meticulously, Aluqa first removed her rings, then the gloves, finally returning the rings to her fingers. "I'm Bruce's replacement, Elena Hartwise. Perhaps they called to say I would be arriving? We heard about the last shipment's mishaps. I was sent to personally oversee this deal and make sure our purchase would be . . . completed." She finished with a patronizing giggle.

The man in question, Bruce, had been delayed by a third team. Aluqa finished putting her rings back on, then took a moment to admire them before giving the woman in white her full attention.

"Mishaps?" Miss Zito's previous biases had disappeared. She was sitting up straight and all ears now. "Surely your employer doesn't blame us for the stolen merchandise. We were the victims as well in that situation. It has become almost impossible to guarantee shipments these days. That is why we currently offer in-person transactions only, and the reason our guard has doubled."

"*Hrm*. Still." Aluqa's petty judgment was bleeding out. "The authorities could not locate the thieves you described, nor find any traceable evidence of the robbery."

(she's loving playing this part. but the funniest bit is she is the one who stole the shit in the first place)

"True. They also searched our premises and didn't find it, either," Miss Zito spat, scowling as she added softly, "If you were implying something."

Aluqa held firm and rolled her eyes. "Very well."

With a snide scoff, Miss Zito made it clear her skin had been successfully gotten under. With several hearty snaps, she called over her assistants. "I don't like how this is going, and frankly, I don't think I care for you, Miss Hartwise."

"Mutual, my dear."

Leigh was enjoying this. *(it's quite entertaining)*

Miss Zito stood. "Let's get this over with."

As her assistants approached, a blankness in their eyes became apparent. *They look like supermodels in the nineties—all emaciated and sad.* Morose skull visages were crafted by their sunken cheeks, appearing perpetually anesthetized, while at the same time each seemed ready and willing to help with anything and everything their boss might require. After receiving instructions in Nordic from Miss Zito, the assistants jetted off like pale, phlegmatic bunnies.

A pallet with a crate on top was soon wheeled into the room from the back hall, its left rear wheel squeaking like a wounded animal walking on a broken foot.

"Johann will help you to your car," Miss Zito said.

Aluqa motioned for Leigh to follow the assistant pushing the cart. Together, they left the others and journeyed down the long, shadowed hallway toward the van. The box on the cart was enormous—around six feet tall and three feet squared at its base—looking as though it had been built to withstand being run over by a platoon of tanks. *(whole lot bigger than i was expecting)* Yet Johann pushed it along as easily as a grocery store shopping cart, softly grunting in a steady rhythm, countering the squeak of the cart's wheel. His clumped lips chattered but without seeming to form words—more like random spasms rolling across his face. The small Grief gem on Leigh's bracelet indicated he was an UnEarth Human, but she couldn't be sure which species. *If I had to guess, I'd say Scythe.*

When they reached the front courtyard, they found it barren and quiet; the van and Member Soundkin were nowhere in sight. The black gate at the far end stood open, and the door guards had vanished. Leigh and Johann halted in unison and looked around. Neither seemed to know what was going on. *I don't like this. Where is everyone?* When a scream erupted from deep inside the gallery, back from where they came, Leigh and Johann shared the same confused glance.

The shriek was abruptly cut off by the jolting blast of a gun. At the sound, Johann tensed and charged back with Leigh in tandem. His grunts heaved with frenzied belligerence, damp with saliva as they sped away. Aluqa's shouting then filled the hallway—primal, sounding as though she were being mutilated by a wild animal. With a cold snarl, Johann left Leigh in the dust, bursting ahead with inhuman swiftness. She charged after, reaching the back room just a few seconds later, where she found Johann's backside.

Stopped flat, he was gazing at the scene.

Miss Zito lay sprawled on the ground, dead, with a bleeding hole between her eyes. The third assistant was also dead, lying next to her atop a growing pool of blood. The final assistant was nowhere to be seen. Behind Aluqa, Member Bulltress stood as still as an indoor tumbleweed, sneering over her shoulder at Leigh. Loosely gripped in Aluqa's right hand was a smoking handgun.

When Leigh entered the room, Aluqa threw her hands up with a flippant grin. "Innocent! The woman attacked me! I have a witness," she declared directly to Johann, who still hadn't budged.

Taking slow steps into the room, Leigh tried to come around him without startling the guy, who was starting to look less like an eager assistant and more like a bodyguard who'd failed his task.

"Truly, we can remain calm and talk about this like civilized creatures," Aluqa said, her tone subtly waggish.

Without comment, Johann walked to Miss Zito's body and knelt to check her pulse.

It wasn't obvious to Leigh how to react in this scenario. Abject murder had not been on the evening's menu. Either the plan had gone completely off the rails, or this was exactly how things were supposed to go, and she had been an unknowing patsy in Aluqa's true plan. The professor thought she'd been aware of all the sneaky tricks being pulled tonight. She thought she had been allowed into the deeper levels, but it was clear there were still many doors left to open in the maze that was Aluqa. In this moment, a frigid indifference was present in the enigmatic woman, clashing with the obvious rush she was getting.

"I had to defend myself," she said, sloppily hiding the gun behind her back. Aluqa and Bulltress then shared a glance, staving off laughter like schoolchildren.

Johann rose, glaring hard, revealing vile, putrid thoughts aimed at Aluqa.

The sensitive Grief gem on Leigh's bracelet was burning brighter. That meant Eve was intensifying and concentrating nearby. She signed, "We should leave," but neither Aluqa nor Bulltress seemed to care. They were rightfully focused on the irate Johann, who appeared ready to boil over.

Boots on tile flooring bore down from the hall into the rear of the gallery. A bevy of sunken-cheeked guards arrived, their eyes hidden behind dark sunglasses. Besides being strikingly similar to Johann in size and shape, the newcomers also shared his unceasing twitch.

Piling in, they assessed the situation while Aluqa approached them calmly. "Now, folks, before you go getting the wrong idea, there's a perfectly reasonable explanation for what you're seeing. As I've just reminded your compatriot here, we need to make sure to keep ourselves in check—emotionally and physically speaking. Perhaps one of you could call the authorities? There may still be a chance to save her."

The guards approached Miss Zito's body.

"Zito is dead?" one asked.

"Zito. Yes. Leader," Johann answered. "Killed by they." He pointed at Aluqa and company.

"Zito was leader. If leader is dead, who leads?" asked another guard.

Leigh's Grief gem became an opaque bulb and was starting to get warm. *Better end this before things get out of hand.*

"Instructions were given," Johann said to his teammates. "Look for new leader. Kill those who removed old leader."

"Really," Aluqa offered, light as air. "You're taking this far too personally."

Another pair of boots came charging in from down the hall. Out of the shadows, Skraga appeared, breathless and in obvious panic. *Where's the rest of Team Two?*

"Scythes! Full-grown, pure fucking Scythes!" she screamed once she caught her breath. "They got Vasberad! We need to move! I'm so sorry!" Charging in, she grabbed Aluqa like a Secret Service agent evacuating the president.

But Aluqa was not ready to go. "Nonsense. There are no pures nearby."

"No time to explain, boss, and I regret having to do this—" Skraga took her by the wrist and hurried Aluqa away just as an earsplitting screech rang across the gallery, echoing chaotically through the back rooms and hallways. High-pitched and stinging, it pierced Leigh's eardrums like a piece of charcoal being jabbed into them and twisted. The scream sent a chill up her spine, even without the accompanying fear. At the sound, Aluqa gladly followed Skraga's advice.

"Very well, lead the way!"

As the party departed, Leigh turned to see each gallery guard pulling an orange-colored orb from their chest pockets. One by one, they smashed the objects against their foreheads like thick-shelled eggs, enveloping themselves in a blazing orange light that oozed like molten lava.

Oh no.

[*This is certainly a most unfortunate turn of events.*]

Leigh recognized the orbs immediately, recalling a chilling passage from one of Dr. Emul's journal entries. These colorful, oblong objects were known as Dread larvae—the initial stage of life for all Scythes born on Fovos.

"That's what I was trying to tell you!" Skraga screamed as they hightailed it away. "They got those Dread baby eggs!"

The ooze steamed and boiled as the light seeped into their skin and coursed through the gallery guards' bodies, revealing ferocious internal changes. Bones and organs disappeared in the blink of an eye, lost to a swirling soup within their torsos and limbs, while screams of agony were expelled by vocal cords churning and mutating.

From the black doorway through which Skraga had arrived, a sound like thumping feet approached, rising with wild intensity and the force of a locomotive. With a shriek, a hulking darkness careened into the room, its claws and limbs flailing like tree branches in a frenzied wind. Its screams were pandemonium, twisting and pinching nerves with radical frequencies.

The shadowy beast immediately sprang into the air—soaring toward Aluqa—revealing features akin to a gigantic burnt-umber praying mantis. Its limb movements were unnerving and erratic, cracking and snapping. A chattering was evident among its screams, evoking a dozen fingers snapping with malice, growing shrill as it sailed closer.

When a shotgun blast went off, the creature collapsed to the ground, mangled but not dead, flailing and limping. Bright orange blood dribbled from its wounds. Skraga stood firmly at the door to the main showroom, holding a sawed-off shotgun—previously hidden under her coat—and keeping the door open for the others.

"Let's go!" she shouted as the team hurried past the looming showpieces. Leigh then remembered that the van wasn't going to be where it was supposed to be, and she had not yet mentioned it to Aluqa. Their only chance would be to charge through the courtyard and make it through the open gate into the street. *Hopefully, these things won't follow us into public.*

Through the showroom's glass wall, the courtyard came into view. The van was still missing, but no one seemed to care and kept sprinting anyway. With a pattering *thump-thump-thump*, dozens of heavy feet neared until it seemed they were directly upon them. Then, bam! Like it had been struck by six demolition balls at once, the wall behind the group exploded. Sparkling hail crashed down like a wave as Leigh risked a glance backward to view their pursuers. *I've never seen a pure Scythe. Not going to miss the chance.*

With tremendous speed, the beasts stomped through a cloud of dust into the room, using four tall legs that stabbed crude, clawed feet into the debris-spattered floor. Long-limbed and gangly, they had skin like a brown cactus lined with black barbs. The split-open mouth at the end of a stem protruding from where a head might be was shaped like a Venus flytrap, fluttering open and closed, searching for meat, but with no eyes present. Those, two tiny orange beads tucked into what might be called the creature's shoulders, had irises of soft yellow and zipped back and forth, seemingly without focus. Yet Leigh could tell they were just as effective and precise as a bird of prey's, having immediately locked her well within their sights.

The Scythes were upon them with overwhelming ferocity. Skraga slowed the creature in front with another shotgun blast, allowing the group to barely escape out the front door, with Leigh exiting just as a limb coated in thick, coarse hair reached for her—the last to make it through. With a shocking bang, the Scythes hurtled into the glass wall of the showroom, which jostled and bowed but held. As they pounded on it with their barbed, ruinous claws, the sounds of the Scythes stymied by the glass were welcome. But the feeling was squashed by the sight of the black gate shut at the end of the courtyard. With a terrific crash, after just a few seconds' respite, the glass barrier bulged to its maximum yield, gave way, and shattered, raining thick chunks onto the escaping party. The Scythes were free, and a table spread had been laid out before them. Team One would be torn apart in a matter of seconds.

What can we do now?

[*It would seem there is nothing.*]

Leigh wasn't sure any of her tricks would bring an Aidaas Scythe down. The best course of action seemed to be to halt in place, close her eyes, and accept her fate, but her feet kept running, and soon she was hurtling herself into the gate with the others. Wanting to see her own death coming, she turned around. The nine-foot creatures had become one swooping brown shadow, mountainous, their silhouettes fused into a vile horror of agony and death.

But the sight was blocked when Aluqa stepped forward, pushing past Skraga to place herself between the monsters and her team. Like arachnids racing toward a fresh catch, the beasts barreled at them, while Aluqa stood tall and held her ground. Raising her hands, she activated the gems in her rings. They began to glow all at once, and a brilliant multicolored shield materialized, extending outward to surround her in a protective barrier. The soap-bubble quality of it reminded Leigh of the spheres she'd seen the Medolians create for protection or travel. With a striking clap and flash of light, the Scythes collided with the barrier and became stuck upon it, as though a magnet had seized them. But undaunted, they pressed forward as if it were merely a torrent of water, fighting through the pain made evident by their screams. The Scythes would break through, and Leigh had no idea how to help prevent that. A shield such as this (*possibly made of Mallos, but how, I haven't got a clue*) was beyond her understanding or current skill. She was as frozen in place by its power as everyone else, lost in awe.

Crying out, Aluqa revealed her own agony. Never having appeared so outwardly helpless, she seemed to be nearing the end of the ride—for her and the Surface. But then came the turn.

When the Scythes were nearly within arm's reach, Aluqa snapped a blue gem off her right index finger ring and hurled it to the ground, where it shattered, blasting a shock wave that reacted with the Eve shield like sodium in water. When the wave struck the Scythes, their screams were silenced. Somewhere amid the flash, they were immobilized, transmuted into brown slabs of stone, mere inches from annihilating Aluqa and the others.

Creeping vines and budding plants grew out from the statues, audibly setting, crackling and hissing like cooling bags of popcorn right out of the microwave.

"Everyone okay?" Aluqa asked, facing her team and catching her breath. "Sorry if I scared you. I had to wait until we were in the right situation."

Leigh was speechless, even for a mute, having trouble processing what she'd just seen.

"I'll only be okay once we're out of here!" Skraga yelled, her apparent terror intensified when the gate began to open, causing her to shriek. Standing on the other side were Members Steelbrook and Impressa, looking easygoing yet triumphant. Beside them was the van, with Soundkin leaning out the driver's window, smacking her gum. Lining the curb behind the van were two more identical vehicles, with drivers who were both Higher members Leigh had believed were still back at Station Five.

Looks like there's a lot I didn't know about tonight.

The freight captain's body, possibly alive, possibly dead, was laid out on the lawn, his folders and papers scattered next to him.

"Pile on in," Soundkin said, following with a toot of the horn.

Leigh didn't remember anything about the ride back other than Skraga's wailing over the Cavalier who had been killed during the operation. The Scythes and their human forms morphing into bug-like monstrosities consumed the professor's thoughts. She'd read about the changing chambers of Trivium, the largest of which was located within the Tribunal. The transformations were said to be horrific and took years, but what had happened tonight occurred in a matter of seconds. The image was burned in her mind, not out of fear but fascination. Yet one question remained unanswered: How did the guards have the Dread larvae in the first place? Those were rare and never used lightly by Scythes. But tonight, they had expended them like quick-performance enhancers. *Why would they risk so much just to save some rocks?*

Leigh also couldn't help repeatedly going over Aluqa's actions and the way she'd humiliated her by keeping her in the dark about the night's true plan. What was supposed to be a smash-and-grab for a single rock had turned into a multiple homicide, and they were now returning to base with three vans' worth of plunder instead of one. *It's impressive. Just wish I could say I was a real part of it.*

When the convoy returned to the compound, Skraga took over unloading duty while everyone else was dismissed. In her room, lying on her bed, Leigh went over the evening's events further. What she'd seen from Aluqa was impressive, to say the least. *She really is an UnEarth creature hunter. The stories were true—no doubt about it.* Her power and skill were no longer in question, and the thought of somehow gaining the same or even greater power made Leigh's imagination run wild. Aluqa was an obvious veteran of the UnEarth conflict and had tricks up her sleeve that the professor could only dream of, but Leigh wanted to do more than dream; she wanted to possess those tricks and all the others Aluqa had yet to reveal.

[*But in order to do that, I would need to stay and remain diligent. Those lessons would most likely take years.*]

(*why? i was doing fine on my own before, without anyone else to teach me. there were lots of times i could have died or been caught and wasn't*)

[*It is likely that was mostly beginner's luck. I have no idea how much faster I could learn from another, because I have never allowed myself the chance to do so. No teacher was ever respectable enough in my eyes for that kind of veneration.*]

(and i did well anyways! i made it to the top of a field most couldn't even find their way into if they had a map with a big red X stapled to the inside of their—)

[*Irrelevant. I am no longer in a scholarly profession—this is a war scenario I am entering.*]

Deep down, the professor still believed she was a free agent. Even with all she'd done for the Surface and Aluqa, every night she went to bed thinking of herself as an individual force acting against UnEarth. But that was most likely a mere continuation of her own foolish delusions.

She had been back in her room for a little more than an hour when Aluqa knocked on the door.

"May I have a word?" she said, entering the green-walled room without waiting for permission.

"Of course," Leigh signed, standing from her bed to show respect, though she couldn't muster a warm expression.

"Tonight was a success. What Skraga just unloaded can expand our defense grid and upgrade all our systems. The Surface will be greater than it was before. And you—being a part of that—deserve your share of the credit."

Leigh signed thank you, placing her fingers on her lips with a flat-palmed hand and moving it outward.

"I realize you are unaffected in most ways, but I would understand if tonight . . . let's say, confused you."

Leigh signed, "Actually, I learned a lot."

"I'm pleased to hear that. Humility is a lost quality. You have no idea how many Cavaliers I've lost over the years on their first mission. That's why we test rooks so thoroughly. Only those we know we can rely on make it through. Normally, the process takes years, but not with you."

Based on her tone, Leigh half expected Aluqa to reach out and tuck a bit of hair behind her ear.

"I want to tell you something," Aluqa continued. "I regret yelling at you earlier. I was upset about something that was not your fault. It was mine. I had never properly explained how you are to address me in the presence of others. When we are alone, I value your candor and input, but when others are near, you are to place yourself below me in every possible way. Do you understand? Your thoughts should not flow without my permission. At least, it must appear so. Can you handle that?"

Leigh held still, suddenly unable to breathe.

"You don't have to answer now. But take the time to think about it," Aluqa said. "You'll see that what I'm saying is true."

Leigh signed, "I was . . . merely surprised by the aspects of the night I was not briefed on."

"And here I thought you were one of my brightest." Aluqa's new tone suggested she was now fantasizing about tearing Leigh's hair from her scalp instead. "That was purely for the good of the mission. If the Scythe had sensed you were prepared for the van to be gone or his boss to perish, it would have alerted him and ruined the plan. Member Silverthorn, please."

Leigh gave a slight nod. *Of course, how did I not think of that myself?*

"I know you're upset, but I really owed you no explanation at all," Aluqa said.

Leigh typed into her Gauntlet. "Not for using me as bait?"

"I would never let anything bad happen to you. You're too important to me. And in case you'd forgotten, we lost one of our own tonight. Do you know what they did to Vasberad before devouring him? Or do you care? Our enemies are austere, and there are many ways to be killed by creatures from UnEarth that would make Hell seem like an eternity in a sauna. Pain and trauma exist that I would not wish on anything or anyone I've ever come across, no matter what they had done."

"I have an idea what's out there."

"You've read some books and scrolls, but you don't know anything. To experience such things is an entirely different animal. And know what? The animals are becoming feistier. More primal. Desperate. Clinging to survival."

"Aren't we as well?"

"Yes, but what separates us from them is the lines we are willing to cross. Now, tell me what you noticed about tonight. Did anything about Miss Zito's guards and their response surprise you?"

Leigh typed: "The Dread larvae?"

"Precisely. Can you tell me why?"

"They are rare."

"They are *valuable*. Yet, I've never seen so many in one place, and *never* seen them wasted in such haphazard fashion. Each of those larvae could have grown to be a pure Scythe. Creatures of Fovos are exquisite worker drones. They're cheap and easy to feed and keep alive for thousands of years of indentured service. Valuable. This means what we stole tonight was much more than a financial opportunity for Miss Zito. It was her livelihood. Stones like the ones we procured tonight are becoming like an endangered species, sought as though no others exist."

"I noticed we only stole high-shaded rocks. Is there a reason only those are disappearing?"

"No one knows for sure. Not even the Cardinal. We use Rapture-soaked materials in most of our Eve tech, but a little goes a long way. Besides, the high-shaded stones began vanishing hundreds of years ago. Far before any such need. Whoever has been taking them has been doing a good job hiding it for quite a while.

Many believe that it is Hywyn, justifying it as a reclamation, but I have it on good authority that they are seeking the missing rocks more fervently than any."

"So they don't know where they are either?" Leigh signed.

"No, they don't. Not even Hywyn and its icy grip have complete control of life. Other powers are at play here, lurking in the shadows."

"Why are you telling me this?"

With a smirk, Aluqa rose and motioned for Leigh to follow her into the hall. Without much choice, Leigh stood and went with her, led to a new section of the mine she'd never known existed, located in the farthest reaches of the east wing.

Behind a door labeled 9XG, which featured no handle and opened automatically when Aluqa drew near, was a white room similar to an autobody shop, but as clean as an operating room. A machine to the left, painted deep blue and the size of a garbage truck, crushed rocks delivered to it by a tube and conveyor belt and sent them through a series of pipes into the next room. A window across the wall revealed what was on the other side. Beyond the glass, a single platform rested in the center of the room. Atop it lay a case made of thick glass the size of a large tackle box. Inside was a gleaming mound of silver powder that dazzled with reflective rainbow light.

"Welcome to the processing center and storage," Aluqa said. "This is where the minillia is siphoned from the rock."

The room beyond, open and empty, made the pedestal look minuscule, but Leigh couldn't help but gaze at the box filled with powder. "Is that all of it?" she signed.

"Only a fraction of a fraction of a gram per kilogram. If we'd been mining for plutonium, we'd have gotten enough years ago," Aluqa said. "And we will need every speck."

"What for?"

"You know what for. For the reason you came here and joined us. The real reason."

Leigh caught Aluqa's gaze, trying to read her face while giving away nothing with her own.

"Your rings," Leigh signed. "It's how they work, isn't it?"

Aluqa laughed and moved close to the window. "You are a clever one. Yes, the closest thing to holding Mallos in your hands. We have to keep it behind a barrier at all times. It is quite radioactive in dust form."

Leigh approached the window and gazed at the box. "Will it be enough?"

"When it comes to minillia, a little goes a long way. The possibilities are practically endless. But one would need to know how to utilize it—otherwise, every grain would be for naught. Lucky for us, someone does. Did you know the Cardinal trained under one of the greatest Hywynite minds in history—the Moekun, Vecter of Auwndwo? You know this name, yes?"

Leigh shook her head.

"Don't neglect your reading. The Moekun is a singular position on Hywyn and considered a great responsibility. They are tasked with venturing out of the confines of Hywynite culture to delve into the reaches many on their world of Rapture would call depraved. The leaders of Hywyn know that knowledge is often only gained by stepping into such places from time to time, and so they rely on the Moekun to inform them of emerging weaponry or advancement opportunities as well as any new technologies at home or abroad. The Moekun were also known for their nilunisinam, a sort of Eve alchemy, where combinations of different shades were tested to see if any benefits or discoveries could be found. Once placed in the role, they remain for life, and Vecter has been the Moekun for going on sixteen millennia. For six of those, he worked with an assistant who would later be banished in the Purge and sent to Earth."

"The Cardinal," Leigh's Gauntlet said.

"He is cunning and powerful, having learned that the ends can most definitely justify the means from his former master. There would be no Surface without him. It began with him, and so too can it end."

"What are you saying?" Leigh signed, sensing a sudden weakness from Aluqa.

"When he arrives, everything will change," Aluqa said. "I know you know this. But I don't think you understand just how much."

"Tell me."

"I would if I could, but I can't tell you everything. There are some things I must keep to myself, at least for now. But I will tell you to watch out for yourself at all times."

"Why?" Leigh asked. "Because of the members he's bringing? Is this an assault? If so, why are we sitting around rather than preparing for it?"

"I do love your fire. It's infectious. But Leigh, tell me something . . . do you even know how to kill an UnEarth creature?"

"A deep wound to the neck. Or between the eyes. Whichever it has. No attack is for sure, but that will get you close."

"I have stabbed many an Eve creature where you described, and rarely had fast success. Yes, their brains are important, but I find those of UnEarth are most concentrated here." Aluqa touched Leigh's chest. "Their essence lies where their hearts would be if they had any. That is where you can end their lives without question."

"And will I soon . . . need this?"

"Who knows? Not even I can see everything, and we're headed into uncharted territory. The two American men being abducted for the Joseph Mandate has derailed everything at a speed like nothing before in UnEarth. Now, the storm is suddenly all around me, and I don't know if I've prepared myself in time. No matter how many times I tell myself I have. No matter the number of times I check the boxes. Oh, how I envy you. Feeling nothing. Nothing but duty. Nothing but drive. It makes you as wonderful as you are. And it will come in useful in the coming months."

"I still don't know why you're telling me all this."

"Because I want you to live. Because you're important to me. And because I'm afraid of losing you when the road gets bumpy ahead."

"I'm here for the long haul. Truly."

"Good, because there is something I must speak with you about. It is dire and will . . . expose me. Therefore the only way I will tell you is if you swear to me I can count on you."

"I've sworn that multiple times."

"And I want it once more. Tell me you are here for this cause and these people who stand by your side. Tell me you are here for me, and not for yourself."

"I'm a Cavalier. You don't have to worry about that."

"I hope so. What I have to say isn't easy. Soon . . . I'm going to have to do something—something I don't want to. You're going to have to watch it happen and it will shock you and hurt you, but one day I know you will understand. Possibly, one day soon. But before I go through with it, I need to know that you have forgiven me first."

"Forgiven you? For the . . ."

"The thing I will do. You need to forgive me for it now. It is absolutely necessary for our cause, and it will help bring UnEarth and the Tribunal to its knees. I know you will want this, and so I know you will ultimately approve of it, but I need you to tell me you have forgiven me. That's the only way I'll allow myself to do what needs to be done—if I know you truly understand."

"But I don't. What is it?"

"I can't tell you. It would ruin everything. You'll just have to trust me. Now, do you forgive me for what I must do to protect the cause, as well as those within it?"

Leigh couldn't say yes to that. [*The logic makes no sense.*] But it was also so completely ridiculous that there seemed to be an air of legitimacy in it. *She's too smart to say something so crazy unless she meant it. Maybe she sees something up ahead, just like she did tonight, and needs this in order to do what must be done.* The moment tumbled over her. The look in Aluqa's eyes as she waited for an answer made Leigh rush to provide one.

"What's this about?" she signed.

"I'll tell you after you answer my question. Do you forgive me?"

Leigh nodded.

"No, say it."

After a flash of uncertainty, Leigh signed, "Yes," making the knock-knock motion with her right hand.

"Thank you," Aluqa said, releasing a labored breath she'd been holding. "You don't know what that means to me. Now, I'll tell you what I can. First, it is true. The Cardinal has indeed made a discovery and built a machine capable of imbuing human flesh with Eve, and is bringing it here from America. You and the Cavaliers will be among the first to go through it, making you Eve-compatible in order to strike at the very heart of UnEarth society. This attack will mark our finest hour and cement the legacy of the Surface in human and UnEarth history alike, forever. Congratulations, Member Silverthorn, you've found exactly what you were seeking. I hope it will be to your liking."

LA ROSE NOIRE

Charging inside her parents' home, Casey grabbed her backpack and the first set of car keys she could find. It was only as she dashed out the back door that she realized the keys were not for any of the dozen or so cars parked in the driveway or on the front lawn—cars that might have been useful—but for her dad's RV on the other side of the house. But there was no time to go back and find a new set; the Lipmayer home was under attack.

When she reached the basketball court, the mysterious Medolian woman in the wide-brimmed hat was already soaking wet, arms out, staring at her clothes. "What is this?" she asked. "You've soaked my things! They're completely wet! Do you know how many things I've got in here?" She held up her wicker bag. "Quite a few!"

Galinthia and Fabian were staring at the siblings who'd thrown the balloons, sheepishly gawking, not knowing why they'd done what they just did.

"Uh . . . sorry . . ." Richard said, turning beet red. "Our sister told us to."

His confusion and embarrassment were well justified. He and the others had no idea that the water balloons were a contingency plan against the Medolians (*mostly Galinthia*) should they act up or threaten the Lipmayers. Inside each balloon was a mixture of water and six tablespoons of common household bleach, enough to dampen a source of Eve energy in more ways than one. *Thank you, Professor Evans.* Leigh had thought up the idea, which was included among several pages worth of DIY UnEarth home defense strategies in her notebook.

"Keep hitting her!" Casey shouted as she charged toward Fabian and Galinthia.

The new Medolian woman's bewilderment evaporated when she raised her wicker bag, seemingly to attack, and a look of sudden worry crossed her face. A sputtering noise like a struggling engine was heard before dying away. *Guess she knows her powers are gone.* Casey's siblings continued the assault, keeping the newcomer stunted. Without her Eve, she was reduced to fighting off the barrage with her hands, choosing to protect her bag.

"What kind of sorcery is this?" she called.

"Miss Casey, what are you doing!?" Fabian shouted. "We had the situation under control."

"Come on! This way!" Casey led the Medolians to the side of the house and opened the door to the RV.

"This is futile," Fabian said. "Please, we can't let you get involved!"

"Too late. Get inside. The train's leaving!" Casey pushed them inside before following, slamming the door, and leaping into the driver's seat. Sputtering to life, the RV lumbered away. In the rearview mirror, she watched her siblings continue to pelt water balloons at the Medolian, who had taken to swatting them away with her hat while trying to chase after the RV on foot, shouting dire words Casey couldn't make out.

"Who was that?" she asked Fabian while taking a sharp right turn. The RV heaved and moaned before dropping back to equilibrium. Her parents' house disappeared from the rearview mirror, and Casey began to panic at the thought of what might happen to her family now. There hadn't been enough time to say goodbye, let alone tell them what was really happening.

"Omalind," Galinthia answered with a sneer. "One of Philomena's devotees. What was it you did to her? What sort of assault was that?"

"It was a . . . special serum. One for taking down . . . well, others like you."

Driving as fast as possible on the dark, tree-lined roads was spiking Casey's system with frenzied adrenaline.

"Those devices were at the ready?" Galinthia asked, leaning over Casey's shoulder.

"Uh . . . yeah." Casey hoped she wouldn't kill the driver, or would at least make it a quick death. Instead, Galinthia playfully punched her in the shoulder, a move that would surely bruise for weeks and nearly made her squeal.

"Well done, human! I had no idea your survival instincts were so advanced. You must have hated and feared us a great deal. That's fantastic!"

Casey sighed in relief while trying to maintain the RV's speed and subtly rub her aching shoulder. "My family—will they be okay?" she asked.

"The Tribunal is after us," Fabian said. "Your family doesn't know anything, just as it should be. Omalind is a dedicated Sentry with no killer instinct. They will be unharmed. Just a mere mind wipe."

"A mind what!?"

"Fear not! Memory erasure is a precise science and one of the first lessons taught to all new Sentries. She will erase only the last hour or so. No problem. Dad, Mom, and the rest will be none the wiser."

That sounds risky and awful, but what choice do I have? Casey had to take his word for it and hope for the best. Her heart sank at the thought of her mother losing the memory of their conversation. As far as Holly would know, they had not yet reconciled. *And she and Dad are going to think I ran away again.*

"How many of those liquid grenades did you have at the ready?" Fabian asked.

"Not enough to keep her at bay for long," Casey said. "We need a plan."

"How did she find us in the first place?" Galinthia asked, taking a seat.

"I'm not sure," Fabian replied. "We weren't giving off strong signals."

"So, we can't Shift, and wherever we go they'll follow? That means we're basically stuck."

"We could bomb the portal residue," Fabian suggested.

Casey truly hated the sound of that. *It can't mean anything good.*

"With what?" Galinthia asked. "We don't have an object large enough to—"

In the mirror, Casey spotted the Medolian's eyes drifting down and around the RV. "What are you thinking?" she asked them.

"It could work," Fabian said, speeding past the question. "However, we have no destination."

"The safe houses will be compromised," Galinthia said.

"As well as the eateries friendly to Medolians. But what about one that isn't so friendly?" Fabian suggested.

"What do you mean?"

"I've been thinking. We still don't know exactly who or what we can trust, or where. So, let's go somewhere we've never been able to trust at all. A place that truly despises us. The one place no one would ever expect to find a Medolian—La Rose Noire."

Galinthia scoffed so hard she nearly choked. "You're serious? The Rose? The only place less friendly to us right now than the Tribunal?"

Fabian changed his demeanor to match his coming sales pitch. "Think about it. Daphne has no loyalty to Tribunal business. Once she hears our story, she's sure to come around. Plus, if we're this nervous to go there, think about how scared Philomena, Asmund, and Omalind will be. They'd never risk a search of the Rose."

"That doesn't make as much sense as you think it does," Galinthia muttered, bitterness in her voice revealing that he might have made a point.

"Daphne? What's the Rose?" Casey asked.

"An UnEarth club here on Earth governed by a Wyst named Madam Daphne," Fabian answered.

"Who also happens to vehemently hate our kind and has an army of acolytes at her beck and call," Galinthia added.

"Come on, let's try," Fabian begged. "Besides, no matter what, we'll have you there to protect us. Won't we?"

"We?" Galinthia raised an eyebrow.

Fabian folded his arms proudly. "Yes, Miss Casey is coming."

The big, sad, cuddly Medolian locked onto Galinthia with his bright, wet eyes and fluttered his long, swooping eyelashes. She looked seconds from vomiting but relented all the same. "Fine. But I have to reiterate, if you take me there, I'm not responsible for who I kill and will feel no guilt for doing so."

"Sounds fair to me," Fabian beamed.

Casey was still trying to catch up. The RV was damn hard to maneuver on the tight curves, and if she was following the conversation correctly, that meant they were about to go from a potentially hazardous situation into a for-sure hazardous one. But she expected Fabian wouldn't have suggested visiting Madam Daphne if he didn't think it would prove useful. *I think the bar she runs is a sanctuary for Purged UnEarth Humans. They would probably see the Medolians as cops.*

Casey wished she had spent more time with the passages in Leigh's notebook that detailed La Rose Noire. *How do I always pick the wrong stuff to focus on when I study?* "Great. So, we have a plan? How do we get there?"

"That will require a Shift," Fabian said, "which we can't do without leaving an easily traceable signal. But there is a trick that will erase the trail. I've only done it once, but Gale has used the technique on several occasions."

"Not in close to a thousand years," Galinthia said, sounding unsure. "We haven't run away from anything in a long while."

"It will work. No one is better at blowing things up than you." Fabian slapped her on the back, nearly popping Galinthia's eyeballs out of her skull.

"Why do I get the feeling there's a catch?" Casey asked.

"We need to detonate a large piece of Earthly material to do so," Galinthia said with a sick glint lighting her eyes.

"You're talking about my dad's RV?"

"If that is the name of this vehicle, then yes."

"You said detonate?"

"We don't have time," Galinthia said. "I can already sense Omalind's power coming back. Human, stop the car."

"My name is Casey!" She pulled over to the side of the road. "This better be worth it." Standing and joining them in the living area, she took one last look around the RV. *Sorry, Dad. I'll try to repay you if I can someday.*

With a glowing hand, Galinthia touched the RV wall. A gleaming aura spread through the matter like a paper towel soaking up neon tie-dye. As the light spread, a sound grew all around them, crackling like hundreds of feet of tinfoil being crinkled up closer and closer into a mountain around them. Casey hurried to touch the Medolians before Fabian Shifted away.

"You ready?" he asked.

"Yes!" Casey lied, more afraid of the RV than the Shift, even though nothing could ever prepare her for the bone-rattling, shocking, and blaring sensation that was teleportation through the Eve. But the strain on her physical being was nothing compared to what it did to her mind. *It sounds strange, but my brain feels independently afraid while in the Shift.*

The RV was near fully soaked in raw, heavenly light, and the sound of the mounting energy sent a feeling of imminent death upon her, telling her she would be blasted into eternity any second. When the Shift came, without thought she thanked God. The light faded quickly, and Casey suddenly found herself in France. The sound of the RV bomb had ceased. She imagined the crater it left behind was the size of a football field, at least. *The highway warrior's final ride. She was a good boat. Thank you for your sacrifice, girl. Rest easy in RV Valhalla.*

The new scenery was nice to look at but did nothing to curb her anxiety over her family, despite Fabian repeatedly assuring her no harm would befall them. Casey then noticed Galinthia was still wearing her brother Wayne's Red Wings jersey.

"Worry not," Galinthia said. "Your sibling presented me the garment. As a show of goodwill, I believe."

"And Gale returned the favor, offering him one of her knives," Fabian said.

"Wow, that was too kind of you," Casey said while subtly panicking at the thought of her younger brother with a Medolian dagger in his possession.

"It is kind, especially for Galinthia. Very unlike her. As though she delighted in young Wayne's company. Though she has thousands more daggers where that one came from."

Galinthia snorted. "You speak too much."

"Thousands? Where do you keep them?" Casey asked.

"With me at all times," Galinthia murmured, sounding done with the conversation. Casey had no idea how she could be holding thousands of daggers when there were only a dozen or so visible on her belt and sash but did not want to pry.

"Now, where is this place again?" Fabian asked no one in particular. "It's been a few hundred years since we—"

"Perhaps a local might point us in the right direction?" Galinthia suggested, sounding disgusted with herself for doing so.

"A splendid idea!" Fabian said. "But who shall we ask?"

As though on cue, the sounds of raucous conversation approached: many voices and shouts. A bevy of men covered in sweat and spilled drinks turned the corner a few yards down the street. Their arms were wrapped over one another, and some were trying to carry a tune, but their drunkenness and belligerence were apparent only to Casey, it seemed.

"Perfect. Here are some folks we can ask," Fabian said merrily. "I do hope they know."

Casey couldn't help but squirm when the mob of men spotted Fabian, already on the approach, and turned to move in on their group. "Uh, maybe we should find someone else to ask?" she pleaded, trying to reach for his arm to pull him back.

The group of men appeared burlier the closer they got, but Fabian strolled toward them with the ease of someone who had just seen an old friend. "Hello! Yes, you there. Hello!"

Joking back and forth in French about the English speaker who must have looked silly to them in his cloak and traditional Kurdish clothes, the group of men in a mixture of soccer jerseys gawked and laughed and snorted. As the gang overtook the trio and surrounded them, Fabian began politely asking questions in their native tongue. When Casey looked to Galinthia for some reciprocated concern, she found the Medolian seemed not to care, looking as though she had not even noticed the group's presence or had fallen back into another trance. Casey, however, was having trouble containing her unease. One man with eyebrows too small for his forehead had gotten inches from her face, filling her air with the repellent stench of cheap vodka.

"Fabian, these guys aren't here to help us," she said.

"What do you mean?"

"I mean they probably want to rob us or just mess with us."

"Would you like that?" one of the men asked in messy English, pulling back the hair over Casey's ear and leaning in close for a sniff.

"Get off me!" she said.

Why isn't Galinthia doing anything? Shouldn't she be ripping their legs off or something? But the men only grew more brazen, touching Casey's backpack and the tips of her hair.

"Hands off!" she shouted.

The men's eyes went wide with surprise before they laughed. Casey was about to scream for help when Fabian suddenly grunted like a mama grizzly bear and held up his cell phone. The naivety had drained from his face.

"That was unwise, young man." Glowing with canary-yellow light that permeated the men, the beam of energy from the phone suddenly burst like small fireworks within them. The soccer fans barely had time to react, clearly too drunk to comprehend what was happening.

"No one touches Miss Casey!" Fabian bellowed.

The light within the men dissipated quickly, and they were left frozen in the middle of the road, each staring forward with shock, as though they'd just received a phone call and been told a personal tragedy took place. In a matter of seconds, tears bubbled up around their eyes, and vicious wails escaped their mouths, contorting their faces so much Casey feared they would all just keel over in the street.

"Now get out of here!" Fabian boomed.

The soccer fans ran away, crying harder than she had ever seen grown men cry in her life, scrambling over one another like they'd all just tripped in front of the entire school at an assembly and split their pants open, all on the day they didn't have any clean under-wear and went without.

Casey was both shocked and euphoric as she watched them go. "You can . . . do that?"

Fabian kissed his phone before putting it back in his pocket. "Just a quick injection of Eve. Presto. Pure emotions. Kiss sound decisions goodbye."

"Only works on humans, though," Galinthia said, sounding dis-appointed.

"Why didn't you do anything about them?" Casey asked her.

"I'm not supposed to react anymore to humans in cities. Fabian says things get too messy when I do."

Fabian nodded. "She's to ignore them at all times."

"Probably a good idea," Casey agreed.

With no clearer idea of which way to go, they spent the next fifteen minutes wandering the industrial roads of Marseille. When Fabian finally began to recognize landmarks, he said, "I think we're getting close. Miss Casey, put on your Eve gem."

With a weighty sigh, she put on the Grief-gem necklace. *At least it's getting easier to adjust to each time.*

Turning a corner, they soon found themselves staring down a bright, color-soaked cul-de-sac. A broad wall of neon at the end lit up the entirety of the street like a carnival fun house. The central fixture was a fedora-wearing cat that removed the headwear and then put it back on as the lights cycled. *This is France? Feels more like Miami.*

"Ah, there it is," Fabian said, sounding less reassured than one usually does when they find their destination. "The Rose. See? Knew it was around here somewhere."

"Let's get inside before Omalind shows up," Galinthia said.

"Great." Casey started down the lane, taking glances at the dark shops on either side that appeared not quite legitimate, as though facades, hollow inside, with prop merchandise in the windows. She then found she was walking alone, several steps in front of the Medolians, who were trailing behind, their eyes scanning the area through narrow lids.

"So, what do I need to know?" Casey asked. "How should I act in this place?"

"As unhuman as possible," Galinthia muttered.

"Whatever you do, don't call us Medolians," Fabian said, his fingers twitching on his cell phone. "We want to get as far in as possible before being found out."

"Can't UnEarth Humans sense each other? Won't they know you're Medolians?" Casey said.

"We can fake it. Our Mallos gives us access to all the shades of Eve. Because of this, we can change our signature to appear to be one of the other types of UnEarth creatures. Think of it like a smell. We can identify each other that way. I can easily appear to be a Lostros, and Galinthia can look like an Archie—no sweat. Of course, we could look like any of the UnEarth creatures, but as I lean Grief and she Wrath, it just makes sense."

"With luck, they'll never know who any of us are," Galinthia said.

"Do we even have a plan?"

"In order to speak with Madam Daphne, we'll need to get through the platinum hall. I just hope that Bai-Shalk bodyguard she usually has around is taking the night off."

"I assume humans are not welcome here, either," Casey said.

"They are not," Fabian replied. "Hence your misery gem."

As they got closer, Casey noticed that the majority of the patrons out front for a smoke break were dressed in similar fashions, usually either vests or overalls and not a pair of shoes to be seen. None of these traits were shared by either Casey or her travel companions, and it slowly began to dawn on her just how out of place they appeared.

Sure hope Galinthia and Fabian know what they're doing.

The trio approached the club and the guards at the entrance, who wore bright cyan ties. When they arrived and neither of the Medolians said anything, Casey decided to speak first. "Hello," she said, hoping it wasn't too bubbly. The doorman, whose eyes were hidden behind sunglasses, nodded and let them pass smoothly. Casey carried on with unsure knees, expecting to be grabbed and eaten or arrested at any moment.

Following the entry threshold into the club, she found herself in a long, dark hallway. At the far end, a dance hall was bursting with chaos, like television static at max volume come to life. The bombastic noise could have been described as music (*but certainly not by me*) and shook Casey's gut into knots as they drew closer.

As she took the final step out of the tunnel, the world of light and sound struck like a punch to her everything, sending her already volatile emotions to wild extremes—from radically despondent to true bliss, then back again. This occurred through the full breadth of her feelings while lasers struck her face and shadows danced like fire swirling around her. Things like scolding heat, cold flashes, snarling teeth, and scaly skin passed like spooky, fucked-up ships in the night.

Casey wouldn't be able to take this for long. The Rose was too much for her senses. *All of them! Let's get this over with!* Turning around, she found Galinthia and Fabian several yards back, still near the entrance. They had stopped moving forward soon upon entering, wincing and holding their ears and plugging their noses as though this place were even more intense for them than it was for Casey. *Try to look a little more conspicuous, why don't you!* After retrieving them, she clutched them tight and led them farther into the hall, trying to stick close to the bar and tables, where the crowd of creatures was thinner. "What do we do now?" she screamed.

"I'm not really sure," Fabian replied, his eyes bouncing about, signaling loudly that he might be expecting an ambush.

How is it I'm better at this than he is? "Great." Casey's words were lost in the clamor. "No plan, and everyone here wants to kill us." She began to shout, "What we need to do is get away from all this—"

The music abruptly stopped, leaving complete silence and Casey all alone, shouting, "—noise!"

The lingering space after the outburst seemed to settle like a balloon drifting to the ground after popping midflight. Casey's breath caught itself in her throat.

A moment later, as though on cue, the patrons around the trio backed away in unison, acting out a plot. Their colored eyes floated in the darkness like flies. Spotlights erupted and turned on Casey and the Medolians as a tall woman appeared out of the crowd, wearing sunglasses and a chauffeur's cap. A team of four dressed just like her, in impeccable suits and cyan ties, followed and formed a towering and imposing line.

Galinthia snapped to attention and drew her daggers, readying for an attack. "We've been had! I knew this was a bad idea! Didn't I say that? I know I did."

"Don't blame me!" Fabian shouted. "It was Miss Casey who wanted to come here, not me."

"Excuse me?" Casey screamed.

Unmoved by Galinthia's defense, the security chief stood her ground. "You're going to follow me."

More guards in suits surrounded the trio. In response, Fabian pocketed his phone and threw his hands up.

"Do you know who you're talking to?" Galinthia threw a dagger at the chief, who appeared to blast it out of the air with a form of goo projected from her hand. The dagger clattered to the ground, soaked in a cyan mess.

"Don't struggle," the chief said. "Unless you want me to like it."

Before Galinthia could respond, a tender voice filled the entire club. "Medolians!" The crowd parted farther around Casey, Fabian, and Galinthia. Looking toward the front of the dance floor, Casey spotted a tall woman with more curves than she thought a body could possess, walking to the edge of the balcony overlooking the room. The bulbous, glossy, puckered lips stretching across her face were a fierce, life-preserver orange.

"That's her," Fabian said to Casey. "Stay by me. I don't want anything to happen to you."

Casey perused the crowd around them, who looked suddenly hungry for her flesh. "No problem."

"Greetings, Madam Daphne!" Fabian said boisterously.

The woman belly laughed and wiped away a tear with a tentacle that appeared from over her shoulder. "Of all the things I thought I'd never see! For you to slip up and arrive here? So foolish, it's unbelievable. Of course, that was before I heard the news—the state of things in UnEarth. How wonderful and fitting, isn't it? Your own house has finally turned against you. The seekers and jailers are now running from the fate they forced onto so many. It's so yummy I could eat it for every meal. When I heard Izaiah's flock was on the run, I thought one or two might eventually show, pleading for sanctuary. But"—she laughed a little more and wiped away another tear with a second tentacle—"I just didn't think it would be so quickly. Like tamed rodents, you jumped into my lap. And I find that . . . quite funny."

"I'll show this lady funny," Galinthia said, readying three daggers in hand.

"Down, Gale." Fabian marched forward. "And so right you are, Madam Daphne. And may I just say, I truly love what you've done with the place." He looked around. "What is it—exactly—you've changed?"

"Nothing."

"See—nothing. Right. That's what I love. Classic."

"This won't work, Medolian."

"Whatever do you mean?"

"Your kind have jailed and killed my brethren for ages. My friends. And now you use a plan such as this to gain my help? Our help?" Her hands and head tentacles presented her club and its patrons. "I suppose this is my fault. I should never have helped you by revealing the location of Nigel Roe. I only did so because I was so tired of the man—I simply wanted to see him in jail for a few hundred years. Eve knows he deserves it. Alas. Chief Mary, dispose of these intruders so we may continue our evening."

"Gladly!" The tall chief in sunglasses and her team began to move in on Casey and the Medolians as Madam Daphne sashayed away.

Jumping into the air and waving her arms, Casey screamed as loudly as her lungs would allow. "Wait!"

Madam Daphne stopped and turned, blinking several times and squinting to spot Casey. "You? I almost didn't see you. Who are you, little thing?"

"My name is Casey. It wasn't the Medolians' idea to come here. It was mine." She took off her Eve gem. "It's my business. I think we can help each other."

The crowd gasped when the gem came off. A thud on the ground suggested one of them might have fainted. Madam Daphne, however, remained unaffected.

"Ah, yes. A human," she said. "Seems my recent mistakes continue to come back to haunt me." She then shouted to the gallery, "Are there any Archfiend or Scythes who'd like a snack? Albeit a small one. With plenty of fat."

"I'll have you know my BMI is down to twenty, proving that a good majority of many people's total masses are not necessarily fat." Casey blew her hair out of her eyes.

Madam Daphne nodded, seeming impressed. "Didn't know that. Thank you." She motioned to her patrons. "Any takers?"

The silhouetted crowd roared, filled with snarls and hungry growls. Casey panicked, jumping forward and waving her arms again. *Don't eat me!*

"Wait! I'm here because . . . I'm looking for my friend!"

The crowd was stayed, seemingly hinged on the calm expression Madam Daphne wore. Casey guessed if her eyes wavered even a little, the floodgates might drop. *I don't think I would last long, even with Medolians on my side.*

"A friend of yours?" Madam Daphne said. "I can tell you, child, they're not here."

"If you would just listen for a moment," Casey pleaded.

"I'm tired of listening. The pleasure of my guests has been violated long enough. Chief Mary, I no longer want them in chains."

"I'll notify the cleanup crew," the chief said.

"She's been looking for Aluqa!" Casey screamed. "Aluqa Morinnean! You know that name, correct? I think my friend got mixed up with the Surface. We want your help to bring the whole thing down." Casey was just winging it at this point.

"You are not friends of Morinnean?" Madam Daphne asked with a peaked brow.

"No, Madam. In fact, it's my belief that my friend joined Aluqa to learn about her. To use her. Leigh is too independent to join someone like that for real. She's up to something."

Madam Daphne yawned. "This does not convince me. But it does make me curious. Do you have more to tell?"

"Of course!" Casey lied, while trying to believe it enough so the UnEarth Humans surrounding her didn't know it. "Tons. That is, I do if you let the Medolians and myself stay here with a guarantee of our safety."

Madam Daphne folded her arms and rapped her fingers repeatedly. The expression on her face was a mixed bag, but Casey guessed she didn't like being talked to by a human in such a way— or at least wasn't used to it.

The silence lasted long enough to again convince Casey it was all over until, with a healthy chortle, Madam Daphne finally said, "Perhaps we can be friends after all." Calling to her guests, she announced, "My esteemed fellows, please return to enjoying your stay. Bring the music back up. And you three"—she pointed at Casey, Galinthia, and Fabian—"may join me upstairs for a drink."

FASHION & ACCESSORIES

Pain ricocheted through his hand. Bam! The bones in Bennett's knuckles screamed. Bam-bam! The rigidity of the target stole each punch's force, draining him twice as much as it normally would. Bam! To get a satisfying ding from the metal took everything he had with every swing. Bam! But it was worth it. Bam! Yet this couldn't continue much longer. Bam! His body would soon collapse, out of energy and usable hands. *But I'm still angry!* Bam! *How do I release this on something without hurting anybody else? Should I just stomp around really hard?* Bam-bam-bam!

He dropped down onto both knees in his cell, panting and heaving. Blood dripped from his knuckles onto the spotless stone. They wanted to hit more things but were already pulsing, swelling, and far too raw. The bars in front of him were splattered red, with murky streams crisscrossing their way down.

After being tossed back into his cell by the Iolanze guards following one of the most brutal and overlong trial sessions yet, Bennett had been overcome with rage, a kind far greater than any he'd experienced fighting overseas. It took him easily, twisting his mind into knots and causing his fingers to curl as though grasping for something to destroy. The cell bars seemed as good a target as any, and when he threw the first punch, he found it to be rather satisfying. Especially so when he began imagining the thick bars were Van-Mortus's face, aiming each blow straight at her glowing red irises, hopefully blinding her for life.

She and her prosecution team had never lobbed so many bombs in a single day as they just had. Over twenty-two hours, Bennett was subjected to creatures continuously lying on the stand about Alex's and Izaiah's characters or about having known Alex while living on Earth as UnEarth Humans. Yet another torture on top of the many the teacher was already enduring. If there were any mercy left in the universe, Alex would have fallen asleep early in the session and not heard a word of it. *Izaiah . . . I don't care about. He can hear it. Doesn't seem to care anyways. The guy is untouchable. It's impressive actually. But still, fuck him.*

Of the three men on trial, Bennett was the only one sitting pretty, a fact that had annoyed him for months and since escalated into outright frustration. Like a kid in class desperate to be called on by the teacher, he found himself wishing to be mentioned by the prosecution, even just once. *Only thing I hate more than some asshole parking too close to my truck is feeling invisible.* On the rare occasions he was acknowledged, Van-Mortus typically praised him, which only grated on his nerves further. For the first time, he longed to be accused of the many wrongs he'd committed. *There are probably assloads of laws I broke during the Joseph debacle! Shit, you guys could probably even make some up. Go ahead! They're not even gonna try and accuse me of fake crimes? That's . . . low.*

In life, Bennett spent much of his time seething over bureaucracy. The feeling of powerlessness while battling any system always left him fuming. Yet, for some reason, he had assumed the systems in UnEarth would be better—free from fraud and extortion. *Why did I think that? No matter which way you look, everything is stupid. Why would this be different?* His rage had been bubbling to new heights lately, and as he grew angrier over the injustices he was powerless to stop, his already turbulent Rapture became more intense, filling him with a bristling coldness and rigidity. *Strange. Usually, it's the opposite with my anger and Rapture.*

But the Eve within him had been feeling different for a while now, especially today. When Bennett looked at his hands, he noticed that his fingertips and up to his elbows were tinted cobalt, a frozen blue. Parts of him had looked like this before, but this was the first time it had happened without triggering his Rapture at the same time. The shade was also evolving, drifting away from the sky blue he was accustomed to and leaning toward a deep royal hue. It reminded him of his lawyer, Roland—particularly his hairpiece—which stoked Bennett's anger like a heavy sack of dried, minced logs being shoved into a steam engine's firebox. Every word ever said to his counsel had been ignored, especially his pleas on Alex's behalf, who now seemed impossible to save from the executioner's axe. *Asshole. Using me as a career booster.* So how could Bennett help his brother? *I can't.* That felt like a second cage around his first.

Floating and wobbly, Roland's face appeared before him. Bennett squinted to see it and knew it wasn't really there, but that made no difference, because it was still aching to get hit. The face floated over to the cell bars and began laughing. Then Van-Mortus's mug appeared, fading into view beside it, followed by Axios. They were all laughing at him. Finally, Izaiah joined them, pointing and cackling with his wide, foul, nearly toothless mouth.

Fuck you all. I hate you all so much. God, I just want to pummel your faces. Make 'em all dent inward. Make 'em gooey and mangled. Oh, it would be so satisfying. They all shouted back in unison, *"Then do it, why dontcha?"* Bennett was on his feet in an instant, bouncing and shaking off the wear on his fists. Hobbling over, he began heaving them at the bars like a madman. It hurt but felt good. The pain was worth it and was getting him what he wanted, all too easy to endure. The faces needed their pummelings.

Goddamn hypocritical assholes!

He punched harder and the faces began to move and switch and swirl and spin upside down. He punched even harder, trying to finish them off with one blow. And the strikes began to ring, and a powerful thud was behind them, like solid pieces of iron were striking an anvil-shaped bell. The blue skin on Bennett's arms began to radiate light and swell, the veins twisting through them inflamed with luminous power. He punched even harder. Azure fire erupted from his hands and forearms with each strike, making everything he had previously produced look like cigarette lighters low on fluid. Eve sparks jumped into the air after the blinding flashes, as if the bars were being struck by welding torches hidden deep within his knuckles.

Seven and a half minutes of nonstop pounding later, two High Celestial guards finally tromped down the hall and into the outer track of the cell, wielding protracted shock spears. From the safety of the outer track, they could have used them to prod him into docility, but they didn't seem keen on that approach as they began unlocking the inner cell door.

"Wondered what was taking you guys so long," Bennett spat, cracking his neck and trying to catch his breath to prepare for a fight—one he eagerly leaped into once the cell door opened. But the guards had him crying uncle in less than five seconds, his head smashed into the floor by a massive crystalline foot.

"Will the prisoner be still?" one guard asked.

"Dr'przznr wn't!" Bennett screeched from under the foot, his face half-flattened into the ground.

Bam! His head was lifted and pounded into the floor. Then again. Bam! The foot came back, mashing his dome from the top with a crunch.

"Will the prisoner be still?"

Bennett was seeing only stars and currently incapable of comprehending what had just happened, leaving his response as merely the drool dripping out of his mouth.

"The prisoner is still," the other guard said after a moment lost to the soldier.

Satisfied, the guards left the pitiful human behind and stepped out to disappear down the hall, though this went largely unnoticed. The stars were shining brighter all the time, flashing like infuriating strobe lights. The fight it took to roll onto his back required all his will and an unknown amount of time—jarring for a man with a near-perfect internal clock. It must have been several hours at least, sprawled on the cell floor, staring at the ceiling through his swollen vision while his thoughts gradually became cogent.

I don't know why I held out hope. They're going to kill Al. I'll probably get life in prison, but who cares? How come Izaiah won't step in and help? How can he just sit around doing nothing? What is he waiting for?

By the time he'd healed fully and his vision had returned, Bennett was feeling anxious and antsy, wanting to spring up and dash in circles like a crazed cat at three a.m.—possibly to let off the feeling of helplessness he was accumulating inside, as well as the Rapture that seemed to be increasing around him whether he was trying to produce it or not.

Fighting the voice within him aching for justice, Bennett endeavored to calm himself and push his Eve as low as possible. But the Rapture just seemed to keep growing, not only within him but also all around him. If the jail's sensors picked up another surge, the guards would be back. The right half of Bennett's face didn't want that. He struggled all the harder to bring down his power; the storm in his gut quieted, but even as his Eve subsided, Rapture continued to grow from somewhere in the room, leaving him utterly confused. *What—where is it coming from?*

An audible hum suddenly became apparent. Turning his gaze down, he found the source of the sound, as well as the excess Rapture: Hannah's belt buckle.

Just what is going on with this thing? Reaching for it, his fingers were inches away when a sudden chill rolled over him. The sensation was familiar, like the smell of an old friend stuck on an article of clothing you borrowed and never gave back. *Kinda hard to return something when its first owner is long dead.* The short time he'd spent with Hannah returned to him, along with the fear and uncertainty of the Joseph Mandate—feelings that had all been eased when she was around but then amplified tenfold after she'd gone.

Kinda crazy how fast you can become dependent on someone.

The aura radiating off the buckle offered a similar comfort to having her nearby. But the signal had never been this loud or bright, and this time he sensed a vague desperation from it—an air of warning or a call for help seemingly emanating through its cadence.

He didn't know why, but Bennett came to the brilliant conclusion that he would be able to connect to it telepathically and possibly understand the message more clearly by entering a meditative state. *I saw a thing about it on UPN20 a couple of years ago. Some dudes in Malonashia or somewhere can—like—break boards with their minds. Or maybe it was cracking eggs. Cool either way. Those dudes were rad.*

Sitting cross-legged in the middle of his cell, Bennett rested his hands on his knees and took several deep breaths into his gut before shutting his eyes and making his first attempt. *Okay . . . what would Hannah tell me to do?* Nothing obvious came to mind, so at first, he simply tried listening to the hum of the buckle. The sound had been steadily growing but soon began to change, making leaps in intensity. A few minutes later, the randomness of the noise was beginning to find form. What kind, he had no idea, but it seemed promising. There might be a chance he would be able to make contact after all. He allowed himself to get excited. But the signal suddenly petered out, and the buckle quieted itself.

No, come on, I can do this. Don't go away yet.

The excitement was summarily killed. *I know better than to celebrate prematurely. What the hell's wrong with me?* He took several deep breaths, his heart stilled. He listened once again, trying to find what was hidden in the sound. Time passed, and Bennett allowed himself to lose track of it. All he considered was his breathing and the hum, which continued to grow. The constant stream gradually became a river, then a thundering shore of turmoil blaring until he thought he might go deaf or his head might explode. A stifling weight pressed on his chest and mind, and a part of Bennett began to wonder if he wasn't about to kill himself by accident like some autoerotic-asphyxiated dumbass. But there were far worse ways to go, and this thing would be seen through to the end, come Hell or high water. He pushed on, no matter how stupid his corpse might look when they found him.

His mind drifted deeper, deeper still into the sound, until the weight of it eventually broke, as though he'd passed under a waterfall into a calm, hidden lagoon that lay behind it. Bennett realized his sense of reality and his body were drifting away. In no time, his corporeal self was entirely lost.

In this new place, the idea of vision or sight had not yet crossed his mind. He was without location or landscape, floating in nothing as well as remaining nothing. For a good long while, he lingered there, not only because it was the most peaceful place he had ever found his consciousness but also because it was simply nice to be out of his jail cell.

Gradually, a sense of something akin to broad musical tones began washing over him. But after a moment, it became clear it was not music he was hearing (*no way, no guitar, no drums—totally sucks*) but more like small variations in time and space that produced a tone as they passed. They were like different time zones forcing their way past him, and something told Bennett he would be able to grab onto one.

After much experimenting, he figured out the trick was to try to match the frequency of the tones with his own. Tuning himself just as he would the strings of a guitar, he fought to match the frequency that repeated most often. As it sped by, he began to feel himself pushed, as though struck by a rushing wind. But he couldn't connect. Just like a surfer falling off his board again and again, the wave passed him by, and Bennett was forced to go back and wait for the next opportunity.

When he finally caught it, he knew beforehand. Just a split second or two, but enough to trust without a doubt that he was about to go for a ride. And go for a ride he did. As he latched onto the speeding wave, a shot rang through him, starting from the base of his neck and running down to his legs.

The transition pushed him past a barrier into a new, wondrous way of experiencing reality. But in this new place, darkness was what he found—empty, endless nothingness. Bennett fought to keep from panicking and tried to go with the flow, pretending he'd simply shut his eyes. This lasted for what seemed like half a day. Then the slow, steady thump of a heart began to reveal itself.

Without him realizing when or how, he was suddenly aware of his body. It had returned. The heart was his.

Darkness gradually faded and gave way to light. He could look down and see himself, even if it was foggy and out of focus. *Everything's like a pixelated dick in a Japanese porno.* But there wasn't any ground yet. Not until the world formed around him, which it seemed to do without his noticing. Suddenly, walls reaching thirty feet into the air surrounded him on all sides. Their soft blue gradually darkened until Bennett felt he was standing inside dusk, while above him the sky became a dismal gold.

The huge hallway appeared to be inside a castle, one made of cobalt bricks a yard in length. Intricate lines of glowing neon blue, some thinner than a human hair, ran along the edges of the bricks, only occasionally diverting from logical square order to add flourishes and accoutrements. There was no proper ceiling above, only occasional arches and sections encasing junctions.

A distant thunder seemed to rumble all around him: broad thumping and distant whooshing, possibly the cries of enormous creatures. But it wasn't a storm he was hearing on the horizon. Bennett would have known these sounds anywhere. They were the song of battle. This must have been a truly phenomenal one, as the very ground shook and trembled as though it were afraid of what was occurring miles away.

Putting one foot in front of the other was a new sensation and took some practice, but Bennett quickly got the hang of walking once again. The hall had no curves, and its walls were featureless, so he just kept going in the direction he was already facing. Feeling like a child toddling around in a world of behemoths, he found the colossal size of the hall made the fact that it was empty all the more puzzling and unsettling.

After a brief hike, muffled thumping that had seemed part of the war sounds became clearer and nearer, soon evolving into the trudge of what could have been armored horse hooves in a steady march. The dissonant clanging grew, echoing through the passage until it seemed directly upon him, and a blue glow appeared around the corner. A troop of enormous warriors tromped around the turn in unified precision. At first, Bennett thought to run, believing it was the Barium Guard, but these were not all High Celestials; there were several Faire among them, as well as a row of Pseras bringing up the rear. The troop's armor was also different from the Barium Guards', being gold rather than silver, appearing heavier and adorned with dents, gashes, charring, and scrapes from combat—unlike the Guard, whose armor had likely never been assaulted by anything nastier than a feather duster.

The whoosh of rigid wings approached, along with a rising note seemingly sung by a choir in the sky. Bennett looked up as a broad silhouette swooped in and blotted out much of the light from above. With one final flap, the figure slowed and landed on a parapet above the marching troops. The armor of this newcomer was more extensive than the rest, its gold brighter, and the helmet they removed from their head was distinct among the troop.

Gotta be the commanding officer. I'd know one anywhere.

With their chest out, the figure stood tall above the others, their gaze fixed on a hidden distance. A sense of worry about what they could see that the others could not was subtly etched into their stance. On numerous occasions, Bennett had seen his own commanding officers appear similarly, carrying the weight of not only the war but also their troops' lives with them. *And they always looked like that just before things got to their worst.*

The longer Bennett stared, the more he felt that there was something familiar about the Celestial commander. Then it hit him.

No way . . .

"Hannah?" he said quietly under his breath.

The winged creature in silhouette turned and fixed their glowing eyes on him, giving Bennett the sensation he was smaller than a cockroach.

Landing with grace, the figure dropped from above, the soft clang of their armor like distant wind chimes. As they marched steadily toward Bennett, he anticipated the fear of being approached by a giant but felt none. As they neared, their aura became clear. It was a little different, but still hers. There was no doubt.

"That one," she said, pointing her huge, glowing stone finger at him. "You have left formation."

Bennett didn't know what to say. He stuttered like a guy caught with his dick in the housekeeper.

"A desperate time, this is," she said. "We cannot break order."

"Of course, I'm sorry," Bennett said.

"Rejoin the Pseras—in the rear."

"Yeah, I just . . . I was told to stay up here."

"By whom? I—"

Before Hannah could finish, a bellowing, ferocious tidal wave of sound struck the castle, so powerful and deafening that Bennett thought a literal typhoon had appeared out of nowhere. *Or a god-damn nuke went off! Good thing there was no flash. Fuck.* At the sound, the Celestials pivoted to an attack-ready posture, as though by pure instinct. Bennett covered his ears, but it did little to stop the tumult, which became more the roar of a wild animal the longer it lasted.

What the fuck kind of animal can make a sound like that?!!?

Lifting her spear, Hannah called out to the others with a drawn-out word spoken in Hyl. Like robots in unison, the troop returned to marching position and set off at a brisk pace. To avoid being trampled, Bennett kept near Hannah at the front.

"Where are we going?" he asked.

"To lower bailey. Western battlements support."

"Right . . . the bailey and the battlements."

"A peculiar creature, you. Did you not heed the briefing?"

"I never paid much attention to those, honestly."

"So strange. Pseras usually listen the closest."

"I'm the worst one. I just want to know what's going on."

"We must fortify. The beast approaches with every grain in the glass."

"The beast?" It was starting to dawn on Bennett that he might have been living inside a memory of Hannah's. *Oh! Now I get it. This must have been the war she fought in Hywyn.*

"So, this is Inferius," he dropped absentmindedly.

Hannah stopped the march. The others behind them halted on a dime. "You had forgotten?" she said. "Tell me, what are you? You are no Celestial."

"I'm nobody," Bennett said. "Just a Psera, like you said. Happy to be here."

"I think not." Hannah stared intently from three feet above. Two other Celestials, likely her chief officers, joined her at her side. A wall of blue and gold loomed over Bennett.

"What is this creature, General?" one asked.

"I'm not sure," she answered.

"The spy. This one must be," another said. "Inform the council we have found it."

"We do not know that," Hannah said. "Decisions will not be made until we do."

She and the others waited for Bennett. He danced between a few responses as the Celestials drew closer and grew bigger. This obviously wasn't going to end well.

Uh . . . how do I make this stop?

It seemed his adventure was over when the rustle of huge wings approached again. Another Celestial, this one in far lighter armor than the rest, swooped in and landed on a perch above.

"Appriso," the newcomer said. "News. This, from the front."

"Share with haste," Hannah beckoned.

"Uhl'k has increased speed. Reached the capitol threshold. This, sooner than predicted."

At first, Hannah said nothing, and the troops did not react. Though their stares remained blank, it was somehow clear that the news was devastating.

I mean, it sounded pretty devastating to me.

Hannah turned to her troops. "With haste of Michael. To western terrace!" she shouted, lifting her spear.

The Celestials under her command followed. In a wave, the front of the battalion spread their wings and lifted off through the open roof into the air beneath the golden canopy. With a swift motion, Hannah scooped up Bennett into one arm before taking off.

Soaring high above the castle, he saw a metropolis of glistening Rapture spread out below them. The world he was seeing within the buckle was still too foggy to make out any details, but the wonder he felt staring at a Hywynite landscape from above—even a blurry one—with its myriad shades of luminous blue, from baby-blanket to deep navy, with trimmings of lavender and indigo, was enough to take his breath away.

The giant armored limb wrapped around him was ice cold, yet it might as well have been an electric blanket and a mug of hot cocoa. Within seconds, he began to feel the safety of Hannah's unshakable presence, like everything would be okay. Gliding through the air, he felt a dreamlike sense of wonder come on. *Shit, I could start singing or something!*

But no sooner did his self-awareness kick in than a sudden sense of doom crawled up his leg, as though Hannah might drop him.

The blue of the city below grew muddier, and a haze of orange and red filtered in like the edge of a dust storm. A queasy unease filled Bennett as a shudder of Dread passed through Hannah.

That doesn't make any sense.

On the horizon he found a rising pall of crimson. A brush fire seconds from climbing over a hill could produce something similar, but other than that, Bennett hadn't the faintest idea what could be just on the other side.

Then the stomps began—earthquakes he could see, with waves speeding across the city and countryside, shaking loose bits of dust and sending rock and glass tumbling. BOOM. The next did not come for another forty-nine seconds. BOOM.

Whatever was coming scared the shit out of him and made Bennett want to puke his guts out.

"It is here," Hannah said just before another ferocious wave of sound tore across the landscape. It was clearer now. *That's definitely a roar.* But one so large it seemed the whole planet was roaring, and along with it came a broiling heat flooding the air.

Just after, a human scream broke through, overpowering the roar. It was one he'd heard before and had just spent more than a year overthinking, one that haunted both his dreams and waking life: the scream Hannah released when she and Joseph unleashed their final attacks on one another.

With the scream, everything around him was erased, dashed out of existence, sending him spinning uncontrollably until he found himself suddenly standing in a landscape filled with a swirling white haze. The crushing gravity was not unlike the Still Room in La Rose Noire, though a much more turbulent version.

The scream was still echoing when the same voice spoke up as though right next to him, their mouth to his ear.

"Who's there?"

It sounded like Hannah's voice in some ways but also didn't. Bennett wasn't exactly sure who it belonged to.

"Who's there?" the voice called again, this time from several yards away, sounding even angrier. "I know someone is here."

"Yeah, I am. Hello?" Bennett called back.

More echoes and wind. Blinding flashes.

"Who are you? How did you find this place?"

Putting up his new hands to show he was not a threat to whoever might be out there, he said, "It's Bennett. Hunter. Are you okay? Where are you? I can't see you."

"No, you shouldn't be . . . get out of here!"

"I'm not here to harm anyone. I'm here because I heard a call. Does somebody need help?"

"I don't know. I don't know you. You're not . . . I don't know you. You're not supposed to be here!"

"Where is here?" Bennett asked.

"I said get out!" The area around him thundered and shook. Her rage bit into his senses.

"I'm sorry, but you *did* call me. So is there . . . I don't know, anything I can help you with?"

"Help? Why would you help me?"

"I'm pretty sure we know each other."

"You're wrong. You don't belong. Just leave me alone."

"I will. Just tell me your name first."

"My name?" The voice seemed to drift farther into the void. "How would that . . . no. I don't know what you're asking."

"Your name. You do have one, don't you?" Bennett shouted, just in case she'd actually moved farther away and couldn't hear him.

"I'm not sure. I . . . NO! STOP IT!" The ghostly voice was suddenly beside his ear again. "Why is this happening? Why now? I don't want this!" The foggy void stirred, churning all around him.

"I said I mean no harm!" Bennett pleaded. "Please, I'm just trying to talk to you. Can you come out? Let me see you?"

Her voice was all around him now, weakened and dry, muttering like a drug addict on the subway. "It's always been like this. Like a dream. I can remember so much, there's a lifetime's worth, yet my eyes . . . they've always been closed. I'm sure of it . . . I'm sure of it . . ."

"You don't have to be in the dark," Bennett said. "Follow my voice. If we find each other, maybe we can see each other."

The environment around him underwent another radical transformation. The storm of white fog reached a chaotic zenith before darkness rolled over. At first like a rain cloud overtaking him, a shadow condensed and swept in front, forming a column. A shape then began to glow as it continued to take form. First came a head, then legs, then arms, then broad wings spread out before him like sails on a glorious ship.

Heavy, rocky steps clomped forward, making Bennett feel tinier with every boom.

"Hello?" A broad, powerful voice with a shimmering echo spoke. Bennett again recognized it: Hannah's voice after her transformation into her ascended form. A thunderclap struck, and suddenly the silhouette was smaller, human-sized, its wings gone.

The shape moved through the fog, and a woman emerged, naked, with long jet-black hair. As she neared, her face and hair began to change. Clothes appeared and disappeared, one morphing into the other before she entered a clearing a few feet away.

Bennett couldn't help gawking. It *was* her. But she was not the Hannah he knew. *How could she be?* Her leather jacket, boots, and jeans had been replaced by a caped suit of golden armor. The unwavering confidence in her face was gone, replaced with timid eyes drifting about, as though an attack might come at any moment.

"Did we barricade the southern cauldron?" she demanded. "Ai remains vulnerable."

Bennett wasn't sure what to say or do. She seemed to be looking through him. His mother used to do similar things when she'd sleepwalk. Phrases would escape, but they didn't mean anything. The difference here was that this angel clearly thought she was in the middle of a fight or was at least looking for one.

And I don't know what will happen if I die in here. Is it like that movie The Matrix, *and my brain will kill me? That would suck.*

"Is that really you, General?" Bennett asked cautiously.

"Of course it's me. Who else would I . . ." She halted, seeming to come to, gazing at her hands, then at him, then back at her hands. Her voice turned soft. "I'm . . . I'd forgotten what form I . . . or did I ever . . ." Her words trailed off and never recovered.

"Do you recognize me now?" Bennett asked.

"Should I?"

"Do you remember Joseph or Chloe or Alex?"

"I have no idea whom you're referring to. Explain yourself."

"Like I said, my name is Bennett. I'm here because you taught me how to use my Rapture, and by doing so, I found you."

"I taught you? You're a pure human, aren't you?"

"Yeah, at least I think so. I'm full of Rapture and my molecules are weird, but I probably count. I'm no Celestial—I can tell you that."

"And now . . . you're in this place, which . . . what is this place?"

"I was hoping you could tell me."

"I'm not sure. Before this I was . . ." She grabbed her head like she was hit with a migraine. "Where are we!? What is this? Am I dreaming?" Her eyes burst open in remembered terror. "Wait. Joseph. I think . . . the nameless Archfiend."

"Yeah. That's right."

"But then . . ." Her eyes darted back and forth, working through it; Bennett could tell she was close but struggling. "It's a fog. They're like memories . . . these feelings." Her jaw clenched.

"You're there. Keep going, and don't ask me to explain any of it. If there's any other way I can help, let me know. Like maybe I can . . . hold . . . something for you."

Hannah's tension suddenly seemed to flow off her like a bag of bricks had finally been released from her shoulders and plummeted to the ground. She peered at Bennett with eerily calm eyes. "I'm not the real Hannah, am I?"

"Don't think so."

"Hunter?"

"That's me. Nice to see you again, by the way, Teach."

"You're right. I do know you." She looked at her hands and the armor covering her body. "Human hands . . . Makes sense, but that still doesn't explain where we are."

"Inside your belt buckle."

"I'm in no mood for jokes, Hunter."

"I'm not jokin' ya, sister."

"Explain. Quickly."

"You know, the one with the planets on it or whatever. After all the crazy shit I've seen with you people, this one's hard to believe? Look, your buckle ended up with me, and I heard a voice. I figured it was like *Techno Knights of the Round Table*, and if I harnessed my chi or whatever like these dudes I saw on TV, then maybe I could make contact with whoever was in here. But honestly, I'm kind of fucking shocked it worked."

"What is Techno Knights of the Round Table?"

"Oh—cartoon I used to watch on Sundays with my brother. Each of the knights had a special sword with the soul of an ancestor inside it. When they closed their eyes and said a magic chant, their ancestor would show up like a ghost and help them defeat the monster. Oh, and they all had robot horses and tanks. It was awesome."

"I see. But if we're inside the buckle . . ." Hannah's eyes were darting back and forth. "How could we . . . really? Wow. So, it is possible." She laughed boisterously, revealing a deep-seated sense of absurdity.

"This really is a surprise to you?" Bennett asked. *I didn't expect that at all.*

"In some ways," she finished, shaking her head. "We always knew that Earthly objects soaked up Eve. Nothing new there. But some have long speculated that since we are made of Eve ourselves and are fully realized creatures, those vessels of Eve might somehow be sentient or, rather, contain a consciousness."

"Just like on *Techno Knights.*"

She gave him a hard glance.

"Sorry," Bennett said. "Also, sorry that this is how you're finding out you're inside an article of clothing."

Buckle Hannah paced, her fingers jammed under her chin. "That showboat. Hannah . . . She must have pushed as much Eve as she could into the buckle before detonating." She looked at the ground again, wide-eyed, before laughing. A single tear made it halfway down her cheek before freezing.

"I'd say you're taking this rather well," Bennett said.

Stretching her jaw wide enough to eat a basketball, Hannah suddenly screamed, blasting him back several feet. Rapture and wind burst from her in a wave before she collapsed and all became silent again. "I don't want this—I don't want this. What am I? A stain or memory? A remnant of someone else?" She locked eyes on him. "You woke me. Why?"

"I'm sorry."

"You could have left it alone, done anything but this."

"Not sure I was supposed to. You really don't remember calling out?"

"No, but I believe you." She rose from the ground and approached him. "I'm actually impressed you were able to find me. It means you're learning. And your shade is deeper than ever."

"I had a good teacher."

"You sure?"

"Yeah. What I never understood was, why me? I mean . . . she could see my soul, right? Literally. She knew who I was. Knew I was garbage. Why did she waste her time? Why did she let herself get killed just to come along with us idiots? Why save us?"

"Maybe it wasn't about you. Maybe it was about something she needed to figure out in herself. All pasts are full of mistakes. If they aren't, someone was cheating. She saw potential in you. That's it. From what I see, you still had yet to prove yourself when she bought it."

"Do you remember it? Like, the moment?"

"No. But I know enough to make a good guess. That second of time is a dark scramble. I can get everything else—the smell of Joseph, the look in his eyes, the feeling in Hannah's heart, knowing she had to put down this one last monster, no matter what. I can see everything until just before. The end is too chaotic to understand. It's as though . . . I don't know how to explain it."

"Well, I saw it. Whatever she did, it did the trick. Joseph was killed. As in gone. Space dust."

"As well as her. Like I said, she killed herself."

"No. She saved us by—"

Hannah roared and stomped the ground, releasing a heavy bang. "She killed herself and left me behind. It happened. It can't unhappen now. I know what I'm talking about . . . I'm her." She turned away, her shoulders heaving with each breath. "I'd like to be alone now, please."

"Don't you want to know what's happened since?"

"Not interested. Maybe when you leave I'll go back to sleep or wherever I was before. Just, please, let me try."

"I haven't told you about Chloe, or Izaiah, or Mara."

Buckle Hannah sat still for a moment before turning back around. "Tell me."

He proceeded to catch her up on everything that had happened leading up to today, including when Chloe took over following Joseph's death, Alex becoming the Ire, and their arrest at Winston's, culminating with the trial. "The sentencing is next week," he finished.

"You know what, maybe being in here isn't so bad. I don't have to deal with that kind of drama anymore. In a way, I'm living Hannah's dream existence. Ha!" Buckle Hannah did a little dance. Her legs didn't move much, but it was still something Bennett could have never imagined the Hannah he'd known doing. Seeing it made him surprisingly morose.

"You know, all this would have been a lot easier if you were there. Maybe things wouldn't have turned out so crappy. We could have really used you."

"Eventually you get tired of hearing things like that, kid—look at me. I'm not your Hannah. I'm her five minutes after she gave suicide her best shot. Which I—we—had been contemplating for a lot longer than I'll ever say. This person here in front of you is the wiser Hannah. Knowing what I know now, I never would have done what she did."

"That's great, but now my friend and I are on the hook for it."

"I don't see how that's my problem."

"And I still don't see how it's mine, but here we are. The whole thing has been a setup from day one."

"You're angry over how the court is treating you?"

"Look, I'm not an idiot. It's great knowing my head's not on the chopping block, but I faced my fear of death a long time ago. I don't think Al has. Right now, I want to get my brother, an innocent man, as far away from this place as I can."

"I'd wish you luck, but I don't think it would do you any good. The UnEarth court always gets what it wants. Nobody is better at neutral judgment than Axios. The Counselors will make their recommendations, which she will take into account, but the final decision rests with her. With no senators given a vote, there's no systemic defense. I'm sorry."

"Well, I can't just sit there when they say they're going to kill him and not me. It's wrong. My Rapture and I both agree on it. We want to do something about it. There has to be a way to help. Maybe even just to keep him alive a little longer. I don't care about Izaiah or the Medolians. Just Al."

"This must be hard for a human to hear, but you will lose at least half of the time. Probably more. It's fact. Losing is hindering, but you must carry on. You can't throw up your hands and cry unfair."

"I know. I get losing. I've lost a little bit, but every other time I lost, I did it because I wasn't good enough. I tried and came up short. But here, my hands are tied. I can't try. They've taken away every weapon I have. I might as well smother 'em with the hair under my nutsack."

"What kind of garbage is that?" Hannah's eyes were now wide, staring daggers into the puny being before her. "You've got to be kidding me. This is the man Hannah thought might be worthy? I don't see it. Where's the quality?"

"I'm not giving up. Just explaining the situation. I'm open to suggestions."

"To do what?"

"Level the playing field. Let them see how stupid it is to treat Al and I so different."

"That's a cloudy goal, unfocused. Find something more direct. In this case, you need something disruptive."

"Yeah. Something that will wake people up."

"Court is a place of politics. You need to be proactive in everything, which is a little hard when you're at the end of a trial."

"I need something that will make them see me and Alex as the same. Maybe my cred could help pull him up? And maybe at the same time wipe the smirks off all their fucking faces."

Hannah appeared to like that. "Okay. Start with what you have to work with. What's in your cell?"

"A bucket and a rag."

"Not much. You could also use your Eve—but just once. They'd shut you down immediately after. So whatever you do, you'll have to do it quickly. Make it count."

"You know these people better than I do. What would really affect them? Make them take notice? Make them listen?"

"In your case, it would take something extreme."

"That's fine. I've fucked up entire governments before. A court system should be fun and easy."

Hannah side-eyed him with suspicion. "This sounds like a dangerous path, but . . . I'm willing to brainstorm the idea. Let's say I find it intriguing. Also, I have an eternity to spend in this place, so it's not like I have anything better to do."

FOUND IN CONTEMPT

As with every day of the trial, the guards came to collect Alex, but on this day, he was spared the pain and indignity of the nevrose helmet. That first step was skipped, allowing them to proceed directly to chaining him to the rock slab on wheels. He didn't know what to make of it but kept quiet. Was it a gesture of goodwill or part of some sick prank yet to reveal itself? Perhaps something planned by Ariel Van-Mortus? As he was wheeled into the Weya-Vein corridor, it dawned on him that he'd never been outside his cell without the mask. Staring down the dank, shadowy walkway, he felt a biting chill pass through him. He wasn't ready to face the world this way—not today, of all days, when his fate would be made official, marked in black and white. Though his conviction had long been a foregone conclusion, today was going to be arduous, and he did not want his face exposed, revealing his inner thoughts and human emotions. *Why couldn't they have just kept it on? I didn't ask for this.* Alex almost broke down and begged for it to be put back on, restraining himself only because he knew his words would fall on deaf ears.

Down the hallway, the hands of the other inmates came into view, gripping their cell bars. The heights and colors of skin and nails varied, ranging from gray to pink, and from grungy to clawed. Alex's heart pounded in his chest at the thought of facing them all, one by one. Especially when the first person he would set eyes on was the one who had made his time in this place an affair on par with what those who fall down a gorge and break their leg—only to die of exposure while nursing a gangrenous femur—must feel. Oaleen was the one who bullied him more than any other. *Except for today. She hasn't made a peep.* As he was rolled forward, his neighbor came into view, draped across her cell's bars.

He had no idea what he'd expected, but the sight of her was somehow like a *Magic Eye* image, distorted with a hidden shape that could only be revealed by continuing to stare. His mind caught up with his eyes as he took in her features: long, oily, jet-black hair; rags smeared with soot and grime; her body filling the gaps between the bars like a dirty sheet hung on a sewer grate. She wasn't nearly as tall in person as her Eve signature suggested, and the burnt red skin with scales he had expected was, instead, a soft porcelain white.

Alex's and Oaleen's stares met for only a flash, her red irises catching the distant glint of a torch at the end of the hall, before she turned away and raised a fist of solidarity through the bars. "Stay tough, Barker. *Ch-ch*. We'll see you soon."

Struck by her words as well as her eyes, Alex nodded, both screaming and laughing inside, wondering why he felt a rush of endorphins upon hearing something so marginally positive from someone like her. His body and mind had been prepped for an assault, so what had happened? He didn't feel battered; he felt bona fide.

Yeah. Tough. Why can't I be? Alex had never been tough in his whole life, not even a few times. Wallowing in his chains, he'd forgotten what words like that meant, but today he had a chance to change that. Today he would finally see himself the way they did—the little people of Trivium City. Using what strength he had left, he tried to straighten his spine, lift his head, and pull his shoulders back.

Oaleen's cell was then out of sight behind him, blocked by the slab he was chained to, and he was left with only a heavy impression—one that instantly transformed him. In that moment, he decided the rest of the day would not frighten or break him. Van-Mortus would not touch him. Loredosai's comments would burn up like meteors in his atmosphere. Axios would find no fear when she peered into his soul. He was the Ire boy, the monster. *Why not act like it?*

The guards wheeled him along at breakneck turtle speed into the main hall through the two thickest metal doors Alex had ever seen or could imagine existing. *It's a wonder they open and close at all.*

Compared to the rest of the Iolanze, the Weya-Vein was quite small. Traveling the route outside was a brand-new and lengthy experience for him. He was now free to see the sights without the nevrose mask—things he never expected to encounter, such as the jail kitchen. *Always wondered what that smell was.* It turned out that the Iolanze guard had been sneaking him in and out of a secret back entrance for several months, forced to do so ever since a particularly ruthless attempt had been made on Alex's life, when two protestors had managed to sneak inside the Tribunal.

Making it to the outer Tribunal steps, the same crowd as always was waiting for Alex and his escort, but the wall of indignation he usually felt when leaving the jail was not present today. No one was shouting. Nothing was thrown. A silence held the area in perpetual limbo, as though it were within the eye of a storm, waiting for rain to wash over it again and a new phase of the hurricane to begin. The citizens of Trivium City looked at him just as he was now looking at them—with sullen faces, tired, desperate for the end of this whole charade. Today was not only the day he would learn his fate, but the day they would as well. Their own hopes and fears answered.

Seeing them with his own eyes, he realized he'd always pictured them as human, wearing Earthling clothes. But these were the people of Trivium. More than half were pure Eve creatures bearing no resemblance to humanity. Yet seeing them for the first time— really seeing them—made them seem all the more human. The look in their faces was simple: pure fright.

I'd be afraid of me too, which is why today I'm running with it. Alex bared his teeth and snarled at the crowd, drumming up a bit of Wrath in the process. It was little more than a bad vampire impression, but the docile crowd was stirred into an uproar like a bunch of pachyderms who'd felt mice crawl over their feet. The other side of the storm had been reached. An explosion of curses and roars in response filled the area, bouncing off the concave wall of black stone behind them. At the display, Alex allowed himself a small chuckle. *That was kind of fun.*

With disorder brewing, the guards doubled their speed, loading him into the carriage. When Alex found Bennett in his usual seat, it felt good to wear a smug grin as cocky as the ones the soldier usually got away with.

"Hey, Al."

"Hey, yourself."

"Got 'em in quite the uproar out there."

"Hated the quiet."

Bennett laughed and motioned at Alex's maskless face. "I dig the look."

"Trying it out."

As the carriage pulled away, a spark of Wrath within Alex caught his attention. He thought he'd turned off the gas once inside the carriage, but a sizzling heat in his chest remained. The scars of the bull insignia were beginning to smoke and smell of burning flesh. Of the many times before, this was the first when Alex liked the feeling of the essence of destruction lingering and growing within him.

Reaching into his pocket, Bennett retrieved a Lyllup Dragon. He handed it to Alex, as he had every day of the trial so far. But today he did not want one.

"No thanks," he said, shaking his head.

"Atta boy," Bennett said before popping the Dragon into his own mouth. "Really proud of you."

The clomping of the Celestial guards' feet on the streets and the chiming of their armor resonated along every corridor. Walls of citizens stood in total silence as they passed, which was even more threatening than the days when they used to shout and throw things. This scenario felt more like they were waiting for the go-ahead to pounce on Alex's lifeless corpse, but all he could think about was what Oaleen had said to him: *Just stay tough. Just stay tough.* His mind wrestled with it—hard-core-style, underground, in a cage match with thumbtacks spread on the mat. *Just stay . . . tough.*

"Don't worry about today—I have a plan," Bennett said, his eyes locked on the UnEarth creatures outside the window.

Alex didn't respond, mostly because he didn't know what it meant. What sort of plan could Bennett have at a time like this? The trial was over. He'd had six months to do something that might help them out. *It couldn't be an escape plan, could it?*

It may have been the effect of the Lyllup Dragon on him, but Bennett had never worn an expression quite like the one on his face: like a kid with a pocketful of M-80s ready to be flushed down a few school toilets. *What's he planning?* It remained quiet in the carriage for the rest of the trip to the Molm Compound, which was much slower than usual, thanks to the surprising turnout of brooding citizens clogging the streets. Once the path to the Mullen Tados gate was cleared, their carriage, as well as the one carrying Izaiah behind it, made its way to the interim courthouse.

For once, there was no ceremony in sight to welcome them into the building. Today was somber from top to bottom. When the crowd finished shuffling inside, the doors were closed and barred shut. But Jobaya had not yet arrived, and Alex's lawyer had never been late before.

Wait, we can't start. Not everyone's here yet.

Asking the guard posted at the defense's table for information was useless; Alex received only a blank stare. He got much the same treatment from Roland.

"You're not going to look for the guy?" Bennett asked after Alex. "He's a lawyer, just like you."

"No. Not just like me," Roland said, leaving it at that.

"I hope I get the chair and you get the biggest loss of your career, you self-righteous, walking-astrology-crystal ass-plug," Bennett practically shouted. But his lawyer continued to ignore him.

Guess those two aren't on good terms.

Alex feared that the worst must have happened to Jobaya. There was only one guess as to who would have been responsible for his disappearance. Looking at the prosecution, he found Van-Mortus facing his way, her eyes calm and confident, the hint of a self-satisfied grin on her lips. *What did you do with him, lady?* Alex's Wrath showed more signs of life. If anything had happened to Jobaya because of him, then there was a good chance today he really would become the Ire again and destroy them all.

A few moments later, when the proceedings began, the important individuals were introduced, and for the first time, Alex got to see with his own eyes the rulers of the worlds of UnEarth, minus those of Fovos, Arros, and Hywyn. Axios was then announced, and all were left standing. Loredosai reached the end of the introductions and took a moment to collect a new scroll with the day's beats.

During what was sure to be the only moment of quiet before their worlds were turned upside down, Alex and Bennett shared a glance.

"Good luck, guys," Bennett said.

"You too, fellas," Izaiah added with a smack of his lips.

Alex couldn't think of anything to say and just nodded.

"Gentlemen, respect, please," Roland said with demeaning frigidity.

The day's session began much like any other, with a banality to match the best of them. To Alex, it was a numb blur. Knowing there would be no more sessions after today scared him to death. He wished to never see the end of the trial, to always be looking up at Axios with panic in his heart. That would at least mean his head was still attached to his neck. Then Alex calmed, remembering everything that had happened so far in the trial, and how none of it had been fast. He felt reassured. *Yeah, I'll probably die of old age before they can put together an execution.*

To his surprise, after only a few hours of listening to speeches in alien languages, it appeared as though things were wrapping up. *Already? To an UnEarth person, that was like five minutes.* But today the prosecution had no open scrolls on their desk. The Counselors' usual hustle and bustle had been reduced to a Monday-morning-in-an-accounting-firm's level of energy, and none of Roland's assistants were out on errands. This really was the end. Van-Mortus was given her place to speak, of course, one final time for good measure, but the usually loquacious lawyer spoke for relatively few moments. *It was still nearly an hour.* Her oratory was grand as well as subtle, and—even to Alex—utterly compelling. An emphasis was once again placed on Arros and her people sharing no responsibility. In fact, according to Counselor Van-Mortus, the Archfiend community was the greatest victim of them all.

"In closing, Your Honor, Counselors, I feel we've laid our case out to its length as you would a scroll to its end, and the facts could not be any clearer, even if seen through a tra glass pane," Van-Mortus said. "The evils that befell our world two years ago were the work of a cadre of souls, chief among them Alex Barker, Izaiah Ezekial, and Bennett Hunter, bearing responsibility in that order. We, representing the people of Trivium, request the death penalty for the two former and time served for Mr. Hunter."

A handful of the Counselors scribbled down the recommended sentencing as cheers and gasps rang through the gallery. *Time served? . . . Time served?!!?* Alex was furious, but when he turned to look at Bennett, he found the former soldier looked even madder about it than he was. In fact, Alex had never seen so much hatred fill Bennett's eyes before, nor had he seen him clench his jaw so tight that straight lines of tension formed across his face.

The floor was then opened to the defendants themselves, giving them one final chance to make a statement on their behalf.

Pointless, and we all know it, but whatever.

Loredosai pointed a blocky blue finger. "Defendant Izaiah Ezekial, you may speak."

"Oh good!" said the Medolian with a chipper bounce. "I do have something prepared. Been working on it for a while, in fact."

Standing and letting his bones crack and settle, Izaiah addressed the Counselors first. "With the Counselors' permission, of course." The head Counselor nodded. Izaiah continued. "Thank you. Your Honor, my fellows of the gallery, I stand before you today a humble man, defined by past failures, with a hope you will find something in these words that will undo each and every one of those failings. What I wanted to say was . . . a soup, a salad, and a sandwich walk into a bar. The soup says, 'I can't stay here—what if someone uses me as an ashtray?' The salad says, 'I can't stay here either—places like this toss me out back for the bugs!' And the sandwich, he just shrugs it off and says, 'Don't worry about it, I—'"

"Not the sandwich!" Loredosai cut him off. "Do *you* have anything of merit to say regarding your defense?"

"Me? Of merit? Oh . . . sure. I was getting to that. I just wasn't sure which order was more appropriate, joke first—then speech—or vice versa?"

"The courtroom is not a place for jokes," Loredosai grumbled.

"Quite right!" Van-Mortus followed up. "You make a mockery of this sanctuary and our profession!"

"Well, I don't know 'bout that," Izaiah said with a chuckle. "But it seems to me this room has been in need of a good laugh since day one. Especially those fellas over there." He pointed at the section of seats mostly filled by Dread-shaded creatures. "I mean, what's wrong? Don't any of you fart every now and then?" He gave a boisterous laugh clearly intended to sweep up others with its charm. But there just wasn't enough charm to pull it off. No one joined. Izaiah cleared his throat.

"Right. Moving on to more important things. I gotta tell you, it's hard to really know what it is I'm being charged with. As far as I thought, I followed the rules and did as I was told. Now, you say I didn't, but nobody said how, other than the fellas being switched at the last second to be sent to Hywyn and Arros. But, I tell ya, I stand by that. I do. I can't tell you why, but I do. I'd like to tell you, but I feel like most ears would choose to be deaf to my words, so I'll just make the same point I've been making. Don't take this out on the fellas. Look at 'em. Really look! Look where they are. They're just human. Let them be free of our world and its problems. Hold me accountable as their supervisor. That, sure, I can see where you're coming from. But send them back to Earth. They deserve to be free until they die. That's all." Izaiah sat down as silence filled the chamber.

Don't think anyone heard a word he said, but it was nice of him to fight on our behalf.

Loredosai moved on to Alex. "Human defendant Barker. You may speak with your voice, hidden no longer, if you wish."

Alex nodded and took a deep breath, wishing they would have detached him from the stone slab first. He tried to speak as loudly as possible, which proved difficult. "With the Counselors' permission." It was granted. "Thank you, Your Honor, distinguished rulers and senators." His voice was weaker than he thought. "I just want to say I'm . . . I'm sorry for what's happened to you and your city. I wasn't there for that part, but I know a lot of people are afraid of me. They should know there's no reason to be. I'm just a man. A human, like Izaiah said. No one special, even. I didn't ask for the Wrath. Someone else put it there, in me. It was so . . . strong . . . and nothing I tried could make it stop. But it's gone now. I know you can see that. You've always seen that."

"That will be all," Axios said out of nowhere, seemingly blindsiding the court, judging by the Counselors' and Loredosai's reactions.

"But I'm not done," Alex replied, surprised by his own boldness and raised chin.

"The honorable Axios thanked you!" Loredosai said with all the might his voice could muster. "Your time is up."

"But it wouldn't stop . . ." Alex continued unabated. "You said the Ire was mindless. But I was still in there. And not just me."

Loredosai looked at Axios to gauge her reaction. She was listening. Silenced. He made no protest and allowed Alex to continue.

"There were other voices. Not just mine. They wanted the fire and pulled me down the hole. I was there. I felt the burn, every second of it. I just couldn't do anything about it. Do with that information what you will. There. I'm done."

"Well done," Bennett said amid the ensuing quiet.

"Thank you."

Axios's piercing gaze moved on to Bennett. With her hands clasped together, resting on the desk in front of her, she waited patiently.

"Bennett Hunter, you may speak if you wish," Loredosai said.

"I wish!" Bennett shouted quickly, slapping both hands on his knees and pushing his chair away from the table.

Before standing, he gave Alex an overblown grin, as though to say, *Watch this*, beaming with an aura of Rapture that had never seemed brighter or more resolute. Once on his feet, he slowly brushed himself off before addressing the court. "Thank you, Your Honor. It is truly a pleasure to be acknowledged by such a stuffy, ancient, backwards society." He paused like a comic holding for laughter, but none of the UnEarth citizens seemed to understand what he'd said, staring blankly. "Ah, slow crowd, huh? Okay, no surprise there. Wouldn't have pegged you all for the brainy type. Or the filled-with-any-kind-of-decency type. I mean, how do you people sleep at night? Blaming Alex and Izaiah for other people's

bullshit is crazy, much like every aspect of your so-called 'civilization.' Which—ugh—don't get me started. Wouldn't know where
to begin or where to stop. I mean, no privacy? That's sick, y'all. Ya
sick fuckin' freaking fuckin' fucks."

Stepping away from the defense's table, Bennett moseyed into the aisle, raising the volume of his voice with each sentence.
"You think you're soooo great. Well, you're not! You're made from
our leftovers, what we're done with after living the shit out of our
short, totally fun, big-tits-and-jet-ski-filled lives. You're just our
gross extremes, scraped off the hair around our assholes. That's you.
But the worst part? I know nothing I'm saying right now is actually sinking in. I can see it in your dumb little faces—you don't really
care. You've made up your minds about everything. Even about me.
You think just 'cause I have a certain shade of bullshit in me—and
it's the same bullshit you've got in you"—he pointed at Roland and
his assistants—"that means I'm not to blame? What the fuck kind
of logic is that?

"Al and I didn't decide what Eve got put in us. The guy never
did a Wrathful thing in his whole life. But me? Shit. What haven't
I done? And yeah, they slapped my wrist a few times, but fuck,
man, I got off light. I killed almost a hundred people, and they
patted me on the head and said, 'Good job, you did your country
proud.' We tortured people—people with families and kids and
shit—people who had nothing to do with anything, just being in
the wrong place and wrong time—and laughed when they begged
to be treated as human beings. *Laughed!* After drowning people in
their own piss. After starving 'em. After dressing them up in makeup and dresses. Just fucked-up, evil, immature shit. And that's just
when I was in the Marines. Back home I was just as bad—walking
around, starting shit just to start it, trying car doors on every street,
seeing which ones were unlocked, taking whatever I could, even if

I didn't need it. Went through women like fuckin' breath mints and treated 'em like fuckin' dogs, thinking it made me a badass, 'cause I'm a fuckin' idiot. Fucked up some dude's truck at a party just because he looked at me funny. Snatched up tips I gave to strippers and threatened 'em if they said anything. The list goes on! Fuck, how much more do I need to say? You're treating me like a goddamn angel when there's literally one sitting right there." Bennett pointed at Alex.

"The only one in the room, as far as I'm concerned," Bennett continued. "Any fuck who calls themselves holier than thou can go eat a dolphin's balloon dick. That goes for the court, too. *So much talking in one room for months on end, and yet not a single goddamn thing actually said!* Pardon the God talk, by the way, just this place makes me want to explode like a fuckin' irony-filled goddamned piñata. Do you guys even know what those are? No, of course you don't, because piñatas are cool."

Halfway through his rant, Bennett began checking the rear entrance. Soon, the reason why became clear when the door opened and a squat blue form waddled into the courtroom: a Psera Celestial. Alex watched him progress down the center aisle, growing increasingly curious. *What's with this?* Over his shoulder, the stout creature carried a large bucket. *And what's in that?*

Bennett dramatically addressed the entire court. "You assume Al is a monster, but the only monsters I see here are you people! All of mankind's worst stories about hideous beasts revolve around things like you—the unwanted things that go bump in the night. But again, I don't expect you to care or understand. However, I do think there is one thing you will understand." Bennett and the tiny Celestial met halfway up the aisle.

With an affectionate hand on his blocky shoulder, Bennett knelt and said some unheard words to the creature, who did not seem to react. Bennett then tried to take the bucket from him, which the Celestial *did* react to, reaching for the bucket after Bennett had snatched it out of his grasp. He took two waddling steps to follow Bennett toward the front of the courtroom but then seemed to realize he was headed toward Ariel Van-Mortus, Roland Archshandr, and Judge Axios. The small Celestial stopped and backtracked, keeping his head as low as possible. *This guy makes me look like Neil Diamond.*

Returning to the front of the room, Bennett was showing lots more teeth through his beard, obviously relishing the opportunity to go big. His already deepened Eve signature was beginning to feel as domineering as that of a full-blown High Celestial.

"That's my friend, Brick, and he gets treated like *shit* around here. I know this because he is forced to retrieve mine, and I happened to notice only the little guys like him—what do you call them? Pseras—have to go around picking up other people's personal waste. Also, the little flying bugs like Alex's kick-ass lawyer, Jub-Jub—I think—who couldn't be here today, and we—all—know—why! I'm looking at you, Miss Van-Mortus. And don't even try to pretend like you don't. You're so obviously evil—I know you did something to him, and so do you, because you couldn't handle someone like *that* being better than you, could you? So you smoked him out! Well, I've got news for you, lady—what goes around comes around!"

Bennett's eyes darted about during a brief pause, and when no one said anything, he continued, "Yeah . . . my point is that no big, bad High Celestial would ever debase themselves with the chores you give my boys, Jubya and Brick—"

"Inno," the small Celestial said, his voice resonating like a bass note struck on a vibraphone. Bennett faced him up the aisle, gaping in stunned disbelief.

"Really? That's a fuckin' cool name, dude. But back to the High Celestials—they're far too good for that kind of work. Or at least they think they are. I like my friend Inno a whole lot more than them, and he agreed to help me here today."

Inno hung his head, as though trying to escape the moment. Bennett passed the defense's table with the bucket, and Alex caught a whiff of something truly revolting wafting through the air.

Bennett, uh . . . what are you doing? A bout of nervousness settled in him.

Bennett continued loudly and proudly, "This here is a bucket, and what's inside is delectable. One week's worth of my own grade F-F-F shit. Waste from my human bowels and *very* human asshole. Thought to be the worst, most horrendous thing my species is capable of producing. So please, consider what I am trying to say to all of you here in the Senate, to all your home-world rulers, to all of UnEarth, and especially to you, Judge whatever Axeebus, when I do this . . ."

Bennett held the bucket out in front of him with straight arms, as though about to punt it downfield. Following his aim, which pointed directly to the side, Alex noticed that the only things over there were the great statues of the dead leaders of UnEarth, brought here from the Tribunal to loom over the trial. These were the same statues the people had effectively prayed to every day to begin.

"That's your boy, Michael, right?" Bennett asked, positioning his feet as Alex felt a swelling of Rapture so potent it was like someone shining a flashlight in his eyes. "Greatest of the great? Yeah? Well, here's what I have to say about that."

With a flash, the bucket in Bennett's hands was encased in a protective Rapture sphere. Letting it go, his leg swung so fast that Alex saw only a blur, and a cobalt explosion erupted, shaking the entire building, shattering the glass windows above, and rendering Alex momentarily dumb.

A white streak tore across the room with a vicious howl, like ten thousand bottle rockets in flight, before a second explosion of blue obscured the statue of Michael. The detonation sent a wave of snapping cold through Alex.

As the cloud of blue and white dust faded, the statue of Michael initially seemed to be missing. But Alex quickly found the lower base, mostly intact from Michael's diaphragm down. The rumble had subsided, and even though a ringing remained in Alex's ears, he sensed not a hint of sound from the gallery.

Dude . . . no way.

When he turned to look at Bennett, he found an expression of utter stupefaction on the soldier's face, his kicking leg still lofted in the air. Slowly, Bennett's gaze drifted to Alex, his wide eyes startlingly present, looking like a kid who'd just crashed his dad's Porsche by accident and had a blast while doing it.

"Whoa . . . holy shit," the soldier said.

With a clang that filled the silence like the first clap of someone trying to start a slow clap, the shit bucket landed in Michael's lap and spun like a top, spilling waste all over his legs and throne as it did. A hushed clatter of debris began to rain down over the statues and part of the room, and when the bucket finally came to a stop and the rain ceased, another incredible hush took over, like a tide receding before a tsunami.

But the space was quickly filled with distraught sighs and breaths, quivering voices on the verge of passing out, and shouts of panic mixed with unintelligible rage. The gasps echoed like sea spray crashing against a shore, and as it grew, so did the look of pride on Bennett's face.

The former teacher couldn't wrap his head around the event, let alone imagine its implications. Did something just happen that would turn the tide? *Did . . . did something just happen at all? Or did I just imagine all of that?*

Finally setting his leg down, Bennett directed his attention up at Axios. "I'm all finished, Your Honor. Sentence the fuck away."

When he took his seat, Bennett looked more at ease than Alex had ever seen a human being. This stood in stark contrast to his lawyer, who was blue in the face—even for a Celestial—his jaw hanging in cartoonish surprise. Bennett cracked his knuckles, relaxed and stretched, smacked his lips, and propped his feet up. The people in the chamber clamored for decency and normalcy, screaming, bellowing, and shifting in their seats. Not even Çilrex could bring them to order. Loredosai called for silence, his feeble voice all but lost. Bennett had broken any chance of order permanently. The Celestial guards on the outer rim of the room watched, spears clasped in hand, fidgeting with uncertainty about how to respond.

The moment was incredible. Alex wished it would never end. He also wished he knew what it meant. Listening to his inner voice, he realized he felt good no matter what would come of it. For now, that was enough. Regardless of his intentions, Bennett had told these people what he (*and I*) thought of their legal process, and he'd done a good job of it. A little sensationally, perhaps, but still, it was something Alex would never forget. He was damn proud of his big brother.

NEWS FROM THE MAINLAND

With her morning coffee and croissant in hand, Casey's heart rate slowed. Thanks to these mundane items, she could center herself—something she had been needing a lot of lately. Strolling down the sidewalk in Marseille, it was easy to look up at the beautiful blue sky or fill her lungs with the crisp morning air, as though it might soon run out. All was normal and human—and, most importantly, boring. *Fast becoming my favorite word.* Nothing but earthly ingredients was in this soufflé. Couriers on bikes raced up and down the lanes. Cars honked once or twice, but otherwise, no other egregious noises intruded. Nothing mind-numbing or extreme existed in any direction, the complete and utter spiritual opposite of La Rose Noire. A pastry and a cup of bold seasonal brew were hers—all hers—and the weather was pleasant. What more could a person want?

The bench she sat on every day around this time was empty. *Score.* With her rear end planted, she had no problem finding peace, if only for fifteen minutes. Nothing could stand in her way. But, just like yesterday—and all the days before that—no matter how hard she tried, she couldn't truly let her guard down and relax.

Although it appeared as though she was surrounded by human civilization, the lines between UnEarth and regular Earth had blurred in the last few weeks. How could everything around her truly be humanity's world when creatures like Madam Daphne had so much influence and control over it? Any alcove could have contained a spy tucked in like a worm in a crack, studying her, belonging to one of the shady organizations Leigh had warned her about multiple times.

And it's always been this way. Just no one knew it. Or very few.

UnEarth Humans had always been on Earth, but the Purge was what had ballooned their numbers. "We are everywhere," Madam Daphne told Casey. "Buried into almost every community. Most of my brethren wanted to find solace from their fellows. Accepting their fate, they set out to live among humans until they perished. The problem was most had no idea how long that would be. Once we assume human form, our lifespans seem to be endless."

Casey had likely met dozens of UnEarth Humans in her life and never known it. As long as she didn't, she had been left alone, just like everyone else. But she was no longer part of that blissfully ignorant club. Cursed by her knowledge, her life had become a wasteland of paranoia, and it likely would stay that way from now on.

This was why it was so important to spend as much time away from La Rose Noire as possible. Marseille, easily the most beautiful city she had ever seen, was not only a pleasure to roam but also a necessary vitamin shot to her mental health. She spoke no French and stopped admitting to being North American after the first day but was still reinvigorated to be out among the people. *The very human, normal, and yes, boring people. But not bad boring. Crap, was that mean?*

Big shocker: it turned out UnEarth—a society built on extremes of emotion—had the potential to be described as a "bit much." The music in the Rose was louder than loud and faster than fast. The food was like eating from superconcentrated packets of space meals meant to be diluted in an ocean of water first, always accompanied by major stomach issues. The hot flavors convinced her that a hole was being burned straight through her jaw. The sour ones made her face scrunch up like a dried prune from just their smell, even at a distance. But the worst were the sweet flavors—overwhelming assaults on her tongue, primarily in the foods from Lanwyn. Traditional cakes and candy, Casey's longtime favorites, were already beginning to remind her of effusive UnEarth desserts.

To her credit, Madam Daphne did her best to accommodate Casey's human digestive tract. Food and drink were brought in from the outside just for her, and nearly anything she desired was fair game, even if it came from the finest chefs in Marseille. The gesture was more than appreciated, as were all of Madam Daphne's efforts to make her feel more comfortable and at ease.

A room had been made for her, a nice size, a little larger than the one she had shared with her sisters growing up. The only issue was the decorating. Madam Daphne had surely ordered it to be furnished for a human, but apparently had given the task to someone who didn't know much about adult women, making the space look like a seven-year-old who dreamed of being a princess lived there. Plush furniture that could swallow a person whole and pastel colors filled every corner. It was a less-than-enjoyable place to spend her time, but so was the rest of the club, where the UnEarth Humans acknowledged her about half the time and sometimes took so little notice that they walked right into her. Most would be annoyed until they recognized her as the human under the protection of the magnate of the Rose; then all anger and bitterness were quickly erased.

Madam Daphne explained to Casey one evening over dinner, "Your shade is almost nonexistent. My guests just aren't expecting humans. It's nothing personal—they simply don't see you."

From what Casey understood, sharing a private meal with the madam was an extremely rare occurrence, and had never been bestowed on a human before. Yet she had eaten in the private dining room by the lady of the Rose's side almost daily since arriving in France. Madam Daphne seemed to savor watching her eat and drink, as though it were her own satisfying meal—almost exactly like Casey's mother used to.

Getting to dine with the madam like this made up for all the years she had spent trying to eat lunch with the cool kids and failing. It made up for it and then some. Getting to stroll into the upstairs office whenever she wished was a power trip she never saw coming, and the sensation of blowing right past the pool players in shadow (*who are arguably the coolest people I've ever seen*) and making her way to the madam's desk was a rush right to the loins. Casey would never admit it out loud, but she had never so badly wanted Leslie Broahnik to walk in the door and see her. *Sure, you got to be first-chair clarinet in seventh grade and play the big solo and get Logan Binds and his friends to swoon over you, but you never got to be best friends with a powerful madam from the afterlife, did you, Leslie? Huh? Did you? Nope, sure didn't.*

Every few days, a fresh concoction would be offered: one of Madam Daphne's attempts to create drinks for a human palate. The flavors began as intense as the rest of UnEarth food and drink, but over time had softened. By now, Casey looked forward to whatever new exotic beverage would be presented.

During these dinners, Casey and the madam had shared lengthy discussions, where the lady of the Rose revealed much about the history of the UnEarth Humans, especially in the last two thousand years, following the signing of the Covenant and the great Purge. Casey's eyes were opened to their lives on Earth, to which they were sentenced as punishment. They were now seen as a people torn from their homes and way of life, made to pretend to be another species just to survive—an existence far more unkind than she had originally given them credit for. *It's hard enough trying to survive in the human world when you're actually human. I should know.*

As nice as the dinners and the distraction they provided were, Casey was desperate to get back to her family. The problem was she couldn't get a clear answer from the Medolians whenever she inquired about moving on. Either they were too nervous to talk about what was happening to them, or they genuinely didn't know who was out to get them or why. The danger they were in was still unclear, and if they wanted to stay low for a bit, something told Casey it was a good idea for her to do the same. Being nearly eaten by Oyel Pattel had scarred her permanently. Going out into the world without bodyguards like the Medolians felt like suicide. For the time being, she was stuck in the Rose.

Taking the last bite of her croissant, she tried to savor it for all it was worth. Her time limit of an hour away was almost up. She would need to return soon, or Madam Daphne would have a squad out after her. Closing her eyes, she took the last few sips of coffee—delectable and gone too soon. With her eyes still shut, she absorbed the cool breeze and sounds of society. Eventually standing, she folded her donut wrapper and stuffed it into the paper coffee cup. After placing them in a bin at the end of the lane, she started back.

Turning the corner to see the cul-de-sac where the Rose lay, she found the group of smokers was not out front. A staple of the club's outward aesthetic, they were not just addicts out for a puff. Cigarettes were benign to those of UnEarth, who usually preferred to smoke ik, a dried weed from Fovos, chopped up and rolled into mondo cigar-size cigarettes called "ik sticks." There was also no reason for them to vacate the building, as all forms of smoking were allowed in the Rose. The smokers out front were, in truth, an early warning system in case humans ever came looking for trouble or unfriendly UnEarth factions sniffed about. Madam Daphne had told Casey all about her issues within the Purged community, which sounded a lot like the turf wars from *West Side Story*. But the smokers were gone for the first time since Casey had set eyes on the Rose. Even the neon cat above the front entrance was turned off. Something felt awry—not quite wrong, but off enough to put Casey on full alert. The street leading to the Rose was also empty, draping the walk in a ghost-town eeriness. As she approached the entrance, her unease grew, marinating in the silence of the lane.

Opening the front door, she was struck by the bombastic music of the platinum hall, and for the first time, it brought comfort. But as she traversed the entry tunnel and stepped through the threshold, she found the hall—normally packed so full of bodies that there were no gaps to pass through—was only half full. Those creatures left on the dance floor were the very drunkest, with the most vacant of stares. Of the bartender stalls, only two were still serving drinks, but even they looked distracted. Drawing closer, Casey figured out why. The barkeepers had their noses buried in the latest edition of the UnEarth newspaper, the *Exodus*. The majority of the creatures on the outskirts of the club and those sitting at lounge tables were doing the same. Even a few on the dance floor were reading and grooving at the same time.

Beyond the platinum hall, the Rose passages were filled with UnEarth Humans deep in passionate discussion while gripping copies of the paper. Something had obviously occurred, and whatever it was had sparked a fire deep within the hearts of the Eve people.

Then it hit Casey—*the trial. It must be news about the trial.*

Hurrying to the spiral stairway leading to Madam Daphne's office, she began to climb. *The trial couldn't be over already. Could it? It's only been about six months.*

Several times, members of Chief Mary's staff stampeded by, seeming busy on some errand, noticing Casey even less than usual and forcing her to dodge out of the way. Upon reaching the office, she found the wide double doors open for the first time. There were still guards posted, but they too had their noses buried in copies of the *Exodus* and didn't seem to be denying entry to anyone. Moving past them, Casey received only a fleeting glance.

Gathered around their boss at her desk were Madam Daphne's advisors, as well as Chief Constance Mary. Their sullen faces resembled those of five-star generals discussing a recent enemy attack on a strategically important base. The lady of the Rose was perusing a mess of papers on the desk when Casey entered.

Likely having sensed her, Madam Daphne looked up and beamed. "Oh, there she is! My sweet human love. How are you, my darling? You look so adorable today. Is there anything I can get you? Are you hungry? I'll have someone bring in a treat from town immediately. How many donuts do you desire? Two hundred? Three?"

"Just had one. That's plenty for me. Thank you, though."

Madam Daphne waved her over. "Come closer. Sit by me, you adorable thing. Isn't she the sweetest?" The entourage around her nodded without glancing up.

Casey made her way past the security guards in green suits and pool players in the shadows before arriving at Madam Daphne's side.

"I'm so relieved you're okay," said the madam. "I worry so. The idea of you being out where I can't see you, alone, gives me the mulah'noo. So nervous. So fragile and helpless."

"I'm fine. Really. I'm from the human world, so there's no need to worry," Casey said. "But thank you for caring." Looking over the papers on Madam Daphne's desk but unable to read any of it, she asked, "So, what's going on? There's no one keeping watch out front."

"Yes, when today's *Exodus* arrived, everyone got a little excited. All parties have resumed their posts, and I'm sure nothing foul besieged us. But thank you for being so attentive. I knew it would be a good idea to keep you around."

Casey glanced over the papers on the desk, but when she got to a stack of scrolls on the far right, Chief Mary snatched them up before she could get a good look.

"I'm afraid I need to cancel our dinner this evening," Madam Daphne said. "Something has come up."

"No problem," said Casey. "Can you tell me what it is?"

Madam Daphne snapped at one of her assistants. "You. Bring her a drink."

"No, I'm fine, thank you." Casey declined with a wave.

"You're sure? I don't want you to be the least bit uneasy or negatively affected by the news. It might be jarring, as it involves the two human males that Izaiah brought uninvited into my home. It seems the trial is over, as miraculous as that is."

So, it's true. From what Casey had gathered, the trial was expected to take years, possibly decades. "Death?" she was almost too afraid to ask.

Madam Daphne nodded.

"For all three?"

"Apparently the Raptured human, Hunter, was as good as exonerated, near to getting away with time served, but instead chose to make some sort of public display and destroyed the presiding statue of the Great Michael. He had some proud exhalation of power and made a big mess in the courtroom. Eve knows why. No one seems to know what message he was trying to get across. He used a bucket of his own feces in the act, so it's anyone's guess. Even without knowing his true intentions, it was enough to see him thrown into the Weya-Vein. Now all three of Izaiah's team will share the same fate."

Casey almost laughed. "Bennett did what?" *Why would he do something like that? What was he trying to accomplish?* "He got himself sentenced to death . . . on purpose?"

"It would appear that way," Madam Daphne said. "This trial proved extraordinary in many ways. Sentencing a Medolian to death is unprecedented. Many of us aren't even sure how such a thing can be carried out."

"That's right, huh. Do Galinthia and Fabian know?" Casey asked.

"You'll have plenty of time to tell them. Best to wait for the right moment."

"I'm telling them?"

"Who else would?"

"But I wouldn't know what to say."

"Say exactly what I've just said to you. Not much else to it. I believe in you. You got this, you wonderful, lovely thing. You're sure you don't want something to eat?"

"I'm sure. But there's something I don't understand. If that was the big news, why is the Rose shut down?"

Madam Daphne radiated joy and pride. "Nothing gets past you, does it?"

Casey looked around. "In fact, if I didn't know better, I'd say you've just been kicked into gear and are getting ready for some sort of attack. Or maybe you'll be doing the attacking."

"Your guess is correct—we are preparing for something. You see, this trial . . . our whole society is going to be altered by it. Even more so than it was by the inclusion of humans in Tribunal affairs. Unlike many of my brethren, I embrace change for all it's worth. As long as I can benefit from it, I'm open to nearly anything."

"I don't follow. That's all taking place on Trivium. What could you get out of this?"

"The question is, what are *you* going to get out of it?"

"I don't follow."

"I'm sorry to have kept you waiting. Truly. It's obvious you began to doubt if I would hold up my word and help you find your friend. I didn't want to tell you anything until I had solid information, lest I get your hopes up. Our sources have informed us that Aluqa and the Surface intend to carry out a mission during the execution ceremony. If the outlandish rumor is true, they plan to send a team into Trivium and make use of the occasion, likely accomplishing something dramatic, if the woman sticks to her nature."

"Aluqa wants to go to Trivium? Why? And how? I thought that was impossible."

"It should be, dear. But all of reality can be mastered with time, especially when you have one such as the Cardinal giving aid. Like many, Aluqa Morinnean has long sought the means to infuse pure Eve into flesh. If successful, the molecules within the Surface members would be compatible with the frequency of the lower reaches of UnEarth. Morinnean could send as many as she likes. The reason I tell you this is we believe your friend will be with them."

"You confirmed she joined? Are you sure?" Madam Daphne became silent and looked away. "How long have you known?"

"A few days. A week at most. There was no point in telling you until just now."

"Are you kidding me?"

"I'm not one to kid or make jokes. I find doing so tacky. The spreading of Jubilee should be done with a glass, not words. Now come over here, young one. I have something you may appreciate." Madam Daphne held out her right hand. An envelope was placed in it. She opened it and handed a small stack of photographs to Casey. "Photos of your dear professor, pinning her to a recent string of robberies of UnEarth materials, including from one of my own facilities. Many pounds of Fervor steel and gems of all shades were taken, as well as a good amount of thorough blackmailing material for our contacts in Bulgaria. There will be more, but regardless, I do not like being inconvenienced, no matter how small."

"I mean no disrespect," Casey said, "but I think you made a mistake by not telling me." Her words sent a shudder through the group of security guards and advisors.

Madam Daphne waved her hand, calming them before any could get heated. She then gave Casey the same look her mother did when she was tired of her shit. "I have not yet decided how I am going to respond to such an aggressive act on Morinnean's part. Attacking an official Tribunal event is brazen, even for her. Especially so, considering she is a human, which makes it twice as offensive. Some would say deserving of her own death sentence. I'm no friend of the Tribunal, but Aluqa is going too far this time. I'm still drawing plans, but there might be a way I can stop her and the Surface, and you can get your friend back."

"I'd like that, too. Whatever you need from me, you've got it."

"That's the spirit."

"Thank you for thinking of Leigh. I know she is nothing to you and your plans, but . . . she's important to me."

"And that's why I care. I see no reason to crack a large number of eggs in my endeavors. Reducing damage whenever possible is paramount. The poor thing was brainwashed into joining Morinnean's second-rate cult. You have my word—every effort will be made to ensure your friend is returned safely. Unfortunately, when this counteroffensive begins, you'll have to stay behind and wait for word. But you will have me for company and will be able to oversee the operation at my side."

"I understand, and thank you. But I'm still confused about something—why would Aluqa risk going to Trivium for the execution? Do you believe she is going to try and stop it?"

"Possibly. It would make sense to save the humans if that is who you're sworn to protect. Though I truly doubt that is the case. If I know Aluqa, she will be there to send a message, and that message will no doubt be secretly about herself. No bigger stage to do it on, as Gabriel himself is said to be attending. I should have guessed. The potential drama alone is like a worm on a hook to that woman."

Casey felt weak hearing the lord of what was ostensibly Heaven being talked about in the same way one discusses an RSVP for a wedding. *Sometimes I start to think this is all make-believe again. But the smells always bring me back, let me know it's real. Always the smells.*

"I'll be sending my own delegation to Trivium to prevent whatever despicable act she has planned," Madam Daphne said. "No proud UnEarth creature could allow Aluqa's plan to see the light of day."

"That's great to hear. How can I help? Just because I can't get to Trivium doesn't mean I'm useless."

"You help us all just by being you. Also, please make sure to keep a close eye on your Medolian colleagues. There's no telling what will happen now. We may be attacked by unknown UnEarth forces. But this is not a fortress—it's a haven for peace. We would stand no chance without the help of the Medolians."

"You can count on me," Casey said.

"I knew I could. Thank you, dear. Now, if you'll excuse us, we have much to discuss and will be doing so in our native tongue, and I'd hate to make you feel excluded."

"That's all right. I get it. Thank you, Madam Daphne."

Casey was escorted out after the madam promised to inform her of any additional developments. Surprisingly, she even apologized for not telling Casey about Leigh sooner. "I'm trying to balance many plates, my sweet."

Before excusing herself, Casey reassured her she understood.

It felt good to have some momentum. *Finally, something is happening.* But that didn't mean the news of the trial was welcome. Casey didn't want Alex and Bennett to be killed, no matter how mad she was at them. If Madam Daphne was able to do all that she promised regarding Leigh's rescue, maybe she could help them as well. But Casey didn't like putting all that hope into one basket. She resolved to implore the Medolians to assist Madam Daphne and travel to Trivium to stop the execution. *There's got to be a way to convince them. Isn't Izaiah their leader? His head is on the chopping block, too. They must still be loyal to him in some fashion.*

Casey set out to find Fabian and Galinthia, feeling wild nervousness settle in her stomach. Fabian would likely be polite, but there was no telling how Galinthia would respond. With any luck, she wouldn't be holding her daggers when Casey arrived. But that seemed unlikely.

There was ample time to think of what to say, as finding the

Medolians took more than an hour. *This place seems a lot larger on the inside than it does on the outside.* Gale and Fabian could have been anywhere, really, as they were just as free to roam the grounds as Casey. The regular patrons of the Rose, once instructed by Madam Daphne to accept the Medolians and treat them as guests, had done just that, no questions asked. All Medolian hate appeared to be gone, at least for now. As such, Fabian and Galinthia had made themselves at home quickly.

If I didn't know any better, I'd say they like it here.

Casey first tried the usual spots. Fabian could often be found near the kitchen or any quiet place nearby to eat the food he'd gotten from it. Eating was the only time he could be seen off his phone, and even then, only for the first few minutes. Gale's usual hangout was a kingdom room called the Blaze Barrel, which was exactly what it sounded like: a humongous barrel filled with fire, constantly rotating, allowing things to crash and explode, adding to the inferno. There was plenty of space for the huge dumpsters of debris dropped in from above to crash about and for those in the barrel to roam and destroy. The whole thing sounded like madness, where guests were free to do anything they wished. Deaths in the Blaze Barrel were common. Murder was fine. Survival of the fittest ruled for Wrath-shaded creatures. To Galinthia, it was recreational heaven on Earth.

Within the halls of the Rose, there was much less meandering, as though a jolt of electricity had surged through the UnEarth community of clubgoers. Most had a somewhat thrilled look on their faces. A few, mostly Grief-leaning types, appeared worried or saddened, but they were the minority. A group of Jubilee creatures Casey passed by had an endless supply of mockery for Izaiah, the "worst joke teller in existence," praising the "embarrassment to all of Jubilee" being given the ax.

"Literally!" a Beaubon Human woman shouted, slapping her knee twice. The group around her burst out in obnoxious laughter.

Eventually, Casey found Fabian and Galinthia together in the Lounge of Lamenting, one of the more benign kingdom rooms, with a small cocktail bar smothered by the sounds of rain and horrid woes and moans. Fabian looked completely at home as the cold downpour from above drenched him, while Galinthia lay sprawled across a bench, her face covered by her arm. The rain pattered and sizzled on her skin before evaporating into a faint mist. *She must have just come from the Blaze Barrel and needed a cooldown.*

At the sight of them relaxing, without a thought or care in the world, Casey became more than a bit angry. *Hope they've been enjoying themselves. Are all Medolians as lazy as these two?* When she told the duo the news of the end of the trial and the triple death sentence, neither seemed to care.

"No, really," Casey said "Have you not read today's *Exodus*?"

"Bunch of Mallos-hating propagandists. Why on Earth would we read that tripe?" Galinthia asked.

Fabian tried to soften the blow. "I think what my counterpart is saying is that the *Exodus* is often rather sensational in its reporting. I wouldn't listen to what others say. It's been far too short a time for the trial to be over. My guess is it will take another five or six years."

"Are you sure?" Casey asked.

"Yes," Galinthia muttered.

"Why would Madam Daphne be making all these moves if it was all for nothing?"

"We've never understood these Purged types. Nothing they do makes any sense," Galinthia said.

"For all we know, this is what Madam Daphne was already going to do, regardless." Fabian yawned, looking seconds from drifting off to a nap. "I don't sense all that much surprise from everyone. If anything, I'd say there's more excitement and a sense of purpose."

Casey tried not to scream in the Lounge of Lamenting. She'd hate to ruin someone else's horrible experience. "I don't understand how you can be so casual at the thought of your former leader dying."

Fabian chuckled at that, and Galinthia released a rare full-blown laugh.

"Izaiah's not about to die," Fabian said, wiping away a tear.

"How do you know that?"

"Because that man has been trying to kill himself for tens of thousands of years—nobody really knows how long—and it still hasn't happened. I doubt anything could kill him, honestly. He's as much a part of this world as the rocks and stumps."

"Can I please go back to sleep now? Your can-do attitude is just not what I need," Galinthia said.

Casey left them alone, feeling mostly confused. She had done as Madam Daphne asked but without any confirmation she'd gotten the appropriate response. Who was correct? Was it the madam, who believed the news and knew big things would start happening soon? Or were the Medolians right, and as usual, nothing much would come of this? All parties seemed so sure, and the human caught in the middle of it all—Casey—didn't know whom to believe. The more preferred option was the Medolians' point of view. The idea that everything in the *Exodus* was being blown out of proportion was a lovely one. But if that were true, then why couldn't she shake the feeling that absolutely everything was about to go horribly wrong in the worst possible way?

JAILBREAK

Leaving the Molm compound following the final trial session, Mara felt empty. Worse, she felt worthless—a dried-out husk in danger of being carried away by a harsh breeze. Though, at that moment, it didn't seem like the worst thing.

Someone was out to get the Medolians—to slow them down and divide them. They had already managed to pull Philomena to their cause, along with her disciples. Who knew when the other Sentries might follow? *We'll all be bowing to Loredosai before we know it.*

The attack on her kind was clearly coming from somewhere. Van-Mortus may have been the hammer, but someone else was wielding it. The most obvious suspect was her only true superior on Arros. Many speculated that the Fallen One had been killed in an Archfiend uprising centuries ago, but none of these reports could be confirmed. After witnessing her work, Mara wondered if Van-Mortus wasn't the actual ruler of Arros, merely keeping alive the story that Lucifer was staying out of sight—all so she could rule without pushback from the Alus Conclave.

Lucifer was a well-known schemer. However, the King of Arros's plots in the past had all revolved around a militaristic approach, rather than courts and legislation. It was possible he was trying something new, but Mara found that creatures rarely acted against their own nature. At present, she had no reason to suspect that he had any designs on the eradication of the Sentry Force.

But who, now, specifically gained from the removal of the Sentries? And when had they gotten to Senator Bo? Mara had still not seen him since her petitioned letter was read in court, and so far, he had not sent word. Was it out of embarrassment? Had he been duped? *If so, it was likely while drunk. I always assumed his nightlife would be his downfall.*

However, there was no time to wait for him; Trivium was no longer safe. Mara wasn't exactly fond of Earth, but the world of humanity was now the only place where Loredosai and his Guard could be avoided—*at least for a while. Who knows what tricks Hywyn will pull to skirt the law?*

But there was something that she needed to do first before she could leave the planet for good.

I hope I'm not being a dullard for trying it.

Her boots made hardly a sound on the brick walkways. With swift steps, she propelled herself through the darkest back alleys and side streets of the Hikkwe district, running not just from the trial and her duties along with it, but from any association with UnEarth—possibly forever. The stench of corruption in the Senate was so potent that she wondered how she could be the only one smelling it—*or the only one failing to ignore it.*

The Tribunal had gone too far this time. This was madness. Never for a moment had she considered the possibility that Izaiah would be found guilty, let alone sentenced to beheading. Nor had she imagined he would be so blasé about it. *How is it that I care about it more than he does? Such cruel pranks the universe employs.*

Once again, the responsibility was falling on Mara to fix everything. Tonight, that meant pulling off a jailbreak. If her plan somehow worked, it might then be possible to gather the remaining Medolians and create an effective resistance on Earth. However, there was also a good chance it could lead to a new kind of war; yet she saw no other option.

She knew it was possible to gain access to Bennett and Izaiah in their jail cells and release them, but she was less confident about her chances at freeing Alex Barker. The Sackulli-Karni was designed by Alice the Builder to be impenetrable. *Of course, she never met a Medolian. We showed up after her time.* Though even if she could reach him, Mara was not convinced that was a good idea. Barker's power had proven itself to be great, but also unpredictable. He had none of the training of his Raptured partner and none of the experience of Izaiah. High-stress situations—as this was sure to be—mixed with his volatile emotions, were far too large a risk; *he could end up burning the whole city down if pushed even a bit too far in the wrong direction.*

But Hunter, who had until now been slow to figure out his Eve— and had never seemed all that useful to begin with—surpassed all of Mara's expectations in an instant, forcing her to swallow some of the more unpleasant things she had thought about the sordid man since saving him from the Wraithians in an African desert. The triumphant display he'd made only a few short hours before had impressed her greatly and, frankly, made her envious. Long had she wished to speak her mind so freely to those who oppressed her people, but she had never dreamed of doing anything so brazen as to destroy one of the presiding statues, let alone the Great

Michael. But since Bennett did not have a long life to live, he apparently seemed willing to sacrifice it for his cause.

His power had exploded to a level matching some of the fiercest Celestials Mara had ever faced in battle. Something about the signature of the attack also reminded her of Hannah. This likely meant Hunter had picked up the technique during his short time with her. *Impressive. He must have retained the information and trained a great deal while incarcerated.* But the stunned silence in the crowd after the destruction of the statue was not only brought on by the deed and its rebellious intentions. The people of Trivium had also been rendered stupid by seeing such a display of power from a lowly human peon.

Expelling Eve from the body in its pure form was not something most UnEarth creatures were capable of. Their power was immense but stored inside their cells, granting them their natural abilities. Only a rare few could hurl it in such an explosive fashion, meaning the people had witnessed something that completely challenged their view of the world and their significance in it. If one human could get to such a place, who was to say that more were not on their way? What would this mean for UnEarth and the station it enjoyed over the human world? Even Mara, who was thrilled to see the people of Trivium taken for such a ride, was subject to a trill of Dread upon witnessing Bennett's prank gone wild.

It was still unclear what the true intention had been in his slinging of a bucket of feces through the statue following his confessions. If he had hoped to offend the people with the poo itself, that showed how woefully little he understood UnEarth society, which viewed feces not so much as an offensive mess but as a resource to reuse. It also showed how blind he was to the people's devotion to Michael. Destroying the Great One's statue was insulting enough, but Hunter had said a lot more with that act than Mara guessed he knew. Objects being seen as representing creatures and cultures was a pervasive aspect of UnEarth society. Most of the different shaded species could be identified by the tool they used in their trade as easily as by their physical appearance. By flinging a bucket used exclusively by a Psera Celestial, Hunter had given the people the impression that the Pseras were part of his defiant act against the memory of this world's most legendary leader, making a statement alongside him. A snowball had been kicked down a hill because of the bucket—one that would develop into a rolling mass of intolerance aimed at the lowly "subset" of Celestials, something the foolish human could have never seen coming.

Presently, as she exited the Hikkwe neighborhood, Mara's goal was to reach the Tribunal without being seen. Forced to wait until the interim courtroom was completely vacated before leaving (*ridiculous protocol*), she sped down the streets, now mostly cleared out after the people had watched the procession of the guilty pass on their way to the Iolanze.

Getting through Trivium took her through Greb-Gek, a Dolorosian neighborhood, and Trib Town, a suburb primarily Lanwynite in makeup. Just a couple of neighborhoods more, and she was in Trinity Plaza.

Like night and day from the grim precinct she had viewed just yesterday, the activity in the area surrounding the Tribunal had become electrified. Only once before had so much color and movement encircled the jet-black building, which stood like a sleeping volcano in the heart of the city—and that had been at the signing of the Covenant. Multiple delegations from the worlds of UnEarth scurried about, having meals, lugging boxes, bags, crates, and belongings up hotel stairs, chatting and sauntering every which way. *Now, where did you all come from?* With a quick check,

Mara sensed activity increasing around both the city's northern and southern Eb Gates. Creatures were already beginning to pour through, even though news of the execution had only been made public a few hours before. *Almost as though they were ready and waiting for the go-ahead.*

It took time to navigate the crowd without being detected or using any Mallos. Twenty minutes later, she was across Trinity Plaza, headed for the entrance to the westernmost section of the Tribunal: the Iolanze. Within a large nook in the structure, down a loading ramp, was a rarely used side entrance. Once inside, Mara took inventory of the Barium Guard presence. The force appeared to have doubled yet again, and there was a surprising amount of activity for Celestials. The Guard was preparing for something, and she could only guess what.

Keeping her power as light as a morning mist, she flew swiftly down each hall, her gray cloak flapping and waving yet remaining silent as a mouse. Fighting a Celestial one-on-one was not necessarily a major concern, but the wise thing was to avoid a direct conflict as much as possible—at least for now. It proved difficult, however, not to wonder how many of them she might have to tangle with legitimately down the road if things continued the way they were. *Keep your thoughts here. No mistakes.* Just before she made her first turn, a pack of Barium Guards stomped near. After slipping into a dark crevice, she waited for them to pass.

Making her way upward, she neared the frontmost section on the primary floor, where the light-security wing resided. For nearly two years, an entire cellblock—one of eight—had been occupied by only a single inmate. What should have been at least a marginally well-guarded area appeared practically deserted, likely because the jailers knew the prisoner would either stay in his cage or he wouldn't. Mara waited until the two guards left their posts for a tour of the perimeter. Sliding out from her shadowed hiding spot near the ceiling, she dropped to the floor and found the old Medolian wearing a gray knitted cap with two brown stripes, hunched over a side table so heavily that Mara couldn't see what he was doing.

When she took her first step, he spoke with a full mouth. "Y'know, s'm'thng t'ld m' y'were gnn' pk rrr'nnn t'show up."

Mara stepped around the cage to see him spoon up a huge mound of green mush into his mouth, mashing on it like a toothless rottweiler. "Thank you for coming to visit me so often, by the way," Izaiah said. "Do you know how many visitors I've had since I got in here? None! Zero! I'm not kidding."

"Fret not. I believe you," Mara said, moving to the cell door, taking it in both hands, and ripping it cleanly off with one pull. "Come along. This is our one chance."

"Somebody probably worked hard on that door. What a shame."

"Now!"

"Excuse me, but just the heck is going on here? I'm eating, Sentry Mara. Awful rude, don't you think?"

"I'm in no mood for games, you daft old toad."

"I'm not playing no games. Really, the cook made such a nice meal, I'd hate to leave it behind. I might be a little selfish tonight, if that's all right."

"By not escaping jail?"

"Why not? It's been nice to see you, though. Even if I can sense an awful lot of disgust in you right now. Kinda sourin' the food, but that's okay. I don't mind."

"Is this a form of punishment? You finally get me to debase myself and ask for your help, and this is how you treat me?"

"You asked for help? When?"

"I . . . well, of course that's what I'm doing!"

"Oh, forgive me, I've never heard it put that way before. But I'm afraid I can't give any help. At least, not any you'd like. But you ask me, you don't need any. Now, you should get going. I'm sure you can sense that you-know-who is coming."

For the past thirty minutes, she'd been trying to ignore it: a gargantuan Celestial power that had arrived on Trivium. Every second, the signal was getting closer to the Tribunal. Even those with dull senses would be overwhelmed at first glance. *Gabriel. He's really here.* Mara had not actually been on the same planet as him in over two thousand years, but his power still felt as though several armies had appeared wrapped in a single, fifty-foot package. There was no time to waste trying to argue with Izaiah. If she had to remove him from his cage by force, she would.

Darting into the cell to take him, she began by knocking the bowl and spoon out of his hands with prejudice.

"My pudding!" Izaiah gasped.

"We can't let them do this to you!" Mara roared into his face. "Get up. We must rally the other Medolians."

"No, you need to. Like you said every time we meet, my time as a Sentry is done. Should've been long ago. My journey's headed in a different direction now. Steeply, too, I think."

"You're really going to let them do this? Let them kill you? And the humans?"

"Seems like they want to kill us awful bad, doesn't it? To tell you the truth, I'm not too worried about the fellas. I'm sure you'll get them out of here. But I'm still waiting for someone to tell me why so many people want us dead. Until they do, I think I'll stick around. I know how important it is to you that we Medolians follow the rules and set a good example. So, I'm doing that. Thought you'd be proud of me."

"Not after the lashing the court gave our entire race for the last six months. How can you just sit idly while they discredit every-thing about us? About you?"

"Have you ever considered they may be right? At least about me? I mean, a lot of what they say is true. The Sentry Force isn't what it used to be. Mallos doesn't seem to be flowing off Earth like it used to, and I can't figure out why. Believe me, I've looked. Doesn't make any sense. I think something in the Eve's pipes got broken somewhere. If you figure out that mystery, maybe you can be the one to finally regrow our species?"

"You speak as if you're already dead! What kind of Sentry would allow such things to pass? And to befall those he claims to care for? You have the power to wipe away the entire Tribunal and rebuild it with humanity's inclusion, just as you've said time and again. Yet you choose to sit and wag your tongue."

Izaiah chuckled. "That's all kinds of sweet. Appreciate the vote of confidence, but you're wrong about something. I'm not, uh . . . well, y'see . . . I'm all tapped out. *Poof*, y'know? Have been for a bit now. Feeling it for years, but then came all the excitement with the Joseph Mandate. By the time the fellas and I were being arrested by the Barium Guard, I was trying to drink from an empty cup."

"I don't understand. You're saying your power is . . . gone?"

"Been fading for a good while now. The last two thousand espe-cially. My knees have been getting the brunt of it, but I've been . . . well, y'know, just plain tired. Things have been hard lately. I know you know that as well as anyone."

"But you're one of the oldest creatures alive," Mara said, her jaw unsteady. "Strength of Eve increases as a creature ages. This is a known rule."

"Guess once you get up to a certain point that rule stops being true."

"None of us knew. You have always kept your strength inside, so we assumed . . ."

"Yeah, I figured that, but didn't plan it. Talking about it seemed kind of silly. I'm not exactly proud of getting my butt kicked by Loredosai and getting thrown in here, but it just goes to show that even if we last forever, it don't mean we last forever."

"None of this matters," Mara said sharply. "I don't want to hear any more. Please. Just come with me. We will find a way to restore your strength."

"Did you even stop to think if that's something I want? Look, I'm just doing what I always do, going with my gut. Right now, it says I should eat. If you're feeling peckish and would like some, I suppose I could share a little."

Mara was dumbstruck, her feet unsure of what direction to send her. Her piece had been said, and it hadn't made any difference. Deep down, she'd suspected this was going to happen, but she was still surprised when it did.

"Oh, Mara. Your heart's in the right place. It always is," Izaiah said. "Only thing you've yet to master—your belief in yourself. You've always been headed down this path. Now it's time to accept it in your core. Not just at surface level, but to actually step into the shoes and begin walking. They're not the ones you were expecting, but that doesn't mean they're not yours."

"What are you talking about? I cannot be a true Warden Sentry with the Senate and the Iolanze encroaching on all sides, not to mention the Alus Conclave and possibly dozens more hiding in the shadows. I need something greater than me. I need help."

"It won't be easy, that's true enough, but the fact that your fear didn't stop you from asking for help shows you're the right one for the job."

"I never said I was afraid."

"Didn't need to, but it's nothing to be ashamed of."

"Why won't you stand for us when we're under attack like never before? Would you let us be decimated all over again?"

"That's not fair." A quick breath of Wrath swept through Izaiah. "You think I wouldn't have stood there with my kin and shared their fate? Batia tricked me. For the first and only time. She sent me away that day. If I'd known what they were planning, I would have gladly been lost to the Eve if it meant sending Uhl'k back where it belongs. Becoming Warden was never on my to-do list, believe me. And to be honest with you, I never really believed you were all that keen about it, either. I might be wrong about that, but now that you've seen what it's about, you can focus on the task at hand and make sure our people are never cut down again. Now, I'd suggest you get a move on. Gabriel's getting awful close."

The lord of Hywyn was not just getting close; he had already arrived. Izaiah was just being nice. Mara needed to leave two minutes ago.

"Sorry I wasted your time, kiddo, but I gotta see this one through. We're Medolians after all, creatures of balance and fairness."

"Those are human fables! There is no fairness in this universe."

"No, see, you're wrong about that."

"We all need to make choices that help ourselves in the end. We need to survive."

Izaiah chuckled to himself as though he were thinking of something else and hadn't heard her. "Tell you what, think of my actions as an experiment. Once and for all, I'm going to find out if I'm really capable of making my own choices. But you need to move quickly if you're going to get to the fellas in time. Please tell them I say hello, and maybe goodbye too, just in case."

"You're making my defection tonight meaningless."

"No. That was the right thing to do, and you know it. You can do anything now. You're free to go after what you want. So, tell me, what is it?"

"I want justice."

"Neat! Then go find it. No one's better at finding things than you. You're the Medolian who caught a Beaubon in the Amazon, after all."

"Why do people insist on repeating that? The task was not particularly challenging."

"Still, just keep your legs moving. You'll eventually find your way. Don't forget that!"

Suddenly, a cold chill struck Mara, and a mountain of Rapture loomed over her, making her feel as though she was standing in the shade of a tsunami. She and Izaiah both jolted when Gabriel entered the building.

"Time's up," Izaiah said gravely.

He had never been more correct, and Mara was done with this back-and-forth. If he wanted to stay, then she would have to accept it. Before finally leaving, she asked, "What if your gut is wrong?"

"Way I figure it, I've managed to live this long doing things that way. Don't see anyone else around as old as me to compare it to. I don't know . . . might just keep on doing what I'm doing."

Mara had always seen the Jubilee-tinted man as a fool handed too much power and responsibility. Now, she wondered if there was more to his unserious ways than had appeared at first glance, or second, or even ten-thousandth. Having nothing left to say, she left Izaiah in his cell, still unsure if he was telling the truth about his lost power. Either way, he'd made up his mind and presented a more thorough argument in favor of his pudding than he'd ever put forward in court to save his own head. *Eve knows why, but he's right where he wants to be.*

Unable to Shift to the Weya-Vein, Mara made her way through

the Iolanze, sticking close to the ceiling and utilizing the many catwalks throughout the Tribunal. The Ulga Vloc, the cellblock where Bennett had been transferred, lay deep in the belly of the building, near the core, where the Iolanze connected to the Senate chamber and the Caechus, the headquarters of the Counselors.

Trying to outrace Gabriel to the other side of the jail and ten floors down proved harder than anticipated, all thanks to the increased Barium Guard presence. Mara had to pull out all the stops. It appeared she was moving quickly enough to reach Bennett in time, but Gabriel's signal was so blinding that it was hard to tell exactly where he was in relation to her.

A shortcut then came to mind. Ducking down the hall leading to the laundry, Mara was forced to wait for another pack of guards to clear out. When an opening came, she snuck through a side door meant for Veen assistants and Beaubons. The back hall led to a food distribution system for the Ulga Vloc. With no obvious signals nearby, the rest of the trek was smooth sailing.

Opening a rusty door at the end of a short jog, she entered the processing and distribution room. A rotating arm on a cylinder heaved itself round and round, moving a barrel of slop with a pressure system and myriad tubes protruding from the bottom, running along the catwalk and disappearing into the walls. Like a huge, grotesque metronome, the slop slapped back and forth with impeccable steadiness.

Navigating a network of footpaths meant to give maintenance workers access to the food pipes, Mara found a nook with a glimpse into the upper level of the Ulga Vloc. Inmates sentenced to death but deemed no credible threat were strung up in several rows of stockades below, held by a strong elastic material made from Fovos weeds. Just enough to keep them alive for their big day, the condemned inmates could move only a few feet in each direction, eliminating any chance of escape.

Mara made her way past another junction station and a steam engine that looked to be a power amplifier for the gear shaft. What was normally an unruly orchestra of noise from the inmates in the cages under her feet was surprisingly docile tonight. They, too, could sense what was coming for them. Searching for his Eve signal, she found Bennett in cage number two, unfortunately the farthest away. Just before she got into position, a mere leap from his cage, Mara's plan was gutted when the doors opened and the lord of Hywyn stepped through.

No! I can't be too late.

The coterie accompanying him stood no higher than his knees, while the wings of the pure Celestials reached only to his mid-thigh. The ceiling of the Ulga Vloc stood only a few feet above his head. A murky shade of blue, some parts of the titan's gemstone body appeared nearly black. But his size and his hue were not all that set the High Lord apart from his brethren. Unlike their rectilinear wings, bent at high degrees and square angles, Gabriel's wings were curved—long a point of embarrassment. It was no secret that Lucifer had also been born with curved wings, and any soul unwise enough to mention that fact within earshot of Gabriel or any of his council was not known to last long. At least, their life wasn't. Their physical body, however, would last nearly forever, encased in bylahtach, a heavy Hywynite metal.

Like most Celestials, Gabriel was a creator. In his art, primarily sculpture, he enjoyed using living beings as not only his subjects but also his medium, especially those who'd wronged him. According to the story—long known throughout UnEarth—his intent was to make his enemies and the very knowledge of their betrayal last for eternity. In the gallery outside his throne room, he kept them; and there they remained, petrified, as they had been in life, enemies of the crown.

Mara froze in place like a possum. One wrong move could cost her her life. The lord of all Hywyn was no one to trifle with, to say nothing of those accompanying him.

First was Loredosai, who, despite his relatively small size and less-than-grandiose voice, had earned his place as the commander of Hywyn's forces through cunning and brute strength. Mara had never fought him personally, but her mentor, Batia, had warned her on several occasions to avoid a direct conflict with him at all costs.

On Gabriel's right was Auelli of Uati, obscured by a large burnt-umber cloak. Their genus, the Clavus Celestials, were the rarest and most elusive of the species, birthed only in a single region of Hywyn: the mountainous province of Uati. To say they were a rare sight on Trivium was an understatement. If one or two did ever happen to visit, they traveled almost exclusively via flight high above everyone else's heads. Having any kind of conversation with a Clavus also proved nearly impossible, as they lacked mouths or vocal cords and communicated exclusively via ESP, telepathy. Some believed they could read the thoughts of other UnEarth creatures as well, which may have led to their general treatment as outsiders by the UnEarth community at large.

The people of Uati wanted nothing from their brethren other than to be left alone, but the icy grip of the Magnus Council would never allow a portion of Hywyn to remain outside their rule. Therefore, to maintain the illusion of a united Hywyn, a Clavus delegate was always required to serve on the High Lord's guard. Auelli had been filling the role for the last thirteen thousand years and was now considered as much a part of the royal delegation as Gabriel himself. Even the Rapture lord knew the strength of the Clavus and had his own part to play in maintaining peace on Hywyn.

This was the first time Mara had seen Auelli in person, though she couldn't actually see much thanks to their cloth coverings. *The closest I ever got to viewing a Clavus up close was in the final days of Inferius, but I was just a little distracted back then.* Other than that, she'd only ever viewed them from afar, soaring through the sky—the draped warriors of violet.

On his immediate left, the third member of the High Lord's entourage was a Faire Celestial named Hedia of Wyando, a faithful servant for even longer than Auelli. Not only Gabriel's interpreter, Hedia was also his voice, speaking aloud each and every word the High Lord would have said himself if his own voice—a thing of UnEarth legend—wasn't too powerful to be used outside his throne room. If the stories were to be believed, it was said to be capable of leveling whole neighborhoods with a single word.

Mara found it surprisingly difficult to relax and keep from tensing up in his presence. Gabriel was no Medolian, but his senses were not to be underestimated. Any slight fluctuation in her aura might have been enough to be noticed by any of the royal retinue.

What she couldn't figure out was why Gabriel had arrived in the first place. It seemed impossibly beneath him to take such an interest in a human, even one who had defiled the statue of his predecessor. But Bennett was not just any human. He had been infused with Rapture and had received Hywyn's full support during the trial, which he'd squandered. The grudge the High Lord held was projected, crystal clear, by his heavy march past the cages containing scores of inmates as silent as the dead.

It would have been easy to leap down onto him as he passed by underneath, his head just a few yards below. The High Lord peered into the pen containing Bennett Hunter, who was unconscious, strung up among dozens of other condemned souls. Moving with the speed of a garage door, Gabriel folded his arms and observed as his faithful servant, Hedia, began asking Loredosai questions in traditional Hyl. The notes sounded like church bells ringing in succession, predominantly vowels. Conversations between two or more Celestials in their native tongue could last an entire night, but that was not tenable for Mara's plan. She would be discovered before then, and likely caught. There was nothing more she could do to free Hunter.

Adding a splash of insult, her senses picked up more Celestial troops arriving at the city's Eb Gates. A force was amassing, and her time here was running out. With no options left, she sneaked away as carefully as possible, moving in tiny, measured motions until she was outside the Tribunal. Then, ran until she was clear of Trinity Plaza. Then, until she had passed the next two neighborhoods. There was no real direction or goal—just running. *I need help.* But no one came to mind whom she trusted.

Eventually, someone would spot her and turn her in. "Wanted" tapestries were likely already being sewn with her face on them. Defecting to Earth was truly the only option now, even if it meant the official end of her time as Warden Sentry—the thing she had wanted for longer than she could remember, all she had ever worked for. The ache of letting go so soon felt like throwing herself onto a pile of jagged ice shards. But sometimes, there were far more important things than titles and status. *A fact that breaks my heart, if I'm honest.*

YOU'RE IN A LOT OF TROUBLE, MISTER

A glob of spit struck Bennett's right shoulder and oozed down his back, coalescing with the rest of the spittle rained on him today. There'd been so much that he hardly noticed it by now.

"This humie thinks he can disrespect us like that? An insult to Michael is an insult to all of us," the disproportionately ugly creature, Splaad, said, sounding on the verge of tears.

Since Bennett had arrived the day before, the insufferable Derd had been lobbing heated insults, complaints, and loogies at him at a surprisingly consistent rate, almost nailing it by the hour.

"You and the Pseras both! I always knew they were no-good schemers!" he continued. "They hated Michael, too? That's fine! 'Cause we'll run 'em all down and squash 'em and send 'em into the void!"

This guy is testing most of my better Rapture qualities.

Bennett remained steady in his defense, which consisted of merely nodding, and thought, *That's fine. I made this bed. I can sleep in it.* Besides, it wasn't the endless animosity and bile being hurled his way that bothered him; it was how right Splaad might have been. The bucket prank (*I call it a statement, but whatever*) had gone completely off the rails. What had given Bennett some much-needed pride and satisfaction for a few short hours had turned into a nightmare scenario when word spread through his cellblock that paranoia and distrust of the Psera Celestials had already begun mounting outside. Some of the undersized blue people had been told to take indefinite hiatuses from their work until things "died down" (*whatever the fuck that means*), while others had been suddenly and completely removed from their jobs and posts altogether, with no explanation given.

I thought the fucks in here were just fucking with me when they told me everyone would see my using Brick's bucket as a joint statement with him. It was even harder to get my head around his whole species or race or whatever being blamed for the statue, too. How the fuck does a civilization get so fucked up that they would—wait . . . who am I to talk?

He couldn't stop thinking about Inno. *I still call him Brick in my head.* Feeling justified by his punt that day, when Bennett had turned around to find a devastated look of disappointment on the small Celestial's face. Now, all he could do was wonder if he had put Brick's fate into jeopardy. *I'll never forgive myself if something happens to that little guy. This plan is looking more and more like a bonehead move. Why can't I stop being such a dumbass? Other people make it look really easy to not be one.*

His constant worrying about Inno and the rest of the Pseras was made considerably worse by the sheer discomfort of being held in the Ulga Vloc pen. The claustrophobia of the cage was nothing compared to the sensation of being held in an awkward fixed position, unable to move freely. *It's why I could never snowboard. I hated being locked in.* Slime-caked slings around his elbows and knees kept Bennett in a leaned-forward state, as though he were in a constant process of falling down, strung up like some marionette puppet, just unable to touch his feet to the floor. The sensation caused a perpetual state of nausea in him. Stretching in a long line on his left and right sides were the other creatures on death row, hung like dead chickens from hooks in a slaughterhouse. Another row of fifty or so condemned were in front of him, while three were behind. The other five cages in the Ulga Vloc were all exactly the same, packed to capacity.

Thanks to the elastic quality of his sling, he was allowed enough movement to reach his water trough and bag of feed, but only just long enough to get a single bite or drink before the tension yanked him back to a resting position. *Meaning no recess or bathroom breaks. If I need to pee or poo, I just pee or poo. Right here. Good stuff. Lots of fun.* Already he wished he were back in a jail cell on Earth with some nice sheets with which to hang himself. But that wouldn't have helped Alex. *Not that I can help him much stuck here like this. Guess I sort of underestimated things a tad.* The soldier had fully expected to be sent to the Ulga Vloc after his statement but had forgotten to do any proper research first. Long gone were his days of space, leniency, and treats, replaced instead by hate, resentment, and gooey elastic restraints.

The large number of condemned packed into the cages like sardines was primarily due to the mass executions the city organized as both entertainment and justice. Few felonies could escape the death penalty if the circumstances were right, and any insults to the court during one's trial resulted in the same sentence. In good old medieval fashion (*which I appreciate*), the perpetrators were executed by beheading, usually averaging a few dozen each month. *But ours will just feature Izaiah, Al, and me. Aren't we special? I won-*

der if they'll be selling popcorn or big legs of meat. Can I request one of those as my last meal?

Escape was still the goal, as Bennett wasn't quite ready to lose his head, but he'd had zero opportunity to talk with Alex so far. *I was sort of banking on being able to do that somehow. If I can't get a message to him before next Wednesday . . . might not be so good.*

Chained to a slab on wheels, the soldier had been taken into custody in the exact same way as Alex, and though he'd never admit it, he rather enjoyed the metal mask sucking his Eve dry. *It was wonderfully quiet in there. Nice and cool. Good place to get lazy and dumb.* Part of him wished he had always had one. All of him wished he still had one now. Thinking would have been easier. Trying to concentrate and come up with a backup plan for their escape was next to impossible as the clatter of food and water buckets toppling over blended seamlessly with the multitude of snorting, farting, growling, and chewing sounds from the creatures feeding. And if the constant barrage of baleful moans filling the halls like some roaming fog wasn't bad enough, the smells and their molestations were plenty to keep his brain from functioning. There would likely be no plan, and no speaking with Alex beforehand, but at least Bennett's brother wouldn't have to go to the executioner alone.

It's all I can offer at this point. Unlike Izaiah, who could have stopped all of this. What is going on with that guy? If he had a plan, it makes no sense to keep everyone in the dark. And if he doesn't have one, then what the fuck?

Bennett's stomach turned, and a sudden need to go to the bathroom overcame him, raising Dread at the thought of the sensation about to move down his leg and the smell that would amalgamate with the others floating about the cage. But he couldn't complain. Bennett was not a victim and knew full well he deserved this. Somewhere deep in him, he even enjoyed it: being punished for once in a long life of never facing the ramifications of his misdeeds. Going to jail on Earth had never been all that affecting, but this place might have what it takes to get him to rethink how he'd lived his life.

The flame of Rapture within him was also affected, feeling robust and reinforced since the end of the trial, no longer an ice-cold chill of rigidity but a warm sensation now. No denying it was still the essence of Hywyn, but it felt different, like the distinction between the smell of a ribeye and a pork chop. Both were of the same idea but from different places.

With the rhythm of a park swing swaying back and forth in a dull breeze, the flame seemed to react with the belt buckle on his waist, which began to pulse and glow the moment he was thrown into the pen. Ignoring it had become impossible, as the signal grew so loud that even his neighbors started to take notice. Hannah was calling, and he was too chickenshit to answer. *She knows something's up. I've kept her on hold long enough. Better get this over with.*

Closing his eyes, he took a deep breath and thought of a tranquil lake with a small rowboat at its center. The craft wobbled, agitating the water around it, but the greater body remained undisturbed. No rippling waves propagated. Bennett exhaled and focused, sending the sounds and smells of cage number two to the unseen, unfelt back of his mind, calming the small wooden boat. Soon, it was as still as the lake, and his meditation trick did its thing, facilitating a smooth transition into the Rapture realm where Hannah dwelled.

The boat and the lake faded, and Bennett was nowhere for a moment, without a sense of time. When he came to, he was walking through a darkening mist, as though night had overtaken the white plane he was expecting. Through the obscuring fog, buildings began to emerge on either side, boxy with rounded corners.

A sky then faded into view, a burgundy as deep and dark as a glass of cabernet.

Trivium City?

Booms like thunder and fireworks began thumping all around him, causing Bennett to duck for cover. Flashes lit clusters of gray clouds hovering above, revealing two dark patches careening across the sky: silhouettes in the rough shape of people. One was alight with blue brilliance; the other, outlined with flashes of blood-red. Around the warrior in red flapped an encompassing shadow of mangled wings. *I know this place. This night.* Bennett had lived this before, but from a different vantage point. Taking place overhead was the closing bout between Hannah and Joseph, shaking the very foundation of the city.

Looking on with a rehabilitated sense of wonder, he was met with a familiar voice approaching on his right.

"This is my favorite part."

Buckle Hannah's boots crunched gravel as she emerged from the shadow of a bistro, her leather jacket ensemble returned, gaze locked on the battle in the sky.

"What is all this?" Bennett asked.

She shushed him, her eyes glazed over as though she were in a movie theatre watching a gripping drama she'd already seen twice. "Here it comes. Look—look . . ."

The combatants reached the point where a stalemate was revealing itself. Buckle Hannah pointed up at her counterpart. "She's starting to realize her little trick isn't going to work."

"What trick?"

"Never actually had a chance to try out the transformation during a real battle before. Never needed to. Wasn't even sure how long she'd be able to sustain it, if she could even get it to happen. It takes a completely calm mind. Digging that far down without using anger is tough. The toughest thing she'd encountered until Mr. Nightmare there."

The look on her face began to morph, now reacting to the battle more like an athlete watching a tape of their championship game. The pride was unmistakable. *She's reliving it: her greatest moment.*

Then came the point in the battle where Joseph and Hannah were seconds from giving their all: the apex. The energy spheres grew into blinding light and Eve. Hannah's raging cry blasted across the cityscape.

But the images and the memory were extinguished just before the explosion. The world within the buckle transitioned back into the white wasteland where Bennett first discovered Buckle Hannah. All sound of the battle had vanished, leaving only a grating ringing in his ears, despite their existing in astral form.

"We know how the rest of it goes," Buckle Hannah said, her gaze still aimed high.

"Reliving your physically bodied life?" Bennett asked, keeping his distance.

"I never had one of those. I'm just looking for any place she could have done better."

"She?" Bennett was a little stunned. *Who does she think she is if not the real Hannah?*

Ignoring his question, she continued gazing into the white above. Bennett tried a different approach.

"Find any screwups?"

"A few." She turned to look at him for the first time since his arrival, striking him with her crystalline blue irises. "I take it the sentencing went well."

"What makes you say that?"

"Your Eve. It's grown. You've got a nice core settling in there."

"I do? I mean, I guess I felt pretty good after my confession. Then after I—"

"This is just from a confession?" Hannah asked with mild amazement. "Interesting . . . I always knew that was a good way for humans to increase their Rapture, but damn. You must have had a lot of mud on your wings."

"Eh?"

"Means a lot to confess."

"Ah. You could say that."

"Then the sentencing went as you intended?"

"Can't you see my thoughts?"

"Nobody can read another person's thoughts. Not fully. Every brain and body—which together form thought—has a unique way of processing information that can't be read by another consciousness. But I can still sense your Eve and what you're feeling, which is plenty."

"And what am I feeling? Not kidding. Genuinely asking."

"More guilt than I expected."

"Thought so. Things went about as well as we could have hoped. My shit was in even worse condition than I expected it to be. But unfortunately . . ."

"No one was offended and simply thought you were stranger than before?"

"Oh, no. They were plenty mad. Just not about my crap. The bucket got Michael square on the kisser, and—"

"You threw it at Michael?" she asked, as if she'd just seen him sucker punch a nun.

"You too? What is it with this guy?"

"That's no guy. That Celestial was one of the bravest, most selfless creatures the Hannah you knew ever had the pleasure of serving. The lord of not just Hywyn, but basically of all UnEarth."

"Then why didn't you tell me that? Making me look like a jerk out there."

"You said you'd aim for a statue, not *the* statue. I take it the people then thought you were implying Michael should have labored with the Psera Celestials rather than lead?"

"Not exactly. Kinda hard since the . . . well, you see, the statue may have gotten a little damaged by my kick, which honestly was so soft."

"You're lying like a lake of fire. What did you do?"

"I didn't do anything! But the bucket may have hurt it, you know. Superficially."

"I can maim you in this place."

"I blew it up into a thousand little pieces."

Her eyes went wide, and a look of tickled shock crossed her face. "That's no small thing. Did you reference the Psera whose bucket you used? Before or after?"

"I might have mentioned Brick and his breed. I think it's bullshit how they get treated."

"There you go. It's no wonder. That was the only item the people could grab onto. A lot was probably lost in translation, too. You didn't consider the fact that only a portion of the creatures in that room spoke the same language as you. You chose not to think about who your receiving audience was."

"Okay . . . that's true. Guess I thought my intentions would be clear once they read my Eve signature."

"They probably didn't want to. I doubt many paid attention."

After grilling Bennett a little while longer, Hannah admitted she was more amused than mad, and even commended him for following through with his plan. "Took guts. Even if it was stupid." Listening to the tale he told, she seemed primarily interested in the different reactions of the senators and Judge Axios after his poop-bucket protest, soaking up the gossip in a way that continued to surprise. *Her mannerisms are so different. So carefree. The stoicism I got used to isn't even there . . . and I'm not even sure if I like it or not.*

"Then I was sentenced to die," Bennett said. "Now I'm trapped in a goo sling in cage number two."

"Exactly like you wanted. So now what? Doesn't seem like you can do anyone any good where you're at."

"Well, how was I supposed to know what this was going to be like!? Seems like you could've warned me."

"Warn you that putting yourself on death row was a bad idea?"

"Yeah! I mean, I figured there would be some way to talk to Al. We can do this—we just need some luck to come our way."

"Once again, your naivety is getting the best of you. Alex may have become the Ire, and you may have survived it, but you fail to see how little you really are in the grand scheme of things. You and Barker stand no chance against the Barium Guard, and you won't be able to hide, either. If you take your signatures down too low, your bodies won't be able to exist on the Trivium plane. You'll fall apart. This plan has no beginning, middle, or end."

"If we get him mad enough, Al can—"

"It wasn't anger that broke Barker's walls and allowed the Ire to take hold. It was sadness. Deep, world-breaking grief. He'll never become the Ire again. He can't lose his greatest love twice. I know you've thought of this. You're no rock-skull, and you've got some fight in you, but you still lack proper training. The advice the other Hannah gave you was fine, but I'd say you were more lucky than competent in your battles with the Archfiend. The Guard is something else entirely. I've seen Loredosai's troops do incredible, horrible things—sometimes to creatures twice their size and age. They are nothing to take lightly."

"If that's all true, I guess there's nothing left to do but sit back like a good little Celestial and wait to die."

"We all have to face that at one time or another, and looking the truth in the eye is hard sometimes. No shame there. You're just not in any way capable of escaping."

"Yet."

"Excuse me?"

"You said I'm not capable. Sure. But what if I became capable?"

"How do you expect to do that?"

"You said time works differently here. In which direction? I get more time in here than goes by outside, right?"

"That's one way of describing the phenomenon. But it's only in your mind. You wouldn't truly be—"

"That's fine. We can do it. I can do it. This is doable."

"What is? I despise the direction of your tone."

"I promise I'll train like you wouldn't believe. I can get strong enough. If you'll just help me. Teach me to use my Rapture. Teach me to fight like a Celestial. Teach me Ou-I."

Hannah blinked twice. "How could you possibly know about that?"

"Folks like to talk loud in the recess yard. You catch things."

"What do you want to know about an ancient Hywyn fighting style?"

"Every last goddamn thing. Show me what I couldn't learn from Hannah before she died. Show me how to be worthy of her time and sacrifice. I didn't ask to be a part of any of this. I never wanted the Rapture, but I've got it now. Might as well lean into it. Help me make all this bullshit worth it."

"By training you?"

"Yes, and if you refuse me, I'll simply remind you you're not actually a person and just a belt buckle, so it's not like you're busy, and it would be really rude to say no."

"To what end? Have you already forgotten the state of your outer body? Is this nothing more than a stall? If so, you'd do well to run to the executioner's blade as soon as possible."

"You can see my feelings, right? Well, look. I want this. I'll do it. Al and I can get belligerent and fight our way out. And even if we fail, that would at least be preferable to rolling over and sticking my neck out. Come on, I want to give Loredosai and his guys some grief. What do you say?"

With a soft chuckle, Hannah seemed to consider it. "I admit, that sounds fun."

"I'm about to die, General. Please, help me again. This will be the last time. If I fail, then I'll be dead, and you can fall safely asleep, never to be disturbed again. At least . . . until the next person puts the buckle on. Just think of it—a lifetime of new faces to meet. I bet that excites you, doesn't it?"

Hannah's expression went blank. "Point taken."

The first day of his training reminded Bennett of when he was a kid learning to ski, spending most of it on his ass in the cold. Many of the exercises were similar to the warm-ups he used to do back on Earth, which was mildly disappointing—until he found out how taxing they were on the white plane.

"Thought you'd have some ancient calisthenics," Bennett said. "Get me some Heavenly biceps. But angels do push-ups too, huh?"

"We'll get to the rest later. For now, a nice primitive push-up will do fine," Hannah said.

By the end of the first six-hour session, he couldn't believe his level of exhaustion and Bennett began to question yet another of his decisions. But true to his word, he stuck with it and worked harder than he ever had, doing everything asked of him. *Feels like going through boot again.* Getting back to raw basics was reinvigorating, scratching an itch he didn't know he had.

"Your mind has a long way to go," Hannah said. "You may have worked out most of your muscles all your life, but never your main one."

"Ouch."

Each session began the same way: Hannah would ask Bennett his primary goal. His answer was always the same: to get strong enough to get him and Alex off Trivium in one piece. The lessons she offered ranged from breathing exercises to mental tricks used for solidifying the body. Much of the material had nothing to do with utilizing Eve, but focused more on how to carry one's mind and let thoughts stream freely, at peace with needs and feelings.

Seeing how Hannah carried herself and getting a glimpse of her Celestial mind was its own lifetime's worth of lessons. A rigid confidence supported her every action. Bennett imagined there had never been a moment when she lacked complete self-assurance. He, a lowly man, knew enough to identify it, but that level of composure was difficult to comprehend. Not to mention her unending stamina. *Though to be fair, she is just a belt buckle now and isn't actually moving any arms or legs . . . But then again neither am I . . . So how can I be so tired? I'm not even running, just thinking about it . . . weird.*

While the weakness of exhaustion had followed him onto the white plane, Bennett felt no sensation of hunger or thirst and had no need to go to the bathroom. Gradually, he began to stop considering the state of his body back in the real world. After what must have been several days' worth of training, he had no desire to go back and check on himself.

Wonder how long I could stay here. They might chop off my head out there before too long. Suppose I ought to head back soon . . . heh.

When Hannah did allow breaks between sessions, she sat back and relaxed, offering stories about UnEarth, Celestial life, and the old wars. The big picture began to reveal itself. The war of the Celestials and the Archfiend had been going on for too long to comprehend, and yet Hannah had been involved in a good portion of it. A few instances let slip details about her time during Inferius, much of it spent fighting the armies of Arros and Fovos on the other worlds of UnEarth. But once the Beast was unleashed, everything changed. The last eighty-six years of the conflict were spent back on Hywyn, defending the capital city of OA and the throne of the High Lord from Lucifer's army.

The creature the Fallen One controlled was described by Hannah as something "out of a six-year-old's nightmare—a walking mountain of flame and death. The very ground beneath its feet was eaten away as it traveled, leaving ravines behind the same way a slug leaves trails of slime." If anyone but Hannah were to tell him the story, Bennett would have thought it was all bullshit.

"Lucifer's plan was almost perfect," she said. "There was nothing we could do to stop Uhl'k's approach, only slow it down. But Aveyl had not planned on the Medolians doing what they did. If not for Batia and the others' sacrifice, the citadel would have fallen."

"You're serious? The entire Celestial species couldn't stop this thing?"

"The Beast is not an animal but a force—unlike anything you've seen. Once it sets foot on a planet, its steps can be felt no matter your location. Its presence immediately begins altering the atmosphere. Nothing is as terrible."

Mental note: don't ever try and see the Beast of Arros.

But story time would rarely last long. Then it was back to work. After only a few sessions, Bennett was doing things he'd never even imagined. The Rapture was revealing itself as a tool limited only by his creativity and will. *Finally starting to understand the phrase "the best offense is a good defense." That shit never made sense to me.* Every notion he'd ever carried about raw force being the only variable that could win fights was replaced by a desire to master problem-solving and think outside the box for alternative options.

"Rapture wants strategy," Hannah stressed. "Only Wrath wants blind aggression."

"Okay, that makes sense," Bennett replied. "I gotta admit, you're a better teacher than outside Hannah was."

"Really?"

"Yeah. She spoke in metaphors'n shit. Talking about cleaning mirrors or something. I don't know. I had a hard time following her."

"The glass pane thing? *Ugh.* She always did think her words were precious little gifts for the masses—to be given rarely and cryptically."

"Can you please explain something? Does this mean you don't see yourself as her? Or vice versa?"

"I may be able to remember her whole life, but the first time I woke up was when you found me. As far as I'm concerned, those memories are someone else's life. That doesn't mean she and I didn't want the same things—I'm just the one who gets to actually enjoy our shared dream and live out the rest of my days how she wanted. Here. Nowhere. With no obligations."

Bennett didn't know what to say to that and kept quiet. For the remainder of their time together, he never brought up Buckle Hannah's self-identity again. If she wanted to be treated as a different person, he had no reason not to.

On the eighth day, prior to a lesson, she said, "Nothing today. You need to go check on your body."

Oh yeah.

Remembering his physical form the same way he remembered a forgotten cousin at a family reunion, Bennett agreed. But when he tried to exit the buckle plane, he found it just as difficult as it had been to find his way into it in the first place. *Felt like I couldn't remember how to walk for a second.*

When his consciousness finally made its way to the surface and popped into his body, the sudden onslaught of stenches from cage number two made a hunk of vomit charge up his esophagus, which he choked back down. Not much had changed around here. Trying to pull his frame up to a more upright position, Bennett felt weak, but surprisingly strong of spirit. His limbs were easily movable, and there were no signs of atrophy. *Looks like the training is paying off.*

"Well—well. So, you're not dead?" Splaad said, spitting some more on Bennett's back.

"How many days was I gone?" the soldier asked.

"Days? *Hrmph.* Try an afternoon. Why? You want to run away? Be free of this place? Well, too bad! You still got plenty of time with us before you get to rest for good."

Splaad kept on yakking, but Bennett wasn't listening. *An afternoon?* The implications were enormous. To him, it had been more than a week.

A childish glee came over him. With this time, he could get strong enough and then some. How powerful he felt after just a week of the basics was proof. *I could get strong enough to tangle with Loredosai, no problem. We'll be home by this time next week.* Alex would have nothing to worry about and could raise his daughter in Arizona until he was an old man. Meanwhile, Hannah would show Bennett all her remaining secrets, and he could assume the role of the bearer of her torch. *Maybe I could go around the world saving people and doing good deeds? Like some angel superhero? Have to come up with a cool name, like . . . the Holy Fighter . . . or something better. A lot more badass. Maybe Magnum. That's a cool word.*

His mind was racing and starting to hurt—his first headache since being imbued. *Probably dehydrated.* He fought toward the drinking sack suspended above his head. The water was like drinking pure pollution, a stark contrast to the bright, clear, misty-mountain-fla-vored aqua delight he'd enjoyed in the low-security wing. *That's fine. I asked for this. Besides, I'm not staying long.* It was a struggle, but he gulped down as much as he could, then strained his neck to force his mouth near the feed bag to get a bite of the dry oat-and-nut mixture that tasted like cough medicine and earwax, washing it down with a few more sips of water.

There, I did it. Self-care achieved.

With dinner down his throat, he settled in and prepared to head back into the buckle plane for another week of sessions with Han-nah. The excitement he was experiencing, as well as his heart rate, first needed to be quelled before he could transition over. Closing his eyes, he pictured the rowboat on the lake in his mind. It was already nearly still.

Getting back in was nowhere near as difficult this time around. *I'm nailing this shit.* A certain giddiness flowed through him as Bennett dove deeper, waiting for the buckle realm to open up like a curtain before a stage production. There were sure to be many more techniques and tricks that Hannah had yet to show him, and new ways to kick ass with his Rapture.

Maybe she'll finally show me how to turn people into stone? Or maybe how to kill an Archfiend more efficiently? Or maybe she can teach me to do the same transformation that she did? Be a super crystal version of myself. I would kill to hear my voice sound like that.

Bennett felt like flexing and shaking his ass while he waited pa-tiently to see the white land appear. But after a few moments, he suddenly realized he had already arrived in the buckle realm and just hadn't noticed. The transition had finished, but surrounding him was only darkness, and he couldn't sense Hannah anywhere.

"Hello?"

Holding his hands out in front of him (*at least I think I am*), Bennett tried to step forward, feeling no ground beneath his feet. Sounds and sights then began to filter in: light air flowing in a tight corridor and dust settling. At first, he was convinced his eyes were playing tricks on him or having trouble adjusting, as gray and blue globs began to appear. Lines then formed and became organized. Shapes coalesced, and he was soon standing between two buildings. Brick was laid in the walls and beneath his feet. Finally, his feet worked, and he moved forward. The alley he was in revealed itself with every step, becoming more familiar. Upon exiting it, he found he'd returned to Trivium. The sky was full of stars, much brighter than the ground on which he stood, as though the cosmic light couldn't reach the planet's surface.

Okay . . . what am I doing here? What is this?

Walking around for a bit, he found a forbidding amount of nothing. There were no shops open or citizens strolling by, no talking, no advertisements or shop signs shimmering with fluorescent luminosity. Even the wind seemed to have left town. The whole thing felt as artificial as a military training course.

And I bet that's exactly what this is.

He prepped for an attack. With a thought, plate armor slid over him. But this was slimmer and more streamlined than the set he'd made for protection from the Ire. A sword also appeared in his right hand, a mixture in length and weight between a Roman gladius and a European longsword.

Thought up this bad boy last time I sparred with her. Treated me pretty well. Think I'll do even better with it today.

If he had to guess, Hannah was planning a sneak attack in order to test his battle readiness. But Bennett was not concerned. *How many places can a Celestial hide? I'll be ready.*

A signal then appeared. Rapture-tinted and potent, it carried the same weight as a pure High Celestial.

She's in her original form. Okay, check.

But it disappeared. The signal left no trace. Then it reappeared on the other side of him before vanishing again. The whack-a-mole game persisted as the signal drew near, and Bennett braced himself. Swooping sounds soared by. His gaze hopped back and forth. *Where is she? Where is this coming from?* His head instinctively aimed high. The Celestial attack would come from above.

A rumble in the ground arrived just seconds before, like an earthquake centering its attention on him, hard to tell its direction of origin. His first thought was of some subway tunnel operating below. But the growl was too hectic and bubbling. That couldn't be right.

Motherfu—

Ground and rock blasted around him in a bombastic explosion, a blue glow deep within it. A huge force surged against Bennett's feet, hurling his body through the air until he smashed against a wall and crashed to the ground. Chunks of stone landed on him, striking like dumbbells lobbed at his head. Most of him was buried under a mound of debris.

His ears were ringing again. He couldn't even hear, but he felt where she was—airborne now, veering in to attack again. *So that's how we're doing it? Fine. Time to change tactics.*

With a fierce discharge of Rapture from his shoulders, Bennett cleared the rock pile off of him and rose to his feet. There wasn't much time to get ready; Hannah was closing in. But at least I can see her. Straining to focus, he conjured a heavier set of plate armor—one made to take hits—which slid over his body and locked into place like train cars connecting, shielding nearly every inch of him.

With his hand out, he conjured a robust handle that connected to his wrist gauntlet, while a thick shield of luminous cobalt manifested just in front of him. The dimensions were likely enough to handle a blast from a tank, and as it solidified, Bennett wondered if he'd made it too heavy to even lift. Inserting the handle into two slots on the back of the shield, he locked the mechanism with a hefty clang.

"Here, tweety bird."

The Celestial was still diving and turning, trying to throw him off, keeping her distance. *Come on, I'm ready to dance.*

His gaze swept back and forth, keeping Hannah's Eve signature in his crosshairs. But as she took a steep dive near the ground, Bennett suddenly lost her. When she reappeared, her signature and visible form had separated—or at least appeared to. It was all too fast. She was too close. Which one was the real one?

Shit. Now or never!

Slamming down his shield, Bennett set his trap, driving the bottom tip deep into the ground and bracing behind it. Just as Hannah drew near, dozens of spikes a yard long flung themselves out from the front face of the shield.

Bring it on!

He'd gotten her. He had to have. She was far too close. The spikes were aimed directly at her face.

But the split versions of Hannah coalesced with a flash, reappearing a few safe yards away, swooping clear of his trap. A gust of wind flowed over him, and a bombastic laugh escaped Bennett's throat.

She's running scared! Hannah soared away and circled him from above.

Lifting the shield free from the ground, he aimed the blue spikes forward. *Yeah, come on and try it again.*

She fluttered back and forth, seemingly playing, until a glint near her began to twinkle. It could have been a firefly for all Bennett knew—swirling around, getting closer, then farther away. Closer, then farther. Was it light reflecting off her armor or blade? For a moment he lost complete track of Hannah and focused only on the glinting orb.

What the hell is that?

Then he realized what it was—but too late.

If his dodge had been even a split second later, it all could have been over. A Celestial spear impacted his spiked shield, exploding with blue fire and a colossal boom. Chunks of Rapture iron blasted everywhere, ricocheting off Bennett's armor as he leaped for cover. More debris struck him—some glancing off, others trying very hard to bury him once again.

Rolling and rising from the ground, he prepared to retaliate when something hit him so hard his brain started to ring. He had no clue what it was, but it felt solid and heavy. Blue light flickered around him, and he caught a glimpse of wings before everything went gray, and he was suddenly off his feet.

The ground and his face collided, sending a caustic agony through him that froze his senses, reminding him of playground injuries where shock and fright sometimes overshadowed the pain. His mouth opened, and a dry siphoning sound escaped—no air in his lungs. It took what felt like an eternity of writhing on the ground to get them full again, but that did nothing to prevent him from sounding like a dying vacuum when he tried to speak.

"Whaaa thaaaa faaaaaa?" He managed to roll himself onto his

back, stinging his whole body with the impact. *Ow.* His right arm managed to rise a few inches, intending to lift his visor but unable to, sinking back to the ground with a clang. *How am I even still . . . conscious?*

The thumping of stone feet approached, and a wide, dark shadow loomed over him. The wings of the general spread above, catching the golden light of Doloros.

"Is this a game to thee?" her enormous Celestial voice bellowed. Bennett couldn't gather a response, his head so full of stars. "I am but one Celestial, yet you believe yourself capable of defeating hundreds?"

"I haaaad yuuuuu," his frail, raspy voice whispered.

"Those words are nothing," Hannah replied. The massive blue form stepped back a few feet and folded its wings. With a whooshing sound coinciding with a steady transformation, it shrank until it was a silhouette the size of a woman.

"I felt that cockiness. Legitimate conflict should not be exciting. Legitimate strength should not be, either." Hannah stepped into the light, her usually wrinkleless brow furrowed into a tight stack of folds. "You're wasting my time, even when I have none to waste. So, knock off the bullshit, remember that you're not just a guy who can jerk himself and others around on Earth anymore, and wipe that smirk off your face. You're not ready. If nothing changes, you never will be."

She turned her back to him and stepped away, leaving Bennett with, "Get out of my sight. I want to sleep. Go back up top until you figure out if you're really up to this. And don't come back until you're sure."

THE CHAMBER

An alarm was blaring, piercing through the chaos. Leigh was assaulted by blue and white strobes, passing by another rotating light attached to the wall. The hall was bustling, everyone scrambling with last-minute items, the commotion intensified by the wailing clamor. Leigh was among those hurrying, trying to keep pace with Aluqa, who had never moved through the station's halls so quickly, tarnishing the graceful, floating visage she worked so fervently to preserve. The rooks in their path parted as easily as bamboo when she and her entourage drew near. If they didn't get out of the way in time, Skraga would let loose with hollers of "Out of the way!" or "Rooks clear!"

Getting into Aluqa's entourage had never been a goal for Leigh, but when the opportunity arose following the heist of minillia, it seemed foolish to say no. At the very least, it might have been a chance to get closer and learn more from her. It didn't take long for Leigh to appreciate the opportunity. For the past nine days—a very busy nine days—she had acted as Aluqa's most trusted advisor.

Taking the position came with the unfortunate task of escorting misbehaving rooks to the Ketinolum, which Leigh now knew contained a Cavalier with a brilshak, the same cattle-prod torture device they had used on the freight captain. Since her days as a rook, she had come to see the wisdom in sending the bad apples for punishment, making it clear to the others what would happen if they lowered the quality of the entire organization. *I was able to be trusted to not be an idiot when I was a rook. But can't say the same about the rest. Aluqa is right, they need regulation. They actually crave it.*

Taking the unworthy rooks by the arm and escorting them to their penance was never an issue for Leigh, and she did so promptly whenever ordered. Even on the day she was forced to walk Danika, her old roommate—a bubbly soul who loved her rock collection—down the dark hall. *She begged and pleaded, but should have known it wouldn't do any good.*

[*The poor thing was pitiable. Definitely not Cavalier material. Not even much of a rook, if I am honest.*]

The remainder of Leigh's time had been spent in service to Aluqa, mostly running errands, including delivering all of her meals to her chambers. When another charity gala required Miss Morinnean's presence, Leigh was brought along as her assistant and date. The professor had been fully integrated, yet Leigh somehow felt she knew even less about Aluqa than before. Complicated and often aloof, the leader always ate alone and never allowed anyone into her private quarters. With each new interaction, Leigh had to wonder which Aluqa she would encounter: the great healer, warming one's chest, or the punisher, here to teach and reprimand those who tarnished her legacy. Guessing her motivation from moment to moment was a crapshoot—*and I was never all that fond of gambling.*

Aluqa's excitement for the Cardinal's arrival and the machine he was bringing seemed as thin as tissue paper, even when it was obvious that she was just as desperate to get into UnEarth as anyone. The lackluster way she answered any questions Leigh tried to ask about the Cardinal's creation begged the question of whether they were headed towards a curse or a blessing.

She still won't tell me anything about the plan they cooked up for attacking Trivium.

[*I have no idea what to prepare or how to proceed. It would seem I am flying blind.*]

Each word dropped by Aluqa seemed to hold the potential to be a part of a much bigger puzzle, randomly distributed from her mouth. During inspection strolls, she would often whisper under her breath, then raise her voice to offer something unrelated and confounding, such as, "Because by then, it won't matter. The war will have already been won."

On that day, Leigh typed into her Gauntlet, replying with, "What war?" though Aluqa seemed not to hear and continued muttering to herself. It sometimes felt as though Leigh were following a senile invalid around, waiting for a crumb of knowledge that would never come, such as where a hidden treasure was buried. But this was still the woman from the stories of the great UnEarth creature hunter, and Leigh had already witnessed her prowess the night she killed a swarm of pure Aidaas Scythes. However, since that night, something had changed. The leader of the Surface appeared more worn with each passing day, her skin growing patchy and dry, her cheeks sinking as if weights had been placed on top of them. Something ominous was building in her mind, and whatever it was, she was keeping it all to herself.

I don't know what she is afraid of, but it's here now. Leigh studied the side of Aluqa's face as they moved down the hall. Her head was so closely shaven that parts of it were rubbed red. The gown draped over her was a cerulean masterpiece of simplicity, its billowing sleeves stopping shy of her forearms, allowing the multicolored rings on her fingers to glisten. A regal power flowed through her hurried steps, assuring Leigh she had made the right choice in the woman she chose to follow. *I couldn't do whatever she's about to. No way.*

[*But that does not mean that she is perfect and will not need me and the others. Whatever comes inside, the Cavaliers will have to be ready to jump in.*]

Presently, they were headed to the main hall, along with the rest of Station Five, mostly trailing behind them. Everyone was required to attend the arrival of the Cardinal and his people.

"The barracks is ready?" Aluqa asked Bulltress, the fourth in their entourage.

A pack of rooks slammed on the brakes just in time to avoid crashing into them.

"Ready," Bulltress said. "Our guests will be good and cozy. If not, I'll chop off some of their arms. The rest won't make a peep about it."

"Pleasant as always, but no limbs are to be chopped off, am I clear? And what about the gold? Did you search every nook and cranny?"

"There's not so much as a speck of gold or yellow or orange anywhere on the premises. We triple-checked. Even got rid of the corn. The Cardinal's eyes will be spared."

"Wonderful," Aluqa said. "And the mine, Skraga? How did we do?"

"Hit six barrels, boss," Skraga replied, sounding exhausted, hoarse, and completely downtrodden. "I told them to run on minimal crew until final shutdown."

"Wasn't the record five barrels? Well done, Member Grassrock. You should be proud."

"We should have hit seven, boss. Could have. I'm sorry. I hate letting you down." Skraga ended with a sniffle.

"Oh, my dear Skraga," Aluqa said, "I'm fairly certain I don't deserve you."

When Aluqa entered the main hall, everyone inside froze. The looks on their faces were priceless, caught somewhere between swooning for "my hero" and kids who were just caught drinking their parents' booze. While slowing only slightly, she let her gaze drift about, giving them all a moment with her glistening brown eyes, reminding them who their trusted leader was. When she came to a halt near the main doors and turned around, the alarms ceased. There were residual murmurs among the members, but the majority were fervently waiting for what she might say. Taking her position behind her left shoulder, Leigh waited along with them. When Aluqa turned over that shoulder, catching Leigh off guard, she whispered, "Just like you, I now have no fear. Because I know I am already forgiven. It is a wonderful feeling. Thank you."

She smiled and lightly kissed the air before turning her attention to the waiting rooks and Cavaliers who had gathered in formation facing the doors. The upper members looked on from a platform off the second-floor grated walkway, effectively a balcony section. Like a high-tier guerrilla military preparing to greet a general adorned with hundreds of medals, the Surface members stood at casual attention, some with stern faces and high chins, while others appeared a little more . . . "loose."

"Get them ready," Aluqa said to Skraga.

"Thysia!" Skraga bellowed at the crowd.

"Thono!" the station members shouted back, jumping into a slightly tighter attention formation.

Aluqa took the guardrail in front of her in both hands. "Here we are, at this moment. You, my great Surface, videnties all, have prepared for this day with impeccable determination. I am humbled to stand before you. Through these doors will soon enter the cofounder of this organization. Many of you have never met the Cardinal, as he has been on an extended mission expanding the Surface into the Americas. But he and his people are to be welcomed as though they are the very same members standing beside you. We all have a shared purpose, and with the power the Cardinal has brought with him, and is graciously sharing with us, we will finally have a chance to see that purpose fulfilled."

The members began to cheer as another alarm went off with a trilling shriek, this time a muddier, lower vibration. It was the alarm of the main doors.

Aluqa chuckled and lifted her head to shout over the noise. "Make me proud!"

The machinery in the doors suddenly moaned, and a hiss of steam escaped somewhere within the assembly. Slowly, the doors began to open. Scanning the faces of those gathered, Leigh observed a mixture of reactions among the members of the station. Fans of the Cardinal were obvious, like little kids about to burst with excitement at the prospect of seeing their Great One in person for the first time. A few—mostly those who seemed more intelligent than the average member—looked as though they were about to witness a river break through and flood the station.

As the doors opened to reveal the wide tunnel on the other side, a stomping of feet in march approached. A group of thirty men and women emerged from the shadows a few dozen yards away, dressed in impeccable blue uniforms. Across their chests was a symbol featuring two thick vertical columns, with short bisecting lines crossing each column, as though a capital H had been broken in half and messily reassembled. Many of them wore sunglasses, and their postures were rigid, faces as emotionless as Celestials. As they neared the main doors, their heads slowly scanned from side to side, seemingly searching for imperfections.

Or threats.

(i feel like i saw these guys on one of Megadeth's album covers)

From behind them in the tunnel, two massive objects came into view in the light. Looming behind the thirty members were two hulking storage containers being driven in on trucks. The members of Station Five looked on with awe and confusion as the trucks pulled in and parked just halfway through the doors, stopping with heavy clangs and sagging to rest. The new arrivals halted and locked their hands behind their backs, stomping into place in front of the trucks.

Whoa, what the hell am I looking at? Are these even Surface members? This is an underground mine, not a diplomatic envoy, people. Let's calm down.

[*It is already worrisome to see such rigidness, and that comes from someone who adores order and austerity.*]

The line of the Cardinal's people parted as a tall, bald figure approached from the rear. When he stepped forward, Leigh set her eyes on a gray-skinned man with impeccable posture and thin limbs. The many layers of robes in varying blue shades he wore were trimmed with silver and white. What little skin wasn't covered was unnaturally smooth and hairless, tightly wrapped over a skeletal structure made of flat planes and hard lines. *(and this dude was definitely on an Iron Maiden album cover)*

What immediately struck Leigh was the lack of light radiating from his Eve-creature eyes.

[*I take it he has been drained of his Rapture almost completely.*]

At his side was an advisor, a bulky man with a short, tight haircut of bleach-blond hair and a scrunched-in face, wearing what looked like a deep blue tactical vest over his uniform. On the other side of the Cardinal was Pahlanksha, their hair and matching suit now fully magenta. A tablet was clutched in their hand, and they appeared tired, the warmth in their eyes faded, like a person jet-lagged from a business trip. The past few weeks, they had been away from the station, which was normal—nothing worth questioning. Pahlanksha would often leave for weeks on end to accomplish their task of recruiting for the Surface. But Leigh assumed they operated exclusively in Europe and would have never guessed they'd been with the Cardinal in America.

What were they doing for him over there?

The Cardinal reached the front of the company, and his people closed the line behind him. His eyes, which were all too human, glanced around the main hall, seeming unimpressed. With his head drifting about as though it were aloft in zero gravity, it was clear his attention was not yet on anyone or anything in particular, especially Aluqa.

Softly to her entourage, she said, "Let's go," and Aluqa moved out.

Leigh, Skraga, and Bulltress stayed close as they approached the Cardinal and the two beside him. Even though she was meeting teammates, Leigh felt like she was approaching rivals at a championship match before the coin toss; though the blond man with the vest was mostly to blame. Pahlanksha managed to toss a small wink Leigh's way just before the parties halted.

Aluqa and the Cardinal met a few feet from each other.

"Cardinal Royce," Aluqa said with a nod.

"Miss Morinnean," the Cardinal replied in a throaty, dry voice, speaking in a slow, drawn-out cadence, gradually acknowledging her bit by bit. "My dear creation, that of number five. This has deteriorated. To further pronounce, the smell has degraded. A field of offense is created. This is thanks to you? Wonder, I, how much worse does it get?"

"The station is in fine condition, as is our organization. No issues of note are present," Aluqa said. "You and your delegation are most welcome and honor us with your presence."

"It is mine—I assure you. That which hath the honor," the Cardinal said.

Leigh examined the details in the Cardinal's face. The few nearly imperceptible wrinkles in his skin followed geometric patterns, tracing straight paths. As purple as eggplant, his angular lips sat four inches below where a reasonable person might expect them to be, well south of his philtrum, stretched like a pull shade.

"Prepared to completion? The gathering task?" he asked.

"It is," Aluqa said.

"The count which is final?"

"Three thousand eighty-five barrels."

"Impressive. This is, in the last days, though a marginal number still."

"Member Grassrock is to thank for the increase in production," Aluqa said, motioning to Skraga, who jumped to attention.

"Ah, it was nothing," Skraga said, turning bashful.

"This truth rings," the Cardinal said. "You, that one, were capable of increasing to this degree all production, all along, yet did not do?" He glowered at Skraga, like a Siberian tiger in slow pursuit.

"Oh, uh . . ." She closed in on herself and began rubbing one of her arms. "I guess I never, I mean I didn't ever think that—"

"Enough," Aluqa interjected. "We are immensely proud of her and her team's achievement, as well as Member Bulltress, whose team rehabilitated the south wing for your company's barracks. And you remember Member Silverthorn." She presented Leigh.

Locking eyes with the Cardinal, Leigh remained stoic. She could read nothing in his gaze and suddenly felt smaller than a speck of dust. *Is he judging me or looking through me? I can't tell.*

"Do not. I," the Cardinal finally said, turning away from her.

"The Surface members of Station Five are the finest I've ever had the pleasure of serving," Aluqa said boldly. "I believe you will find the entire facility has been well maintained."

"Admirable, nearly, that you find that belief valid. The seeing shall be done by myself," said the Cardinal. "That alone shall fulfill the need for proof."

"As you wish," Aluqa said.

The Cardinal returned his wandering, judgmental gaze to meet her eyes. "This room is needed—you will vacate. Assembling of the gift will commence. Eight o'clock will begin. This is the ceremony."

"We will be here," Aluqa said.

"Pleased," he said. "Now, I will be excused. Rest will commence. Undisturbed, are they? My quarters remain so?"

"Yes, your quarters are as you left them," Aluqa said. "Skraga, if you could please escort the Cardinal—"

"No sense or need," he said, extending a stiff arm, palm facing Skraga. As he crossed to leave, he forced Leigh to step aside to clear his way. His long legs had taken him halfway to the door when he halted and tilted his chin up over his left shoulder to address Aluqa curtly. "Morinnean, visiting my chamber, you may do. The time is one hour."

"Yes. I will," she answered, her voice suddenly chilled with tension.

Departing the room a moment later, the Cardinal left behind his advisor in the tactical vest, with a name panel reading *Opal Graine*, who forced his cramped lips open enough to smile, revealing a mouth filled with silver.

"That will be all," Opal said, his words messy like a chubby kid getting his face squeezed by a manic aunt, ushering the heads of Station Five out of their own main hall.

Aluqa's face was obscured, but Leigh could guess the expression she was wearing: one of annoyed, simulated graciousness. "Let my people know if you need anything," she began.

"We won't," Opal said without disturbing his squished grin.

Pahlanksha, who had also stayed behind, neither supported nor opposed what Opal was saying. They looked as though they had been forced to listen to a lot of nonsense from him for several hours and likely just wanted some peace and privacy.

"Let's go," Aluqa said finally, sounding utterly disappointed, and turned to Skraga. "Send them back."

"Station Five, you're dismissed!" Skraga bellowed at the members, who dispersed, rubbernecking at their counterparts from America and the hulking containers on the trucks behind them. Aluqa's team was the last to leave. Just before the door closed behind them, Leigh noticed that the Cardinal's people had already begun unloading the containers from the trucks. Then the doors slammed shut.

The members had been dismissed for a little over three hours when a vibration from the Gauntlet on her wrist buzzed. A message had come through her beeper. The number was Aluqa's. It read: *My Chambers*. As she had done dozens of times that week already, Leigh went to the second story of the east wing and knocked on Aluqa's door. But this time, instead of the door opening just a crack, enough to get only a glimpse, a booming voice called from the other side.

"Come in."

The voice was Aluqa's, but the power behind it resonated as if she were speaking from inside a grain silo. When Leigh opened the door, she stepped into a quaint, softly lit apartment designed for ultimate simplicity. The white-and-silver walls were accented by wood and navy-blue furniture, warming what might have otherwise been a sterile atmosphere.

Turning to her right, a vicious, harrowing face appeared. An enormous mouth cavity stretched wide, open and pointed her way. The long, jagged, razor-sharp teeth filling it resembled some horrid deep-sea creature, matching its body, which seemed to swim through the air. If she'd been able to feel fear, she would have screamed. Leigh stepped around the form to find a whole skeletal structure, stretched and kinked like a snake, with ten clawed arms tinted a deep gray with black spots. Support beams drilled into the floor and wall held it in an attack posture.

Previously an Archfiend, it belonged to the Aili clan. Leigh knew their body type well, having seen dozens of them in the forest near her parents' cabin in Montana the night Joseph took the stones. Studying it, she found a hole the size of a fifty-cent piece in its breastplate.

Just like she said—chest.

Numerous skulls of UnEarth creatures decorated the wall. [*Including the others scattered throughout the station, I count two hundred three kills. How many more trophies could there be?*]

At the center of the assemblage of skulls was a small shadow box. Inside lay a dirty, pointed shard from a broken plate aimed straight upward. Inscribed on the small plaque on the box's frame were the words *från mormor. Swedish. I think it says "from grandma."*

"Thank you for coming," Aluqa said from somewhere out of sight. "Don't let any of my pets scare you. In here."

Entering a side hall, Leigh moved to the bedroom and found someone standing in front of a long mirror. It took a moment to realize it was Aluqa; as her posture had gone from wilted to erect and bold. A striking confidence radiated from her stance, and the sunken crevices in her face had filled in, becoming smooth surfaces with a luminous sheen. The bags that had been accumulating under her eyes for the past few weeks were all but erased, as though wiped away.

Most unfamiliar of all was the voice coming from her, no longer peppered with sawdust or scratching the ear. This was a steadfast, boundless tone, seeming to resonate from within the very earth surrounding them.

With a slight smile, she admired herself and her rings in the mirror. The cerulean dress had been discarded, replaced by a white ensemble with black accents.

"Could you?" she turned, revealing her gown's unzipped back.

(shit, that's what you wanted?) With a nod, Leigh moved to zip the dress, but could only get it halfway up, when the zipper stopped near Aluqa's shoulders. *(damn, girl)*

[*I do not remember her being so . . . broad.*] With a grunt, Leigh strained, hoping the dress fabric was tough enough. When the zipper was fully raised, Aluqa released her breath and settled into it, her face softening as she gazed at them both in the mirror with a mix of wonder and melancholy.

"You really are special," she said. "You know that, right?" Leigh nodded, glancing at Aluqa's arm and noticing a soft patch of bruised skin with a black dot at its center, near her inner elbow. The obvious track mark was quickly ignored. "You're the only one I trust. On this whole planet. The only one who's proved themselves. Truly. The only one who's known suffering. What you endured with the nameless, it's something no one should ever have to experience. You've completed your penance for the world. It should ask no more of you."

Lifting her hand, still gazing into the mirror, Aluqa gently kissed

Leigh's knuckles and rubbed her thumb over her skin tenderly. "Though, sadly, I will. Nothing will ever be enough, I'm afraid. Not until the end, which is a wonderful place. I'm sure of it. I dream about it often. So often, I've started wondering if it's even there. But if I haven't found it, that just means I haven't fulfilled my duties yet. This means neither have you."

Leigh signed, "Will you tell me what's about to happen?"

"You know I can't. But please don't worry—I'll keep you safe no matter what. I would let this planet we love burn to the ground before I let anything bad happen to you."

A quiet moment followed. Aluqa and Leigh locked eyes, holding fast. It wasn't clear if Leigh should respond or simply nod. *Why is she saying all this? Does she think we're about to march to our deaths?* Eventually, her hand was released and Aluqa took a final glance at herself in the mirror, straightening her dress.

"The end must be out there somewhere. And I wouldn't want to find it with anyone else. Only you." She turned around and smiled down on Leigh with her lips shut tight. "Now, let's go find it."

When the time came to reassemble for the Cardinal's presentation, Aluqa departed her chamber with her coterie, finding the rooks of Station Five lining the halls near the east wing. None dared enter the main hall before her. Some looked like kids on Christmas waiting for Mom and Dad to wake up so they could open presents. As the leadership passed by, the others joined the parade.

Following Aluqa through the doors into the main hall, Leigh was struck by the stench of industry: rust, metal shavings, packaging materials, industrial glues, soldering wire, oil, grease, and air filters. Then, there it was, just in front of her: the machine in the center of the room, a slumbering colossus. Finally, the professor was looking at it—the thing from her deepest dreams—but a protective tarp kept her from knowing anything about it other than it was as tall as a Winnebago and a little more than half its length. Not staring was impossible as she followed Aluqa across the room and up the stairs to the second-level platform, where they settled into the square balcony nook overlooking the hall.

Pahlanksha was already there, waiting patiently with their hip leaning against the right-side railing. It looked like they'd had a shower and some good rest since arriving. The new suit they'd changed into was casual and gray with mint-green accents, and their long hair was pulled back into a tight bun. With hardly a nod, they acknowledged Aluqa and company.

Their arms crossed loosely, they resembled a kid at a sleepover who didn't want to do what the other kids were doing. *Wish I could read them better.* They knew as much about the Surface as Aluqa, maybe even more in some areas, and nothing seemed to phase them, as if they always knew exactly what was about to happen. But today—what was surely supposed to be an exciting day of achievement—they looked especially nonplussed, which was not encouraging. Since returning with the Cardinal from America, their true allegiance seemed unclear. Leigh wanted to believe Pahlanksha would never let Aluqa and the others fall into harm's way, but there was no way of knowing.

I mean, they did give me a wink. That's not nothing. Might not be something, but it's not nothing.

The rooks and the remaining Cavaliers filed into the hall silently, assuming the same positions they had earlier but pushed back several feet to make room for the mammoth hidden object. Moments later, as if choreographed, the Cardinal's people marched through the doors and took their places lining the perimeter of the room. With everyone inside, the doors slammed shut.

From several yards above, Leigh studied the rooks. Most looked either excited or nervous, and she couldn't blame them. They had no idea what was about to happen. Rumors about the Cardinal's visit had been spreading for weeks, but no one really knew what the machine was or what lay ahead.

When one of the Cardinal's aides whispered something in Aluqa's ear, she nodded and approached the balcony stage. "It is time," she announced. "Now, my members, I give you the Cardinal."

The door on the ground floor opened, and the Cardinal entered with Opal, still clad in a tactical vest, close behind. The members remained quiet as he leisurely marched into the room, his head and shoulders high and proud, up the stairs, and onto the grated platform, coming to rest side by side with Aluqa, facing the others below.

Placing his hands behind his back, he took a moment before speaking. "Sons. Daughters. Children of the Surface. Cardinal Edwin Royce, this is my title. Upon seeing you, the heart inside me fills with joy and pride. Longing for the presence of you, I have. In capable hands, you have been. This, I know." He motioned to Aluqa, who barely acknowledged it. "For great time, I have been away. This indicates, wrongly, I care for you not. The opposite. This is truth. This absence reveals the care in me, so deep, for you. In your persons, to myself, is viewed the hope of humans. We have been fighting, some of us long, to save this world from UnEarth. The tyranny. Until now. This moment. But what is? Great change. The human delegates', this trial. This has found an end. Three prisoners, convicted. All. Condemned. Execution. This act occurs. The time is six days."

A murmur rippled through the crowd. The Cardinal allowed them a moment to react while Leigh's eyes narrowed. She could barely believe it. This seemed way too soon for the trial to be over.

She was surprised that she felt so strongly against the idea of the executions. Yes, she wished ill of Alex Barker and Bennett Hunter, and the Medolian Izaiah, but the UnEarth Senate was wrong if they thought anyone was to blame for Joseph's actions other than Joseph himself. The nameless demon had been a driven and selfish individual, and he would have hated seeing the glory go to anyone else. Leigh wouldn't have it any other way. He and the Medolian Chloe could take all the blame just fine. The trial made no sense to begin with and solved nothing.

"It's true," Aluqa said. "It is done. The trial was observed by every creature on every world of UnEarth. Nothing has ever captured their attention in the same way. The execution will be one of the largest gatherings in the history of Trivium City. In attendance will be the most powerful creatures in all of UnEarth—not just politically. The lords of the Eve. Even the greatest of them."

A louder gasp went through the crowd. Leigh nearly doubled over. *She couldn't possibly mean . . .*

"Yes," Aluqa said, raising her voice over the chattering rooks. "The great High Lord himself. Gabriel."

The noise in the hall became a torrent.

(you've got to be kidding me)

[*It is almost unthinkable. He has not left the throne room in—*]

Raising her hands, Aluqa quieted the members. "Yes, it's true. Somehow this was enough to make him rise from his throne for the first time in nearly two thousand years. Word is he was heavily invested in the trial. Hywyn made every attempt to pardon Hunter, which failed. Our sources tell us the High Lord may even be on Trivium as we speak."

The Cardinal interjected, overtaking her. "A gift. This is. We are handed this, to strike. Created, the Surface was, to search for this. This moment."

Aluqa jumped in again. "The Cardinal is saying that we'll make the UnEarth scum regret using humanity as they do—starting with their greatest leader."

The crowd cheered, clearly energized but still uncertain about why they were being told this. There was little they could do about the news.

"Long ago, we promised you we would find a way to let you into their world, where we could continue the fight," Aluqa continued. "Until now, we have let you down. But, my friends, I am pleased to say the day has finally come. You have long wished to walk through the lands you've read about and see these things with your own eyes before you destroy them. Now we will give you that chance."

"Your journeys, far and forlorn," the Cardinal added. "But higher, farther, there is. Always. If desired, seeing the level of next . . . to give the self to fight. For Earth. This is the reason."

"This may be the greatest act the Surface will ever commit," Aluqa declared. "The whole world and every creature in the cess-pools of UnEarth will know what we have accomplished. Each and every one of you—every mind and pair of hands—will put a hole in Trivium so large it will never recover. And you, the greatest minds and hands humanity has ever known, will do this as one. None shall be higher. None shall be lower. You will no longer be rooks or Cavaliers but the Sanctioned—an unstoppable force. One that will march to Trivium City and eradicate the lords of Un-Earth with a single blow."

The crowd murmured. A few shouted as if they'd just found Jesus. "Yes, I know it sounds implausible, but it is true. And I will prove it to you." Aluqa stepped aside. "Cardinal Royce, if you would."

Nodding solemnly, the Cardinal motioned to his people. "Rise."

With no sound at all, the tarp over the machine was lifted, re-vealing what looked like a huge metal doorway without a door—a gateway into a stout hallway. The walls of the hall were blank, but inside the machine lurked what Leigh imagined was something akin to the guts of an MRI machine: crude robotics and circuitry. The outer shell was thoroughly Celestial: immaculate, pristine, shimmering blue steel. Only one variation came in a wide, raised lip at the halfway point.

"The gateway," the Cardinal announced. "Merely human, no longer. Following the act. Those who travel through. Something else—you become. Powers you will have—but comprehend not. All of this, soon."

The Cardinal then called out to one of his members on the ground floor. "Bartholomew."

A man stepped out of the lineup and approached the machine, flanked by a crew of three waiting at the mouth of the chamber. His eyes were unwavering, with the focus of an Olympic diver poised on the board, deep black eyebrows clenched tight.

When he reached the machine, he halted and turned his chin up toward the Cardinal. "Yes, sir."

"Lucky. The first. This is you," the Cardinal said.

"Yes, sir," Bartholomew replied, his expression blank but a faint eagerness evident in his voice. "Lucky. I."

"Worthy. Go. The time is now."

Bartholomew moved to the chamber and approached the doorway as the machine came to life, like a lumbering beast awakened from a nap—guttural and roaring. Lights and steam poured from the open mouth, ready to devour him.

"Bartholomew," the Cardinal boomed, "long wished, in you, the chance. This is correct? The fight against oppressors?"

"Yes."

"And yet, you, no tools."

"No. No tools."

"What tools? This would be the want—power and might. What shade?"

"Rapture."

"This is good. The strongest. By long and far. Bartholomew, that one, this has been the wish. The power, this can be given. This, by I. Requirement, there is one—this is trust."

"The trust, in me. There," Bartholomew said.

The Cardinal opened his arms wide, as though offering a hug to his acolyte. "Then forward, that one. Son. Mine."

The three members at the mouth of the chamber, wearing medical gear, approached Bartholomew as he removed his jacket and shirt.

During the process, the Cardinal spoke. "Sons. Daughters. Mine. We bear witness. Rebirth. Man, Bartholomew. That one will approach. Fear is not found. The first step is this."

Bartholomew held still as one of the medical team gave him a shot from an injection gun. The liquid inside appeared to glow a dull blue. *(the hell is this shit?)*

"The tonic. Choose your shade. This will," the Cardinal explained.

Bartholomew didn't react as the injection was administered, and soon the syringe was empty.

"With tonic in body, Bartholomew will commence. Rapture will cement. The chamber does this."

Bartholomew entered the metallic blue mouth as the machine activated. Leigh refused to let herself even blink, determined to watch as closely as possible until the very moment he disappeared.

The blare of the machine did not deter the Cardinal. "Now, in the heart. The chamber will change. Compatible with Eve. This will be him, and you."

The clamor in the room swelled, like a fleet of jets taking off in a middle school gymnasium. A few seconds passed before a blast of blue light flooded out of the chamber. Bartholomew's footsteps, from unheard to resounding, echoed like monstrous boulders being heaved to the ground.

The light flashed and pulsed, giving off heat while a smell reminiscent of mothballs and rain began to fill the room. Then it shut off, and the machine powered down slowly, quieting like an air raid siren.

Bartholomew emerged from the other side, his chest heaving. A soft blue glow radiated around him. After a few steps, he halted, and a plume of steam was released.

"Boy, the feeling in you. Describe this," the Cardinal asked.

"Impervious," Bartholomew replied.

"To us. Show this," the Cardinal commanded.

Two of Bartholomew's teammates moved around the chamber toward him, each wielding a sledgehammer. Stretching his arms out wide, like a man preparing for a belly flop, he let them swing at will, the hammers crashing against his skin, cracking as though they were striking a concrete wall covered in ice. His face remained blank throughout the assault. After five or six swings each, the men stopped, and Bartholomew lowered his arms. Though his skin glimmered with a slight, frozen blue, he bore no bruises.

He's not even shivering.

Even Leigh's jaw dropped. The guy had indeed been given the powers of the Eve. Not only that—he'd chosen his shade. The members from Station Five approached the gateway like thirsty travelers finding a gushing hydrant in a drought-ridden desert, awe in their eyes, hands slowly rising to touch it—unlike the Cardinal's people, who hadn't budged an inch since arriving.

"You have been shown," the Cardinal said, pride swelling in his voice. "Now, you see. Now, you go."

The Station Five crew raised their hands to the Cardinal and

Aluqa, shouting in belligerent declarations over one another. Nine Cavaliers charged down from the second story to join them, and Leigh was about ready to go too. This was surreal. But something felt off. It was too perfect, too seamless. She remembered that Alex Barker and Bennett Hunter had both struggled to harness their Eve powers, yet Bartholomew had adapted almost immediately.

As though he'd already been through the machine once before.

[*It would stand to reason. Tests were surely conducted prior to their traveling here.*]

Sure . . . Leigh eyed the Cardinal's people. The sunglasses they wore now seemed less about uniformity and more about concealing possibly glowing, Eve-powered eyes.

Was I right all along? Is this an invasion?

Leigh glanced at Pahlanksha, hoping to see if her skepticism appeared justified. Based on their body language, it seemed it was.

Aluqa addressed the crowd, many of whom now had tears streaming down their faces. "Now, please, my friends. Let's not lose perspective. We have this tool, yes, this miracle, but what's important is what we do with it. Smart, tactful—this will be our way. With the power of UnEarth flowing through your veins, you will take the fight to them when they are most vulnerable. You and the members of the Surface from the stations around the world will attack all at once, swarming the High Lord by the thousands. Then, we will unleash our weapon—the secret attack developed by the Cardinal himself to kill creatures of the Eve. They will not be able to suppress it."

A chilled hush swept through the people.

"I regret we cannot tell you more about what will happen, but spies are lurking in every dark corner. Only the Cardinal and I know the full extent of the assault's design. The details will be given to you just prior to your departure. This is the only way to ensure success. You will not be given more than you can handle. You all will be able to help."

"The Surface will act—this as a wave. Cleanse the Tribunal. This will be done," the Cardinal proclaimed. "Civil war will come. Destroyed, from the inside. To reshape. Regrow. But separate. Forever apart."

The members cheered once again.

"This will take full commitment. Are you ready?" Aluqa asked. They roared in response. "Good. In five days, it will begin. Contemplate your shade. The choice is yours. All are within your grasp. But do not take this lightly. It may be the most important decision you ever make."

Later that night, after the station had become so quiet a rat's fart could echo down every hall, Leigh lay in her bed. The great question was supposed to be on her mind: which shade would she choose? Aluqa had instructed her to give them all equal consideration, but she had no intention of doing that. She'd always known what shade she would choose. While the others would likely spend the next five days going back and forth until they drove themselves crazy, Leigh would patiently wait to give the answer she'd had for two years.

When there came a knock at the door, her first thought was *(this is it, the ambush. the Cardinal's people are here to kill us all)* But upon opening it, she found Pahlanksha standing there. Leigh looked at them questioningly, then shrugged. Letting them in was her first instinct, but she quickly reconsidered and kept the door ajar, blocking Pahlanksha from entering.

"Am I disturbing you?" they asked.

Leigh signed no.

"May I come in?"

Leigh lightly shook her head.

"I understand. See, smart. Box of bananas, what did I say?" They lowered their voice to a whisper. "You've figured out this game quickly. I kind of wish you hadn't, but that's also why I'm here. I probably don't have long. She keeps a close eye on you. Hopefully, the Cardinal's presence has distracted her enough. She got today's dose of his juice but usually goes back for more. I'm here because I think you should hear something—something she doesn't want you to know, but you deserve to."

Leigh began to slowly close the door, but Pahlanksha pushed it back open.

"I get it. She's wound you around her finger so tight you can't imagine letting go now. Nobody understands better than me. But the mission she and the Cardinal are sending you on is not what they say."

"What do you mean? The machine doesn't really work?" Leigh signed.

"Oh, it works," Pahlanksha said. "That's not the problem. The members will all get exactly what they've been promised—whether they like it or not. But the whole thing is a farce. None of this plan is truly about killing Gabriel and the Senate. That's just a smokescreen, a possible cherry on top—one the Cardinal knows won't really work."

"He doesn't want revenge?" Leigh asked.

Pahlanksha laughed quietly. "All that man wants is for his daddy to take him back."

"But Celestials don't have dads—" Leigh started to sign.

"An expression, Professor," Pahlanksha cut her off. "What I'm trying to tell you is that you need to be extra careful in the next few days. Don't let your guard down for even a second. Never let your possessions out of your sight. I'm not entirely sure how it's going to come, but I know it will. You're going to get swept up in it, and I, unfortunately, won't be there to help you."

"Why?"

"Because I'm leaving tonight—one last trip. And sadly, our paths may never cross again."

"Why are you telling me this?"

"Because this whole thing has been about you."

After Pahlanksha's last word, a low, resonant yet feminine voice spoke up from just down the hall.

"Such a late hour for a meeting. My my."

Drifting like a ghost, Aluqa rounded the nearby corner and approached Leigh's door, her head held high, eyes wide—revealing the whites above her irises, confident and direct, with a trace of frenzy. Pahlanksha straightened and tightened their expression, avoiding the approaching leader's gaze.

"What's the news?" Aluqa asked, squinting and lifting her shoulders.

"Nothing," Leigh signed.

"Really? It didn't sound like nothing. Though I couldn't make any of it out. Is this true, Pahlanksha? Was it nothing?"

Pahlanksha beamed and spun to aim the smile at Aluqa. "Nothing the Cardinal wants you to know."

"Is that your new excuse for everything?"

"Just when it's true." Pahlanksha let out a soft giggle.

Aluqa's chin slowly lifted higher, her eyes locked on them. "Then I'm sorry my presence has gotten in the way of your duties." She offered a bite-sized smile of pettiness.

Stuffing their hands into their pockets, Pahlanksha stepped away, locking vaguely manic eyes on Leigh. "Not at all. We were done. Weren't we? Done, yeah? Goodnight, Professor."

When Leigh and Aluqa were alone, the leader turned to her. "It's truly sad how quickly they can be turned. The Cardinal's people. He's been pilfering my best for years. After just a few months over there, just . . . poof. I hardly know them anymore. Pahlanksha has been a loyal friend for many years, but not even they can withstand the influence of Royce. Take their words at face value at your own risk. That's all I will offer. Now"—Aluqa took Leigh's hand and kissed her knuckle once more—"I'll say goodnight."

ASKING FOR A FRIEND

Waking up in the morning and rising from bed was the best part of any day in Felix's eyes. Each new sunrise brought an exciting array of choices, meals, challenges, and sights to behold. Life on Earth was an uplifting joy—every minute of it. It didn't matter that very few pure humans felt the same way; that was only because they didn't know how good they had it. They had nothing to compare life on Earth to, having known only what he called paradise. But Felix was aware of other places where life might exist. None were as pleasant, and some could be called darn near unpleasant.

I know that one all too well, know what I mean?

Mornings were at their best when all required tasks were completed at the same time every day, in the same order and in the same way. Felix could be particular about this. First, he would clean his feet before stepping onto the ground, using a soapy bucket of water he always made sure was kept beside his bed. Next was making his cot and tidying up any last-minute messes in his home, which consisted of said cot, a small end table, and a blanket; to him, an abundance of riches.

He even had a short stack of books next to his pillow, gifts from the owner of the business. However, they mostly served as a stable platform for other items. Felix didn't quite grasp the excitement surrounding reading. People often described looking over perplexing jumbles of letters, or "words", recounting something they could just go look at with the same eyes they were using to read the jumbles with in the first place; but something about that loop had always unsettled him. A few gracious souls had tried over the years to teach him the meanings behind those jumbles, but nothing they said ever made any sense, and Felix found himself never caring much or trying very hard to change that.

They always claim reading sparks up imaginings and colored thoughts, but I've never had a problem with those. So, I'm not sure why I would even need to try it. Books were fun to look at when they had pictures, though. *They're like little paintings on every page!* Those he adored. Before his Purging, Felix had never even seen a painting, and had fallen completely in love with the art form upon his arrival on Earth. *We don't really have things like that where I come from.*

With phase one of his morning routine complete, Felix moved on to the next, and most important, phase—*Breakfast!* After taking the single step required to enter his tiny kitchen, he scooped up a cup of uncooked rice from the bag given to him by his boss. Human standards for their food were higher than the peaks of the Pilomines, which meant they often tossed out perfectly good stuff. Much of that good stuff often found its way into Felix's pantry. Many bags and containers even had healthy molds, mealworms, and colonies of little crunchy critters already thriving inside, saving the time and energy it would take to cultivate those himself, and providing Felix with an endless supply of nutritious meals.

The dumb-dumbs don't even charge me for it. I admit I'm pretty smooth when it comes to dealmaking. There's an art to it, after all.

Stepping out of his domicile into the back hall of the Quin-to-Zyan Massage Spa and All-You-Can-Eat Buffet, he turned and locked his front door with a turn of the padlock attached to it, which could have been easily ripped off by any reasonably sized nine-year-old. The location within the building where his front door resided was so ambiguous that it did not have a proper name, such as "entryway," "foyer," or "hallway." At best, his plot of land could be described as "that place over there." The door had been installed on two cheap hinges on a support beam shoved into place with just a pressure fit, next door to the broom closet and cleaning supplies. His proximity to the bottles of bleach, soap, and mop bucket worried his boss and landlord, as it could potentially agitate or poison him, but that couldn't have been further from the truth. Noxious chemicals were as good as potpourri to Felix Niel.

He tried to hurry along. Often, he was what Missus Topsic called "late"—whatever that meant. *I can't exist late. I'm always me. Living the same as I always do.* Felix just took it to mean he was supposed to be at work a little earlier than he thought he was.

Being somewhere according to what the sun and moon told you was bull-hooey. *Even the word is strange. Time . . . tiiime. Tie-mmm. Just weird.* Others described it as a large fabric that allowed people and things to live forward. *A big fabric? And nobody bats an eye? Things don't go in this direction or that. They just are. Some people, I tell ya . . . just another excuse to make us look at numbers all the time. One thing I hate about living away from home—everyone's obsession with these numbers and letters. Know what I mean?*

His commute consisted of a dozen or so steps on soiled yellow tiles. Walking through the curtain at the end of the hall transported him into a new world, one filled with misty, scent-engorged air and tranquility bells playing on a constant six-hour rotation. The atmosphere was intended to make the human customers as docile and relaxed as possible. *It's just great! I get to watch them come in stinking of Grief and leave with Jubilee coming out their holes.*

The first thing to do was fetch his custodial cart and wheel it to the restocking station to load up on the day's supplies. By now he had it all down to a science. Even though he had no idea how many of each item he was taking, he knew what three rolls of toilet paper and five rolls of paper towels looked like.

Apart from Felix's janitorial duties, he was also tasked with re-heating the rocks in the saunas each morning. The only problem was how he was supposed to do it. Missus Topsic specifically hired him because he was an Archfiend; one blast of Wrath could keep the rocks steaming all day. *Amazing savings on the electric bill.* However, Felix loathed having to turn on the hateful energy to do it.

By lunchtime, he had changed the urinal cakes, washed the front and rear windows, polished the pipes in the washroom, and continued his meticulous project of scrubbing the outer wall—a concrete texture so gnarled and rough that he was stuck using a toothbrush and a bucket of soapy water with a spritz of lemon and vinegar. The mess in the main bathroom was a bit larger than usual for a slow morning but proved to be no problem.

I'm sure the boss won't mind if I take my lunch now. Heading to the kitchen, Felix was given his raw chicken breast for the day. Hurrying back to his closet, he happily ate the meat with handfuls of rice from the bag next to his bed. After enjoying his lunch, he washed it all down with a gulp of Earth water from the sink, the taste of which he still couldn't get used to. *It's so light! And dare I say . . . wet?*

With lunch over, Felix excitedly returned to work for the second half of the day, proceeding to clean three massage rooms without any surprises. Upon entering the fourth, he noticed a patron was still inside, obscured behind the changing curtain.

"So sorry, my mistake," he said, ducking away. "I'll come back later. Not a problem. Know what I mean?"

An authoritative woman's voice arose from behind the curtain. "Stay where you are."

Felix froze. A primal part of his core had been struck. The voice was familiar; he knew it, but couldn't place it. *I suddenly have some heebie-jeebies going on.*

"Something I can help you with, Miss?" he asked, then recited from memory, "Here at the Quinto-Zyan Massage Spa and All-You-Can-Eat Buffet, we understand that some clients expect a more full-service experience. However, if you are intending to approach me romantically, I must disappoint you—not only am I not interested, but that also goes against company policy."

"Shut up, you idiot. It's me," the woman said, her voice bordering on booming.

"Ma'am, we have a zero-tolerance policy on employee abuse or harassment. I'm afraid I'm going to have to ask you to—"

"Felix, listen to my voice. Use your senses."

The truth caught up to him like a smack to the back of the head when he realized there was a faint hint of Mallos in the room. Then he caught her scent. *No. It can't be. Why would she be here?* "Mara?" he squeaked. "What are you doing?"

"Don't use my name! Shut the door. What do you think I'm staying hidden for?"

Felix did as told. "I suppose to preserve decency. What on Earth are you hiding from? I thought other people were supposed to be on the run from you."

"Because I refused to stand by the court's decision. As you can imagine, there's nowhere I can safely go now. I'm on my own and need to find the other Medolians—or at least a way to prove our innocence before our name is smeared further."

"I see . . . That sounds fascinating. Would you mind telling me what all of that was supposed to mean?"

"Which part?"

"All of it. Every word. Starting way back at the beginning. None of the things you said in that order made any sense. I heard something about a court case? That sounds kind of boring. Did you come here to bore me?"

"Tell me you're not serious."

"I am being serious, if that's what you're asking me."

"Haven't you been following the news? You've paid no attention to what's been happening since Joseph? What have you been doing for the past two years?"

"Has it really been two years? I thought it had just been one. Wow. You're looking at what I've been up to—no Tribunal or Abyss bombs on my mind. Just keeping my head down. Best thing I know to do."

Mara hung her head and pinched the bridge of her nose. "Batia, grant me strength."

"Are you a customer?" Felix asked. "Or are you here to cause trouble or make an arrest?"

"Have you heard nothing I've said? Do you not understand? I'm here to collect you. It's time to fight once again." Mara quieted herself and slowed her roll. "We need to get going, so grab whatever you need quickly. We don't have much time."

"Collect me? What kind of thing is that to say?"

"Just as Hannah did. Right? Come now, we need help. You're duty-bound."

"So that's what you're asking for? You've got a funny way of doing it. And by the way, you've got that backward. I'm the one who collected Hannah. So you can stop yapping about my duties."

"You say that as though it was providence that you got her involved."

Felix felt foolish for that one. "I don't understand why you're here. You always treated me poorly, remember? I do. Centuries of it. I have no desire to go with you."

"I feel nothing for your cries of leniency. Don't you think Hannah would want you to?"

"Stop it. That's low, even for you. Don't use her against me. You never approved of our friendship. Admit it. That's why I saw so little of her until she divided from you."

"Trust me, she would have wanted this. You may not have been paying attention to your home world while you were here wallowing in your Grief, but I've been in the thick of things, and let me tell you, they are growing dire. This is no time to put your head in the sand. Now, come along. I can explain more on the way."

"Bad? It's *been* bad! Nothing's been right since Hannah left. And nothing felt right for a dozen dimes before that. Humans and their technology are getting out of hand. The Eve is getting rotten—more so all the time. Nobody's talking to anybody! I can't figure out why everyone wants to go around making messes all the time. I guess I'm not one to talk, being a Fiend and all, but still . . . I guess none of it makes any sense."

"Would you shut up already? Have you no pride? What would Hannah think of seeing you like this?"

"That's the last time I let you say something like that to me. It's been a pleasure to see you again, Sentry Loren. Please ring the bell there if you need more towels." Felix started back into the hall.

"Oh, stop being so stubborn!" Mara snapped. "You know she'd still be alive if not for you. Just admit it so we can move on."

That sent Felix's Wrath soaring, enough to cook a thousand sauna rocks. Hatred bubbled to the surface, manifesting as steam rolling off his skin and a sudden, painful growth of his fangs. Stomping back into the room, he slammed the door behind him, roaring with his true Archfiend voice.

"*Take that back!*"

"I will not." Mara folded her arms and relaxed her posture.

Before he could respond, the door behind him burst open, and Missus Topsic's cowboy-hat-topped head poked inside. The curly wig she wore that none of the employees would admit to knowing about was sitting lop-sided. *She must've just come from a nap.* "What is the meaning of this, Felix? I said small bursts of Wrath! You want to scare the humie customers? Settle your ass down."

"Sorry, ma'am."

"Now stop bothering the nice Medolian lady and go clean the benches in room six. Had a Lostros with a skin condition. Wear gloves. Bring extra everything."

"Yes, ma'am."

Missus Topsic tipped her hat to Mara. "Our apologies, Warden Sentry. We're not accustomed to receiving such esteemed guests from the Tribunal. Your services will, of course, be free of charge today."

"Thank you," Mara said, her tone brimming with more satisfaction than Felix liked.

When she finally stepped away, tossing Felix a few more accusatory glances, Missus Topsic left the massage room door open.

"Great, now it'll be awkward passing her in the hall. Thanks a lot," he said.

"She knows who I am? I don't believe I've ever seen her before," Mara said.

"Guess so. But I didn't know you got promoted. That's . . . nice. For you . . . I guess."

But Mara wasn't listening to him, her eyes glued to the open door, watching it like it owed her money. "Your manager, what sort of creature is she?"

"What do you mean? She's not an UnEarth Human if that's what you're asking. Just does business with 'em."

Mara listened for a moment to something Felix couldn't hear. Then her face went white. "She's ratting me out. We don't have much time. You need to decide if you're coming with me or not."

"Very not. You're on your own with whatever it is you're doing."

"How could a creature remain as slovenly as you for so long? You'd think you would have accidentally evolved a little. I see no reason for you to refuse this task. It's not as though I'm trying to save my own skin. I'm past that. This is about saving Alex Barker's and Bennett Hunter's lives. You do remember them, right?"

"Of course! I was the one who saved those two from becoming science experiments. What happened to those boys? I always wondered."

"They're about to be put to death."

"What? Why?"

"Because of the trial I just spoke of! Pay attention!"

"You never said that specifically. I would've remembered if you had mentioned those boys. If that's the case, let's go save 'em! Why not?"

Within moments, Felix was charging down the hall, intent on quitting and running away on a new adventure. His unnatural fear of Missus Topsic meant his resignation would have to be delivered passively; he was simply going to walk out the back door and hope it took her a while to notice he was missing. Passing his living space on his way toward the back door, he felt a swell of excitement. Embarking on a new mission brought back memories of his short-lived adventure with Hannah. A kind warmth filled his chest, a smoldering flame stirred by purpose. He and Mara exited the building into a bland suburban mini-mall at high noon, surrounded by chipped asphalt bleached gray by the sun and stacks of signs for fast-food restaurants.

"Where is everyone else?" Felix asked, his sense of purpose suddenly deflated.

"Everyone else?" asked Mara.

"Yeah, you know, the others along for this adventure. Where's the team?"

"There is no team. Why do you think I came to you?"

Felix's heart sank. "Oh, I thought it was a team effort. Never mind. I have no desire to work with you alone." He started back into the spa, trying to imagine Missus Topsic's footpath to guess if she had checked on sauna number one yet and noticed him gone.

"You've got to be kidding," Mara said, slamming the door in his face with a well-placed Mallos sphere. "Does your pride mean so much?"

"No, but my sanity does. I can already tell what working with you will be like. Doesn't seem like fun, know what I mean?"

"How is that supposed to make me feel?"

"It's supposed to wake you up! You have no idea how you're perceived by others and have never taken the time to think about it. Being around you is like chewing on seashells. I can't figure out why Hannah enjoyed it."

"That's a bit harsh. I know I can be strict, but—"

"Ha! Is that what you call it? You practically forbade her from seeing me, didn't you?"

"It wasn't . . . exactly—"

"See! Told you. Forbade. Like I was some bad influence."

"You were."

Felix was ready to hit Mara with a clever comeback (*just as soon as I think of one*), but when Missus Topsic burst out the back door, wielding a broom high above her head like a cavewoman with a club, he yelped like a startled chimp.

"Felix! Get your Imp butt back in here."

It wasn't the physical threat she posed that frightened him, but the thought of how awkward it would be to work with Missus Topsic if he stayed, now that she'd seen him try to escape. He could never face that kind of social interaction. Without much delay, he shouted, "Run!" and he and Mara bolted down the street. Missus Topsic's voice faded, yelling something beneath the sound of his and Mara's feet on the pavement. *She sounds so hateful! I'm genuinely shocked.*

He glanced at his new Medolian partner. "If I come along with you, I don't want any more surprises. I'm not going unless you're serious about saving those boys."

"I am," Mara said. "Though their safety is not all I'm after. I need to get to the bottom of whatever nefariousness has taken hold of the Tribunal. With any luck, we will be able to help many more than just the humans."

"Nefariousness? Now there's a five-rube word."

Once they were around a couple of corners, they slowed to a walk, though Felix couldn't help but notice Mara acting as though they were still being followed. To regular humans, she would have already appeared a strange character thanks to her attire, but this cartoonish behavior, coinciding with it, was like holding up a lit flare in a movie theatre.

"I don't think you have to worry about Missus Topsic coming after us. I know she's scary, but she's not *that* scary," he said.

"It is not your employer that worries me."

"Okay, well, maybe we could, uh, appear a little less spooked anyway? I feel like that might just draw more attention to us."

"They could be coming at any minute. If I start to sense an incoming Shift, we're going to have to get out of here. I have to be prepared."

"A Shift? Like a Shift-Shift? Does that mean Medolians are chasing us?"

"It means we should hurry."

"Jiminy! Mara, what have you dragged me into? I don't want to be chased by any of your Mallos pals, thank you very much."

"Can we please just get to the nearest Eb Ring with as little discussion as possible? There's one in a market nearby."

"I'm not done talking about this. That's a bit of a bomb to drop on someone, isn't it? Does this mean my life is in danger? Do they have a good reason for coming after you? How do I know I can trust you?"

That stopped Mara in her tracks. "Excuse me?"

"I'm sick of everyone turning out to be bad. I'm through with it, so how do I know I can trust you?"

"I don't know what to tell you. I've never had to defend myself in such a way. No one's ever accused me of being untrustworthy. In fact, I'd never really considered it."

"You didn't? Hmm . . ." Felix could sense no lie. "Okay. That works. I'll tell you what—I'm going to be your friend in Hannah's honor."

"I'm so blessed."

"Don't sneeze at getting a friend. You've been in need of one for some time. You only get so many in life."

Mara said nothing and picked up her pace. Most of the humans they passed paid them no mind, even with her unusual behavior.

"You really have no idea what's been happening?" she asked Felix. "Do you not speak with others in the UnEarth community to receive updates?"

"Sure, I make chitchat here and there. But I often don't hear what the other person is saying. It's all kind of a blur, you know what I mean? I just like being polite and smiling."

Mara scoffed. "I've been with Barker and Hunter the entire time, dealing with the fallout of that night, watching them put on trial with Izaiah. It's been a tiring, bewildering affair."

"The old guy actually let them put him on trial? That was sure generous of Izaiah Ezekial."

"He also let them sentence him to death. The entire Senate seems corrupted, except for Senator Bo. I've known him for two millennia. He's a noble Nashwynite. He *must* be going along with this against his will. If I could just reach him and talk one-on-one, I know he would tell me the truth and give me a target to neutralize. But since I'm on the lam, there's no way to contact him. Not through proper channels, anyway. We need to find out who's pulling these strings so I can start cleaning house."

"Cleaning house, huh? Now you're speaking my language! So, we want to talk with this Bo fella? Got it. And you say he's a senator? Sounds like a big deal. I know how dirty they can be, but if you say he's on the up-and-up, that's good enough for me. But if the rest of the Tribunal can't be trusted, maybe we should enlist the services of someone who treads an opposing, opposite, other-sideways path? Huh?"

"What in the name of Michael's wings are you trying to say?"

"If we can't get to this Bo through proper channels, what about an improper one?"

"I don't know if I like the sound of that."

"Let's just say I know someone who might be able to help. But it will be risky talking to him, you being an agent of the government and all. Might be best if you hung back."

"But I'm no longer an agent of the Tribunal."

"No-no, that doesn't matter. Not to these types. If anyone gets a whiff of Mallos nearby, they'll think a Sentry's close."

"I'm not hanging back. If you're worried about others knowing I'm a Medolian, I can assure you I'll mask my energy. All they will see is a Wyst."

"Yeah . . . the thing is—just because your energy signature won't read as Medolian, doesn't mean people won't figure out you're used to being an authority figure."

"I'm not allowed to be viewed as an authority figure?"

"Not when you're looking to meet with the types who hate those types. Unscrupulous folk are always on the lookout for narcs, and . . . well . . ." He motioned at Mara's person.

"Do you think I don't know what that term means? I am not."

"I mean . . . your body language alone . . . the suspicious stares—the battle-ready tension. Did you ever think of putting your staff away? I know you like it, but it's sort of a deadly weapon. Know what I mean? The humans just see it as part of a costume, but that thing is terrifying to UnEarth creatures. Everyone's heard stories of the things you've done with that."

"Her name is Nual."

"Okay, we've all heard the stories of the horrid acts you've committed with Nual."

Mara slid Nual off and glanced over it. "I guess she does stand out. Fine." With a swift motion, she reduced the staff to white light before it dematerialized into the naturally occurring energy field swirling around her body. Dematerialization was a trick only Mallos users could do. Mara's staff, imbued with Eve, dissolved and re-formed with ease, which always made Felix wonder why she didn't do it more often. *Must be a comfort thing. Like a blankie.*

She presented her empty palms, as if to say, *How about now?*

"I can still tell that if you caught someone breaking an UnEarth statute, you'd make sure they were reprimanded—aka, a narc."

Felix could feel Mara's resentment in her silence. Soon they reached the market where the Eb Ring was located. As usual, it was buried deep in the rear. Similar to the Klaas Fete—a haven for UnEarth Humans on Earth—this market was only a third as large, without a caged fighting arena at its center. When Felix and Mara entered, the looks on everyone's faces said they knew a Medolian had just walked in. His second-hand embarrassment kicked in at how she carried herself, obviously believing she was fooling them. *She's probably arrested half the people here and doesn't even remember them.*

When they passed a small clothing boutique, Felix veered off. "Wait, let's stop for a minute."

"Why?" Mara asked.

Felix shuffled through a rack like a mother trying to find something respectable for her teenager. "Because we need to get you something different to wear."

"Wear? Is there an issue with my garments?" Mara asked, glancing at her reflection.

"You've been wearing the same tired rags for three thousand years. It's time for something a little less recognizable." Felix flipped faster, not knowing exactly what he was looking for, but certain he'd know it when he saw it. After a few minutes with no luck, he settled on the best he could find.

When Mara stepped out from the bathroom wearing the ensemble—a pair of yellow slacks and a frilly pink blouse tucked in—Felix almost burst out laughing. The sight of her in pastels was simply jarring. With the rest of her gear safely stashed in the same energy field as Nual, they purchased the clothes with rubes from her pocket and moved on.

After they exited the store and walked only a few feet, Mara suddenly grabbed Felix's arm, her grip tense with paranoia.

"What is it?" he asked.

"I heard someone nearby speaking about Medolians. Someone must have spotted us."

"I think you're overreacting. They all knew already."

Taking him by the wrist as though she hadn't heard him, Mara hurried them toward the market entrance. "We can't risk using an Eb Ring now. Someone might follow us."

"That's fine. Where we need to go is only a few stops on the train," Felix said.

"The train? As in the human train?" Mara squeaked, her tone filled with nausea.

Getting her onto public transportation took longer than Felix had thought possible. Every move Mara made suggested not only that she didn't understand the most basic human customs, but also that she didn't care enough to make any effort. Her revulsion toward mankind was worse than that of even the nastiest Purged Archfiend. At least one item could be found to criticize every ten or fifteen feet. Everything—from standing in queues to pay phones—was labeled "worthless human things."

Once on the train, Felix found two open seats, but Mara refused to sit, choosing instead to remain on her feet, vigilant and keeping a close watch on everyone else in the car, which the humans were obviously made uncomfortable by. When they arrived at their stop, Felix hopped off and led them out. Salty sea air—good and thick—filled his lungs, mingling with the scents of the wharf. Though he wasn't a fan of water, he made this trek once a month to satisfy the part of himself that still craved fresh meat. Many on the wharf were happy to hand off buckets of fish trimmings at no charge.

Seeing the fishing boats lined up, along with sailboats aiming their masts at the sky, was something Felix adored. Passing the fish market, they made their way to the far rows of the dock, where a scattering of boat parking was dotted among gas stations, garages, and repair shacks. They soon came upon a ship called the *Bythan-thrope*, a worn craft with a third of its brown paint job stripped off.

When he neared the boat, Felix excitedly shouted, "Boris! Aye!"

"Boris?" Mara asked. "As in commander? Of Aul-Wa? I trust you're joking."

"This is why I didn't tell you who we were coming to see. I knew you'd act not nice about it." Felix cupped his hands around his mouth and shouted again, "Hey! Get on out here!"

A worry began to settle in that Boris wasn't home. *But where else would he be?*

Mara turned away from the boat as though disgusted by the sight of it. "What use could a creature such as him be to anyone?"

Felix tried shouting a couple more times, but the *Bythanthrope* remained stubbornly uninhabited and quiet.

"It doesn't make any sense. He never leaves this ship's side," Felix said. "He's been rebuilding the same one for a thousand years. He always said so." Just as he was about to call one last time, Mara tapped him on the shoulder.

"Wait." She was pointing at the ship's anchor chain disappearing into the darkness below. Felix stared but didn't grasp what she meant, making Mara roll her eyes so hard he worried they might fall backward into her head.

"Lift it," she said.

Doing as told, but not fully understanding why, Felix climbed onto the boat and hoisted the anchor. Slowly, the chain rose, wet

and dripping. But when the end arrived, instead of a lone pointed anchor, a man emerged from the water along with it. He was
mountainous, even while curled around the anchor like a koala,
wearing a dark gray sweater and tall fisherman's overalls. As he
rose from the water, he remained asleep, dripping gallons back into
the ocean.

"There he is. Come on, big guy. Wake up," Felix said, hurrying to
meet the three-foot-wide-shouldered man before his eyes opened.
*Don't want him seeing a Medolian first. Rapture types especially don't
care for them . . . at least in general. Though I hate to generalize.* The
sailor stirred but quickly returned to a deep, snoring slumber.

"We don't have time for this." Mara strode over, her steps heavy,
and touched his shoulder, sending a blast of Mallos through him.
With a jolt and a yelp, he woke with fists clenched. Boris unraveled
himself from the anchor and leaped onto his boat, seeming dazed,
as though waking from a drunken stupor. "What's going on here?
The Meds? Why? Who let them in? Wait a minute. . . Felix, is that
you?" Boris's battle-ready stance dropped away. "You here to scrub
the deck again?"

Felix laughed shortly. "No, Boris. Not today, unfortunately."

With a hefty cough, and after slapping his ears one by one, dis-
lodging another few cups of sea water, Boris glanced at Mara. "Yeah, I thought that was Mallos. *Ick*, nasty stuff. What's one of them
doing here? Heard your lot were assimilated as agents of the Barium Guard or something. Or is that why you're here? The ingestion
is all complete and now you're on duty? That's fine. You can look
around all you want, but you won't find anything sticky."

"What makes you think the Tribunal would have any interest in
you?" Mara asked. "A dishonored war hero? They threw you out.
Why would you be of any concern to them?"

"Ah, don't be like that. I work hard to keep my business as unscrupulous as possible. But if you lot don't know about it, that means either I'm way better at this than I thought, or you're way worse."

"This is pointless," Mara said, walking away. "This nonsense won't help us."

"Hang on." Felix dashed over and stopped her. "You haven't heard the plan yet. Boris and his friends are no friends of the Tribunal. This will be okay." He turned to Boris. "Tell her what you and your crew do."

"Tell a Medolian? Mate, I ought to kill you just for bringing her here. I wouldn't even come down this way for a dime or two if I were you. I'm going to tell everyone about this. We're all going to want to kill you."

"She's decommissioned. Ran away!"

"Yeah? For how long? Where else is a Medolian going to go except back to the Tribunal? It's only a matter of time. As if they would let her off the leash for long. In fact, if you are telling the truth, and she is rogue, then being near you is probably the worst thing I could do. Good way to get myself caught." Boris turned and started toward his wheelhouse.

As he began to whistle, Felix was reminded of how powerful a Celestial whistle could be. Their lung capacity, even in human form, was unmatched among any creature in the six worlds of the Eve. During her walks with Felix on Earth, Hannah often whistled, doing so for weeks on end without even stopping to answer a question with words; her song conveying all he needed to know.

It was one of the most beautiful things I've ever heard. Unlike the drivel that was currently coming from Boris, who was making an attempt to flee the scene.

"Tell her. Please. I wouldn't ask if it wasn't important." Felix clasped his hands together and dropped to a knee.

Boris stopped and turned back around, snorting like a snout-nosed creature, then stepped out of the wheelhouse. "I can feel that desperation. Stuff makes my skin crawl." With a sigh, he spat a huge gob of mucus over the side and began busying himself around his boat, wearing a grimace. "I run goods."

"No kidding," Mara said. "I could have told you that."

"Come on," Felix pressed. "Goods and . . ."

"Sometimes people."

"People?" Mara asked, eyebrows raised.

"Not what you're thinking. UnEarth Humans," Felix clarified.

"That's forbidden. The Tribunal needs to know of any travel an UnEarth creature makes on Earth."

Boris chuckled. "Hence the unscrupulousness."

"Are you with the Cypress Cilian Group?" Mara asked.

"Guilty."

"Then not only do you smuggle UnEarth creatures on Earth, but you also smuggle them back to their home worlds. I've lost many a vigilante because of you. Been looking for the center of your operation for a while. We're not even sure who your leader is."

"We know. And it'll stay that way. You'd probably be surprised to learn how much we know about the comings and goings of the Tribunal. Helps us run our business."

"You have spies?" Mara asked.

"And how."

"Any chance you'll drop names?"

"Is that a joke?"

"It was worth a shot."

Boris turned to Felix. "You sure she's not a Tribunal stooge anymore?"

"Sure, I'm sure!"

"The thing about big shots like Mara Loren—the ones who dream of greatness—is they never notice all the 'little' people around them. Especially Medolians. They do whatever they want and call it balance. But us? We got 'thrown out,' as you put it. Even though we got Purged, we still have to live under your rule, as well as the humans' rule. Does that seem fair to you?"

"It was never my rule," Mara said. "Vanity is not one of the chief traits of Medolians, I assure you. Their actions are kept in check by their peers, just as yours are. Medolian Sentry arrests of UnEarth creatures are minuscule compared to the human world's arrests. The majority of those I'm sent to find are already in human custody. It's often made my job much easier."

"That supposed to make me like you?"

"I don't care if you like me. Or if you hate me. Being a Medolian, you get used to the nicknames and malice. As you mentioned, no one really trusts us."

"No, just the new lot. We trusted the Sentries when Batia was in charge. Back before Inferius. She was a solid piece of granite, straight as a beam of light."

"You speak as though you were best friends."

"I'm pushing twenty K, young one. I knew most of the old lot. In fact, I was close with many of the Sentries. One might even say I know more about the Medolians than you do. Seems I heard you've always been one to avoid your brethren like the plague. Something about being too good to spend time around inefficient losers who just aren't as competent as you?"

Mara looked ready to respond with a loaded retort but instead released a beleaguered half-breath. *Guess he got her with that one.*

"You know, for someone who was once the Warden Sentry, there seems to be an awful lot you still don't know. You might want to—" Boris stopped when he noticed Mara's expression: like a shepherd informed their flock was lost to a flood.

Boris winced. "Oh, you didn't know? Rats. That was not my intention. To deliver negative personal news. Apologies."

"Your spies told you this?" Mara asked, her voice flat.

"No, the *Exodus*. It's all over the latest issue—your betrayal of the Tribunal and attempted jailbreak. I was wondering, why didn't you get the kook Izaiah out of there?"

"Because he wanted to stay."

"See, that I just don't get. Couldn't the guy have gotten himself out immediately? What's he playing at? Must be such a confusing life, being born a feeble old man from the get-go. Almost makes me feel sorry for him. Huh." Boris stared Mara down. "So, you want to know the name?"

"Philomena," Mara said solemnly, her head hung low.

"You guessed it."

Felix raised a finger, confused. "Uh, excuse me, what's that?"

"The Medolian who took my place as Warden Sentry," Mara explained.

Felix rifled through things to say, but they all felt too small. Even he understood how long Mara had vied for that position.

"Speaking of authority types," Boris said, "might I suggest we adjourn this meeting somewhere more private? UnEarth folks walk this dock, and the last thing I want is to be seen conversing with the Miliandre." He stepped back into the wheelhouse. "Might I suggest out at sea?"

"At . . . sea?" Felix yelped. Being this close to the water was already causing him a minor panic attack. He hadn't been on a human watercraft in almost three hundred years and had not planned on ever doing so again. Water was a mystery he had no desire to solve. It was heavy, cold, clingy, and stifling. It also reminded him of folks from Nashwyn, the UnEarth creatures he got along with the least. But when Felix looked at Mara, he realized his fear was not the biggest obstacle to getting them on the boat; her scornful look was.

Downright chilling. Guess she didn't like something he said.

"What's wrong?" Boris asked.

"I hate that name," Mara replied.

"Which one? Miliandre? What's that mean?" Felix asked.

"It's Hyl," Boris shouted. "It means the bossy middle child!"

Felix braced for impact, turning to see if Mara's cheeks were scorching red.

"Uh . . . I'm sure it's just a playful nickname," Felix said, hoping to quell a fight before it began.

Mara's arms folded so tightly it wouldn't have been surprising if they had started steaming. "I'm not getting on that boat. Not with a creature like that. We'll take our chances on our own."

An immense raised thumb was held out from the wheelhouse. "Not too fond of you, either, missy. You two can climb aboard and try to get what you're after, or stay here. I don't care either way. It's no wind out of my sails." The boat engine came to life with a coughing fit and puff of smoke before being put into gear.

"Don't you think we should go along with him?" Felix said to Mara, surprised he was advocating for it.

"I don't believe for one second that man will be useful. We should never have come here." Mara appeared resigned to stay on the dock and let Boris putter away. *This isn't turning out so great.* As the boat began to pull back in reverse, Felix saw their window closing. *Time to make an executive decision.* Against every instinct he had, with a running start, he sprang through the air, landing on the boat with as much grace as a drunk swan with no feet.

"What are you doing?" Mara called.

Felix turned back to the shore. "You asked for my help. I say we take his." He and Mara locked eyes in a staring match, which ended up being one of the most intense challenges he'd ever faced. Conquering his fears, Felix held her gaze until he actually won. With a scoff and a roll of her eyes, Mara leaped the thirty feet to join them on the boat.

"I still think this is a bad idea," she said. "And just remember, you're the one who can't swim."

The *Bythanthrope* set out from the marina into the softly rolling waters of the bay. Slowly, the shore and buildings drifted away, becoming merely a line of mush on the horizon.

Only to me, though. Mara could probably still read a newspaper stapled to the dock.

The farther they got from land, the more Felix clung to the wheelhouse. Without meaning to, he soon found himself curled into a ball on the cabin floor, where he could no longer see the water and could imagine it wasn't even there. *Except I can still hear it.* After a few minutes, Boris killed the engine and sat down next to Felix with a moss he fished out of a cooler attached to the side of the boat. Both Mara and Felix declined a drink when offered.

"We who live by the sea don't trust folks who won't share a drink with ya."

"Seems you've really taken to the Earthman sea life," Mara remarked, taking a spot leaning against the wheelhouse doorway.

"Sea life pulled me in. There was no helping it," Boris said. "Like many of us who fell from UnEarth."

"Why is that?" Felix asked, trying not to sound petrified. "Doesn't make sense to me. None of the other worlds have an ocean like the one on Earth. Thank goodness."

"But you see, that's exactly why!" Boris exclaimed. "The seas of the Earth . . . I tell ya, before the Purge, none of us had ever seen anything like it. Not like the lava seas of Arros. Or the brine seas of Nashwyn, with their clarity, calm, and buoyancy. But this beast here—the multiheaded ocean of the Earth—you ask me, it belongs more on a world like Fovos, if there were any large liquid bodies on it. Even the sand oceans of the Dread world are tame compared to this. I've seen whole fleets of stout sailors, human and UnEarth Human alike, disappear over the horizon, never to be seen again. Swallowed by the sea—the thing we're currently riding on top of. The whole time you're out here, you're wondering if it will notice and get mad. It's a foe unlike any I've ever faced. It's dark, deep, and terrifyingly easy to lose yourself in. I respect it."

"That's very fascinating, but we didn't come here to hear your story," Mara said bluntly. "We came to procure your services."

"Hold on there, Miss Medolian," Boris said. "We're a good ways yet from talking business. You two haven't told me anything about what you're doing. If she's on the run like you say, I imagine you'll be wanting to disapp—"

"I'm not running from anything," Mara snapped. "I'm getting to the bottom of who wants my people gone—and why."

"That makes me even less sure I want to do business with you."

"Since when are you so discerning?" she asked.

"Since a wanted Medolian defector woke me from my nap. But now that I'm aware you want to hire me, I'll need some standard details. Think I'll let you figure out the big ones."

"We're traveling to Nashwyn," Mara said.

"I see. As you mentioned earlier, we do ferry to the home worlds. But that comes with a heavier price tag."

Felix raised a finger, ready to negotiate, but Mara chimed in first.

"Whatever you charge is fine," she said.

Boris offered a smile that was half a wince as he tossed out his empty moss can and reached for another.

Felix leaned in toward Mara. "Are you sure? These guys can charge you an arm and a leg, if you know what I mean."

"Rubes won't be a problem," Mara said resolutely, leaving it at that.

"Well, okay then," Boris said. "Though I should mention, seeing as you are special cargo, and things in the underground are shaky at the moment, there will be an added premium. I'm sure you understand. It's expensive risking your life for the greater good, isn't it?" He beamed a petty smile.

"What do you mean 'shaky'?" Mara asked, her tone sharpening.

"Strange happenings have been going on ever since Inferius. People talking to unusual types. Odd connections being made. Many in the underground think another UnEarth war is brewing. Not sure between who, though. Another war would be profitable, especially for those with sway in the Senate. A lot of folk are already preparing for the worst. Getting people places safely is becoming harder. Lucky for you, Nashwyn is still one of the easier worlds to get to."

Felix felt a jolt of Dread hearing that, but Mara just laughed it off. "Nice try."

"You don't believe me? About which part?" Boris asked.

"You think UnEarth senators are secretly conspiring to restart the war? For what purpose?"

"Since you're headed to Nashwyn, you can drop in and ask your old mentor, Bo. If anyone would know, it would be the Wyst."

Mara scoffed and laughed, but gradually seemed to realize he was serious. "What do you mean? Why him?"

"Why, indeed," Boris said. "Who else besides Van-Mortus and Speaker Binahq could run the show? They have the fanciest titles, right? Yet numerous measures they presented sank to the depths without a trace. But not Bo. Who's the real person you need on your side to get anything in the Tribunal done? Nothing since Inferius has been approved without the signature of the Nashwyn senator."

"That's because Bo is the most fair-minded. The people trust him, as well as the Wysts. No other world is as inclusive."

"Then why has your boy been backing Van-Mortus's every whim for the last fourteen hundred years?"

"He's never backed Van-Mortus. She receives her orders from Aveyl himself."

Boris looked bored with the conversation. "Look at the Lutrescent treaty, which gave control of the Lutrescentian Fields on Lanwyn to a private Trivium business—Mulhauser Wane. If you didn't know, it's been investigated for fraud more times than I've seen an eel's backside. The treaty was backed by Rowse and Mistress Tennile. It never would have gotten through if Van-Mortus hadn't gotten Bo to cosponsor it."

"That was a special circumstance," Mara insisted. "The Scythes were starving, and the Beaubons controlled a surplus."

Wait—what's going on? Felix was having trouble following along.

"Okay then, what about Covenant amendment three ninety?" Boris added.

Mara pondered in silence for a moment. "The reduction of dependency on the Counselors to conduct the census?"

Boris took a loud sip of his drink, locking eyes with her.

"You must be joking," she said.

"Arros spends six hundred years vying to get the revision on the books, failing time and again. Then, out of nowhere, Bo gets behind it, and the amendment passes. Boom. Every time Van-Mortus advocates for something, Bo sees it done. Simple as that. They've just done an amazing job making sure people like you don't notice. As long as everything seems like business as usual, it'll sail right through the Tribunal."

"That's coincidence. There have been plenty of motions that haven't made it onto the books."

"Doesn't make what I said any less true," Boris countered.

"But why? What would Bo gain by playing both sides? Van-Mortus has nothing to offer him. Arros is poor and destitute, while Nashwyn has always thrived."

"If I can get you to his planet, maybe you can ask the senator yourself."

"Does that mean you've taken the job?" Felix asked eagerly.

"If you can actually pay," Boris said, "which I will be expecting up front."

Standing, while remaining hunched to avoid hitting his head on the ceiling, Boris belched and crushed the can of moss in his hand. A burst of blue light from his palm transmuted the can into a dark brown material. He tossed it into the water, and it landed with a robust plop, disappearing in no time.

"Let's get you ready for the trip," he said.

"Ready? How?" Felix asked.

"It's going to take some doing to get you into the processing station," Boris said. "Neither of you are claustrophobic, are you?"

Felix and Mara each raised a hand as though ready to be called on by the teacher.

"That's unfortunate," Boris said, grinning. "This is going to be a very unpleasant trip for you, then. Oh well."

LITTLE DOOR, BIG HANDLE

A bristling energy had swept through La Rose Noire ever since the trial's end. Everyone but Casey seemed to have a mountain of tasks to tackle. Boxes and crates arrived by the truckload, stacked along the halls and crammed into corners. Most contained food and beverage supplies, but some were more ominous, filled with assault rifles and body armor. *I opened one by accident—promise— and almost screamed! What kind of rescue mission are they planning?*

New faces roamed the halls as Madam Daphne's forces grew by the day, increasingly filled with dangerous-looking individuals. Tomorrow, they would head to Trivium to thwart the Surface's attack on the execution. If all went according to plan, the madam's people would find Leigh and bring her back to the Rose alive. Casey hoped Chief Mary had her soldiers in check—because the added security actually made her feel less safe. *I was feeling plenty secure before, aside from some of the meaner creatures here, but I just steer clear. Am I missing something? Are we expecting to come under attack?* Everywhere—everything in the Rose had changed, except for the platinum hall, where nothing ever changed and the party would continue until the end of time, if allowed.

With all her aching heart, Casey missed her morning donuts and leisurely strolls through a quaint, autumn-kissed French town. That reprieve from the club was necessary not just for her sanity but to remind herself she was still on Earth, not some alien planet. But for the past four days, she had been grounded, restricted from leaving the Rose. The outside world had been deemed too great a threat by the madam.

Since her house arrest, Casey had taken refuge in a small, cupboard-like space she discovered at the end of a dimly lit stairway in the lower enclaves of the club. It appeared recently abandoned, ripe for claiming. She found some snacks, a few books, and blankets, transforming it into an impromptu home. The bedroom Madam Daphne had given her felt like a puke-filled kiddie carnival by comparison. Every moment spent there made her feel like she was being watched, a sensation she couldn't shake. Cozy and offering distance from the sensory overload that was the pink room, the cubby at the bottom of the stairwell was as good as gold.

Often while catching up on sleep, she heard Chief Mary's boots echoing above. One day, the chief's security forces began patrolling in body armor, their movements clanking like maracas. Once the door guards started carrying rifles, it became clear this pseudo-army was evolving into more of an army-army. Casey couldn't help but notice their gun magazines faintly burned with cyan light from within. *Fervor bullets? What the heck could those even do to someone?* She repeatedly halted herself from worrying about Leigh becoming one of those unlucky enough to find out.

How could she let herself get so mixed up in this mess? And how could I go and do the exact same thing?

Ever since the sentencing, rumors had circulated. Some claimed the Tribunal had dispatched hit squads after the Medolians, opting for outright elimination. Others whispered that the Sentries were orchestrating a retaliation, planning to assault Trivium en masse to rescue their leader. Casey could attest to the latter being false; she had two Medolians in the Rose with her, and neither was preparing for anything other than their next meal or maiming contest. *They especially wouldn't lift a finger to save Izaiah. I swear, those two are four times as lazy here as they were at Mom and Dad's.*

Presently, after finishing a snack from her last delivery of Earthling food, Casey balled up the wrapper and stuffed it into a box she'd turned into a makeshift trashcan. Today had been especially dull, and patience was never her strong suit (*in fact, I'm downright terrible at it*). She decided to venture out into the Rose to see what was happening. Speaking with Madam Daphne and asking for an update seemed worth another shot, despite being turned away at her office door every day for the past four days. There was no reason to think today would be any different, *but still . . . squeaky wheel.*

Ascending to the next floor, she found the hallway empty—a rarity these days. But it wasn't long before a squad of Chief Mary's crew stomped by. Stepping aside, Casey noticed the guards' eyes on her, a targeted gaze she wasn't used to. She'd become accustomed to being ignored by UnEarth creatures, so their attention felt strange. Glancing down, she realized she'd forgotten her Grief gem today. *Damn, I left it in the princess doom room. Don't feel like going back in there to get it.* But that made the guards' scrutiny even odder. *Um . . . were they told to look out for me, or something?*

As she approached Madam Daphne's open office door, sounds echoed down the spiral stairway. At the upper landing, she found the usual guards, who squinted to see her coming. The tallest spoke into his radio, sounding more agitated than yesterday. "*Ugh*, the human is back."

Knowing the drill, Casey stopped a few feet away and waited. The door opened, and Chief Mary stepped out.

"Miss Casey, Madam Daphne sends her regrets once again. She is far too busy for visitors. She must also cancel your dinners for the rest of the week. She hopes you're doing well." The chief extended a basket filled with likely delectable treats. "From the human world."

Casey didn't really want it but felt she had no choice but to take the basket. Gripping the handle, she said, "Thank you," and was about to leave when she decided to get a little cheeky. "What if I said it was an emergency?"

"I know you're lying. So, what good is it?"

"Where am I supposed to go? She put me on house arrest."

"For your safety."

"I want Madam Daphne to tell me that."

"The madam cannot be disturbed. She is planning for every contingency in the coming operation—the same one that might locate your professor. I thought you wanted that."

"Of course I do, but I've heard nothing in almost a week—"

"You'll receive word when it is appropriate."

"Am I to just sit around until then? Like a prisoner?"

"If you're looking for a task, prepare the Medolians. We will be moving out soon, though I can't say when. I want them ready at a moment's notice. They will play a vital part in this. Without them, the madam's plan fails."

"Why doesn't one of your guards do it?" Casey asked. "What makes you think the Medolians will take orders from me?"

The chief's annoyance was palpable even behind her blacked-out shades. "You brought them here. They are your responsibility.

That's all I'm going to say, peon." With that, she stomped back inside and closed the door.

Sulking away, Casey muttered, "What am I, Fabian and Galinthia's keeper? You'd think creatures thousands of years old wouldn't need so much hand-holding."

After more than half an hour of searching, she was about ready to head back to her nook. Neither Fabian nor Galinthia was in their usual spots, and no one in the halls would stop long enough for her to ask about them. *Most of them get startled when I say hi. I can't believe I forgot my Grief gem. This seems pointless without it.*

As she wandered through the seemingly endless murky halls, she ended up back where she'd started. Resorting to other techniques, she expanded her search to places she wouldn't usually expect to find the Medolians. *Where else could they be? It's not like they would just vanish without telling me first. Right?* Making her way to the second floor, she checked the kingdom rooms. Without the ability to go inside, it did little good. For a half hour at each door, she attempted to ask those emerging if Galinthia or Fabian were inside. No one who saw her or heard her gave a clear response. Best she could tell, the answer was no.

Moving to the upper levels, where the private guest rooms and sub-kingdom rooms were located, Casey resorted to trying random doors, checking each handle's temperature first to ensure she wouldn't encounter a fire or Human Archfiend on the other side. *Or something worse I have yet to meet.* After another hour with no luck, she decided it was time to tell Chief Mary the Medolians had flown the coop—at least from her sight.

Rounding a corner, Casey glanced in each direction, planning to turn back, but something inexplicable caught her eye: a door, similar to her cubby door, but a miniature version of the others in the hall. It came up just above her chest. She'd encountered varying sizes of doorways throughout the Rose, but this one tugged at her attention. Its proportions mimicked a normal human door in miniature.

The chances that the Medolians were inside were slim to none, but curiosity had already sunk its insatiable claws into Casey. She opened the door, finding a hallway dimply lit by sporadic lights above. Every instinct told her to turn back, but her body couldn't help stepping inside all the same. Her childhood love for ant tunnels and prairie dog holes came flooding back. The desire to know where this path led was overwhelming.

But why is it so dark in here?

Even the murkiest larger hallways had foggy sconces illuminating their paths, but this miniature corridor resembled a lava tube with holes in the ceiling every few yards, letting in muted remnants of light scattered down through deep cracks in the Earth.

As she ventured deeper, a fork in the path emerged, barely visible in the dim glow. Casey hesitated, hearing the faint echo of voices drifting down the hall from the right. Their words were too soft to make out, but their tone was casual, and it sounded as though they were standing in a large room. Despite what her ears, nose, and better judgment screamed, she pressed on to the right.

A grotesque odor soon enveloped her as her feet began to crunch over debris littering the ground. Most of what she could see in the murk looked like trash, but scattered patches of dark matter, reeking of decay, suggested that something more organic was strewn about. Bones cracked underfoot, filling her with terror but also—surprisingly—an unshakeable resolve. *What am I, crazy?* The smell of dead wildlife was then overtaken by the recognizable scent of wet clothes left out for days. It then hit Casey: *Am I in someone's house?* UnEarth Humans claimed nooks and crannies all the time, just as she had done with her cubby. The animal remains scattered about were likely leftover meals.

Glad no one seems to be home . . . at least so far.

A section of the hall opened into what might have been a reading nook, now converted into a private living space. Empty moss bottles littered the floor around a mound of blankets and pillows. The area was free from rotting things and bones—though the odor was reminiscent of an entire county of angsty teenagers' bedrooms.

Soon, Casey pinpointed the source of the echoing voices. A vent in the ceiling projected the words of two men as clearly as a radio. Normally, she would have moved on, respecting their privacy, but then one of the men said something that made her freeze.

"Hope your end's been as bad as mine," said one man. "This operation gets any bigger, and we'll need to take over a few more local peon residences for beds and plunder."

"She's even bussed in the scrappers from the Burin clan. Didn't think the madam would ever call in that favor."

The first man had a higher voice, but sounded larger; Casey imagined he had a big nose (*for some reason*). The second man had a long drawl and sounded like he might have been blinking or flinching a lot. Through the vent, she could only see the very bottom of their feet, which provided no clues other than one of the men was rather fidgety. *Probably Blinkie.*

"How's your department looking?" asked the second man, the less fidgety one.

"The madam wants a lot and keeps adding to the list. It's getting kind of hard to keep up with the changes."

"Gotta be ready. Who knows what surprises Morinnean might have planted for us? Booby traps and whatnot."

"You seem worried."

"You kidding? The human could never contend with us. This

time next week, Aluqa will be dead, and the Surface will be burnt to the ground. Once that happens, no more human resistance on Earth. This planet will be ours for the taking."

No more human resistance? That's what all this was about? What does that mean for Leigh? And for me?

Casey pressed herself against the vent, listening intently as the men continued discussing the preparations.

"It surprises me that Morinnean is making such a huge mistake."

"I can't believe she's sending her entire upper and lower caste. Makes me think the whole thing is a ruse. Nobody's that thick."

"Royce's pet always manages to have a trick up her sleeve. Makes me glad we're not on the assault team. Security and mop-up suits me just fine."

"Would be fun to see the station when they first break in, though."

"No kidding. Who knows what the human's got hidden away? The madam has been waiting for a moment like this for a long time. Morinnean's been a nuisance for more than a century. Time to put that dog down. No doubt it'll be easier now that we've got our hands on a couple of Medolians."

"*Bleh*, speak for yourself. I can't stand the thought of them being here. After all these years—all our chants of 'Medolians dead on sight!,' we just let the first ones to show up waltz right in? I wanted to puke when I tasted Mallos again."

"Now who's thick? It was the luckiest thing that could have happened. Think ahead, for once. That small, round human dropped two of the most precious treasures in the universe right into the madam's lap."

"But the round humie gets free rein of the place. Little runt. Cassie or Katie or some human name. You ever notice how all their names end in 'eee'? Like babies, you know? When they're fresh and small. It's like they want to stay in their larval form indefinitely. But a peon shouldn't roam these halls free of fear. I never understood how we were supposed to keep her from being eaten. Most don't even believe me when I say those orders are from the madam. They think I just want to eat the humie myself. Which I do, so it's hard not to feel like a hypocrite."

"We won't have to pretend for much longer. The execution is in less than two days. I heard the doc finally perfected his machine just in time."

"Neil-Shemaine? I wouldn't trust it. His track record speaks for itself—poorly."

"He's been gathering intel on the Meds the whole time they've been here. Feeding the toy he's making. I heard it works even better than anticipated. The Sentries are as good as ours. Then we can finally eat the fat little human. I've called first dibs on those thighs."

The men laughed together and Casey's lunch threatened to come up. How could she have been so stupid? The signs were there. What could someone like Madam Daphne want with a human like her? Why would she care about Leigh, who had allied with her enemy? *It was all a setup. She just wanted to get close to the Medolians so she could take something from them. But what?*

Had Fabian and Galinthia already been captured? Was that why they were nowhere to be found? If so, the guards wouldn't have been speaking so casually. *They must still be out there! I have to warn them before it's too late!* She listened a moment longer, but the guards offered little new information, instead starting an argument over who would have killed the most humans had they been part of the upcoming invasion of the Surface.

With time running out, leaving seemed justified. As Casey turned to retrace her steps down the narrow, dim hallway, she was suddenly halted by the sound of scurrying feet—larger, much larger than a rodent. Flappier, thumpier, not clawed. It was more like . . . *heavy, fur-covered sandals?*

Her skin went cold as she spotted a shadow outlined in fur charging toward her. Heavy grunting and labored breathing washed over her, stealing her breath away. She fought to regain it, only to have it snatched again by the creature's cackling laughter.

The blood drained from her face and legs. Her eyes widened to their fullest. Never before had such raw survival instinct surged through her. And yet, she couldn't muster the will to move.

Hazy light flowed in from above, glistening off saucer-sized lenses that never blinked, their warm green irises fixed dead ahead. Floppy feet stamped louder, echoing through the narrow hallway. Grunts and gurgles mixed with choppy snickers, creating a cacophony that filled the air. Casey's mind froze, her instincts paralyzed like a gazelle caught in the predator's gaze, accepting its fate just before the jaws of a lion closed in. But gazelles typically fled first, giving survival a fighting chance. At the very least, she should have dove into the bushels of blankets and pillows, seeking cover. Yet something deep inside told her it was too late. There was nothing she could do, so she chose nothing.

The padded feet slapped the floor, the sound dry and wrinkled, lightly coated with dust. Then the first glimpse of a maniacal face emerged, a grin stretched wide like a balloon ready to pop, teeth gleaming under the feeble light. The raw intensity of its breath suggested a desire for a struggle of dominance—or a mate. Or both. Sloppy, fervent words spilled from its foam-encrusted lips. "Gotta find it. Gotta get it. Get it—get it!"

By now, the creature was too close for any chance of escape. Options evaporated. Casey was unarmed, and the thing was clearly seeking her. This was apparently the lucky guard who had struck gold in the building-wide search; their prize would be assured, enshrining them as a hero. The only question that remained: Would she be taken dead or alive? *Maybe it'll just be my bones they deliver. That could be different.*

Resigned to her fate, Casey closed her eyes, trying to block out the sounds of the clamoring beast. She craved a moment of peace before the end. *I'm sorry, Mom. I failed you.* The creature's breath grew heavier, the thumping of its feet echoing in her ears, and she clenched her eyes tighter, willing herself to disappear. At the very least, she wouldn't have to see that twisted smile in the dark before it all ended.

Hope I don't scream too much.

SURR

Through the small window on Alex's cell door, flashes of neon green poured inside with each strike of lightning. The ensuing thunder felt like a herd of invisible buffalo stampeding by, but what was truly disconcerting was the silence between strikes. If there was any wind blowing outside, Alex couldn't feel it in the Sackulli-Karni, and there wasn't even the patter of a single raindrop on the roof. Storms on Trivium, of which there had been many lately, were completely dry.

Nearly every night this week had hosted one, but tonight's seemed especially aggressive. For hours, Alex had been enduring the pounding and shouting from the Trivium sky. The largest blasts of fury pulled screams from him, but by now his voice was cracked and flimsy, with nothing left to properly express his terror. It was as if all of Trivium were trying to tear down the walls of the Tribunal to get to him. *So come get me.* Alex was tired of the tension and outside threats. Once that gavel had come down, his life was ostensibly over. This period he was existing in was limbo. He was not a living creature by any stretch of the imagination. Life in a cage, held by chains, was no life at all. Any camaraderie or sympathy he thought he might receive from the other inmates—now that he was officially on death row—was nowhere to be found. *I can't take much more of this.*

On several occasions, he had been mere moments from finally falling asleep, only to have one of them shout something like, "Drifting off to visit the missus?" Then they and the others would laugh, following Alex's panicked, startled cry. Death was looking sweeter by the minute. But the inmates and their taunts were not the worst of it. Ever since the sentencing, there had been more onlookers than ever visiting his cell. The people wanted to see the Ire boy before the chance was gone. He was like an endangered animal in a zoo, deemed too dangerous to live, set to be eliminated by the state.

The brief flash of commiseration he'd felt from Oaleen had never resurfaced. When he was rolled back to his cell following the sentencing, she refused to meet him at the bars or even look at him. *When I caught a glimpse of her, she looked disappointed.* Even days later, what he'd felt from her was still getting to him.

Does she think I was somehow defeated? That I wasn't tough enough? What else could I have done?

Word of the convictions and death sentences had already spread throughout the jail even before his return. The news had apparently been shouted throughout the streets of Trivium. You'd have to have been under a rock not to know how the trial had ended. From what he gathered, the people began cheering and celebrating the instant the news washed over them.

Alex spent the next day curled up in silence, feeling only pity for himself. Oaleen, for once, seemed completely unwilling to speak with him, not even to insult him, which he found himself oddly missing. The continued silence chilled him even more than the face of death staring him down. Finally, late one night, his cell neighbor spoke out of nowhere in a somewhat indirect way.

"This putrid marriage idea. Explain it to me." Her voice echoed softly in the hall through the small window on the door of the Sackulli-Karni.

"Are you talking to me?" Alex asked incredulously.

"Who else would I be talking to? You think Tobs has ever been married? *Chhhr*—No, human. You. The ilthaugh—what my people call the peons. The Barker. Explain to me why one creature would attach themselves by law to another in such a fashion. Such a merger, a loss of self. And the gravitas behind it. The ways of your world must have changed, because last I remembered, creatures being traded from family to family was called marriage. Yeah?"

"I suppose things were that way once. But that was a long time ago," Alex said.

"For you, maybe. But then I heard the way you talk about your wife and the marriage you had, and it sounds like a completely different thing. It makes my head hurt to think about . . . and then I get angry. Then violent. But I'll try to behave. So, tell me about the marriage you had. What version was it? The formality kind, yeah?"

"No, my marriage was not just a formality."

"Okay, but the way you talk about her—this unblemished creature—it's ridiculous, like she never had runny shits or anything. I'll never understand beings like you that put others on pedestals. *Ch-ch*—You're worse than a Mal-Drimo. Why not put your own self up there? Seize the moment and your life, before someone else does."

"I didn't put my wife on a pedestal."

"Yes, you did. *Ch-ch-ch*—You ever listen to yourself? Your whole existence was based on this one other entity. This other life-form.

Not you. To cling to. *Arck!* You needed her and her presence at all times—otherwise, your body became useless. You still need her now. I see it in your signature. *Ch-ch-ch-ch-ch*—Your Eve is only full when you think of her. What kind of grown creature would willingly become so reliant on another?"

"We were a team."

"A team in what?"

"I don't know. Life."

"Raw existence? Okay . . . yeah. I see it. But to me, it means weakness. In my world, there aren't any two-creature teams. Your clan is your only team. Your millions of brethren are the ones who make you strong, and all are expected to be able to fend for themselves. We see reliance on others as a failing. As for whatever this 'love' nonsense is, I don't even know where to begin telling you how little I understand that."

"If that's really how you feel about life, I feel sorry for you. Really."

"Explain it, human."

"You can't imagine the joy you might feel from seeing the same face every morning? A face you trust and find comfort in, one you can't get enough of looking at? You'd rather be lonely? Going through life with no one else?"

"I've never been alone. My clan was full of others who looked like me and smelled like me. Others who thought like me. If I were to make a deduction, I'd say you couldn't stand the thought of facing the world without someone to share in your misery should you fail. I think that's what love is."

"You say that like it's a bad thing."

Oaleen laughed once, though she seemed caught off guard and had nothing to offer in response. Secretly wanting to make amends, Alex decided to try and appease her.

"It wasn't about what I could get out of my life with her, or about what I could take. It was about what we created together. What we had. She and I were one. One creature. Two halves of a whole. Greater than our individual parts."

"Ah, so like a parasite. Fovos is full of those."

"No, this is different. This is was one person who knew me inside and out. No secrets. My good and bad were laid bare. And she loved me enough not to hold any of it against me. In fact, that made us love each other more. We had a great thing going. We'd gotten far, were ready to move on to the next stage together, then . . ."

"Let me guess—tragedy?" Oaleen said. "That was a new word for me when I got to Earth. New concept. See, that's what I found gross during my time on that mudball. Your obsession with preserving everything. You're nearly as bad as the Celestials. I don't get your preoccupation with having perfect little boring lives. It makes me uncomfortable. *Ch-ch-ch-ch-ch*—it's like you think nothing ever ends, or breaks down, or runs out."

"My life wasn't perfect. In fact, it was awful sometimes. I lost people. Just surviving in human society was terrifying enough."

Oaleen laughed so boisterously her shade cloud pulsed. "That's some of the funniest shit I've ever heard. I spent four hundred years on Earth, and most of it was a cakewalk compared to the places I've seen things live in this solar system. To hear someone who's only lived in these recent centuries, on that planet, with all the human comforts and technologies, complain is face-numbingly laughable. Your people just read about problems in your little booky-boos and news pamphlets. You don't really deal with any yourselves. The fact is, your lives are fine for the most part. All you really do is go from one place to another to get food and then travel back home. That's it. Then repeat it with the monotony of waves rolling on a shore. And as for losing people . . . what else do you think being a living creature is? I have news for you—you all die! How is this a surprise to any of you?"

Alex screamed at the wall and Oaleen's signature with all his might, "Because she wasn't supposed to leave yet! Because we were supposed to have a home and a child. I was supposed to help raise Patty. Melissa was supposed to see her walk and fall down and live. We were supposed to just be parents, like other people got to be. I just wanted to love someone and not kill them for once. First my parents, then my grandpa, then my wife. Everything and everyone I've ever shared my life with has been taken. And now, I don't even believe I'll get to be with her when I die. And I stopped thinking she's out there waiting for me. I don't think there's anything waiting for us out there. Not anymore." Alex stopped himself. A tear slid down his cheek, leaving a cold trail. "Didn't mean to go all human on you."

"No," said Oaleen, a little softer than usual. "I felt some new things from you just now. Things I've never . . . just whispers, but, I don't know. From your point of view, I could see how things like a wife could have been a big deal. *Ch-ch*—Husband too, I guess."

"Thanks, I think," Alex said.

That was wholly unexpected. For the first time, he felt he might have gotten through to her. He wanted to continue but speaking with his voice in the shape it was in had drained him. With the thunderstorm continuing its assault on his senses, keeping his eyes open was getting trickier. "I'm going to . . . I think I'm going to try and get some sleep," Alex said. There was no response. *Did I offend her?* "I'd just like to be alone for a while, I think."

"You are alone, Barker," was all Oaleen said.

Then there was quiet in the Weya-Vein while the storm continued. Alex did not pass right out as his mind drifted into a fog of half-sleep. With each flash, his consciousness was kept aloft like a bobber on the water's surface. The storm must have dipped for a time, as he lost himself for a bit, only to be awakened by a violent resurgence of lightning an unknown amount of time later. Thunder cracked like the whips of lion tamers, and a sudden wind erupted, this time strong enough to be felt in the Sackulli-Karni. The lightning from the storm lit up the small window in Alex's cell door repeatedly, creating a pulsing white square that could have been a flashing motherboard component as far as he knew in his daze.

For over an hour, this new leg of the storm raged. Thunderous cracks shook him with each strike, jolting him back from whatever fatigued state of mind he seemed to want to crawl back into. When his arms grew too tired to fight against the chains, his ears began to ache. In a vain attempt to fight the pain, he dipped his head from side to side, passing his vision over the cell door. A scent then began to find its way to his nose. Its musk was human and somehow familiar, evoking a memory he couldn't clearly recall. When a stout shadow appeared in the door's window and then disappeared, he shook it off as a figment of a weary mind, only to have the shape reappear again. Squinting, Alex vaguely made out the outline of a head, possibly hooded. The green lightning illuminating the cellblock surrounded the form in a veil of light, burning bright on its edges like an eclipse of the sun. But when he closed his eyes, Alex found no color or puff of Eve. Nothing was there, surely; yet when he opened his eyes again, the silhouette remained.

I must be going crazy.

Between two claps of thunder, a man spoke, startling Alex. The voice was old, with a high tenor and thrashed vocal cords, as though a withering fire of brittle, dry wood were speaking.

"What do we have here? So, this is the boy?" the voice asked, with an elated air from the darkness and anonymity. "I've heard so much. My eyes delight in viewing the one that all the fuss is about."

"Who are you?" Alex asked, peering to see the man better but unable to make out any solid features.

"A fan." The man's teeth were bared, smiling, gray in the dim light.

Wanting only to dismiss this stranger as he had done with all the others who came to see the Ire boy, Alex surprised himself when his own feet began taking steps closer to the cell door. The chains holding him, fixed to the pulley system in the ceiling, increased their tension, yet he pressed onward. Nearing the outer ring and the cell door, he found its window filled only by blackness. No Eve signature was anywhere to be found.

A lull in the storm then arrived. Shadow overtook the block for nearly a minute, and Alex could find nothing of the man. When his vision began to adjust, filled with murky grays in the black, a lightning strike filled the hall and the Weya-Vein with a tsunami of light, blinding him and revealing a pair of eyes at the cell door. They were wide open, peering through the window, embedded in a face like a drooping sad clown mask. Slings below the eyes carried bags of bruise-colored skin. Yet for how dead the man's face was, his eyes were exceptionally present and alive—analyzing, studying, wide awake—a manic quality leered behind them, as if the person behind the clown mask were screaming for help while gagged.

"And your name?" Alex asked, having reached the limits of how far he could walk before the chains flung him back. It was cumbersome to remain, and he still wasn't sure why he'd walked to meet the man in the first place. No one had ever come to him like this, alone, in the middle of the night. Oaleen had woken him up plenty of times to tell him how much she hated him but had never come to his door to do it.

"Of course, my name," the man said. "Why do my manners depart when their moments arrive? You're no more an animal to be gawked at in a cage than I am to those who walk the streets of Trivium with shackles in their eyes, fleeing where they tread. My name is Surr."

"Nice to meet you, Surr."

"Likewise, Mr. Barker. You've no idea the wonder I feel at your presence in the flesh. Can you come any closer? Any at all? I wish for a better look at you. This gaze is doing me wonders."

Another blast of lightning struck. Its corresponding thunder followed almost immediately. But this one was much louder than the rest, as though a tank had fired a shell just outside the walls. The chains holding Alex shook and danced in the shock wave.

As requested, Alex pressed himself as far forward as he could toward the cell door. By now, he could lightly make out the shape of Surr, a hunched man covered in rags.

"There you are. A beautiful boy," the man said, his fragile voice racing up Alex's spine like a lizard escaping a freezer.

"You're not staff. You're an inmate," said Alex.

"Correct. I, too, am in chains. Barred from my old life—which I hardly remember. Sometimes it seems the chains are all I will ever know."

"But where are your chains now? You're not housed here in the Weya-Vein. How did you get here?"

"My life has been long. Does that surprise you? Much of it spent roaming and discovering. The Iolanze contains many secret passages, all of which I've since learned, hammered into my mind as deep as only the sharpest chisels could carve. I could navigate them with both eyes and both ears plucked like feathers from my head. But few have ever learned of me. My reputation here is . . . not. An apparition. A fog. Never noticed. The guards know not that their routes, which have never changed or paused, are stalked."

"If you can move around so easily, why not escape?" Alex asked.

"Escape to where?"

"I don't know. Someplace you're not a prisoner. Somewhere you're free."

"*Hrm.* Interesting. Tell me, where in life is this freedom? Can you eat it? Can you hold it in your hand? Yours to let live or crush into dust? This freedom, in all my years, I've never seen it. No creature is allowed to truly live. Each falls under the rule of another. I believe in little else."

"So, you see being in here as no different than being out there?"

"Something like that." Surr snickered, laughing with a dry, congested breath. "You think I'm odd for the choices I make, yet I look at you and ask a similar question. Why do you choose to stay, Ire boy?"

"I can't leave whenever I want."

"You can't?"

"Of course not."

"But you are the herald and creator of the Ire, are you not? That which could tear into the heart of the Tribunal, rip it out, and march safely out the other side to wherever it wished in all the realms."

"I don't know where you got your information, but it's wrong. The Ire wasn't like that."

"No? Yet my sources assure me."

"I wasn't in control when it happened," Alex said. "It just . . . took over."

"I see. Explain how such a thing could happen."

Alex hung his head. "Is this what you came for? To learn about the Ire and the person inside it before he dies?"

"Death is in your immediate future?"

"You must not have been keeping up on current events."

"You speak of your execution? Yes, a shame. And yes, you figured me out. My curiosity was once again an obvious detriment. I needed to see it for myself. Excuse me—I meant you—Mr. Barker. Not it. Though you do seem to speak of the Ire as though it were an it."

"That's exactly what it was. The thing was . . . like being chained down in the path of an open spillway. Moving one way or another was impossible. Fighting was impossible. There was nothing I could do to stop it. Not on my own, anyways."

"This force sounds formidable and terrifying."

"You have no idea."

"I see. Then why do you think such a thing would allow itself to be extinguished?"

"Allow? What do you mean?"

"You said yourself you are not the Ire. It was something else working through you, correct? But this force surely wasn't destroyed. Killed? No. It was merely put away in a box. If it is truly outside of you, what makes you think it won't just take over again? Perhaps as some defense against the executioner's blade? If I was any sort of intelligent force of nature, such as the one you describe, I would go quietly into neither night nor day."

The thought struck Alex like a hammer over the head. When his focus waned, the chains forced him back several feet before he caught and steadied himself.

"Careful," said Surr. "I do hope my words have not given you distress, young man. Think nothing of them. It's become clear I should never have come. Not sure what I was thinking." His silhouette and beaded eyes drifted away from the door. With no

Eve signature or body to see, he had vanished completely into the darkness, as though he'd never existed at all.

"Wait!" Alex called. "Come back, please."

A moment of silence passed before the man's eyes reentered the window. "Don't worry, I won't leave you."

Alex stepped forward. "Thank you. It's nice to have someone to talk to that doesn't berate me."

"I understand that notion well. No disrespect is intended when I say I wasn't expecting the Ire boy to show such . . . humanity. Such fear . . . I have to confess, son, I'm in a sort of awe. Your accomplishments are profound for someone so young. Never before has a human been the subject of so many songs among the peoples of UnEarth."

"Songs?" asked Alex. "I didn't accomplish anything—"

"Hush, child. Praises are being rained upon you by an elder. Learn to relish in the downpour. Since the Ire arrived, my entire cellblock has been raving about it. About you."

"But I thought the UnEarth people feared the Ire."

"We believe the one capable of creating the Ire to be a creature above all. Capable of destroying an entire planet. Or . . . we did. The others will be so downtrodden to hear the news—you were just as much a victim of the Ire as we. I now see how lucky all of Earth is that your counterpart, the Rapture boy, was there to stop it. His name again, what was it? . . . Ah, yes, Hunter. An apt name."

"Yeah . . . we were lucky to have him."

"I hope I can meet the Hunter before his end. That story would surely prove to be enough to satiate me for another few dimes."

Alex's chest was getting warm, which came as a surprise. "It wasn't just Bennett," he said.

"But Hunter walked into the maelstrom with no guidance or guarantee of safety. It seems lucky you were taken over and he was the one with no choice. To make such a dangerous decision . . . takes great strength and courage."

"Yeah, but nobody else knows what it was like being in there. Having to live with that fire burning in you. Having to live every day since."

"Tell me," Surr said solemnly, his muted eyes fixed on Alex's.

"It was . . . everything I thought Hell could be. Just pain and burning . . . The intensity was buried so deep. Shocking you frozen while it . . . I don't know, I can't describe it." Alex turned to walk away. "I changed my mind. I don't want to talk about this anymore."

"'Tis no problem, child. But that does not mean it is not a disappointment."

"I'm sorry?"

"You were the Ire!" With a sudden jerk and baleful voice, Surr shrieked, joined by a crack of lightning and thunder. "You, child, for a brief moment, were more powerful than even the greatest of UnEarth! You could have stormed the gates of Hywyn yourself. Only the Beast of Arros could have stood as your equal! And now here you stand, trying like mad to remove yourself from this purity of greatness? No—not what I imagined at all. I will now be forced to lie to the others upon my return as not to tread on their wants and dreams."

What is he talking about? What greatness?

The Wrath in Alex was creeping up now. *Did he come here tonight expecting to get the Ire's autograph?* Trying to put a positive spin on that night was insanity at its peak. Absolutely no one in a sane world would have been interested in that.

"I will let them keep their notions of the Ire," Surr said. "Prisoners have so little as it is. I'll also do this for you, so your story may never be tarnished. The creatures of UnEarth fear you. That would be a truly terrible thing to waste. You are above them all. Even Gabriel. He has grown leisurely, like the rest. Those of UnEarth don't know how to adapt at the speed of humanity's progression. They are sensing an end. My boy, you are not a freak. You are a culmination."

"Of what?"

"Everything that those who would control others fear. The weak overcoming the strong."

"No one is afraid of me. Not anymore."

"And yet, they behave with hostility toward you. This is fear manifesting. Your fear of them makes you let them walk over you. Their fear of you makes them want to squish the threat before it can harm them. Fear is a whirlpool where twisted emotions fight for dominance to reach the center, where, in a tempest, they collide."

"Well, I'll be dead soon. And I won't have to worry about any of that."

"Wrong attitude, Mr. Barker. Tsk-tsk. Have you never given any thought to your legacy? To your life after life? Think of what others will think of you long after you're gone."

"That doesn't matter to me now. I just want this all to be over."

"The man who cares not for his afterlife cared not for his life when alive. These were the words of my mentor. Again, this is disappointing. And here I had such high hopes for you. Of course, that's what I get for placing a human on a pedestal. Things have been quiet for a while. Stagnant. Festering. Then you showed—the man who killed a Medolian."

"I told you, it wasn't me."

"I see that now—what you truly are. You are without hatred, Mr. Barker. A rare one, indeed. I see why Izaiah chose the path he did. He knew the true key to the Wrath in a human was not to find one with rage who might misuse it immediately, but rather one draped in benevolence—to let the fire sink in first. But the Medolian could do nothing for your sadness. The Wrath used this to burrow its way further."

"I've heard this before—my grief caused the whole thing."

"The Wraith Chloe knew exactly what they were doing by ending Melissa's life in front of you. She and the Brothers of Gehenna wanted the Earth destroyed along with as much of the universe as they could muster, one way or another. If the Brothers had been able to complete their transference and reach critical mass, the blast would have spread throughout the cosmos, turning it to ash. But they did not plan on the Ire making a choice that day."

Alex's head was beginning to hurt. "How can you know all this?"

"That doesn't matter. But I ask again, is it true?" Surr pressed. "Was the Ire acting outside of you or with you in concert? Who was the piloting force?"

"I don't know! I don't know anymore . . . Can you please . . . can we not?"

Surr waited a moment. "Your shame is like nothing I've ever felt. To think that an evolved creature could despise themself so much . . . it breaks the heart. You may learn to love yourself one day as you loved your wife, Alexander. Imagine the possibilities then. For it was your great love that first created your great strength."

Alex let the thought sink in before asking, "Did you say greater than Gabriel?"

Surr revealed his gray smile. "That is why the High Lord has come. The reason he visited you the other night—to see the one true threat to his rule before it is snuffed out for good."

I thought he came to pity me. Could a creature like that really fear me?

"Yes," Surr said, as though he'd heard Alex's thoughts. "You've caused a Celestial lord to experience fear. Even in my time, that is rare. You're something else, Mr. Barker, even if you don't know it."

The implications were staggering. Alex lost his balance and skidded backward on the lumpy ground. As he regained his footing, the chains above dangled and chimed wildly. But when he looked at the cell door window, he found it empty. Exhaustion caught up with him, forcing his stance to give way. He was dragged back to the center of the room, rehung like a marionette. Gradually, the swing slowed, and he checked the door again—Surr was still gone. A fight for consciousness overtook Alex.

"Where'd you go? Surr?" he asked, but there was no reply. *I didn't hear his footsteps.*

The fog in his mind closed in as the window to the outer block remained empty. Surr's breath in the darkness never returned. For what felt like hours, Alex pored over what he had said, until suddenly, morning arrived. The storms had ceased, and he found himself curled in a ball, wondering if it had all been a dream. He called for Oaleen, asking if she had seen where Surr had gone or if she had heard the end of their conversation. If the mystery man had really been an inmate as long as he claimed, she would likely have known him by name.

"I can't remember the last thing he said to me," Alex said.

"What in the Eve are you blabbering about?" Oaleen said, yawning like a lioness.

"You didn't hear any of our conversation?" Alex asked. "You couldn't have been that fast asleep with the storm."

"Heavier the storm the heavier I sleep." She yawned again. "Haven't had a good one like that in ages."

"You're not playing? You didn't see him? Or hear him? Surr? That was his name. Ring any bells?"

"Surr? You sure you weren't just talking to yourself, making up friends? I'm starting to think you're losing it, Barker. Think about it—how could anyone get in here? Did you forget this is the highest-security jail wing in all of Trivium?"

"But he was standing right there! Why would I make something like that up?"

"I don't know. Maybe you want attention. Or maybe you're finally losing it. Or more likely, you dreamed it."

"But it's just . . ." Alex trailed off, not wanting to add anything else that might embarrass him. *Like that's possible.*

"Just what?" Oaleen pressed.

"Just . . . I can still smell him."

HARVEST AT THE ROSE

The purest terror clawed up Casey's spine as the smiling, fur-covered creature charged from down the darkened hall. Grunts and frenzied breaths drew near. "Gotta find her . . . gotta find her," the thing repeated in saliva-drenched bursts. Its bright eyes, the size and color of tennis balls, never blinked, locked ahead. Long nails clattered on the floor like the largest rat in existence scurrying toward a human-sized block of cheese. Every tendon in Casey's body snapped tight, as though stricken by sudden, extreme cold. Death was upon her, and nothing, it seemed, could prevent it.

Just stay still! Staying still is great! Remember how much you like to sleep? Her heart even joined in, stopping for a brief second as the panting thing grew close enough to grab her. *Or slobber on me.* Then, as suddenly as it had appeared, the creature was gone, headed down the low-ceilinged hall in the same direction. Its footfalls hadn't skipped a beat.

An overwhelming stench of moss engulfed her before fading. As the breath and steps of the creature became softer, and her heart and lungs and basic functions started again, the realization finally struck: she was alive. Excessively sweating, but alive.

I . . . I'm in the clear? I have to be. Not that she was ready to calm down just yet. That was a Human Beaubon that passed (*though it looked more Beaubon than human*), complete with a stare like a runaway crack addict. She'd spotted a flash of cyan clothing: the uniform of a member of Chief Mary's security. The path through the miniature hall must have been a shortcut. *But that smell . . . She was probably drunk.* Just like the clubgoers who'd run into her many times before Casey started wearing her Grief gem regularly, the UnEarth woman hadn't even known she was there. But the pitter-patter of the Beaubon's feet had since vanished completely, giving Casey an opening to hurry back the way she'd come as covertly as possible.

Finding the Medolians was all that mattered now, if Madam Daphne hadn't gotten to them already. The guards' overheard conversation had confirmed Casey's worst fear: the past six weeks had been nothing but a setup. The madam was not planning to help get Leigh back at all but only wanted the Medolians. For what, Casey still didn't have the faintest idea.

But what can she really do to a Medolian? There's no way the chief has the kind of weapons that can bring down one of them. So, what's the plan? The guards had mentioned how lucky it was that Casey had brought the Medolians with her to the Rose, but nothing more. *If those two get hurt because of me, I'll never forgive myself . . . if I live long enough to, that is.*

Reaching the end of the dim hall, she opened the half-scale door and peered out. The coast was clear, but raised voices were arguing somewhere nearby in French, the direction of which remained disappointingly unclear. With a quick breath, held as if her life depended on it, she darted out, choosing right as her direction and hoping to everything good and holy that she'd picked the best way. When the arguing voices began to fade away, a touch of relief caressed her, quickly slapped away when she rounded the next corner and found a trio of Rose security guards a little more than a dozen yards away.

Stoically sitting at their feet was a creature much like a leopard, but aquamarine and vibrant orange, with both colors fighting for dominance like a tiger's stripes tossed into a laundry machine. The surface of its skin was without pores or hair or blemish, directing light like a shark's, while long tendrils flowing from the top of its head stood in place of ears. Whatever it was, the creature was as beautiful as any butterfly or rainforest flower she'd ever seen, but Casey knew a drug-sniffing dog when she saw one. Most of the terror she'd just shed came rushing back.

Her feet—reliable as ever in their old-man sneakers—planted her, allowing her to backpedal as quickly as possible. But just before she disappeared around the corner, the leopard creature's head began to turn her way. The guards had not noticed her, but she had no idea about the animal. With no desire to find out, she darted into the closest open door she could find. Stepping in, she strained to close it silently as the air in the shadowy room choked her. The smell was abhorrent to all decent values and ideas of purity. Every ounce of Casey was offended, even the pockets stowing arsenic. The stench was organic and sour, and biological. *I can taste it! I can taste it! It's like ten basketball locker rooms after doubles scrimmages—but on my tongue—and all at once!* By some miracle, she had not vomited, as though she'd found a smell so disgusting it broke her receptors and rendered her system null. More than anything, she wanted to leave and never find out what was causing the stink because most of her already knew but couldn't risk the hall or the Nashwyn leopard.

As she ventured forward, black shapes and the grunts and moans of alien coitus drifted by. Screams like baboons devouring a swarm of bats sprang up. Bursts of cyan light blinded like camera flashes. Mouths connecting crackled like radio static, releasing small sparks of rainbow light. When Casey's shoe slipped on some thick unknown substance, she reached out to catch herself, grasping something coated in goo. Before an apology could be made, the creature she'd grasped let out a pleasurable squeak.

"Don't be afraid to give it a little oomph back there. Thank you."

Casey pressed on, desperately searching for an exit, bouncing off bodies left and right, growing more woozy by the second, feeling myriad bits and bobs graze and/or slump over her as she passed. The far wall arrived not a moment too soon, and she planted her spine against it, making her way. Among the frenzied shadows, there came a glimpse of La Rose Noire security and their Nashwyn leopard, searching the orgy. The leopard's movements were steady and sleek, keeping its belly only a few inches above the floor, as though ready to pounce. Casey hurried, sidestepping and running her hand along the wall. When it gripped a door handle, she thanked the Lord. When it turned, she thanked Him again.

Slipping out, it seemed impossible not to let in a noticeable burst of light. Casey found herself in a service hallway for the transport of trash bins. No one was in sight. Closing the door behind her as quietly as possible, she hightailed it away. In a stroke of luck, this was somewhere she had been before and knew the way, but there was no hiding in a hallway as plain as this, and the next junction was a good dash away. For all she knew, the Nashwyn leopard might have been sensitive enough to feel panicked footsteps through the floorboards, making running an idea not worth considering.

The junction came, and Casey rounded it. No one was in front

of her, and no one was screaming behind her. *Yet.* The nook she'd
claimed at the bottom of the stairs was not far. *I need my things.*
Then we're getting out of here. After dodging another security detail,
she managed to make it safely. Taking a moment to collect herself
and drink some water, she packed supplies into her backpack and
set out to find Galinthia and Fabian.

Few places remained to search, and with many of their usual
haunts already checked off, coming up with an idea of where to go
was tough. But while stalking the halls, she discovered more doors
of varying sizes. After finding the first, it was as though a veil had
been pulled back, revealing yet another level of the mysteries of the
already mysterious Rose. Using the doors and the tunnels beyond
the half-scale doors, she was able to travel surprisingly quickly and
out of sight. *Fabian has to be somewhere with food I haven't checked*
yet. But I've been to the diners and dining rooms and the kitchen. And
the butcher. So . . . that would leave . . .

Like a stinging, dissonant piano chord struck behind her, stunning and petrifying, Casey realized where he must have been all
this time. *Of course! Why didn't I think of it before?* Five minutes later, she was in what was known as the "backyard" of La Rose Noire.

Twenty yards up, a canopy of vines blotted out most of the cool
moonlight trying to fall on the area, which sprawled over at least
an acre. What light made it through fell as beams of blue haze,
illuminating the gazebos and vegetable garden with a ghostly glow.
Following the paths paved with luminous green cement, Casey
began to worry she'd come to another dead end before spotting
a huge Doloros squash snoring so loudly it shook like a broken
washing machine.

"Fabian! You need to get up," she cried, scrambling over.

Curled into a ball within the mostly eaten gourd, the Medolian was smothered head to toe in a pulpy yellow-green mass. "Huh?" he mumbled, peering up through half-closed eyes.

Casey's whispers were so panicked they were even louder than casual conversation. "We need to get out of here. Come on!"

Fabian began to stir, but slower than a passing cloud, chewing on remnants still in his mouth. As though only now noticing her, he gave Casey a pleasantly surprised smile. "Say what now?"

"I just overheard them. Madam Daphne isn't helping us. She's been setting us up. They've got the whole Rose security force after us. Come on!"

"Huh? After us? To do what? Is there another meal on its way? Ooo, I hope so!" Fabian finished with a monstrous yawn, expelling a cavern's worth of bad breath.

"I'm not messing around! They're coming! We need to get Galinthia and get the heck out of here."

Just as she finished speaking, an alarm began to blare over the entire complex. Its long, droning wails seemed intended to wake the dead.

Fabian spat out a mouthful of seeds. "Huh? What's that?"

"It's what I told you!"

"When?"

"Just now! They're going to take us, and I don't know what for."

"You weren't kidding? But why? Wait, no . . . I get it. What did Gale do now? Did she kill someone she wasn't supposed to? Or was something expensive broken? That's all right. Just tell them to fill out an official A6-4 Medolian erasure and log the proper scrolls with—"

"No, she didn't! Or, I don't know, probably, but that's not what they said. They want you and Gale. They said I brought you to them. I don't know what they want, but we shouldn't wait around to find out."

The benign expression on Fabian's face suddenly turned sour. "*Hmm*, I do sense an awful lot of malice in the building. What is that Wyst up to?" Without taking the time to wipe himself off, he rose to his feet and revealed his phone from his pocket. With a flash of yellow light from its camera, the gourd debris was stricken away, and Fabian appeared as though he'd just taken a shower and had his clothes dry cleaned.

"Come on! Hurry," Casey cried.

"Very well, Miss Casey. Though I won't be able to Shift. Not unless it's an absolute emergency. We'll have to get out of here the old-fashioned way."

"By sneaking?"

"No. By letting Gale use brute force and do whatever she wants. It's always worked for us in the past."

Casey had no reason to argue with that. If it meant their safe escape, so be it. *I just won't look.*

She stayed close on Fabian's heels as they charged away, and hardly ten seconds had passed before he suddenly seized as though being stunned by a taser. Stiffening up like a board, he stumbled one step before managing to catch himself. Every muscle in his wide frame was suddenly clenched, as though fighting an invisible force keeping him in place. At the same time, a high-pitched noise rolled over the garden, reminiscent of a chorus of rusty flutes holding an off-pitch note.

"Fabian?" Casey cried, running to face him. She found his gray eyes wide with terror. His leg twitched like a dog having a dream, as though he were fighting to speak but could not. The color in his eyes began flickering, fluctuating between all the shades of Eve. "What is happening to you?"

The high-pitched ringing grew louder and nearer. Casey searched in all directions, peering into the foggy distance of the vegetable patch. She soon found a cluster of cyan eyes creeping toward them. Chief Mary and her security forces slowly revealed themselves beneath a beam of moonlight. The two guards on either side of her carried what looked like brass knuckles blazing with aquamarine light.

"What have you done to him?" Casey screamed, blocking the path between them and Fabian.

"What the Medolians have done to countless creatures," Chief Mary said. "I've muted him."

Casey then became aware of another sound: large metal wheels rolling over the rough terrain of the garden path. Splitting up the middle, the security team made room for a six-foot-tall silver beast. Its face was a smooth metal plate bolted to the frame. Extending from the plate, pointed toward Casey and Fabian, was a cone of brass-colored metal. The swirling grooves around it made it appear to be a roiling flame that defied gravity, burning straight outward, adorned with bolts and wires. The machine sounded like a dishwasher running on high with a couple of live raccoons inside. This was blanketed with a crackling like radio static yanked up several steps in pitch.

Veins began bulging from Fabian's face, neck, and hands, while his teeth ground so hard a white powder formed on his lips. "It's . . . it's . . ." he stammered. "It's inside of me."

"Very good, Mr. Medolian." A salty voice spoke from the darkness beyond the machine and security team. "Release him."

The sound of the device cut off, and Fabian collapsed to the ground with a low thud.

Stepping into the light with a dramatic wave of her head tentacles, Madam Daphne offered a self-satisfied laugh. "Intelligent for a Mallos creature. Your interior is what ails you. Though more specifically, what I've put there—a masterpiece, if I do say so. A perfect blend of the old and the new."

"Madam Daphne!" cried Casey, remaining by Fabian's side. "What is happening? Why are you doing this?"

"Don't play dumb with me, dear. You're far too easy to read. You know exactly what's happening. Deny not the world to save your own feelings, love."

With a strained grunt, Fabian began to rise to his feet, his muscles quaking, his knees on the precipice of collapsing.

"No, you poor Grief-tinted dullard, not yet," said Madam Daphne. With a twist of her wrist, the machine released a trumpeting blast, and Fabian was thrust to his knees once more, wheezing for breath. "Maybe I gave you too much credit. After all, it was you who placed yourself in this position in the first place. Willingly, too. Medolians, *yecht*. Your very smell offends me. A species that stands for nothing, creating chaos only to fool others into believing it's balance. You name yourselves Sentries yet care nothing for the greater UnEarth community."

"You know what I think? I think none of you one-sided ninnies are capable of seeing the big picture," Fabian choked out, losing the battle to rise to his feet.

On another signal from Madam Daphne, the machine's power was increased, forcing Fabian even lower, his nose pressed within inches of the floor.

"You still don't remember, do you?" Madam Daphne expelled with gratuitous resentment. "Of course you don't. I simply can't believe it. My life, reduced to this, set down a path of darkness, and yet the gatekeeper who led me here remembers none of it."

Fabian's back was sizzling. "I made you open a nightclub in France?"

"Do you know not of humiliation? I was a priestess, you shapeless, formless, nothing of a creature. Do you know what that is? Of course you don't, I can tell by your dopey stare. On Nashwyn, a priestess is one of the chosen, those who know the true spirit of Shek'twi, the very heart of the planet. We are tasked with the protection of my people's most prized treasure—the menagerie—the Bin'Talio. I had power. Real power. I commanded armies. Then, following a simple act of betrayal, I ended up here. This . . . place. This pile of waste they call Earth, the muck that stripped my Eve from me. You know, it was the first time I ever knew the sensation of nakedness. Shame had found me. I finally recognized this concept, and it frightened me. How could it not? Set loose in a primitive world of savages with nothing to call my own. Do you have any idea what that's like? And then, following hundreds of years of strife, grasping to survive, along come a pair of smug Medolians who tell me I've broken one of their 'laws' by simply eating food."

Fabian managed to raise a pointed finger. "Wait. Yeah . . . I do remember you." His words slurred and blurred together. "We took you in because you ate someone's . . . pony."

"It was meat. I was starving. A human's needs are beneath my own."

"Look, if every UnEarth Human went around doing whatever they wanted all the time, eating whoever or whatever, humanity would catch on, especially this latest bunch. If they do, they'll start changing how they live and throw the Eve out of balance. The Tribunal won't let that happen. I doubt you want it to, either."

"Spare me this mindless sophistry. I'm not here to bargain with you, Medolian. I'm letting you know why your immediate future will be markedly unpleasant."

"Stop this!" Casey screamed. "Can't you see you're hurting him?"

"Why, yes. I can." With a smile aimed at Casey, Madam Daphne gave another signal to increase the machine's power. When the sound reached a fever pitch and Fabian began to cry out, she clapped and giggled with glee, sending a shudder through her head tentacles. "This is even more fun than I was expecting! Like a swine raised and nurtured, only to be slaughtered when ready. Oh, Medolian, I can't wait to see what makes you tick. We're going to learn wonders from your carcass."

"Whatever you're doing, whatever you want, we can work this out!" Casey shouted.

"For a human, you are especially unwise," Madam Daphne said. "Though nowhere near as dull as the Sentry—*tsk-tsk*—eating and gorging himself, never paying a single rube or franc. No questions asked. Never wondering what might lurk within."

No. She wouldn't.

"The food . . ." Casey said. "You poisoned it."

The lady of the Rose turned up her nose. "The madam would never craft a poison! Such a thing is beneath me. At least, not a fatal one. If it were part of a creature's request to find pleasure and passion, so be it. But no, I did much more than simply poison the Medolian. I laced every treat and salty morsel he ingested with billions of these." Revealing a jar from between her breasts, Madam Daphne turned it over, letting the light play in its shimmering sand-like interior. "Earthly bacteria instilled with Eve. A wonderful, unexpected result of our preliminary work infusing Eve with living flesh. The fat Sentry never even knew of the clusters of my little babes growing within him. Now, they've permeated every inch."

Chief Mary smacked the howling machine as if it were a prized bull's backside. "With this, my N'trinto canon, we can make those clusters do all sorts of things. Observe." She motioned at two of her crew, who broke away to retrieve Fabian.

"Don't you touch him!" Casey shrieked, lashing out before being seized herself and held in place.

Madam Daphne clasped her hands and beamed the same way she would have at a newborn puppy stretching before a nap. "You are the sweetest dream. I really mean it. Just so cute I want to burst!"

Approaching Casey, she took her lightly by the chin to turn her nose up. "Little one, I know you may not believe me, but this is for the best if you truly care for him. The Medolians would have eventually ruined his confused mind. Now, you can live in peace, knowing only comfort and pleasure. Look at you, you precious, fragile thing. I pity and adore misbegotten creatures such as yourself. I can't help but care for them. I promise to give you everything you want and ask for very little in return. And as an added perk, should you ever get out of line, my punishments are considered to be both fair and mutually beneficial."

The Rose security hoisted Fabian from the ground, where he winced, moaned, and gurgled, shaking as though he were being subjected to soundwave torture that scrambled his mind. His lips and teeth danced, chattering his words like rain patter while his eyes remained locked on Casey. *He's trying to tell me something!*

She reached out to touch him but was pulled back immediately by the chief.

"I wouldn't do that if I were you," Madam Daphne said. "Where would you go? If he tries to Shift while the machine is on and the bacteria are activated, they will implode all at once. You'd be lost to the Eve along with him. A waste of perfectly useful specimens, if you ask me."

"You're a real-life monster, aren't you? Proof they exist. Well, I'll never be your little pet, you hear me?" Casey roared. "Never! So get it out of your skull because you seem to think you can control others, but you don't. Nobody does, and I've never understood why that concept is so hard to grasp."

"What a wonderful simplification. But you fail to understand, child," Madam Daphne said. "I did not just fill the Medolians with tricks. Did you really think your own meals would come any more free of cost? Did you think I was letting you sail on my back?"

"You put something in . . . me?" All the dinners Casey had shared with Madam Daphne flashed through her mind.

"Something special was brewed just for you, tailored as an antithesis to everything you cherish and admire, to all your personal warmth and happy thoughts, and most of all, the summation of all that you love. The compound kept inside the capsules floating within your bloodstream is one of my proudest achievements. It can be released at a moment of my choosing."

"I thought you said you don't use poison."

"My creation won't kill you, dear. If released, it will fill you with the most potent unpleasant emotions you are capable of feeling. Everything good and blissful and comfortable would be taken from you, replaced with its shadow. It would be an excruciating darkness from which there is no return. This, one of my finest masterpieces, if I dare say, was made for you, because I care. Because you're worth the energy, my darling. Now, come take your place by my side."

Casey wiped away a tear, brought on not by the threat she'd just received, but by the realization that it had come from someone she'd started to trust and see as a friend, possibly even a mentor. But no, the lady of the Rose was all too similar to humanity: full of greed and deception. "You don't get to play with our lives like this," Casey said weakly.

"Young thing, I get to do whatever I want. I'm Madam Daphne, one of the most prominent Mal-Drimo. That's why you're so fortunate. Of all the counts and countesses, all the emperors and all the kings and queens, you have been the lone human to change me, to make me finally see that your species can be useful for more than just acquiring resources. They can also be desired for their company, and not just as sexual objects. I admit I have a genuine fondness for you. So young and fresh and blind, just traipsing and stumbling. I will cherish you and make sure nothing bad ever happens to you again as long as you live, yes I will. You have my promise."

Casey stayed firmly in place. Chief Mary would have to carry her over because she would never willingly join Madam Daphne at her side.

"Fine. But you made me sad." Madam Daphne held out her open hand. A remote control was placed in it by Chief Mary. *Is that the remote to release the poison?* Casey froze like a deer caught in headlights.

"Wait," her weak voice muttered.

"What is it, darling?" Madam Daphne asked.

"Before you do that, I want you to tell me the truth about one thing."

"You want to know about your friend, is that right? How did I know that was going to come up? You never fail to disappoint, do you? What I told you before was the truth. We found your professor. I've known where she was all along—I just had no intention of doing anything about it. She made her choice, and she'll die with the rest of her cult."

"Die?"

"They plan to travel to Trivium and perish in a mass suicide. Can you believe it? All of them. Somehow, they think that will help their cause. Aluqa Morinnean is about to commit the mistake of all mistakes."

"This is about you and your grudge against Aluqa?"

"That woman has been a thorn in my side for going on two centuries. If she is going to leave her base of operations unguarded, I see no reason why I should let others pluck the fruits I've earned with sweat and tears."

"Two centuries? That's impossible. She's human."

With a dire look, Chief Mary leaned into Madam Daphne's ear and whispered something. The lady of the Rose listened but appeared unconcerned.

"Nonsense." She readdressed Casey. "Aluqa may have been born a human, but with every kill she became more like us of UnEarth. Her cells are no more human than my own."

"What did she do?"

"She made a deal with a devil long ago, or in this case, Celestial."

"The Cardinal?"

"Clever, you are. She and Royce first met in the early nineteenth century. She was a plague, traveling the world hunting my brethren. But when she made him her target, she failed. For reasons unknown, he spared her and gave her what she needed to acquire the gift of long life."

"What was it? What did he give her?"

"His blood. Even Human Celestial blood is soaked with Rapture. Little by little, his was added to hers. The human somehow survived and grew an empire that reached heights to rival my own. But it would not last. The Surface has faltered, and like all humans, in her desperation, she was bound to make a mistake. And it didn't take long. When she embarks on her crusade, the human resistance on Earth will be reduced to nothing but a memory in the wind. UnEarth will take control of this planet with ease."

"You couldn't possibly stop all of them. Aluqa has members all over the world. Tens of thousands."

Madam Daphne laughed once. "She might, if she worked half as hard at recruiting as she did perpetuating that silly myth. The Medolian Mara Loren has done far more to suppress an UnEarth uprising on Earth than Morinnean, and she disappeared days ago. The Surface lost stations one by one, until all that was left was Aluqa's primary. Her membership numbered one hundred forty-two as of yesterday. Mostly frightened, feeble-minded trash she uses as labor. And with the Cardinal frequently recruiting for his own projects, the Surface has never been able to gather the numbers needed to enact real change. But one thing Morinnean has always known is strategy. She knows how to do a lot with a little. It's rarely worth it to engage with her in battle, but I have never taken my eye off her, biding my time to strike. This is it. With her resources added to my own, and now two Medolians under my thumb, I will be able to control all of Earth. The Tribunal can scream and shout all it likes."

"You're a real piece of work, aren't you?" Casey said.

"Yes, my darling," Madam Daphne agreed happily. "A work of art." She lifted the remote to press its button in full view, when—blam!—it was knocked from her hands and shattered on the ground, stabbed through its heart by a red-and-brown-handled dagger.

A Wrath-tinted Mallos sphere rocketed into the group, with Galinthia planted on top like a skier in a downhill dash. The sphere dissolved just before she landed flat-footed, crouching, and drew daggers with both hands, her eyes blazing with crimson intensity.

"You're all about to expire. Hope it was worth it."

Madam Daphne, clearly more annoyed than threatened, said, "Why does everyone suddenly think they're permitted to say such things to me?" With smooth, even steps, she approached Galinthia. "Put away the rage, Wrath Sentry. You've had plenty of time to play. Now it's time to pay."

"Are you betraying us, Wyst? Consider your answer," Galinthia snarled.

"Careful!" Casey screamed. "She can stop you with that thing."

"Machines fill no Sentry with fear!" Galinthia responded. "Nothing of the Earth may harm us. Lay down your weapons or succumb to a slow fading."

"I'm serious!" Casey screamed.

"Betrayal? Really?" Madam Daphne said. "Medolian, if you ever thought we were on the same side, then I seriously question your intelligence. Perhaps the large one was the brains of the operation. I shudder in excitement at the thought of a world without your kind. Whoever is spearheading the attacks in the Senate—Van-Mortus, one can only assume—is doing the worlds of Un-Earth a great service."

"You sick, Fervor-spewing—" Galinthia sneered, lunging with the speed of a hawk in flight. But Chief Mary blocked her dagger blade, gripping Galinthia by the wrist. With a hideous shriek, the chief revealed tall yellow fangs and eyes blazing with aquamarine light. Blue-green flooded her complexion as she struggled with Galinthia, her strength seeming to increase the more she changed, until the machine screamed once more and her foe crumbled to the ground, joining Fabian.

Casey was utterly helpless, unable to move. The chief, now twenty-five percent more Wyst than woman, seized her once again. A rancid fish smell poured from her throat.

"Please! Let them go. I'll do whatever you want," Casey pleaded. "You want a pet? You got it! Dress me up however you like, just don't hurt them because of me."

Madam Daphne rolled her eyes. "I swear, I've never been asked so many ridiculous things in one day. It's tiring. Chief Mary, you may take the Medolians away. If it would make you feel more comfortable, you may remove their limbs. I doubt we would learn any more with them attached. Better safe than sorry."

"Good idea, boss," the chief said with a prominent grin.

"No!" Fabian bellowed from the ground with a sudden swell of energy. "You won't have Miss Casey, and you won't have us!" Shaking like a withered sapling in a storm, he fought to stand, a canary-yellow Grief-tinted light radiating from him like a thousand candles. With thumping, plodding, desperate steps, he marched toward the machine. "Get out of here! Get to safety! Go, you two!"

His feet cracked the path beneath them, crunching and sinking. Chief Mary turned up the power on the machine, and her team began piling onto him like defensive linemen onto a running back, but he could not be fully detained. Fabian's steps continued steadily toward the machine.

Just before reaching it, he stole a glance at Casey and Galinthia. "Make this count! It's been my pleasure, my friends."

With a roar, Fabian opened his arms wide and fell forward, hugging the machine and creating a Shift portal at the same time. The white explosion that followed would be something Casey would never allow herself to forget.

TO NASHWYN

Once the last guard in the warehouse dock had departed and their signature was gone, Mara lifted the lid of her crate and found herself in a vast, murky room, with green and dirty-gold highlights gliding along the walls in the distance. The shipping dock and warehouse had been a tizzy of energy during the day, but now lay as silent as a tomb. The crates in which she and Felix had been hiding, usually reserved for shipments of molspuk squid from Nashwyn, had been intercepted by Boris's Cypress Cilian Group while en route. *Just a lovely scent to soak in for days on end. Just lovely. Can't get enough.*

With the speed of a strong wind, she rose and zeroed in on Felix. Lifting the lid of his crate, she found his dirt-and-hair-encrusted face gazing up with petrified red eyes.

"Is it over yet?"

"Yes. Time to go."

After helping him up, Mara hurried them toward the rear door, per Boris's instructions. *If this all goes according to plan, I'll reconsider how I feel about the big Celestial.*

In the back reaches of the receiving facility, huge, fleshy tubes with purple and pink rings around the spouts sucked up and spat out packages of all shapes and sizes. Many crates could be seen going this way and that inside the tubes, disappearing into the dimly green semitranslucent walls. *The MMS of Nashwyn. Their mailing system.* After a series of twists and turns, dodging suck-and-blow tubes along the way, Mara and Felix burst from the exit into a sunny day in the city of Diodre.

When her eyes adjusted, the cityscape—a lustrous conglomeration of green and yellow with aquamarine filling every gap—seemed to pulse and breathe like a single creature. Backdropped by a mulberry-pink sky fading into lilac, the glossy, naturally moist sides of the Nashwyn skyscrapers flickered in the sun. Their spires, ribbed like prophylactics made for her pleasure in various artistic angles and frequencies, were often topped by bulbous sections of some sort—shapes reminiscent of inverted raindrops that Mara would just as soon not think too much about. Bubbles as large as brownstones were interspersed among huge vines and tube structures hanging from branches, extending throughout the city like a kelp forest in a world of giants.

Intermixed throughout the structures were travel tubes, winding and twisting like crazy straws installed throughout the skyline. At any given moment, thousands of citizens of Diodre were in the tubes, jetting at speeds fast enough to pull the hair off a gopher, if one were to be caught inside for a remarkable reason.

There was no denying the unremitting beauty of the city. Even Felix seemed to appreciate it in his own way—at least, as much as a man could while keeled over, looking ready to pass out at any moment.

"Lovely. Can we move on, please?" he said, gulping and hiccupping right after.

If he's having this hard a time now, how is he going to remain conscious once we descend to the true Diodre city—the one underwater?

Those who came to visit the planet but were not compatible with aquatic living could enjoy much of what Nashwyn had to offer from the dry upper portion. But Nashwynites were first and foremost creatures of the depths. Though there was a metropolis up here in the thick, damp air, a far greater one rested below.

"Let's get to it. This way," Mara said.

The warehouse they were escaping was located at the end of a large octopus-like arm of the city's floating platform. Mara inhaled the smells: salty, tangy, sour, and crisp, filling the two-hundred-percent humidity air. The sights: brooks foaming and bubbling everywhere, glistening greens as far as the eye could see. The planet of passion, though gorgeous to behold, had always carried a signature she'd never had a taste for, like the awkward smell of another's dwelling that you never bring up. But today, it was giving off less outward Fervor than she remembered. Feeling a certain "weakness" in the planet's life force was surprisingly disheartening.

"So, we're going to see this senator?" Felix asked, trudging behind her. The noises escaping him suggested he was on the verge of puking.

"Yes. Boris has only ever been trouble, but he's right that Bo is somehow in the middle of it all."

"I don't get it. Why don't you trust Boris? Hannah did. If he says this Bo fella isn't such a great guy, I say we listen. Celestials don't lie very often."

"That Celestial is a trafficker and has no idea what he's talking about. Bo is a distinguished statesman and has been in that role since before the Purge. The people trust him—not just on Nashwyn, but in all of UnEarth. And if you summon Hannah from the dead to defend your stance one more time, I'm going to toss you into the brine and leave you on this planet."

"Sorry. Just sometimes I don't know what to think about things until I try to see them from her perspective."

Mara knew what he meant but had no desire to let him know that.

"I trust Bo because he was the mentor I never had in the Sentries. Izaiah Ezekial took no matters seriously—always cracking a joke, even when I asked for help. Even when it would hurt. Yet he had no real idea. Izaiah is far too dense to read people. It's likely he's long forgotten how it was to first learn to control Mallos. Mastering it took me a long while. Almost to Inferius's end. I was finally getting the hang of it when Batia . . . I wasn't a natural like Chloe, and Izaiah didn't help. His advice was always 'Just go with it' or 'You just need to feel it.' But Bo actually put forth effort to communicate with me and hear what I was saying. He saw potential in me."

Mara wanted to pick up their pace, but Felix was moving as sluggishly as a donkey on tranquilizers.

With a blistering groan, he suddenly collapsed to the ground like a toddler in need of a nap. "I can't do this. Why does it smell this way? I feel like I'm standing in a petri dish in full bloom. The squid crate was better!"

When his cries did not die down after a few moments, Mara shouted, "Okay, fine! We'll get you a stasis suit."

That quieted him enough to get him back on his feet and shuffling onward. The nearest store with suits was five blocks away, forcing Mara to carry her partner the last leg of the trip. The selection was poor, as only one suit could fit a human adult, and it was previously owned and in rough shape. *At least it's cheap.* Mara would be paying for it, after all.

Once Felix was snug in the suit as his bony frame would allow, he stepped out, and Mara felt her first urge to giggle in a long while. Stasis suits reminded her of the tethered diving garbs humans had recently developed in the nineteenth century—*clever little primates*—and seeing Felix inside one was quite amusing.

Taking it for a test run, his movements were clunky but also faster, and he no longer required as many breaks. A hopeful cheer spread through Mara at the thought of their mission continuing unabated. But that was squashed when a cry of passion suddenly rang out from behind them.

Mara spun to find a Poa-Lo-Fey Wyst approaching, gesticulating and waving wobbly arms that looked potentially deadly. Their genus was known for both prowess and aggressiveness, as well as a desire to flaunt it. This one was puffing her chest and showing off her fins while chanting in Lexine. After hearing the tenor of her pitch, Mara groaned and pinched the bridge of her nose. *Why me?*

"What did they say?" Felix asked.

"She's challenging me to a contest for dominion over a prize."

"What prize?"

"You."

"What does she want me for?"

"Do you really want to know the answer to that question?"

The Poa-Lo-Fey roared, flaring the tendrils on her chest and shoulders to the maximum, signaling she was ready to begin. Mara knew her type well. This situation was all too familiar. *It used to happen whenever Hannah and I came to Nashwyn.* The Wyst was past talking; nothing would satisfy her until Mara fought her. *This is the very same aggravating shit that made me never want to come back here.*

"Remember, you made me have to do this," she said bitterly to Felix.

Too quickly for the Wyst to react, let alone defend herself, Mara sent a punch into her chest, channeling a burst of Fervor. Having no idea what hit her, the Wyst crashed into the street, halting several carts and the huge dryn slugs pulling them. The slugs reared back, releasing monstrous hissing and gurgling noises while discharging the contents of purple bile sacks from their undercarriages.

Staring in surprise and seemingly aroused wonder, the nearby public began grunting like gorillas to show their admiration. *I always hated that, too.*

"Wow," Felix said, gaping along with the rest of them. "I didn't know you cared."

"Let's get out of here." Mara led them away from the crowd, hoping no one had recognized her and blown whatever slim chance they had to pull this off.

The deeper they traveled into the city, the more comfortable Felix became in his stasis suit—but then a little too comfortable, as he began making detours to check out every shiny thing that caught his eye, which Nashwyn was unfortunately plagued with. Eventually, the duo reached a district called Swinnlax, an affluent business-oriented block in one of the busiest parts of Diodre. All along the green-and-turquoise path were colorful wonders to be seen, ranging from artists and performers to vendor carts.

Mara's new partner had no trouble mingling now, as the Wysts seemed just as fascinated by the Human Archfiend as he was by them. Several times, she had to pull him away from conversations so they could carry on, making the trip a plodding one to reach Itilipsinian Square, the high government plaza of Nashwyn— what the people had dubiously dubbed the sip-sip, or "place of heavy sucking and fucking." Primarily, the ruling elite were located in one of the many towers under the water's surface, but Bo's office was not in the depths. Being made to live in human form to serve as a Tribunal senator, his office was located above the surface, surrounded by breathable air.

A dark nook provided a prime spot to regroup and allow Felix to catch his breath. *The weight of the suit seems to be taking its toll.* They remained in the nook for a good portion of the day. The warnings Mara had received did not fall on deaf ears; she wanted to take a good long look at things before making any moves.

It was nearly dusk when a convoy of luxury-class dryn slugs arrived in front of the building. Senator Bo and his entourage exited the cabins, gabbing and spilling drinks, chewing on food from trays carried by attendants, and made their way inside, disappearing from view when the doors slapped shut behind them with a suction-cup slurp. But he was not lost to Mara. She knew Bo's every move as he and his crew made their way to the top floor via a private elevator.

"He's in his office," she said to Felix.

"Gotcha. So, what's the plan?"

An aching desire in Mara urged her to simply break into Bo's office and accost him in front of his team and guests. But at least three other Medolians were no doubt searching everywhere for her, and this setup would've made a wonderful trap. Nashwyn was a likely place to check for her, though as yet no natural Shifts had transpired in the city or on the planet. *Hopefully they're busy searching Earth in vain.*

"So, how are we doing this?" Felix asked, likely sensing her hesitation.

"There's no way in from up here. The building is too guarded."

"So, we're giving up?"

"No, I said we can't get in from up there. But we can from the lower city."

"You mean in the brine?" Felix asked with a gagging, weak moan.

"We got you a stasis suit. What more do you want?"

He had no argument, and instead just let his mouth hang open like a cabinet door on a single hinge until they reached the nearest entrance to the undercity, which was never far no matter where you were on Nashwyn. Semicircle cutouts in the cucumber-skinned ground contained shallow pools that led to the brine. Much like an underground subway entrance, a steady stream of riders flowed in and out, as brightly colored as Mara had ever seen. Na-Nala Wysts lumbered by, clumsy once out of the liquid and forced to walk on land. The Poa-Lo-Fey tended to storm in and out with a volatile splash, while the Bai-Shalk, sleek and slippery and almost always addicted to speed, came and went without appearing to disturb a single water molecule, like traveling spirits, leaving only razor-thin trails.

Felix walked slowly to the edge of the entrance, leaning to peer into the brine. Others sidestepped him, the slow foreigner in the way. Mara did not want to make a scene and attract any Mal-Drimo Wysts, who couldn't resist coddling a poor, pathetic thing, which Felix clearly was. Passing quickly ahead, she sucked in an enormous breath before entering the aquamarine liquid, leaving him with no one he knew around him to complain to. Once he mustered the courage several moments later, he followed Mara into the undercity.

For accuracy's sake, it should be noted that the water covering ninety-eight percent of Nashwyn's surface was not, in fact, H_2O, but a culmination of the runoff from all the living things that had ever existed on the planet, sustained still by those who currently did. Life on Nashwyn secreted liquid easily, readily, and freely. The oceans were, in fact, a giant soup of this nutrient-rich biomass, which Mara tried not to think about whenever visiting the under-city. Like most humans, she found the idea revolting.

The city life of Diodre'Ipsil surrounded them. Light passed to the eye easily through the brine, illuminating advertisements for products as well as traffic signs. In this portion, there was no need for travel tubes. Some remained solely for secure or private channels, but most travel was done as the Wysts and their ancestors always had: by flipping their fins. The creatures of passion were tremendous swimmers, gaining an increase in their natural abilities while submerged. Collisions between travellers were rare, as commuters followed ocean currents in coursing streams, for the most part neat as a pin.

The entrance they'd passed through led to a large shopping center. This one, known as the Kefell Bloom, was filled with yellow light, soaking the green-and-blue walls in brilliance. Nearly every type of Nashwyn business was accounted for. Every flavor of food or garment style could be found somewhere within the Bloom's four-mile stretch of towers descending into the deep.

Though wildlife was not an issue—most of it stayed away from Wyst cities and their lights—some species had evolved over the years to live among the people in a codependent relationship. Many were sluglike creatures tolerated either because they expelled a pleasant-scented gas, had barbs with narcotic-level venom, or, sometimes, because they were pretty and decorative. Other wildlife, such as the udilla, resembled larger seahorses with webbed arms and legs. These scavengers would often steal a Wyst's lunch if attention wasn't being paid.

Every few feet, there seemed to be some sort of artistry on display, from poets to musicians. Many colored their bodies with paint, while others attempted to paint passersby as a form of performative art. Almost no one objected, letting them do as they pleased, which was probably why the painters appeared so surprised when Mara dodged away, dragging Felix with her. All wanted a chance to paint the Archfiend in the stasis suit, but that would have proved far too annoying and delaying to allow.

Mara's breath was out. Releasing what air she had left, she inhaled the brine, waiting for her body to adjust to breathing something quite a bit thicker. *I avoid this part as long as possible.*

An old elevator was somewhere nearby that she hoped was still functional. *Looks like they've changed a lot of things over the years. That better not be one of them.* Many changes were nice to see, like the expansion of cuisines offered, but some were not.

Nashwyn guards—which Mara hadn't seen in the flesh in nearly two thousand years—were suddenly all over the place, accompanied by a bevy of propaganda smeared across the walls. Banners hung by the government featured cherry-picked quotes from Speaker Binahq and Ariel Van-Mortus that suggested Hywyn and Arros were instigating a new war. The same banners also urged all Wysts to rally to Nashwyn's cause and join the corps. Mara had seen similar messages from every kind of government across Un-Earth, all aimed at keeping their armies stocked. It made sense, but something about these banners was unsettling. *I've never seen the Queen's Council go to such lengths. Why would they decide to use fear on their people like this? What do they gain?*

In the deepest bowels of the mall, below what was essentially the food court, little was housed but service hallways and subordinate offices. A satellite HQ for the Vigilia Patrol was located down here, but the space had not been used for anything other than storage for at least a thousand years. Only a handful of souls roamed the area, which Mara carefully avoided. Soon, they rounded a soft corner into a desolate hall and found the freight elevator she had been searching for. A flat green wall, with purple veins flowing like rivers on an atlas, was cut down the middle by a deep gash, encased by huge folds of tissue on each side.

"Thank the Eve," she said, pressing the dark green freckle to the left side, which called the elevator.

"Oh, I see," said Felix. "Fun! I like lifts. Will this take us all the way to the top?"

"No, but it will get us far enough."

After sneaking their way through the building via two different elevators, Mara managed to get them onto yet another. The third was more like those on Earth—rectangular and made of sturdy metals and cured Nashwyn polymers, and featured a marble floor. After swiping the security leaf she'd stolen from the guard at the first transfer, they ascended. This elevator would get them far, but not all the way to the top, where Bo's office resided. The only access to that floor was via his private elevator, which was under much stricter security.

"How do you know about all these elevators?" Felix asked.

"I once aided an operation to smuggle a Nashwyn politician out of the building when several rebel factions were attempting to assassinate him. This was the route used."

"I see. Sort of ironic, then, huh?"

"I suppose. This is where the heights are going to come in. But don't worry, you will not fall."

"Comforting," Felix said.

With a long, high-pitched note announcing the floor, the elevator door opened to the third level from the top. Most everyone had gone home for the day, which played wonderfully in Mara's favor. But the floor wasn't fully abandoned yet. Guards were coming, easily sensed, forcing her to quickly direct Felix and herself into the room at the end of the hall on the left, where Bo's office resided, two stories up. The guards' senses wouldn't be perceptive enough to see her; Mara knew that, and luckily Felix's stasis suit shielded his Eve signature from view. Soon, the guards passed and took the elevator down several floors.

The empty office they entered appeared to house a host of clerical workers' desks. A gigantic enclosed fish tank sat at the far end, containing floating balls of color with translucent skin. These were espods: creatures perfectly content to float around all day, serving as decoration, unaware of who they were or what their surroundings were like. Next to the tank was a window peering outside to a cloudy, rose-tinted day.

"Here's where we get clever," Mara said.

Outside the glass, Diodre stretched out below, a garden teeming with Eve, nestled beneath a wisp of pastel-yellow clouds. When Mara opened the window, a warm breeze touched her face. Ducking down, she climbed onto the thin ledge outside.

"This is what you meant when you said don't worry?" Felix nearly screamed.

"I promise I will not let you fall. Come now, follow me."

Shaking so much that the stasis suit chattered, Felix inched toward the window. When he was just a few inches away but still unwilling to peer out, Mara took matters into her own hands. Clutching the chest of his suit, she yanked Felix out into the air. Luckily, he was smart enough not to shriek. With a couple of well-placed jumps, Mara landed them on a ledge outside the top level. They slipped inside through the window. Once it was closed behind them, Felix was left hyperventilating.

Mara set him down gently. "Apologies."

"If you're going to manhandle me, can I at least get a warning next time?"

"I did warn you."

The room they were in was a side storage connected to Bo's office by a heavy door. The lights were off, allowing Mara to spy on three signatures in the next room. All were laughing along with the senator, including someone with a Grief signature and another with an especially potent Dread signature. Neither were pures, and Mara didn't recognize either of them, but the Grief signature seemed young, maybe less than a K, while the heady Dread signature sent a surprising shiver cascading down her spine.

"We're going to hold here a moment. Wait until he is alone," Mara said.

"Whatever you say," Felix responded.

Mara's attention remained fixed on Bo's signature. His aura was calm, relaxed, even confident. She didn't sense any of the guilt or doubt she had expected. After all, he had reportedly fled from the trial to Nashwyn in shame. *Several eyewitnesses sensed it.*

Mara's Wrath erupted out of nowhere. The urge to break through the wall, tackle Bo onto his desk, and start asking questions took over. But she couldn't risk it without knowing who the other two in the meeting were. She was in no mood for surprises. Sitting down, she focused on the wall intensely, gradually noticing a voice speaking directly to her. Felix had apparently been going on about something for who knew how long.

"What are you saying?" she asked. "I told you, we're waiting."

"I . . . I mean, I know that. That has nothing to do with what I said. Did you even hear what I asked? Have you heard anything I've been saying?"

"No. Repeat it."

Felix hesitated. "If you didn't hear me, why did you respond like you did? You answered like something was already my fault."

"Will you just tell me?" Mara moaned.

Felix held up a yellow folder containing a stack of flattened shells—the Nashwyn equivalent to sheets of printer paper. "These are strange."

He stood next to a file cabinet, one among dozens filling the room. Pieces of a broken lock lay at his feet. Mara approached him, just fast enough to appease him.

"You broke into a cabinet?" she asked.

"So, all the things you've been doing are fine, but I break one little lock and it's a big deal?"

"Just tell me what you found."

"Well, something isn't right with these. What do you call them? Forms? Sheets? Things with writing—know what I mean?" He held the shells out for Mara, who gave them a cursory glance.

"Count forms for the census?"

"That's what they are, huh? Interesting," Felix said.

"No, it isn't," Mara replied.

"You sure? The Tribunal postponed the census until after the human trial, didn't they? And it seems like they delayed it before one other time, too."

Mara was already losing interest. "We're all very impressed with your knowledge of current events. Now, put this back before you blow our cover."

But Felix was not retreating; he continued eyeing the sheet with slant-eyed bewilderment. "Look, I know I'm not the brightest bulb in the tube sock, but if the census was postponed, then where did these names come from?"

"You don't even know if those *are* names. That's what not being able to read means, remember? Just tell me what you're getting at before I miss something important."

"I don't have to be able to read to see if something is off," Felix said. "Why can't you? I thought you were the Medolian who found a Beaubon in the Ama—"

"Cease that tired story!" Mara managed to temper her voice, pushing back the bitterness that threatened to spill out.

Felix held the shell inches from her face. "Look at the sticker. Here. See how it's peeling at the corner? I've seen these kinds of papers before when I used to deliver packages for the Tribunal as penance for Inferius. The stickers they use stick on a whole lot better than these. And see the signature? It's a copy—a stamp. Just compare it to the others." He flipped through some pages to prove his point. "They're all the same. See it?"

What Mara had initially dismissed now whispered for her attention. She began to examine the forms. "These are identified as property of the office of Claude Malcom Rowse, Fovosian State Department. Why would the Wysts have their paperwork?" The dates and signatures jumped out at her. "These are dated for next year." Fully intrigued now, she snatched the shell from Felix and perused it. "Why would Bo have these?"

"See, I told you something was funny with them."

"But how did you know to look in the file cabinet?"

"You mean you don't smell it? How *did* you catch that Beaubon, anyhow? There's a Wrath stink all over these forms. Cabinets, too."

Mara felt like a poor excuse for a Sentry for having missed it. The forms did indeed carry a faint hint of Wrath, along with Dread. *But what could that mean?* She turned her attention to the dozens of other filing cabinets in the room. A new drawer was broken into and opened. "Crop numbers for Fovos." She tried another. "They're all full of forged census documents."

This was obvious foul play, but the exact nature of it wasn't clear. Wrath filled Mara's heart as she turned to face Bo's energy signature in the next room. "I'm tired of waiting for answers."

In one swift movement, she materialized her staff and channeled Wrath through it, forming an orb of red-and-white light.

"You sure you don't want to think this through first?" Felix asked, ducking for cover, likely knowing his words were in vain.

When Mara released the blast, it struck the wall and tore open a gash before fizzling out, just as it began consuming the desk on the other side. Leaping through the hole in the blink of an eye, she lashed out at the Human Lostros and Human Scythe seated opposite Bo. Both were hardly able to stand before Mara transferred enough Mallos into them to render them unconscious. The two guards who charged into the room seconds later were quickly contained in a single Mallos sphere and tossed out the window, where they fell harmlessly into the brine. *If they can dive even a little, they'll be fine.* With all obstacles out of the way, she turned her attention to Bo, who remained seated calmly at his desk, an amused look on his face as if he'd just witnessed a musical number made exclusively for him.

He clapped boisterously, but only once. As usual, the senator was adorned in feathers that shook and jingled—today, blue and purple with orange accents. "Wow! Truly breathtaking. Do you have any idea who you've just laid out on the floor of a sitting Tribunal senator's office? Do ya?" He began singing, "Because I don't think you dooooo!"

Mara wasted no time. She sped to the other side of his desk and seized Bo by his feather-encrusted vest. "You and I are going to share words."

"Whoa-whoa-whoa! That is real jaminskin you're handling there. Straight from Xinthi. Do you have any idea what it costs? You look like some horrid, ogrish creature at the moment. Do you know that? Truly barbaric. How I could have ever associated with you, I'll just never know."

Felix finally scurried through the hole in the wall to follow. At Mara's glance, he scampered to the door to keep watch.

Letting go of Bo's vest, Mara stepped back, her eyes locked on him.

"Better." Bo composed himself and whipped back his luxurious black locks. "Now, why don't you make us a drink before we begin? I suspect we'll both need it. I know I will."

Pushing back from his chair, the senator stood and faced the not-so-mini bar to his left. Eight shelves lit with emerald light housed a variety of beverages, the bottles ranging from glistening glass art to bolted metal boxes oozing with volatile libations.

With a blast of Mallos, Mara turned the entire setup into a sagging mess of aqua-tinted, translucent goo steaming like a mound of hot rags dropped in a frozen wasteland. For the first time in perhaps his entire life, Bo appeared genuinely shocked.

"Of all the horrible decisions you've made today, I guarantee that was the worst one."

Mara hit him with a hard stare. "Missed you at the end of the trial."

"Yes, well, I've been needed here. As you can see, the panic in the streets thanks to the nameless demon and his girlfriend has not died down."

"Why have I never noticed it before?" Mara said, moving in slowly. "I now see what it looks like when you tell a lie. I must have never wanted to see it. How naive of me. You are a politician after all. One of the best."

"Thank you, darling. But you're the one creature I could never lie to. I promise. Cross my heart."

"That's also a lie."

Bo's jaw danced a little. "Yes, I suppose it was. Ha! Well-well, look who finally woke up and joined the table for senior creatures. I hope you're not expecting more accolades or candy. Maybe a ribbon? Unfortunately, I'm fresh out."

"Tell me why you did it. You knew they would use my words against me."

"I do and say what I must to get the job done. Duh."

"Your job is to destroy the Medolians?"

"My job is to do the bidding of whoever provides the rubes. Life needs those in order to be lived. Remember? That's the way we do things now."

"Don't try to run away from this. Why would someone want us gone? Who? The Sentry Force has been nothing but loyal to the Tribunal and the people of UnEarth."

"Oh, wake up! What world *doesn't* want to get rid of the Medolians? Whoever controls the Earth controls the Eve flowing to UnEarth. If the Medolians are out of the picture, the sovereign worlds can tilt things to whichever shade they like, as much as they like."

"That's not possible, even if we were gone," Mara said. "It would take thousands of years or a huge invasion force—one bigger than UnEarth has ever seen. The people do not want to destroy the humans. Doing so would have disastrous consequences throughout the Eve. Everyone knows that."

"You and I both know Hywyn would love to get their hands on Earth and make it pump nothing but Rapture like a broken oil main. They're a bunch-a power-hungry saps. But you choose to ignore it. Don't underestimate how far the Magnus Council will go to remain in power. Ever."

"And yet you played along with everything. It's true, isn't it? Nothing gets done in the Senate without Bo's stamp."

"Guilty."

"Even when it might get Izaiah killed?"

"Maybe especially then. I have about as much loyalty to that man as you do. It was a shame your teammates perished and we were left with just him to carry on as the senior Sentry leadership. What with Illyana gone—vanished—never to be seen again, and you being far too young and naive. Even you yourself exclaim how much worse things have gotten under Izaiah's leadership. You might even say this is me completing my obligations to the people to the fullest."

"And what about me?" Mara asked. "What about when my turn comes? Will you have the same tenor?"

Bo groaned and rolled his eyes as if he'd just heard a fart. "You will all be given the opportunity to swear fealty to the Barium Guard and serve under Loredosai. It's a tender offer. Trust me. I can't believe we even talked them into doing it. So, no stupid theatrics, okay? Just make the right call when the time comes, which should be soon. Fair warning."

"I think we should go," Felix said, sounding jittery.

Mara knew he was right but wanted more from the senator. "We're not done." She raised the yellow folder of shells to Bo's face the same way Felix had to her. "Tell me, man of the people, why do you have census names locked away in your files?"

Bo's Eve signature transitioned sharply when his eyes landed on the form. The beating of his heart elevated, and his Fervor noticeably declined. "We are facilitating storage for our friends on Fovos," he said, the lie glaringly obvious once more.

"Are you?" Mara said. "Interesting. Are all the forms here fraudulent, or just these?"

"You don't even know what you're looking at," Bo sneered.

"You're right—I don't. But it's got me curious. I think I'm going to keep this. As a souvenir." She folded the shell and slipped it into one of her side pouches. "I wonder if Reyo would be interested in seeing these. Does she know what you're up to?"

"You won't get far with this course of action."

"We'll see."

"No, it's true. I made you, and I have the power to unmake you. You're already a fugitive. What will you do now? How could you possibly help your situation? The Barium Guard will find you, and if they don't, the Violet Knights will be next. You won't last a year. But what I can't figure out is why you would risk coming here. What did you have to gain? It's embarrassing for me. I teach and I teach, and you still act like a little brat. Coming here was a huge mistake. If you don't realize that, I will literally have to disavow ever knowing you."

"I did learn one thing just now . . ." Mara said. "Never trust a Wyst."

"You're only proving how pathetic you are. It's all very upsetting for me. Do you know how useful it was to have a loyal Medolian at my beck and call? Guess I'll have to find another. Shouldn't be hard, though. Those of Mallos have no real identity or purpose. They exist to help or hinder others. The Medolians are tools to be used for the greater good of billions of other UnEarth creatures. On that, Hywyn and I agree."

Mara reflected on the last two thousand six hundred years, starting when she first met Bo. How many jobs had she done for him, unknowingly aiding whatever shadow cabinet operation he was part of? And now he was in some sort of agreement with Fovos?

"Whatever Mistress Tennile promised you in return," Mara said, "you won't get it."

"I think I know a little more about deal-making than you, sweet lady."

"But you know nothing of the greed of others because you're so focused on your own. Tennile is subservient to Lucifer-Aveyl. She supported the Alus Conclave throughout Unos and Inferius. She desires the dominance of the lower shades only. They are insatiable, both of them. You will lose. They'll see to it."

"Things have changed," Bo said. "Arros is no longer an issue—or won't be soon enough."

"You're the one being naive," Mara said. "Fovos and Arros have the only pact that has never been broken. Tennile and the Scythes fear Lucifer and his mastery of Uhl'k."

"Then you've underestimated me," Bo said. "Just like everyone else I've ever passed in my life on the way to the finish line. All too lucky I provided a pleasant backside to gaze at."

"I'm not kidding—I think we should go," Felix said urgently, waving his arms. When Mara ignored him again, he added, "People are on their way. Can't you feel that?"

Mara knew; she just didn't care. She wanted to squeeze Bo's face until everything he knew spilled out. *What else? What isn't he telling me?*

"Is that Wrath I see in your eyes?" he said with a self-satisfied smile.

"Mara! Listen to me." Felix stepped away from the door and leaned in closer. "We need to go. Trust me on this. He is stalling."

"Stalling for what?"

"I don't know. But I know a bullshitter when I see one," Felix insisted.

Only then did she notice Bo's somewhat staggered, off-center stance behind his desk. *Is he hiding something?* Stepping around, she pushed him aside and knelt, discovering a blinking light on a small rectangular metal device attached to the desk's underside.

Unsure what to make of it, she waved Felix over. "It's from Earth, right? Those electric, blinking, lighted bulbs?"

"Lightbulbs?" he asked, eyes widening.

"Yeah."

With one look, Felix's eyes went wide. "That's human technology. Electronics. No. Bad—very bad."

"Human? But how did—" Mara glanced at Bo; a childlike sense of delighted mischievousness was smeared across his face.

"He's sending a signal we can't hear or see," Felix said, his voice rising with anxiety.

"To whom?" Mara asked, at the same time sensing an incoming Shift. In fact, multiple signals were approaching. The room erupted with white light, and the power of Mallos flooded in. Without even sensing their energies, she knew which Medolians had arrived to do the bidding of the Senate.

How could I have been so stupid? Gripping her staff, Mara materialized her usual clothing, burning away the ensemble Felix had picked out, and stood ready to face whatever was incoming. When the storm of white light faded, she found herself facing Philomena, Omalind, and Asmund.

The Rapture-tinted leader, Philomena, with her long, gleaming straw-colored hair, wore the same aloof yet judgmental expression that Mara had always known her to have. To her right, Omalind's eyes were hidden beneath a wide hat. On the left, Asmund held his head high, catching light on his scarred cheekbones while staring with wide, psychosis-stained eyes. The three traitorous Medolians formed a wall between Mara and Felix, blocking any clean escape.

Taking a step forward, Philomena revealed her bare feet beneath her cloak for a brief moment. "Former Sentry Mara Loren, you have been accused of crimes against the UnEarth Tribunal and are to be arrested by the ranking member of the Sentry Force. Any resistance will be countered."

"I see you had no issue assuming my title," Mara said.

"It was given up by its former owner."

"I'm appalled you wouldn't do the same. Have you not been paying attention?" Mara said. "Do you not see what's happening?"

"Cleaning house? Evolution?" Philomena said. "Don't be afraid of progress, elder. That's what got you into this mess. Now, come with us. Without resistance."

Off to the side, the senator snickered loudly.

"You're being fools," Mara said to the other Medolians. "They'll use you to destroy the Sentries."

"The one who did that was you!" Asmund moaned, breaking his silence and revealing his brown teeth. "You and Izaiah. I've been doing some reading of the old scrolls. We know what the Sentry Force used to be. Don't we, Philo?"

"We do, and it will be restored to its former glory," Philomena said. "First step: test the loyalty of all Medolians. Starting with you. So, what will your answer be? This might be your last chance to save yourself, elder."

"It is not I who is in need of saving," Mara replied. "You'll rue today, pupil."

With a wave of her hand, Mara released a blast of Mallos. The energy erupted as a concentrated shockwave, mimicking a Shift but merely serving as a flare. All three younger Medolians lunged for it, hoping to catch her in the act of escaping. Asmund even began making a portal of his own but had to double back, looking as if he'd slipped on a banana peel. While the trio was distracted, Mara launched herself and Felix over their heads, landing just outside the door to the hall. Wrapping them both in a Mallos sphere, she catapulted them down the hall and through the window capping the end.

The barrier expelled debris as Mara's sphere shot like a bullet toward the ground and the city of Diodre. Behind them, the others were immediately in pursuit, following in their own spheres. The sensation of having Mallos on her tail was a new and unpleasant experience. She'd never had to run from her own before, and it quickly became clear that she wouldn't lose them in the air. Her only advantage was her knowledge of this planet. Like a bird of prey diving for food, she dropped Felix and herself into a crowd passing through a lower city entrance.

"Far out," Felix said as they landed.

Shutting down her Eve, Mara masked herself as much as possible and kept her head down as the other Medolians approached. The brine entrance they had dropped near was busy, packed with a sea of bodies coming and going from the undercity. Slipping into the crowd, and then into the water, she and Felix kept up with the throng, which sped up considerably once submerged, entering the densely populated area known as Twil'K.

Unabated, they traveled with the cluster, while Mara kept track of Philomena and the others soaring above. Even after they passed, she was unable to drop her guard. Genuine worry was a feeling she had rarely experienced since the war. What she felt now was likely the same as what other creatures must have felt when being hunted by her.

Philomena was not to be trifled with, and Asmund was known for his loathing of his fellow Sentries. They would not rest until their prey was found. The good news was that Mara had all the same tools they did at their disposal, and then some. All she had to do was make wise choices, and they would be able to get out of this. But that would take time they didn't have. The execution for a sham trial was about to commence. Someone wanted the Medolians gone, and she suspected Izaiah had a good guess as to who.

"We have to stop the execution," she said quietly to Felix. "We can't let Izaiah's head come off. He might be the key to this whole thing."

"How are we going to do that?" he asked, his nervous eyes peering through the glass of his stasis suit, watching the sky above the water's surface as though it might fall on them.

"I don't know," Mara said, "but unless we do, we may never find out what's really going on."

With the Medolians patrolling the air and ground from above, and Wyst forces likely looking for them in the lower city by now, there seemed to be nowhere they could go without being spotted. She and Felix were stuck for the time being in the market, surrounded by sylari (*fish*) guts. The smell and frenzied commerce being carried out would keep them hidden, but there was no telling how long that would last. The execution was in less than twenty-four hours, and Mara wasn't sure if she would be able to survive getting out of the city, let alone make it back to Trivium in time to stop it.

Well . . . maybe it's time to think outside the box. What's something I haven't tried yet?

EXECUTE

The wonders of Trivium surrounded and engulfed her: the prodigious buildings, proud statues, colorful people. Somehow, after spending so many nights awake imagining—yet never believing it possible—she had arrived. Leigh Marie Evans was finally seeing UnEarth with her own eyes. But all she felt in this moment, and every other since arriving, was fury.

It should all be burned to the ground. Everything.

[*Surely the materials used to build it are just as flammable as those on Earth.*]

I don't see why not. Wouldn't be hard to find out.

The civilization had a far more modern-human atmosphere than she'd expected, though much of this was due to the blazing lines of light and letters of brilliance blanketing the city. Like the fluorescent bulbs radiating in the hearts of New York and Tokyo, the signs and marquees of more than half the Trivium businesses pulsed with Eve in every shade under the dusky maroon sky.

Despite the abundance of light sources, the building faces were dark. Few were particularly tall, yet the urban landscape loomed, as though aching to consume her. *(feel like i'm looking through a fish-eye lens)* The structures were muted, dismal shades. Absolute white and black were nowhere to be seen among the brick and mortar making up the majority of the city. But the missing color was replenished in spades, thanks to the creatures making their way through the lanes and stopping for meals. The UnEarth Humans hid as little of themselves as possible here, letting their Evebeast selves shine through. Tails, nubby growths, and extra limbs were allowed to protrude at their leisure. Skins ranged from human tones to cyans, greens, reds, oranges, and blues. The sunglasses usually worn on Earth were abandoned, letting every eye radiate with its shade. Even attitudes and behaviors were different: they appeared more relaxed, free to laugh together, and looked more human than they ever did on Earth.

(i would punch every one of their throats if i could)

One key area where Trivium surpassed the cities of Earth was—surprisingly—in how well-kept everything was. The signs of wear and tear of normal everyday life were nowhere to be seen. No rat holes, no rain streaks, or crumbled brick. Only near the buildings and citizens unmistakably of Wrath did things start to get messy, and even then, they were cleaned up relatively quickly. But the city did carry an ancient air, similar to the countless tombs and temples she had plundered over the years. Every street, down to the pebbles in the footpaths, was scarred with memory, even if none showed outright. This society had been thriving since before the first brick was laid at Uruk, considered one of the oldest cities in the history of mankind. And yet, to the creatures surrounding the professor, this place was still young compared to those on their own home worlds.

The crowd moved along, her in their midst, their disgusting, gro-

tesque bodies rubbing against her and smearing the occasional fluid. Her research meant she knew them all, and even though it was
incredible to see the myriad genuses of Eve creatures in the flesh,
she hated them. The belligerent loathing she felt for them consumed her every thought more than anything she'd ever despised.
The sea was slowly but surely making its way toward the capitol on
Aurau Avenue, one of four main roadways leading to the Tribunal,
and somewhere among this mess and throng were Aluqa, the Cardinal, and the other Sanctioned, mixed into the mass like her. It
had finally happened. Humanity had successfully invaded Trivium.

Commerce had not been halted for the big day; in fact, it seemed
to be bustling. Alien languages were being spoken all over. If someone tried to converse with her in some Arrosian dialect she was
expected to understand, it could potentially jeopardize the whole
operation. Leigh knew many words in Klepc'ti, but the language
came in many flavors, depending on which clan of Archfiend you
were speaking with. One wrong step would be noticed. *Let's hope
all the rooks are having an especially cerebral day. Lord help us if one of
them gets stopped and questioned by a Barium troop.*

In the distance to her right loomed the curved, pointed spires of
the Bibliotheca, something she thought she would only ever read
about and regretfully wouldn't be able to see more of on this trip. A
few yards away, to her left, was an Arrosian contrict—essentially a
hot wings hut that looked exactly as she thought it would. The fire
crater behind the kitchen billowed far more smoke than expected,
filling the lane and obscuring her vision for several blocks. The
smell rolling off the blaze was like turds and black licorice seared
to a crisp, laid atop a slice of ribeye. At first, she was mortified, but
not two minutes later, she began to think it might have smelled
tolerable, then pretty good. Soon it was something that seemed

worth trying. The Eve in her veins was changing her, and not just her sense of smell and taste.

I fucking hate it all.

Her every waking thought was fury. Leigh's fists had never been clenched so tightly. Each structure passed was a missed opportunity for justice, to tear down that which oppressed. A wandering fire was looking better by the minute. [*Because Trivium and all its inhabitants deserve it. And I deserve to bear witness.*]

The burn was fueling her. Her chest heaved with each breath and strike of her heart against her breastplate, pumping as fast as a sprinter's feet on pavement. Her choice of Wrath was proving to be everything the other Sanctioned wanted to avoid. True, it hurt just as badly as she thought it would, reaching nowhere near the heights of pain the Abyss brought on, but the Wrath was also bringing gifts to the party. Leigh's confidence had never soared higher, and nothing in Trivium City could bring back any fear. Bitter rage was all she knew, which came in handy in situations like this. Such resolve had never found her. Every promise she had ever made to herself—about not following others and continuing to take her own path—was long forgotten, trampled by the force of righteous indignation.

They thought I was mad to choose it. No one else joined in.

On that day, the day of their imbuement, with the execution just seven hours away, Leigh had been in her private bunk, patiently waiting for the inevitable. No distraction would have worked, so she didn't bother looking for one. When the time came and she opened her door, Aluqa's face was there to greet her, not twelve inches away from her own.

I should have guessed.

"Sleep well?" the leader asked softly.

Leigh simply grinned and made the *after-you* motion. A chuckle broke from the master of the station before she turned and per-fected her posture, lifting her chin and touching all ten fingers together at chest height before making her way down the hall. The glow of her many rings sprayed the blue walls around them with color.

"What shade have you chosen?" she asked Leigh as Skraga and Bulltress joined their march.

Leigh typed into her Gauntlet. "I've chosen Wrath."

Aluqa didn't say a word. Neither did Bulltress, while Skraga let out a gasp and muttered, "Whoa."

Of all seventeen Cavaliers, the professor was the only one to choose the shade, along with a handful of rooks. The others might have feared what would happen if they were injected with the spiritual force of destruction, but something far worse had al-ready flowed through her. A man-beast had forced her to taste the Abyss, the cruelest and previously unknown shade. The pain of the energy was still fresh in her mind, like every nerve in her body had gotten a tattoo with a rusty nail—like she had been tossed into a pit to fall lower and lower, away from all light and warmth in the universe. The power was the essence of damnation, rot, and indif-ference. It was that which broke her core, rendering her the numb woman she'd become. But the Wrath was different. The nameless had unfortunately taught her that. To destroy was part of life, like it or not.

Cavalier and rook alike gathered outside the main hall, forming a line. One by one, members began passing through the Cardinal's machine. Their screams and cries for help quickly stacked up into something resembling a mega haunted maze attraction. All that was missing were heavy rain and guys with chainsaws, their blades stripped off. Flashes of light from the chamber blotted out all others in the main hall as it force-fed pure Eve into the flesh of the rooks, now members of the Sanctioned.

When emerging from the other side, only a handful remained standing. Most collapsed into heaps of sweat-soaked panic or laughter-riddled mania. Unfortunately, three died in the first half hour. There was little anyone could do for them. The vast majority had chosen Rapture, and those Sanctioned seemed to have trouble moving their feet once the power set in. *Their brains can't even process how to use their limbs now without the right emotional input. But none of them read, so they wouldn't have known to expect that.*

A few stellar examples did appear, exiting the chamber with little issue, some even with their heads held high. Those who stood firm began trying out their new abilities immediately, unable to resist. The Rapture choosers had become impervious to harm, while the Grief choosers were too heavy to lift yet capable of lifting anything. Those who chose Fervor gained a boost in speed and flexibility rivaling any Olympian. Nearly all crashed into walls, other members, and the chamber itself before getting the hang of it.

Even those who emerged dead sick began to have fun with their Eve once they started feeling better, joking and playing around, taking joy in figuring it all out. *Kind of silly, but they need to get used to it if they're going to pass for UnEarth creatures.* However, the Cardinal's people put a stop to the frivolity as soon as their leader took notice. With a stern lecture, the Sanctioned from Station Five were reprimanded and put into square line formations, like his own people, to await the imbuement's conclusion.

Processing the Surface members from Europe and America took several hours. [*I cannot imagine how long the other stations must be taking, considering we have the Cardinal for guidance, and they do not.*] Yet even with the help, sending every Sanctioned through took so long that Leigh began worrying they might not make it to the execution in time.

Being at the rear of the pack, second to last among the Cavaliers, she didn't have to endure the wait with nothing to do and nowhere to go. When the line had worked through and the member in front of her, Rampart, had finished his walk—having chosen Grief and successfully marched away with his dignity intact—she was finally up. Stepping onto the platform marked by two foot indicators instructing where to stand, she locked eyes with the preparatory member in medical scrubs. The mask on her face left only her eyes to communicate with—blue as a glacier's ass. No signs of callousness were to be found.

Blue Eyes approached, a syringe case in hand. Soon would come the only part of the process Leigh had been dreading for days: the shot of glowing liquid that determined which shade of Eve would be imbued, à la the presentation of Bartholomew. But when Blue Eyes took out the syringe—a volatile red gel burning inside the vial—Leigh swore she saw no needle on its end. When Blue Eyes pressed it to her arm, there was no prick or pressure. Leigh made no quick movements but once again locked eyes with her. Blue Eyes gave no sign of anything wrong. When Leigh took a quick breath as though to speak—*a habit even a mute can't break*—Blue Eyes tapped her arm twice with a quick "Shhh."

With the vial somehow emptied and the red glow gone, the scrubs wearer pulled away and quickly put a bandage on Leigh's shoulder, tapping her arm twice, this time harder, as though saying, "*atta girl.*" The "needle" was quickly disposed of, and a bright smile was sent Leigh's way via Blue Eyes.

"You're all set. Best of luck on your walk, Professor." The mask barely jostled as she spoke.

But moving on seemed too easy. Leigh kept a questioning glance on Blue Eyes, who nodded toward the chamber before turning her back. "As I said, you're all set. Don't fret—you'll make it to Trivium just like everyone else."

Leigh sensed no lie. A wave of relief crawled up her legs. *The shots did seem like a strange part of the process, but why am I allowed to go in without one? Will I still get the Wrath?* Scores of questions were begging to be asked, but if the situation was as secretive as she sensed, it seemed a better choice to play along.

[*But I must acknowledge the very real possibility that without the shot, I will simply die inside the chamber. That woman in the scrubs is from the Cardinal's Surface, and I can think of at least two reasons he might want me dead.*]

(pretty goddamn bleak. and accurate)

Stepping onto the platform, Leigh stared down the short walk. The gray walls lined with flat-faced panels reminded her of some of the caves she'd charged headfirst into over the years in search of artifacts—to discover new worlds long forgotten, to open her own and everyone else's eyes.

The masked woman still wouldn't look at her. *(what the fuck, Blue?)* A decision needed to be made now—to go in or not—and with no more clues as to what had just happened. *(i think someone either just blessed my ass or damned me. fifty-fifty)*

[*Generally preferable gambling odds.*]

Leigh began. The first two steps were easy. The rest could only be described as a gauntlet of misery and insidious torment. Once inside the chamber, a barking shriek tore into her ears, mixed with heavy-duty machinery. The effect was immediate and hindering: a scalding sensation of heat—not on her skin but from within—as though her skeleton were broiling like red-hot steel, ready to be hammered into shape. Every muscle in her legs strained to carry her forward, slowing her down and threatening to shove her sweat-soaked face into the ground. Flashing light and chaos passed on all sides and through her as her mind twisted back and forth, sending Leigh to another place free from pain. But the Wrath soaking her flesh would not be ignored. The fire had already risen through her, filling her head with images of all the things she loathed and feared, and making her eyes water, blurring her vision. Her knees wobbled, threatening to buckle. Yet her steps continued, and when the professor began to believe there would be no end, she found herself passing through the exit and thinking, *(that wasn't so bad)*

Am I really out? Is it done?

Cool air touched her cheek. A hissing sound revealed itself as her ears adjusted. The loudest thing in the room was her, skin sizzling and clothes steaming. Grunting with a primitive ferocity, she shook her head. The cloud that rose from her long hair drifted over the room. The jaws of the other members hung open, their vivid eyes wide and captivated. Streaks of crimson coursed through the professor's veins, rising and falling, some visible deep within the tissue of her swelling muscles. She stood before her peers, sizzling like a roast pulled from the oven, her bristling red irises glowing like LED lamps.

Aluqa approached her with a sense of both caution and curiosity. "How do you feel, Member Silverthorn?"

"Angry," Leigh replied, her voice emanating from her core. Through her broken vocal cords, the voice of Wrath was deep and cruel, reminding her of Joseph, as though he were speaking through her.

Her emotions had not been missed since they left; they had been revealed to be a hindrance. But the loss of her voice would never cease to be mourned. Everything she was had been fragmented more by the loss of her primary tool than by the hand of Joseph. Somehow retrieving it had always been the dream, but never a real goal—always seeming foolish to chase something so impossible. Then a miracle happened, and she'd found it, but this was not how she wanted to regain her voice. This sound coming from her was a thing she hated almost as much as she did the people of UnEarth.

With a proud exhale, unsurprised, Aluqa left Leigh at the chamber to join the others in the ranks. The last to go through the machine was Skraga, who not only strolled through flawlessly and casually, but then asked immediately after exiting, "Wait, did I do it wrong? Nothing feels that different. I'm so sorry—I think I broke your machine, Mr. Cardinal, sir."

It turned out the supplements she had been ingesting for some time had acclimated her enough that a full imbuement of Eve was nearly a literal walk in the park for the woman from New Zealand.

"Sorry I ruined the finale, everyone!" Skraga shouted as Aluqa and the Cardinal approached the railing of the second floor. This time, no one else shared the platform with them. Leigh, Skraga, Bulltress, and Opal had all been ordered to remain below, now among the anonymous Sanctioned.

Spreading his arms, the Cardinal took in the crowd, heaving a huge breath through his frostbitten nostrils. "Feel. Power of Ouna. UnEarth. The strength is this. The strength is you."

"Sanctioned!" Aluqa shouted. "The tools of UnEarth's destruction, to be used for the greater task. The most dangerous force in all the cosmos. Under your new strength, the Tribunal itself will kneel."

The Sanctioned cheered, grunted, and shrieked, becoming frenzied. Their eyes shone with Eve light, each fully prepared. Leigh's was not the only fire lit by her shade. They were ready to give their lives, if necessary. *And so am I. Whatever it takes.*

(burn it down. absolutely)

"My friends, we have kept you in the dark for too long," Aluqa began. "How can you be expected to execute a plan of attack if you do not know the plan to begin with?" At her slight smile, a few members who chose Jubilee began snorting and hooting, only catching themselves after they'd already made fools of themselves. "Yes . . . thank you," Aluqa said, continuing.

"This attack will be great, my friends, but it will not be one of swords, bullets, or rocket grenades. I know some of you have dreamed of something similar all your lives, but in truth, these weapons will only get you so far. What good will killing a few foot soldiers do? This question is what first joined the Cardinal and me and created the Surface. His development of a certain weapon, more a dream than truth, has continued since our coalition's founding. Never before seen by any of his kind, capable of killing any UnEarth creature, this dream weapon uses the same principle as a radio put in tune. UnEarth exists on another frequency, which we can use against them and render their nervous systems inert. In short, we will use sound to melt their brains."

The Sanctioned were stewing with excitement, aching to gossip or gasp, but the scolding they had received from the Cardinal earlier had sealed that bottle tight. Aluqa continued.

"With this weapon in hand, each of you will march through Trivium to the execution grounds and take your predesignated locations around the Civis Sedibus, the royal bleachers. There we will wait for the opportune moment when the High Lord is at his most vulnerable, and I will activate the weapon myself. Then we will all bear witness to the creatures who oppress us crumbling to nothing."

"This is truth," the Cardinal added.

Bags of clothes were then distributed to the Sanctioned by a dozen of his people. The disguises were obvious: made to turn them into UnEarth Humans. No hats, but many members had their hair dyed by the Cardinal's people and styled with spikes and swoops. Leigh wasn't thrilled about any of it. *I saw this coming but was never fond of vests.*

[*They serve no purpose. None.*]

But the worst of it came when the Cardinal's people collected shoes from random members. More than half were going to lose their footwear to ensure a suspicious number of human-shaped figures didn't show up in Trivium City all at once wearing something most UnEarth Humans couldn't tolerate. Leigh held her breath as they approached her lane, picking people here and there. By accident, she made eye contact with the woman making the choices, who slowed only a fraction before moving on, touching the shoulder of the man directly behind Leigh. Releasing her breath, she danced her toes in her shoes, feeling deep loathing for the woman who almost took them away.

The same members who provided the UnEarth Human makeovers then distributed what looked like bulletproof vests to the Sanctioned. As they did, Opal shouted over the others with his scrunched face.

"These packs will transmit your health data back to the station. It is imperative that we know how you are doing. Every vest has been outfitted with a multireality GPS, so if you run into trouble, we will be able to locate you and retrieve you safely. The computer in your vest is very fragile and tucked away in your front pocket. Be careful with it! Don't let it get damaged. But most important of all, these packs will protect you from the weapon's signal. Do not remove it for any reason once you are on Trivium. If you do, we will not weep for your corpse. However, if you follow all our instructions, you will come back alive and victorious. This, the Cardinal has assured you."

When Leigh received her pack, she studied it, finding a sort of

Rapture-infused tech built into the chestplate. A single blue light blinked gently in the lower corner. But what truly caught her eye was her bracelet's Grief gem, which began fluttering with its glow in multiple shades when brought near the pack.

Interesting.

Slipping on the vest and locking it tight with what looked like modified airline-belt clamps, she wondered if this thing would ever come off her body while she was still alive. [*The number of things that can kill us today is much higher than anyone here realizes or is willing to admit.*]

"You will now receive the most important object you will ever be handed," Scrunched Face said, his silver teeth twinkling. "More than all the money you've ever earned or even your own life, this is the most significant thing that will ever happen to you."

The third delivery came along, and Leigh was handed something that made her head tilt to the side instinctively. A perplexed wave washed through her, scattering her anger for a brief moment. A gray plastic handle was in her grip, with a six-inch-wide, one-inch-thick disk attached to the top. Her eyes were reflected in a strip of platinum around the disk's edge. She turned it over and around, trying to see what she was missing. There was no trigger, flashing lights, buttons, or bullets. This was . . . *I have no idea what this is.* Glancing around the room, she could see she wasn't the only one.

Aluqa waited for everyone to have their tool in hand, cradled like cavepeople holding sticks with their last bits of fire. Once she was done sighing, she spoke. "The most powerful tools are often the simplest. In your hands are transceivers—a weapon that can be taken onto the execution grounds without detection and will end the life of every UnEarth creature within earshot. All you need to do is keep it out of sight and safe until the time is right. Then, hold your torch aloft proudly. Let them see us with their own eyes before we shut them forever."

A few cheers broke out among the Sanctioned anyway.

"Discovered a frequency, have I, using human technology. This discovery came at great loss," said the Cardinal, silencing everyone. "War begins. This comes again. But not. This is also possibility. The Sanctioned can do this."

The Cardinal's people suddenly pounded their chests and pressed their fists hard enough against them to juice a tomato, shouting in unison, "Evo! Aio! Eio!"

Break—mend—bend? What does that mean?

(and how did they all know to do that just then?)

The Cardinal put up his hand, and his people returned theirs to their sides. "Evo, aio, eio," he said.

The meeting concluded soon thereafter, the only remaining order of business being how they were going to get to UnEarth in the first place. *A really minor detail, when you think about it with half your brain missing.* But the Cardinal once again proved to be two steps ahead.

On his signal, when the main doors to the hall opened, a blast of light and sound flooded inside. A raging storm struck Leigh in the face, and she knew instantly a Shift—or something like it—was nearby. *(and making my fucking blood boil)*

What looked like a portable Eb Ring, eight feet in diameter, rested on the back of another truck.

(did he have one of those just lying around?)

[*They are supposedly difficult to obtain.*]

The direction each Sanctioned was sent was intentionally staggered to ensure they did not all arrive at the same station on Trivium at once. Over the course of half an hour, every member stepped through the white storm inside the ring. All except Pahlanksha, who had remained absent. Leigh was near last to go, just ahead of Aluqa.

"I'll see you out there," Aluqa said, grazing Leigh's bracelet with her fingers.

"Me too," Leigh replied.

Out of belligerence, she screamed during the Shift through the gate. Chloe's Shifts had been far smoother rides. *Well, sure, I know that now that I have something worse to compare it to.* Traveling via Eve Gate was her least favorite mode, and Leigh used her newly functioning voice box to vent her frustrations.

Upon landing at Trivium's northern gate, she found her legs as stiff as ironing boards and breath could not enter her lungs. For a second, she thought she'd arrived inside a giant roll of plastic wrap. As creatures skimmed by on arrival, her shoulders were shoved again and again. While she was figuring out how to move, a pair of thumping hooves approached her from behind like an elephant in a stampede. Before she could be crushed, strong hands suddenly took Leigh by the shoulders and yanked her to safety. The breath she'd lost caught up and jumped back into her a moment later.

It took every ounce of effort she had not to glare at Skraga for saving her life.

"Funny seeing you here," Member Grassrock said, releasing Leigh only once she kicked herself free. "Guess we're not all as spread out as we would have hoped."

"Guess not," Leigh said.

"Hey, I thought you couldn't talk."

"Guess I can, for the time being, at least."

"Okay, that's good, right? You don't sound good, though. In fact, you sound terrible, like you're about to die."

"Thank you, I agree," Leigh said, feeling a mix of hate and fondness for Skraga. *She might be the one person I don't want to maul.*

Their march to the execution began. Staying relatively close to Skraga so they could check up on one another, Leigh felt more secure in case the worst happened and a fight broke out or the Barium Guard spotted them. For a Grief-filled person, Skraga appeared chipper, wearing her awe on her sleeve as she gawked at the sights. Because of how apologetic she was every time she bumped into someone, begging for their pardon, she didn't stand out in the crowd at all.

Presently, Leigh was nearing the center of the city, no more than a mile from the execution grounds. Several blocks back, around the time the crowd turned away from the route to the Tribunal and onward to the arena, she'd lost track of Skraga. Scuffles were suddenly breaking out along the way between Eve creatures—grunts and shouts, drinks spilled—growing squallier as the march continued. Her fingers clamped tighter around the plastic transceiver hidden inside her rags. Her baby, the only one she would ever have. Leigh would protect it no matter the cost to herself, until it could do its duty. The thought of it made her salivate.

As huge Celestial guards began appearing on the sides of the road, wielding tall spears and overlooking the procession, Leigh felt a glimmer of what life under majority Hywyn rule might have entailed. Keeping her head low and thinking nasty thoughts, she passed each guard, hoping for the best. *They would never suspect humans were here, would they?* More likely, they were there to keep the audience for today's show in check. Even the Cardinal's vests and transceivers were so far proving to be invisible to the people of the Eve.

Soon, the mass of creatures—ranging from bright-green-haired simians with overly large heads to slippery, web-footed aquatic life—squished in around her before passing through a bottleneck into a tall black archway that looked to be made of chipped stone. She then entered a courtyard five hundred yards wide, laid out like an open clamshell made of blocky, symmetrical shapes and cobalt steel. It was a fight not to get stepped on and squished by the mob.

Music filled the air, both from an overhead PA system and from individuals performing around the outskirts, culminating in a muddy clamor that grated on the ears and the soul. The bleachers facing the execution platform rose toward the heavens—the roof of the clam's mouth—its steelwork foregoing all unnecessary adornments. Across the yard, at the edge of the clam's mouth, the killing deck platform was raised about fifteen yards, broad and flat, little more than a sturdy floor high enough to easily see things die on. A tall backdrop of dismal gray stone behind it blocked any view of the outer city. Center stage right was a sword displayed in what looked like blue ice, at least ten feet in length. At the sight of the blade, Leigh's mouth began watering. She didn't know which she wanted to see more: the sword being used or the transceiver in her hand activated.

The bleacher structure facing the killing deck was a monolith stretching into the sky. The highest chair built into it—a testament to simplicity—was also the largest. It was utterly laughable that something so big could be made for only one creature. *(that thing could comfortably seat a nuclear submarine)* Above the viewing box hung the banner of Hywyn, itself much larger than those of the other worlds. The five other shade leader boxes were placed on either side of the Celestial lord's, cascading down. Beneath the banner of Arros sat the second largest. *Must be Lucifer's seat.*

[But even if he is still alive, there is very little chance he will make an appearance.]

True—what with Gabriel here.

(mister "high lord" probably would've stolen his thunder)

The Wrath pumping through her couldn't even convince Leigh that she wanted to see the actual dark prince in the flesh—the creature that had terrified her mother's every waking thought until the moment she died. *And I hated her for it. But now look where I am, staring at a chair made for the guy. I have a rough guess of how big his butt is.* The Fallen One, despite his abominable reputation, was an average-sized High Celestial. Even knowing this, she was still taken aback by the modest size of his throne.

Seeing the sheer magnitude of the seating platform, Leigh began to wonder if the transceivers would do the trick or not. Gabriel's chair was far higher up than she'd imagined. *Really living up to his title of High Lord. I hope the frequency can reach him, or else this will all be for nothing.*

The lower half of the clamshell lid was lined with hundreds of rows of private box seats, most of which bore the markings of Hywyn. On the ground floor of the courtyard, surrounded by tall black walls, it was standing room only.

Makes me nostalgic for seeing concerts. A couple of the times I saw Dio remind me of this.

Leigh broke away from the horde moving for the stage and approached the royal bleachers. The crowd was thinner, but that would not be the case for long, as the venue was filling up quickly with bodies, some of which were ostensibly giants.

Several other Sanctioned passed by, closer to the middle of the structure. All were rooks Leigh recognized, their eyes aimed down as if out of anonymity or shame. *(what could they be ashamed of? what we're doing today is the proudest thing we could ever do)*

Soon, on the other side of Gabriel's throne, Leigh continued another minute before settling into her position, as marked on the map she was handed just before departing. With her back against the base of the bleacher structure and the scene building before her, a rough estimate put the number of attendees in the low hundred thousands. Eegreds, the giants, towered over the crowd like pillars scattered throughout. On the outskirts rested actual pillars, utilized by thousands of creatures scaling their faces to get a better view of the stage. Leigh had to hand it to UnEarth engineers for doing such a good job making sure everyone had a clear view. *(but i still hate them)*

A chattering energy flowed throughout the courtyard like a flock of birds tied to a post. The people were excited. This was obviously a great day for the citizens of UnEarth, which made Leigh even angrier, somehow finding a new threshold. Without at first realizing it, she began cradling and softly petting the device under her robes.

The purest release and middle finger to an oppressive authority—the *oppressive authority.*

Aluqa and her plan would be successful. *I'll see to it.*

The courtyard was almost full now. The seats across the bleachers were shuddering with anticipation. Soon, it would begin. The writhing Scythes and Archfiend on the viewing towers had covered every inch of the gray stone with flickering orange and crimson. Less than an hour later, when the square was packed beyond capacity, there came a hush, but it was unclear what had officially prompted it. A figure then appeared on the platform, blazing with a blue so brilliant they might as well have been covered in mirror sequins and hit with a spotlight.

The pure Celestial woman stood inside what looked like, again, a low polygonal clamshell, this time just big enough for her. When the Celestial spoke, the sound was amplified, emanating as clearly as if she were standing within a few feet. With broad, powerful words, the icy, Rapture-laden—and frankly loud as hell—quality

of the voice forced Leigh to resist the urge to climb up the platform and try to make the Celestial's head explode somehow.

[*There has to be a way.*]

She caught only the gist of the announcements: the date and
time, names of the members of the Senate and court responsible
for the day's event. This part alone took over ten minutes. Next
came the introduction of the high-profile individuals who'd come
to witness the execution, of which there were three hundred and
forty-nine. Notably absent was the senator from Lanwyn, Afton
Laffler.

(i wanted a chance to off him myself with my bare hands)

Then came the thumps of the granddaddy of them all, ready
to make his debut. When Gabriel's name was called, a shadow
passed over the crowd, blotting out light as though a blanket had
been pulled over them. Leigh craned her neck to view the tower of
blue appear atop the royal bleachers. With his wings aimed out—
pointed and angled at their ends like some medieval dragon—he
seemed to be laying claim to the entire populace beneath his feet.

The stories and bits of information on the High Lord did him no
justice. Peering down from on high was an overpowering presence
beyond comprehension. The Rapture soaring off the behemoth,
like radiation from a brick of plutonium, sizzled over Leigh. Gabriel's body was made of gemstone flesh, but a much darker shade
of blue than most High Celestials'. Foggy and ashen, in a certain
light, his tint drifted close to cyan, especially under his arms and
the backs of his legs. But he was no less grand because of it. The
High Lord's face was sharply chiseled, a visage angled slightly forward and down, with an elongated nose and chin. Permanently
dipped low and jutting, the brow above his gleaming, frigid eyes
draped all but his glowing irises in shadow.

A petty bitterness dripped from the creature, crashing down the

bleachers onto the crowd like a waterfall, clashing with his outward air of steady poise, power, and grace. Leigh understood it and
respected him for it, but also hated him completely. *And I hope he
can feel it.*

With slow steps, the High Lord made his way to the front of
his throne. The hushed people stood as still as pillars of salt, as
though admitting they were all his subjects, while his gaze drifted
over them. When his thundering steps stopped, he took his seat
with deliberate patience. The instant his butt touched the chair, the
crowd took a collective breath.

On the stage, the speaker waited for the go-ahead motion from
one of Gabriel's keepers, who had joined him by his side and sat
in their own chair beside the throne. The speaker then gave a long
speech about the sanctity of the Tribunal and the power bestowed
upon it by the Eve to do what was deemed necessary. It was then
time to bring out those fated for death.

(frickin' finally)

A shudder passed through the crowd like a silent wave at a football game. This was what they had been waiting for, aching for,
for two years. Isolated cries, roars, squawks, and squeals broke out.
This barnyard dance was set to pop.

A moment later, a huge mess of gears behind the stage started
up. Wheels that sounded mammoth and possibly made of stone
turned, and a low, pulsing moan was accompanied by a soft whirring. A platform then rose into view with a host of shapes standing
on top. It was not hard to spot the condemned, the only human
shapes present. Though they were too small to make out any details, it was clear all three were wearing gray masks that obscured
their faces and were surrounded by Celestial guards and a con-
temptuous-looking Wyst, whom Leigh assumed could only be
Volirhm Kalos, the Tribunal's lead executioner.

Seeing Izaiah Ezekial, Alex Barker, and Bennett Hunter chained to rolling slabs made Leigh feel all but nothing. She couldn't even muster abhorrence for them. They were just something else happening that had nothing to do with her. She was not there to stop their deaths. In fact, the frequency of the Cardinal's weapon might have been strong enough to kill them, as they had become more UnEarth creatures than men by this point. [*They were ignorant and weak. That is why they find themselves on that stage.*]

Sorry, boys, you're on your own.

The crowd, however, seemed to have more than enough hate for the condemned to make up for Leigh's indifference. Booing and hissing with bloodlust in their eyes, the people reacted viscerally when the humans were revealed and wheeled to the center of the stage. The executioner approached Izaiah first. Apparently, he would be the one to lead things off, which the crowd raucously approved of, starting into several rhythmic chants that grew like roaring flames. [*And I agree. Speaking from a strictly logical point of view. Kill the Medolian. Kill the biggest threat.*]

The speaker began a list of the convicted men's crimes, which Leigh paid close attention to. *I want to know everything they got him for.* But her focus was so drawn by the presentation and the ever-present urge to activate her transceiver that she hardly noticed the soft tugging on her robes, which had begun just a moment before. When it grew to a full yank on her shoulder, she finally looked, ready to lose control on an unlucky soul, but found only Aluqa standing beside her. The brown of Aluqa's eyes had been flushed away, replaced with a diamond-blue radiance. The sheer intensity of them shocked like a jolt of static, weakening Leigh's Wrath. Morinnean's smooth-skinned face wore a playful expression, as though surprising an old friend she happened to spot by coincidence while on vacation in another country.

Leigh half expected her to say, "Darling, so good to see you. You look wonderful." Instead, she said, "Hello. Lovely day, yes?" with a banality that almost sent Leigh stumbling.

Signing messily, Leigh replied, "What the hell?" as she forgot about her voice in that moment.

"Here you are. This is where you were supposed to be, and you are. Just like always," Aluqa whispered excitedly with a titter, exposing her teeth, which faintly glowed blue as though under a black light. "Member Silverthorn. Come. This is the way."

With a childlike laugh and a firm grip on Leigh's wrist, Aluqa led them off to the left, away from the base of the royal bleachers platform, through the crowd as the speaker continued on stage. At first, Leigh tried to fight it. *(no! we're going to miss the attack!)* But Aluqa was unbeatable, her grip as firm as cooled lava. There was no point in resisting, but Leigh's Wrath decided she would put up a fight the whole way, regardless.

The slowly escaping duo soon reached the far wall and exited through a side gate. Outside the courtyard, the crowd was just as dense as the one inside, all waiting for some cheers to announce any good news. Further away from the execution grounds, Aluqa dragged Leigh through an archway-laden path near the Ishwill Gardens. Following a brief, struggle-filled trek, she rounded a pillar, one in a series along a path supporting a travel tube, and halted.

"What about the others?" Leigh bellowed, finding it hard not to while fighting to reclaim her wrist.

"They will always be remembered, from this day until the last. The great, cleansing wave of the Surface," Aluqa said. "But that's not your fate; that remains ahead." From around her neck, she revealed what looked like an expensive garage door opener. "Given to me by the Cardinal. The remote to activate the transceivers." Aluqa chuckled slowly, her voice filling with bass. "But like all things touched by the Cardinal . . ." Between her hands, she crunched the remote like a paper cup. The pieces that fell out were not circuitry, but chunks of thin folded steel, like foil shredded by a dog.

"A lie," Aluqa said, just as screams from inside the arena swelled and flooded Leigh's ears. Wailing, choked with terrible pain, a desperate, terrifying pain. A blaze of color—the whole prism— flashed with a single burst as blinding as a miniature sun in the courtyard. The voices were then cut off by a boom.

It pounded like a boxer's glove against a heavy bag. The blast struck her eardrums. A shock wave rushed into her like a gale-force wind. The ground shook so violently that clinging to a pillar's craggy surface was all that kept Leigh from rolling an ankle. Even without heat, the exposed side of her face burned as though hit by a spray of steam. The crowd around the arena gasped and shrieked as smoke and dust rose into the air, before a panicked, stunned atmosphere assumed dominance.

What . . . what was that? That wasn't . . .

Drifting about, Leigh's gaze quickly found Aluqa, already aimed her way, unaffected, a pillar of untouched elegance in the dust-filled mist. "There was nothing I could do for them," she said with a callous, serene apathy. "They would have understood . . . Yes. They would have . . . the act. This happens again. In you. The time . . . this is soon."

DEAD MAN WALKING

There was no thunder that night. The week prior had been riddled with it, but that evening was quiet. Quiet and cold, and nothing more. The upper cellblock of the Weya-Vein slept like a tomb. Alex thought he had suddenly become deaf, or that sound itself was steering clear of him. *Everybody else is.* Even the chains strung on him and those swooping like knotted vines from above were as silent as falling leaves. Perhaps they did so on purpose as a form of mourning; for tomorrow their captive would be permanently removed.

Come sunrise, Alexander James Barker would be taken to a different location, where his head would be removed from his body, and peace would come to this and many other lands thereafter. But all he could think about was how he might see her when it happened, how Melissa might be there waiting for him, her eyes, her voice. Perhaps she would be the one sent to pick up his head from the ground and bring him to Heaven, if such a place existed the way he still wanted it to. Or perhaps she would drop his body off a cliff into the fiery void while keeping his head with her in Heaven; that way, he would always see paradise but would never feel it. *Why does my imagination think of stuff like this? How is this helpful?*

Since the sentencing, Alex had tried to force himself to forget all he'd learned about the soul from UnEarth. No matter how scared he was to see her, he needed to believe he wouldn't fade away once dead, that there was more to do, even when his body would be long gone. He needed to believe that one day he and Melissa would be reunited with their daughter, his family together at last, and he would get the chance to talk with her and ask her all about her life. Alex had only that to hold on to as he watched the light of the moon through the square window on the door travel across the walls and bars of the cellblock.

He took a slow, deep breath, making sure to inhale through his nose and exhale through his mouth, trying with as little force as possible to relax. *By all that's holy, I'm going to truly relax for at least one minute of my adult life before I die.* His recollection of the re-laxation tapes his wife had gotten him was fuzzy by now, but he hadn't forgotten the mantra. *Breathe. Just stay calm. Breathe.* The next part about everything working out fine had never sat right with him for obvious reasons now. He considered skipping it, but just to cover his bases, kept it in. *Everything will be fine. Just stay calm.* He repeated the phrase in its entirety for nearly half an hour.

When his heart suddenly sang, he startled himself, and Alex somehow knew deep down, from the darkest, lowest recesses of his psyche, that he believed he would still live on after his head was removed. *I survived death the first time. There's no reason I won't go on. And Melissa will be there waiting. I know she will.* He continued repeating the mantra until—with a pop like a pebble dropped into a pond—his mind cleared.

There it is. Whatever it is. Whatever it was, a sweet, blissful nothingness found him. It was slightly chilly and refreshing, as though he were the pebble. All but weightless, part of him bitterly knew he would somehow screw this up and lose the feeling, but after a good thirty seconds, Alex dared to open his eyes. The feeling largely stayed.

"Been waiting for that," Oaleen muttered out of the blue after being little more than a ghost for nearly two days.

"What?" Alex replied.

"You're resigned. It's been happening over the last couple of hours. At peace with your death. This is good. Must have thought of something significant or made some deal with yourself. This is exactly the way, *ch-ch-ch*. You should be proud. I've only seen it in a handful of creatures outside my species. Most of those were in here, not on the battlefield. Kinda funny. It's impressive, though, arriving at such a place. Didn't think any human was capable, let alone—*ch-ch*—you."

"Thanks," Alex said with a little mustard on it.

"Shall I guess? The wife?"

"You have more shit to throw at me? Even now?"

"As I've told you, I don't understand the use of this phrase! Fecal matter is a fine gift in many societies. But I felt what you meant. The answer is no—I will not 'give you shit.'"

Alex waited before answering. "You won't berate and belittle me at all?"

"I said no. Can you not hear?"

"Why? You ridicule everything else I say."

"You're hours away from your own beheading. What could I possibly have to say to you? A peon does not occupy a large portion—*ch-ch-ch*—of my thoughts, believe it or not."

"You're not the only one who can sense things. Us humans have senses too. I can tell you want to say something. Must be burning you up inside, not insulting me constantly."

"Got nothing to say to a dead man."

"I've been dead this whole time. We both knew that from the first day they rolled me in here. Hell, I knew it the moment giants with spears crashed through the roof to get me. Either right there or after a trial, which, frankly, I was surprised happened at all. But my head was always coming off. Never stopped you from insulting me every hour on the hour before."

There was no retort. Alex's jaw hung open, ready to argue. *Wow. Is this really happening? Did I just win?* He chose the same path he did when he won arguments against Melissa and didn't press it. Feeling guilty (*because of course I do*), he asked, "What about you? Have you found it? Peace with death?"

"I was born with it."

"Makes sense. But if you're born ready to die, what is it you're ready to die for?"

"Excuse me?"

"What cause? You're giving your life. What for?"

"Is that not the greatest thing one can give?"

"But I thought you didn't see value in life."

"Of course, I do, which is why I spent so many years removing those who took more than their fair share, allowing a larger number of creatures to partake in newly freed resources. All creatures are allowed to live out their prime and step aside when the time is right to make room for new life. This cycle is well known to my clan."

"Make room by dying?"

"You do understand it."

"Sounds like your equation goes from zero back to zero and ignores all the meat in between. Where does the meaning of life fit into your view?"

"I hardly know what you mean. Life is not a number. Life just is. Nothing can truly change because nothing ever truly becomes. The cycle will keep chugging along forever, even after you and your 'meanings' are long gone."

"If your life has no meaning, why not just kill yourself?"

"*Ak!* You're a fool if you think such childish notions are useful at a time like this. Your argument is inert."

"Like you said, I'm a dead man already. I can argue anything I want."

Oaleen scoffed, then said distantly, as though trying to hide it, "You wouldn't be a dead man if you didn't want to be."

"Excuse me? I didn't catch that."

"You want nothing more than to die. *Ch-ch-ch-ch-ch*—A power lies in you capable of bending the cosmos to your will, and you choose instead to mope. It's beneath any creature."

"Choose to?" Alex shouted through a coarse throat. "Why are we doing this again? Even if I could, why would I want to become that thing again?"

"Why wouldn't you? With that power, you could take your freedom with one hand! The Ire could break down any wall, march away, and tell the entire Celestial-controlled institution they call UnEarth to swallow a yellow rod. Then . . . no one could kill you. No one would have to watch you die. But you've never found it. You never found any of the same rage. Not even close. After everything that's happened to you. I can't fathom how it was you in the first place. You, Barker, the opposite of Wrath in almost every way. But there was enough in you, wasn't there? Just enough for one great release. But that was it. You're done. A broken weapon ready to rust and fade."

"I think I'm going to be sick. Is that what you were doing all this time?" Alex desperately didn't want to believe it. "Trying to bring that nightmare back? Really? What the fuck is . . . what is wrong with you? You wanted to see me change that badly?"

"I need not pretend to say hateful things to you, Barker. My disdain for your signature has only grown since the day you entered my life. We here in the Weya-Vein pity you. Your quaint human mind and words are like an infestation we've tolerated as best we can, knowing you would soon be gone. Once the Sackulli-Karni is empty again, and your stench has departed, we'll be able to rest."

"You know, amid all that judgmental nonsense, I think I just sensed my first lie from you."

A splintery growl echoed down the stone cellblock. "Incredible fortune you're set to die, or I would tear down this wall and pull you apart, limb by limb."

"I'd like to see you try. There's nothing scary about you, and I should know—I'm usually afraid of everything."

A harsh puff of steam escaped Oaleen's cell and drifted through Alex's door. "Barker, the ways you test me . . . you must be my final punishment before I become nothing."

"In fact, the way you and everyone else from your world spit on Earth and humans, I'd say you're jealous."

Oaleen laughed, then dropped to a lower tone. "No."

"Not even a little? Because I'm thinking back now on most of the things you've said to me, and I think they could be interpreted as envious hostility."

"Ridiculous. I would have been angry with you regardless."

"Ha! So you do admit to being envious of humans."

Oaleen choked on her scoff and spat it into the hall. "Your world is the bunny slope. A tepid waste of space. What do your people have that I don't? Parents? We have mentors. Siblings? I have millions of them." There was a pause and a softening of her tone. "However, there is one thing . . . My ilk would never say it normally, but they all wonder what it's like to . . . have a family. Offspring. To grow a being created from your traits alone. When you die, it will be as though you continue on. That . . . is a strange and intriguing concept."

"Including you?"

"I've sometimes wondered. Such immortality shrieks of true greatness—what all Archfiend desire. The One Voice would be proud."

Alex had never considered Oaleen's Archfiend life in such a way and was frankly a little stunned. He'd mostly been bluffing when he goaded her with his accusation of jealousy.

"I understand you were set to be a parent yourself," she said.

"I was."

"Commendable. And you felt ready to assume the mantle?"

"I did."

"With no trepidation? How did you know?"

"Because it was in my DNA. But that doesn't mean I was calm and collected. I was absolutely terrified. Though it helped knowing I'd found the woman I wanted to have children with. As long as I had that, I just . . . knew it."

"Sounds like more superstitious nonsense."

"Might be."

With an uncharacteristic interest in prolonged discussions, Oaleen asked several more questions about human parenting behavior, ranging from when hunting responsibilities kicked in to under what circumstances rearers were allowed to eat a disappointing or underperforming child. Laying out Earth values without openly insulting the Archfiend and her culture was like walking a balance beam with an elderly armadillo in his trousers.

Eventually, the conversation turned to discussing her upbringing in Arros. Alex asked the question, never expecting anything more than a snarl for an answer. Then Oaleen began divulging what might have been the deepest secrets of the Archfiend, revealing what it was like to be born in a lake of fire and find her way to the surface. Once she landed, how her body solidified, and she became an adolescent Archfiend ready to do the bidding of the One Voice. How survival called at every second, demanding she play the part of a dutiful member of Clan Niel, along with the bevy of savagery that came with it.

"I've done evil. I don't deny it," she said. "I just sometimes can't help but feel like I was fated to. Always on that path. I don't remember any big turns I could have made."

The teacher soaked up all he could, learning about the Archfiend as the night went on, gaining a new perspective on the Wrath. *Wish I'd known some of this a lot sooner. You all might not be so bad. At least, not all of you.* He found himself wanting to know more, and perhaps wanting to discover the desire within himself to appreciate that part of him. *Had similar struggles with my white American and Bangladeshi backgrounds. Always sort of hard to feel pride for either.*

The life of Arros was starting to sound as simple as that: bustling, demanding, exhausting, violent, but also perfectly natural. *Can't say that doesn't also describe my home planet to a T.* Alex did his best to remember the names of the great Arros generals Oaleen spoke of with utter passion, the planet's legendary heroes of the past. The Archfiend, much like humanity, had a history riddled with conquest and colonialism, of political powers trading land and influence for millions of years. Somewhere amid the conversation, Alex found he couldn't get enough. His love of history alone did him in. Then, before he knew it, the sun was moments from rising, interrupting them with its misty light creeping into the block.

Well, son of a gun. She distracted me all night.

The beauty of the sunrise faded quickly. It became the worst he'd ever seen. He hated it; he wanted it to leave. He wanted his talk with Oaleen to never end—for obvious reasons, but also because he now desired to stay with this new version of her, which felt like the most genuine one, as well as a stranger. He'd forgotten what it could be like to have a real conversation with someone, how time could ooze by, and how all cares could be dulled simply by their discussion. Nights like that with Melissa were some of his favorites, though he had no real memory of them at all. But the coming of today's sun meant everything was minutes from ending.

Maybe it is for the best. One last good feeling before biting the dust.

Plodding thuds of Barium feet marching through the halls began growing softly within the Weya-Vein. As the steps neared and the echoes grew louder, the jail awoke, stirring into a frenzy more bombastic than anything Alex had yet experienced. Inmates stomped their hooves and hooted and squawked, their voices churning into a nightmarish blend. Wiggled by the vibrations, the chains above him chimed. By the time his escort reached the Weya-Vein, the whole building had been sent into hysterics.

The door to his cell opened. Blinding sunlight poured in. Before Alex could discern how many had arrived to take him, his vision blacked out. The nevrose mask had never been clasped on so quickly. Just before everything went dark, he spotted Loredosai a handful of Celestial steps away in the hall. He and his Guard were arrayed in ceremonial war armor, plated in silver and platinum with fierce blue inlays and rigid, symmetrical linework.

Inside the nevrose helmet—his senses cut down and emotions largely rendered null—Alex didn't care nearly as much about his impending execution. *State's gonna do what state's gonna do. I can't change it. No one can.* But now any final words he and Oaleen might have shared were impossible. Among a lifetime of people he would never see again, he was most upset about losing this new friendship. *She was the only person I could have looked in the eye one last time. This is starting to feel really wrong. Will I even get a chance to say any final words without the mask, or will they just cut off my head while it's still on?*

Alex's body was then removed from the chains by new, even rougher Celestial hands. *These guys make the last ones seem like luxury resort masseuses.* Like a bag of oranges thrown against a wall, he was attached to the rolling slab. Rapture surrounded him like a storm cloud rising. *There must be a hundred of them here today. Lucky me. Just going to keep on saying it. Lucky fucking me.* Surr and Oaleen rushed back to mind, the two who had believed in him, who tried to tell him he was stronger than he thought he was. *Even the mighty Celestial guards are afraid of me. Their signals are shaky and flecked with anxiousness.* He then began to consider there might actually be a way out of this. *If I could just get the mask off and get mad enough, there's a real chance I could show them all something they'd never believe.*

When loaded into his carriage at the end of the trek, Alex found no sign of Bennett, which meant they must have been traveling solo today. *Figures.* Immediately, they departed. This would be a much shorter trip than the one to the Molm compound. Alex sensed, albeit nearly imperceptibly, the crowds of creatures in the streets, passing like loathsome electronic billboards behind a black sheet of fabric. There was Jubilee and excitement in several shades, as well as Dread and Wrath. Grief was nowhere to be found, except in what were likely pure Lostros. Soon, a looming wall of Eve drew near that Alex correctly guessed was the crowd filling the execution grounds' stadium.

The frigid chill of the Barium Guard surrounding the stadium was nothing compared to the bone-deep, piercing, leg-shaking, inescapable freeze radiating off a stupendous Rapture signature nearing on the opposite side. A single individual—Alex was sure of it—which could only mean the High Lord.

The ground rumbled and shook increasingly as the carriage neared the end of the journey. The pounding feet of the thousands in attendance churned his empty stomach. *Kind of relieved there was no last meal, if I'm honest. Don't want to even imagine.* When the sound of the crowd became too much for even the mask to deaden, the carriage came to a halt and Alex's slab was loosed within seconds. *You guys really are in a hurry.* A cold wind struck his skin as he was wheeled away, made all the colder by the looming silence of those stationed at whatever this loading dock was. None of the signatures surrounding him made so much as a click of the tongue. But the emptiness was soon extinguished by a familiar voice.

"Al! Hey, Al!" the voice screamed from under a nevrose mask of Bennett's own. Alex couldn't help but smile and feel catharsis at his approaching Eve, which until now he'd assumed was just another Celestial, certainly not the signature of the soldier he knew. Something was drastically different about it. This guy's Eve was sturdier, more organized, while burning far brighter with deeper blues. *What the heck happened there?*

"I can hear you, Bennett," he said.

His partner's signal grew near, and with a soft, heavy thud, their slabs were staged within a few feet of one another.

"Good, because we're going to have to think fast on this one," Bennett said.

"Does that mean you've got a plan?"

"Sort of. And I can hear the sarcasm in your voice."

The clattering chatter of Fovos beetles pulling another carriage arrived. Izaiah's brilliant apple-green signal was inside the box.

"This fucking guy," Bennett said from the lowest gutter of his throat.

In moments, the slab was loosed and wheeled over to join the others. Muffled words escaped the old Medolian's mask, which Alex could not make out, and neither he nor Bennett responded. Izaiah said nothing else after.

It was probably the setup of a bad joke.

"Look, Izaiah, if you're going to do anything, now is the time," Bennett said after a moment, continuing to surprise Alex with his stoicism. "I don't know what you're waiting for, but Al and I would love to keep our heads on today."

"Oh, don't look at me for anything, fellas. I'm just happy to get out of that cell and get some fresh air!" Izaiah yelled, his scratchy voice echoing within a tinny metal space. "Wish I could help. Honestly, I do."

"That's almost word for word what I thought you were going to say," Bennett said, his tone like a dry sponge.

"Guess that means we're on our own," Alex said.

"I figured it would be like this," Bennett said. "Tell me something, Al, how mad can you get?"

"Have you taken a look at where we are?"

"I mean it. Can you get hot? And I mean nuclear scorch. Burning even by Arros standards."

"I can. Get on with the plan."

Bennett gave an amused chuckle before saying, "Good. We'll need it. When I say so, bring as much rage as you can."

"And that's it?"

"That's it."

"Fine," Alex said. "You better not screw this up like last time, though, and wait too long."

Bennett bounced nothing back, and Alex felt pride in how he'd conducted himself. *Surr and Oaleen were right all along.* Though the soldier's silence likely meant he was just going over the supposed plan in his head. As far as Alex still believed, their chances of getting out of this were slim to nil at best. Bennett and his cynicism likely knew this as well, yet his confidence appeared absolute, as though he were hiding something up his sleeve, some tool. This man was not the guy who'd flung a bucket of his own shit in court last week. This man had seen and done things since, indicated both by his voice, but also by his signature, which had matured like a flower in bloom. *Could it just be from his time in the upper levels of the Weya-Vein?*

The condemned trio remained mostly quiet for the next twenty minutes, except for Izaiah, who let out a fart one might expect from a hippopotamus. Soon, however, the jail slabs were rolled up a short ramp and halted again. The platform where Alex now resided was built so soundly that the vibrations of the guards' footsteps were easily mistaken for heartbeats. Through the Rapture surrounding him, he barely made out the shadowy image of enormous chains on either side of the platform, leading up to what must have been the greater part of the structure. Once their full escort was loaded, a vast machine of gears and pulleys was activated, thundering all around, swelling louder as the platform neared the top, while the Wrath within Alex rose to break free. *This damn helmet. Oh-ho—if I wasn't wearing this fucking thing.* The words of Oaleen from the night repeated in his head. "The Ire could tear down any wall." *That means I could. The Ire was me, right? That's why I'm here today. It was proven in a court of law.*

Every day spent in the Sackulli-Karni served as kindling. All the waiting and anguish spilled out, flooding his thoughts, and the anger came, requiring only the faintest of summons. The deadening effect of the nevrose helmet began to wane. With a crunch, the elevator platform reached the top, where the sheer force of the roaring crowd struck the condemned, drowning Alex. The sight of them was like looking through sunglasses at several thousand gleaming lightbulbs inside a dense cloud. The sea of Eve stretched out for hundreds of yards before rising in the back like a tsunami wave threatening to crash over the stage. Atop the bleachers structure—what Alex first mistook for the morning sun—Gabriel's signal blotted out most of those in attendance around him.

Rolled near the edge of the execution platform, the condemned were placed beside one another, facing the crowd. Alex was on the far left, while Izaiah was on the right, closest to the executioner's sword. *Guess that means I get to go last. Again . . . lucky me.*

A booming voice was already speaking, a Celestial in some sort of box facing the people. Alex had no idea what the creature was saying, only that it seemed unpopular. Then he heard his name. *Ah . . . right.* The bile-filled roar that followed would be glued into his mind for as long as he lived, however long that would be.

"Don't worry, we're getting out of this," Bennett said after a moment.

Thanks to his deadened emotions, Alex was in no danger of laughing. "I thought Izzy was the one who made the bad jokes."

"Hey!" Izaiah said, sounding destroyed. "I jotted down some new material during my stay in the cell. Mostly setups. I can't seem to write a finish that doesn't offend the people I tell them to. But I think some of 'em might be pretty good."

"I'm sure they are," Alex said.

"Are you two done?" Bennett shouted. "I don't know about you, but I'm getting out of here." A torrent of Rapture appeared within him, solidifying in a way that reminded Alex of Hannah's signature; on a smaller scale but with no doubt.

Guess he's been practicing. Or stumbled upon some blue steroids.

"That'll put the sprinkles on your donut! Well done. You oughtta be careful, though, Bennett," Izaiah said. "They're liable to cut you down."

"That's literally why we're here!" the soldier retorted, continuing to grow his power. "Come on, Al! Join me! I know you can do it. Find your strength!"

Now? It appeared Bennett was wasting no time, and Alex was only too eager to play along.

This helmet won't stop me. Come on!

A spare tank of gasoline found its way into his fire via catapult, and images of Melissa's body, Joseph's horrid face laughing up bits of carcass, and the helplessness Alex had felt the night he was shot ran rampant through his mind. Two Celestial guards on the platform moved closer to him and Bennett, keeping an eye on this new development, though they weren't immediately alarmed. The little humans would never be able to break out of bonds made for pure, strong UnEarth creatures, never in all the lifetimes of creation. But if that were true, then why did Alex sense nervousness in them? The crowd was no longer interested in what the announcer had to say, beginning to take notice of Alex's and Bennett's growing Eve. A storm of hissing and barking filled the courtyard, rising toward what felt like a roaring downbeat.

Completing the announcements, the Celestial speaking from the box finished with a single name: Kalos. A hush spread so suddenly that it was as though the crowd's favorite golfer had just stepped to the tee. A chant then broke free of the silence, growing louder. This prompted the tall Wyst to leap to his feet and pump his fists like a professional wrestler about to jump into the ring. The Poa-Lo-Fey had a head shape not dissimilar to that of a hammerhead shark, with long tendrils flowing off the ends. These could be whipped back and forth to intimidate foes or hype up crowds. Following a series of ritualistic shouts and guttural grunts, Kalos took the hilt of the sword awaiting its wielder in a stone base. The throng exploded with applause. *So, he's a rock star.*

With a sound that tore like a microscopic incision on Alex's eardrum, the sword was pulled from the stone. Its silver-and-white blade shone like pure moonlight through heavy mist. There was obvious Rapture of at least two tones in its signature, one of which was violet, sending a feeling through Alex like someone he loved was nearby and everything would be all right. The rest of the sword's signature was hard to discern, seeming to fade into pure energy that both blinded with white and appeared to be nothing at all: a void. The reveal of it sent the crowd into even more hysterics than Center City Philadelphia after a fourth straight Super Bowl win.

First up was Izaiah. Two Celestial guards approached him slowly while Kalos continued his song and dance, and Bennett and Alex continued powering up.

"More, Al!" Bennett bellowed.

Alex screamed, clenching his muscles and resisting the scalding heat rising into his helmet and the blistering sensation on his face and head. Volirhm Kalos had since posed in the shape of a swan, his sword extended like a grand wing—the statuesque finale of the executioner's preshow number. Finally making his way to Izaiah, he aimed the blade at his neck.

Even while facing an instrument he'd likely seen fade countless creatures over the millennia, Izaiah still refused to budge. *He's not even trying to stall with a joke?* That enraged Alex even more, feeding his fire. *Why won't he fight back? What is he doing? WHY?* A flash of heat rolled up from his toes. At the same time, Bennett's Rapture spiked, sending waves cascading through the stage floor. His signature had flared like a stovetop burner on high. *He's actu-*

ally going past me! The soldier had never surpassed Alex's Wrath, and he wasn't about to let that happen now. Clenching his whole body, he roared. Exponentially, their energies grew back and forth, side by side.

"It's working!" Bennett cried.

The Celestial guards watching them finally intervened, though rather lazily. The one closest to Alex smashed the blunt end of their spear into his gut, but the pain only amplified his Eve. Soon his skin was sizzling, and the metal mask began to feel soft. The guards and close spectators started shouting, likely desperate to figure out what to do.

An innumerable number of condemned creatures had no doubt put on a similar show over the years, giving brute force their final confidence. But there was little chance any of them had actually set themselves free. And like everyone kept saying, Alex and Bennett were nothing compared to a pure. But if that were true, it made little sense when the executioner—still flexing his arms, his blade lingering over Izaiah—was seized by a guard and dragged over to Alex instead.

The teacher's vision rose to the glowing silhouette of Fervor. When the announcer bellowed something in a panic, the executioner swiftly raised his blade, which Alex could see with his own eyes as the nevrose mask began to melt off his face. He found himself eye to eye with the Wyst set to kill him, who suddenly appeared too stunned to strike.

The wrist restraints were starting to give. Within seconds, Alex would be free from his bondage. Bennett's own power had become like a crashing sea in a bay of colossal rocks beside him. Momentum, it seemed, was in their corner. *Are we really going to do this? We are, aren't we?*

Alex lost himself in thoughts of imminent victory when, suddenly, the world blinked and shook, spinning wildly.

For a few moments, his entire presence seemed lost.

Something terrible and shocking had just occurred. He knew that much, but his mind was miles from catching up. Fear and agony washed over him. The only thing Alex knew was that the Eve he'd amassed was gone—poof, like it had never existed at all, leaving him empty. Before being snuffed out, the Wrath in him seemed to seize, as though crying out in agony.

The blast gradually made itself known. *An explosion. Yeah, that's what that was.* The stone slab he'd been attached to had been hurled like a rag doll—flying end over end, skipping across the ground until it violently slammed to a halt.

Debris continued to fly, striking him with pieces big and small. But soon, everything died down, and the boom faded. The last bits cracked against walls and wreckage, and a quiet took over, except for a steady, piercing ring in Alex's ears. It seemed that whatever had happened was over and done, yet he felt suspended in an addled state, lofted without his feet on the ground—a dangling kite in the eye of a storm.

The shackles remained clamped around his wrists and ankles. The metal slab had not only failed to crush him into jelly, but it also seemed to have prevented any major injuries when he'd landed. As Alex came to, the realization of his narrow survival kicked in, mixed with the misery of jagged rock, broken glass, and wood jammed in his sides, legs, and arms. He couldn't help but scream and clench his fists until his palms burned; the tension helped ease the hurt. As he began to struggle, the bands holding his wrists suddenly gave, as though a mechanism inside the slab had released automatically. His feet were also liberated. Wiggling free—forced to squeeze out from under a jagged stone clawing into his side—

Alex rolled away just as an avalanche of rubble made one last attempt to crush him, missing by less than a foot.

Rising to his feet, he hobbled away as quickly as he could, becoming engulfed in a cloud of gray. Limping forward, his wrath gone, he felt lighter, as though he'd lost weight without appearing any skinnier—a wet sponge that had been squeezed and left on the counter. He had experienced this sensation before: it was much like how he had felt on his first visit to Trivium, as though, at any minute, his body might start falling apart atom by atom—*and like my feet aren't touching the ground. I hate that part.* Only getting his Eve back would help, but, like trying to strike a match in a thunderstorm, he could not reignite it within him.

Between chunks of rock and metal were the limbs and mangled bodies of UnEarth creatures—crushed and burned, with sunken flesh as though they'd perished weeks before and been left to wither and jerkify. Able to claw his way to the top of a debris pile, Alex found before him a bleak, dust-covered landscape. Drifting smoke filled the air so thickly he could hardly see his own feet. The royal bleachers loomed high in the distance, a dark, broad shadow hovering over the gloom. Gabriel's seat, the only one high enough to be clear of the haze, appeared empty. If the Celestial lord was still in it, he was giving off no light.

More limbs and mangled bodies passed under his feet as Alex traversed down a hunk of the platform. "Bennett!" he called, not caring who heard, grabbing hold of something before a sudden attack of lightheadedness made him stumble and crack his head open on one of the slanted columns.

Catching his breath, he noticed the wall he leaned against was made of yellow-tinted stones the size of SUVs, with green cement between them: one side of an archway to the back entrance of the execution platform. Passing through the arch, he found the shriveled corpse of the Wyst executioner with a splintered hunk of wood extruding from his abdomen. His sword was embedded into the same wall he'd been pinned to, just a few feet away, his severed hand and arm still gripping the handle.

Good riddance, ya jerk.

"Al?" Bennett's voice arose, no louder than a whisper, from somewhere behind him.

"Bennett?" Alex hurried to find him, meeting up with him just a few yards away next to an empty jail slab. The locks and bands were open. A nevrose helmet lay on the ground next to it.

"Good, you're alive," Bennett said, his voice worn and grizzled. His own helmet had been removed, though Alex didn't know how. "Couldn't find your signature."

"Does that mean you were worried? Yours is gone, too."

"Yeah. My guess is those were Mallos bombs of a sort, or at least made to replicate a Mallos surge. Makes sense. Today was a perfect target."

"How did you get all that? It was an explosion, for Pete's sake."

"I felt it. You didn't?" Bennett asked with even more throat sand. Alex motioned at the empty slab.

"Not mine," said Bennett, shaking his head. "This was Izaiah's."

"Where did he go? They didn't cut his head off, right? I was sort of busy getting angry, but I'm pretty sure that didn't happen. And I didn't feel a Shift."

"Me either. But I don't really care where he is. The bombs scared everyone off for a bit, but I bet they'll start coming in to search for survivors soon."

"Yeah, I can smell them already," Alex said. "Whatever set off the bomb, do you think there will be more?"

"I think they would have gone off by now. Suicide bombers tend to go all at once. Anybody who missed their chance usually doesn't do it after the fact out of embarrassment. They'd rather hide and run away—probably to a new continent."

"How do you know—"

"Educated guess."

Bennett started away from the stage arch toward the exit from the grounds. "We need to find somewhere to lay low. Wait for our powers to come back."

Alex followed at a brisk pace over the scorched and wreckage-ridden lot behind the stage, hoping they were headed toward greater Trivium, somewhere not so out in the open. Bennett's senses and ability to navigate were well trusted by now, so when they began making turns and winding through the cluttered neighborhoods to the east of the Tribunal, Alex kept quiet, channeling the agility of a silent barn rat seeking food in the night. At any moment, a blue-winged nightmare could come crashing down on their heads.

They had yet to pass another living soul, excluding the wheezing bodies of UnEarth creatures taking their dying breaths. Then faces began to poke around corners and appear in windows, but it seemed no one was paying a modicum of attention to the humans; the explosions had sapped it all.

They're completely dumbfounded—like they never thought anything like this could happen here.

The cries and moans of pained creatures began to grow. Wounded individuals passed by, leaned against broken walls, or simply sprawled in the road. Each of them was asking for help, and Alex had to resist the urge to give it. But when he saw a Psera Celestial trying to walk on one leg, disoriented, he couldn't help but slide under their arm to help support them.

"Hi there," Alex said to the Celestial, who stared as if they were being assisted by a cross-eyed chicken.

When Bennett eventually turned back and saw what was happening, his hoarse voice failed to scream. The Celestial his partner was helping continued to stare, but when Bennett returned, they must have put two and two together. Wailing like they had a broken leg, the sound the Psera released echoed through a series of drainpipes before bursting from their mouth.

"Wait! I'm trying to help you!" Alex pleaded, but the Celestial continued howling, drawing the attention of everyone nearby.

When Bennett arrived, he shoved the stout Celestial aside and seized Alex by the arm. "You idiot."

As they turned to leave, the crowd began to shout about the humans who were not only alive but making an escape. This was just as several Barium Guards flew by overhead, their wings spread wide. Fear never had a chance to settle into Alex, as it was clear the Celestials were headed toward the execution grounds, paying the crowd no mind. This didn't dissuade the mob, however, and as Bennett and Alex made their escape, the people continued yelling, marching slowly after them.

Breaking away, the humans ducked through several side passages and alleys with low clearances. The shouts of the guards faded but were soon replaced by the clang of a whole squadron's worth of Barium armor, swelling in approach, filling the stone walkways. With a sharp turn, Bennett snuck down a tight inlet, which ended quickly. On the left was a building like a smooth box, likely a Celestial home with no visible way to climb its walls. But the one standing opposite looked far more promising: an old wall with bricks of various dark autumn shades, made of differing shapes and sizes. Halfway up the wall, a slanted open window sat at the top of an ornate, latticed structure of black wood interspersed with gnarled gray vines.

"Let's climb," Bennett said, starting up.

Carefully gripping the structure and making sure to steer clear of the barbs on the vine, which were close to half an inch long,

Alex took his time climbing after him. When Bennett neared the open window, he peered inside and instantly ducked away, his face flushed white, looking moments from puking.

"What is it?" Alex asked in a panicked whisper.

"Hang on," Bennett said, taking a second before inching his way back up. Peering over the sill with extreme caution, he eventually let his shoulders loosen. "I think it's okay. Just don't freak out when you get up here. You'll see."

After Bennett disappeared into the window, Alex diligently climbed the rest of the way. When he rose above the windowsill, he was forced to stifle a startled yelp, nearly throwing off his balance and sending him plummeting. Standing in the dead center of the room was a tall, thin woman dressed in a black gown, her wispy hair aloft, tendons protruding and clenched tight. Frozen in place, no more breath in her than a stump, her exposed skin had shriveled up and cracked into slivers, akin to bark. A long, gangly arm was stretched out toward the window, its hand reaching with curled, clawed fingers of yellow-green.

Together, Alex and Bennett circled and studied her.

"The bombs must have done her in," Bennett surmised. "Looks like a Scythe. Maybe she got literally scared to death? Or maybe the radiation fried her?"

Those guesses all sounded good to Alex, or at least plausible.

They searched the room, which was mostly obscured by a thick layer of yellow-and-orange-tinted dust on every surface. The broad, faded, rug-laced floor was outlined by portraits on the walls of terrifyingly, disturbingly, and depressingly ugly people. A modest chair was set against the wall on the left, facing directly toward the most stupefyingly ugly man surely to have ever cursed the face of many planets. Beside the chair was a long wooden trunk with dozens of differently sized, golden-rimmed compartments. In the corner was what looked like a coffin—black, with a shredded texture that made it appear as though it had been constructed by paper wasps.

Nearing the coffin, Alex made out a soft chattering sound and leaned closer, trying to find the source. As his ear found its way to the wall, just under a charcoal portrait frame, the sound opened up into a sea of writhing clicks and taps, thousands and thousands of traveling legs just on the other side.

"You wouldn't think there would be anyone else home," he said with a nervous swallow.

"Looks like a good place to lay low," Bennett replied.

"But for how long? They're going to be looking for us, and Izaiah's gone."

"What would you rather do? Just charge through the city? With all those guards out there? In the middle of the day? And I don't know about you, but I feel like shit. That bomb . . . we're lucky it didn't kill us."

"If we just keep the momentum going, we can fight our way through. Come on! We almost had it on the execution platform. I can feel it. It's there, waiting to come out. I can do some damage. Let's do it."

"I don't doubt you could, but we should be smart about this. We should rest. Regain our full strength. That will be the most effective option. I doubt they'll start tearing down doors looking for us. They probably assume nobody would take us in and that we're headed for the nearest Eb Gate. Let's wait for darkness. Get as far as we can before having to do things your way."

"What do you mean? I thought it was your way," Alex said.

"Used to be."

"What changed?"

"A lot, Al."

Guess I can't argue with that.

COVET

The tapping of their feet on the stone walkways echoed around them as dark snow began to drift onto their heads. Aluqa moved from one shadow to the next, leading the way as if she'd known the back streets of Trivium all her life. The unending ringing in Leigh's ears from the explosion made it difficult to focus on the back of Aluqa's glistening shaved head. All she could do was try to keep up. They had been running for fifteen minutes without stopping.

The maroon sky behind them was thick with a rising cloud of smoke, while swooping Celestials patrolled and surveyed the streets. Panic rippled through their formations, usually immaculate, as they searched for direction. *Celestials don't know what to do if the enemy isn't right in front of them.* The Barium Guard was busier than they'd likely ever been. Leigh guessed they had only just begun drawing up contingency plans for another Joseph-level event in the last few months, let alone preparing for an attack of such destructive magnitude in a heavily populated area. She still had no idea of the extent of the damage, but the blast she'd felt

would have been the stuff of nightmares had she not been imbued with Wrath. Set off within a stadium filled with creatures,
the death toll was undoubtedly monstrous.

*(good. fuckin' monsters deserve to be treated as such. slaughter 'em all.
that was just a taste)*

[*But what I am truly interested in is what toll it took on the Un-
Earth leadership. Who among them was killed? With any luck, they all
perished.*]

*They goddamned better have. The Sanctioned didn't get themselves
blown up for nothing. Poor bastards never even saw it coming.*

[*I know I did not.*]

She watched the woman ahead, uncertain of what to make of her.
Moments after the blast, Aluqa had produced a syringe from her
dress, resembling those used to inject the Sanctioned. Inside was a
shimmering blue liquid, but it looked different from the concoction Blue Eyes used—duller and more opaque. When Aluqa injected herself, raw power burst from her eyes and coursed through
her veins, glowing—a blazing light—eliciting a low gasp. Since
then, her speech patterns had become as broken and embryonic as
her Celestial partner's.

Pahlanksha had mentioned that Aluqa received doses of something from the Cardinal during her visits to his quarters. It stood to
reason this could be a more potent form of Eve than what the lowly rooks and Cavaliers had been given. If Leigh's theory—which
was still in its early stages—held true, this injecting of Aluqa with
Eve had likely been ongoing for some time. [*It would certainly help
explain how she has appeared to live for so long.*]

They exited a barren alley into a courtyard laden with orange and
green. Thumps and shrieks echoed as masses of people scrambled
to escape. Leigh dodged behemoths and floating cocoons, keeping
Aluqa in sight as they crossed the yard. All the while, she replayed

the mission in her mind, from the beginning to this very moment. The blue-eyed woman in the chamber had failed to give her the shot of "Eve" from the syringe. *Wonder what it really was.* That was the only difference between Leigh and the others. *I should have blown up with them.* It was not the vest that had detonated, nor the device she'd been told was a transceiver. [*That could only mean it was them—their bodies. The Cardinal turned them all into walking grenades.*]

(what the fuck?)

Though she was furious, much of her ached knowing she was not there to see the giant explosion the others had created. It may have killed them all, but such a force would have been a marvel to behold. *And be a part of. So much destructive power. So much death.* Yet, as she ran, sticking to Aluqa like a heat-seeking missile, the effects of Wrath began to fade, and sadness crept in at the thought of Skraga blowing herself up. It seemed a monumental waste. The entire Surface had participated in the attack, which meant Earth's defense force had just committed a mass suicide bombing. If even a few of the UnEarth leaders survived, the planet the professor called home would be left at the mercy of the Tribunal and any potential retaliation it sought.

But all that concerned her now was why she hadn't been among them and where Aluqa was leading her like a lemming with four brain cells.

Aluqa remained gleefully five yards ahead as Leigh began to piece together their gradual turn, block by block. Her memory allowed her to visualize the Trivium landscape from above. In five minutes, they would reach Trinity Plaza. A short hike beyond that lay the central governing body of UnEarth: its brain and heart. *That has to be it. She's turning south. What else is this way?* This trip was offering much more sightseeing than Leigh had anticipated.

She's leading us to the Tribunal.

Her plan was slowly revealing itself. The explosion had created enough chaos for them to move unimpeded, but Leigh couldn't fathom what they could accomplish there that would justify the lives of the Sanctioned. Each time she glimpsed the ziggurat through the gaps in the skyline, it loomed larger. It was unlikely to be fully populated at the moment, making it improbable that Aluqa intended to carry out another attack meant to annihilate UnEarth lives. *(doubt anyone important is left in there)*

So, what in the world could we be doing?

The Wrath in her veins made Leigh angry, not stupid. Setting foot in the UnEarth Tribunal was not only a monumental proposition, but could prove exceedingly dangerous, especially now. Numerous security protocols would have likely been activated after the bombing. The best move was obviously to walk away, abandon this ridiculous life altogether, and maybe become a nun. If Member Silverthorn left now, while the city was still reeling, she might have reached an Eb Ring and returned to Earth. But she knew there was no real hope for that. Leigh would press on to see where this path led, which now seemed to point straight into the Tribunal itself.

Her chance had arrived to survey the inner workings of the world she loathed more than any other. The knowledge and experience would be invaluable and irreplaceable—*(if I make it out)*

[*It is a dangerous choice, I agree, but this is the way Aluqa is going. Therefore, it is the direction I will be going.*]

Soon, they passed the last eatery at the end of a lane, and Trinity Plaza spread out before them. Aluqa had taken them around the northeast side to the Caechus, the Tribunal's third primary section, which housed the Counselors and the archives: the Armarium. The recent damage was evident, with chrome scaffolding, planks, and walkways crisscrossing the building as it underwent extensive repairs. The devastation Joseph had wrought before his inevitable downfall was far beyond impressive. *Wish I could've seen it. I deserved to watch him die.*

Aluqa stepped behind a building of rust-colored brick and halted, staying just out of sight of the Tribunal. As she surveyed the plaza—surely far more desolate than usual—Leigh kept her gaze locked on the back of Aluqa's head.

"I sense your confusion," Aluqa said, her voice soft yet deep, filled with bass. She turned to face Leigh, a knowing grin on her lips. "Your hatred and your love for me."

"They're all dead," Leigh said with her charred, Wrath-filled voice.

"This is truth. One final act. This, one of defiance."

"Final? They didn't know. They thought—"

"Never could have known. This, they. None of you. How could you understand? None of you . . . children, awash in a sea. Fearing to tread. This would have been wise."

"What are you talking about? Our forces have been severed. How can we continue this war without an army?"

"Ha!" The laugh expelled by Aluqa was robotic, devoid of merriment. "Army? Is this unseen? Point it out. The wish is mine to see. One hundred and fifty-eight lives. That was the strength of the Surface."

"Huh? One hundred and—"

Leigh felt as if she'd been struck in the chest by a rock with a note tied to it that simply read "*Duh*." There were no other Surface stations. Station Five was it. The Cavaliers totaled seventeen. The rook facilities and the mine weren't kept in poor condition to maintain control—they were simply inadequate. The other stations didn't keep radio silence for security; they didn't exist at all.

"The forties. Forties, indeed. This was the time of greatness. Seven stations there were," Aluqa said. "The strength was grown, several thousand strong, but not enough. Never. A drop of the needed. The drain called. But before Surface could give out, forever, or be ended. This, by him. The Cardinal. I wished to let them find what greatness they could. To find death and bring many along. The enemy. This is who they took. As all Sanctioned wanted."

Leigh studied the vest Opal had given her. *(there's no such thing as multireality GPS, is there?)*

[*Of course, there is not.*]

"What do you mean 'ended'? He was planning on killing them all anyway?" Leigh asked.

Aluqa laughed again. "Not just them."

"Tell me what happened. I know you must have had a good reason, but why did you give them toys and promise they would get to see the massacre? They knew nothing of their—"

"Nothing of massacre. This is known by you. Nothing of my lies. This is known by you. The purest—these are my lies. Told for salvation. All Surface was to be sacrificed, one way or another. The burden of false ignorance. This was my chain. This knowledge. The Cardinal could never know. This . . . disaster. For years, the secret was kept. I knew nothing of my betrayal, and so it was told. But events needed to be molded. This was my time and energy. An idea. Its creation. To . . . make most of it. To stave off inevitable."

"Inevitable?" Leigh bellowed. "You say that as though we are powerless. You've killed hundreds, if not thousands, of them by yourself. You're the only one who can teach us."

"Thousands. Yes. But a pure Celestial . . . never."

"That can't be true. You were great enough to spare the Cardinal's life all those years ago."

"The Cardinal allowed the lie. This, because he cares not for human thoughts. So it was told, my sparing of his life. But I did not. He spared mine."

Leigh considered this quickly. "It's his blood, isn't it? In your needle. He gave you his blood. Made you his pet."

In a flash, a cold hand gripped her neck, like an arctic river rock crushing her windpipe and cracking her bones. The blue fire in Aluqa's eyes flared.

"In comparison with the greatest, that of Hywyn, of Rapture, all are powerless. Whatever victories are attainable—these should be taken. This is what I have done. This is what shall be done. This, by me. And you."

After releasing her icy grip, Aluqa moved to the edge of the rust-bricked building's corner to peer out over the courtyard. "Soon, I will end it. But first, we begin."

Before she could step out, Leigh planted her feet and said, "No."

"Your pardon, Member Silverthorn?"

"Don't give me that. You just turned the whole team into chowder and can't tell me why. If you think I'll follow you now, I—"

"I did not destroy them. The Cardinal did this," Aluqa said sharply. "I maintained silence. The deed was carried out, as my truth stated. The risks were great, as my truth stated. But should I deem an explosion necessary, this will be accomplished by you. No questions will be asked. And you will relish in the fire. Is this understood?"

Leigh balked but stayed quiet, simply shrugging. *(a good fire does sound pretty fun. boss lady is right)*

"Forget not, the choice. This was yours. Without me, there was no path. No plan. My creation nourished you. Soon, you will repay this. This act will be the most destructive UnEarth has ever known. All, by you. This fire will reach across even soaked shores and fields of snow. Now, come."

With a swift turn, Aluqa slid around the corner and disappeared. Without much of a second thought, Leigh followed. *Shit—knew exactly which buttons to push.*

Stone structures, the deepest red can get before turning black, were symmetrically dotted throughout the paths in the courtyard leading to the Tribunal. The obelisks, pointed and angled at the top, provided minimal cover, but Aluqa utilized every foot, keeping herself and Leigh firmly obscured. The colossal house of government grew more menacing and imposing with every step. Its barbed spires gleamed like polished ebony reflecting the maroon sky.

Aluqa and Leigh soon crept to the foot of the stone steps leading to a pair of grand teardrop-shaped doors. Two watchful guards stood on high platforms, one on each side of the main stairs, their heads rotating and eyes scanning in perfect sync like security cameras.

Stopping behind a decorative stone block near the lowest step, Aluqa stole a glance. The guards had not yet made a fuss. "Yes, their sight is amazing. But what good is it if they are not told what to seek?" She smiled again, but there was nothing cheerful about it; nothing human.

"Worry not," she said. "I allow nothing bad. Nothing to you." From her pouch, she revealed two tones, the relaxation tools of UnEarth, nearly twice the size of the one Leigh had. "You know how these work." Aluqa handed one to Leigh, who nodded.

Gripping it tightly in both hands, Leigh felt the Wrath within her simmer and spread out, relieving the pressure that had built. Unlike previous occasions when she'd used a tone, she could now feel the Mallos flushing through her, could taste it. The neutral Eve was both stifling and freeing, like jumping into a pool in winter. The air seemed to be sapped from her lungs, and the longer it lasted, the more naked and exposed she felt. Yet there was something familiar about it, a reminder of carefree childhood days when the changing scents in the air signaled the approach of a new season, and the biggest problem she faced was needing to come in from play.

She gripped the tone tightly and took her first step to follow Aluqa, daring not to glance at the guards as they ascended. The sound of their footsteps felt deafening, but in reality, the two women moved as quietly as house cats. The tones worked well enough that the guards paid no mind as they approached the upper half of the steps. Slowly and steadily, sticking as close to the wall as possible, Leigh ascended. The Celestial guards never faltered or turned their gazes down, and soon Aluqa and Leigh found themselves on the upper level, a mere fifteen feet from the door.

Not knowing how to operate the doors, Leigh sighed with relief when they opened automatically, emitting only a soft whoosh. Feeling a tug on her arm, she hurried inside after Aluqa, and the doors began to close immediately behind them.

When the seal shut, it felt less like a door and more like the lid of an isolation tank, sealing them in with a vacuum grip. A dampened silence enveloped her, and she turned to find herself gazing down a gigantic hall of dark blue-cobalt stone. The ceiling and rafters above were interlaced with shadows, broken by hanging tapestries and enormous scrolls stitched with the languages of UnEarth. The minimalist adornments and trim made the immaculate hall seem more like an art museum awaiting its first exhibit than a house of politics.

The descriptions she'd read about the Tribunal's interior could not have been more obtuse if the authors had tried. They measured its size in relative terms, claiming, "The ceiling is higher than a football field!" But they failed to convey the profound insignifi-

cance that washed over a lowly human who stumbled inside. The
feeling of self-worth being squeezed out of them like juice from
a lemon. The words described a place where angels, demons, and
everything in between brokered civil discourse and created laws,
but they could never capture the overwhelming sense of timeless-
ness and stillness that filled the air. The history of UnEarth, locked
away in her mind, swam through every scenario and individual
that might have passed through these halls. Thanks to the Wrath
coursing through her, she loathed this review, yet it was still undeniably fascinating.

Luckily, for the moment, the halls were empty. No assistants,
Pseras, helpers, or Counselors were in sight. Aluqa slipped away,
and Leigh followed, unsure of their final destination now that they
were inside. Perhaps they were headed to sabotage the offices of
the Counselors? Their journey through the Caechus continued un-
interrupted for ten minutes until they reached Ronnimus Hall,
which would lead to the Counselors' chambers—if they took the
door on the right. When Aluqa skipped the sixty-foot entrance
made of deep red-brown rock and continued to the next left,
Leigh realized instantly where they were headed. It all started to
click: this path led to the Armarium, the repository of the Tribunal's most precious treasures. Everything from iconic weapons of
great wars to original copies of vital documents were stored inside
for archival purposes.

Twice more, she and Aluqa had to grip their tones to sneak safely
past a patrol, but soon they stood outside an entrance that looked
no different from the others they had passed. Above it, a bulbous
nameplate made of blue-gray steel spelled something in Hyl that
she couldn't pronounce but recognized as Incicto in English. A
platform loomed above them: another guard post. This one was
empty. *Guess threatening Gabriel's life did the trick.* As they passed

through the threshold without detection, Leigh began to question the effectiveness of the Barium Guard at all. *(not that i wish otherwise at the moment. just funny)*

Their contingency plans must be only a few bullet points long.

The atmosphere of the enormous room beyond seemed to close in around them, further dampening the sound, as if all noise in the Armarium was killed before it could propagate.

"We have the place to ourselves. Two little humans," Aluqa said, releasing her grip on her tone to become fully visible again. Leigh did the same, and some of the Wrath returned, but not as much as before. Slowly, she began to feel like her old self again. However, the more she regained her composure, the harder it became to focus on their task, as the pressure on her muscles and the tightening sensation of her skin intensified.

(my teeth feel like they're going to start falling out of my head any second)

Leigh and Aluqa strolled through the halls of the Armarium. Tall columns reaching to the ceiling divided the enormous shelves running the length of the room into sections. The shelves, reminiscent of grocery store aisles but fifty times bigger, contained crates with elaborate locks, igniting Leigh's excitement yet again over mystery boxes. She yearned to peek inside each and every one. Some shelves openly displayed their contents, flaunting actual treasures like gold trinkets and rubies housed in glass cases and open-topped crates.

Statues and busts of long-dead politicians gazed down at them from high and low as they entered the central lane, where Leigh's attention was immediately captured. On the far wall to the left stood a full-size statue of Michael, pale gray with smooth, subtle features. In his hand, held high, was a spear, bathed in light from a stained glass window behind him. The twelve-foot weapon appeared to be made of polished ice, a translucent sky blue. *I know what that is. It is the weapon Michael wielded for forty-thousand years—Ahnim.*

(until it got used on his own ass. i'm surprised they would give it its own special little stage and make such a big deal out of the very thing that killed their all-time favorite guy)

Below the stained-glass window, displayed on a monumental plaque, was a helmet of weathered gray steel large enough to house a small sedan. *That's gotta be Molm'Ursuth's helmet.* Covering every inch of its exterior were wide, firm spikes, designed for battering enemies. [*He was not known as the Iron Flood for nothing.*]

(i was kind of expecting more, though. not much scary about a giant, inverted waffle maker on a big fat demon's fat head)

The value of the contents of the room was immeasurable; yet, as Leigh suspected, Aluqa strode past it all. Somehow, none of it seemed worth a second glance, and soon they came upon the entrance to the Sercilium, a gateway of white stone. As they stepped inside, a series of panels on the surrounding wall caught Leigh's attention. Each panel bled into the next, depicting the great war, Inferius. The obviously heroic Celestials and other members of the Alliance dominated the lower shade armies, portraying major turning points, including Michael's slaying at the hands of his "twin," Lucifer-Aveyl. The images divided the story into two halves on either side of a short pillar at the center of the back wall. Atop the platform rested a foggy blue cube, bathed in a ghostly spotlight Leigh couldn't identify. Inside lay an object, hidden in obscurity, square in shape and about the size of a watermelon.

"There it is," Aluqa said, revealing a small gray puck from her bag that looked to be made of pumice.

"What is that?" Leigh asked.

"Similar tools you've used, but of Rapture."

"But is that . . . Mallos?"

"Correct. Concentrated. Extremely rare. You might say decades needed—to tear out the heart of a mountain. This—only this finds enough." Aluqa planted the puck on the side of the enclosure and spun to Leigh, suddenly and forcefully grasping her face in both hands.

The leader pressed her lips against Leigh's, opening them wide when Aluqa's tongue slipped in, writhing over and under her own. Fury rushed through the professor in a heartbeat but was quickly overtaken by raw, uninhibited passion. Her hands had to be held at bay, clenched tight to keep from seizing her idol. No doubt she would have accidentally scratched or opened some skin. Their mouths would have been molded together if made out of clay. When saliva began to cascade from their chins to the floor, Aluqa suddenly pulled away and sucked up all she could from Leigh's cheeks and the gap between her lower lip and chin, not letting a drop fall. Spinning back to the glass cube, she spat her mouth's contents onto the gray puck. Once drenched, the thing sizzled like a firecracker about to go off as a high-pitched whine grew.

"This is it, Member Silverthorn. Everything we deserve."

Her heart racing, Leigh was so flustered she hardly noticed being hurried to safety behind one of the six tall pillars in the round room. Aluqa then plugged Leigh's ears, keeping her eyes locked with the professor's. A feeling of safety poured in, immediately followed by righteous loathing. The shriek of the puck was cut off by a small explosion, followed a moment later by the sound of cascading glass raining onto the floor.

"That wasn't so bad," Leigh said, earning a sly smile from Aluqa in return before she slipped around the pillar.

After a moment, once Leigh had collected herself, she saw an unassuming stemless cup resting in the center of the square case.

Its crystalline body was murky, streaked with two shades of blue. On one side, it was so vibrant that it seemed to let you peer into a cloudless sky on a sunny day. On the other side, a dim, lifeless color charred near a burnt umber or shadowed gray, depending on the light.

Many in the anti-UnEarth online community still believed that something as drastic as the first legal declaration of armistice in the history of the realm of the soul could be forged by something as trivial as a scroll etched with ink. But Leigh had known for a while that wasn't true. The Covenant was not a written document at all, but a vessel. Placed ceremonially within its walls during its creation were two Celestial feathers: one from Michael and the other from Lucifer-Aveyl.

I mean, I knew what I was about to see. But still . . . that's it? The Covenant is a Manhattan tumbler?

Without a moment's hesitation, Aluqa made her way to the box, stepping over the broken glass. It took two hands to pick up the cup, which was both larger and smaller than Leigh expected.

The pieces of Michael and Lucifer were still luminous, even after all the years of separation, offering the faintest glimpse of what it would have been like to stand in their presence. It was a scent she would not soon forget. The destructive fury of the Fallen One was apparent, but nowhere near as raw as she imagined. The sensation told her he was a more reserved and meticulous destroyer than the stories suggested. But the energy of Michael was hard not to focus on, diverting her almost completely. Its scent was what Leigh imagined mornings in northern Alaska were like: the awakening of a frosty chill. And yet she also sensed peace and the warmth of lying in a meadow draped in sunlight, surrounded by the scents and sounds of life at its purest.

But Aluqa's face was not filled with awe as she held the cup aloft.

Instead, it was filled with malice. The light in her eyes fluctuated, seeming brightest when her speech patterns were at their most rudimentary.

"Can you really believe it? How insignificant. Part of me expected to be unworthy. The precious Covenant would know. Stop me. But no. Here it is. This. That which has directed all our lives. Year zero. When Gabriel and Lucifer drank. When the armies of Alliance and Die Muneris could not end a war, yet a cup . . . Some say poetry. I say idiocy." She smelled the rim. Her irises ignited. "UnEarth society, all. Built around an object. This. So revered, all assumed none would steal. And so far true . . . of UnEarth creatures. But to me . . . an opportunity."

Aluqa stretched out her arms and held the cup to Leigh. "Your responsibility. This, Member Silverthorn. Protect it. Keep it. Until task-complete."

Leigh's fingers trembled as she gripped what was essentially a glass bucket in both hands, unable to help but also immediately smelling the rim, finding no scent. With a screeching Velcro tear, Aluqa removed a thin bundle from her vest. It flipped open and unfolded, transforming into a backpack. Its square shape was ideal for the cup—custom made. Leigh placed it inside and put the bag on.

"Don't let me down," Aluqa said.

A small flash of the weight she was carrying sped through Leigh. Not only the weight of the fate of UnEarth but also of Earth and all humanity. To say nothing of her own devotion to Miss Morinnean and the powerful desire to live up to her expectations. "Never."

(speaking of weight. damn, this thing is no joke. did i just strap a log to my back?)

The first steps took a few tries to get going. *(seriously, the fuck?)*

"Stay behind me. We'll need to move fast," Aluqa said, turning to run.

But when she faced the door, a tall figure stood before it, blocking the way: a silhouette, a rolling mist fraying its edges. Leigh knew well the frame of the Cardinal, but this creature's shoulders were at least a foot broader, his once lifeless eyes now aflame with azure, growing in intensity, his once gray skin now stained the color of the ocean. Close at his side stood Opal, his posture somehow even more erect, arching his back unnaturally, a bright azure glow of his own pouring from his eyes and streaking through the veins in his neck and exposed forearms. With his chin held unnaturally high and tilted at a slight angle, he appeared only semi-aware of the moment. [*Perhaps he is having an adverse reaction to his imbuement?*]

(yeah, the guy's looked better)

When the Cardinal spoke, the power and potency of his ageless voice stunned Leigh, as though it had finally been unfurled, revealing its true self for the first time.

"No further."

Aluqa growled and stomped her foot in frustration. "Quicker than expected. Rather annoying," she practically shouted at the Cardinal.

"Mutual." The Cardinal drifted into the room, his arms tucked behind his back. Opal followed, but with steps that made him look more and more like an antique wind-up soldier.

Definitely having some sort of processor issue.

"Detestable brazenness," said the Cardinal. "You think yourself great enough to thieve such treasure. Your flesh belongs not—in this city or sanctuary. A relic more sacred than your mind comprehends, this you bastardize. Be returned. This, to me."

"A snake. A false face—pretends to despise those who cast you out," Aluqa said. "But in truth, anything—absolutely anything—this would be given by you. If only to return."

The Cardinal remained quiet while Opal huffed and puffed, his eyes growing angrier and more absent by the moment, his head drifting farther to the side.

"Command your pet. It will retrieve the dagger," the Cardinal said with a slight nod in Leigh's direction, acknowledging her for the first time. "This will be in my hand. This will end the conflict. Morinnean will be released. The word you have—this is mine."

Leigh caught Aluqa's gaze. *He doesn't want the cup?*

(the Wraithian dagger. always with that goddamned thing)

"You will not touch her," Aluqa said. "The proud Royce . . . I know how you pine for forgiveness. Yet you succeed only in forgetting. Hywyn changes its mind, never. An exception—you . . . no."

"I will be welcomed. Raised to viceroy," the Cardinal said. "Gabriel will bend a knee. This, when he sees my gift."

"Gabriel's dead," Aluqa said.

"Yet you tell others to wake. The High Lord regains strength. This, now. Also, desire for retribution."

"Surprised not that he lived," said Aluqa. *(neither am I)* "Real prize is mine. I will watch UnEarth wake to no Covenant. No signs of who took it. The realms tear one another asunder. This, through fear and mistrust."

"Child, once I deliver Erelerim and you to his feet, Gabriel's ear—mine for eternity. First, I ensure Hywyn invades. Occupy Earth. Take control, once and for all. Peons fall under the wing—a change. More peaceful, Rapture-tinted. Life proper. Earth will thrive. Hywyn, galvanized, ever nearer to purity."

"Nice plan. Won't bear fruit," Aluqa said, taking her first steps toward the door and the ones blocking it. Leigh instinctively kept pace, unable to help but feel thrown off-balance by the suddenness.

(okay, are we just going for it?)

[*This does not seem like a sound strategy.*]

With his long, slender arm, the Cardinal reached into his robe and revealed a remote control. Aluqa's powerful march was halted instantly.

A deep, tense inhale coursed through her nose before she asked, "The real trigger?"

"Yes," the Cardinal said. "In activation of Sanctioned. This button detonated. Pride would have been felt. This by you. All were in designated stations. An effective attack. The chaos will bring change before order regains."

Thinking of the other Surface members dying in the explosion sent Leigh's blood boiling. She couldn't hold her tongue. "Order will never return to UnEarth, Human Celestial. We'll make sure of it."

A slap suddenly struck her face, zapping her cogency for a flash. The hand that hit her might as well have been a T-bone steak fresh from a freezer. Leigh caught Aluqa's disappointed glare just before she turned back to the Cardinal.

That's what I get for speaking out.

"Wrath creature speaks not for us. But you will stand aside. This, or be dealt with," Aluqa said.

"We stand not aside," the Cardinal said.

With a press of a large green button on the other side of the remote, Opal suddenly jolted. The utility vest he wore buzzed and flashed with strobes of blue from what had looked like decorative light reflectors until now. Releasing a tight, strained grunt, he suddenly lurched and began twitching. His shoulders curled inward and he froze a beat before jutting out with an aggressive snap. Scrunching his face to withered-raisin levels, his neck continued curving upward until his chin was at a high forty-five-degree angle, posture as rigid as a skyscraper. A good foot of height had been added to him, as well as what looked like two hundred pounds of muscle or possibly concrete.

Panting slowly, Opal breathed with a vibrating chill while the vest continued to pump rhythmically, a buzzing hum mixed with a low pulse. The behemoth's jaw remained jutted and partially open. Any humanity left in his eyes had been blotted out by the light pouring from his sockets like road flares. Standing side by side with the Cardinal, now equal in height, he appeared to be awaiting instructions, which were promptly given.

"Take them." The Cardinal's finger pointed out his prey, just in case.

It may as well have been a stampede of bulls coming at them. As Opal lumbered forward, his steps pounded like cinder blocks thrown onto the pavement, and Leigh began to imagine herself as a smear of red guts on the ground. The Rapture in his veins was fierce, and its energy was upon them just before he himself.

But just before being trampled, Leigh was jolted by a bang when the incoming truck was tackled out of the way by a yellow blur going fast enough to make her think an actual car crash had occurred. The blur was soon wrestling with Super Scrunched Face while at the same time shouting profuse apologies to Aluqa.

"I'm so sorry I'm late, Miss Morinnean!" Skraga shouted amid her struggle, tears streaming down her face. "I got lost on the way!"

Leigh nearly shouted with furious joy at the sight of Member Grassrock, who appeared completely unharmed, and the realization struck her that Skraga must have known about Aluqa's hidden agenda to infiltrate the Tribunal all along. *(damn. that girl can keep a secret)*

That explains why she was waiting for me at the Eb Ring. I had a protective shadow today.

"No apology necessary, my dear!" Aluqa said to Skraga. "You were right on time."

The muscle-bound woman of Grief and Opal were locked, seemingly going back and forth in domination of the bout.

Skraga has the heart and experience. She should be okay.

(but i want to help her! i just can't leave Aluqa)

Leigh fixed her gaze on the side of her leader's face. Aluqa's focus had not budged from the Cardinal, with eyes that looked far more wrathful than the Rapture in her should have allowed. Her and Leigh's path was still blocked, and the Cardinal made clear his intention to continue doing so when he stretched his arms wide enough to cover the whole doorway.

"You don't leave. Not unless dead," he said.

Aluqa lunged suddenly, reaching for one of her rings. Leigh couldn't see which one. But his outstretched paw was too quick. A clang sounded when the gem she'd grabbed was knocked free. The Cardinal's long phalanges seized her and wrapped around her neck and wrist. Under his grip, her tan skin began to turn blue, the color spreading all over. Wet, sluggish coughs escaped her. Aluqa's life was already being choked out.

Feeling a thousand miles behind, Leigh snapped free the smallest gem on her bracelet: the yellow Grief-soaked piece. With a running start, she leaped into the air and reached back, rock in hand, trying to gather all the momentum her frame was capable of before slapping the side of the Cardinal's head as hard as she could.

What was no more than a startling firecracker to the people of Doloros—much like the white poppers of Earth—was a far more dangerous thing to those of Hywyn. The scream that the Cardinal released when struck was proof positive he'd been hurt badly.

The pop was so explosive that Leigh was instantly thrown to the floor. Before she could hop to her feet and dash away to try again, something struck her—she only realized it was the Cardinal's foot a moment after landing several feet away. The searing pain in her spine and left kidney arrived at around the same time.

With one hand, the broad, stretched, blue-gray menace held on to Aluqa, while his other was grabbing at the black mark Leigh had left on him, which might as well have been a third-degree burn, judging by his wails. Seeing stars, Leigh stumbled a few times before being able to rise. The pain thumping through her pulsed her Wrath and sparked small flashes of joy.

"A peon! Peon! Nothing more!" the Cardinal shouted. "A waste." For the first time, his gaze was fixed on her. *Think I liked it better when he didn't acknowledge my existence.* "You will remain. Wait. Still needed, that which you possess."

The Cardinal turned his fury back to Aluqa. "You. Suckling my life force. This, for a century. Now . . . I give to you all you can take. This and more." The Cardinal's face was changing, becoming more Celestial-like by the minute, contorting into a long, cold, wicked, contemptuous glare. "Humans and hubris attempt to move onto a stage. But higher than themselves. Much. Your species sees not. This—the truth. You are a garden to be tended."

Aluqa's body had stopped moving, and her eyes were shutting. The spreading blue in her skin had almost completely overtaken her, while a suspicious glow in her abdomen was beginning to spread. There wasn't much time.

Only one thing I can do.

Touching the broad steel-gray disk from her bracelet, Leigh focused. She'd never tried to do this under extreme pressure before. Clearing her mind, she imagined every inch of the Wraithian dagger, down to the last detail. The final necessary ingredient was to activate the disk, which took only a little bit of willpower.

It may have been that Leigh's heart was racing and her instincts kicked in, revealing her hidden, super-powered self. It may have also been because she was in the real UnEarth, fused with Eve, if only temporarily. But for whatever reason, when she touched the disk with two fingers and trained all her yearning onto the dagger, its hilt began to appear surprisingly quickly, sliding out of the gem like a firecracker snake from a black puck. Once out a few inches, she took the handle in her grip and pulled. What had been the hardest part the last time she'd practiced was over before she knew it. The whole of the handle pulled free, burning at its edges on the stone before the serrated blade itself appeared.

Eight feet away, the Cardinal was crushing Aluqa's windpipe, only now taking real notice of Leigh, who attempted to pull faster but was unable to sacrifice focus for haste. Finally, the blade came free from its hiding place with a pop and a tiny flash of white light. Leigh's arm collapsed to her side, causing her to nearly stab herself as exhaustion took over, in addition to the dagger feeling at least a couple of pounds heavier on this planet.

The professor hesitated before attacking. Rule number one was never to use the dagger on an UnEarth creature, period. But that cautionary guideline was being overridden by Aluqa's face turning a drowned, ghostly shade of death. It was the face of the woman who had saved Leigh's life on more than one occasion, the woman she trusted more than anyone else and most wanted to be, and the face was as close to fading as Leigh would allow. If there was ever a time to test the weapon out, this was it. It didn't matter that she had no idea what would happen if she mixed Wrath and Rapture within herself. Making the bargain was as easy as breathing.

Gripping the handle tightly, fighting the weight, Leigh crouched and hurled herself at the Cardinal, aiming the blade like a bayonet at his abdomen. But his stretched frame spun at the last moment, thrusting Aluqa between them. Again and again, Leigh threatened to attack while he kept her at bay with his limp shield.

"Aul! Wa-h'ah! The blade comes free," he said with rigid elation.

When she moved her feet and the blade, his eyes remained fixed on the weapon, his awe blending with his stony stoicism. Leigh wasn't sure whether to attack him or throw it like a stick, hoping he would chase after.

He extended his hand. "Good. The one who found it. Evans. Professor. Great of feats. Fight not for this one, Morinnean. Betrayal befalls they who do."

"You're the betrayer!" Leigh shot back. "A liar and false face, just like Aluqa said."

"Peon, you have no sense of lies. Now, hand me the blade. This, now. Move slowly."

Leigh did just that, nodding and moving like molasses, clearing her mind of any sign of the double cross she was planning to pull at the last second after pretending to give up the dagger.

Aluqa's body began to droop. Leigh moved faster, getting within a few feet, when suddenly Aluqa began to laugh softly, choking and gagging on her last breath at the same time. The wad of ensuing spit leaping onto her lips was not wasted. In her right hand, she held aloft another gray puck and smeared it across her pursed mouth.

The Cardinal's eyes were easily hijacked, bulging. Reaching for the puck with a boisterous shout, he gifted Leigh the perfect opening. Darting in, she lunged and thrust, sinking the blade into his side. Even with all her righteous force, she was only just able to penetrate the Celestial's skin. With both hands, she pressed forward. The jagged blade caught after several inches, which proved to be enough. The scream that erupted from him was like a Chinese gong made of evil nickel and copper ringing in her face. But the storming howl began to fade as a frigid chill made itself known in her hand before swimming up her arm. Her breath caught in her throat, suddenly frost.

When the gray puck, which had fallen to the ground, popped, the wave that escaped sent all three curling in pain. A shocked gasp escaped the Cardinal, who'd been standing just above it, the closest to the blast.

After the sudden wave of Mallos passed, a weight poured onto Leigh's chest, which spread to fill every inch of her as the dagger blade continued to pump. It soon felt like she'd been encased in concrete, unable to move even an inch. Her heart, pounding in her ears, started to slow, as though struggling to pump quicksand. Rapture oozed like icy honey into her veins and took over, all the way down to her toes, extinguishing the red in her eyes and replacing it with Celestial blue. Her skin dipped several notches darker and paler until she looked as though she'd died weeks ago after being trapped in a walk-in freezer.

There was no way to be ready for the power of Hywyn, even after experiencing the Wrath, which was essentially emotions she'd known since childhood. The emotions of Rapture were a whirlwind of only the most complex portions of the psyche, as well as one's true best self. By all accounts, she'd reverted to a newborn. These emotions, most of which had been forgotten long ago, brought tears to her eyes. Not of joy, nor of sadness or loss, but so much more. It was as though she were comprehending and experiencing life in this universe for the first time, turning around and acknowledging all of creation after only marching aimlessly forward since her birth. The overwhelming sense to preserve and protect everything in existence took over.

A rigid, broad, cold, forceful feeling filled her. An obstinate sense of right and wrong crept through, a deep stubbornness previously unknown, even to herself. Her sense of self was obscured, as though she was now too ashamed to remember any of her past life and its countless flaws. Only perfection would do. As everyone knew, things that weren't perfect didn't belong and were to be corrected.

The Cardinal was the current wrong.

Still six inches in his side, the dagger continued pumping Rapture into Leigh like oil from a well, and the Celestial's face was drained of color in a handful of seconds. The glow of his skin transferred to her, increasing the already insurmountable pressure. Just when she felt she might collapse or burst, without any real awareness of the effort, Leigh managed to retract the blade. The deafening bang that followed may have been entirely in her mind.

Stumbling to the side, the Cardinal reached out to snare her by the arm. "You . . . what have you done?" His fingers were quivering like thin branches in the wind as his head drooped to his chest, then slipped to the side.

Utilizing every ounce of the newfound strength in her fists, Leigh balled them up and cracked him in the jaw as hard as she knew how. Rock on rock, the hit sent shivers through her, exploding with blazing blue-over-blue light. Immediately after, she and the Cardinal both collapsed.

Staring at the roof, she lay motionless, colder than she'd ever been in her life. Yet her jaw could not even chatter. Her body would not allow movement and thus the expenditure of energy if it was not somehow ultimately constructive. That same body was feeling heavier by the second. No way she would be moving anytime soon. But the good deed had been done.

The Cardinal remained on the ground, rolling slowly side to side, moaning, holding his wound. Then the brassy, booming force of his voice waned and began to fade entirely.

Lying on the ground, Leigh could see little, her vision restricted to the direction in which her head had landed. Out of the corner of her eye, Aluqa peeked into view, rising to her feet and stumbling toward her. *Thank goodness she's alive.*

(always knew the leader would make the winning play)

As Aluqa knelt beside her, Leigh expected to be lifted, removed from the indignity of the ground, perhaps raised and heralded for her great sacrifice. But Aluqa's hand swept entirely over her and seized the Wraithian dagger instead. Standing with it gripped tightly, she moved away from Leigh without ever looking her in the eye.

The bout Skraga was locked in had taken a turn for the worse. Member Grassrock was not only losing—beaten to a bloody mess—but was currently being held in the air by Opal, laid out. She might as well have been a sacrifice to a primitive god.

A wailing cry burst from her as Opal looked poised to shatter her spine over his knee. But Aluqa was within striking distance like a shot. The Wraithian blade was plunged into Opal's neck, right at his jugular. Blood spat out, dark and thick, streaming beside lines of brilliant ink gleaming like blue lava. A gasp escaped Aluqa that shouted ecstasy and agony and terror. Holding the blade still for a moment, she shut her eyes before yanking it free from Opal. He never made a sound before dropping Skraga to the ground.

The man with the scrunched face and hulking body shriveled up, curling into a fetal position before falling over, shrinking to a size even smaller than he had been before. He never moved another inch after.

A scream then erupted from Aluqa as her back arched. Her arms flexed as though clutching invisible ropes, shaking as her entire frame began to grow. A crackling and stretching sound accompanied the changes in her skin and skeletal structure, forcing itself into flatter planes and straighter lines.

When Aluqa went silent and opened her eyes, they were once again glowing with brilliant blue. Her expression then molded into something like a vacationer relaxing on a beach. "So that's what it's like. Brilliant. And exactly how I hoped. All has happened as I foresaw."

Aluqa lingered near Opal's body for a moment, though she seemed to be unaware of it. After taking a long look at her hands— blue as an ice pack, with veins burning bright—and the dagger and rings decorating her fingers, she turned to Leigh and smiled. This time, it felt genuine and much more human.

Rising from the ground, Skraga gripped her arm tightly at the elbow. Blood was dripping onto the floor from her inner pant legs. Something unseen was bleeding. "We did it, boss! Just like you said." She tried for a small wave but winced immediately and returned to nursing her arm.

Leigh wanted to rise and join them in celebration but still could not move. The pressure in her skull pushing on her ears and eyeballs was making her partially deaf and blind.

Skraga dashed to her side. "I'm sorry I wasn't there to help you. But don't worry—we'll get you out of here, safe and sound, Silvey. You, me, and Miss Morinnean."

Her arm swept under Leigh, who was disappointed she was about to be carried but also grateful at the same time. *Let's just get this over with.* But with a stifled grunt, Skraga suddenly fell forward and landed like a log that had been tipped over. Her face scraped along the ground as she settled on top of Leigh's waist, pinning her to the floor. Attached to the back of Skraga's head was a shimmering black gem flashing with sparks of magenta—the same one missing from Aluqa's left pointer-finger ring, the only one Leigh had never been able to discern the shade of.

The leader stood over them. The smile had not left her chiseled, corpse-blue face. As Leigh gawked, unable to process what had just occurred, she felt Skraga's life force drain away. Her Grief signature faded at the same time as her heartbeat—which Leigh could now see and feel within her—slowed to a crawl before stopping entirely. The scream that Leigh tried to force out came only as a haze of mist and a hushed breath. *(what is she doing? Skraga was doing as told!)*

"Tsk tsk tsk. Amateur. Green," Aluqa said. "Should not have gone for full strike. Especially not concentrated junction. Ribs. Thought you knew. A small stab in the wrist. Enough."

Why are you doing this?

"I did not have to do much. Expelling little energy . . . the Celestial creed." Using the Wraithian blade, Aluqa cut the shoulder straps on Leigh's backpack. "Truly special—you were. But, guards arrive soon. Two minutes. Thus, I leave. To the Eb Ring hidden within the Tribunal. This, not even you know of. My first plan—we leave together. This—I expected. In such case, I take the dagger later. But now . . . works fine."

The backpack containing the Covenant was jolted and pulled out from under Leigh.

Aluqa then began edging toward the door.

"Could've been more, but time to move on. Thank you for retrieving Erelerim. That which could kill him. Glad—I was—that you made your obsession. After reading emails and electric journals, I knew you would. I needed to wait—let you do. Turned out you were loyal, always, even when unaware. I won't let sacrifice be in vain. Farewell."

Following the pitter-patter of her feet that faded to nothing,

Leigh was left lingering in the purest silence, simply trying to find her breath with the weight of not only Skraga's body on her but also that of the Rapture, a pressure that pushed all the harder the more she fought it.

No telling exactly when the Cardinal had gone completely still—well dead by now. The dripping treacle of time had given Leigh swaths of space to hate herself for being so trusting. *And dumb.* She now questioned her own perfection. It broke the professor's heart, and yet she had no hate for Aluqa, feeling something for the woman more akin to *Oh you poor, lost child, who knows not what they do. Who led you astray?*

But she got away with my prize. I broke my rule and look where it got me.

[*Hence, rules should never be broken.*]

Her arm twitched. *Wait, what was that?* Then it moved enough to slide off her to the ground. Like a rain cloud opening for the sun after a long and abysmal storm, Leigh's mind seemed to spring wide with clarity, having made a breakthrough with the Rapture. *I think I'm starting to . . . get it.*

First up was fixing the imbalance of offense Aluqa had just committed: a conscious being had wronged another conscious being.

Her fingers began to rattle.

Perfection had been tainted and molested, and for it, someone would absolutely stand to be punished.

Her elbow joint managed to snap shut on command.

The fact that Leigh was the victim did not matter. Any creature betrayed in such a manner after giving all of themself to another would be treated the same.

Wiggling her toes and rotating her ankles came next.

There was no dilemma. Aluqa was to be corrected. Decency demanded it.

This surging sense of purpose fed the strength needed to lift Sk-raga. As she fought to free herself and to scream, a new voice crept up Leigh's throat like a wind from deep within a cave. A riotous cry broke out, broad and low as a Celestial. The power of it shook her body and Skraga's. *How can this . . . I sound like an ocean liner horn.*

The more she roared, the stronger she got, and soon Skraga's body was rolled off, allowing Leigh to place herself on her stomach. *Okay, Aluqa said they would be here in two minutes. That could only have been a minute or so ago.* Slowly but steadily, she was able to pick herself up off the ground and set her feet. The more she focused on justice, the easier it got. Taking lumbering steps, she felt like a mess of rocks in a trash bag stumbling around.

Moving behind the Covenant display case draped in blue glass shards, Leigh found a handle underneath the corner of a heavy rug. *(to the inch. gotta love Celestial design and craftmanship)* Not only was Aluqa wrong about Leigh not knowing about the secret Eb Ring within the Tribunal, but she had the entirety of the Tribunal's secret escape tunnels memorized, thanks to a map she'd discovered among the books in the library Aluqa had granted her access to.

This particular hatch was installed for the security of the Covenant and had only one feature: it could not be opened from the other side. This was to prevent thieves from getting in but allowed the cup to be quickly removed should any nefarious force attempt to steal it by invading from the outside. Lifting the trap door and taking one last glance at Skraga's body, she collapsed into the tunnel below and shut the door. The carpet corner fell back into place with a thud.

Beside her now was a gold box about twice the size of the Covenant. [*Whoever arrived first in the Sercilium was expected to break the glass and put the cup in the box. This is a transit system.*]

After smashing the box's glass top with her balled fists and climbing inside, Leigh curled up and fit in as best she could. Her body was still poking out all over the place, but with any luck, it would work anyway. Above her, a single Celestial guard stomped into the room, having only just come to check. With a chilling bellow, they sounded the alarm, and Leigh pulled the lever beside the gold box. Like a shot, it darted off down a thin track built into the floor of the tunnel. Cool air flushed on her face as she sped through the dark.

The wails of the guard quickly faded, and Leigh was soon several hundred yards away. Her Eve trail was likely still lingering in the air, and it would not take them long to realize someone had gone down the trapdoor. With only one official exit, they would likely be hurrying to try and cut her off at the end of the track. *But I'm planning on being good and gone by then.*

The box on the cart traveled into the lower reaches of the building, and in no time, she arrived at the end, gliding to a gentle, perfect stop. The square wall in front of her opened, spilling white light into the tunnel, and Leigh peered into the Il In Ano, the secret Eb Ring chamber within the Tribunal, to be used only by the most senior leadership and their close staff in dire situations.

Walls of silver-and-gold brick were framed with deep blue girders and bolts. The swirling white light playing on the walls and ceiling radiated from the space inside the gold ring at the room's center. A gentle bubbling and sloshing filled the air, as though an idle boat were waiting to speed off once given the go-ahead. The noise was far more tolerable than the blaring roar that accompanied the large-scale Eb Ring stations. But the sound also meant the ring had been activated. Aluqa may have already gotten away.

Squeezing out from the tunnel into the room was a slow process. Like a dollop of batter falling from a wooden spoon, Leigh spilled onto the floor. The whooshing white noise grew from a babbling brook to a rushing creek. Finding the will to lift her head, she let her eyes adjust and discovered a human figure approaching the ring, strapping a guide helmet on.

Aluqa.

She was just yards away from the gateway border but not moving at full speed, seemingly having trouble properly attaching the helmet while clutching the backpack containing the Covenant. At the sight of her, a torrid storm of Rapture filled Leigh's legs, then her abdomen, then rushed up her spine to her neck. With duty, purpose, and, most of all, surprising speed, she was on her feet. [*Fix the wrong. Fix all wrongs.*] With thundering steps, she charged to the center of the room.

Aluqa jumped, snapping to attention when she turned to find Leigh. Unmistakable shock crossed her face before Aluqa squatted in a defensive position. "You adapted? That's . . . well, impressive." Laughing, she turned back and hurried to the gate.

Leigh would be there soon, but Aluqa was too close to the storm. *I'll be too late.* That could not stand. The wicked were to be punished—to be halted. With nothing more than instinct, Leigh thrust out her hand and released a blast of Rapture from her fingertips. The burst of light struck Aluqa in the shoulder, soaking into her and swirling around her frame, slowing her in place.

Long, slurred words escaped her lips. "Immmm-pssssble! Yuuuu cnnn't beeee cuuuhhpble ivvv thissss."

Leigh couldn't have agreed more. She had no idea how she'd just done that. All she knew was her will to prevent Aluqa from escaping punishment. [*The wrongs shall be righted.*] The freezing power had discharged from her as easily as a thrown baseball, one created entirely by the purest—yet most complex—emotions she'd ever felt. *(could get used to this)*

Reaching Aluqa, Leigh slowed and approached cautiously. Though she appeared firmly held in place, it was also likely Aluqa was faking it, waiting to strike. Stepping in front of her, Leigh looked over her leader, somehow seeing her for the first time, beneath her skin. The head of the Surface was having the utmost trouble moving, still inching toward the gate with fear beaming from her eyes and very little light left in them.

"Your Eve is leaving you," Leigh said, her voice biting and shimmering.

Aluqa turned a full shade whiter at the sound.

"Do you know why the Rapture leaves you? Because you are beneath it." Reaching into Aluqa's waist sleeve, Leigh retrieved her dagger before taking off Aluqa's guide helmet.

"For this and your offenses, you will be punished." The bag containing the Covenant was slipped off next. Aluqa was clearly fighting with all she had but could not get through Leigh's stasis lock to move at full speed.

One hand was somehow able to get ahold of Leigh's wrist, but the grip was weak—stunningly weak. So much so, Leigh did not break it immediately and stared instead into Aluqa's eyes with her own, twice as vivid and blue. It was a curious sensation. It seemed a wonder she could have ever followed one so clearly hiding under innumerable layers of false bravado, smoke, and mirrors. *She's not worthy.*

Bothering to break the grip seemed pointless, so Leigh simply walked away toward the Eb Ring.

"Yuuuuu can't!" Aluqa yelled, slumping low. "I mmmmud you! Evvvver-thing you are . . . zzz thnksss t'meee!"

Leigh turned around. "This is truth. I am grateful." She then signed, "Farewell and good luck," before putting on Aluqa's helmet and turning to the Eb Gate.

But just as the white storm filled her vision, a condensed fog filled her mind. Before she could take her first step, Leigh's eyes rolled over, and she collapsed.

FINDING THE LIGHT

Fabian was gone. The flash of light that had taken him also managed to destroy the machine that had held him and Galinthia in place like prisoners in snares. Shreds of the Grief-tinted Celestial's clothing, torn and ragged, was intermingled with the remnants of the machine, which had been warped by his Shift into essentially a huge tinfoil ball with some girders and jagged scraps jutting out every which way. In the whole mess, there was no sign of a body. *No blood. None at all. But . . . do Medolians even have blood? I'm sure they do, right? Does that mean he could be . . .*

But the way Galinthia had reacted told Casey he'd vanished for good. Never before had she appeared so confused, so debilitated, or so weak. Her brow clenched in a way it likely never had before, creating a brand-new crease. Grasping the thousands of years she and Fabian had spent together became painfully easy, thanks to the baneful look in her eyes.

In truth, it was all happening too fast. The boom and flash had caught everyone off guard, especially Madam Daphne and her forces, which were pushed back several feet. The energy given off by the explosion staggered anyone present who wasn't pure human, seemingly affecting the strongest of them most of all. Casey was the only one left standing upright when it was all over.

Galinthia didn't remain down for long but was still largely immobilized, gaping with a hung jaw at the remnants of the machine, her eyes darting back and forth as though trying still to find him in there. "What does . . . But he didn't . . ."

Desperate to console her, Casey had absolutely nothing to offer other than, *We can do as he asked and make sure his sacrifice wasn't in vain*, but kept it instead to herself.

Near the base of the pile of wreckage, a blinking yellow light caught her eye. *His phone!* While Madam Daphne and her team were recovering, Casey charged toward the smoking pile and retrieved the device, pocketing it before hurrying back to Galinthia, just as Chief Mary was being helped to her feet by her crew. The glow in her eyes had dimmed, and her features had become markedly more human. Even Madam Daphne had been altered slightly, her cartoon-proportioned curves slimmed, and her life-preserver lips deflated by a dozen or so psi.

As though somehow sensing exactly how much beauty she had lost, she threw her hands and tentacles in front of her face as she cowered away. "Get them!" she shouted, disappearing behind her security. "I'm not losing two Medolians!"

Chief Mary—dusted off and ready for action—charged at Casey and Galinthia, followed closely by her team.

"Can you get us out of here?" Casey shrieked at Galinthia, whose eyes—unlike everyone else's—had reclaimed their brilliant Un-Earth glow. Her gray irises were soaked with a fiery red, and the sadness and shock on her face had since burned away, replaced with unequivocal hatred, aimed squarely at Madam Daphne.

"I can," she said to Casey, a deep, primal sense of both calmness and ferocity lacing her words.

Then came a flurry of movement. Galinthia seemed to fade into her attack, hot wind and red light sweeping around Casey as though she had stepped into a dust devil in Death Valley in July. Fleeting glimpses of flying daggers, along with pained grunts and cries, accompanied the squall.

Galinthia's arm suddenly wrapped around Casey's waist, and before she knew it, she was being carried away.

Nearly a dozen bodies in green suits lay lifeless behind them, brilliant aquamarine blood spreading across the ground. But many were still standing. Chief Mary and those who had survived Galinthia's volley were quick to give chase.

Hurrying Casey through the garden, the Medolian attempted to create a Mallos sphere around them but suddenly seized up and collapsed halfway. The ball petered out, sending them both rolling to a stop on the pavement. Casey rose and scrambled toward her. Gale lay face-down, eyes open, staring bitterly at the ground and gritting her teeth.

"What's wrong? Can you fly?" Casey asked. "There's a way out of here—we just need to get above the canopy!" she shouted, her gaze darting to the security team closing in.

Galinthia shook her head. "Can't explain it. Whatever that Wyst did to me, I can't get any Eve flowing right. We're stuck on foot."

Before Casey could get Galinthia back up, Chief Mary and her backup—eight or nine guards—arrived. Rising with a burst of power, Galinthia immediately engaged the team. With dagger throws and energy blasts of red fire, the Medolian kept them at bay, playing defense while struggling to keep them off and retreat at the same time. Dodging and hurdling over fallen security bodies and rogue airborne batons, Casey did her best to scurry ahead of the chaos.

The madness around her mounted as the Rose security seemingly grew stronger, while Galinthia noticeably slowed. Casey managed only a few more yards before one of Chief Mary's crew snatched her up and hurried her away.

"Gale!" she cried, quickly silenced by a hand over her mouth.

The guard carrying her was hightailing toward Madam Daphne, and Casey began glimpsing a nightmare future as a living doll, constantly dressed up and gushed over, when a dagger blade struck her captor's spine and ejected through his chest, spraying her with blood. Mid-run, he collapsed, but before Casey could hit the ground, a sphere of white and cobalt blue formed around her, cushioning her fall and raising her to her feet.

Galinthia was racing toward Casey to reach her before Chief Mary and the others did, approaching from a side path. There were now only three guards on their feet along with the chief, but the fierceness of Mary was every bit Galinthia's match.

The Medolian resumed her onslaught of daggers and energy bursts as she ran. Each dagger fired was summoned back to her holster to repeat the process. To Casey, it looked as though she had multiple arms or was—perhaps—an octopus completing dozens of tasks per second. The death and horror surrounding her were manifestations of all that lurked in the deepest, dankest recesses of Casey's psyche, but there was no denying the efficiency with which Gale could put them down.

When the briefest of openings came, the Medolian leaped toward Casey, collected her, and tried one more time to rocket them out. But it was still no use. The attempt left her panting for breath as Galinthia let loose with a bellowing curse in a dark language that churned Casey's stomach.

Not even two seconds passed before the Rose guards were upon them again. This time, Galinthia did not bother keeping a free hand; she scooped up Casey like a bride on her wedding night. At the same moment, a slew of Rose reinforcements began streaming into the garden ahead, flanking their position.

Galinthia took every path she could, trying to reach the outer wall, but was repeatedly cut off. The replacement guards did not suffer the same weakness as those caught in the blast that killed Fabian. They were at full strength, giving chase like a pride of hungry lions.

Bangs echoed, and bullets flared with cyan light, whizzing by and burying themselves into the plants and trees of the backyard. Explosions of dirt, wood, and liquidized matter burst all around them, sending a few small drops of the cyan goo onto Casey's hand. The stuff began burning like cold lava instantly. Flinching and stifling a scream, she couldn't help but wipe it on Galinthia's clothes, but the Medolian did not notice, far too busy trying to find a path to the back or side walls while the Rose security did an irritatingly good job of goaltending. Before too long, it became obvious they were being boxed in.

Galinthia began retracing old routes, going in circles, her speed rendered useless and her ideas clearly running out. It then struck Casey that there was one direction that was not being guarded: the path back into the Rose.

It was too crazy not to work. She shouted into Galinthia's ear, "Go back through! Inside!"

Without skipping a beat, the Medolian veered right and bolted for the rear entrance to the Rose. A lone Wyst guard stood in their way but was easily bowled over by a quick sphere surrounding Galinthia and Casey, which tore down the door and cut a circle out of the wall. The Mallos sphere waned and faded immediately after, sending Galinthia stumbling and Casey crashing to the violet-and-turquoise-tiled floor. Both were able to rise before security arrived.

Galinthia slumped like a boxer entering the fourteenth round, her back heaving as she fought for breath. There was no way she would be able to carry Casey anymore. In fact, she looked nearly ready to give in and surrender—something that once seemed impossible. But Miss Lipmayer was not ready to give up yet. Becoming a dress-up doll was not part of any future she wanted.

"This way! Come on!" she shouted, taking Galinthia by the wrist. The Medolian stumbled along, following without protest down the hall.

But Chief Mary and the others were upon them quickly. No more bullets were fired, thankfully—likely because the interior of the Rose was not to be damaged, and neither were its guests. UnEarth Humans making their way to the backyard gawked and guffawed as they passed, backing away from the charging human and Medolian just in time.

Galinthia was once again forced to fend off their pursuers while Casey piloted a path through the hallways. *Can't believe all that time I spent aimlessly wandering around here is finally paying off!* Two turns were cleared successfully, while Chief Mary and her team dodged flying daggers, leaping out of the way like a troupe of juiced-up trapeze artists. Soon they were passing the kingdom rooms—the Still Room, the Blaze Barrel, the Lounge of Lamenting, and the others—narrowly avoiding the clutches of Rose security at every step. The few patrons who lunged at Casey to collect her for the guards received immediate daggers to the heart. Of the thousand or so blades thrown thus far, none had come close to harming Casey, as though she had a protective bubble surrounding her. The savagery and precision of Galinthia were like no other.

Soon they were entering the platinum hall from atop the primary stairs at its center. When they spotted several lines of Rose security guards in the middle of the dance floor—glowing batons in hand, ready to kick ass and take said ass into custody—the duo stopped flat. Chief Mary and the others pulled up behind the escaping party and formed a barrier on the opposite side.

"Where do you think you can go?" the chief said. "Right now, Madam Daphne is retrieving another remote control to activate the misery within the human. The Medolian can't Shift away. You can't fight us all. Face it, you're done."

Galinthia glared with a raised lip but was panting too hard to respond, clutching her breastplate. Casey, meanwhile, was busy trying to think of a way out of this. Nothing was making itself immediately obvious.

Chief Mary then laughed and gave her crew orders in French. They began encroaching.

There's gotta be something. Come on—come on. Then Casey saw it: their ticket out. Looming above the dance floor, attached to the rafters, hung the huge machine like some sort of industrial pump. The thundering device shook and heaved with each rotation as it sent gallons of fluorescent liquid ooze pumping through the dozens of tubes extending from it. At the end of each line was an UnEarth Human hanging from the rafters by hooks inserted throughout their person, with at least one IV stuck in their arms and/or legs, injecting them with a pure shot of home-world nectar.

Casey leaned into Galinthia's ear. "Bring it down."

Without hesitation, Galinthia launched a dagger burning with crimson fire in the direction Casey pointed. The engine's mount was pierced like a stick through a paper bag. With a shriek from its rusted-metal frame, the machine broke free and plummeted toward the dance floor. Most—but not all—of the security were able to leap out of the way before the impact, which boomed and rattled the thousands of liquor bottles on the shelves behind the bartender stations. Glass and debris filled the air like splashing water.

While Casey cowered away from any potential shrapnel, Galinthia acted, seizing her by the waist once more and, with a monumental cry, bounding the thirty-five feet to the bottom of the stairs, then the nearly two hundred more to the top of the felled engine. *Wow, this thing is a lot bigger when you get up close.* Casey managed a glance back to see Chief Mary and her crew trying to catch up, but they were long gone when Galinthia made a third and final leap, landing them at the doorway to the club exit. Together, without a look back, she and Casey charged down the entry tunnel and into the night of Marseille.

The cul-de-sac ahead was dim other than the neon light of the cat above the Rose, and no one was in sight—not even the smoking section. Casey's sneakers slapped the pavement as she and Galinthia ran as fast as they could, but the human began to lag immediately, and Galinthia was forced to carry her once more, charging off at nauseating (*but only at first*) speed.

Over Gale's shoulder, Chief Mary and her crew exited the club just in time to watch their prey scampering away. At the sight of their dejected, bitter faces, Casey let a smile find its way to her.

And good riddance!

Opening her mouth wide, she took in the air. It was so . . . human. The lights were far less intense, and weren't fizzling with kinetic energy, ready to pop. The streets were quiet and serene, even for an industrial area. A palpable sense of freedom washed over her as she was carried away by her knight in crimson garb in desperate need of a wash.

Galinthia did not stop running for at least five minutes, charging past and over the people of Marseille, who froze in shock at the speed and agility of the strange woman in a gray cloak. But she was without a destination. Her rabbit-foot breaths tapped Casey's forehead. *She's trying to run it off. I know exactly what that's like. Poor thing. I can't imagine what she just went through. But if I try to console her, she'll probably get offended.*

Casey sniffed up a tear, resting her muscles and her eyes for a bit to collect herself before trying to figure out where they were. "Gale, slow down. It's okay. We got away. Let's ease back."

The Medolian seemed not to hear her, and Casey then began to notice her heart and entire chest were pumping wildly, literally heaving.

"Gale, are you okay?"

But the Medolian continued on, primal as a rodent, mouth sneering, beginning to mutter angry words under her breath. Then the words breached the surface, a form of pissed-off-sounding Latin. Her rage was boiling over and... *It's pretty clear she doesn't know how to deal with this!*

"Gale, listen to me. Calm yourself. You're going to have a heart attack. You need to channel this, focus it, and—"

With a monstrous heave, Galinthia hurled Casey four stories into the air, where she landed on a gravel rooftop. Crashing and rolling on the rough bed of pointed rocks, emitting a scream that would make a banshee ask for lessons, she heard Galinthia roaring her own heart out down below. Rising above the roof edge just in time, Casey spotted the Medolian charge into a warehouse, straight through a huge metal roll-up door. The few windows on the side of the building lit up as though hundreds of flares were ignited inside all at once.

A titanic rumble swelled out of nowhere, shaking and chattering the larger stones in the gravel. This was more than an earthquake;

Casey's gut and instincts knew that. *Down*, they screamed, and down she went just before an explosion shook the very air, and scorching heat blasted like a surging ocean wave. The area was awash in a deep ruby red, mixed with the yellow and orange flashes of searing flame. Hunks of debris spewed out, ricocheting off the lip protecting Casey.

Once the last bit of wreckage had fallen, she cautiously peered over the edge. The block below had become a dimmer version of itself, blanketed in black ash, sans one of its biggest warehouses.

The hundred-yard-square building was now no more than a cardboard box with its top and sides ripped off messily. Judging by the crater left over, most of whatever was inside had been completely vaporized. At the center of the bowl stood Galinthia.

A furious red glow around her began to wane as her shoulders heaved. After a brief moment, she seemed to straighten up, and suddenly a Mallos sphere was around her, rising and soaring over to meet Casey on the rooftop. Galinthia dropped down a few feet away, taking one final breath of released frustration.

"We can resume our escape," she said.

"Did you get it all out?"

"Yes, I believe so."

"Because it's okay if you need to. Just don't blow up any more buildings."

"There were no humans inside."

"Well, okay, that's good at least. People's things can also be important, too, but we can discuss that another time."

"Shall we resume our escape?"

"Tell you what, find us a park, somewhere dark with trees and bushes."

As suggested, after leaping back down to ground level, Galinthia carried Casey until they came upon a small city park, no bigger than a municipal baseball field.

"Will this do?"

"Sure, it's fine. Thank you for getting us out of there," said Casey.

But Galinthia was not listening. Her head was pointed back the way they came, with sadness and confusion draping her face. *She really doesn't grasp what's happened.*

"I'm so sorry about Fabian," said Casey.

"That idiot. Fool. Grief-filled simpleton. Why would he do that? How? We would have broken free. We would have—"

"He did what he did so we could get away," Casey said. "And we did, thanks to you. He would be proud."

Galinthia released another wave of anger, but smaller this time— not much worse than the hot winds Casey had dealt with in some scorching deserts around dig sites.

"How could he? How could he? It doesn't . . . he just . . . became nothing. I couldn't see him. I heard his scream, and then . . . he didn't say anything else. It was like the stories of Die Muneris and those who vanished. The silence."

Casey knelt next to her. "I'm only alive because of you. How can I repay you?"

Galinthia caught her gaze. At first, it seemed she might scold Casey or tear her apart or set her on fire as some retribution for her lost partner. *Probably a dagger through at least one eye.* "He did what he did to make sure you were safe. Fabian saw something in you. I will not reject that, and you owe me not. His death will not be in vain. I shall continue his will. You'll live as long as I am able to ensure it. Madam Daphne will not end her pursuit of us. We are joined now. But I need time to regain my strength. That means we need a plan."

Casey stood to meet her and waited to hear Galinthia's genius.

But when no idea was put forth and Gale's gray eyes stayed locked on Casey placidly, she realized it was she who was supposed to be talking.

"A plan? You want me to come up with one?"

"Escaping the Rose was only possible because of your lead," Gale said. "Continue."

"Continue . . . to lead? I'm sorry, but you got the wrong idea. I'm not trying to lead anyone. I just want to go home. That's all."

"Very well. I trust your parental units kept my room in order. Let us depart."

Casey wanted to slap herself and make sure this was happening. "Are you sure you wouldn't rather just fly off and leave me now? You did your part. You got us out of there. I can't ask any more of you. If you want to leave, you can. You're a free being."

Galinthia's eyes narrowed in confusion. "You do not wish me to journey with you?"

"No, I didn't say that, I just . . ." Casey stopped herself. Here she was, speaking with a Medolian who was listening to her every word and asking what their next plan of attack was. *It's bizarre. What do I do? It would mean I would be in less danger if I went with her, right? Or more? Hard to guess.* The responsibility was so heavy it sent her mind spinning.

Galinthia remained silent, waiting on Casey's word. Her rawest emotions seemed to have been successfully purged, leaving her face as bare as a freshly cleaned plate.

"I suppose . . . we should start by getting someplace safe," Casey said.

"Very well." Galinthia scooped her up into her arms as though a keyword had been uttered. "Now that we are joined, I feel I should know your name. Tell me, what is it?"

Casey nervous-laughed, but when she realized Galinthia was serious, she did not bother making a fuss. *Not when she's holding me in her arms like this.*

"Um, it's Casey."

"Very well. Human Casey, where shall we depart to?"

Okay, this is feeling like a lot within a little. I need to think. No ideas came to mind other than to say, "West," which was mostly Casey's inner atlas talking; and off they went.

Galinthia charged for miles, switching back and forth between long bounds and tight sprints, first out of the city limits, then along the coast of Marseille, starting northward and then west, over rugged ground with the Mediterranean twinkling in the distance all the while. As she went along, Galinthia's strength seemed to grow, and her steps became broader and less erratic. Eventually, the ride became so smooth that Casey nearly drifted off more than once.

After an hour of travel, she finally said, "I think we've gone far enough for tonight." *No way Madam Daphne's remote control could reach us here.* "I don't know about you, but I need to sleep."

In a dense cluster of bush-and-tree-covered forest, Galinthia set her down. A fire was created in no time. On a makeshift bed of leaves, they rested as the sun began to warm the color of the sky. The duo did not speak for a long while, as Gale's stare never faltered from the fire, and Casey eventually drifted off to sleep using her backpack as a pillow.

A startling cry from Galinthia shook Casey awake sometime later. Not knowing exactly how long—though the sun had moved into the latter half of the sky—she found the Medolian leaning against a tree, her hands gripping her head as if a bug were inside and she were trying to dig it out.

"What is it?" Casey asked, hurrying over. "It's not Madam Daphne's machine, is it?"

"It's Mara," Galinthia said through gritted teeth. "She's been sending a signal all morning, but . . . I can't read it. It's all noise. Gah! A stabbing wind filled with occasional words."

"Mara Loren?" Casey asked. "What do you think she's trying to say?"

"She appears to be in distress. Possibly calling for aid. The signal is being sent from somewhere far away—probably an Eve world. But I can't decipher it. The Lady of the Rose inhibits my abilities still."

"If you need to go help your boss, I understand," said Casey.

"Mara is the most powerful of us after Izaiah. She's never asked for assistance before. This could very well be a trap."

"You think she would set a trap? She seemed like such a softie under all the scowling."

"I've never understood the Fervor-tinted. She craves control and yet seems to loathe it. There have been several messages from her of late, most of which were quite cryptic. She originally warned us against returning to Trivium, but has been the Warden Sentry for two years now. The Miliandre has always longed to be a voice in the Tribunal. She may no longer be on the side we want her to be on. This may be her way of bringing us in to appease certain creatures. Something strange is going on, and I cannot tell what. That has a tendency to anger me."

"Are you going to go to her?" Casey asked.

"I couldn't even if I wanted to. The signal is coming from Un-Earth, but I cannot see clearly where. Besides, I will not risk Shifting until whatever Madam Daphne has placed in me is gone. I doubt any of the others will arrive to join her, either. It's too short notice. Medolians tend to become transfixed with certain states of being and do not register anything that falls outside their sphere of what they deem important. It would seem Mara is on her own with whatever she is dealing with, just as she usually prefers it."

The signal from Mara continued for another half an hour before stopping. Never able to get a clear sense of the message—at least not one she could convey to Casey—Gale seemed to be subtly tortured the entire time it ran.

"It's gone. Thank the Eve," she said with a sigh. "Either Mara ceased the transmission, or something else did."

"What do you think it was?"

"I know not. But nothing in any world is as it was. Much has changed. Fabian and I had no concept of who we could trust. All we had was each other. But now, I am alone."

"You're not alone," said Casey, smiling as warmly as she could.

"What is wrong with your face?"

"Nothing. Sorry."

"You are a strange being, but Fabian was right to trust and care for you." Galinthia rose to her feet. "Now, let us be off. It won't be safe here for long. My strength has returned enough that I can fly. Our destination is up to you."

After putting out the fire, Casey retrieved her backpack and joined Galinthia. The opaque energy of a Mallos sphere wrapped around them, and they were suddenly in the air, gazing down at southern France.

"Which direction?" Galinthia asked.

"Do you know the way to my family?"

With a modest grin, Galinthia nodded. "I do. Brace yourself." At blinding speed, the Mallos sphere flung itself out over the Mediterranean and climbed into the sky. The world streaming by underneath so rapidly that it became a mush left Casey's brain feeling much the same way.

Forty or so minutes later, North America appeared on the horizon. Casey had a rough guess of which way was Michigan but no real idea. *It doesn't look like the map from here—just a bunch of jagged coastlines with tiny lights.* Thankfully, Galinthia seemed to know the way.

"The scent of your home is strong. Especially that of your siblings. It will not be hard to locate them."

Soon the Medolian sphere was swooping over Lake Erie and the forests and cities of Michigan. The sphere dipped closer and closer to the ground, and Casey began to spot landmarks. Her feet wiggled with anticipation.

When they arrived at her parents' home, nestled in the forest, things seemed peaceful. Casey noticed the front porch light was still on, despite the day being half over, but gave it no second thought. Setting them down on the front lawn, Galinthia dispersed the Mallos sphere. With giddy excitement, Casey charged toward the front door, shouting to greet her family.

But Galinthia reached out to prevent her from running, and she said gravely, "Hold."

Casey studied the house. Her gut suddenly agreed, but without any evidence. "What? Is something wrong?"

Galinthia was staring at the house with the attentive suspicion of a police escort in a crowd. "I sense none of them."

"They're not here? Well . . . maybe they all went out to eat?" It was a rare occurrence, but it did happen from time to time.

Galinthia shook her head and stepped in front of Casey to block the path, as though to protect her from an attack that might come from the front door.

"I'm sure there's nothing to worry about. They'll be back soon," Casey said, trying to convince Galinthia and herself. *They're just out shopping . . . all sixteen of them.*

Before Casey could formulate a plan to check things out, Galinthia marched up the steps and into the home. *Or we can just do it that way.* Casey couldn't help but call out the names of her parents and siblings and nieces and nephews as she followed, even though Galinthia would have already been able to sense their life forces if any were present. *Unless they all started bathing in bleach.*

"I don't see any sign. Where could they be?" Casey asked.

Galinthia darted upstairs, and Casey made her way to the kitchen. Stepping inside, she saw something that made her heart sink to her feet. Carved into the far wall were the words; *We hav dem. U no y. Com n get.*

I did it . . . the one thing I said I . . . oooo, Case, it's official—you're the worst person on the planet. No one close. Nobody. Not even the guy who dressed up like Uncle Sam and beat that church lady to death. At least he only killed one innocent person . . . that I know of.

They searched the rest of the house from top to bottom. There were no further clues as to what had happened to the Lipmayers.

"A puzzle. Usually, I find some sort of hint. A speck. But there's nothing," said Galinthia.

"Who? I mean, who could have done this? The message on the wall says we know why, but I don't!" Casey shouted through tear-soaked eyes.

"Whoever it was," Galinthia said, "they will regret this act before their unpleasant end."

THAT WAS LUCKY

Having just said goodbye to Hannah—the one residing in his belt buckle—Bennett woke from his meditation. He'd entered the white void to update her on his and Alex's situation. The look on her face when he arrived suggested she never planned on seeing him again.

He only stayed long enough to give her the basics, what she couldn't glean from his emotions. It was around twelve hours to his consciousness, but only a matter of minutes in the real world. Though he could have stayed longer, he was anxious to get back and get the day over with. All the help she could give him had been gotten. Anything more would take a span of time he didn't have in the reality containing his body. With a bland "good luck" and a shrug, she saw him off.

As he returned to the surface, Bennett had already forgotten how much the Scythian home they were hiding in felt like the belly of a monstrous ship at sea. Strained creaks, wavering moans, and drawn-out gurgles emanated from unseen, unnatural organs, as if the whole structure were breathing. *If I'd ever been swallowed by a tree before, I might have something to compare this to. But I never was. Not once.* The owner of the home remained where she had apparently been shocked to death by the explosion at the execution, planted in the middle of the room, facing the window with a terrified expression. She was shriveled and dried up, more a husk than anything.

Near the window, Alex peered out over the neighborhood while keeping himself scarce. "Welcome back. Didn't peg you for the spiritual type. Was that a meditation thing?"

"Sort of."

"You were pretty gone. Where'd you go?"

"Doesn't matter," Bennett said, joining him by the window.

Darkness had nearly overtaken the city, matching the somber quiet that had blanketed it a few hours before. Nearly nine hours had passed since they found the Fovosian home to hide in. But now, the silence was breaking under the approaching ringing chorus of the Barium Guard's armor and the echoes of doors being kicked in and homes being tossed, steadily growing louder.

"They're getting closer," Alex remarked, standing from his crouched position where he had been stretching. Since their arrival, he'd hardly sat still, bouncing on his hands and feet anxiously. A broiling heat of Eve simmered within him, sizzling like coals at the heart of a fire. An anxious desire for action was clear in his signature. *Even without seeing his soul, I'd know he was aching for a fight.*

"Yeah. Safe to assume they'll be clearing this neighborhood next," Bennett said.

The majority of the forces seemed centered on the northeastern section of the city, which made sense, given the Eb Gate was in that direction. With this small band of Guards approaching, it might be possible to depart just before their arrival, riding that wave as far as they could get. If Bennett and Alex stood any chance of reaching an Eb Ring and escaping the planet, they needed to remain unseen for as long as possible. *Doubt we can avoid detection completely.* Bennett had seen the sniffing animals from Nashwyn from afar; they looked effective and possibly vicious. *The only reason we haven't been caught is because the explosion at the execution has them busy.*

So far, he and Alex had been fortunate, but it was soon going to be time to sink or swim. The creatures hunting them had something they didn't: endless patience. They would wait at both Eb Gates for as long as it took to catch their prey. On little more than a hunch, Bennett guessed there would come a time when a weak point in their security briefly opened. *More a hope than anything.* With three rings per Eb Gate and their gargantuan size, there was a chance the humans could sneak through. A small chance. Maybe not subatomic, but small. But they had no other options. Bennett was being forced to work wonders with very little. With Izaiah missing, there was no one in the city they knew or trusted, nowhere to go. *We have to do it now. Tonight. If it doesn't work . . . we might be stuck here for a long time.*

"What do you say we leave a little early?" Bennett suggested.

"You mean now?"

"Yeah. Let's use the fading light to our advantage. I know I have a hard time finding a target when everything gets muddy and gray."

"Guess that means we oughta get going."

"Guess so."

"What's the plan?"

"Get to the Eb Ring without detection," Bennett said. "Don't worry about grabbing a guiding helmet. If we get spotted, we'll have to fight our way through. In a dire case—which is highly likely—running may be the best option. I know we both turned up the juice on the kill stage, and you feel strong, but there are hundreds of Celestials out there. We can't assume we're badasses. That leads to stupid decisions."

"Run?" Alex's eyes lit with confusion. "That doesn't sound like you. Or fun."

"You go looking for fights now?"

"Since when do you not? Don't you want to test your strength? And don't pretend like you didn't do something to get stronger recently. Was it that meditation? I felt it."

"I'm just saying, let's be cautious."

"You're saying you don't think I can do it."

"It's a suicide run, Al."

"Then how come you don't think you're in danger, huh? I'm getting pretty good at reading signatures, believe it or not, and I can see you're only worried about my strength, not yours."

"That's partly true. You haven't used Wrath in a long time. I mean, look at you, you're flesh and bone."

Alex glanced at his arms, initially threatening to pitch a fit. Instead, he laughed and nodded, as though just now realizing how thin he had become. "True, but you're forgetting one thing. You're talking to the Ire boy. I killed Chloe. I've been sitting in chains for two years. All that rage had nowhere to go. Now it can. Believe it or not, it would give me great pleasure to unleash my fury on some angels. If you need help out there, just let me know."

"Look at this guy. You know, if those bombs hadn't gone off, I would have shown you a thing or two. Let you see what an Eve user really looks like."

"Bring it on, fancy pants," Alex said. "Who do you think did it, by the way? The bombs?"

"Whoever it was, they weren't aiming for us. My guess is they were going for Gabriel. Some political faction or rebel fighters, most likely. Makes sense. It's the first time he's put himself out there in thousands of years. Perfect chance to take a swing at the big guy."

"You say that like you used to do the exact same thing. You did, didn't you? Of course, you did."

"Not me personally, but let's stay on task. We've got a hell of a job ahead of us."

Bennett closed his eyes. Gabriel's signature had risen from the darkness like a phoenix over the course of an hour, shortly after he and Alex arrived at the Fovosian's. The Lord Celestial's blinding aura now burned as a monstrous flame a few miles away. If Bennett didn't know better, he'd swear he felt Wrath hiding somewhere deep in there. *He's mad as shit. That's for sure. Probably because he can't find us.*

At the moment, Gabriel's strength was slightly less than before, but the dip might not last long. "Glad the Barium Guard is being kept busy," Bennett said. "They're probably trying to wrangle any stragglers. Maybe someone who didn't blow their pack like they were supposed to, or suspicious civilians wrongfully accused— which I would bet the left half of my dick is happening. I don't think there's going to be a better time than now."

Alex cracked his neck. "Then I say we make these people sorry they ever used us like toys."

"Digging the confidence, Al."

Alex clenched his fists. Beneath his jail shirt, his chest scars ignited with scorching red, steaming and crackling. To his UnEarth senses, a blinding fire churned before Bennett.

"Pump the brakes. We're not quite there yet. Let's head downstairs and get ready. Don't want to alert them early. I noticed we were just off the Iliksheen. That road leads to the North Eb Gate. We'll stay ahead of the Guard on patrol but not too far ahead.

These Celestials have fixed routes they use to search the city. This will keep us clear for a bit. We'll continue to keep our energies low until we're close. Then make a break for it."

"How do you know all of that?"

"Doesn't matter. I do."

"Works for me." Alex extinguished his fire and followed Bennett out of the bedroom and down the hall of the Fovosian home. Taking the black, crocodile-skin-like banister in hand, they descended a steep stairway cautiously to the ground floor and moved into the front entryway. The rest of the Human Scythe's home was walled with uneven, warped planks of gnarled, textured brown material. What little lighting there was came from softball-sized beetles clinging to the walls and ceiling, whose abdomens lit brighter with murky orange whenever something larger than itself drew near.

Upon reaching the front door—a cramped slit in the front wall that featured no window—Bennett paused. "Okay, don't forget—sneaky. No loud noises or sudden movements. Keep your Wrath as low as possible, and most of all—"

A vicious scream cut off his words, like a parakeet blitzed on meth. The sound came from behind, stabbing Bennett's ears. He turned to see, crawling out of the darkness of a hole in the ceiling over the stairs, a long-limbed creature on the approach. Its jittery, wiry movements were like a lizard on a branch, with the speed of a house cat. Clawed fingers and toes at the end of thin appendages kept it securely locked to the ceiling, while orange eyes gleamed behind long, straw-like hair. Its panting breath sounded like a pile of ash being sucked through a pipe, expelling gobs that screamed intermittently as it got closer.

At first glance, Bennett thought he was seeing a new monster that must have been hiding inside one of the many crevices or short tunnels in the home or maybe crawled in through the open window upstairs, just as he and Alex had. Perhaps some horrid Fovosian pet protecting the home. *But I checked every room!* Then he saw the creature's face and felt like an idiot. This thing was the woman they'd found and thought was dead, now crawling across the wall like a crab, her skin—the dead bark—flaking away, changing her more into a frenzied brown insect by the second.

She was playing dead. Like a possum, of course she was. The Scythe retched curses in a foul language as she sped closer. Taking a moment to pause, she locked her bug-eyed stare on them just as a seam at the center of her face opened to reveal a wet horror underneath that Bennett had seen before, or something similar, with Nigel Roe.

At ten yards away, she leaped off the wall and splayed herself out, claws and mandibles aimed at her prey. But the entire Scythe was blotted out by a yellow-and-red flare that lit the room with a flash of Wrath. When the light dissipated, the soaring Scythe had become a chunky mass of zooming cinder. Bennett leaped out of the way, letting the thing crash to the ground, where it broke apart like spent charcoal.

Alex posed with his palms out, fresh smoke dancing around him in ribbons.

"Did you just throw a fireball?" Bennett asked.

"I told you I could get strong," Alex said, murder in his voice and red in his eyes.

Before Bennett could reply with "Hot damn," a mess of long, ringing shouts from Celestial throats sounded an alarm from somewhere in the neighborhood—somewhere close. The landslide of noise might as well have been announcing their execution a second time.

"Asshole fucking nipples. There goes stealth mode. Okay, plan D. Quick, hit me!" Bennett snapped.

"What?"

"You've got destruction—I've got defense. You do you and let me do the same. Come on! Trust me."

"You want me to attack you?"

"That's exactly what I'm saying. Viciously. You have to mean it."

Alex stood dumbfounded for a moment or two longer than Bennett liked. *Come on, Al. Do I have to do everything?*

"Even with all that Wrath? You going to do it or not? Or do I need to bring up the night you watched your wife die alone in the hands of a monster? A monster you could have killed, by the way, because—you know—you did. Oh, and did I mention that while it was happening, I did nothing about—"

The hit that connected with Bennett's jaw sent him to the floor and almost knocked his lights out. Reality jittered for a second like a TV losing signal. The burn began to settle into his cheek as his mind surfaced from a fog. The pain, white hot and staggering, made him shake, but it also drove him. Getting back up, he held his jaw to help him face Alex, who appeared, in a word, angry.

"What you wanted?" the teacher asked.

"Yeah. Damn. Give me a second. Okay. Okay . . . Again."

As requested, Alex lashed out with a flurry of hits. More prepared this time, Bennett did as his training with Hannah had taught him and treated each punch from Alex as a barrier from a goal. His Rapture responded to the Wrath by swelling and solidifying. A terrific blue electric haze appeared around him, beaming with frenzied light. The red fire over Alex did much the same.

"More!" Bennett shouted, becoming like an immovable block of granite, the hits swaying him less and less, their thuds tightening.

Alex continued thrashing. The Wrath and Rapture clashed and swirled and sparked like hammered iron. Smoke and pulsing light filled the home with scorching intensity. After only twenty sec-

onds, there came a zenith and a vicious boom. Two glowing sources of Eve, burning fires of color and force, shone among the dust
in the air: vicious Wrath and sturdy Rapture. Where fire burned
on Alex, centered on his hands, a new set of armor appeared over
Bennett, similar to the set that had formed the night of the Ire.
But this was a new design he had conjured himself, bulkier and
burning much brighter than the last, which had been brought into
existence purely by his instinct and subconscious using Rapture as
they saw fit.

"Looking good," Alex said.

"You ain't seen nothing yet." Turning his palms up, Bennett focused. With a mix of extreme low and extreme high frequencies,
a noise like scraping metal over a huge empty jug crescendoed.
Moving his right hand away from his left, imagining the object he
wanted to create as clearly as possible, he applied the appropriate
shade of Rapture. Slowly but surely, a form began materializing in
his hands. At first, it was a rod with a primitive handle; its color
was a deep blue, halfway to black, yet still managed to glow with
starlight radiance. At the forty-one-inch mark, a rectangular head
the size of a cinder block capped the rod. Bennett held aloft the
sledgehammer he created. Basic, but able to do the job just fine.
*It's the first one I've ever done with my real body. Considering, I think
it's pretty good.*

"Have to admit, that is damn cool," Alex said.

"Isn't it, though?" Bennett slid back his helmet's face covering.
"Ready?"

Alex answered by bashing his fists together, exploding charcoal
knuckles with fiery sparks.

"Let's see what we're made of," Bennett said, turning toward the
front entrance.

When he and Alex charged out of the home onto the gray-bricked road, the Barium Guard was already approaching and would be upon them soon. Reinforcements would also be arriving from the air any second. *I can sense at least five. Already not looking too good.*

"This way!" Bennett bellowed, leading them away from the largest of the approaching clusters. Alex's speed proved both shocking and incredible. *Damn well hard to keep up with.* To do so, Bennett utilized another trick he'd learned.

Bursts beneath his heels let him bound forward at superhuman levels, moving along like an ice skater, pushing off the ground every dozen yards or so. When he began threatening to leave Alex in the dust, the teacher increased his speed even more, challenging Bennett to keep up. The crimson fire around him grew to a scorching blaze, nearly blotting him out completely.

Through the city, they made their way along barren streets, traversing back roads, passing groups of citizens who either stood in shocked silence or called, "They're here! This way! Come quick!"

The guards in pursuit had coalesced into a globular behemoth of Rapture energy driving after them in the streets like an avalanche—a bubbling swarm with dozens of heads, and more Barium swooping in all the time. *Guess they let everyone know where we are.* According to Bennett's previous calculations, completed with Hannah's assistance, there was almost no conceivable way he and Alex would be able to make it off the planet if they encountered even a fraction of this size of force this early in the trip, and the Eb Ring was still a depressingly long way off. *At least a couple of goddamn miserable miles.*

Bennett began looking for a fortification in which to take cover or any possible escape routes. *She didn't tell me about any of that. Just the fastest way there!* He and Alex were going to have to start improvising. A large banner strung between two tall poles caught his eye. "Al, light it up!"

With a fiery explosion under his feet, Alex leaped onto a nearby balcony and flung himself onto the pole like a flying squirrel. A blast of Wrath from his hands lit the banner aflame and sent it swaying and crumbling into the mass.

Leaping through the air and landing next to Bennett, he asked, "You really think that'll slow them down much?"

"You got any better ideas?"

"We could stop and ask what they want."

"Leave the jokes to Izzy."

From an alley's passing shadow, two Barium Guards appeared. *How did I miss those?* Dodging out of the way just in time, Bennett and Alex dove forward before doubling back to attack a different Celestial each. The blue warriors were caught completely off-balance, as though neither imagined the escaping humans would dare stop to face them.

With a hefty swing, Bennett connected his hammer with his Celestial's jaw, sending them soaring backward, crashing into a barrier wall outside a home. In the corner of his vision, Alex was busy pummeling his enemy, who was having a hard time laying hands on the dancing fire monkey at their feet. With a massive punch that burst into flames on contact with the Celestial's chin, Alex sent the Guard soaring into the one Bennett had just knocked down. Giant crystalline wings and arms and legs clamored to get free from the knot they'd been mashed into.

Wasting no time, Alex and Bennett were on the move again, dashing down the street. The two and a half seconds it took to deal with those guards had narrowed the gap between them and their pursuers considerably. The chances of success were dipping lower than ever. *I'd guess we have three or four seconds now.*

From a different alleyway on the other side, more broad blue menaces appeared, making Bennett sneer. *We don't have time for this!* The two guards swooping in and raising their spears were about to meet a wrath of a different sort: the kind from a Rapture user. Bennett readied his weapon for a powerful strike capable of taking them both out with one hit. *Been saving this one.* But a flash of white and red blinded and slowed him just enough to make out Alex's horizontal body soaring into the guards like an Olympic diver, tearing a burning gash from both their sides and even a bit out of their wings. The sound they each emitted would most likely be categorized as a gasp but was best described as a long fart into a tuba. The Celestials did not fall, but were so stunned they didn't move. Alex leaped back with an explosive burst of fire to meet Bennett on the main roadway. Only one second had been lost.

"Not bad," Bennett said, taking notice of a sudden looming shape in the middle of the city: the remnants of a Pilomine mountain peak. The small mountain, the only one left within the city limits, loomed like a monolithic traffic cone and seemed to appear out of nowhere on the left. He and Alex then dashed by a road that looked to head straight for a tunnel through the peak.

That's our ticket!

"Al! This way!"

Taking the turn, they made their way at breakneck speed toward the tunnel. However, the sudden maneuver proved to be a time killer, as the first wave began to dive in from above.

"Keep going for the tunnel!" Bennett shouted, spinning in time to face the first Celestial to attack. A spear tip soared toward his head, which he deflected to the side with his hammer, gripped wide with both hands. Bouncing off the balls of his feet and toes, he backpedaled and fended off the blue Goliath.

After a fight with patience, when the Guard finally drew close enough, Bennett went for the gut with a heavy, low swing just to the side of the abdominals: a weak point for Celestials not many knew about—*but Teach did.* Dazzling, wide eyes full of unspeakable surprise blinked as the Celestial keeled over holding their abdomen. The next hit from Bennett to the back of their cranium put them face-first into the pavement with a thud.

As the rest of the first wave swooped in, Alex unleashed a round of scorching fireballs that exploded against the troops' armor. The collision of Wrath and Rapture created a clamor like a rockslide coming face-to-face with an iceberg at the edge of the sea.

Bennett swung his hammer in a wide arc, knocking away the incoming spears. He held the next wave at bay long enough for Alex to slice through the air like a cannonball, breaking several of their shields in two. Leaping forward after landing like a jackrabbit, Alex rejoined Bennett, who had begun dashing toward the tunnel entrance.

The teacher then overtook the soldier, leaping off protruding walls and low balconies, enjoying himself, by all indications.

"Waiting on you!" Alex shouted, now several yards ahead.

Little asshole. What looked like an overpass careened into the lane, leading into the tunnel: a subway line, as well as aqua travel tubes. The overhead structure proved a minor obstacle for the airborne Guard, but still gave Alex and Bennett just enough time to zoom safely into the tunnel.

Close and low with powerful gusts from their wings, their pursuers sounded right behind them. The tunnel was large, but not enough for the Celestials to fully spread out, corralling them to one or two at a time. The bluster of their cries and jangling armor compounded into a blaring roar, flooding the air. *Why do I feel like every church bell on Earth is after us with a kitchen knife?*

Populated primarily by foot traffic, the tunnel also contained ample carriages and merchant carts hauling goods. Some of these had roofs sturdy enough to leap from, allowing Bennett and Alex to pass over the slow traffic, which had halted upon the entrance of the cascading choir of ringing metal that was the Barium Guard in hot pursuit.

If they could stay ahead of the Guard, Bennett could only hope that wherever the tunnel ended, there was no one waiting. At the moment, the only strong signals he could feel were directly behind them. The coast seemed crystal clear ahead.

But not from the back! Incoming!

Like he had been struck on the ass by a bus, the soldier careened forward into a carriage. Upon impact, it was shredded into sharp black crystals that threatened to pierce the gaps in his armor. Using his hammer to help him stand, Bennett flung himself free of the debris and faced his attacker.

The Celestial was none other than his very old friend, the Guard who'd escorted him every day of the trial—the one who originally placed him in nevrose chains.

"Well, hey there, Wiener," Bennett said.

Swiftly, Wiener Whistle attempted to engulf him with their huge frame. *Guess they still want us alive. Otherwise, it would be a sword.*

"I've had enough of you, and things are different now." With a heavy swing, Bennett's hammer collided with Wiener Whistle's chin, sending them hurtling into the next carriage.

Damn. Didn't think they'd be thaaat different. Thanks, Teach!

"Al! The roof!" Bennett shouted, pointing desperately and starting back toward the tunnel exit, hoping Alex understood what he meant. Luckily, he did and proceeded to blast the framework supporting the tunnel. Steel girders whined and snapped with ferocious screams. Alex then blasted the stone itself, which at first seemed to have no effect; the Wrath simply vanished upon the surface, as though absorbed by the rock.

With a groan, and after Bennett swore he heard Alex say "motherfucker" under his breath, the teacher launched into the air again: a reverse meteor. The booming tube of smoke and fire tore through the rock overhead, which began steaming and hissing, scorching red hot, breaking free and crashing to the road, colliding with Celestial Guards and knocking them out of the air. With another explosive pop, Alex came blasting out the other side of the roof. More rock fell, starting a cascade that knocked out more than half of the initial force pursuing them. But it did not take long for the stream of pursuers to flow free again.

Dashing away, again utilizing carriage roofs, Bennett knew the Guard was not far behind. This jailbreak was looking hopeless. But then he saw it: the dim gray light at the end of the tunnel. *We're going to make it?* There were no large signatures he could sense on the other side. No one was waiting. His and Alex's stride continued to increase, bounding at breakneck speed, leaping so fast he didn't understand how he was processing it all. This was starting to look too good to be true. The Guard in pursuit was close but losing ground to the humans hurtling away with strobing bursts of red and blue, and would not reach them before the exit. It appeared the tunnel roof trick had worked. Bennett allowed himself to believe they might actually do it. The doorway to freedom grew larger and larger. He began to see buildings and people out and about and hints of burgundy sky at dusk. The tunnel mouth came, seemingly open wide, ushering them onward. Free air began to fill his lungs.

This was when the end came down upon them. Two gigantic legs and feet appeared out of thin air. The ground ruptured directly ahead. Rapture had fallen like a sun—glorious and blinding. The shock wave stopped Bennett and Alex dead in their tracks and flung them to the ground.

Why you? Fuck! Why did it have to be you?

High Lord Gabriel's curled wings flapped once overhead, generating the wind of six Black Hawk helicopters before folding closed. The dust and debris kicked into the air never truly settled; small and medium bits lingered and drifted lackadaisically.

Bennett and Alex were ants to the creature, who was somehow even more gargantuan up close, and a pure, deep terror struck the soldier. Not just in his mind, but with pulses of toxic Dread trying to find their way to the very surface of his Eve signature. This was new. *What the hell is this guy?*

The structure loomed over them with a head held so high it was hardly visible at this close range. On the lord's stoic face were subtle hints of anger, possibly even contempt. Bennett thought his lips looked as though they might shift, revealing his mythical voice that could kill them out of spite. But the High Lord remained silent, hardly taking the time to look down on them—his victims— while reinforcements piled up behind him. The pursuers in the tunnel caught up, blocking the escape on all sides.

"Shit, what do we do?" asked Alex.

The fires of Wrath and Rapture around them burned as bright as ever. Their fight was not done, but as Bennett studied their situation, he could not come up with any solutions. A heavy breath and sigh were all he could muster. *Come on, you old goat, what have you got left, huh? What would Hannah do?* But in the absence of an immediate plan, Alex took it upon himself to act in lieu of any such thing. With wild ferocity, he leaped at Gabriel's chest, cocking back a powerful blow as he zoomed through the air. His fist burned like a miniature sun, a tremendous strike poised to land— at least, it would have been, had Gabriel not swatted him from the air with a flat palm, dismissing him like a fly hovering over a plate of potato salad.

Alex slammed into the ground with a deafening crack, disappearing into a cloud of dust as he bounced away. Gabriel then shifted his focus to Bennett, who was already charging his hammer with every ounce of raw Rapture he could muster. *I know I'm nothing compared to this guy—practically already a smear on the bottom of his boot. But if I'm dying today, I'm making damn sure he remembers me!*

Gabriel's gaze passed through Bennett as though he were already a ghost, the Celestial's hand reaching out to him like a child taking a toy from a shelf. The appendage opened, transforming into a cold, suffocating vise, ready to imprison him once more. A surge of petty anger ignited within Bennett at this sense of helplessness. Yet instead of weakening his Rapture, the emotion fueled it. The hammer in his hands swelled with radiant light, vibrating and pulsing with energy, ready to dance.

Deep in his bones, he felt it as Gabriel closed in, hand outstretched—he knew was ready. This attack would work—somehow, he just knew it.

When Gabriel's hand began to encircle him, Bennett launched off the balls of his feet and swung with all his might, drawing all the energy that Hannah was able to teach his dumb ass to find. The blow landed squarely on Gabriel's cheek. Blue sparks erupted into the air, illuminating the dark tunnel. Yet the towering figure hardly staggered; the High Lord's head moved only a few feet.

That was enough, however.

Next thing Bennett knew, he was soaring through the air, propelled backward and smashing face-first into a building. After a moment, he picked himself up and dusted himself off, peering through the hole he had created in the wall. There, a cloaked figure loomed over him, radiating a Rapture signal unlike any he had ever encountered. It was both riotous and forceful, yet so ethereal that it seemed to fade in and out of existence. The mystery warrior was clearly Gabriel's bodyguard, swooping in to protect the High Lord.

Before he could pick up his hammer, claws of royal violet pierced Bennett's wrists, dragged him outside, and pinned him to the building like wall tacks through a poster. Beneath the assailant's hood, Bennett glimpsed a stark, shadowed face, also violet. No mouth was visible—only a long, flat plane. Pure white eyes, shimmering and glossy, devoid of pupils, flashed up at him once, making him feel even smaller than he had beside Gabriel. The purple warrior remained silent, exuding an air as cold and unyielding as a glacier drifting through a river of ice.

Bennett still had plenty of fight left in him, kicking back with all his might, but every swing missed its target. That was when he realized the violet Celestial had no legs; their body stopped at the hips. They lacked proper arms as well, using their expansive wings to perform the functions of hands, much like certain species of bat. Bennett struggled to kick higher, aiming for the torso or perhaps some ribs, but his bulky armor limited his reach, preventing his legs from getting anywhere close.

"Hey! No fair!"

Lifting him away from the wall by his wrists, the cloaked Celestial carried him back to where the short fight had begun. Gabriel loomed over every nearby building, arms crossed as the humans were delivered to his feet. Loredosai brought in Alex, who, despite his fiery struggles, couldn't break free from the grip of the commander of the Barium Guard. Then, Bennett was handed over to the High Lord, who reached out and clasped him in one hand, cracking his bones like a chorus of Harley engines idling in neutral.

"Put me . . . *gek* . . . down . . . you freak!" Bennett managed to cough out. The hand clutching him felt like the most permanent structure he'd ever encountered; nothing he did could make it budge an inch. As he was lifted high into the air, closer to the lord of Hywyn's face, he began to notice the smallest imperfections—chiseled lines and divots, signs of wear and tear. His basketball-sized eyes gradually revealed swirling streams of energy within them, resembling blood vessels busy at work.

Peering into those eyes was the hardest part. Bennett knew he wanted to confront the face of the one literally holding him in bondage—*before he squishes me like a bug*—but honestly, he wasn't sure if he had the strength. *I've never looked into the eyes of a judgmental building that wants to kill me before.*

Gabriel studied Bennett with a slight tilt of his neck, then lowered his hand, gripping the left shoulder plate of Bennett's armor. As the titan began to pull, the metal crunched under his grasp.

"Whoa, whoa! What are you d—" Bennett's words were cut off by a tight gasp. Screaming torment shot through him as a fire-poker sting seized his shoulder. For a second, he thought a nerve in his spine had been severed. His eyelids flew wide open as the High Lord slowly peeled away the plate, rubbing it between his fingers as if studying it. The broken chunk crumbled to dust from the grinding and faded into nothing.

The white-hot agony was unending and unwavering, crawling through Bennett and clamping onto his throat, lacerating his nerve endings with scabrous claws. Piece by piece, Gabriel began to remove his armor. A cold rush accompanied each agonizing tear, pulling taut and snapping, detaching fragments of his psyche. The chill in his limbs was invasive and unwelcome, devoid of any Rapture. The pain ran deep—a pure, heart-stabbing sensation, ice-ridden and so shocking that it rendered him motionless. *Am I a corpse already? Is this what it feels like?*

With his arm and leg plates removed, Bennett was left with only his helmet and chestplate. Deep down, he convinced himself that these final pieces would remain intact, that somehow this assault would stop. It always had before. He'd faced tough spots in the past, but he always managed to escape. There had always been someone there to help him, just as he'd helped others—*Arghhhh!*

His Rapture took a sudden nosedive, but it wasn't because of Gabriel, nor his pierced wrists, nor the anger swelling within him. It was because of a lie. He'd never helped others as much as they had helped him. Bennett knew that, yet he couldn't admit it. To him, life had always been a test: the survival of the fittest. Deep down, he believed it was smart to let others support him while giving little in return. But both he and his Rapture knew that was just bullshit, born from his own selfishness.

As Gabriel reached for the helmet, his fingers clamped down, and Bennett was struck with the grim realization that no one was coming to help. Alex was down, held in place. So was he. Closing his eyes, he braced himself as best as he could. The helmet lifted, tethered by spirit-made tendons that forced Gabriel to pull just a bit harder. A resounding snap echoed through Bennett's skull, shaking him to his core and blinding his senses until the singing misery dissipated. The helmet was tossed aside, fading into nothingness. Moments later, the same routine followed for his chestplate.

Soon, the Rapture armor was gone, leaving Bennett as exposed as a newborn, the blood drained from his face, his lips trembling. The High Lord looked down on him now with visible disdain, his hand poised to crush the life out of him. Instead, Bennett was treated more like a stress relief doll: pumped a few times, just enough to make him vomit on himself, before being unceremoniously released. He crashed to the ground next to Alex. The two humans were then restrained once more—the cloaked purple warrior for Bennett and Loredosai for Alex.

The captain of the Guard let out a foghorn laugh. "You two thought you would make it to freedom, huh? Your Earth?" He attempted a larger, more boisterous guffaw, but with his high-pitched voice, it came out awkwardly, prompting Bennett to chuckle, spitting up more vomit.

This time, there was no reason to fight back. He'd given his all, and the strength and speed of Gabriel had proven absolute. *Guess he lives up to his job title.* The lessons with Hannah just hadn't been enough, exactly as she'd said from the start. *Eh, it was fun while it lasted.* Bennett and Alex exchanged smirks as they came under the shadow of the High Lord.

"Nicely done, Al."

"Almost had it, didn't we?"

"And without one bit of that Ire bullshit."

"Hey, yeah . . . you're right." Before Alex could hold his shoulders high, he and Bennett were forced into kneeling positions, surrounded by hundreds of Celestial guards, more swooping in every second. With arms crossed, they waited silently, the Rapture tree line they created deafening with a hubris-stenched rigidity.

Blocks of robin's-egg-blue stone were brought in and placed before each man, perfectly sized to bend human-sized creatures over and lop off their heads.

"So, we're back to this, huh?" Bennett drawled, a bit of drool escaping.

The crowd parted for a small troop of Psera Celestials. Above their heads, they shared the burden of a massive sword—at least thirty feet long and five feet wide. The blade was like a bar of ice, deep blue at its center fading into a stunning violet on its outer edge. The end featured no point at all, just a flat edge meeting at square corners. Though it was one solid piece of Rapture-soaked metal, something told Bennett this wasn't a tool for creation. *Unless it's trying to create dead silence.* He couldn't imagine what a sword that big would do to his body. *Probably some Bugs Bunny–type shit.*

"How many times have we been on our knees about to be killed now, Al?"

"Honestly, I've lost count."

The Faire Celestial at Gabriel's side launched into a chorus of sounds, likely a sanctimonious speech in the native Hywyn tongue, but to Bennett, it just sounded like bells clanging in his head. Judging by the body language and tone, it was his guess the guy was going on about how much of an honor it would be to get killed by Gabriel. *How he hasn't bestowed this honor for a while, or some equally stupid shit, yadda yadda.*

Hocking up a quality loogie, Bennett spat at the High Lord's feet. "Here. Some polish. Don't let those boots get dirty, now."

"Yeah." Alex spat his own, a small and disorderly spray mostly hitting its mark.

A subtle yet audible gasp rippled through the surrounding Celestial ranks. Each of them turned upward to Gabriel, awaiting the High Lord's response. Without so much as a blink, he continued. Calmly, he grasped the handle of the sword as it was raised to him by the Pseras. What must have been several tons of death instrument was lifted as if it were a broom handle, held high and presented to his subjects. In perfect unison, the entirety of the Guard folded their wings over themselves, obscuring their faces as though unfit to see it. A low tone resonated from the backs of their throats, sounding like dozens of empty water jugs tossed to the ground.

"God, you fuckers are weird," Bennett said.

"The great Gabriel, the Oarlam, Arname of Ai, Overseer and Lord on High, will now install justice," the Faire Celestial finally proclaimed proudly in English. *For our benefit. Yay!* He then gestured grandly toward the High Lord.

Gabriel took one small, six-foot step toward Bennett. *Guess I'm first. More yay!*

"Bring it on, you big, beautiful bitch. Show me what you got."

Pierced once again by the violet warrior's wings, Bennett was held to the block by his arms and shoulders. A primal scream escaped his throat, which quickly morphed into a laugh, hopefully showing how ready he was to be obliterated.

"Destroy me! Let's go!" With the little movement he had, he turned back to his brother. "See you on the other side, Al."

"I know you don't really believe that. But I hope you're wrong," Alex said.

"I hope I am, too."

Raised high in the air, the sword's shadow passed over Bennett, then along the ground. Each moment hung like a glider aloft, making it hard to know if time was flowing or not. When the shadow of the blade returned, a clang rang out, and the shadow was suddenly gone. Bennett then began to realize he was still alive and that his head wasn't rolling on the ground.

The blade had been swung; he was sure of it. But there was no pain, no squish, no boom. Instead, a profound silence enveloped him. *Huh?*

A new Eve signal suddenly flashed to his attention—one he knew well by now.

Craning his neck, he spotted a drifting, flapping cloak of dark gray. A robust and galvanized mix of Fervor and Mallos swirled together in her Eve signature. Bennett had never felt such relief at sensing the presence of the Medolian Mara before. *Well, where the hell have you been?*

She hovered in the air, gripping the blade of the High Lord's sword and halting it midswing. Before Gabriel could react to the intrusion, the Medolian launched a Mallos-infused kick into his head, exploding like a missile impact and sending him flying. The High Lord crashed through several nearby buildings, his wings flailing in vain as he tried to save himself by stabbing into the ground. An earthquake followed, rumbling as glass shattered and dust sprang into the air before he finally came to a stop.

While Bennett struggled to process what he'd just witnessed, signals of Mallos began to pop up all around them. At first, it seemed like an error in the fabric of reality. There had never been this many sources of neutral Eve in one place at one time before. The Barium Guard seemed to share in Bennett's confusion as figures bathed in light began to materialize. Streaks of blue darted this way, crossing paths with strobes of yellow and orange going that way. A brash line of green and cyan cut through it all, followed by a swirling stream of robin red. Blasts of myriad shades fused with Mallos sent Celestial guards soaring to and fro, sometimes colliding mid-air and sending their spears clattering to the ground. Spheres of Wrath and Jubilee exploded like bombastic fireworks as figures zipped through the fray inside their own spheres—large enough to play a life-size game of pinball with. Bennett couldn't tell how many had arrived but guessed a half dozen or so.

The panic in the Guard was palpable as their heads whipped about, desperately searching for targets to hurl their spears at. Loredosai and the violet warrior were equally ineffective, as they were forced to hold the humans in place. Gabriel was on his feet in no time, taking a brief survey of the chaos before launching an assault on Mara, who remained lofted in the air, awaiting him.

What followed was a dance at hyperspeed, showcasing Gabriel's incredible agility, especially for one so large, as Mara's Mallos sphere zipped around him like a giant firefly.

Momentum favored the surprise-attack, the Medolians knocking down blue brutes left and right, but the Barium Guard quickly regained their footing. With powerful bursts from their palms and wings, the Celestials managed to slow one of the Sentries just long enough for Bennett to catch sight of a short, wiry man wielding what resembled a medieval gardening rake with three sharp claws. He wore a gray cloak and hood, much like the others. Wrath wove through his Eve signature, which, while the dimmest among the signals present, still held considerable weight compared to the might of the Celestials.

A cold chill swept through the intersection with every swing of Gabriel's fist, spinning him around like a washing machine drum. Try as he might, he couldn't catch Mara. With the grace of a leaf caught in a storm, she darted in and out, waiting for the right moment. When the opening finally appeared, she unleashed a flurry of swipes, her blade glancing off the shimmering aura surrounding his massive form, skillfully avoiding being snagged from the air. A bellowing shout rang from her when she swung her staff again, tearing through the Rapture barrier with a sound like stacked sheets of glass being cleaved, and dug into the High Lord's side. His expression after was not a flinch of pain but more deeply rooted confusion.

She pulled the blade free and floated back a few feet as Gabriel's hand grazed the wound, which began to pour Rapture like a widening crack in a dam. Even Mara seemed surprised that her attack had worked.

A pain Bennett had nearly forgotten roared back to life as the violet warrior released him, pulling their wingtips from his limbs and zooming off to intercept Mara's path to Gabriel. Without a moment's hesitation, Bennett began reconstituting his armor and summoning another hammer. The entire set formed in a mere four seconds.

Turning to Loredosai, Bennett shouted, "Let go of my brother!" and swung. The Celestial dodged, but Alex was released all the same. In a beautiful orchestra of brutal improvisation, the two rushed Loredosai, landing a powerful punch to his face. The blast of Wrath and Rapture fused into a blinding burst of white light, sending the commander of the Barium Guard flying into a cluster of his own men, toppling them like blue bowling pins.

The other six Medolians joined Mara in a tight circle, their formation shrinking until they stood back-to-back with Bennett and Alex, surrounded by an encroaching Celestial force. Gabriel stomped into the center, sending shuddering quakes through the ground. A standoff ensued between the seven Medolians and two humans facing the full might of the Barium Guard, not to mention Gabriel and his royal bodyguard. *Talk about David and Goliath. Heh-heh. Get it?—Ah, fuck you.*

Mara faced the High Lord, her frigid expression unwavering. "Lord Gabriel, the Medolians of UnEarth have a message for you. We're taking the humans, Barker and Hunter, back to Earth, which, as of this moment, is the sovereign land of the Medolians. No other UnEarth creature shall set foot on that planet ever again. If they do, they will answer to us—me, first and foremost. Earth is now the sole domain of humanity, the Purged, and Medolians."

Bennett stole a quick glance at the others accompanying Mara, noting their not-quite-organized formation. *Body language is a little hard to make out with this bunch.* He didn't recognize any of them; Izaiah, Fabian, and Galinthia were absent. Instead, he was surrounded by a tumultuous mix of powerful Mallos signatures, each representing new faces and fresh Eve energies, making it difficult to distinguish one from the other. *Guess the other Medolians did exist, after all. I always thought they were part of Izaiah's fantasies. Wonder what that little asshole is doing now. Fuckin' wiener shit.*

"In addition," Mara continued boldly, "the creatures of Mallos will no longer be forced to serve the Tribunal or anyone from Un-Earth. Our people are Sentries no longer. These are the terms we are establishing, and they are nonnegotiable."

Bennett sensed a wave of jitteriness ripple through the Medolians. *I doubt any of these guys have ever seen Gabriel in the flesh.* The sour blue giant glared down at Mara, his crystalline face set in a stone-cold judgment.

To Bennett's sheer delight, she topped off her declaration with, "We are leaving now." With a flash and a wave of her hand, she dissipated her staff.

Ooh, I could feel the pettiness and reversed snobbery. Love it. Good job, Mara.

"Here it comes," she whispered to her team.

Here what comes? Bennett glanced at them for clues. The Medolians braced themselves for something, trying (and failing) to conceal their anticipation. Just as he began to piece it together, he noticed Gabriel take a deep breath. *Wait . . . he's not going to . . .*

Just before the word crossed his lips, Mara shouted, "Now!" At her signal, she and the Medolians united to create a protective bubble shield over themselves, Alex, and Bennett.

The timing was impeccable, almost synchronized with the near-irresistible force unleashed by Gabriel's utterance of the word, "No."

It was indistinguishable from the bombs that had interrupted the execution, but this was neither Mallos nor solely the force of Rapture. The torrent released by his voice was a hurricane, flooding Bennett's mind with swirling chaos. A piercing, needle-point pain lanced through his skull, amplifying the sound to an almost incomprehensible volume. Inside the Medolian sphere, the word transformed into a cacophony—simply the holy-shit, most-loud-est-est fucking thing he had ever heard. Without the protective shield, it would have ripped the flesh from his bones like a leaf blower aimed at moist, tender brisket.

The Celestials, however, appeared largely unaffected, standing their ground like statues, far too cold and lifeless to be considered alive. In the stillness that followed the blast, as the debris settled, the bubble shield folded down, exposing the humans and Medolians. Mara exclaimed, "Let's move!"

Bennett wasn't done trying to pick his thoughts up off the floor—they'd been blown out of his head by Gabriel's voice—when the Medolians swooped away with the speed of falcons diving for prey, carrying him and Alex along for the ride. The Medolian who had grabbed him with such force that he felt he'd been hit by a car was a woman who appeared to be in her late forties. There was no time for pleasantries, but her Rapture-tinted signature was robust enough for Bennett to trust her.

Alex was scooped up by a tall, lanky, Dread-tinted Sentry, whose signature felt shakier in comparison. The squad fled the area with tremendous speed, weaving left and right like a flock evading predators. Yet, despite all of Mara's maneuvering and tricks, they struggled to find a path clear of the Celestials. Azure guards swarmed at every turn, launching spears that whizzed past them, striking at the Medolian spheres, which thankfully managed to slip free of their grasp.

Blue wings surrounded them, flapping and thumping all around as the spheres sped onward. Behind them, Gabriel's signature took to the air, filling the sky and encroaching like a zeppelin flying at

Mach 1. When Bennett turned to look, the enormous creature barreled through its subjects like an eagle slicing through a swarm of fruit bats. *If I didn't know better, looks like he's about to scream at full volume.*

The blue colossus arrived, blotting out the sky like a third moon over Trivium before diving down—a free-falling mountain of Rapture. Several Medolians fired geysers of Eve into the air, but the attack amounted to little more than a lightshow, barely affecting Gabriel. Then, from the side, with a tremendous pop and a flare of aquamarine light, a Fervor-tinted Medolian soared through the sky and collided with his left wing. The impact sent the sphere bouncing away, sailing into the distance. Though staggered in flight, the Celestial giant did not slow down.

In fact, I think he's speeding up!

"Can we go any faster?" Bennett whined to his carrier, who seemed not to hear or understand him.

When Gabriel started to get especially big, Bennett realized the High Lord was targeting him, aiming squarely in his direction. He caught the Celestial's dead eyes, which felt like they were stabbing into his soul. A gigantic blue hand reached out toward the sphere, an almost beachball-sized target for the giant.

Wonder what this is going to feel like.

Bennett held his breath, wincing in anticipation of being swatted when suddenly, a Fervor-and-Mallos-tinted boot struck Gabriel in the face with the force of a freight train, sending him spiraling out of view, truly knocked off course this time. The buildings he crashed through crumbled, tumbling to the ground in a catastrophic domino effect.

"Go!" Mara screamed, shaking out her leg and foot.

The Medolians needed no second invitation; they bolted from

the scene so quickly they seemed to leave ghostly mirages in their wake. Mara quickly caught up and resumed leading the way.

As they retreated, even after he sprang from the ground to continue his chase, the High Lord began to fall away. For once, he became a reasonably sized figure, shrinking more with every passing moment. That was when Bennett caught the briefest glimpse of victory. The other Celestials were falling behind as well, unable to keep up with the Medolian spheres. Mara's attack had nearly done the trick. *I wonder if she broke her foot on that dude's face. Sure sounded like it.*

Only the violet warrior managed to keep pace, spraying welding-torch fire from the tips of their wings, striking at the spheres as they grasped for the escapees. However, the Medolians' constant volley of rear projectiles kept the warrior at bay. It seemed increasingly unlikely that the violet warrior could halt this breakaway all on their own. The Eb Gate loomed too near, and the Celestials were too far away to catch them. Gabriel was rebounding quickly but would never reach them in time.

There's no way he could, right? Are we going to do this? Are we home free? Holy shit. Okay . . . don't jinx it!

Joy entered Bennett's heart. He couldn't help it; a song swelled in his lungs, begging to be let out. *Definitely some Springsteen. Nothing else makes me as happy.* Glancing at Alex, he hoped to share a joyful expression as they were whisked away to Earth, safely tucked in for the trip, each with their own special Medolian—the most powerful of UnEarth creatures—acting as their personal escorts and soon-to-be best friends.

Bennett's gaze locked onto his brother, who appeared to be experiencing the same tumultuous thoughts. Alex had his eyes closed, a relieved smile breaking through his expression. Just then, a brilliant shape materialized in the air beside him. A cloak of shimmering blue, soaked in Mallos and Rapture, fluttered around Alex for a brief moment before he vanished—missing, no longer in the sphere. Bennett blinked several times, convinced it was a trick of the light, but then Alex's signature abruptly reappeared in the opposite direction, closer to their pursuers.

A couple of hundred yards behind, Bennett spotted him suspended midair, held by a woman wrapped in blue. Her glittering blonde hair and silver clothing, both trimmed with sky blue and violet, flowed like streaks in an oil puddle. *The other Medolians! The other three. Philomenabrown-or-whatever! Of course*—the agents of the Senate had not been accounted for.

Why didn't anyone think of that?!!? And why aren't any of you reacting?!!?

The blue Medolian was soon joined by two others—one tinted with Fervor, the other Grief. When Bennett turned to Mara to see what she would do, he instantly realized, by the look on her face, that there was nothing she could do for Alex—or would. They would not be stopping to go back. All Bennett could do was scream belligerently at the top of his lungs, making no coherent sense but doing it anyway, desperately reaching out. But the teacher was already a tiny figure in his view, shrinking by the second.

The moment came and went too quickly to process, and suddenly the once-savior Medolians were moving on, and behind them, Alex was being handed over to Gabriel like a trinket retrieved from the floor. *He was right there! How could they let him get grabbed like that?* Bennett's disbelief, quickly morphed into a deep-seated sickness, a noxious dread that grew more potent as he and Alex drifted apart. He wanted nothing more than to vomit until the sphere he was riding in was full.

Most of the escaping party didn't even seem to notice the abduction, frantically fleeing as if the Medolian boogeyman were hot on their heels.

"What about Alex!?" Bennett screamed, fighting against the futility of the situation. "What about Alex, damn it!"

But the Medolian carrying him remained silent, piloting the sphere after Mara without deviation.

"Keep going! To the gate!" she shouted as the towering gold rings of the Eb Gate came into view.

As the Medolian spheres swooped down toward the station, Bennett tried once more, "Al! We can't leave Al!" But by now, the other Medolians had already begun disappearing through the closest ring. He would be following suit in no time. Backpedaling felt like a natural reaction, but it did him no good in the sphere.

"Don't take us through! We need to get Al!"

The white storm in the ring approached, ready to take him, and he felt a crushing sense of powerlessness. Not even during the entire shit show that was the Joseph Mandate had he felt such an egregious weight of despair as in that moment when he was taken through the gate and Alex, his brother—the one he'd promised to take care of—was left behind.

MILK & DONUTS

Foggy midday light was the first sensation to appear, softly filtering through closed eyelids. Fresh air kissed her face, stirring Leigh as she found the gentle whisper of bushes and trees—their oceans of leaves crackling and rustling in the breeze.

She groaned, the sound dry and raspy. Her throat was parched, her lips cracked. An all-encompassing thirst consumed her. A deep, relentless pain throbbed throughout her body, centered above her eyes, where a dull ache pulsed with each heartbeat.

Lying on her back, she felt something soft beneath her, but that was all she knew. Blankets cocooned her, and a plush pillow cradled her head. *Was I asleep?* The scent of wild grass in the air mingled with a musty, swamp-like odor reminiscent of moss clinging to a tree trunk.

As her eyelids struggled to open, her irises were flooded with stinging white light, forcing her to shield her eyes with her hands. The sun blazed overhead, flickering through the branches of a

towering oak that loomed above her. Its thick trunk stood beside
the bed.

Where am I?

Rising was out of the question at first. Her limbs were too
weak. It must have taken an hour of lying still before she gathered
enough strength. Thirst eventually drove her to move. As her eyes
adjusted, she was able to look around. The bed she lay in—more
comfortable and engulfing than any of the expensive mattresses
she'd ever bought—had a frame with tall corner posts of brass and
was, indeed, sitting outside. *(the hell?)*

She hadn't dreamed it. All around her was a scene of nature more
majestic than any photo she'd ever seen in National Geographic.
(did i just wake up in a Bob Ross painting?) Lush green swaths blanketed a field surrounded by tall trees creating a perfect perimeter
wall. At the center of the clearing sat a glistening pond, its edges
lined with tall stalks of golden grass slowly dancing in the sunlight
bouncing off the water's surface.

Is this Earth? Where was I before? Can't quite . . . picture it.

On the other side of the bed, she found a small table with a glass
of what looked like the most refreshing water the universe had ever produced. Without a second thought, she found the strength to
reach out and take it. The glass almost slipped from her weak grip
a few times, but she managed to get her lips around it and gulp.
Streams ran down the sides of her mouth. It was empty too soon.

Setting it down, she sat for a moment, letting the water soak
into her sponge-dry throat and lips. The pressure in her skull began to lessen, the disorientation subsiding, but the feeling that she
was dreaming persisted. Only then did she notice the other items
on the table. Her personal effects—the Gauntlet and gem bracelet—had been placed in such a way next to the bed that she knew
it had been done with care. Instinctively, she wanted to reach out

and take them, but her body needed a few more minutes with the water.

When she finally turned to glance behind the bed, she saw a cabin made of vibrant orange autumn wood. A layer of dim grime had built up on the surface over what looked like centuries, especially in the nooks and crannies, but it couldn't fully diminish the color, which remained alive and resolute. Something about the cabin's construction, basic and straightforward enough to convince you its blueprint had been drawn in the dirt with a stick, made it both timeless and pure, yet amateur and clumsy. The wild brush and vines consuming it were doing their best to pull the structure into the forest, but it seemed not to have budged an inch, looking as sturdy as new.

Focusing did nothing to help her remember how she'd gotten there. *I was . . . with Aluqa. In her group. Europe. In the mine. The Surface.* She gripped her head as the ache came shooting back. The faintest glimmer of something she used to know as emotions was there, whispering. Then she remembered: hate and anger, the fire of the Wrath. It had flowed through her, making her belligerent, incensed, despising, and a hundred other things she'd never felt before. But now she couldn't feel any of it. The memory was far less potent.

Then the cold hit her. The last to flow through her was the Rapture, something even more amorphous. What she remembered of it was mostly pressure, both inside and out. The force and its expectations were impossible to live up to. But there was no sign of it now, or of the Wrath, or any other prominent, ordinary emotion. It seemed she was back to her old self. Or rather, her new self—the one who'd gotten used to being a numb rock.

Little by little, it came back: the memory of the Covenant and taking it from Aluqa at the Eb Gate. *The Cavaliers. I was one of them—right.* A long face appeared in her mind. His eyes erupted with blue as he reached out for her.

The Cardinal.

Most of the rest of the memories returned with a bang. *The explosion. The execution.* Shutting her eyes tight, she wrestled with it. This was the worst regretful hangover of her life, by a mile. *And that's saying something.* Thinking of what she had said and done, and thought and felt while "on" the Eve, was not pleasing. When potent emotions first found their way back into her, she thought she'd missed them, and welcomed the opportunity to at least feel something again. But this person she was now—the one moving forward from all that—saw them as a crutch, and not even a sturdy one.

[*Worse still, they are the very thing that creates UnEarth in the first place.*]

I'm not making any more juice for those assholes. Feeling nothing is fine with me.

The truly last thing she could remember was stopping Aluqa before she could step through the Eb Ring. [*I barely made it to the gate room, I do not see how I could have made it off Trivium alive. Such a great concentration of Eve would have killed anyone.*]

She began to look around at her surroundings, a new idea brewing. (*i mean . . . shit—it probably did kill me*) This place was starting to look suspiciously similar to the way her mother used to describe heaven. But that couldn't be it. That was ridiculous. Then she began to hear a sound—something like giggling. But that didn't make sense, either.

(*what the fuck is . . .*)

Movement suddenly appeared off to the left. A young woman came prancing around a tree into the field, her arms aloft. She was laughing and bouncing, reaching for what Leigh eventually saw was a swath of butterflies fluttering away. It took a moment of staring to realize she was seeing Skraga. Alive and well, the woman had shrunk by at least one hundred fifty pounds. The muscles were gone, her bulging shoulders along with them. This woman who'd replaced her appeared fragile enough to make a sheet of paper look bulletproof, but she was undeniably happy. The smile would not leave her face. Leigh couldn't ever remember seeing one quite like it on her friend.

But none of this added up. Skraga had collapsed and stopped breathing in the vault. And she hadn't looked like this, like her old self. Something was off, and the scene was starting to feel more like a cliché Heaven scenario by the minute. I just can't believe that. Leigh swung her legs over the side of the bed. Her bare feet touched the ground. *I don't feel dead.*

(would i be this tired if i was?)

Near the foot of the bed sat the backpack she'd been given by Aluqa. *Which she stole back from me.* Plopping to her knees, Leigh crawled to it and opened it up. There was no large glass cup; the Covenant was gone. [*I know I did not dream that.*] There was also no sign of the Wraithian dagger. *What the hell is going on? Wait a minute, that's it. Hell.* Then she began to realize that scenario— good old damnation—sounded far more likely. [*I would have never made the cut into Heaven by any metric.*]

Yet those cottontails don't exactly threaten the same way as fire and brimstone.

(not that i'm complaining)

She wasn't explicitly worried about her missing items, but who-ever had taken them should have known she would stop at noth-ing to get them back, emotions or no. The most likely scenario was Aluqa being somehow behind it, but nothing about the area around her screamed Morinnean. As Leigh sat in the short grass with the backpack in her lap, thinking over every possible scenario, a sweet cherry voice came filtering through the chattering leaves.

"I'm coming!" Skraga was charging through the tall grass in the field toward the cabin. "Hold on, I can help." Panic was in her voice. "Did you fall out?"

By the time she reached Leigh and saw the look on her face, Skraga lost her worried air. "You okay? I thought you'd thrown yourself out of bed."

She had let her hair down, revealing a long mane that Leigh had no idea had been curled up into tight buns on her head. Like a drug addict who'd gotten clean and begun a journey to a healthy weight, her eyes were eerily present, lofted over pale, bruise-colored patches of wrinkleless flesh. Folds of loose skin on her arms gave proof of the bulging muscles that had recently stretched it. But even with the changes, she was still very much Skraga, her bright and generous gaze aimed Leigh's way.

Though her jaw does seem to be sagging a bit.

Opening her mouth to answer, Leigh coughed on the words. No sound escaped. The voice she'd gained through the Wrath and Rapture was gone.

"What's the matter? Can't you talk?" Skraga finally arrived, panting, and knelt next to her. Leigh shook her head and pointed at her throat. "Oh, I thought you could again. Guess we've both been through some changes since we got back, huh? What about your computer talker?"

Leigh shook her head. The Gauntlet was fried.

"Oh, well, I only remember a few of the hand words you taught me, so I'm not much help there. But you know what? I'm not going to apologize for it. Nope, I won't." Skraga smiled, radiating pride. Leigh returned the gesture with a respectful nod.

(atta girl)

"So, I s'pose I ought to speak for the both of us, then. Okay, first thing—we're not on Trivium anymore." (*no kidding*) "And you've been asleep for a long time. I was afraid you were gonna die, but then you just kept hanging on."

Leigh motioned around at the area with a questioning glance.

"Oh, yeah, I don't know where we are either," Skraga said. "But it's nice, though, isn't it? We bring you outside every day to get some sun. You know, since you were so cold. The old guy thought it would do you good. I think I agree with him. Either way, it worked!"

Leigh gave another questioning motion and mouthed, *What old guy?*

"Oh—Scruffy! That's what I call him. This is his house. Funniest guy I ever met. You'll love him! I never laughed so hard. And not in a good long while . . . too long, in fact. Kinda forgot what laughing was like. But it's great, so that makes you kind of sad again, doesn't it? Which I don't like anymore, so I go back to laughing, and that makes it all better. Scruffy helps, too. He'll be back soon. He promised, and so far, he always keeps those."

It was hard to know what to make of all that. Apparently, someone called Scruffy had helped get Skraga and Leigh off Trivium. And helped take care of them. But there was no one left from the Surface who could have fit that description. Leigh was assisted back into bed and tucked in by Skraga. Despite wanting to know more, she had used up all the energy she had for the moment and didn't have enough to fight off the sleep trying to roll over her.

"You just rest, Miss Silverthorn," Skraga said. "Sleep is always good. I'll keep watch of you 'til he gets back."

Simply hearing the word "sleep" sent Leigh's eyelids into shutdown mode, and without knowing it, she drifted off into another deep slumber. When she woke again, the sun had moved into the back third of the sky, its light tinted a hazy auburn. Skraga was nowhere to be found. There was so little sound and movement around the pond that it would have been easy to assume time had stood still, if not for the calling of a few birds hidden in the trees.

Amid the tweets and whistles, one grew in volume, but it was not like the rest. This one was far less majestic. Then it became clear it was not a bird but the whistling of a person. Around the same time, Leigh began to hear the sluggish scraping of feet on dirt.

"He's here!" Skraga shouted, appearing out of nowhere from Leigh's left, running off to the right. Following her trajectory, Leigh found a hunched shape ambling up a faint path through the flowers toward the cabin. As he got closer, the man grew more disheveled, separating himself further from the beauty around him until he appeared just as covered in grime as the cabin. But like the cabin's radiant wood, his whistling broke through the image. The tune could not be described as Dixie, or pop, or show tunes, but something that reached down to a primal core inside Leigh. Much more ancient, without steady tempo, verging on pseudo, bullshit jazz— somehow elemental. The hairs on her neck rose upon hearing it.

Carrying a large wicker bag over his shoulder, causing him to grunt with every step he took, the mystery man lifted his head when Skraga shouted, "Scruffy!" on her way to him.

Wrapping her arms around him, offering a warm hug, she took the bag off his hands before helping him the rest of the way. No stronger than the old man, she also had trouble with its weight, but carried the bag without a peep. Leigh had risen from the bed and begun trying to find her legs when Skraga and Scruffy approached. The old man waved, smiling with only a few teeth in his mouth, and that was when a hard realization struck Leigh.

Wait a minute . . .

She studied him: his fingerless gloves, doofy face, spotted green coat, emerald-topped cane, and a gray knitted cap with two brown stripes. All were exactly how Casey had described the previous Warden Sentry, Izaiah Ezekial, the Medolian creature with immense power disguised as an old man to better infiltrate our world. *But it couldn't be, right? There's no way. He got killed at the execution one way or another, I'm sure.* The Heaven idea was gaining even more steam, but Leigh wouldn't allow it. His kind would have been even less deserving of infinite bliss than her. The Sentries were the ones who, for so long, had enacted the plans of the Tribunal in its subjugation of Earth. In so many ways, they were the tightly laced boot worn by the foot of the oppressor.

The Wrath was waving at Leigh, scratching at the door, begging to be let in. But she didn't know how to do that, even if she wanted to open herself back up to it.

He brought Skraga and me here? But why? We were already on Trivium, practically inside the police station. Is this place one of the Medolian safe houses? It was always an inevitability the authorities would catch up with her. Leigh just thought she would feel more accomplished at the end of her journey. Or, at least, had gotten further down the road.

Once close, Skraga introduced the newcomer. "Well, here she is. Member Silverthorn, meet Scruffy. Scruffy, meet Member Silverthorn. Told you she'd heal quick."

"The professor, yes. Wonderful! Glad to see you up and about," the man said with startling joviality. "Looking plenty strong, too." He held out a dirt-caked, half-mummified hand to Leigh. She gave a weak shake. "Like she said, call me Scruffy. Sophia here was right on the money with that one. Awful nice, this lady. Together, she and I have been keeping watch over you."

"As well as each other," Skraga said. The cheeriness of the moment was making it impossible to believe.

Izaiah was too genuine to be real. This display wasn't what Leigh had expected, not after all her reading, even after Casey had described him in exactly this manner. *That part of the tale just seemed too . . . I guess . . . similar to Casey to have been true.*

[*But there is no doubt. This must be Izaiah. Just look at him. There is no coincidence that can create this scenario.*]

The man before her didn't exactly feel like a creature bent on enslaving an entire planet. There was zero malice. This man felt more like a great uncle whom no one ever talked about but had some amazing stories once you got to know him. Yet that made her extra defensive. With her Eve senses gone, she could no longer feel his emotions. He was a mystery other than her basic ability to read body language and tone, but all input there was running counter to what she believed.

"I understand you can't use your voice anymore. I'm sorry, that's a shame," Izaiah said. "I suppose it's my responsibility, so I will be the one to apologize to you for it. My old pupil, Chloe, did a lot of things that hurt a lot of people. None of it makes me proud, but it's on me, nonetheless."

"Your pupil is why she can't talk?" Skraga asked, her upper lip curled in confusion.

"Unfortunately, yes," the old man said. "Remember, dear, when I told you I knew a thing or two about UnEarth? I've been a part of that world for some time. I'd hoped that getting you both off Trivium would start me on my long road to penance. Now, let's eat some breakfast before the milk gets warm. Sophia, sweetheart, would you mind getting the table? Looks like we'll need three chairs today."

"Sure thing!" Skraga bolted up the cabin steps, stumbling on a few, barely regaining her balance, and disappeared inside.

Izaiah remained, leaning on his cane, his bright gray eyes fixed on Leigh. The grin on his face seemed as permanent as a Buddha statue. She was sure he was studying her as much as she was studying him. No degree of blankness on his wrinkled, bearded face could convince her he wasn't plotting some surprise arrest or punishment.

"Do you want to hear a joke?" he asked after a moment.

Leigh wasn't sure if she did, or what to do. She shrugged.

"I'll take that as a yes. Okay, let me see . . ." Izaiah reached into his coat pocket. Leigh readied for the worst. Out came a small green notebook with a pencil tucked inside it. Rifling through its pages, he chewed on his tongue as he decided something. *(probably which way is best to kill me)*

"Ah, here's one. A favorite. Ready? Here we go . . . What do you call a donkey standing on your roof? —Do you give up? —A confused donkey!" Izaiah beamed as though she might break out in tears of laughter. Instead, she offered a silent, double thumbs-up.

"Oh good. I'm glad you liked it," he said. "Look, here comes Sophia with the table."

From inside, Skraga brought out a rusted folding table and set it up on the short grass a few feet from the bed. Three folding chairs—all from different sets—were placed around it.

"Let's eat," she said.

"Don't have to tell me twice." Izaiah hobbled over quickly. Leigh's instincts kicked in as he passed, and she took his arm, helping the old man to his seat. The bag he'd brought with him was emptied of two jugs of milk, and another large oil-soaked paper bag, which contained a few dozen donuts that had been mashed into one mound during the trek to get them here. Cups and plates, which were also of differing origins, were brought out as Izaiah broke apart the donut block as best he could.

"Here you go," he said, putting a few chunks of chocolate-frosted vanilla, old-fashioned, and an almost intact jelly donut on Leigh's plate. "Little soul grub. Does the body good after a nasty, not-good ordeal. How about that?"

Izaiah sat down with a thump into his seat and reached for one of the milk bottles. "This one's mine. You two can share the other." Popping the top, he chugged a third of it immediately.

"Not a problem," Skraga said. "I couldn't finish mine yesterday."

Once everyone had a glass of milk and crumpled donuts on their plate, the feast began. What should have been enough baked goods to feed a whole office floor's worth of people was gobbled up by the two across from Leigh in a matter of minutes. Never had she seen such ravenous warfare used against a donut. The confectionery stood no chance.

While staring at the display, she lost what little appetite she was beginning to find.

"Don't forget to have some," Izaiah said to her. "And the milk, too. It's as fresh as it gets! Can't say the same for the donuts, but that's not a problem."

He returned to his meal, while Leigh grew agitated with the situation. This was no time for normalcy. Too many questions were unanswered. She waved at him to get his attention.

"Yes?" he asked with crumbs falling into and from his beard.

Leigh made the motion for a pencil and paper, pointing to his coat pocket.

"You want some . . . well, sure, duh, why didn't I think of that?" Reaching into his pocket, he retrieved the green notebook and handed it over. "There's still a couple of blank spaces in the back."

As Leigh flipped through the pages, intent on reaching the end without stopping to look around, she found herself fanning the pages slower and slower. Cryptic symbols and sketches of symmetrical linework seemed to shift, forming different shapes depending on how she held the book. Scattered throughout were writings in too many languages to count, filling nearly every inch of every page. Some thoughts were so small they couldn't be easily read without a magnifying glass, while others were scrawled in large letters—perhaps to emphasize their importance—such as SWALLOWING HOT DOGS? FUNNY?? OR NOT? Not wishing to be rude, Leigh did not linger long on any page and finally reached the back, finding a corner of white space.

Quickly, she wrote, *You're Izaiah, right?* and turned the notebook toward him.

He read it and let out a literal hoot toward the sky. Some landfill breath wafted out, carried gently by the breeze. "I tell ya, I've been known by many names over the years. That's definitely one of them," he said.

"Izaiah?" Skraga asked. "Does that mean you're not Scruffy?"

"No, Scruffy's just fine, my dear," Izaiah said. "Better than fine, in fact."

Leigh wrote again, *How did you find Skraga and me?*

"By checking the ground. Both of you must have fallen down, because that's where I found you. Can't imagine the ordeal you went through first. But we don't have to think about that if you don't want to. Donuts and drama don't mix, ya ask me."

"Scruffy helped me after you and Aluqa had gone away," Skraga chimed in. "But I never met him before that. Did you? 'Cause how else would you know one of his names?"

Leigh wrote, *An old friend knew him.*

"You must be referring to Miss Lipmayer," Izaiah said. "How is she doing?"

Fine. No thanks to you.

"That isn't very nice," Skraga said.

"No, it's okay." Izaiah patted her on the arm. "I deserve it. Trust me. I can take it. Thick skin. Comes with maturing, which I've done plenty of."

"You don't look that old," Skraga said. "Come on."

Leigh rolled her eyes in lieu of laughing.

"What?" Skraga asked.

"Thank you, but I'm a lot older than I look, young lady," Izaiah said with a wink.

"Whoa, like a hundred years old?"

"Maybe a little higher."

Leigh wrote in the notebook, *Oldest living thing on the planet.*

Skraga read it and scoffed, wide-eyed. "Member Silverthorn, that's awful rude, don't you think?"

"Sophia, I promise there's no problem," Izaiah said, continuing to pat her arm. "The professor is many things, including a little judgmental, from what I hear—but a liar she is not. She could be right, even if I don't look it. I've seen all kinds of people come and go over the years—gangs, tribes, cities, herds—each with their time to shine. A lot of 'em no one will ever know about because they didn't leave anything behind, 'cause they had nothing. No stuff, just the basics—food and shelter."

"You were around when people didn't have stuff?"

"Oh yeah. Then along came the Sumerians. Loved their stuff. Then the Egyptians—who *really* loved theirs. Don't get me wrong, though. I spent a good amount of time with them. To me, they were the wheat-and-barley eaters. 'Course, I didn't call them by those names until recently, when modern folks came along."

"What did you call wheat and barley?" Skraga asked, just as

Leigh hoped she would, seeing as she was running out of white space.

"This stuff, and that stuff," Izaiah said. "Beer was an instant hit, even though it wasn't quite the same back in those days. Then bread came along . . . wow. New, exciting, and delicious, that's all I knew. The Egyptians called their bread Blin, did you know? The Chinese called theirs Aju. Don't let anyone tell you different. People are always telling me I'm wrong about stuff, but I was there. And my memory about food is sharp as a thorn. Not so much about wine, though. I admit . . . yeah, I became a little too friendly with that for a bit longer than I should have. But people just kept getting more and more things and stuff, and most of it you couldn't even eat if you wanted to. Silly, y'ask me."

"Wow, so you weren't kidding. You really are old," Skraga said. "Does that mean you're a creature?"

"It does indeed. A person, like you, but one made of different stuff," Izaiah said.

Leigh tapped Skraga on the shoulder to show her what she'd written: *You never asked who he was?*

"Sure, I did!" Skraga replied. "Then he answered, and I couldn't remember his name, and he said he was fine with Scruffy, and that was the end of the story. Good enough for me then, and I won't apologize for it now. Nope, won't."

He wants to arrest us.

Leigh showed the message to Skraga, not caring if Izaiah saw it or not. Skraga gawked at it for a moment before turning to face him. "Arrest us? For what?"

"Uh, I have no idea," Izaiah replied. He and Skaraga turned curious expressions back to Leigh. "Care to elaborate, Professor?"

Her eyes rolled again involuntarily, and she shook her head.

Izaiah continued, "If you were thinking the Sentries would be coming after you for something related to the Joseph Mandate, well . . . hate to be a diminisher, but you weren't exactly . . . well, considered much. The folks in the Tribunal tend to think about their own primarily. In fact, exclusively. That's been one of my pet peeves, which I've been trying to stop for a while now. And even if the Sentries were after you, you wouldn't have to worry. I don't work for those folks anymore."

Once again, Leigh found herself stumped. She wrote, *What were you doing in the Tribunal?*

At the same time, she thought, *It couldn't be a coincidence you were there.*

"It was all a coincidence!" Izaiah answered. "Darndest thing. I was in the Armarium, doing some searching of my own, when I heard some commotion coming from the Sercilium. That's when I found Skraga."

"He pulled the rock off my head," Skraga said, turning the back of her scalp to Leigh with another giddy smile. A three-inch bald spot was centered on the top of her head, exposing a patch of light purple skin surrounding a deep brown mark. "It did this. Funny, right? Then I must have fallen asleep, 'cause I missed helping you and Miss Morinnean get out safely. But now that you're awake, maybe you can tell me where she is. 'Cause I sure hope she's okay. I've been worried about the boss lady."

Leigh shared a knowing glance with Izaiah. *I'm guessing he left her behind in the Eb Ring chamber.* His aloof expression said he obviously knew the truth of Aluqa's fate but had saved Skraga from it. *That says a lot.*

Shaking her head, Leigh tried to look devastated as she answered Skraga's question about Aluqa.

"Oh, okay," Skraga said. "We'll have to go look for her soon. Once you feel good and healthy, of course."

"I'm sure she's fine, dear, wherever she is," Izaiah said, reaching for another handful of donuts. "But I was wondering—that Celestial fella you were with, was it his idea or hers to take the Covenant?"

Leigh remained still, offering nothing. Skraga half-shouted, "It was Aluqa's!"

"Yeah, thought so," Izaiah said. "A dilly of a plan—taking the cup, seeing what happens. But I'm not sure right now is such a good time for something like that, so I decided to take it back. Seeing how it wasn't yours to begin with, I figured you wouldn't mind. You don't need it, after all. Don't take this as me trying to help the Tribunal. Just trying to do the decent thing."

Leigh's pulse quickened as Izaiah reached into his coat pocket.

"But, to make up for it," he continued, "at least I hope it will—you can have this back."

He revealed the Wraithian dagger, its rough blade gleaming in the light, and set it on the table. "I didn't want anyone to get hurt on accident, so I kept this with me. You can have it, though, being the one who found it."

Leigh instinctively reached for it, but as her fingers grazed the handle, Izaiah suddenly snared her wrist and pulled her closer. His voice became softer, more serious. "But I feel I gotta say . . . this isn't any ordinary tool. I know you know this, but sometimes important things need a fuss made about 'em."

Skraga, noticing the tension, put down her handful of donuts and sat up straight, watching the situation with the protective readiness of a family dog around tall strangers wearing hats.

Izaiah continued, "To tell ya the truth, I don't think this thing is safe anywhere. If I had the power, I'd destroy it right now, but since I can't, I figure the best place for it to be is with someone who won't misuse it. Someone with some brains." He released her wrist.

"I'm often wrong about things, but please—please don't make this one of them. Sound good?"

Stupefied at this point, Leigh nodded slowly before taking the dagger and sliding it into her belt. Little by little, she was starting to feel more complete.

"We're all happy, right?" Skraga asked. "I can't tell."

"Absolutely fine, my dear," said Izaiah. "The professor's also developed a mighty thick skin."

Leigh nodded in agreement. He wasn't wrong about that. Using the last bit of white space on the current page, she wrote to Izaiah, *You said you were searching. What for?*

With an excited burst of energy, Izaiah sprang to his feet and hobbled into the cabin. "Glad you asked! I'll show you! One minute."

When he returned, he was holding a small box, slightly larger than a cigar box, made of dark metal with black-plated corners. As he set it on the table, Leigh's heart skipped a beat. She recognized the design immediately—it was one of the many mystery boxes from the Armarium, a box aching to be opened so that the treasure inside could see the light of day.

There was nothing she could do to keep from licking her lips as it was placed a few feet away on the table.

"What's that?" Skraga asked.

"This is something I thought I'd lost a long time ago," Izaiah said, spinning the box so they could see the front. A bulky lock with a square keyhole stared back at them.

Leigh's eyes narrowed. *Looks even more uncrackable up close.*

"Whoa," Skraga said. "Do you have the key?"

"I do not."

"Then how are you going to get it out of there?"

"That is an excellent question, Sophia. I've tried everything I know. But this is one of the ilthinq boxes, designed by Alice the Builder herself. Can't get the damn thing to even wiggle."

Leigh found that impossible and gave Izaiah a look to prove it.

"I know what you're thinking," he said. "He's a Medolian—he should be able to blast it open, or think it open, or something. But I can't. I really can't. Honest."

Leigh shrugged, asking why.

"Because I'm currently experiencing a drought of Eve power. Which may be looking more like a permanent desert. We'll see. But I used my last bit to get us off Trivium. I'd say that puts me out of the game. Luckily, new star players are coming up all the time."

With a soft nudge, Izaiah pushed the box across the table to rest in front of Leigh. "You wouldn't be able to lend us a hand, would you?"

Me?

(what can i do that your magical ass can't?)

She didn't take the box or offer anything more than a questioning glance.

"Do you think you could?" Skraga asked, leaning over the table, resting on her elbows, gazing at the box. Her wide-eyed stare then drifted to Leigh. "Open it, I mean."

An elementary-school pressure found its way back to the professor. Emotions or no, feeling needed and the desire to impress others were hard traits to shut down completely. Even though this felt like a trap of the simplest magnitude, she couldn't help going over some options in her head. One idea seemed promising.

Yeah, that would do the trick, I bet.

With Skraga and Izaiah gazing at her, waiting for an answer, Leigh took the box and gave it a once-over. Giving them the *"one-second"* gesture, she moved to the bedside table and retrieved her bracelet. Breaking off the last fire-red gem, she placed the box on the ground and stuck the gem inside the square keyhole. Finding a suitable rock nearby, one tapered to a point, she took aim, covered her face, and swung. It took two hits, but the red gem cracked open with a hiss. The dark gray metal screamed as the burning ooze inside melted its way through the lock. After a brief but energetic reaction, the red light faded, and the front of the box was left mangled and smoking.

"Even if this doesn't work, that sure looked cool," Izaiah said. "Now, before you get in there, you should know, what's inside is—"

With a solid knock from her boot heel, Leigh cracked the lock in two. The box lid fluttered open before slamming shut again.

"Valuable," Izaiah finished.

Placing it on the table, Leigh lifted the lid to find a four-inch snow globe resting in the direct center. Nothing else was inside.

"Ah! There she is," Izaiah said with a gasp, reaching out for what looked like a trinket of great age but still ultimately a novelty item. Once in his hands, he handled it with the same care he would an egg. His fingers grazed its golden base and foggy glass ball.

"Yes, indeed . . . there she is." With what could have been mistaken for a quick sniff of tears, Izaiah was suddenly back on his feet. "Always nice when things work out. Sophia, my dear, may I ask you a favor?" He approached her as though he were passing a candle.

"Sure, anything," she replied.

"Can you please hold on to this for me? I don't want anything bad to happen to it." He placed the snow globe in her hands. "I'd like to go for a walk around the pond, and it's our newly woken friend's turn to walk me."

Skraga fought off tremors as she took the treasure. "Are you sure, Scruffy? I can tell how important this is to you. Thank you. I will guard it with my life."

"Hopefully, that won't be necessary, but thank you." He turned to Leigh. "What do you say, Professor? Would you care to take a walk?"

With her caution up, Leigh tucked her arm into his and helped him as they slowly made their way toward the water.

"We'll be back soon," he said to Skraga. She waved them away, keeping her attention squarely on the globe.

The scenery was becoming more yellow and orange, with pockets draped in growing shadow. Around the pond was mostly mud, except for a ring of tough dirt circling it a few yards from the water's edge. Making their way with a pace so leisurely it seemed sometimes as though they were standing still, Leigh tried to take in the beauty of the nature around her. She'd spent so much of the last year in an underground mine that she'd forgotten the smell and rejuvenation of flowers or the feeling of grass caressing and tickling her skin.

"Heck of a friend you got there," Izaiah said, motioning back to Skraga. "Fiercely loyal, and with a good heart."

Leigh nodded. On that, she and Izaiah agreed emphatically.

"Shame it took me so long to get to her. By the time I got that black rock off her, whatever it was, she'd been without breath for a good while. I did my best to heal the damage, but I've never seen an injury like that get fully reset. Not even by the best. Brains are just too tricky. Don't think she'll ever be truly back to her old self. But that said, this is the only version of her I've ever known, and I find her delightful. No one else laughs at my jokes as much as she does. Not by a day's trek."

(she does seem happier)

But that doesn't mean the poor thing didn't deserve better.

Leigh did her best to remain stoic and let him take this wherever he wanted it to go.

"Then there's you," Izaiah said. "Sure, you might not be able to laugh at my jokes. Even though I'm fairly certain you wouldn't even if you could. But that don't mean you're not a good person, too. I heard every word Miss Lipmayer had to say about you, and almost all of them were something to be proud of. You're a hard worker, and a harder cookie." *Pretty sure he means "tough cookie."* "Frankly, I don't understand how you're still standing, helping me, instead of the other way around. Your body must be tired after all that on Trivium. Don't think any human's been through what you just were. Pure Wrath to pure Rapture in the same night? Guess you might just be built different."

Leigh was having trouble wrestling with her suspicions of the man and the undeniable craving she had for more whenever someone began raining praise on her.

"I know you're not fond of me," Izaiah said. "Seen enough of that to spot it pretty good. And I don't blame you. Your perspective on this whole thing has been from a dismal place. Sorry I gotta say. One unfortunate truth is, you can't plan for everything, and Joseph fell well outside the boundaries of everything. We failed you, but I also know my team worked harder than they ever have. It doesn't say much, but it says something. I would take your place if I could—be the one who had to deal with the nameless. Never should have been your burden, even though you handled the whole thing as well as a bird flies."

Leigh scoffed.

"I'm serious. Most people would've buckled under the pressure." *(who says i didn't?)* "But you let it drive you. That takes a quality no modern society has a name for, but one group of nomads I spent a good deal of time with used to call 'high click.' Or, rather, they would make a high pitched clicking sound with their tongues, but to them, that counted as a word. Anyways, when they said some-

one has high click, they meant that person will adapt and perse-
vere, but always through consistent change. A person with high
click may be many individuals in their lives. They are ravenous
learners, dynamic pivoters, and yet, always able to keep track of
their end goal, which will never change once set early in their lives.

"I was worried about you both. I want you to know that. You and
Miss Lipmayer. I was assured by one of my team, Fabian, that the
two of you had safely returned to civilization following the Joseph
affair. My friend sadly lost your snowmobile tracks but felt confident you had made it far enough to get help. Unfortunately, there
was little else I could do. I'm not happy with how it turned out, but
it was about the best way things could have gone. I truly believe
that. You can hate me all you want, but I think you're smart enough
to see the truth of what I'm saying."

She was. Leigh had been in charge of too many people's lives
over the course of her career to not know exactly what he meant.
With a slow nod as they neared a circular tract of vines and short
grass, she gave him a thumbs-up. *Consider it under the bridge.*

"Oh, good. I'm glad. That will make everything else I'm about to
say that much easier." Pulling away from her, Izaiah leaned on his
cane, looking over the water. "I'm okay here for a minute. Gonna
take it in."

Leigh stepped away, letting him have some space. The sun was
coming in low through the tops of the trees by now. Dusk was approaching. It was a scene she had witnessed many times in her life
growing up in Connecticut and Montana. But she'd never enjoyed
a scenic moment like this next to a Medolian before. That was new.

"I take it you became fairly obsessed with UnEarth after the
mandate," Izaiah said. "Which I understand. Most people do after
encountering an Eve creature. But it looks like you took it pretty

far, huh? Must be on account of how much you hate UnEarth, especially the Medolians."

Leigh nodded.

"I figured as much. The last few days didn't help, either, I'm sure. It's hard to know where to put your effort after something like this. But the main thing to remember at all times is to remain calm."

Leigh signed, "Easy for you to say."

"No, it isn't," Izaiah replied. When Leigh looked shocked at his understanding of ASL, he snorted. "Oh, yeah, I've seen some hand talk here and there. Tend to pick up languages pretty quick. I might not know a few words, but I'll prob'ly get your gist."

In that case, Leigh signed the first question she had. "Why did you bring us here?"

"Needed someplace secure. Can't use a safe house on account of some trouble within the Medolians. But I wanted to get you healthy so I can ask you a question, which I will do in a moment. But before that, I had something I thought needed to be said. You see, I like you. Even before ever meeting you, I thought you were okay. One of a kind. And that can be enticing to all sorts of groups. So, I get why you ended up with the Morinnean gal's outfit. But to be honest, I'm not too happy about the attack on the execution. Those were some nasty toys your friends set off. Even if they didn't know they were going to be exploding themselves, they thought they were there to kill UnEarth folks nonetheless.

"That being said, I also know the fellas and I are only alive because of what happened. So, I'm conflicted. I know you had Wrath in you, and believe me, I know how persuasive that can be, but I saw too many innocent people get slaughtered that day just to leave things be. Now, don't be alarmed. I'm not going to hurt anyone. As if I could. But I am going to ask you to help me pay for the debt of those lives."

"How?" Leigh signed.

"So glad you asked," Izaiah said with a chortle. "Always so eager. But I can see how tired you are, you know? I can see how badly you want to go home and be done with all this. I get it. I've felt that more times than I can remember. But it always comes back. Always. It's as though once this stuff touches you, you can't get it off. UnEarth stains, and you and I are soaked in it, my dear. I think if you looked down inside yourself, you'd know you're not gettin' out. Not now."

"Get to the point."

"Eager. I like it. I'm offering you a chance to do something that will actually make a difference. Or could, if I'm right. We'll have to see. But I know it will do more than whatever prolonged study session or series of heists you were probably starting to build in your head will."

[*He is not wrong.*]

And I'm dying to know where this man's point is landing.

"The way I'm seeing it, you can handle something more challenging," Izaiah said. "Something that can't be done without great precision. Where not even a single mistake could be allowed. Something that no one else I know, not even me, could pull off, no matter how hard they tried. You might say that a job like this would be perilous, and yet, if successful, could save all of mankind from potential destruction and/or enslavement."

Leigh was sure she appeared dumbfounded, despite having not moved an inch.

"I guess I'm trying to tell you that there's something I've been needing to get done for a while," Izaiah continued. "Just an idea I had. A hunch. But I kept pushing it back on my to-do list. Then Joseph happened, and well, you know the rest. Now, I'm far too weak to do it myself, and I need some help. Namely, yours. I know you don't know me personally, but it's rather important. Otherwise, I wouldn't ask." Izaiah waited for a response to continue. Leigh was curious enough to offer a slow nod, her lingering hesitation masking any clear yes or no.

"I will warn you again, this thing is dangerous. Extremely. As most really important things are. It will take a cool head. Don't ask me why, but I trust you to see it through. The way you handled the nameless demon was really something. Don't think nobody noticed. I sure did." He left another pause. She still wouldn't outright agree or reject him. Not until she had just a little bit more.

"I realize how unfair it is of me to ask this of you. And feel free to tell me to go eat rocks," Izaiah said. "You just got out, after all. Off Trivium and UnEarth. Away from the only place you truly wish never existed. But now, I was just wondering, um . . . would you mind going right back in?"

OF HIS OWN ACCORD

I wasn't strong enough. Just like he said.

The ground was craggy, black, and looked the same everywhere. But the spot Alex had chosen to stare at was special. It was his—an anchor. All he had, a section about the size of a quarter. He would never take his eyes off it. The thing kept him from shaking. If there ever were a god who loved him, he would never be forced to look at anything else and never be removed from its presence. Staying in this spot forever would be a perfectly reasonable way to live his life.

He said we would do it together. But we didn't.

Cold gripped his legs, despite the heat-filled creatures surrounding him. The urine had soaked his pants by now, top to bottom, and he had no more left in his bladder to release from sheer terror. The room he occupied was a living nightmare, its walls and ceiling made of matte darkness. All around him were red, maroon, and scarlet creatures swaying like trees in a gusty forest. Long snouts snarled and drooled acidic slobber onto the floor, but the teacher kept his eyes on the spot on the ground, ignoring everything else.

The spot was good. It was acid-free and had never done him or anyone else wrong. Right there, with his spot on the ground, he was safe.

You left me here. Left me with nothing.

Clangs everywhere—the chatter and clinks of metal. The collar around his neck, connected by a chain to all those around him, held him loosely in the dense cluster of Archfiend assembled in three lines. The pures, for the most part, were docile, seeming resigned to the situation. Their snarls and drools of acid were no more a threat than humans yawning or scratching themselves while waiting in a queue. But the Human Archfiend present—which amounted to only a handful—looked terrified to some degree.

At least I'm not alone.

The humanoids were scattered throughout the rows. Alex was lucky enough to have one in front of him, rather than a pure. *Especially one of the Ostra clan. I wouldn't stand directly behind one of them to save my grandma from a falling piano . . . at the very least, I would second-guess it.* But something about the bald woman with olive skin was curious, possibly off. The enigmatic air surrounding her had grabbed his attention immediately upon their grouping. Her Rapture signature was incredibly low in bandwidth, as well as in general depth. In many ways, it reminded him of his and Bennett's Eves shortly after they had first been imbued.

Among the many curious things about the mystery woman, chief was her smell. She graciously did not give off the sharp, stagnant air and mothball musk of most Human Celestials. *I've come to find it just disgusting. Bennett, especially. Didn't have the heart to tell him how bad he was smelling back there.* The faintest hint of expensive perfume lingered on the woman, along with an earthy, mineral-rich dirt scent. Both were perplexing. And though she was obviously scared, just like the rest of them, the fear and Dread flowing in her veins was something else entirely.

There was no fooling Mr. Barker. Even though no one had said so, he knew for a fact she was no Human Archfiend. She was a plain old, one of eight billion, Earth-born *Homo sapiens*, just like he used to be. The only questions were: Who was she, and what had she done to earn her spot in line? To no one's surprise, there had not been much time to catch up before the prisoners were chained together and marched down a hall. So far, there had not been any opportunities to try and speak with her and ask who she was, but he had a pretty good idea.

There had been rumblings—things he'd heard during his brief stint in the Ulga Vloc before being brought here. It seemed the attack on the execution was being blamed on a resistance cult from Earth. Using technology stolen from a prominent Purged Celestial, they had been able to force enough Eve into their bodies to survive the trip to Trivium. The imbuement was temporary, however, unlike Alex's and Bennett's. Apparently, a handful of cult members were found several miles from the execution site, having chosen to run rather than take part in the attack. Their remains were difficult to identify, as it looked as though their molecular bonds had begun breaking down after only a few hours. Most of what was found was described as "just something sorta gooey."

Somehow, the woman in front of Alex, who was surely part of the attack, had not dissolved. Her signature was low but just strong enough to keep her together. One of the rumors that passed through his cage was that the leader of the suicide cult had been captured alive. This must have been her. It had to be. Only a leader would have been given some kind of special imbuement—one permanent or semi-permanent—or was using some form of synthetic Eve long enough to render her body compatible. *If that would even work.* Her stance was like someone who was important or had gotten used to being treated as such. But however noble and brave she was, and despite the fact that she had brought an entire UnEarth city to its knees, saving Alex's life inadvertently at the same time, she couldn't keep her body from shaking with tremors.

Looming over the chained prisoners—a gold mouth ready to swallow them all—an Eb Ring waited to transport them farther into UnEarth. Any minute now, the gateway would spring to life to take them, but more than Alex had ever wanted anything—except for maybe Melissa back—he didn't want to go through it. He would give back every good thing that had ever happened to him if it meant he didn't have to cross the threshold. It was disgraceful how willing he was to go back to the Sackulli-Karni. He'd be a good prisoner and not speak unless spoken to. He'd eat the slop, the whole pile of it. He would stay in those chains, staring at a different spot on the floor forever, if it meant he didn't have to go through the gateway ahead of him now. What lay beyond was too much for his mind to digest.

For his many indiscretions against UnEarth, he was not being put back in the Weya-Vein, an already traumatizing cesspool of misery, or even put to death—which was starting to feel like the girl who got away. His body was now the property of Ariel Van-Mortus and the Alus Conclave, claimed by Arros. It seemed the Archfiend did want ownership of him after all. *They just took their sweet-ass time getting around to it.*

Alex spent two days in the Ulga Vloc before his transfer. He, along with the mystery woman in front of him, was not to be a prisoner of Trivium. The facility they were being transferred to was located on Arros—the world of Wrath, ruled by King Lucifer-Aveyl, lord of the Archfiend.

Without the faintest clue of what lay before him, all Alex could do was stave off the images of Hell that he'd imagined as a child. Would it live up to them? Or would it be far worse? What horrors could the universe bestow on a mind if it was really trying? If the Human Archfiend around him were any indication, there was plenty of reason to be afraid. Their ilk were usually put in jails on Earth or on Trivium. Pures tended to be the ones sent to homeworld facilities, which meant the Humans present were either especially nefarious offenders or had been victimized by the system in the worst possible way.

Alex continued to stare at the spot on the ground. It helped. But not with the chattering of his teeth. Nothing helped with that. When it did occasionally stop, the tic just switched to his tongue, which flapped like an otter wrestling with a ball. But the spot on the ground helped with everything else. *Just focus on that. Stay there. Don't think about where you're going. Don't think about what's over there—the wild monsters that will want to tear my flesh from my bones, the flowing rivers of lava, or the plants I've heard about that explode with fiery meteorites, burning their way into rock up to a mile away in order to plant their seeds. To say nothing of the billions of Archfiend that call the planet home.*

Then there was Alex's reputation. He knew the Archfiend hated him, resented him, and probably felt several other negative emotions he didn't even know about. The verbal abuse he'd suffered from Oaleen would likely be child's play compared to what lay before him.

But I don't want to go. I can't!

He could practically hear what she would be saying right now if she were here. She would have told him to toughen up, straighten up, and not to take things like this without a good, shitty attitude to match. None of which sounded unreasonable at the moment. Alex was tired of the cold, chilling fear. And his cold, chilling pants. The power he'd had during his battle against the Celestial guards while escaping alongside Bennett was a fantastic memory. He'd never felt stronger or more capable than when he'd torn through them, beating his jailers with the strength they originally thought he'd possessed when he was first arrested. He was a wall that had finally gotten its missing bricks replaced.

Then there was Bennett, and the power he'd gained. Alex still had no idea how he'd gotten so strong. *Maybe he'd been training the whole time he was in jail? Sounds about right. They probably would have given him his own gym. He was given everything else—why not?* With the extra power, the human duo had gotten far on their own. But that final charge for their freedom would likely become Alex's last enjoyable memory forevermore. He hated that it included Bennett, even if he wasn't the one who had actually let him go. That was Mara, and the rest of the Medolians.

He said we would do it together. He lied.

Alex relived the moment over and over again, whether he wanted to or not: the moment when the Rapture Medolian had swooped in and stolen him. Her arm had wrapped around him so suddenly that, for the tiniest fraction of a second, he'd found comfort in it. The faintest memory of loafing on the couch with Melissa had sped by. Then, he was shocked, surrounded by and living in gray. Something had happened, but he didn't quite know what. The moment was hazy. Philomena, a blur of orchid blue and violet, introduced herself formally once she set him on the ground. She then informed Alex he was under arrest yet again, before immediately handing him over to Gabriel.

Once again, Alex was a dot in the High Lord's shadow, as an enclosing wall of blue shrank him down. But this time, one thing was different: he was all alone, abandoned as he was set to be executed once more. *Three times in one day has got to be some kind of record.* Gabriel was all too eager, even for a creature that moved like a tortoise when not in battle. The giant sword was gripped tight in his hands, and Alex was held down as the blade was raised above his head. That was when a savior (*depending on how you look at it*) arrived in the form of a Wyst: Valio-Malo, the lead Counselor. With just a few words, they were able to stay Gabriel's hand and Alex was relinquished to their custody.

It seemed earlier in the day, while Alex and Bennett were hiding in the Fovosian's house, some last-minute strings had been pulled in court, and not even Gabriel had authority over the great Judge Axios outside his homeworld. The High Lord, out of monstrous frustration, slammed his blade into the ground, shaking the whole block, before he swooped into the air, disappearing over the horizon with his entourage.

The memories made the Wrath return. *Bennett looked right at me. As he was being dragged to safety, and I was dragged to face the punishment incurred by not only him but Joseph and Chloe and all the demons that made it to Earth.* None of them would pay for what had been done. None but Alex Barker would.

He lied to me. Again.

Alex broke his gaze from the spot on the ground to take a quick look around at the beasts—imps, fiends. Red scales rolled in the dark, some shimmering, others dull and caked with muck. He'd never really come to terms with the fact that the same energy keeping him alive had created these things—those long, craggy tongues, and penetrating eyes. But wishing the Wrath had never invaded his body was starting to feel tired. *A man can only complain so much.*

The woman ahead of him in line had lost much of the little blue she'd had in her signature, and the missing Eve seemed to be replaced by a dull orange. *Her fear is so intense she's generating notice-able Dread. But Izaiah said that's not . . . possible.*

Alex felt for her, no matter what she may or may not have been a part of. No creature deserved to live in such a state of misery. If he was ever going to try and talk with her, now seemed as good a time as any.

He cleared his throat before speaking softly. "Miss. Hey . . . Excuse me."

She didn't turn around or respond, but her signature jumped just a hair.

"I understand if you don't want to talk," Alex started again, slightly louder. "But this might be our last chance to do it with a semi-normal person before we get sent off to wherever it is we're going."

Her bald head remained facing forward.

"Do you understand English? Parlez-vous français? Please, because those are the only two I know."

"I understand you fine," she said.

"So, she can speak."

"I have nothing to say to you, Barker."

"You know my name?"

"Everyone knows your name. But to hear you now, you're not as I imagined." She turned to peer at him with inquisitive yet disappointed blue eyes. Their shine had diminished since entering the Eb Gate chamber, falling from crystalline to muddy and near black.

"I know. Because I was the Ire, right? Sorry to disappoint. I taught elementary school and liked to make things like airplane models and wood sculptures when I had a life."

"A strange one, then, to carry the weight of Hell."

"You're telling me, lady."

"Do not call me that."

"Then what should I call you?"

"I'd rather nothing. But you may use Aluqa to address me."

Her expression, full of bravado, was a facade. Alex knew it well, after reading the same expression year after year in his class. *There was always that one kid . . . Always that one.*

"I'm not kidding," he said. "If there's anything you want to talk about before we head in . . ."

"I've studied Arros thoroughly since before you were born. There's nothing about the Murag you could tell me that I don't already know."

"Okay, sure. But how are you feeling?"

"How am I feeling? What kind of question is that?"

"The most basic one, I think. Look, I don't know anything about you. I'm not looking to judge anyone. You're obviously a very impressive and important person. But you're still just a human."

"I've been instilled with the power of Rapture. I do not fear. The essence of creation will protect me."

"Whatever you say. But your Eve is shrinking. It might not last much longer in there."

She turned away from him and stood even taller.

"Is your name really Aluqa?"

"No," she said after hesitating. Her signature began to quake, wavering. "It's . . . Lina. But no one else calls me that. No one even knows that name. No one since . . . my mother. They call me ma'am, or boss. The creator. Member on high, chosen to lead Earth against UnEarth. Aluqa Morinnean."

"I think I like Lina better," Alex said.

She nodded. "Me too."

"You know, one thing I've learned in all this is that fear might be awful, but that doesn't mean it's wrong. Sadness, either. They're all part of the life equation. I don't think anyone should feel shame for feeling those things. Or avoid them. If we weren't supposed to have them, why are they there? Pretending things aren't the way they are is like lying. Truth always makes things easier. But maybe that's just me."

Under her breath, Aluqa said something Alex didn't catch.

"What was that?" he asked.

"I said I'm not afraid of going to Arros," she answered, her presence rising with a resounding clarity. "I fear never returning. If I don't die immediately after crossing this threshold, I'll be put through the greatest challenge of my life. But my work here isn't finished. There's still much left to do, and I also need to thank the one who sent me here in the first place. Personally."

"I don't think either of us are coming back once we step through that gate," Alex said, colder than he intended.

"I agree."

They both kept quiet after that.

Then came a chime—a horrible, rattling, cranky, scathing sound that made Alex long for the drawn-out tones of the Celestials and their armor. But this was not their show. This was the domain of Archfiend jailers. Several of the long-snouted dragons on the outskirts hissed, trilling and banging their jagged chestplates.

The mass of prisoners stirred at the sound, riled. They all knew what it meant—even Alex, who didn't fully understand, though he did. The sound meant it was time to get up and go to Hell. But his tendons were suddenly as tight as piano strings. His veins filled again with icy fear while his head boiled. A single word repeated in his mind at the speed of a hummingbird's wings: *No-no-no-no-no-no-no-no-no-no.* It couldn't be time. There had to be something else here to do, something on this side of the portal. Bennett was gone. Izaiah was gone. Melissa was gone. Alex was left with no one.

Because he lied. All he does is lie.

His baby girl was safe at home and would never have to see a place like Arros. He had that. With any luck, she would never hear of UnEarth, and never learn what really happened to him. His grandmother would teach her about the God of the Hebrew Bible and the stories Alex had learned in Sunday school. Looking back on them now, he found a new appreciation for them: Adam and Eve, Noah's Ark, the like. *The really old ones. Even the one about the guy who got swallowed by a fish and spit back out a few days later.* Alex had left religion because of the politics and infighting and power grabbing, but those basic tales didn't seem so bad now. Life was complicated enough and got more so all the time, and after learning what he knew and living what he lived, he just hoped his little girl would steer clear of the truth for as long as she could—just remain happy and ignorant for a while, back where he wished he could get back to.

Don't leave there, Patty. Stay for as long as you can.

A cavernous boom rumbled. The golden ring before the prisoners ignited and filled with a swirling storm of black and murky gray. The mouth was ready and hungry. *Wish that it actually was a big animal. I'd rather be digested than go through this thing.* It was a rare breed: an Eb Ring with a fixed route straight into the Murag.

It shouldn't be me going through this, Bennett. It should be you. We both know it should have been you.

Desperate tears welled in Alex's eyes. His chest pulsed with shallow breaths while his jaw and lips danced. His heels dug into the ground preemptively. He longed to be a Lostros, so weighty no one could move him.

I didn't lie. I never lied!

The Archfiend captains made their way to the front of the conglomeration. Guards surrounding the outer perimeter looked poised and ready to pounce on their brethren and tear them to pieces straightaway if any got out of line.

But you lied, and look at the free pass you got because of it.

Alex considered one last try at being disobedient, at getting killed before being forced through the gate. *That's it.* He found the loophole. *Suicide by cop, UnEarth style.* All he would have to do was raise his Wrath. *No problem. Just remember what Oaleen and Surr said. I'm the Ire—I'm the Ire. I'm the Ire.* But just as he was about to power up, just as he began letting the anger and hate flow, there was a sound like an F-1 engine revving, and the chain on his wrists shot an electric, stinging pain through his body. The prisoner Archfiend around him shrieked and writhed. Alex's whole Eve signature was thrown out of phase. The Wrath was gone—a fire extinguished before it could catch.

That was the moment the chieftain in the front announced the march. The torment from the chain persisted, a relentless freeze that gnawed at him. Whips were drawn and lashed against flesh, their cracks splitting the air. Slowly, the mass began to shuffle toward the gate. With every ounce of his will, Alex pulled, yanking and heaving, desperate to find some shred of strength that the chains on his wrists and the collar around his neck hadn't yet drained from him.

"Come on!" he cried to Lina. "Help me. We have to try."

Aluqa's hubris and facade had been wiped away once the chain gang began moving. Dread filled her like a leak had sprung in her soul. A jittery nod followed Alex's request. Together, they fought the chain, but no other creatures bothered joining. They were smart enough to know there was no point. Alex and Aluqa were dragged along like fish caught in a net, moving toward a compactor, flapping uselessly.

Ever larger, the gate loomed, and the teacher's knees began to buckle. His breathing became so shallow it disappeared. His heart pumped so hard it aided the guards, thrusting him forward, as though trying to smash free from his ribcage and make a break for it.

A smell began to creep off the gate, sifting through the air. Something like sulfur, but a thousand times more potent and rotten. It was laced with death—burnt, scorched flesh. Then came the sharp, acrid sting of gunpowder, previewing the astounding heat awaiting him.

His feet skidded uselessly across the ground, straining to dig in but only flailing like a child. The Archfiend behind him, seemingly having had enough of the human's shit, snapped the chain, forcing him back into line. Hate radiated from the beast, crawling across the back of Alex's neck. A guard's whip cracked against it next, a clawing wound. As the first prisoners were pushed into the gate, violent bursts of sound exploded from within, tearing at the air like hurricane winds, biting into his spine. Among the din, he caught the broken sound of Lina's voice, muttering something only she could understand—something that sounded eerily like a prayer.

Alex suddenly wished he had done a lot more of that. To him, prayers had always been just another word for wishes, and Grandpa Parai had warned him of the evil in those. But right now, he couldn't help but close his eyes and pray. He begged for help. He pleaded with anyone who might listen.

His eyes snapped open just in time to see Lina hesitate before stepping into the Eve storm within the gate. Then she was gone. What sounded like a scream escaped the flash of light—so brief, Alex immediately wondered if he had imagined it.

"Come on! Move it!" one of the slithery-tongued serpent guards yelled in English.

I can't. I can't do it. Please don't make me do it. If I do, nothing will ever be fine again, and Melissa couldn't have been wrong about that. She was never wrong about anything.

The portal drifted ever closer, its roiling heat scorching his skin. The ring's vast entrance swallowed his sight, filling his perception. The churning Eve within the gate was ready to take him, and Alex was ready to force the others to send him through. There was no way he'd walk into that fire again willingly. But as he drew within mere feet of it, something in him changed. His legs stopped their useless fight. A cold, sudden awareness of himself struck.

No . . . I'm not doing this again. No more.

This wasn't how he would allow himself to behave. He wouldn't be dragged to Hell like a whining slab of meat tossed onto a barbecue. He might have been damned, but he was still a man. If Lina could walk through the Eb Gate with her dignity intact, so could he.

He would take the step himself. With his head held low, he planted his foot, ready. Despite his paralyzing fear, he filled with pride. *I'm going to do this, and maybe when I see Melissa again, I can tell her what I did on my own.* A microsecond was taken to savor the pride blooming in his chest, but unfortunately, that brief pause was enough to set off the Archfiend behind him, who seemed impatient to get to prison. A heavy, clawed hand shoved hard between Alex's shoulder blades.

He didn't even know what happened.

Through the portal he went, face-first, and disappeared.

"*Hrm.*" The demon grunted as he stepped through the gate after him. "Enjoy, Ire boy . . . Enjoy."

THE END

Acknowledgments

Thanks go to Tammy Salyer, Miranda Paige, and Zach Bruning. This book would not have been possible without you.

I also wish to thank Todd McFarlane, John Carmack & John Romero, Steve Perry & Stephani Perry, and Ed Boon & John Tobias, whom all share a portion of the blame as well. As such, any & all complaints should be made to their respective agents and managers.

APPENDIX

UnEarth Senate:

Majority Party: Hywyn
Home World Ruler: High Lord Gabriel
Ruling Body: The Magnus Council
Current Senator: Honorable Speaker Binahq
The oldest of the six worlds of UnEarth, Hywyn formed four point one billion years ago out of Rapture, the shade of Eve manifested by the acts and will of creation. For tens of millions of years, the Celestials lived peacefully, creating anything and everything possible, until the other worlds of UnEarth were discovered and conflict first came to the world of purity. Though it took many millennia for Celestials to learn basic combat, Hywyn eventually led the worlds of UnEarth to victory in both major UnEarth wars, Unos and Inferius, and helped found the Tribunal and Senate, placing themselves as the majority party, never to give up the slot.

Second Majority Party: Arros
Home World Ruler: King Lucifer-Aveyl
Ruling Body: Alus Conclave
Current Senator: Ariel Van-Mortus
The second world of UnEarth to form, Arros is made of Wrath, the shade of Eve manifested by the acts and will of destruction. Since the dominant species on the world, the Archfiend, operate similarly to a hive mind, a governing body was not needed for many millions of years, until the first skirmishes with the high shaded worlds of the Eve began. The strongest of these chosen leaders,

Molm'Ursuth, led Arros into the first UnEarth war, Unos, and was defeated by the newly discovered Medolians of Earth, Michael the Great, the united peoples of UnEarth, and Lucifer-Aveyl of Hywyn, who would later be banished to rule as king of Arros, continuing his rule in seclusion to this day.

Minority Party: Nashwyn
Home World Ruler: Queen Regent Bau-ni Reyo (*ruling in stead of her mentee, King Bauq-un Reyo, currently in pupal stage.*)
Ruling Body: The Queen's Council
Current Senator: Minority Leader Mau-auvt Bo
Nashwyn and the Wysts are created from Fervor, the shade of Eve manifested by life's passions. The Wysts were the first higher-shaded creatures to discover the temporary gateways that open between like shaded worlds as their orbits convene. This is how they discovered the Celestials over one million years ago. Though the two species shared few traits, diplomatic relations were pursued, and the worlds began to form the first common UnEarth language. When the armies of the lower shades began to show themselves, Nashwyn and Hywyn joined forces, creating the first UnEarth union.

Of the higher shades, Wysts are the most zealous and likely to enter into a conflict.

<u>Second Minority Party:</u> Fovos
<u>Home World Ruler:</u> Mistress Tennille
<u>Ruling Body:</u> N/A
<u>Current Senator:</u> Head of the Cavern States Claude Malcolm Rowse

Fovos formed a few millennia after Arros from Dread, the shade of Eve manifested by fear and doubt. Existing alongside Nashwyn in the second pocket of the UnEarth universe (*Universe Delta, à la Professor Francisco Emul's notes*), Fovos is perpetually dim, never truly in night, and never truly in day. Most of its life originated beneath the crust, near the planet's core where it's warm, though many of the planet's creatures make the cold, dark surface their home, living among the dead forests and bogs covering its landscape. The Scythe's current leader, Mistress Tennille, has lived far longer than any of her predecessors by siphoning Eve from her constituents, which they have given up gladly for thousands of years.

<u>Third Minority Party:</u> Lanwyn
<u>Home World Ruler:</u> Premiere Meese Linski
<u>Ruling Body:</u> The Leew Union
<u>Current Senator:</u> Afton Laffler

Lanwyn, the world of green, and its tree-dwelling citizens, the Beaubons, were formed from Jubilee, the shade of Eve manifested by joy, excitement, and contentment. Lanwyn and its sister-world, Doloros, both exist in the same subpocket universe as Trivium, which is always visible, especially at night, where it glows like a warm, soft sun.

The Beaubons of Lanwyn, though relatively small, and with a cheeriness sometimes hard to tolerate, have proven themselves mighty warriors and trustworthy companions to the higher shades of UnEarth.

Fourth Minority Party: Doloros
Home World Ruler: Governor Monty Mulmin
Ruling Body: The Klepper Lostros Club
Current Senator: Prime Minister Yaddo
Created from Grief, the shade of Eve manifested by despondency and sadness, Doloros is a world of golden mountains and sand. Though slow to move, as well as to leap into action, the Lostros are strong, powerful creatures, able to lift many times their own, already notable, weight. Though the Lostros fought exclusively for the lower shades in Unos, their loyalty to Arros and Fovos was put into question when Doloros switched sides in the final years of Inferius, helping to turn the tide against Lucifer-Aveyl and the Archfiend's attack on Hywyn, helping to bring about the longest reign of unequivocal peace in modern UnEarth history.

Universe Alpha

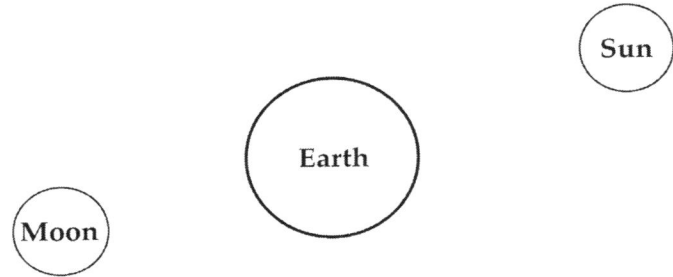

Sun

Earth

Moon

Note: Images not to scale

Universe Delta (UnEarth)

The sun emits Eve, making it visible in Universe Delta.

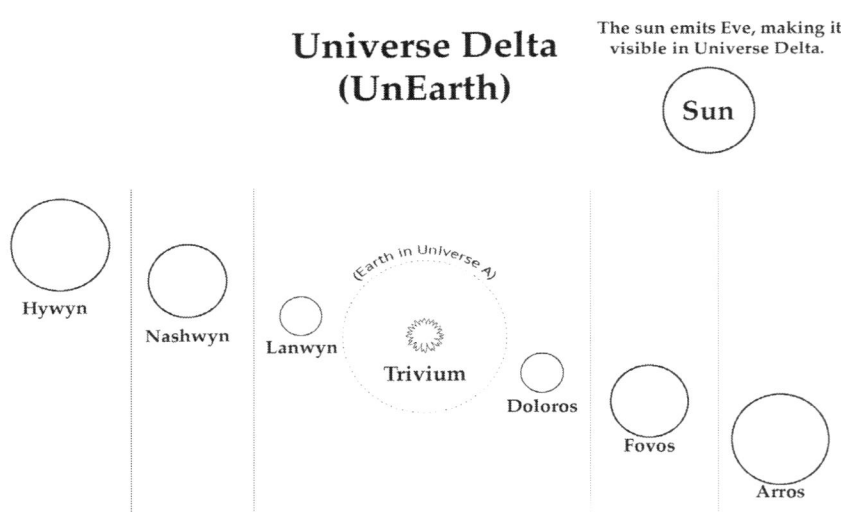

Sun

Hywyn

Nashwyn

Lanwyn

(Earth in Universe A)

Trivium

Doloros

Fovos

Arros

Universe Delta
(UnEarth)

UnEarth World		Eve Shade	
Hywyn	◯	Rapture	
Nashwyn	◯	Fervor	
Lanwyn	○	Jubilee	
Trivium	✳	Mallos	
Doloros	○	Grief	
Fovos	◯	Dread	
Arros	◯	Wrath	

Note: Images not to scale

The Tribunal

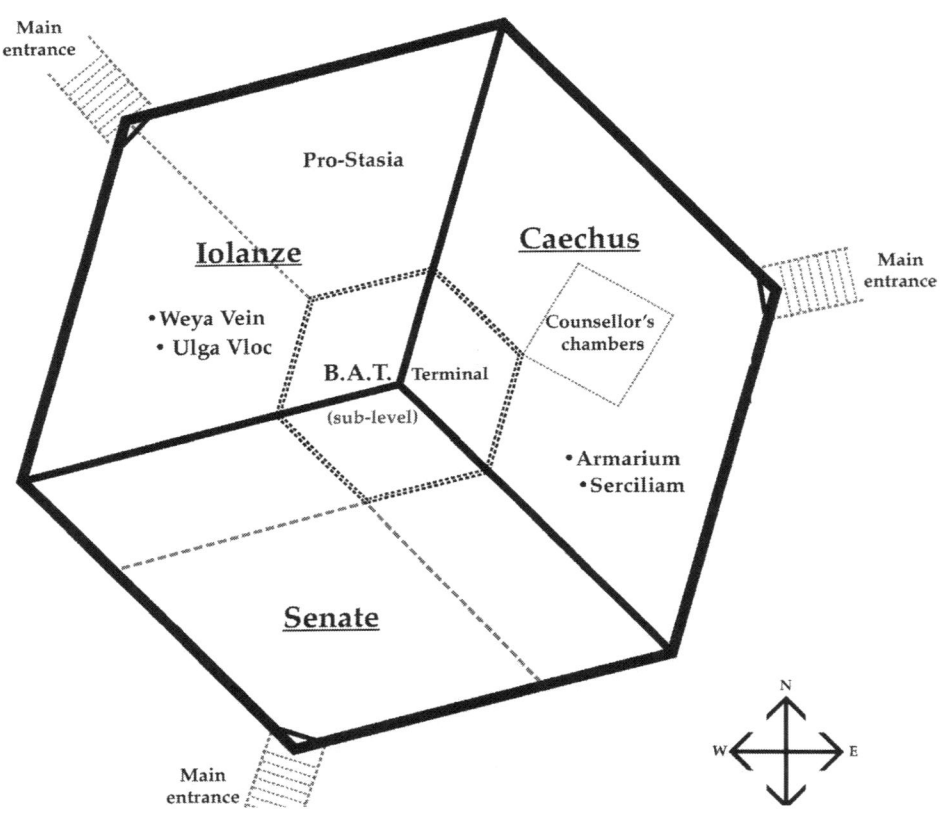

Main entrance

Pro-Stasia

Iolanze

Caechus

Counsellor's chambers

• Weya Vein
• Ulga Vloc

B.A.T. Terminal
(sub-level)

Main entrance

• Armarium
• Serciliam

Senate

Main entrance

N
W — E
S

Trivium City

- Museum of Nature, Science, and Eve

○ North
Eb Gate

Pilomine
Mountains

· Carniyan

· The Biblioteca
· Shira
Ai's Peak · Execution Grounds

· Colossal Competetive
Eve Leagues

⬡ **The Tribunal**

Trib Town Trinity Plaza
Greb-Gek
Hikkwe district

· Mulen Tados
· Miss Massachusetts's
Meatery
○ South
Bellion Eb Gate
Square

Port Wynass Lunsai

Financial Sector

N
W ←→ E
S

UnEarth Timeline

13.8 Billion YA -	- Life begins with the Great Expansion.
5 Billion YA -	- Natural evolution of Universe Alpha solidifies Universe Delta.
4.5 Billion YA -	- Trivium is fully formed in Universe Delta.
500 Million YA -	- First Eve creatures appear on Hywyn.
2 Million YA -	- Temporary portals between UnEarth worlds are discovered.
50,000 YA -	- Michael, of OA and Lucifer, of Aveyl are born the same year.
42,000 BC - **37,000** BC -	- UNOS, the first great UnEarth war, takes place.
28,000 BC -	- "Lucifer's Coup" - Following its failure, he is cast out of Hywyn.
3109 BC -	- INFERIUS begins.
3101 BC -	- Michael is killed in the Battle of Lannion Peninsula by Lucifer.
3026 BC -	- Gabriel assumes mantle of Overseer.
86 BC -	- Uhl'k, under Lucifer's control, makes landfall in Hywyn.
YEAR ZERO -	- Begins with Die Muneris. INFERIUS ends.
YEAR **1** -	- The Covenant is sealed. The Purge begins.
March, **2000** AD -	- First official sighting of the nameless demon by Nigel Roe.
February, **2006** AD -	- The UnEarth Senate votes to approve the Joseph Mandate.
October **18, 2006** -	- Gehenna is opened.
October **29, 2006** -	- Battle at the Tribunal creation of the Ire